Serpents of Summer

Rage of Lions Book Five

Matt Barron

Blade of Truth Publishing Company

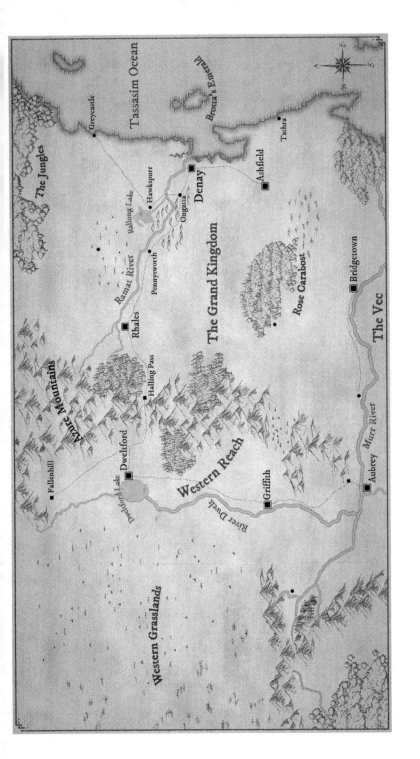

PROLOGUE

"I hope winter comes soon, I'm jack o' this heat!"

"I can stand the heat, it's a lick o' rain I want to see."

"Enough talk, you two," Corporal Gennet, a stocky Claw of the White Lions, ordered his chatty companions. "We're almost back to camp!"

"Ah, give t'anks," muttered wild-haired Treff, the militiaman from the Gilded Coast, just south of the Quenland forests. "I needs me a long drink."

"And mayhap some camp bread," added Treff's comrade Olfrad, a scarred, bald-headed convict from east of Rhales. "I ain't eaten none o' nothin' since last night."

"We'll make our report to the captain before any of that," Gennet told them. "Duty first."

"Well, ain't you the good little sworn yeoman, Corporal," Treff mocked him. "Good and loyal."

"Yes, I am," the corporal replied flatly. "So are you. And you'll stay that way if you want to get ahead in the Lions."

Treff and Olfrad both rolled their eyes. Gennet saw them do it but could not be bothered to defend himself any further. They were two complainers and pains-in-the-neck, but not shirkers, at least not to the point of outright insubordination. They did what they were told when ordered and otherwise looked out for themselves, which was about as much as any ex-convict could be expected to do.

"You two just keep up with me until we're dismissed," he commanded and then started off at a trot over the parched grass. Just ahead they passed fellow militiamen standing picket outside the camp. Fifty men in five lines of ten—the base unit of the White Lions—were positioned in front of the camp at the south end of the vale. They faced Halling Pass Castle and its village at the valley's north end, barely two thousand paces away. The castle belonged to the White Lions' liege lady, the Duchess Amelia of the Western Reach, but until that morning it had been in enemy hands. Corporal Gennet's little patrol had news for the captain on that front.

The corporal led the way into camp, and it wasn't long before they were waiting out front of the captain's tent, a simple square affair made of unbleached cotton cloth like every other tent in the camp. Nobles and knights on campaign typically lived in the largest tents and pavilions they could afford, made of the finest and brightest cloths. "Princes march under silk," was a saying amongst the common folk of the Grand Kingdom. Not so the captain and officers of the White Lions. From the least soldier to Captain Prentice Ash himself, everyone was equipped by the duchess from her own treasury, and the entire company marched under plain canvass. It was a humility that served an important purpose. Since none of the White Lions were nobles themselves, not even the captain, it would be taken as presumptuous for them to have the kinds of bright tents that knights and nobles favored. The sumptuary laws—the laws of fashion and manners that kept the lower orders from presuming on the rights of their betters—were not as strictly enforced in the Western Reach as they were in the rest of the Grand Kingdom, but they still were there. Better not to tweak the nobility's noses; peasant infantry like the White Lions were affront enough to those high-born folk who were convinced that war was the sole province of knights and nobles.

A drummer named Solomon, who also served as the captain's personal messenger, ducked his head into the tent, and Captain

Prentice Ash emerged a moment later. Tall and broad-shouldered, Captain Ash was wearing his quilted arming doublet and trousers dyed the deep blue of the duchess's house colors. He had ashen blonde hair, close cropped, and a full, trimmed beard. Piercing blue-grey eyes seemed to take in everything around him all at once. He was wearing a heavy, slightly curved sword made for wielding two-handed but not the straight-bladed cruciform weapon of a knight's longsword. That was another exclusive right of the nobility that the Lions would not violate. Standing as close as he was, Gennet was pretty sure he could see the tip of a scar poking out of the captain's collar, just where his shoulder met his neck. The corporal knew the rumors—that his commander was said to have a mass of such scars all over his body. He was even supposed to have once survived a one-hundred-and-twenty-lash flogging if the tales were to be trusted. Gennet wasn't sure he believed that; the captain looked like God forged him out of a piece of steel, but even so, men of reputation tended to gather exaggerated tales and legends around themselves.

"You have a report, Corporal?" the captain asked, startling Gennet out of his distracted thoughts. The corporal slapped his right hand to his chest in a fist and trusted his men were doing the same. He noticed the captain cocked an eyebrow. Gennet looked at Treff and saw that he was tugging the forelock. The corporal slapped his man's shoulder and raised his own eyebrows. A tugged forelock was the respect a low born or convict gave to a nobleman. Even a yeoman might be expected to make the gesture. Only a patrician, like a high-ranking guildsman or town alderman, was absolutely excused from the obeisance. It was not so with the White Lions. From the highest to the lowest, they saluted. Treff realized the mistake he was making and switched to the correct gesture. When he did, the captain returned the salute.

"Your report?" he demanded again.

"It's as you said to expect, Captain," Gennet explained. "The noble leader, an earl, and his knights lit out this morning, out the back of the castle. There's a dry wash out there runs away northwest. It used to be a creek, when the rains would come, but it's all dust now."

"How far did you follow it?"

"Just 'til we came upon a dried pond that's no more'n a bowl in the rock now. You could see where there used to be fish. Then there's another gully that switches back south and west, like the local guides told. I figure that's the one the prince and his knights are watching the other end of, back on the road."

The captain nodded. The company currently had five hundred infantry, but they were accompanied by a force of over a hundred knights on horseback. Those were Reach noblemen, the province's knights ahorse. They also currently included a Prince Farringdon, apparently a ruler in exile from some place in the Vec. Gennet didn't understand the whole of it, just that Farringdon was a prince and the duchess let him ride with her knights and nobles. There were other stories that went about the camp of another prince, one from Rhales or Denay, who'd tried to rape or murder the duchess, depending upon which tale you listened to. Gennet didn't know about any of that either, but he was fairly certain that had to be a different prince from the Farringdon fellow.

At any rate, when Captain Ash sent Corporal Gennet and his two men out to scout the flank of the castle and the village at dawn, he had also sent the knights ahorse back down the trail to watch out in case the local guides were right and the earl who'd captured Halling Pass Castle was going to make a run for it. A hundred or more knights should be more than enough to hold the twenty or so men-at-arms the invader earl was said to command.

"Must 'ave been a pretty little creek once," Treff said wistfully, his eyes straying north over his shoulder to the flank of the mountain that hid the secret waterway from view. Once, the slopes would have been dense with bushland forest, but now the trees were black spindles, leafless and dead. Water-starved by drought, the undergrowth had all burned away in a bushfire sometime in the last year, taking the leaves from the branches with it. And now the rains were looking like to fail again.

For another year, winter would not come.

The spring of the previous year had seen the dreadful Night of the Red Sky, when the Redlanders from the far west had used human sacrifice to stop the flow of the Murr River. That waterway was many leagues to the south of Halling Pass, but the magic of that night had spread across the whole land, it seemed, the Western Reach especially, along with the chaos that the battle had ignited. And the summer that followed had not ended. An autumn, a winter, a spring, and now another summer had all been rainlessly dry, hot, and wearisome. Folk prayed for rain and muttered that there was a curse on the land, but there was no consensus about who to blame for any curse. Some said it was because of Daven Marcus, the "Kingslayer King" in Denay, who had killed his own father for the throne, even though he still denied it had happened. Others blamed Mother Church, which had broken into factions, ostensibly supporting or opposing the contentious king or some other peer of the realm but really seeming more interested in fighting their own private war. Then there were those who only wanted to see the old order restored, no matter what kind of man sat on the throne in Denay. These blamed the rebellious nobles for the curse, shrilly condemning every man or woman of birth who did not bow the knee to Daven Marcus. And top of that list of supposed renegades was Duchess Amelia. Of course, there were still the brotherhoods of devilish, painted men ranging about the land as well. It was all irrelevant in Gennet's head. All he knew was that there was no rain, there had been no rain, and he had no idea how much longer folks could go on living if no rain came.

"That will be all," Captain Ash told them. "Take a rest until evening watch is called. Get yourselves some food and a drink."

"Yes, sir!"

All three men saluted crisply, and Gennet wanted to sneer at the other two's sudden enthusiasm for orders and discipline. The three turned to go, but the captain called Gennet back, letting the other militiamen leave without him.

"Trouble keeping order... Corporal Gennet... is it?"

"Yes, Captain," Gennet said, confirming his name, then thought about the rest of the question. "I mean, no! I mean, yes, Captain, my name's Gennet, but I've got no problem keeping order."

"No?" The captain cocked an eyebrow.

"They're straight dealers mostly, Captain. It's just that they're the kind that used to be convicts, you know."

"I do know. I am that kind myself."

Gennet swallowed involuntarily and did his best not to tremble suddenly. How had he gotten himself into this spot? He meant the captain no insult. Hells, if any man in the whole company respected Captain Ash, it was him. Gennet had been a mere halberdier, just another Claw in the line at the Battle of Red Sky. He had been there on the war wagons and gone tumbling when a Redlander beast-man, with bull's horns as broad across as a cartwheel, had used its brute strength to knock the wagon on its side. Gennet still remembered scrabbling about, looking for his lost weapon, when the lone figure of Captain Ash had charged along the line, leaping from wagon to wagon, throwing himself into the gap and fighting off the thundering bull-man, captain's longspear against wicked iron mace. Gennet knew he was only alive because the captain had held the gap long enough for the rest of the Lions to rally.

"I mean nothing by that, Captain," Gennet stammered, trying to not panic as he defended himself. "It's just that there's a type, there really is."

"And you are not that type, Corporal?"

"Me? Captain, no I..." Gennet stopped and thought. What he'd been about to say was not entirely true, and he earnestly wanted to tell the captain the truth. He owed his leader that much at least. "Fact is, Captain, yes, I am that type. I just never got caught. I won't confess to anything, but there's a bailiff or two around about who'd like to get me on a convict chain."

"Indeed? But you are not a transported man?" The captain seemed to have sincere interest in Gennet's story, and for some reason the corporal felt himself wanting to tell it.

"I came across the mountains a yeoman, Captain," he explained. "Free but poor. I couldn't go home, for reasons, and I heard free men could get work in the Reach. I did some laboring but couldn't find anyone to take my side and vouch me into a proper job. The riverfolk have the Dwelt all locked up for work, and merchants don't like men that they can't ask around about. I'm not afraid of hard work, but I was stymied. Then I heard 'bout the Lions and how they were made up of convicts but were taking more men since there was a war coming. I signed up and marched south with you to the Murr and Red Sky."

The captain nodded thoughtfully. Gennet wondered if he would remember him and how he saved his life. If he did, Captain Prentice did not say so. Instead, he asked, "Is that where you became a corporal?"

"I was made line first after the Red Sky, Captain," Gennet said and shook his head. "I made corporal after the Bronze Dragon ambush on the road to Griffith Pale."

"You've seen a lot of blood in service to the duchess and the Reach."

"I have, Captain, but I'm glad of it, I think. I never had a trade, and I was given to roughhousing. Even brawled a bit as a young man, but I've taken my licks for that one. I guess joining the Lions, I found out what I'm good for. I'll get the discipline into those under me, I swear it to you."

Captain Ash gave him a wry smile.

"Good man," he said approvingly. "In the meantime, get to the cook fires and see yourself fed."

Gennet saluted, and the captain returned it. Then the corporal marched away proudly.

CHAPTER 1

"I think this's got to be all the villagers, Captain, and then some," said the blunt-faced Sergeant Franken as they marched through the castle barbican to find a crowd of peasants crammed into the fortification's one bailey. There were so many that there hardly seemed to be space for Prentice and his lead cohort of a hundred militiamen to come in to take possession of the liberated castle. At the sight of armed men in steel plates, buff coats, and brigandines, the crowd shrank back warily.

Following orders they had already been given, the Claws of the White Lions company, halberdiers only this time, filed out in two lines on either side of the inner gate. The clash of their armor and weapons echoed off the walls and was answered by murmurs of fearful uncertainty from the unarmed press of low-born folk.

"We will have to get these people back to their homes," Prentice said quietly to his sergeant and was about to send his drummer Solomon to fetch the chirurgeons traveling with the company to tend any sick or wounded when a voice called from within the wary crowd.

"Is this it then? You gonn' slaughter us like they said?"

"Who was that?" Sergeant Franken demanded, his glare scouring the watching faces.

"That was me!" declared a tall, heavy-set man with hair like matted straw but wearing a clean, homespun tunic and leather bands around his wrists. Prentice watched as the big fellow pushed to the front of the fearful folk around him. The frank hostility in his expression was obvious.

"What's your problem—" Franken started to demand, but Prentice put his hand on his sergeant's shoulder. The two men were of a similar size, and armed and armored as he was, there was no fear that Franken would not win a confrontation. But that was not what Prentice wanted. These were people already beaten down and abused. No point making it worse.

"Who are you? Where are you from?" he demanded.

"Who's to say I'm not from right around here?" the man retorted.

"You have a Rhales accent," Prentice pointed out mildly.

"Alright, fair 'nough. I'm from Tollips Bridge, just south o' Rhales," he said meeting Prentice's eye. "Farmer Ben, they call me."

"And what are you doing up here in the pass, Farmer Ben?" Prentice had never heard of Tollips Bridge, but any mention of Rhales put him on his guard. It was Kingslayer Daven Marcus's original seat of power, after all.

"We fled 'cause the village was burning," Farmer Ben explained. "Me and me family, the wife and the littles. The village was burnin'. We aren't wayward or nothin'. We just wanted to get safe from all the fighting. Figured to get across the mountains, 'cause with the long summer, weren't no snow in the passes. And then we thought t' find a village and look for work. That's what most of us was doin' when the earl's men scooped us up and set us to fetch and carry here...that was like, weeks ago. We's all like that mostly, 'cept for the folk what was born here in the castle village itself."

Heads nodded eagerly behind Farmer Ben, with continued wary glances cast at the armed militiamen.

Refugees, Prentice thought. More mouths to feed than the village farms could support. Was that why the earl was so eager to quit the castle? Surely not. Even if the immediate land couldn't support them, as conqueror he would have been within his rights to just turn them out. He had no obligation to keep them around.

So, what was wrong?

"What is this talk of killing you all?" Prentice asked, his eyes scanning the cowering mass of humanity. What had the invader told these folk to make them afraid of their own liege's men?

"That Earl Yarmass and his bondsmen said you'd be killing us 'cause that's how the witches out of the west get their power. They kill small folk and drink their blood and turn into animals. They said the duchess is a witch, and that she's called lioness 'cause she changes shape and eats men alive. She's an army of painted men who can all change into animals, and they're ravaging the Reach from north to south, pillaging and slaughtering. That's what they said."

Earl Yarmass. At least Prentice had a name now for the invader who captured the castle. As to the rest of the peasant's story, he did not like what had been said about his liege.

"There are some evil men like that in the Reach, but they are the duchess' enemies," Prentice told the crowd. "They come from far in the west and we are her army for fighting them."

"You don't have to fear," Sergeant Franken declared indignantly, as if the peasant's uncertainties offended him. "Captain's done more to fight the Redlanders and the beast-men than any other man alive!" He paused and nodded to Prentice apologetically, apparently realizing he had spoken out of turn.

"Thank you, Sergeant," Prentice said quietly, returning his man's nod. Meanwhile, a tight conference had gathered around Farmer Ben and a tense argument was conducted in hushed tones. At last, another man, smaller than Farmer Ben, pointed to the white lion embroidered on the front of Prentice's brigandine armor.

"That lion? It's hers?" he asked.

"It is."

"And you're her captain? The one they call Ash?"

Prentice blinked in surprise. He had not expected anyone would recognize or have heard of him. If they thought Duchess Amelia was a witch, he could only imagine what rumors were attached to his name.

"I am. What have you heard?"

"My cousin says you do fight monsters and that you beat the king's champion in single combat."

Prentice looked down at the blade at his side, the heavy war-sword that he had accepted from the hand of Lord Carron Ironworth, yielded at the end of honorable combat.

"I did defeat Baron Ironworth," Prentice told them. "He was not at his best that day." And he died for it, slain at the treacherous hands of Prentice's own brother, a Knight of the Church.

Farmer Ben looked at the armed militiamen.

"So, which one is it?" he demanded belligerently. "You a monster or a monster killer? Or is you both? We all seen enough to know one can be the other. So, we need to know. There's enough of the work of witches of late. We'd sooner die than put our necks under another yoke like that."

Prentice doubted that many of the crowd would choose death before servitude, but he was sure Farmer Ben meant every word. Whatever had happened here, the refugee from Tollips Bridge would be dead before he let it happen again. Prentice found he admired the man's brass. With no weapon of his own, in the middle of an intimidated throng who looked like they would shrink from a hissing cat, Farmer Ben refused to be cowed.

"I am here to put a new garrison in this castle, and they will be ordered to hold it against every force not bound to the Duchess of the Western Reach. They will have a sworn duty to defend every loyal Reacherman—peasant, priest, or patrician. And the only liberty they will have will be to dig new wells and to search the high mountain valleys for any streams to redirect and bring water down here until the drought has passed."

Prentice fixed his eyes on the refugee spokesman and let the man search his own features in return. Every word he'd spoken was true.

"I heard she were a kindly ruler," someone else in the crowd said, "but she killed one of her own noblemen at a feast, that's what they say. Slit his throat right there at the table."

"That man was a traitor who conspired to murder her husband and was about to kill her as well," Prentice said carefully, recalling the traitor Sir Duggan.

In truth, it was not the duchess who had killed Sir Duggan, but she had been close enough to be splashed with his blood when it happened. The details were not what mattered now, only the spirit of the action. Prentice explained, "The Lioness is just and judges truly, but her justice is swift and steel hard. Cross her law and you will feel it fall upon you, but she is never cruel. There are executions, but never any torturing—no crows' cages hang from her walls."

Prentice saw several nod grimly at this declaration and it seemed good enough for Farmer Ben.

"If all that's true, there's somethin' you need to see."

He gestured for Prentice to follow him to a doorway that led to a cut-stone undercroft beneath one of the castle buildings. The crowd parted to make a way, and Prentice nodded to Franken to maintain control of the bailey while he took two Lions as escort.

"Some of us been here a fair long while," Farmer Ben explained as he suddenly stopped on the threshold. The anger in his expression was mixed now with grief. His eyes were moist. "Nearly a full season, if there were still seasons, and mostly it was like any other lord's fief in war, if you take my meaning."

"Go on," Prentice told him.

"I been a rogue afoot once, marched off to defend Lord Traste's forests against the bandit dukes years back. Maybe you heared of it?"

Prentice had not and he shook his head.

"Well, anyway, I know what it's like in war when men get their blood up. And men of rank, they don't ask—they take, and pity on you if it's somethin' you can't give up. That's how it was here. More than one bloke come into the castle with a pretty wife or daughter and there weren't much could be done if one of the earl's men took a fancy."

"He could'a stopped 'em!" someone else in the crowd growled with hateful venom in his voice, but when Prentice looked for the new speaker, everyone had their heads down. He did not blame them.

"Yeah well, when it was clear the earl weren't going to do nothin' to stop 'em," Farmer Ben went on, "most of us just put our heads down and tried not to see. Tried to keep our own womenfolk out of the way like."

Prentice suddenly realized he had not seen a single woman in the crowd around him. Had these peasants hidden them all away after Earl Yarmass's men fled in case the new force was as bad as the previous? Or were there even any women left? How brutal had the earl's forces been? Prentice felt his teeth clench as the thought of what might have been happening here made him shake with restrained fury. He had once cowered in a church as Redlander spearmen systematically butchered an entire village outside. That time he had been one of only a handful, hiding and frightened. Now he had an army at his back, and if something similar had happened here, his wrath would be terrible.

"The sacrist tried t'say somethin'," another man in the crowd asserted. The words drew Prentice out of his savage thoughts for a moment.

"A sacrist?"

"The castle's chaplain," said Farmer Ben. "Good man in the main. He preached a sermon about how adultery were wrong and the shame for it didn't just fall on the woman. That taking a woman you weren't married to was a sin."

"But that did not help?"

Farmer Ben shook his head in weary sadness. "Some of the knights took umbrage. They grabbed him and beat him with threshing flails. Then they threw him out of the castle. That was the last we seen or heard of him. Ain't no one said nothin' 'bout liberties after that."

Prentice could well imagine.

"And all that maybe we could've endured. Our womenfolk are strong in heart and only a dog turns on his girl just 'cause some nobleman took liberties. But then the witch came with her riders two nights ago."

"A witch and riders?" Surprise drained much of the rage out of Prentice's mind for a moment. "What do you mean a witch?"

"The lord o' the castle was dead when I got here. The earl and his men killed him and all the men-at-arms when they took the place over. The lady was still alive though, her and her daughter, and they were runnin' the castle still. And the earl's men, they weren't takin' no liberties with them ladies, least not bad like. Then the witch..."

He twitched his head at the dark open doorway.

"She's in there?" Prentice asked, cocking an eyebrow.

"Her handiwork. She's long gone, her and her hooded guards, but ain't no one here ever gonna forget the night she visited."

Prentice stepped into the shadowed portico and immediately knew what he was going to find. The smell of blood and filth that was too dry to rot quickly roiled around him like a fog. He swallowed bile and stepped forward slowly. As his eyes adjusted to the dimness, shadows began to resolve into solid objects. The undercroft had been a storeroom at some time but was empty now. Likely, there was simply not enough to store with the drought. In the empty spaces where barrels and sacks might have been, now there was only carnage.

"They tried to burn the place last night," Farmer Ben said from behind Prentice's shoulder. He was carrying a lit rush-light, and even by its meagre flame, the additional glow revealed almost more than Prentice could bear to see. Ben pointed to a scorched spot against one wall nearby. "Maybe they din't have enough fuel, or the stones was too hardy. Or maybe God just wouldn't let 'em cover the evidence. Someone has to see this, don't they? Someone somewhere's got to bring some justice for this."

Prentice turned and saw that Farmer Ben was weeping. He did not blame the man as he looked at the bodies and parts of bodies strewn about in the stone-walled space. Blood was smeared in ritualistic patterns and runic spells here and there. In the middle, as if in pride of place, were the brutalized bodies of the lady of the castle and her daughter, less mutilated, but no less ravaged than the rest.

"Did any survive?" Prentice asked.

"More than a few, ones that we hid once we knew what the witch was about. She only wanted women, but turned out she didn't want all. Just enough to make this temple to hell's demons."

"Your wife?"

Farmer Ben lowered his head and nodded, ashamed. "I found her afterwards and gave her a burial. It weren't proper, but..."

Prentice put his hand on the man's shoulders. The peasant refugee shook out great sobs of grief.

"Will you swear to the truth of this?"

"We never seen it 'til after. But we heard the screams, and we seen the men come out with the blood on them. Most of us smallfolk were hiding, but some of us kept watch and we seen 'em."

The fury that had abated within Prentice's heart washed free again, like a sudden ice storm, cold and ruthless as forged steel. It was a calm he often felt in the midst of battle, a rational certainty that brooked neither fear nor failure. His eyes searched the carnage one more time, as if to burn the image into his memory, but already his mind was racing with plans, orders that would have to be given and actions to be taken immediately.

Men would die for this abomination.

"Fetch two cloths, sheets or the like, to carry those two noblewomen's bodies," he commanded Farmer Ben, his voice like mountain ice. "Then bring them down the road after me."

"Where are you going?"

"To bring the wrath of God upon this Earl Yarmass and his men."

CHAPTER 2

A messenger was waiting for Prentice in the camp when he returned from the castle, saying that Earl Yarmass's fleeing knights had been captured without battle. Prentice ordered two more of the cohorts from the camp to follow as soon as they were ready while he led his first hundred directly down the road. A full cohort with polearms, swords, and ten gunners with matchlocks double marched to where the Reach knights were holding the captured earl's small troop. Ideally, Prentice should not have needed a single militiaman. However, while over a hundred Reach knights were sufficient to keep the invaders secure, he knew that what he was about to do would not sit well with many of the nobles on his own side, let alone his enemy. He wanted to make sure that if any objected, they lacked the power to stop him.

His enemy. That's what they were now.

He was the duchess's captain, but he was also doing this for himself. Prentice's wife was a former convict named Righteous, and when she had come over the mountains years before, her overseers had raped her so savagely they thought they'd killed her. From that day on she'd hidden herself as a young man amongst the other convicts until, at last, Prentice had puzzled out her secret and she had grown to feel safe enough to be a woman again. In his mind's eye, Prentice could see his wife, bloody and broken in that undercroft. He rarely thought about the men who had raped his Righteous; that was all before he met her. Now the reality of that past merged with this present, and the images of rapine slaughter filled his mind with such rage that he trembled to restrain himself. Every other minute he urged his men to hurry down the pass. This earl would not escape justice.

The column emerged around a rocky spur that separated one small valley from another and found the Reacher knights and their prisoners calmly waiting. Earl Yarmass's twenty men-at-arms were dismounted, as were many of their captors. The atmosphere was relaxed. Several men shared a drink or chatted lightly as squires held unmounted horses calmly off to one side.

"Captain Ash," called a knight with a limp and a hardwood walking cane when he saw the approaching soldiers. "You are well come, but reinforcements are most definitely not needed."

"Viscount Gullden," Prentice acknowledged the man, bowing as rank required. Gullden was the Knight Captain of the Reach. As Prentice commanded the duchess's men afoot, so the viscount commanded the knights ahorse—the bannermen sworn to her service. "You have captured them all?"

"Quite so, and cleanly too," the viscount said proudly with a smile and a nod. He gestured with his hand for Prentice to follow him toward the main crowd of waiting knights. "Turns out they were under the command of Earl Yarmass. Did you know that?"

"I have learned it."

"I wish I had. The man's my cousin, if you can believe it, on my mother's side. Once we laid eyes on each other, it was a simple matter to call truce and give them a chance to offer parole in exchange for quitting the field and relinquishing any plunder."

"They had already quit the castle, My Lord," Prentice said through gritted teeth. "They have no rights to plunder."

The fact that Gullden and Yarmass were cousins complicated matters, and a small inner voice counselled Prentice to be cautious. Wisdom said he should seek another course, but he could not bring himself to do it. The thought of his own wife, torn and beaten, turned his stomach with bile. Even if he could put his personal fury aside, there was Farmer Ben and the other men who'd had wives and daughters taken from them. And worse than all that, there were the brutalized women themselves; *they* deserved justice.

Lord Gullden ushered him past lesser knights to the inner crowd. Prince Farringdon was there—the young man with softly curling brown hair, a crooked nose that had been broken during a grim imprisonment, and a melancholy manner, who nonetheless smiled a greeting to Prentice. The furious captain did not return the smile, though he did nod. Prince Farringdon occupied a position in society almost as complicated as the captain's. As a foreigner, the Veckander prince had little real power in the Western Reach or the Grand Kingdom, but as a prince, his rank was far above that of any of the other nobles present. Because of their history on the battlefields of the Red Sky and after, Farringdon and Prentice shared a measure of respect that also did not fit the normal array of their ranks.

"My cousin, Lord Yarmass of White Trees," Visount Gullden introduced one of the prisoner knights, drawing Prentice's attention away from the prince. "And his son and heir, Sir Haravind."

Prentice could barely bring himself to look at them, but even in a glance, the two men coping with the day's heat in their plate and mail were obviously father and son. One was plainly the younger copy of the other. Glancing over his shoulder, Prentice waved up the corporal of the cohort.

"Do you not tug the forelock to your betters in the Western Reach?" a nasal voice demanded, and Prentice looked back to see Earl Yarmass glaring at him with undisguised contempt. "Armored or not, you are still a peasant, boy."

Controlling his fury by sheer force of will, Prentice refused to answer the condescending nobleman. The summoned corporal rushed forward and saluted, with all thirty of the cohort's swordsmen in column behind him. It was enough to give the gathered knights expressions of misgiving, Reacherman and invader both. The militiamen moved swiftly, and any uncertainty was quickly swamped by the shock of Prentice's next orders to his men.

"Arrest Earl Yarmass and every one of his men. They are the men of rank, armored, but without the longsword. Bind them under the duchess' peace."

Any knighted man of the Grand Kingdom carried the longsword as the symbol of his rank. No one who was not a noble was permitted to carry this specific weapon. When they yielded to Viscount Gullden, Yarmass's knights would have surrendered their own longswords, at least temporarily, as a sign of trust. So, amidst this polite gathering of noble warriors who were officially at war, with their bright heraldic colors and polished armors, the missing longsword was the quickest way to distinguish an enemy prisoner from an ally.

Confusion flashed through the crowd as the White Lions moved to detain the prisoners. Some were knights plainly indignant, while others were more uncertain. Prentice, the low-born man, had no right to take any noble as a prisoner; Captain Prentice Ash, commander of the Duchess Amelia's militia and her chosen counselor, had the favor of the highest authority in the land. What limits were there to what *he* could command?

"Cousin, what is this? Do you plot some treachery, or is it just the lapdog's doing?" Earl Yarmass demanded of Lord Gullden. He pulled his arm away from a militiaman who tried to grab it. "Unhand me, lout!"

Throughout the crowd, Prentice's men produced ropes to bind the hands of the prisoners, but in many instances, Reach knights moved to stop them. They looked to their knight captain to intervene. Viscount Gullden pulled Prentice to one side and spoke with him quietly but firmly.

"This is not how it is done, Captain Ash," he insisted. "The parole has been offered and accepted. It is shameful now to bind these men as prisoners."

"Parole has nothing to do with this," Prentice hissed back through gritted teeth. "These men are being bound for rape and slaughter. They're going to hang!"

That made the viscount recoil.

"Men of rank do not hang!" he declared with a loud voice. Discontented murmurs rushed through the crowd. Hanging was a low-born man's method of execution. Nobles, should they be sentenced to death, had the right to the swift cut of an axe or headsman's sword.

"Hang?" Earl Yarmass repeated loudly. "You'll let this low-born cur hang my men? We will fight to the death un-armed first."

"They won't fight alone nor be unarmed for long," Viscount Gullden added flatly.

Prentice looked back and forth between the two noble cousins. Gullden's expression was one of grim resolution, as of a man forced to an undesirable situation but willing to do his duty. Yarmass was smugger, apparently convinced he had trumped Prentice's attempt to arrest him. Prentice met the man's self-satisfied gaze and felt a nearly overwhelming urge to draw his sword and strike him down. His jaw clenched so tightly with the emotion that he could taste blood where he had bitten the inside of his cheek. He felt his hand on the hilt of his weapon, risky as such a gesture was in this tension, but try as he might he could not remove it. A gentle touch on his shoulder caught his attention and he started, turning to see Prince Farringdon there.

"Captain Ash, you know this is not how it is done," the prince urged gently. "What troubles you so that you would violate the laws of chivalry like this? You are not of rank, but you are wise in these matters."

"Chivalry?" Prentice turned on the prince and the young man shrank slightly from his glare. Women were dead, violated and defiled in their own flesh, and their husbands and fathers were left to wring their hands and grieve, all because of the laws of chivalry that let men of rank take. What was chivalry and glory worth if it protected men without honor? "They must answer for what they did. For every woman in that chamber. For what they did to Righteous."

"Righteous?" the prince repeated. "Lady Righteous, your wife? She is with the Duchess Amelia, Captain. What has she to do with this?"

Righteous? Prentice blinked as the truth of the prince's words sank in. Of course, she was not here and nothing that had happened in the undercroft had anything to do with her. At that moment the sound of marching feet began to echo off the hillsides about. In short order, the next two cohorts, two hundred more militiamen, armed and ready for battle, entered the tiny, sun-scorched valley.

And with them came the little band of peasant villagers carrying two sheets stained with filthy streaks of ruddy-black. As soon as he saw Farmer Ben at their head, Prentice stepped away from both prince and viscount and then turned to face the hostile crowd of nobles as a whole.

"You speak of chivalry?" he shouted at them, his voice echoing around the valleys. "Come, see now, and tell me what chivalry was at work in Halling Pass Castle while the earl's men dwelt there."

He marched toward the men with the bodies, waving them forward. The leading nobles followed behind him, confused. When the two groups converged, Prentice threw back the edges of the cloths to reveal their contents.

"The lady of the castle and her daughter," he announced. "Let any man who doubts my actions come and see my reasons."

"What is this, cousin?" Viscount Gullden asked, his eyes fixed on the grisly sight of the two murdered women.

"I don't know! Perhaps the peasants raped and murdered these women after we left the castle," was Earl Yarmass's reply, but his tone sounded unconvincing, like a badly rehearsed lie. "I don't even know who these women are."

"These were noble women," breathed Prince Farringdon. "The clothes tell the tale." Though the women's garments were little more than tatters now, the remaining bits were too fine to have been peasant clothing.

"And will you truly claim these were only murdered this morning?" Prentice demanded. "Are these bodies only hours slain? Or do they look like what they are—days dead?"

"I don't answer to convicts," Yarmass spat back. He turned to Viscount Gullden. "We did not do this, cousin. You must believe me. These curs obviously plot some revenge and have gone so far as to murder..."

Gullden held up his hand and turned to his cousin. "I want to believe you, My Lord Earl, truly I do. But this? This calls for trial. Whatever else happens, the murder of two ladies of rank like this must be answered in trial."

"There's more than two," Farmer Ben insisted boldly, his forlorn face set with grim determination. "We already shown the captain. More than half the women of the castle, defiled and murdered like this and worse."

"More?" Gullden repeated and he looked at the earl with disbelief.

"They lie," was all Yarmass could manage by way of answer.

"Captain Prentice is right," said Prince Farringdon, his voice as full of horror as the knight captain's. "A crime like this must have a trial."

"Then I choose trial by combat!" declared Sir Haravind suddenly. Somehow free of his bonds, Earl Yarmass's son had contrived to get close to one of the Reach knights, and he drew the man's longsword before he knew what was happening. With surprising strength and speed, Sir Haravind shoved the disarmed man backward and surged at the gathered peasants and nobles. The cloths holding the slain women were dropped as their carriers fled. Sir Haravind swung wildly as he charged, and Prince Farringdon was knocked from his feet as the sword slashed at his head. Viscount Gullden was shouldered aside, and Haravind pushed for his preferred target.

"I might hang, but I'll send you into death ahead of me!" he shouted as he charged at Prentice. "You'll be my herald in the afterlife. The slayer of Ironworth will serve me in hell!"

Prentice had no idea what strange theology the young knight thought he was referencing, but it did not really matter. The captain backed away from Haravind, hands on his sheathed blade and hoping to make enough of a gap between them to give him time to draw the weapon. He need not have worried. In spite of Haravind's declaration, this was not truly trial by combat. He was an armed prisoner assaulting the captain of the White Lions. There was no way Prentice's men were going to stand by for that. Four halberdiers from the nearest line rushed forward, and Haravind found himself cut off from his intended target and surrounded. He tried to use his purloined longsword to drive through the hafted weapons, but the number was too much for him. Even as he pushed one aside, another axe blade hammered against the backplate of his armor. The edge had no chance to get through the steel, squealing as it struck a spark, but the force of the blow staggered the man, and before he could recover, a third of the halberdiers used his weapon's back spike to hook behind one knee. Sir Haravind was sent sprawling in the parched grass and his purloined sword was lost to him. By the time he pushed himself up to his knees, the halberdiers had him pinned with their weapons. A pair of Lion's Roar militiamen who carried the matchlock firearms rushed to stand in front of the fallen knight, their smoking weapons pointed straight at his chest.

"Good steel armor can turn a blade or hammer," Prentice said, approaching the fallen knight, meeting his sneering gaze without fear. "Even iron shot might not penetrate if fired from too great a distance. But let me assure you, sir, that at this range the Lion's Roar will punch straight through you and your breastplate like a nail through a thin board."

As Prentice got a little closer, Sir Haravind spat at him, though the gobbet fell short.

"Coward. I knew the stories about you weren't true," he snarled hatefully.

"The contempt of a rapist?" Prentice answered with a sneer of his own. "How will I endure the shame?" His men smiled at that. Then Prentice leaned in even closer, and a sudden flash of inspiration brought a question to his lips unbidden. "Which victim was yours?"

Sir Haravind's expression transformed to one of vile amusement.

"All of them," he said, as if it were a boast. Then he repeated it as a shout. "All of them. The witch said she'd never seen vitality like mine. I blooded them all."

"That's a confession," Prentice shouted at the gathered men. From Viscount Gullden to the other Reacher knights, it was clear that they were disgusted by what they were learning of the Earl's occupation of Halling Pass. Sir Haravind's declaration was the final seal that made supporting the earl's men impossible. There would be no more talk of parole or chivalry now. "What more is there to do but hang this man?"

"No!" Earl Yarmass cried out, his formerly arrogant tones now dissolved in anguish. "He's my only son. My heir. We all took part in the ritual, each to some degree. He was not the only one."

"What ritual?" Prentice asked, approaching the earl who was now also held in custody by two of his militiamen.

"The witch promised to make him potent."

"Potent?"

"He's sired twice, and both times the babe was stillborn," the earl explained, words babbling from his mouth. "Stillborn and the birth took the mother, too, each time. It's a curse on him, on us, on our line. The witch said she could take the death from him. Make it so he could get an heir."

Prentice felt the bile twist his gut once more, tasted it in the back of his throat. This man had killed women, seen them raped to death, because some occultist promised him a grandson. "You think this should gain him mercy? He boasts of the crime."

"He's a fool lad, hiding his fear behind bravado," the earl pleaded. "And he only did it because I insisted. The crime is mine. Punish me in his stead. I'll confess and hang for it if you'll only spare his life." Yarmass looked past Prentice to his cousin, begging with his eyes for this one mercy.

"My Lord?" Prentice asked the knight captain over his shoulder. Viscount Gullden shook his head, too confused to speak.

"You would give everything for an heir, would you?" Prentice turned back, asking the restrained earl. "Even your life is not so precious to you as that?"

Yarmass nodded.

"And you're sure your son has sired no child?"

"None yet that has lived."

Prentice looked over the gathered faces, all watching.

"Alright," he said. "You in his place. You will hang for his confession."

The earl shuddered in his captors' grips and hung his head. Then he looked up at his son.

"I bequeath you my name, son," he called out. "Our line rests now in your hands." He bowed his head once more and awaited his fate.

"Find the nearest tree with a sturdy branch and hang him," Prentice commanded.

"And this one?" asked one of the four halberdiers still restraining Sir Haravind. "D'we release him?"

"Yes, and the rest of them as well," Prentice said in a loud voice. "After you take them and geld every last one of them."

A hiss of collective discomfort escaped the gathered knights, but no one moved to stop the militiamen as the prisoners were drawn away to be castrated. Haravind tried to fight and was swiftly knocked senseless. Earl Yarmass also tried to fight and screamed about treachery, but he was unable to break his guards' grip, and he was dragged away to a nearby stand of trees.

Prentice made his way over to where Prince Farringdon was sitting up with assistance from a squire. There was a trickle of blood down the side of his face.

"Caught me with the flat of the blade, I'd wager," he said as Prentice crouched to examine the wound. "I was damned lucky."

"Yes, you were."

"A dark business, Captain Ash," Viscount Gullden said quietly as he approached the two men on the ground. "Dark and grim indeed."

"Justice often is," Prentice said over his shoulder. He did not look at the viscount, but his eyes met the prince's gaze, and he was surprised. The young royal had long been a quiet sort, having survived horrors of his own in the occupation of his home city by the Redlanders. Prentice had at times wondered if the man might have been perpetually cowed by the experience, made childlike by the terrors he had faced. Now though, instead of a weak-hearted expression, Prentice saw his own resolve reflected in the prince's eyes. The foreign royal approved of Prentice's judgement.

"I'm not sure everyone will see this as justice," Gullden continued. Prentice stood and faced the knight captain.

"If any voice a doubt, let them go to that undercroft and see what remains there. Then let them wonder if justice was done."

The viscount did not look very comforted by Prentice's words, but he made no further objections. The squire helped Prince Farringdon to his feet.

"The question that remains unresolved, though, is who this witch was," the prince said thoughtfully. "And where is she now?"

"Some madwoman who fancies herself a power in spiritual places?" Lord Gullden offered.

"We can hope so," said Prentice.

"You would hope for such a thing?"

"A madwoman is better than the alternative."

"Truly?" Gullden's tone was full of disbelief.

"Was it like Aubrey?" asked Farringdon, and again Prentice was impressed by the man's sense of his own thoughts. He looked at the prince and nodded somberly.

"What could be worse than what you have told already?" Gullden went on.

"My Lord Viscount," said Prentice, "it could be a serpent-woman, a Redlander priestess with true power, like the ones who make beast-men and who summoned the red sky. If that is who she is, then that means they are further into the Reach than we ever imagined."

The three men stood silently with that unnerving thought between them for a long moment. Then Prentice looked up at the bright blue sky.

"Damn this drought," he muttered and left to command his men back to the castle. Their task was not finished yet. Things needed to be set in order, and he needed a drink to wash the taste of bile out of his mouth.

CHAPTER 3

"**M**ust be this is the hottest church I've ever been in."
Amelia only just caught her lady-in-waiting whisper the peevish comment beside her. It was likely that no one else around them overheard it, but the duchess still bestowed her companion with a stern look. Lady Righteous noticed the unspoken rebuke and ducked her head politely.

You're not wrong, My Lady, Amelia thought, and involuntarily she looked up at the vaulted roof high above them. Normally, she imagined, the nave and transept of Griffith Cathedral would be a cool space, preserved from even the direst summer heat by the height of the vault and the thick stone walls. Today, though, the entire building was filled to the brim with bodies, warming the air with their presence. From the door forward, every pew on both sides of the aisle was filled, first with yeoman townsfolk and then with patricians and the respected of the town. Finally, as the transept blended into the chancel, every available space was occupied by men in armor, the sworn banner knights and men-at-arms of Sir Sebastian, soon to be acclaimed Lord Sebastian, Earl of the Griffith Pale. As she looked up at the shadows among the vaulting beams, Amelia would not have been surprised to see the air shimmer with heat as it would under the midday sun.

Being duchess, Amelia was standing in the chancel with her closest ladies beside her as ahead at the altar, senior churchman High Sacrist Quellion intoned prayers of blessing upon the investiture of the new earl. The previous Earl of the Griffith Pale, Lord Derryman, had been killed during then-Prince Daven Marcus's crusade into the west a few years ago. The earl's older son died of a flux soon after, and the seat had been held vacant ever since—that was, until just recently, when Lord Derryman's nephew, a knight named Sebastian, had returned from the war. Pledged in service to a count named Lark-Stross after his term as a squire, Sir Sebastian had been fighting for that lord's faction, mostly in the southern lands of Rose Carabost and the town of Vanhoe. After several seasons, the young nobleman had negotiated the conclusion of his duty and now had returned to his family's homeland with a significant force of personal bannermen, over one hundred knights ahorse in all. The duchess had come south to Griffith for the new earl's investiture, as well as some other business on behalf of her lands.

Amelia tried to focus on the High Sacrist's words. She was the ranking noble in this assembly and her dignity was on display. What good would it be for her to keep Righteous from whispering like a gossip if the duchess herself was looking about like a gormless gawker? Flanked by two ladies-in-waiting, she felt nonetheless almost alone, isolated from most of those around her. Almost none of the nearby men-at-arms in their finely polished armor and bright heraldic colors were known to her by name. The main body of Reach knights was north with Captain Prentice Ash, hopefully retaking Halling Pass Castle from invaders. These men and their ladies, those that had ladies with them, were newcomers to the west. Of course, once Earl Sebastian pledged his service to her as the final part of the ceremony, all his bannermen would be her liegemen as well, owing fealty to her through him. It was not exactly an unwelcome development. The continuing wars had cost her land many of its nobles and knights. New blood was needed. However, the fact that these men would only serve her through their loyalty to the new earl meant that the service they gave could be easily revoked if Sebastian gave the order. Ever since her husband's death just before the Redlander's first campaign, Amelia had been laboring to win the direct loyalty of her nobles. She would have to begin all over again to win this fresh cadre of knights from the rest of the Grand Kingdom. That was why she had come south to Griffith, when by rights she could have easily insisted that Sir Sebastian come to Dweltford for the investiture. She had meant it as a show of respect to the new earl and thereby his men as well, but as a consequence, it meant she was without the support of a number of her usual advisors, which she did not enjoy.

Prentice, of course, was the main wise counsel on which she relied and had been relying almost since the day she first met him. Although she knew the injustice he had suffered during his years as a convict, Amelia thanked God often that this loyal and capable warrior had come into her service. A newer counselor of a different sort, Lady Dalflitch, fallen countess and former lover of the Kingslayer King, was also not in Griffith, having remained behind to supervise the civil matters of the duchess's holdings. As skilled in administration as Prentice was in warfare, Dalflitch was another loyal retainer for whom the duchess thanked God. By far the most beautiful woman Amelia had ever known, Dalflitch's guile was her actual defining trait, and woe betide any who underestimated her.

Even denied these two sage voices, Amelia had to admit that she was not truly alone, for she did have her other two closest ladies-in-waiting with her—Lady Righteous and Lady Spindle, now standing one either side of her. Despite their titles, the pair were not truly ladies of rank. They held their "ladyships" by dint of service to the duchess alone. If she dismissed them, they would return to being mere members of the yeomanry. Each woman was dressed, as the duchess was, in finely embroidered linen with only the lightest of cotton underdresses; anything else would have been unbearable in the dire summer heat. The dresses were the work of Lady Spindle, a slender, brown-haired, dark-eyed, bird of a woman as skilled with needle and thread as any Duchess Amelia had ever known. If there were such a thing as a seamstress's guild, Spindle would surely be one of their guild-mistresses. The other, Lady Righteous, was strawberry blonde and blue eyed, but just as lean. She was Captain Ash's beloved wife.

For all her craft, though, it was not for her sewing that Spindle was most renowned, nor was Righteous best known as Prentice Ash's wife. Neither woman was the great beauty that Lady Dalflitch was, but they possessed an air of mystery that drew all eyes, for both wore masks of embroidered lace that covered one side of their faces. The masks concealed ugly scars that were the legacy of their true pasts, for while they were now honorable ladies-in-waiting, first and foremost they were ex-convicts and knife fighters of talented savagery. They were the duchess's companions and bodyguards both. Captain Ash called them the Lace Fangs, and any of the duchess's enemies who took them lightly would learn the folly of their mistake before they died. Lady Righteous often joked that while she preferred to fight wearing men's trousers or hose, a dress made it so much easier to hide some steel on her body. Amelia knew that whenever they were with her, even formally dressed as they currently were, Spindle and Righteous always had some "cutlery" close to hand.

The High Sacrist ceased his intoning a moment and looked across to his left where Sir Sebastian was awaiting his part in the ritual. The young nobleman was straight-backed and clean of face, with long, dark hair tied back in the knightly style, and a strong jaw. He was wearing a coat of mail that seemed strangely old-fashioned for a modern knight and, to Amelia's eye, surely brutally heavy in the heat. Over that, he wore a sleeveless tabard in white with three green chevrons on the chest, the basic heraldry of the Griffith Pale. Each of the chevrons had three silver rings upon them, a sign of the family's wealth and their service to the wealth of the kingdom. Finally, the tabard was edged in alternating blue and white diagonals as a mark of sworn fealty to the Western Reach and, ultimately, the duchess herself.

As she studied the fine garment, Amelia remembered that when Earl Derryman had fought the prince for her, years ago and far away to the west, he had also been wearing the simpler and outdated mail coat rather than the typical knight's plate harness. Perhaps the armor style was some form of family tradition. She noted that Sir Sebastian was carrying the same conical form of helmet that Derryman had worn that day. A moment of sadness flickered in her mind as she remembered the enormous nobleman ploughing into the fray to buy her time to escape. More than once, noble men had made such sacrifice on her behalf, and she remembered each one. She prayed she would never forget them and never dishonor their sacrifices.

Sir Sebastian knelt to receive a blessing from the High Sacrist, his helmet on the ground in front of him next to a square of crimson cloth sitting folded upon the ground. Now the churchman turned to Amelia and invited her, as duchess, to also come before him. She schooled her face to a smile, banishing her somber memories to the back of her mind. It would not do to be scowling at a new retainer as he swore his loyalty. She moved out from her pew and stood beside the nobleman on his knees. When he rose, he would be Earl Sebastian and he would never have to kneel to anyone but his liege and the royal family again, except in church. Even kings knelt before God, assuming God was still in the Church. When the religious raised arms against each other and against the throne, where did God stand, exactly? It was a question to vex the soul, and it certainly troubled Duchess Amelia's.

"Your Grace," the High Sacrist said to her, "you stand in the place of the Duke of the Western Reach. Sir Sebastian has humbled himself before God and Church. Do you accept his obeisance also?"

"I do, Excellency," Amelia answered, forcing herself to speak loudly enough for her voice to echo all the way down the nave. Although he was considered to be roughly the social equal of a baron, the High Sacrist, like all churchmen, was officially separate from the social order, and so was not addressed as "My Lord."

"Sir Tarant, bring the sword," the High Sacrist commanded, and one of Sir Sebastian's men, his closest lieutenant by all accounts, came forward holding a longsword by its scabbard. Sir Tarant wore modern white-steel harness, the plates and mail clanking as he moved up beside his leader and held the weapon hilt forward. Sir Sebastian grasped the handle and drew the blade, then he placed it tip down on the folded cloth on the flagstones in front of him. A piece of ritual with a practical purpose, the red kerchief protected the tip of the blade from being damaged on the masonry as Sir Sebastian placed one armored hand upon the pommel and one upon the crossguard, bowing his head as if in prayer. The High Sacrist placed one of his hands on the knight's gauntlet on the pommel and the other on Sebastian's head.

"Sebastian of Griffith and the Griffith Pale, do you pledge now your heart and blade to the throne of the Grand Kingdom and to the rightful king who will sit thereupon?"

"I do," Sebastian pronounced with a deep, strong voice that echoed in the hot, still air. Amelia noted that the High Sacrist did not name a specific king, certainly not Daven Marcus, the Kingslayer. Current political realities and civil strife meant the traditional oaths and pledges needed to be adjusted slightly.

"Do you pledge to defend Mother Church and the one true faith, her doctrines and laws, against all enemies and even the sin in your own heart?"

"I do."

"And do you pledge your loyalty to the Western Reach and to its liege, swearing to take up your sword to defend its lands and its peoples, to enforce its justice and preserve its traditions?"

"I do."

Amelia was not sure, but preserving traditions was not a phrase she remembered from other pledges she had witnessed.

"Duchess Amelia," the High Sacrist continued, "you stand in the place of the duchy and its seat. Do you receive the earl's pledge?"

Amelia turned a scowl upon the churchman. She did not "stand in the place" of the duchy. She sat its seat herself as duchess in her own right. The High Sacrist's repeating of the words implied that she was only a placeholder, ruling the duchy of the Western Reach because there was currently no duke. It was a common enough occurrence for church leaders to use ceremonies and sermons to make social or political comments, as the earlier wording about the "rightful king" proved, so it was likely the churchman knew exactly what he was saying. He was delivering a public criticism of the duchess's marital status. Despite herself, Amelia was incensed. Not so long ago some members of the Church had decried her as a wayward wife, supporting Daven Marcus's spurious claim that he had married her. King Chrostmer had put paid to that nonsense, which led in no small part to the conflict between king and prince that ended with the son stabbing his father to death in front of the courts of Denay and Rhales both.

My land is beset by war, sorcery and drought, churchman, Amelia thought as she momentarily stared daggers at the High Sacrist. *With which spare half a moment did you want me to find a worthy suitor and bat my eyes at him long enough to have him woo me?*

The High Sacrist smiled at her with beatific indifference to her disapproving look, and she snapped her head back to regard the waiting earl-to-be. Delaying the ritual would only play into the High Sacrist's hands. She would speak with him later.

"As Duchess, I accept Sir Sebastian's pledge of loyalty," she said loudly, knowing there was an edge in her voice. A thought occurred to her, and she went on. "Rise, Earl Sebastian. Rise, My Lord, and take up your sword. Wield it for justice and peace in all *my* lands and the Grand Kingdom, in the name of the throne, Mother Church, and the Western Reach."

Those were the correct words of the ritual, and it was not exactly wrong that Amelia would speak them, but as the pledge was being said in the church, as opposed to a great hall, it had been expected that the High Sacrist would say them. Sebastian looked at the High Sacrist, and Amelia also turned to the cleric, returning his serene smile, though she was sure her eyes showed her calculation. It had been one thing for him to imply a rebuke with his ritual words, but to correct her now would look petty, and might *genuinely* exceed his authority. The decorum of the Grand Kingdom's highest society was a ruthless but ever-shifting set of rules.

I've played this game with kings and princes, you pompous snot, Amelia thought, keeping her smile polite. *Try me at your peril.*

With no other polite course of action available to him, the High Sacrist nodded to Sebastian, though his serene smile had faded. The newly invested nobleman stood to his feet, lifting his sword and holding it in both hands.

"Long live *Earl* Sebastian," his man Sir Tarant shouted. "Long live the earl!"

Even with the heaviness of the hot air, the church vault rang with cheering.

Chapter 4

"**P**oor beggars never stood a chance by the looks of it," muttered Markas behind his captain's shoulder. Prentice nodded without looking back at him. They were standing amidst the wreckage of a roadside encampment. Dozens of bodies had been slaughtered and left where they fell, all their worldly goods broken and scattered between them. Flies and other insects crawled over the slain, and Prentice was careful not to get too close lest he disturb them. The pests were annoying enough as it was.

"More refugees like Farmer Ben's lot, I'd say," Markas added. That assessment seemed a good one to Prentice's eye. The dead bodies were a mix of ages and sexes, a few of them children. They wore yeoman's garb, mostly rough homespun, some pieces of leather or linen. Prentice decided to risk the flies and squatted down to study a particular group of corpses, hoping to divine any clues about their killers.

"Looks like at least three groups together, by the campfires," Markas went on. Prentice rubbed his chin thoughtfully.

"Franken was getting me a body count," he told his standard bearer. "Go see if he has that number yet."

Markas saluted and marched off in the midmorning heat. Prentice was not really in a hurry for the count; he already had a fair idea of how many were dead. What he mainly wanted was a moment of quiet. He could have simply ordered Markas to stop speaking, but he understood the militiaman's need to talk.

Brutality like this was hard to absorb. Some men went silent in the face of it, as if it could be shut out of their minds if they just refused to acknowledge it. Others talked, often pointlessly. Prentice did not begrudge a man either response; he just needed time to look and think.

First Halling Pass Castle and now this.

The nearest bodies were clustered around the remains of a campfire, as Markas had observed. Several were merely slumped over where they had been sitting, while others had fallen from their feet. Those might have been standing when the attack started or else had leaped to their feet in the early phases but made no distance to flee or defend themselves. He did a quick assessment of each corpse in turn, nine in all. They had puncture wounds, and two had the remains of broken iron arrowheads in their flesh. The ambushers had struck with bows and taken down nine individuals around this one fire in quick order. The earth under the bodies was stained to rust, the seemingly small wounds having bled out swiftly.

"Got the count for you, Captain," Franken said as he approached. Despite the heat, he was still wearing his blue brigandine, armor, and symbol of his office. The pauldrons on his shoulders were steel, polished so brightly that they flashed like silver in the sunlight. The left pauldron was embossed with a lion's claw, symbol of Franken's specialty in the militia's order of battle. It was the same as any corporal or sergeant's armor, except for one distinction—a polished bronze disc that was pinned to the front of the embossed piece of armor. The disc was engraved with a symbol of a dragon with its claws wrapped around a long cylinder; it was called a Cannon-Taker's Medallion, and it commemorated the courage of a small group who had captured the Kingslayer's Bronze Dragon cannons during the retreat to Griffith. Not even a dozen men in the Lions had such a medallion. Franken carried a fistful of sticks with him, and Prentice knew each piece of wood would have ten marks on it to keep track of the body count.

"My reckoning comes to forty-seven low folk, including the young'uns," the sergeant reported, "and one sacrist. Do you think it was Redlanders?"

"I do not know, Sergeant," Prentice said, standing up and looking about. His first cohort was milling about, sweating in the sun. The order had been given that metal armor could be left in the baggage, and a good number had even shed their buffcoats, wearing no more than their shirts and trousers. It did not leave them ready for battle, but it was a necessary allowance for a long march in the heat of the drought. Otherwise, Prentice knew he would be leaving his men collapsed on the roadside from thirst and heat exhaustion, as dead as these corpses. "You say there was a sacrist?"

"Fresh-faced one, this way."

Franken led Prentice to where a man in a clerical robe was lying half under a broken wooden box. "Man" was a generous description. As Franken had said, the churchman would have been lucky to have been sixteen years old—still a novice, most likely.

"A bitter business, Captain Ash," Prentice heard Prince Farringdon say, and he looked up to see the royal, dismounted and walking his horse carefully amidst the bodies. The injury to the side of his head had received the services of a talented healer it seemed. Already, the wound was halfway healed to a scar.

"Indeed, Highness."

"Have you any notion who might have done this? Some of the knights seem to think it would probably have been bandits."

"Do they?" Prentice was still trying to think, but the prince was not someone he could send away on a simple errand. He scanned the ambush site once more. "Any word from the men set to look for tracks?"

"Not yet, Captain," Franken replied. "Did you want me to chase 'em up?"

"Go do that," Prentice commanded the man.

The sergeant left.

"You do not think it was bandits, do you, Captain?" asked the prince, and Prentice, suppressing a sigh, which would be rude to give in a royal's presence, turned at last to face Farringdon.

"I am not certain yet what I think, Highness. What I do know is that these folk were slain by bowshot, swiftly, accurately, and either near sundown or in the darkness."

"Truly? How do you know what hour they were attacked?" asked the prince.

"The fires. They were stopped for the night and had taken the time to make campfires and settle around them."

"Perhaps they stopped earlier in the day."

"And set fires in this weather?" Prentice let his stern expression show what he thought of that proposition. "Far more likely they left it as late as they could and set them only for cooking purposes. Everyone was gathered to eat."

"So, taken late in the day? That makes sense as you explain it, but how do you determine the rest?"

"The only wounds are arrow hits."

"But there are no arrows," the prince countered.

"There are some arrowheads, though, or pieces of them. It seems likely these ambushers took their arrows with them."

"Why?"

"To hide their identity, I suppose, if the fletchings were distinctive."

"So, bandits then?"

Prentice shrugged.

He thought about how many had died and how swiftly. If the majority of nine folk around one fire had been killed before they even rose, that meant a large number of shots. Accurate shots, too, since a man with a single arrow in him might easily enough make a run for it if he was only hit in the arm or some other meaty part. These shots were all to organs like kidneys or else to necks and faces, judging by the injuries. And then there was the fact that so much of the refugees' impedimenta was left behind. There was little sign that the attackers had made any serious effort to loot their victims. It reminded Prentice of the original Redlander army that had attacked the Western Reach, led by the dreaded Horned Man. That force had taken no loot to make a point. Prentice wondered what that meant for this band of refugees. Prince Farringdon had similar thoughts, it seemed.

"If not bandits, could they be Redlanders?" he asked.

"We have not ever seen the invaders use bows," Prentice responded, and that was the source of his disquiet. This attack had many of the hallmarks of Redlander action—the suddenness of the ambush and the brutality, the lack of looting. Yet, in all their many depredations, the invaders had never shown a preference for bows, or indeed any form of missile weapons. They were exclusively hand-to-hand combatants, at least as far as the White Lions knew.

Sergeant Franken returned with a pair of men, rovers who rode with the company to act as scouts. Dressed in buckskins, open-necked linen shirts, and straw hats on their heads, the lean, wiry men were the best scouts in the Reach. Prentice would have liked a company of them, but more than a handful would draw the ire of the noble men-at-arms riding with him. Military horsemanship was supposed to be a knight's prerogative. In the eastern Grand Kingdom proper, men of the rovers' station were forbidden to even mount a horse in the presence of a ranked noble.

"What have you found?" Prentice asked them.

"They were all on horseback," one of the two said through the length of grass he was chewing.

"All?" Prince Farringdon asked.

"That's what I said, in'it?"

"You found where they tethered their horses?" asked Prentice. He wanted any source of information he could get. The rover looked at his fellow and then they both shook their heads.

"They never did," he said laconically.

"What do you mean?"

"I mean they never tethered 'em. Far as we can tell they never got off their horses except at the end, after the deed was done."

"They shot from horseback?" Prentice asked in near disbelief. The rover nodded solemnly and shrugged.

"Seems to be."

Prentice looked the man straight in the eyes for a moment and then nodded to show that he accepted the men's word. He dismissed them with a wave and Franken led them away.

"Some men hunt from horseback," said the prince, but Prentice hardly heard him. There were crossbows that could be shot with one hand for hunting small game, and such weapons could be used from a saddle. Of course, knights fought with sword or lance and shield from horseback. However, none of these was like shooting a bow, especially something like a warbow that could kill a man or woman with a single shaft. That kind of weapon required two hands, which meant the rider had to control their mount with their legs alone. It was a sophisticated art that took determination to learn and years to master. Prentice had only read about such skills in histories and stories of travel to far-off lands. Until now all the Redlander forces they had faced had been on foot or, rarely, riding in chariots. The prospect that the invaders might now be able to field horsemen different but equal to Grand Kingdom knights was unnerving, to say the least.

"Whoever these attackers were, they were not hunting," Prentice said, shaking his head. "We will have to hunt them."

Prince Farringdon nodded, but Prentice was not talking to him or even really paying him any attention. An assault like this, whether it was banditry, invaders, or something else, demanded swift action. This kind of murder and affray so close to Dweltford could not be tolerated. They would have to be hunted down, and since they were mounted, it meant they would need horsemen to pursue them. That meant he had to speak with the knight captain. The thought made him scowl as he wiped a finger across his forehead and flicked away the sweat.

CHAPTER 5

"He's got a set o' brass balls on him, I'll give him that," Spindle said as she sat in her place beside the duchess at the high table in the Griffith Castle Great Hall. With its tall westerly windows shuttered against the afternoon sun's heat, the cool hall was beginning to warm quickly now that its myriad candles and lanterns were lit for the night's feast. The warmth at the end of the long day was doing little for the mood of the duchess's lady-in-waiting, it seemed. Lady Spindle smiled formally enough beneath her mask, nodding like any other polite courtier at other guests who caught her eye, but her muttered words revealed her true feelings. "Imagine givin' her grace lip like that—and in a *church*."

"Impertinence is the way a lady says it, Spindle," Duchess Amelia corrected her companion. The duchess also had a fixed smile in place, but she was in little mood to connect with other guests. Fair-haired, with unremarkable eyes and soft features, Amelia knew no one was gazing upon her for her beauty. She was a curiosity to them, no more, and the guests were watching her for the novelty of her presence. So, she kept her eyes down and studied her fork or goblet alternately, then took a long moment to adjust the ducal signet ring on her finger, even though it fit perfectly. It had once been sized for her husband's finger, but it had long since been adjusted to fit hers.

"Bloody cheek is what I call it," Righteous added from Spindle's other side.

Amelia sighed wearily.

"It's done now," she said, looking to put the matter aside, at least for the evening. "If there is a need, I will seek redress with the High Sacrist at another time. For now, we must enjoy Earl Sebastian's feast. And remember, this company will include some of the guild master merchants that I need to meet with in coming days, so we will project the correct dignified air."

"Happy, pretty, and approachable, but not trollops," Spindle said, summarizing the duchess's pre-feast instructions. The Lace Fangs exchanged serious glances and nodded, then looked out at the crowd with fixed, pleasant expressions. Amelia nearly burst out laughing. At least it made her smile much more genuine for a moment.

"Arise for Earl Sebastian," called a herald from the far end of the great hall, and everyone stood from their seats as the new lord entered, accompanied by the stern-faced High Sacrist Quellion. The High Sacrist was wearing full clerical garb—a dark robe, ribbons of fine embroidery on the hems, and a large cross hanging from a chain around his neck. His clothing was fine, but Amelia noticed that there was not so much extra decoration as many religious of his rank favored. He seemed to wear no jewelry other than his ring of office, and even his cross was not made of gold.

Stern with himself as well as others, Amelia thought. She took that as a good sign. The man might condemn her marital status, but likely he wasn't doing so just for political advantage. *At least he despises me honestly!*

She raised her sleeve to cover the smile that that wry thought put on her face as the earl and churchman approached the high end of the hall. Everyone at the high table stood now as well, but as duchess, Amelia kept her seat. There was no protocol requiring her to stand. Her rank demanded that she stood for no one less than a prince or a king in her own lands. She had originally planned to stand regardless, as a gesture of respect, but seeing Quellion at Earl Sebastian's side, she changed her mind. She wanted to remind the High Sacrist that she was no placeholder noble. Spindle and Righteous stood beside her, and Amelia used the moment of shifting and movement to fix her expression with dignity once more. She then bestowed her most politic smile upon the approaching earl.

Sebastian proceeded down the hall like a man marching between an honor guard. He had put off his mail coat and longsword in favor of cotton hose and a simple grey doublet, but he still wore his family tabard over that, belted with his swordbelt. As he walked the length of the aisle between tables, he smiled sincerely to guests on either side, nodding occasionally to one or another in a gesture of respect. He was clearly happy, but there was no smugness to his manner. To Amelia's eye he was every bit the young and vigorous noble leader her domain needed. But then, her retainer Sir Liam had seemed the same, and so had Prince Daven Marcus when he first arrived in her lands.

Let Sebastian be as he appears, she thought. *We need no more venal aristocrats here in the Reach.*

When the earl reached the high table, he looked along the length, making eye contact with each guest there in turn. Many he spared no more than a moment. In truth, it would have been impolite to do otherwise in many instances. Even as earl, he should not be making eyes at another man's wife, for instance. When his gaze reached the duchess, he met her eyes with no change in his polite, welcoming demeanor, and he returned her civil smile with a nod that seemed sincere. Then he scanned the rest of the table. As he did so, Amelia shifted her gaze to the High Sacrist and noticed that when Quellion looked at her, his expression was much less benevolent. The duchess bestowed a gracious nod upon the clergyman and then returned her attention to the earl, who was now making his way around the table to his seat at her left. He was lord of the feast, and she was his guest of honor. A steward pulled out the lord's chair and he stepped into his place.

"Duchess Amelia, High Sacrist Quellion," the earl began his welcome, "gathered worthies and noblest friends, welcome to this hall, and thank you for helping me celebrate this great day in my life."

Applause filled the hall and Earl Sebastian received it with aplomb. Then he raised his hands for quiet.

"Now, friends, let us eat. This is a meager season, and the land labors to produce a bounty. Let us not waste this spare moment of celebration with an excess of speeches."

Guests nodded appreciatively and everyone settled to their places. Stewards emerged from doorways with food for the tables. Instead of the typical sides of roasted meats, platters of diverse vegetables, pies and cakes, this night's tables were laid with stews and simple breads. Even soup was rare, and noticeably absent were the river fish that would in other years have been a staple of Dweltside cuisine. The earl was not wrong when he said the land labored to produce a bounty.

And in the north, my dear Dweltford would struggle to provide even this little abundance, Amelia thought, and for a moment she felt a flash of genuine pity for Earl Sebastian. This was a great day for him, possibly the greatest of his life. He had just acceded to one of the highest ranks in the Grand Kingdom. There were now no more than a few score of men or women more important than he. It was a moment to celebrate, but the drought choked the festivity. Yet, despite the lack, the hall was filled with warm conversation, and next to her, Amelia felt that the earl kept a good humor.

Plates were served to the high table, and Amelia delicately tore pieces of bread from a small loaf and dipped them in a gamey-tasting stew that seemed flavoured with some kind of wine and wild herbs. She was enjoying the fare when she noticed that next to her the earl and the high sacrist were engaged in a whispered debate. The words were beyond her to make out until she heard the earl say, "Tush, Excellency. Surely it can wait for a more somber hour."

Amelia did her best to seem that she was not listening, but her ears strained curiously to make out the High Sacrist's response. She need not have bothered, as after a single whispered reply to the earl, the clergyman addressed her directly.

"Your Grace, I was just discussing with the young earl a matter of protocol," Quellion said in a voice loud enough to carry to most of the high table. "Did you truly think it fitting to speak words out of turn in the house of Our Lord? He thinks it was likely only an error, but I wonder. And even if it was so, is that really a justification?"

Amelia tipped her head without looking at the High Sacrist, as if she was hearing his voice from a great distance. Her lips curled ever so gently in the merest shadow of a smile. Did the man really mean to give her a lesson here in the middle of the earl's celebratory feast?

"Do you not think it right for an earl's liege to bestow his title upon him, Excellency?" she asked, studiously focusing her eyes on the feasters in front of her, as if the High Sacrist was no more than one distraction amid many, barely worthy of her attention.

"An earl has his title from the throne in Denay, Your Grace, not from the duchy," Quellion corrected her.

That's twice you've told me off, sacrist, she thought. *I might have to start keeping count.*

"You speak the truth of King's Law, Excellency," Amelia conceded. "But as you rightly observed yourself today, there is no true king seated upon the throne in Denay. Until the time that vacancy is resolved, the duchy must speak to the law."

"Yet the duchy has its own vacancy in this regard," said Quellion.

"Not so, Excellency," Amelia answered immediately, ready for the churchman to pursue this line of conversation. She reached gently for her goblet. "I invite you to come to Dweltford and see for yourself. The ducal seat is not the least bit unoccupied. Perhaps only newly arrived in the Reach, you are not aware of this?"

"When God seeks to punish the land, He gives it women and children for rulers," Quellion intoned. "So it is written in the scriptures."

Amelia paused with the goblet halfway to her lips and turned a look of scarcely restrained fury upon the churchman. Quellion was leaning onto the table so that he might look around Earl Sebastian directly. His face was earnest and stern, and it looked to the duchess that he was searching hers to see if his criticism had hit its mark. She made no effort to hide her feelings from him.

"Are there fewer invaders in other parts of the Grand Kingdom, Sacrist?" she demanded through gritted teeth. "Less warfare and strife? Is the drought less severe?"

"In some places there is yet rain."

"And these places are more holy?"

"They are places where the guidance of Mother Church is not flouted," Quellion insisted. "The righteous traditions are maintained."

"Which part of Mother Church?" Amelia shot back. "Word is that the Church flouts its *own* guidance nowadays. Even the ecclesiarchy cannot agree which righteous traditions should be most honored. Unity certainly falls by the wayside."

The high sacrist recoiled as if slapped by the duchess's critical words, and even Earl Sebastian cocked an eyebrow uncertainly.

Too bad, Amelia thought, recognizing that she had risked going too far with her comments but feeling no remorse. *If you don't want to be slapped, do not provoke the Lioness.*

"You think to judge Mother Church?" Quellion demanded in an indignant whisper. "You, a *woman*, think to judge?"

"Did Deborah not judge Israel when God could find no sound man for the task?" Amelia retorted, barely keeping herself from sneering. "I am sure *that* is written in the scriptures, too."

"You exceed yourself!"

"No worse than you, Sacrist."

"Gentles, please, this is supposed to be a celebration," Earl Sebastian intervened earnestly. He looked from clergyman to duchess, and Amelia was touched by the genuine pain in his expression. She nodded graciously.

"Of course, My Lord," she answered and turned back to her goblet with a resumed smile. Sipping demurely, she waited to see if the High Sacrist would let the matter rest, if he even could. Finally, it seemed that he was willing to accept Sebastian's lead, and the next thing Amelia heard was the earl calling for someone else.

"This is supposed to be a revel," he shouted over the entire assembly. "Bluebird, where are you? We need entertainment."

CHAPTER 6

One of the tables furthest from the dais suddenly exploded in an enormous row of scattering tableware and ladies' cries of alarm. Amelia looked down the aisle to see a man with trimmed grey hair who was dressed in a motley of every shade of blue that could be imagined by man or woman. As he tried to rise from between two ladies at the table either side of him, no matter how the man turned or twisted, one part of his attire or another seemed to catch upon something—a cup, a plate, a fork, even once on a lady's jewel. He apologized profusely while trying to detach one woman's bracelet from the hem of his tabard-like cape, but as soon as he did, the sudden gesture of freeing it sent a silver spoon skittering across the table, causing a fresh shout of alarm. Every attempt to improve the chaotic situation only seemed to result in something worse, and the man in the center simply begged everyone's pardon all the more. While the fracas raised chaos though, it was increasingly received with greater good humor as it was clear the poor fool was always the worse recipient of each next misfortune.

"Is this an entertainment, Earl?" the duchess asked, curious but uncertain of the accident-prone man's role in the evening.

"It shall be, Your Grace, if he can ever arrive," Sebastian said with a nod and knowing smile. Then he turned to call down the hall again at the continuing disruption. "Good Bluebird, master tumbler, can we expect you soon, do you think?"

"Coming, My Lord," the fumbling man shouted back as he tried to step out from his place only to stumble over his own spot on the bench and fall back against the table with a rattle of cups and plates. There was a fresh happy cry from the guests near him, and soon laughter was spreading throughout the hall at his antics.

"We are keeping the duchess waiting, Bluebird," Sebastian called. The tumbler stopped suddenly still, one arm poised outstretched only a hand's breadth from the female guest to his left.

"Waiting? Oh no! That will not do! Not do! Not for the duchess!" The man snapped his arm back beside himself and turned at attention to the high end of the hall. "Fear not, My Lord. Her Grace shall wait no longer. The bluebird shall fly."

With that, the man swiftly ascended his place upon the bench and then onto the tabletop. He turned to face the high table and raised his arms wide, so that the blue motley of his sleeves spread like ill-made wings of some fantastical bird. He then began to sprint along the table, fresh laughter and cries trailing behind him as he came on. Every movement seemed as clumsy as before, but Amelia could see the man never seemed to step anywhere but safely upon the table boards. Although plates, cups and cutlery all rattled at his passing, not a single one was kicked away or even went underfoot. It was a masterful performance—undignified but violating no specific guest's dignity. Amelia shared the other guests' growing amusement. When he reached the end of his table, Bluebird leapt from that one to the next, and the man raced between the next rows of seated diners. Then he was in the air, casting himself from the table end nearest the high table and collapsing to roll across the flagstones like a runaway bundle of blue rags, before popping up straight and executing a perfect bow. Next to Amelia, Spindle clapped her hands in delight, and she was not the only one at the high table, male or female, to do so.

"Forgive me, My Lord," he declared. "I was entangled in the charms of two very fine ladies."

"Do not ask my forgiveness, Bluebird," Earl Sebastian chided, "ask Her Grace." The earl directed the performer's attention to the duchess.

"My Lord?" Bluebird declared, seemingly aghast. "I cannot discuss the charms of other ladies with a duchess. She might think me a letch!"

"I am sure that a man of your age and dignity has nothing but the purest intentions," Amelia said readily. Bluebird raised his eyebrows, as if surprised that the duchess would be so ready to engage in playful banter, then flopped forward in an exaggerated copy of a courtier's bow.

"Truly it is so, Your Grace," he said as he rose up again and half turned to the guests behind him, giving them a pantomime version of a cunning glance.

"Got her fooled, I think," he said as if delivering an aside to the audience. Many of the guests laughed out loud, and Amelia smiled readily.

"An entertainment indeed, My Lord," she said to the earl, and he returned her smile.

"Merely the prelude, Your Grace," Sebastian said and turned to Bluebird once again. The entertainer was capering back and forth in front of the high table.

"Enough, Bluebird," the earl commanded. "Your tumbling is superb and your wit swift, but you know that's not why I hired you."

"Truly, My Lord?" Bluebird asked. "Is there more to my talents than that? I never realized I was so gifted a man."

"Poetry, man."

"Oh yes, poetry. That was the word you used when you paid me my fee."

"He's a true jester," Spindle whispered appreciatively.

"He's funny enough," said Righteous, and Amelia thought she was being unfair. The man was quite clever, and if he was a poet into the bargain, then he surely was gifted.

"You may begin, Bluebird," the earl commanded. The tumbler poet nodded happily and then straightened himself to his full height. Over the space of several breaths, the man underwent a subtle but impressive transformation. All folly and mockery left his expression, his mannerisms, and in their place he stood with a simple dignity, one that even his outlandish clothing seemed not to detract from. With the stance of an orator, he reached out one hand and began to recite.

"Gentles, pray attend to my verse, humble in tribute, to the *Earl Returned from the East.*"

The Earl Returned from the East, it turned out, was an ode to Sebastian, composed to celebrate his accession. It was not an uncommon thing for a nobleman to do, to commission poetry to his own glory, especially in a commemorative context like this. As she listened, though, Amelia was impressed with the solemnity and restraint in each stanza. The poem praised the earl and described his feats as a knight, but none of them were overblown or made to seem excessively dramatic. His victories were realistic, and his failings were mentioned as the parts of a man that he must work to overcome. Of course, the earl was described as successful in each humble endeavor, but the implicit humility was so unusual in Grand Kingdom nobility that Amelia knew everyone must surely have noticed it. It reminded her of Captain Ash and his own dignified resolve. The thought caused her to look to Lady Righteous for a moment, and she wondered at how she must miss her husband. When the poem was finished, there was a pause of hushed awe and then the hall rang with applause. Amelia joined in.

"Was that worth the fee, My Lord?" Bluebird asked pleasantly once the clapping had died down. Earl Sebastian nodded benignly.

"I should think so," he said. "I fear, though, that you may have given me a better report than I deserve. I know I asked you for a commemoration, but this would be a reputation hard to live up to."

Humbler still, Amelia thought, and she studied the earl a moment. He was seeming more and more like the kind of noble her lands needed.

"Oh, my most sincerest apologies, My Lord," Bluebird declared, and he resumed his playful demeanor from before. He turned a full circle to scan his entire audience. "Perhaps a doggerel then to lighten the mood and bring us all back to the merely festive."

"That's a good idea, Master Wordsmith," the earl agreed, and many of the audience smiled and nodded as well.

"Something lighter and more suited to fooling. I call this one *The Gull and Golden Horns.*"

Bluebird launched into a comic verse, and Amelia quickly realized that the "gull" to which the title referred was not a seagull as she had imagined, but a fool, a village idiot who was easily "gulled" by everyone he met. Each stanza told how with every foolish decision, the gull rose accidentally higher in the world, becoming a knight and then a noble's champion. The noble's land was eventually beset by a wild beast with an elk's antlers made of gold. The gull swore to bring back its head and set off on the quest with his faithful, mangy dog.

"He means Liam," Amelia said quietly as she recognized the true story behind the mythic imagery. The poem was the story of her disloyal retainer, transformed into a fey tale. As she listened, she began to wonder which other parts of the poem connected to the story of Liam's ambitions and betrayal. At the very least, she was quite happy to hear him immortalized as a fool who rose in spite of his ineptitudes. It was not an especially accurate characterization, but it was as good as he deserved.

"And thus, with the beast not trapped in the stream that was no more than ankle deep," Bluebird pronounced from his next stanza, and folk tittered as the gull's trap for the beast turned out to be useless.

"The Brook was more than ankle deep," Amelia said more loudly than she meant to. "It was banked with the dead and crimson by that day's end."

Lady Spindle heard her, and Duchess Amelia was surprised when Lady Righteous explained to her companion.

"He's talking about the Battle of the Brook," she said with a scowl. "It's a play about Baron Liam and that means..."

Bluebird had gone on to describe how the gull had fallen in the water and could not get up, splashing like a child in a bath. The golden horned beast was about to kill him when his mangy pet dog leaped into the water and bit the creature's head off. The sudden savagery in the poet's description caused more than one lady guest to gasp in horror, but Amelia had to bite her cheek to keep from grimacing.

"My captain is not a mangy dog!" she said almost at normal speaking volume. No one but her closest ladies heard her, or so it seemed, but she wasn't sure if she was glad about that.

"He's insulting Captain Ash," Spindle agreed. "Calling him mangy."

"Well, I see him without his shirt at nights," said Righteous. "He's got himself some scars, no mistake."

Amelia and Spindle looked at her, astonished at her apparent equanimity. Righteous shrugged.

"It's the truth. 'Course that don't mean I'm not going to slit this blue tit's throat for his bloody *impertinence*. That's the word you said to use, isn't it, Your Grace?"

Amelia nearly burst out laughing and perhaps would have if she had not been sure that Righteous meant every word. She looked askance at her and shook her head subtly.

"It might be what we say, My Lady, but not what we do."

"As you say, Your Grace."

Amelia accepted Righteous's response, though she wasn't sure she believed it. The poem was entering its final stanzas as the gull foolishly took the beast's golden horns and placed them on his helmet, an unmistakable reference to Baron Liam.

Then, in his wounded state, the fool fell asleep, wearing the helmet. When he awoke, he found the beast's lingering magic had caused the horns to bond directly to his head. Mistaking him for the beast returned to life, his mangy dog leaped upon him and killed him, as it had the original beast. Many of the guests found that twist uproariously funny, as the presumptuous gull finally got his comeuppance. The poem ended with the dog running back to the nobleman's home where he was taken in by the lady of the manor and allowed to sleep in her bed until the lord came home that night and turned him out.

"Oh, now she's got to stripe his neck with crimson for that," Spindle said. "Your Grace, he's just insulted you *and* the captain. And Righteous too, being as she's his wife."

Amelia found she almost agreed. With his final words, this poet from the east had implied that she slept with Captain Ash, with her retainer. This was not the implicit rebuke that High Sacrist Quellion's words in church had been, but it still intimated scandal, nonetheless. Was she to be insulted at every turn by these men from across the Azure Mountains? The duchess turned to look at Earl Sebastian to see if there was any sign that he understood these subtle gibes being fired at her. The new earl was smiling as he applauded Bluebird, but it seemed like an honest and earnest pleasure, without the smugness a politicking courtier would usually project.

"Did that suit better, My Lord?" Bluebird asked.

"Much more festive, Bluebird," Sebastian said, "though I suspect you hid a lesson for us in there as well."

"How so, My Lord?"

Here we go, Amelia thought, and she steeled herself for what new censure would be sent obliquely her way. But Earl Sebastian surprised her.

"The gull is a fool, yet he rises," said Sebastian. "He rises and he succeeds. Yet in the end, his foolishness lays him low, and his greatest victory comes by the lowliest of creatures. Someone in this hall has also recently risen in society. I am newly made an earl today, and while I would not disdain any one of my retainers by comparing them to a mangy animal, nonetheless, I depend on even the lowliest of my people for my success. We are all bound together in this land and its trials. We must be ready to sacrifice, to look to our rank and our obligations, and be never too eager to claim glory. We all rise and fall by God's will, and we must accept our place under that will."

"Well said, My Lord," Quellion intoned with a sage nod.

Bluebird opened his arms wide and lifted his eyebrows ridiculously in pantomime surprise. "By God, My Lord, I had no idea there was so much wisdom to be found in my happy verse. Your insight exceeds mine, and I wrote the silly thing."

The hall was filled with guffaws, and Bluebird bowed and capered in every direction. Watching the skilled jester, Amelia did not realize that Sebastian had turned to speak with her.

"I'm sorry, My Lord?" she said.

"I asked, Your Grace, what you thought of the doggerel, or indeed of my commemorative before it?" Sebastian said.

Amelia blinked, trying to compose her thoughts. She had been so ready for a nasty piece of verbal dueling, the kind of social combat that was the favorite pastime of Grand Kingdom nobility, that when Sebastian instead turned the situation into a lesson in humility, she was at a loss for words. Speaking too quickly in order to fill in the silence, the best she could reach for was, "I did not much care for the mangy dog."

Earl Sebastian interpreted her words as an attempt at humour, and he laughed readily, joined by the nearby guests who heard Amelia's words.

"No indeed," he agreed with her, chuckling. "I should not like to find one in my bed either. Thankfully, 'tis only a poem."

Bluebird bowed and withdrew, fading back into the crowd of guests, anonymous despite his distinctive garb. The earl let the dinner continue, occasionally speaking with Amelia but mostly conversing with the High Sacrist on his other side. For her part, the duchess settled into her thoughts and picked at her food as she pondered the implications of the afternoon's ritual and the evening's festivities. One thing was certain to her, though—this Earl Sebastian was a different man to any other young peer she had encountered in her time as Duchess of the Western Reach.

CHAPTER 7

"I mpudent blighter!" Knight Captain Gullden declared as Prentice approached. The nobleman was leaning on his walking stick and wiping his brow with a cloth. Still competent in the saddle, the viscount's many injuries made simple walking much more of a burden.

"My Lord?" Prentice asked, bowing his head.

"Some penny-prophet under the trees over there, playing the wise hermit out here in the middle of nowhere."

The knight captain pointed to a small stand of ghost gums clustered under the ridge of the hill that separated the knight's column from the main body of the militia. The tree leaves were brown, but it seemed deep roots were keeping the plants from dying outright. It was the kind of place a hermit might pick to act the mystic. As he looked, though, Prentice could not make out anyone in the sparse shade beneath.

"Oh, the beggar's made himself scarce," Gullden said as he looked. "Was there only a moment ago. Probably knew better than to stay about after what he said."

"Someone offended you, My Lord?"

Prentice knew his request was unlikely to be well received as it was. His odds would be worse if some yeoman or churchman had just put the viscount's back up. Gullden scoffed at Prentice's question.

"Beggar priest, you know the type. All wild eyes and holes in his cassock. Put out his hand and offered a prophecy in exchange for a benefaction. That's what he called it—a 'benefaction.' Typical grasping cleric."

"The Church does not approve of selling consecrations," Prentice said, parroting the official line that was increasingly disregarded as the ecclesiastical class broke into warring factions. As a formerly condemned heretic, it was always safer for him to make his faithfulness clear. "Of course, itinerant clergy are permitted to beg for their bread, My Lord."

"If only he'd wanted bread," Gullden retorted. "Threadbare fellow rubs his tonsure and puts his hand out, offering a prophecy. Then he proceeds to tell me that I'll fall and die to a serpent."

"My Lord?"

The viscount's simple words caught Prentice's attention. Both he and Duchess Amelia had seen visions of a giant serpent in their dreams in past years—the image of a terrible beast that represented the Redlanders and their fiendish shapeshifting magicks. Typically, Prentice would put no more stock in a roadside prophecy than Lord Gullden seemed to, but with the horrors of witchcraft at Halling Pass Castle and now these slain refugees, a divination of serpents might need more consideration, at least as far as Prentice was concerned.

"I mean, honestly, I *am* Knight Captain of the Reach," Viscount Gullden continued dismissively. "I fight the Redlanders, which includes, of course, their foul serpent-women. What kind of guess is it that I might face one of the sorceresses? I nearly demanded my guilder back, just to teach him a lesson. Damned penny-prophets. Drought can't grow a decent harvest of anything, but these holy ticks sprout all over like weeds."

"I understand your frustration, My Lord," Prentice conceded. "I might set some men to find him, if you do not object."

"If you wish to. Like as not, he's got himself a bolt hole around here somewhere." Viscount Gullden looked about again, then shook his head ruefully. He blinked and looked at

Prentice directly. "Was there something you wanted from me, Captain?"

Prentice drew in a breath to steel himself.

"I have the word of the rovers concerning the slain," he began. The viscount blinked and looked toward the separating hill as if he just remembered that a caravan of slaughtered yeoman had been discovered on the other side. Prentice fought to keep from rolling his eyes. It was why their forces had stopped in the first place, after all.

"Not right, that," said Gullden finally, shaking his head. "Drought's the cause. When food gets scarce, thieves get bolder and nastier. It's common enough in lean times."

Prentice nodded as if he agreed. "I am not convinced they were mere bandits, My Lord."

"No?" Gullden's brow knotted skeptically. "How say you?"

"They were all on horseback, it seems," Prentice answered. The nobleman's expression instantly darkened.

"You do not think to accuse men of rank, I trust?"

"No, My Lord," Prentice said readily, inwardly cursing the man's reflexive pride. "Not unless they were more men from over the mountains like the ones in the castle."

He made a particular point of not naming Earl Yarmass or his son specifically. That did not make much difference to the viscount, it seemed.

"Is it not enough for you that one small group forgot their birth and were seduced away to wickedness? Must you look to lay the blame for every evil at the feet of the well-born?"

"With the highest of respect, My Lord, I do no such thing." Prentice felt an old wariness rise inside himself, the harshly learned self-protection of a convict. He had to fight the instinct to tug his forelock and simply walk away from an angry noble. Never argue with a drunkard or a fool, as the old saying went. If the knight captain was determined to be offended, it would be easier to let the matter go. Prentice was no longer an exiled convict on the chain, however. He was captain of the duchess's militia, and his duty to her demanded he be more resolute.

"These riders who attacked were almost certainly not knights, nor other Kingdom men-at-arms, My Lord," he said firmly but politely. "They used bows from horseback to kill their victims."

"Odd," said the viscount, and Prentice was relieved the man at least had enough integrity to look beyond his emotions and see the mystery.

"I think it might have been the invaders, Redlanders," Prentice explained.

The viscount drew back and frowned at the idea.

"They neither ride nor use bows, Prentice," he chided, using unusual familiarity. "You know this."

"I know that we have never seen them do so, My Lord, but five years ago we also knew there was nothing in the west but endless grasses—certainly not a nation of pagan marauders beyond a shallow salt sea. I am hesitant to say for sure what I do or do not know of Redlanders."

Viscount Gullden scowled, but it was softened into an expression that showed he recognized Prentice's point.

"I am skeptical, Captain, but you make a fair argument. What will you do?"

What will I *do?* Prentice thought. *What are* we *going to do?*

"My plan, My Lord, is to detach a small part of our force to track these bushwhackers to wherever they are laired and deliver the duchess' justice to every one of them. These men are riders, so we will need to send riders to catch them."

"You mean to dispatch your rovers then, I assume," said Gullden, his tone intimating something more than a question.

"I have only a handful of such riders at my command," Prentice answered, eyes narrowing. "The ambushers were easily a large company, more than a dozen, and skilled at horse combat, wherever they come from. It will take more than two or three trackers to capture them."

"I thought your Lions were trained and equipped to fight men on horseback."

Prentice's eyes narrowed in near contempt. It was well known that many nobles resented the way the White Lions were trained to be effective opponents to knights on horseback. However, that did not mean he thought high-born men-at-arms had no more function in the duchess's forces. Especially in a case like this where mounted arms were needed to bring enemy riders to heel.

"You know a task like this one needs a mounted force, My Lord. As knight captain, that is *your* purview—to bring the duchess' justice to lawbreakers and her enemies."

Prentice realized it was a risk to remind the viscount of his duty. Indeed, it might even be taken as an insult, and the nobleman was clearly in a mood to be uncooperative. This was exactly the kind of confrontation Prentice wanted to avoid, but he found himself here anyway. Viscount Gullden's expression turned harshly grim once more.

"Are you always this unyielding in your execution of the duchess' justice?" he asked bitterly. "I wonder that you don't hope to find knights at the end of this hunt to set men of rank against one another yet again. It seems that is a kind of justice you favor."

"I have thousands of convicts under my command, My Lord Knight Captain. They march, fight, and die at my command, often brutally. Did you wish to ask some of them if they feel I am too one-sided in my execution of the duchess' justice?"

The two men faced each other in the bright sunlight, sweat beading under their armor, but the coldness between them was like the depths of winter nights. Prentice had begun this conversation hoping not to offend the viscount. Now, it was all he could do to contain his fury. He did his best to maintain the correct air of respect, but internally he trembled with the effort. Gullden held Prentice's gaze for a long moment, then his own dark expression became more shamefaced, and he rubbed his bearded chin as he looked away.

"Prentice, you know I understand why you did what you did," he said. There was no need for him to explain what he was referring to; both men knew well. "It was a grim business all around and truth to tell...well, I don't see that any other form of trial would have turned out better for those depraved men. But..."

"But what, My Lord?" Prentice almost demanded, swallowing gall.

"But...many of the knights ahorse are not at peace with your actions," Gullden told him. "It is said that you exceeded yourself."

"They were rapists," Prentice replied, his voice harsh. "They were all lucky not to hang."

"Many do not see it that way, and they say so. There has been talk of paying you a late-night visit with drawn steel, 'in the 'part-light', as it were."

They would regret it if they tried, Prentice thought.

"Steel in the 'part-light'" was an expression that meant an ambush in the night, with no more light to see by than that cast by stars and the glittering band of the Rampart in the sky. Prentice had been through more than his fair share of such combats.

"Are you saying, My Lord," Prentice asked, "that because of these grumbles against me around the campfire, you will not order any knights to assist in hunting these butchers down?"

"I am saying, Captain, that even if I did order it, I do not think they would obey."

"Not one of them would see it as a duty to the Reach?" Astonishment cut through Prentice's growing wrath for a moment. Would the knights of the Reach really let murderous raiders range free in the land just because of what he had ordered done in Halling Pass? He might have believed it of Rhales nobles, or even the Denay court now that Daven Marcus sat the throne, but Prentice had grown to expect better of Reacher-men.

"Some might be willing to go," Gullden conceded apologetically. "But they would not, I think, wish to endure the ire of their fellows. You are condemned by not a few."

"They are sworn to preserve the duchy's peace and protection."

Gullden nodded. Prentice waited to see if he would say anything more, but the knight captain merely stood remorsefully silent. A crow landed, cawing loudly, in the branches of the nearby trees, and a flock of smaller birds took wing out of the shade to flee the predator.

"You truly will just let this stand?" Prentice asked at last. "You are knight captain. They must be made to obey."

The viscount shook his head sadly and looked away.

"Prentice, I have decided to take the knights ahorse directly south to Griffith to escort the duchess home from the new earl's investiture."

"My Lord?" Prentice asked, surprised by the sudden change of subject.

"With the bad blood between the militia and nobility," Gullden explained, "and the complexity of the current situation, I think it is the best course of action."

"My Lord, there are good folk massacred in the heart of the Reach," Prentice objected, his earlier anger now giving way to sheer disbelief. "Their bodies rot not a hundred paces from us. The duchess' peace calls out for justice from the blood-stained earth beneath their corpses."

"And I say the duchess' peace is not served but further disrupted by our two forces remaining together."

"Then hunt the marauders by yourselves," Prentice insisted unwisely, his self-control stretched nearly to its limit. "The militia will return to Dweltford."

"The militia..." Viscount Gullden almost shouted, setting off the crow's call once more, and his sword hand strayed to the hilt of his longsword for a moment, as if by reflex. Prentice took a half step backward, suddenly on guard, but the viscount retained his composure and his hand dropped from the weapon's pommel. "The militia is well disposed to handle a problem of banditry and the peace of the Reach."

The sudden possibility of violence quieted Prentice's fury, and he regarded the knight captain with renewed but wary calm. Viscount Gullden was no coward. Prentice had seen the man throw himself fearlessly into combat on more than one occasion. He had become knight captain through such acts of courage. Nonetheless, it seemed he lacked the will to face the disapproval of his peers. Prentice found his respect for the man diminishing, softening like wax in the heat. However, the viscount was still his liege lady's knight captain and thus was entitled to respect.

"When will your division of the company be departing, My Lord?" he asked with a controlled tone.

"An hour at most, I think," said Gullden. "We can cross a goodly distance riding this afternoon. We'll likely be able to make that village with the new-dug wells before sundown. We'll water our mounts there, refresh our canteens for the next leg of the ride."

"Go with God, My Lord," Prentice told him, and he saluted.

Gullden looked surprised but not offended. The viscount nodded and then hoofed away with his walking stick. Prentice bowed his head, closing his eyes and rubbing at the bridge of his nose. He wanted to curse, to draw his sword and find something to fight, to rage against the ridiculous injustice of his world and society. But there was no point and no enemy here to fight, not with a blade at least. Instead, there was the grinding duty of delivering what justice he could in the small increments that were possible, like the slow boring of hard boards, and waiting for the moments when enemies showed themselves plainly and he could hack them down with a sword.

He looked up and for a moment thought he caught movement in the shadows under the trees. Viscount Gullden's penny-prophet perhaps? Prentice considered trying to find the man, to ask him about his divination. Perhaps the churchman was a true seer and might give useful insight to go along with his more generic pronouncements. Perhaps not.

Feeling bitter, Prentice turned on his heel and went looking for Sergeant Franken. He would have to set the Lions to grave digging, to put the dead in the earth. It was too dry to burn the bodies, which would have been faster. A loose ember from a pyre could easily turn into a grassfire that would sweep the parched land for leagues, threatening any nearby farms or villages. He would also have to order his rovers to track the horse-riding archers before the trail went cold. He would command them to stay hidden if and when they caught up to the marauders and just watch and report back once they knew something useful. It would be a perilous duty, but Prentice knew he needed to march the militia back to Dweltford and reequip for a proper expedition to stop these mysterious horsemen. He did not want to lose their trail in the meantime. Knight Captain Gullden was not wrong in one sense—the White Lions *were* charged with keeping the duchess's peace. It would be a more difficult task for men on foot than riders, but regardless, the Lions would have to hunt these horsemen out and bring them to justice. Noblemen might feel divided in their duty between the honor of their birth and the duchess's. Prentice did not. He would see these murderers brought to justice and then he would turn his men to hunt the Halling Pass witch and any more of her cultists.

The Reach would have the duchess's justice, no matter who disapproved. Prentice would see to that.

CHAPTER 8

"Captain Ash, I've been thinking about your wagons."

Prentice looked over his shoulder to see Prince Far-ringdon approaching from behind him. The foreign royal was walking, leading his horse by the bridle, stepping swiftly to catch up to Prentice at the head of a marching column. It had taken the White Lions not even an hour to bury the slaughtered refugees and mark their graves with simple stones. Even so, before the task was finished, the knights ahorse, the noble contingent of the Reach forces, had already ridden off, the knight captain leading away every highborn warrior with one exception—the foreign prince. No comments were made, no explanations given. Prince Farringdon simply joined the militia once the grave digging was finished and followed along with the line of the march like a solitary outrider.

Once the graves were covered and the march resumed, Prentice had sunk into his own self-contained thoughts, brooding over the dead refugees, as well as the dark memories of torture and blood sacrifice in Halling Pass. As captain, there were no militiamen who would ever be so familiar as to try to speak with him as a friend. It was an isolation that could be lonely but suited him well enough at a time like this. The simple sounds of the march, the clank of harness and the shuffle of weary feet, the soft snorts of the wagons' bullocks, the buzzing of insects and the huffing of soldiers in the heat all formed a kind of blanket over the day, a soft orchestration that settled like silence over everyone. Prentice was happy to march under that blanket, his thoughts ordered only by the rhythm of his own footsteps.

Except now there was Prince Farringdon.

"My wagons, Your Highness?" Prentice replied.

"Yes, the war wagons." The prince reached Prentice's side and matched his stride while dropping his voice to a conversational tone. "I've been thinking, and if this is not a bad time, I would like to share my thoughts with you to hear your opinion on them."

Prentice turned to fix Farringdon with a straight gaze for a moment, and the gentle royal met his scrutiny with an open expression. The prince was an enigma to the militia captain. The young man's manners and speech were unmistakably high-born, comfortably royal. He never shirked any courtesies or privileges of his rank, not such that Prentice saw. However, he was equally never disdainful of his lessers. He never spoke condescendingly to Prentice or any officers of the White Lions, for that matter. Just the fact that he had bothered to dismount to have this conversation instead of literally "speaking down" from his saddle was so unusual compared to Grand Kingdom nobility. Viscount Gullden, for example, would not have bothered to dismount to tell the militia captain that he planned to take the knights away to the south. If he had not already been out of the saddle, he would not have thought to show his inferior even that much deference. To Prentice's wary mind, this kind of consideration only made the prince more of a potential threat. There were always some nobles who thought they had the "common touch," to be able to mingle with the low-born. These were the most dangerous nobles of all, because in Prentice's experience, such aristocrats inevitably took offense when the commoners they "touched" touched them back. Then the friendly façade dropped, and some pitiful serf or yeoman found himself flogged for forgetting his place in the order of things. Only Duchess Amelia had proved trustworthy to Prentice's way of thinking, and even with her he was diligent to maintain the boundaries of rank.

So, Prince Farringdon's earnest humility did little to win Prentice's goodwill.

"What about our wagons, Your Highness?" he asked.

"I was wondering how much weight they can carry."

"They carry quite a bit of weight. Is there something you want to add to the baggage?"

"Well, Captain, I thought perhaps some cannon."

Prentice felt his eyes go wide as he made no attempt to conceal his surprise. "Cannons, Highness?"

The prince immediately raised his hands defensively.

"Nothing like the brutes the Denay kings call their Bronze Dragons. Those are enormous, and as I understand it, so ancient no one even knows how they were made." The prince shook his head with a smile. "No, I was thinking something much smaller and easier to move, firing a shot more of this size."

He clenched one hand into a fist, to show his meaning. A *much* smaller cannon than the Bronze Dragons, it seemed. Prentice wanted to scoff, but when he had first seen a matchlock gun, he would never have believed it would have the power to punch an iron ball the size of a child's marble through the hard steel of a knight's armor. The Bronze Dragons were enormous tubes of thick alloy. They required teams of bullocks to move and crews of a dozen or more men to aim and fire. Shooting stone or metal balls half the size of a man, they were perfect for sieges but inefficient on a battlefield and not too difficult for an enemy to outmaneuver.

"The war wagons are already heavy, Your Highness," Prentice said, engaging with the prince's suggestion directly. "Their sides are thick wood and metal-bound to withstand axe and sword. Add the weight of cannon and iron shot to that and they would bog in even hard-packed earth. We'd never get them to move. Not to mention that mounting such weapons on the wagons would require yet more metal to strengthen the frames and take up space which should be given over to the Claws and Roars."

The war wagons were an innovation of Prentice's, heavy carts with reinforced sides that could be folded down to protect their wheels and form nearly solid walls. They could be wheeled onto a battlefield and formed into an instant fortification at a moment's notice, giving a massive advantage to his soldiers. The wagons had proved effective in several combats and had been a telling factor at the floating bridge battle on the night of the Red Sky.

When this brutal summer began, Prentice thought.

"I recognize the problems, Captain," Prince Farringdon responded fluidly to Prentice's objections. "The Dragons, of course, each have their own carriages, impressive constructions in their own right. Why not so with a lesser weapon?"

"If that's your thought, Highness, forgive me, but what do you need with the wagons?" Prentice was trying to be keep polite, but the heat and his own grim thoughts made him unwilling to entertain the prince's fancies. He looked to the horizon and judged that it would soon be sundown. Haste to return to Dweltford or not, the Lions would have to camp another night beside the road.

"What I was thinking, Captain," the prince went on, "was that a smaller cannon on wheels could be towed behind a wagon, hitched. Then the wagon itself would only need a longer and stronger yoke pole and an extra pair of horses or bullocks on the front. A simple conversion, wouldn't you say? Here, if you look at this, it will show my thinking."

The prince reached into his doublet and drew forth a leather folio wallet, which he awkwardly opened with one hand, his other remaining on his mount's bridle as they walked. He fished two pieces of paper from the wallet and handed them to Prentice. The captain took the sheets with a heavy sigh and stepped out of the line of march to let his men pass him while he paused to look at them. On both pages were charcoal drawings of cannons of varying sizes and mounted on different ideas of their own carriages, some two-wheeled, some four. One sketch was very clearly the rear end of a war wagon with a cannon hitched to it, exactly as the prince had described.

"Did you draw these, Highness?" Prentice asked as he surveyed the images.

"Last night," Prince Farringdon confirmed with a nod. He stopped and almost dropped the leather wallet as his horse tried to walk on, nearly pulling itself from his distracted grip.

Prentice did not notice. He was too busy studying the drawings with freshening interest. They were rough, not proper diagrams in ink, but the hand that drew them was clearly skilled and well educated in engineering. There were little notations about angles of construction and strength of materials.

"You drew these *last night*, you say, Highness?" he asked again.

"Indeed, after we made camp. I often draw or write in the evenings. These ideas have been in my head for some time, and I've other scribblings in my journals in Dweltford, but I thought I should have something to show my meaning when I broached the subject with you. I would have mentioned it earlier in the campaign, but the march to Halling Pass was so swift and then the hellish business with Earl Yarmass and his men. I've been trying to pick my moment. What I imagine is a cannon behind most or even every wagon to make a true fortification on your battlefields."

As the prince was talking, the next cohort began to pass, and Prentice waved over their corporal, the man Gennet. The junior officer stepped aside from the march and saluted.

"Send to the drummers; beat the halt and camp," Prentice told him. "We'll set canvas for the night here. The day's been long enough, and we gain nothing by pushing extra hours now."

"Yes, Captain!" Gennet saluted again and turned on his heel, calling for drummers to send out the orders. In moments, the marching column started breaking apart, fetching tents and other canvass from the baggage.

"Your Highness, as we camp tonight," said Prentice to his royal company, "perhaps you would be so kind as to join me and outline more of your thinking."

Prince Farringdon's face lit up at Prentice's invitation. "I would be most glad to."

A quick glance and Prentice found where his own place was being prepared, attached to the side of a wagon, and he led the way to that spot. As the two men bent under their shelter, Solomon trotted up, carrying Prentice's three-legged camp chair with its leather seat and folding wooden legs. The young drummer set the chair up in the shade and stood back proudly at attention, like a formal page in a noble court. He had a waterskin hung over one shoulder.

"Go get yourself something to eat and a drink of water," Prentice told him.

"I'm alright, Captain," he responded without hesitation.

Prentice frowned, fixing him with a hard look. "Do as I command, Solomon!" he said firmly.

The young man swallowed, his expression stricken. "Aye, Captain."

"A good wedge of the pemican and a full drink," Prentice instructed as the lad moved off. "Eat it all and make sure you have the drink as well. Then get back here. The prince or I may have further use for you."

Solomon brightened at that and made off to where others were preparing food.

"He is so eager to please," Prince Farringdon said in a kindly tone.

"He wanted the privilege of waiting on a captain and a prince," Prentice said, "and he'll have it, but not just for the pleasure of it. He's a White Lion and has duties. He cannot do them if he drops from hunger or thirst."

"You are a stern man, Captain Ash."

"War is a stern occupation, Highness."

"Surely he is too young to be a convict?" the prince asked.

"I do not think he is a convict, but he would not be the youngest I have ever known if he is."

The prince shook his head in wonder and Prentice offered him the chair.

"Where will you sit?" Farringdon asked.

"The ground was sufficient for me for many years, Highness," Prentice replied, but he moved to the nearby wagon and hoisted a small barrel up from behind the closed backboard. He hauled it over and planted it next to the chair. "And a barrel is a throne to a convict."

The two men sat. Solomon had left the waterskin beside the chair and they passed it between them, downing the warm liquid thirstily.

"You do not mind the memory of your conviction?" Farringdon asked between draughts. "Most men would not bring up the shames of their past so readily."

"Does the sword fear the memory of the fire that forged it?" Prentice shrugged.

"I hadn't thought of it like that."

"Everyone knows who I am, Highness. My past and my present. Why pretend?"

Farringdon nodded thoughtfully. Prentice handed him the two sheets of drawings, which he accepted.

"So, what are your thoughts?" the prince asked, waving the papers before putting them away.

"Ambitious notion," Prentice said noncommittally.

"I believe it can work. A cannonball the size I am thinking could make carrion out of a line's worth of men before it stopped."

Prentice winced. War was his trade, and while there were evils like witches and Redlanders in the world, it would be a necessary trade. However, most nobles made a game of war, and they treated men like Prentice and convicts like the Lions as mere pieces in that game to be moved about at will and discarded when broken. The prince certainly seemed to have the "common touch," but when he made off-hand comments about wounded men as "carrion," Prentice was forcibly reminded that Farringdon was still an aristocrat.

"Do you know anyone who can make these cannons of yours?" Prentice asked coldly.

"There are men in Masnia who have learned to make some of this sort, iron forged and bound with rings for strength."

"Not cast in bronze like the Dragons?"

"As I said before, no one remembers the technique of that manufacture. I think you already knew that. But as to how to make ironbound cannon, your Masnians in the Fallenhill workshops, they will likely have some ideas."

"Master Yentow Sent is already making the Roar's matchlocks, as well as the Fangs' and Claws' weapons, and all the armor for the company," said Prentice. "He is fully occupied with those tasks."

"Perhaps a journeyman or two might be diverted? The workshops themselves expanded? Or a new master enticed from Masnia."

Yentow Sent would love that, Prentice thought. *And if we expand the workshops any more, they'll be a town unto themselves.*

The prince was still studying him closely, and Prentice realized the royal was seeking some more indication of his reaction. He found himself of two minds. In principle, more weapons on the battlefield, especially ones as powerful as the prince was proposing, would always be welcome. But with the pressures the Reach was already facing, there were precious few resources to spare for experimenting as Farringdon proposed.

"Perhaps in the future, Highness," he said trying to remain politic. "It is not an unworthy idea, but I am not sure now is the right time."

"I had thought you a forward-thinking man, Captain," the prince said defensively. "Not one to fob off new ideas."

Prentice nearly threw a stinging rebuke back at the prince but was interrupted by Corporal Gennet suddenly approaching. Before the junior officer could speak, Prentice held up his hand to stop the man. He would finish what he had to say before he dealt with the next problem. Inwardly though, Prentice was thankful for the moment's interruption as it gave him a chance to put his thoughts in a more polite order. He looked at Prince Farringdon.

"I am unafraid of new ideas, Highness," he said with a quiet but firm tone. "And I have no intention of fobbing you off, but my first duty is to the duchess and her lands. I have wars to fight, castles to capture, and raiders to hunt, all with barely enough food and water to feed the men I need to do it. So, while your ideas appear to have merit, with your indulgence, Highness, I cannot spare more than a few words and thoughts for them now. Perhaps when we are back in Dweltford."

Prince Farringdon accepted Prentice's words solemnly.

"I apologize, Captain," he said, sounding chastened but not offended. "In my eagerness, I spoke hastily."

Although he had given a much more dampened response than the sharp retort he originally thought to give, Prentice knew the prince could still have taken umbrage at being spoken to in such a manner. What was most striking, though, was that Farringdon had been willing not only to apologize to someone so much inferior to him in status as a militia captain but to do it in the presence of a mere corporal.

The common touch or genuine humility? Prentice wondered. Before he worried about sorting out the answer, he signaled Corporal Gennet to make his report.

"Your pardon, Captain. Don't mean to interrupt," Gennet said, "but Sergeant Franken sent me to ask if you're ready to eat since the men are all at their meals and if he needs to set a man to cook anything special for the prince like? Only he come on the march with no squires or anything, and we've not got any cooks or special foods, so...so we're not sure what you expect.

All we got is old hard tack—it's got worms—and the pemican, sir. There's water to wash it down, but it's pretty warm and stale now, halfway to fetid really."

Prentice cast a glance at the prince, who simply shrugged as if the question were moot.

"I will gladly partake in whatever is offered," he said, and Prentice was convinced he meant it.

"I have some watered wine with me, Captain," Farringdon offered when Gennet was out of earshot. "I am willing to share, but it's only the one small skin. It wouldn't go far amongst a company this size. I could split it with you, though, if you would like."

Prentice cocked an eyebrow and shook his head.

"I doubt the company expects you to keep them supplied with wine on the march, Highness, unless your saddlebags are concealing a couple of hogsheads no one knows about."

"I fear not," the prince said with a smile, "but I want you to know I am with you on the march. I have not quit the company of the knights ahorse because they do not care for Veckanders. I owe a debt of service to the duchess, for her justice has served me well. I have my life by her grace's hand, and it seems to me that you serve her justice with the greater loyalty and devotion. I am here because it is the better place to be, even if the food is more weevilly."

Prentice blinked. He wasn't sure he had ever received a better compliment from someone so highly born, except perhaps from the duchess herself. He nodded, not sure what to say, exactly.

Convict life may have been harsh and bitter, he thought as he reached out to massage a sore calf muscle under his boot. *But at least it was uncomplicated.*

CHAPTER 9

T he glowing full moon and Rampart split the night sky, lighting the land to a silver sheen in all directions. Duchess Amelia found herself standing atop a tower in her nightgown, looking out over the rooftops of Griffith. To the west was the dark-water ribbon of the River Dwelt, diminished in its flow but not nearly as drought-strangled as it was farther north near Dweltford. The still surface of the water glittered in the moonlight, seeming brighter than the nearer torchlights of the town watch.

I am dreaming, Amelia thought, recognizing the strangeness of the scene as similar to night visions she had heard of from Prentice. Over the years, he'd had a number of prophetic dreams like this one. The duchess had once had a vision of her own and been the recipient of an odd prophecy she still felt she did not truly understand as well, but this was the first *dream* of this type she had received.

I must be dreaming.

"You are," said a voice, deep like the darkness of the still river water but warm and comforting. She looked about herself on the tower top but could not see anyone. She was alone.

"No, not alone," she heard the voice say again and it sounded as if it came from beneath the tower. Amelia leaned over a stone balustrade and looked down into the streets of the town below. In the dreamlight, the deep shadows between the houses were banished and Amelia could see the snow-white coat of a mighty lion stalking the close-walled alleys and narrow streets. From above, its elegant mane seemed to flow and billow in an unfelt wind and its coat glistened white like the color of stars. Amelia had seen this beast once before in a vision in her own castle great hall where it did battle with a mighty serpent and a flock of wretched, rotten birds of prey. In the manner of dreams, she knew the moment she saw it that the mighty beast was hunting. She looked to the streets to see if she could determine its prey.

"Serpents," the starlight creature said without looking up at her. "Cunning as they have been since the days of the garden, so they are now in the town."

Suddenly, Amelia became aware of a sound like the hissing of snakes and looked behind her to see two long, coiling reptiles slithering over the edge of the other side of the tower. Their iridescent scales were muted in the silvery light; nonetheless, she could see they were multicolored along their sides and their eyes were the darkest of red, like blood that was pooled and drying. They hissed, and their tongues flickered as they surged toward her. Amelia leaned back in horror, her hands gripping the stone barrier that kept her from the desperate plunge.

"Jump," said the lion voice with infinite calm. "You will not fall."

Having no choice but to trust the instruction, Amelia pushed herself up over the balustrade and threw herself over. Immediately, she plunged downward, but not in a fall. Though her motion was still swift, it seemed strangely controlled, as if she were being carried down in haste by a giant, invisible hand. Looking back to the tower top, she made out the serpents as they sprang over the stone rail themselves and, seeming to defy gravity to grip the bricks of the wall, surged down the edifice after her. Amelia found herself deposited in the midst of an empty stone fountain in the dark street. Looking up, she could see the pursuing snakes, coiling and ready to spring at her. Before they could, though, two she-lions burst from the shadowy streets and intercepted the reptiles. With single snaps of their inexorable jaws, the serpents' backs were broken and the danger was gone.

"Lioness, they call you," the angel lion said. "The pride will not abandon you to peril. These little wyrms are the least of their brood, and you will not need to fear. See, though, how they bring you their tribute."

Amelia looked, and the two lionesses, like housecats with a mouse each, approached with their serpents in their mouths and dropped them at her feet.

"When this moment comes, you must see all in one look, for these trophies will be snatched away. You must learn their secret before they are taken. Do not give way to fear."

What does that mean? Amelia wondered, but before she could ask, she heard a sound like hoofbeats coming first from the east but rising rapidly to a cacophony that echoed off the walls of the town and threatened to swamp her with its force. It grew so loud that she pressed her hands to her ears to shut it out, and yet as she looked all about, she could not see its source. The sound of the horses' hooves so thundered about her that she was sure she must be in the midst of their stampede, yet she saw not one. She was about to shout out to the angelic lion to beg it to stop the noise when she looked about and realized she was no longer in the town of Griffith.

The sound ceased.

"What now?" she asked, expecting the angel to hear her, even though she could no longer see the creature nor the two lionesses. There was only the quiet of a peaceful night, though behind her she could hear the sound of water and realized that she was standing now on the west side of the river. The dark, glistening ribbon was winding its way through the grasslands, but as she watched in the dreamlight, the flow was choked away until nothing but a dusty dead riverbed remained. Then came hoofbeats once again, but this time only a single set. Galloping down the dried watercourse came a single mount, but as she watched, Amelia knew it was no mere horse. It was a wild thing, with the serpents' eyes of darkened red and a filthy, knotted mane. Its coat might once have been white or pale, but now it was mange-ridden and stained with muck that could well have been more dried blood. A single twist of horn projected from its forehead, hung with carrion as from a raven's beak or a hawk's talon.

A unicorn? Amelia thought, but this was no embodiment of purity that legend said was drawn to the chaste virtue of a maiden. If it *was* a unicorn, it was a perversion of so wholesome a creature, its majesty debauched, and its power enslaved to evil.

On the creature's back was another serpent, though this one was enormous in comparison to the two that had attacked her at the tower. Its body was as thick around as a strong man's legs, and it twisted itself fully about its unicorn mount multiple times so that it seemed almost to be choking the life from the mythical beast. As Amelia watched, the mighty serpent opened its mouth and began to sing. The sound was horrifying to the duchess's ears and again she pressed her hands to her head. Nevertheless, the singing continued, and more beasts began to come from the grass on either side of the dry river.

First were horses, and Amelia wondered if these were the ones she had heard but not seen before. These came to stand before the serpent, but they seemed reluctant, tossing their heads and stepping back and forth skittishly. The unicorn sprang forward and gored one of the beasts through its neck, killing it instantly. The corrupted fable then lowered its head to begin eating the torn flesh. The rest of the horses whinnied in indignance, but the serpent flicked an impossibly long and muscular tail across their noses and the proud animals were cowed. They bowed their heads in obeisance to the singing snake.

"Poor things," Amelia said.

Then she realized that more animals were coming, drawn by the singing. There were dogs, coming in twos and threes until a wild pack had formed. The serpent whipped at them with its tail, and they barked back, not cowed like the horses. Then the serpent's song drew a smaller mob from the greater pack, and these suddenly writhed, as if their own flesh made war upon them. Some were transformed into horned beasts, and Amelia wondered if they, too, were becoming unicorns, but as their flesh ceased its struggle, they revealed themselves to be hairy mountain rams. Even then, they were misshapen, with uneven horns, missing limbs, and deformed skulls.

"What is all this horror?" Amelia asked herself, and as she did so, the serpent and all its menagerie noticed her for the first time. Each in their own way, the animals began to stalk her. With quickening steps, she backed away but found herself tripping and falling into the dried riverbed. The dusty bottom cracked under her and suddenly she was sucked into the mud beneath. It gripped her, and no matter how she struggled, she could not free herself. The hunting beasts drew closer, and Amelia felt terror rise in her throat.

"Where are you?" she cried out to the angel. "Where are my lions?"

"They are hunting," the angel's voice echoed in the warm night air.

"You said they would protect me," she protested.

"They will."

The hounds began to circle her while the other animals hung back.

"Will they do it soon?" Amelia demanded, seeing the slavering pack as it tracked her scent and watched her closely, their cold eyes full of predatory hunger. "These dogs will destroy me."

"Not all," said the celestial lion. Amelia felt the angel might have been about say more, but there was a sudden eruption of noise from behind the pack of hounds as lions leaped from the grass and fell upon the snake riding the unicorn. A melee of snarling claws and hissing fangs erupted, and the space beyond the dog pack became pandemonium. The dogs themselves, however, kept circling.

Looking about for a way to escape, some way to drag herself from the entrapping mire, Amelia saw two other hounds, different from the pack and keeping apart. Both sat like obedient hunting dogs, waiting on their master. Their coats were clean and their expressions watchful. One had a peacock riding on its back, the colors of its feathers muted in the dreamlight like the iridescent scales of the snakes.

"Here, boys," Amelia called, clicking with one of her hands, seeking to entice the two compliant hounds into aiding her. "You'll help me won't you? Good boys? Just need you to help pull me out."

The two dogs watched her, tongues lolling, but coming no closer.

"Come on, boys. Come and help me. Good dogs."

The hunting pack began to growl, and Amelia whipped her head around to see them ready to pounce. Despair struck her and she put her hand to her mouth to stifle a cry as the hunters leaped. Expecting to be savaged, she had a moment to realize that one of the two waiting hounds had sprung to her defense, fighting off the predators with loyal fury, before she clenched her eyes tight. Then she felt that the surface under her was not the clinging sludge of the drought-stricken Dwelt but the mattress of her own bed. The entrapping feeling of her dream was mirrored by the twists of her entangling bedsheets. Looking about her shadowy room, Amelia realized it was still some time before dawn and she was awake. The starlight coming in through the open window was nothing like the brightness of her dream, but silhouetted against it she could still make out Righteous's form, dozing upright in a chair as she had every night since they had come to Griffith. A warmer yellow light drew Amelia's eye and she looked to see Spindle cupping her hands around the meager flame of a rushlight lit from the embers of the tiny, banked fire in a brazier standing inside the chamber's hearth. Any more fire than that would have made the chamber unbearably hot.

"Is all well, Your Grace?" Spindle asked. "Only you were talking some in your sleep."

"Just a strange dream," Amelia answered reflexively. For some reason she could not name, she did not want to say what she had seen in the dream. It somehow seemed too intimate to discuss in the night hours, even with her ladies-in-waiting. "What is the time?"

"An hour or so before dawn, according to the night crier's call," said Righteous from her shadowed chair.

"Oh, I didn't mean to wake you both," Amelia said apologetically.

"Not to fear, Your Grace," Spindle replied in a comforting tone. "One of us is almost always awake through some part of the night. And if you wake, then best we both be, too."

"You are both so loyal," Amelia whispered, then lowered her head back to the pillow. She did not expect to sleep, but there was no urgent business to hand, and lying still in the predawn gave her a chance to think through what she had just experienced. Some of it seemed to make a kind of sense, but so much was a mystery. One thing she did understand—in coming days she would have to keep watch for snakes. The question was, what kind? How would she know them? And what kind of serpent could sing a song to bind the loyalty of other beasts and even transform them in their very flesh?

That last question was the most important, she was sure, and she had no idea what the answer might be.

CHAPTER 10

Prentice woke well before dawn, and after checking in with the last watch, as well as seeing to his morning requirements, he fetched a short wooden pole from the baggage. By the time he returned to his bedroll, he found Solomon stirring on his own blanket on the ground. Prentice crouched next to the drummer and nudged his shoulder.

"Time to wake up, lad."

Despite his half-asleep state, Solomon was on his feet in a trice. Prentice stood and handed him the wooden pole. Even in the dim light, the youth's expression was excitement tinged by uncertainty.

"Right, Solomon, that belongs to you now," Prentice told him. "You are of an age to be apprenticed, so while you march with the Lions, it's time you learned the Lions' trade. You're not big enough yet for a full halberd or pike, but you can start to learn the skills. Put one hand here, the other there, over and under. Now, feet like this."

Eyes blinking away sleep, Solomon moved eagerly to do as Prentice ordered, mimicking every movement as closely as he could. With his empty hands, Prentice showed Solomon the first drills that every militiaman learned, the foundation of the weapon skills upon which the White Lions were built.

"Forward and thrust," Prentice issued the drill orders like any other corporal. "Step back and thrust. Forward, thrust down and then up." For about half an hour he drilled the youth, until

Solomon's shirt was wet with sweat and the training pole hung heavily in his hands.

"That's enough for this morning," Prentice told him, looking to the horizon to see the sun coming up. "Take a rest and see yourself to some breakfast. Then get ready for the day's march."

Solomon grounded the pole and stood leaning upon it, just as he must have seen hundreds of others do every day of his time with the Lions. He looked like any other militia trainee, just three-quarter sized, and it made Prentice smile.

"You are fully on the path, now, Drummer Solomon," he told him. "Today you began your training for the Claws. When we get back to Dweltford, we will find you a fighting knife and commence your training with that as well."

Prentice pulled his own dagger, a simple but well-forged, cross-hilted weapon. His wife had given it to him the day he faced Baron Ironworth. It had been her idea of a lady's "favor."

"I'll show you how I care for mine," he said, turning the blade competently in his hand. "There's a myriad of techniques that someone of your size can master that will also set you up well for later weapons, like the Fang's sword and buckler."

He handed the weapon hilt-first to Solomon, who took it with the reverence due a holy relic.

"My wife gave me this one," he explained as his protégé studied it in the dawning light. "I will show you how I care for it and keep it keen. There is a lot to learn to be a man-at-arms, not just how to put the pointed end in the other man."

"This really is the blade Lady Righteous gave you?" Solomon asked in an awe-filled tone. "Is it true that she used to be called Cutter?"

"It is, but do not ever let her hear you call her that, or you might find she takes one of your fingers to teach you your mistake."

Solomon's eyes grew wider, and he swallowed loudly.

"Probably better if you stay clear of her, to be honest, lad," Prentice told him, then shook his head. "Of course, once she learns you've received your first dagger, she will not want to leave *you* alone. She will insist on taking a hand in your training, I am sure. She will want you to know all the nasty tricks that a Lion does not need but which work well in back alleys."

"She's really that good, isn't she, Captain?"

"Yes, she is, Solomon. If she tries to teach you something, anything at all, whatever she shows you, you take it to heart and practice it. It will serve you well, you can count on that."

Solomon nodded, his face earnest and serious, as if every word from his captain's lips was a divine pronouncement. Prentice held his hand out and the youth offered the dagger.

"Hilt first, lad," Prentice told him, putting his hand on the weapon and positioning it correctly in Solomon's grip. "Always offer a blade to another by the hilt first. That way they know you are not threatening them with it, and you will not cut them by accident. Now, try again."

Prentice released the dagger into Solomon's control once more. The boy held it a moment and then offered it to Prentice as instructed. Nodding approval, Prentice received the weapon and returned it to its sheath.

"That is everything for now. Breakfast and rest before we commence the march. I will want you strong for running messages when we reach Dweltford."

"Aye, Captain. Do you want me to put this staff back in the luggage?"

"Yes, but Solomon, it is yours now. You will carry it with you every day. If ever it is out of your sight, you must know exactly where it is, for it is your responsibility. Every morning when you wake and whenever your duties are done when we are in camp, I want you to practice what I have just taught you. As you get better, I will add more to your drill. It is what men-at-arms call repertoire. You are going to be tired. Your arms will ache, and your hands will have blisters. It is going to be hard, but you will do it because you can. And though it will take years, before you know it you will be a full White Lion, as skilled and powerful as any of our company."

Solomon beamed as if he had just been promised a life of cream cakes and revels, and then saluted his captain. Prentice returned the salute and Solomon dashed away. Behind him, Prentice heard Prince Farringdon stir and looked to see the royal rising from his own blanket, facing away. Almost certainly the prince knew what had just happened.

"He adores you, I think, Captain," Prince Farringdon said quietly, not turning, as if the topic was too sensitive for face-to-face conversation.

"He is a loyal lad, and courageous," Prentice observed, looking to the prince. "He stood beside me the whole night of the Red Sky, never flinched. He is clever, too, sharp mind, good heart. If there is any justice in this world, he will be the captain himself one day."

"You could be right. A goodly target for a young man to aim his arrow at."

Prentice looked at the prince and shook his head. Farringdon must have caught the motion out of the corner of his eye, for he glanced over his shoulder.

"You don't believe me, Captain?"

"I am not accustomed to men of birth who approve of the ambitions of their lesser, Highness," Prentice replied.

"I have not yet persuaded you that I am different from other men of birth you have known?" asked Farringdon.

"Oh no, Highness. I am reasonably persuaded that you are sincerely whom you appear to be."

"Then why your suspicions still?"

Prentice stepped to the young royal and lowered his tone. "I can see your earnest efforts at camaraderie, Your Highness, but what I cannot see is why. I do not know your purpose."

He looked Farringdon straight in the eye and the prince met his gaze.

"You don't think I might just like you?"

Prentice cocked a skeptical eyebrow. Farringdon saw it and chuckled, shaking his own head.

"No, perhaps not. And even if I did, why would you trust me? I've heard the way the Reacher nobles talk about you when you are not around. They do not much appreciate you, even as they cannot despise your success. Lower-born men, or even high yeomen or patricians, are not supposed to have the ear of a duchess. In the Vec, we are not quite so strict with our social order."

Prentice was surprised to hear that the nobility talked about him, though he realized he probably should not have been. Viscount Gullden had said as much. He had assumed it was only because of the incident with Yarmass's men in Halling Pass. It surprised him that he might have been more mentioned than that.

"So why are you here, Highness, marching with the footmen and not ahorse with your equals who despise me so?"

"Perhaps they despise me as well," Farringdon said, but again he shook his head. "No, I am not so pathetic as all that, no matter what is said about me."

"We both suffer the rumormongers," Prentice conceded. "We might have that in common."

Prince Farringdon nodded, then looked down. Prentice wasn't sure why he was pressing so hard on the prince, but perhaps all he wanted was to have the issues in the open. It was clear Farringdon was seeking to make some sort of connection, and the mention of the duchess's ear made Prentice think that the prince saw him as a path to a closer connection with the Reach's ruling lady. What he still wanted to know was why. Farringdon's quiet manner made him hard to read, hard to judge for motives.

"In the night watches, on my bed, I hear her whispering," Farringdon muttered without looking up. "The serpent priestess who tormented me in the Ditch. We used to joke about it growing up, my brother and I. Joked about the prison, you know? 'I'm a prince's son,' we'd say. 'Offend me and I'll have you down in a cell in the Ditch!' And then I was there, and I knew what fools we'd been. The despair that comes upon a man when the earth closes upon him and the chains hold him to the wall."

Prentice felt bile rise in his throat and his hand threatened to twitch nervously as the memories of his own internment and interrogation at the hands of the Inquisition boiled up in his mind. He clenched his jaw and his fist, fighting back the horrors from his memories.

"I hear her in my dreams," Farringdon went on. "That hissing whisper, telling me how my father and cousins had died, how my friends died. How she planned to kill *me* when my time came. Do you know what that feels like, Captain? Trapped and tormented and longing to die, to get it over with?"

"I do."

It was a simple statement, but Prentice knew he was hiding nothing from his tone. Farringdon looked up, and as their eyes met, a moment of understanding, of true comprehension, passed between them.

"I thought you did," the prince admitted. "I've heard other stories. The nobles are not the only ones who discuss you or your past. Even that is not the whole of why I am here, Captain. In dreams, when I hear the whispers, sometimes I hear thunder—impossibly loud—so loud it shakes my heart in my chest. And then I hear a man's voice and he challenges the witch under the earth. A man comes with his soldiers. Obeying his orders, they rescue me out of the hell of the Ditch. I know I was touched with the madness of a broken man. My faculties were not at my command, but I remember that voice—your voice, Captain. You rescued me, Captain Ash. I owe you my life."

"I did it at the duchess's instruction, Highness," Prentice said, feeling humbled by the prince's straight acknowledgement of the debt between them. "Whatever you owe for your rescue, you owe to her."

"I know," Farringdon concurred, and he turned back to his bedroll, crouching down to begin packing it away for the march. "And I will do whatever I must to see that debt discharged. But I owe a debt to you as well, Prentice."

He paused and looked up. Prentice realized what he was doing. The prince wanted to know if he had the militia captain's permission to use his first name, as a friend might.

I see you, Highness, Prentice thought. He nodded slowly.

"You lost a friend on the bridge across the Murr, did you not, Captain?" Farringdon asked, returning to his bedroll. "Under the red sky? A knight?"

"Knight Captain Sir Gant," Prentice said, and the memory of that moment as he and Gant saluted each other across the shattered gap in the middle of the boat bridge came back to him.

"I do not propose to replace your lost comrade, Captain," Farringdon went on. "I would not insult you with that ambition. But you and that knight were friends, I hear, because you saved his life at an earlier battle, the first of this war. Since you have also saved my life in no less dire circumstances, I would be remiss not to follow that knight's example, wouldn't you say? You can understand the why of that, I hope."

"*You* understand a great deal more than I imagined, Highness," Prentice said. For most of the time since he had been rescued, Prince Farringdon had been thought of as little more than a mute, a wounded mind in a hale body—present but not truly there. Prentice was shocked to realize just how wrong that assessment had been. Even his own shrewd insight had failed him in this regard. Had anyone not underestimated Prince Farringdon?

"People say a great many things when they don't think you are really there," the prince explained, clearly picking up on Prentice's thoughts. "I am a royal of a broken land, prince of a people ground into dust. To most who see me, I am more ghost than man. I am resolved to change that, and to repay my debts."

Prentice was struck by another unexpected memory of Sir Gant—the day they had met. Prentice had not been freed from the chain for more than a week at that time and suddenly, in the duchess's presence no less, there was a knight on his knees before him, recounting a tale different and yet so similar to Prince Farringdon's, and pledging an honor debt like this one.

I used to be good at keeping my head down, Prentice thought. *How did I start attracting so much attention?*

"Very well, Highness," he told the prince. "Within the bounds of my oath to the duchess and the Reach, I accept your pledge, as I accepted Sir Gant's." He offered an open hand and Farringdon, standing, took it. Then, when they had broken their grip, Prentice bowed deeply, as a man of his rank to a royal.

"Debt or no debt, Highness, we will not forget our places."

"As you say, Captain." Farringdon surprised him by saluting, White Lions' fashion. The two men chuckled.

"So how should we proceed with this new understanding between us?" asked the prince.

"With your permission, Highness, similarly to my morning with Solomon."

"You want to put me through weapons' drill?"

"Not quite," said Prentice with a wry smile. "But you will have seen, I trust, the longblade I carry, the one from Lord Ironworth?"

"The champion blade?"

"Yes. Since taking it in a duel, I have done my best to master it, partially because I want to honor the dead man's memory, but mostly because some day now some young madcap's going to get it in his head to challenge me for it and claim the honor for himself."

"The killer of the champion-killer," Farringdon said, and it was clear he could see the soundness of Prentice's thinking.

"I would just as soon put the thing away," Prentice continued. "The Lions' weapons suit me well enough—Fangs and

Claws. But there is an advantage for the duchess with me having it."

"Her champion bested Daven Marcus' man."

"Exactly."

"How then to training, Captain? What use will I be?" asked Farringdon, and Prentice's smile turned knowing.

"I have the repertoire, Highness, but I need a partner," he said. "Someone with whom to spar. Sir Gant was an excellent companion in this regard, but since his passing, no other noble has stepped up. When we are in camp, I join the weapons' drill at times and my dear wife keeps me more than honest. But I need practice against the longsword. Will you do me that honor?"

"The honor would be mine, Captain," said the prince. He touched his fingers to the nearly healed cut on his temple. "And I know I need the practice as well. My father's swordmaster used to say that the longsword was an unforgiving mistress. Neglect her and she will spurn you."

"My friend used to say the same thing," said Prentice. "What say you then, Highness? Shall we try to woo her back together?"

"I think I would like that very much, Captain Prentice. I doubt I have much insight to offer you, with your experience and skill, but my father's master was an excellent sword and I trained with some others of great skill as well, as prince's are wont to do. Perhaps I might have something in my repertoire to surprise you."

Oh, you do, Highness, Prentice thought. *Well and truly.*

CHAPTER 11

"Well, that could have gone better," Duchess Amelia muttered under her breath as she exited the Griffith Conclave Hall. She blinked in the daylight as she stepped through the two copper-embossed doors with their graven scenes of the river trade—boats and boatmen rendered in the polished metal. The main of the guildhall was like any other such civic building in the Reach, made of fired brick and heavy wooden beams, but its front was an impressive edifice of dressed sandstone blocks like those used for castles and town walls. At least it would be, once it was finished. A stack of half-cut blocks sat unattended in the street, and while one corner of the front was completely marked in pale stone, the other still showed its humbler original brick.

The drought's taken the workers away to dig for water, Amelia assumed. There were a number of trades around her land suffering the same labor shortage. *Or the merchants have decided to save their money.*

Nothing choked off men's pride in their own wealth like the fear it might all be draining away. Amelia knew that was why she had received the response the Conclave masters had just given her. She had come to ask them, plead with them even, to make extra efforts to send food north to support Dweltford. Between the ongoing summer and the huge influx of refugees needing to be fed, her capital's lands were no longer sufficient to support the town. The situation was not yet desperate, but it would not be long. Griffith's patrician council, its wealthiest merchants and highest guild masters, were completely sympathetic, as long as nothing specific was expected of them.

Professionally earnest, she thought. *A merchant is every man's friend while doing no one any favors. Silver first, sympathy second.*

"Tell me, Ladies, what do we think?"

Behind each shoulder, the Lace Fangs kept wary watch upon the street as the day's business flowed along. Every kind of townsman could be seen walking the cobbles, from burly day laborers in homespun and straw hats to proud craftsmen with sleeveless doublets bearing the flashing precious metal of their guild pins. All gave the finely dressed trio of ladies in their midst a wide berth. Even if they did not recognize their duchess on sight, the Lace Fangs' ready hostility would have made any approach seem hazardous.

"Think about what, Your Grace?" asked Spindle.

"About my meeting with the town fathers," Amelia answered, her frown making her own opinion of the encounter obvious.

"I think we should have brought Lady Dalflitch with us," Spindle said, sharing her mistress's expression.

"She'd've known how to handle them dandies, that's for sure," Righteous agreed.

"Yes, well cunning as she is, even Lady Dalflitch cannot be in more than one place at the same time," Amelia said, conceding their basic point but bringing them back to the issue at hand. "So, we must make do with our own wit and wisdom."

The Fangs nodded. A pair of workmen carrying sawhorses and leather tool bags tried to slip around the three women to enter the Conclave Hall, but one of them bumped Spindle's hip as he passed, pushing her sideways and almost catching her skirt on the hammer handle sticking out of his bag. He half turned his head and tugged his forelock but did not apologize. Amelia thought to call him back for his rudeness and half expected

Spindle or Righteous to do it of their own accord, but instead, Lady Righteous stepped up close to her and whispered in her ear.

"Perhaps it might be best if we walk and talk, Your Grace," she said. "Doubt you're in any danger, but not everyone's going to know who you are on sight, and three women dressed fine on the street without chaperones? That might draw a kind of attention we don't want to have to deal with."

Amelia had a sudden memory of her dream, and she grew immediately wary. She cast her eyes about, her mind awash with images of lurking serpents.

"A good plan, Righteous," she said, and the three ladies made off toward the north-east quarter of the town where the outer walls also branched inward to enclose a ward that was colloquially known as Griffith Castle, even though it was more of a fort with walls but no keep.

"As to your question, Your Grace," Righteous said as she led the way up the street, Amelia directly behind her and Spindle last in line as rearguard, "I think them merchants did what merchants do. They waited for you to show them where the money was in it for them."

"I offered them tax concessions," Amelia countered.

"I don't know, Your Grace, but I reckon they want no tax at all."

"You think they're *all* that greedy?"

"Might not be greed, Your Grace," offered Spindle. "I think they's in earnest about everything costing more with the drought. And I think they mean to help. They just want to pick *your* pockets for the extra costs, not their own."

Amelia sighed. The drought oppressed everyone, and she was asking the Conclave members to make extra effort on her behalf.

On behalf of my people, she thought, correcting herself. She was prepared to shoulder some of the extra cost. Could they not see their way clear to doing the same?

"I figure that heavy one was sincere, Your Grace. He wanted to help, I'd say," said Righteous.

"They were all pretty fat," said Spindle. "Which heavy one did you mean?"

"The dusky one—hair like black wires and skin all polished dark wood."

"Oh, him? Master Jannomoch. Yeah, he was in earnest, seemed to me. Where's he from anyway? Don't see many of his type in the Reach."

"Masnia, I guess," Righteous said with a shrug.

"He's a Quenlander," Amelia said, correcting her lady. "They're a folk related to the natives of Aucks, though different too, I understand."

"Where's that then?"

"Quenland is north of the Grand Kingdom," Amelia explained. "Some of it owes fealty to the duchy of Gilded Coast. Most of the rest is a kind of hot forest full of these proud, swarthy folk. They are especially good craftsmen, apparently. They build homes of wood that tower high into the forest tops."

"Hot forest?" asked Righteous. "He must feel right at home in this weather."

"Maybe so, My Lady," said Amelia. "But what is this other land he spoke of, Radengon-Beyond-Dwelt?"

"I think it's down south and west of the Dwelt," said Spindle. "Leastwise that's the feeling I got."

"The Reach is all the land from the mountains to the Dwelt. My authority doesn't stretch west of that. I didn't even know there were folk down there."

"Makes sense though," said Righteous, and Amelia stopped in the road, looking at her lady in surprise and confusion. Righteous cast a glance backward, and realizing her mistress had stopped, turned back a step. "Think about it, Your Grace. If you're a Reacherman and you've got your yeoman freedom—maybe you're a freed convict—you can stay in the Reach and enjoy the duchess' peace, or..."

"Or?" Amelia wasn't following Righteous's reasoning.

"Or you can take any tools and livestock you can scrape up, cross the river to the west, and suddenly you're a free bird. You don't pay taxes to no one and you settle wherever you please. And if the Murr goes a long way west, then once you're settled you can sail back down the river to trade anytime you like."

Amelia had never considered the possibility. Settlers beyond the Dwelt, and in such numbers that they would trade back into the Reach? Master Jannomoch obviously had, though.

"Must have seemed like a sweet deal," Spindle was saying. "At least until the Redlanders come down the Murr."

"I think that's what he meant," said Righteous. "That Jannomoch bloke didn't want lower taxes or more money, he wants protection for his trade in this Radengon place. If the Redlanders had to come past them, or through them, to get to us, then they could be in a dire way by now, assuming they're still alive at all."

They want my protection? Amelia thought reflexively. *Then they shouldn't have fled my authority.*

Almost as soon as she had the thought, she shook her head and dismissed it. That was the false pride of Grand Kingdom nobility, the old institution that was mauling itself to death in the civil war. No matter what her rank, Amelia knew it was a mistake to think that way. That was the thinking that treated peasants as property and loyal soldiers as kindling for the fire of war. It was wrong. This land of Radengon-Beyond-Dwelt, whether it was a full country unto itself or a scattering of farmer settlers eking out their private living, was a land in need of protection, the kind of protection her White Lions gave her lands.

"And that is an opportunity," she said out loud.

"Your Grace?" asked Righteous, not understanding. She looked to Spindle, but the other Lace Fang only shook her head as well. Amelia smiled at them both.

"Never mind, My Ladies, I will explain when we reach our lodgings. I'll need pen and ink as well. I must write to Master Jannomoch."

The two women nodded, accepting implicitly that their mistress had reached some decision that suited her, and now they had a duty to escort her to its execution.

"At least it was encouragin' to hear there was one load of goods already on the way up to Dweltford," said Righteous as she led the way again. "I figure that's Lady Dalflitch's doing. She said she had some other merchants in her connections that she was leanin' on."

Amelia nodded. The Conclave Council had assured her that at least one shipment of long-lived foods—pickles and hard tack, that sort of thing—had already been sent north up the Dwelt, with a plan to offload it where the river water ceased to be navigable and have it carried north from there by bearers and pack animals. The Conclave's grasping insistence on exemption from taxes left a bitter taste in Amelia's mouth, but the news of the shipment and the possibility of an expansion of her influence into a new land through Master Jannomoch gave her a sense of optimism overall.

Ahead of her, Lady Righteous suddenly held up a hand.

"Looks like some sort of crowd, Your Grace," she said. "Blocks most of the street. Hands on our silver or the cutpurses'll take it all, I'd say."

"Cut the duchess' purse? Let them try," said Spindle belligerently.

"Don't doubt they will," Righteous counseled. "Let's just keep her grace close and get through quick as we can."

Spindle nodded, and she and Righteous pressed close to Amelia as the trio began to make their way through the thick crowd on the street. Amelia was accustomed to being defended like this at times and the jostling of crowds was nothing new to her, though it was rarer in her life since she had risen to her noble rank. Nevertheless, there was a tense mood to this crowd that set her on edge. She could see by their expressions that Righteous and Spindle shared her misgivings. When Righteous presumed to grasp her mistress's wrist and pull her more forcefully, Amelia did nothing to resist. The crowd was predominantly workmen, it seemed to the duchess, and they were speaking loudly, on the verge of several arguments. Stepping into spaces and gaps, the three ladies negotiated the incipient mob like swimmers watching for rocks in the rapids of a rising torrent.

Quite suddenly, they broke into an open space in the midst of the crowd, a clear area around a white stone fountain, and Amelia recognized the little square from her dream where she had fallen into exactly this dried up water feature.

"Repent your sins lest your curse consume us all!" cried a near-feral voice.

CHAPTER 12

A melia looked to see a sacrist with a roughly shaven scalp that festered with painful-looking sores. He was wrapped in little more than rags, and though he was not as thin as other clergy Amelia knew, he had a drawn and hungry face. He lifted one hand in the air, as if calling down judgement from heaven, while the other pointed talon-like in her direction.

"Do you not see the words of the Lord's wrath written in fire in the very heavens against you?"

Amelia blinked, too taken aback by his words to even think of being offended. The disgruntled crowd gathered around the street preacher, and even a summary glance of their faces showed they'd been riled by his sermon. Hostility seemed their common mien, though whether for or against the speaker depended upon which cluster of listeners she looked at. Some clearly agreed with his pronouncements while others scowled and shook their heads in disgust.

"See while this land blanches and thirsts under this heat, doxies so fine as this stalk your streets, tempting the God-fearing man from his goodwife and hearth with their lace and fripperies. How much silver have you made this day, slatterns, offering lust for coin? How many babes go hungry to line your purses and pay for your fine garments? How many wives wait dejected for the men you lead astray?"

Did he really just call us whores? Amelia thought indignantly. She wondered how often the clergyman confronted well-born women on the street like this. She and her ladies were dressed in fine linen dresses and her Fangs were wearing their lace masks, but surely they were not the only ladies about business in the town. They also had their hair covered and their bodices fully laced. They were hardly flouting decorum like common street-walkers.

Given the heat, I'd much *rather be in my chambers, where I could unlace in private,* she thought.

"Back off, vagabond," Righteous said in a cold tone, one hand out to fend the wild sacrist away as he began to stalk toward them.

"See how the wanton shows no respect for the words of faith?" he said, turning to his audience and stirring them further. "There speaks the mouth of a shrew who has never known the firm hand of a righteous husband."

That pronouncement almost made Amelia guffaw, and she felt herself smirk contemptuously. Righteous's husband had given her her name himself, and if any man in the world had a firmer hand than Prentice Ash, Amelia had never met him.

"Why chastise them?" a voice called from somewhere in the alleyway congregation. "They don't make the drought. You don't even know if they is whores."

"An' even if they is, we've always had trollops," added another voice. "It's not like paid girls ever dried up the rains before."

Amelia was glad that the man's knee-jerk theology had its opponents amongst the crowd, but she felt from the hostile air that those might have been the minority. Even as some were arguing with the street preacher, there was a muttering that seemed to show an angry approval of his sermon.

"There was no drought before, but were they ever so brazen before?" the sacrist countered his challengers. "Did they walk the streets in the day? When honest men like you should have been at toil, not tempted away. No, I say! These are like the fallen woman who disports herself in castles with foreign princes, calling herself duchess and lion queen."

I have never called myself 'lion queen,' Amelia thought. The images of her dream rose in her mind once again and she wondered if this sermonizer was a serpent she needed to watch for. She studied him over Righteous's shoulder, looking to absorb all the details she could, just as the angelic lion had counseled her.

"This *is* the duchess, you daft lout!" Righteous spat back loudly, and the sacrist paused, his face troubled as if in complete confusion.

"That might have been a mistake, My Lady," Amelia whispered to her protector.

The street preacher peered at the three of them as if they were difficult to make out, and the crowd in turn watched him watch them. The entire little square seemed to hold its collective breath.

"We should go, now," said Spindle quietly behind the duchess, and Amelia nodded. That small motion was enough to release the preacher from his fugue. His eyes widened in seeming disbelief.

"The chief harlot herself!" he bellowed, and his voice echoed off the walls. "She has come down from her tower to walk amidst our misery and gloat at the suffering she has wrought. Daughter of Jezebel! Do you rejoice at our grief?"

"You go too far, holy man!" shouted a deep voice from somewhere in the crowd to Amelia's left.

"No, we have not yet gone far enough!" the sacrist retorted. He whirled about, arms raised, as if drawing his listeners in closer. "The Lord has offered up the source of our misery to us that we may purge it and deliver this land."

Amelia clenched her jaw and swallowed her terror as best she could. Her nerves sang like a taught rope in a high wind, and she looked from Righteous to Spindle and at the crowd all around. Her Lace Fangs were deadly, but such a mass of bodies would sweep them away if this wild prophet of doom could stir them up to insurrection.

"We should duck 'em like scolds!" shouted someone, suggesting the low justice punishment for an abusive wife. That drew some nods and approving mutters until another shout voiced an obvious objection.

"Where would we duck them? What water is there for that nowadays?"

"Maybe just string 'em up by their wrists and give 'em a good floggin'!" shouted a third.

"Why by the wrists? Use their necks and throttle the sin out of them!" declared a fourth.

I am in a nest of vipers, Amelia thought, the fears of her dream recurring and making her heart hammer in her chest. She looked back and forth in every direction as members of the crowd started to press forward, savagery in their eyes. One man reached out a hand to grasp Spindle by the shoulder, then recoiled as a flash of steel slashed. Blood sprayed from between his fingers where he gripped the injured hand, and he cried out in terror, pushing backwards against the men crowding behind him.

"Next fool tries to lay hand on Her Grace, or either of us, gets to see what his innards look like," Spindle shouted, her voice shrill but resolved.

"The bitch fights the judgement of God," shouted the street preacher, but the sight of blood seemed to have galvanized the issue. While many of the sacrist's impromptu street flock were willing to be riled to violence against three women on the street, others were not so motivated.

"This ain't right! Duchess or not, you can't just string up women for being out in the day," counseled an older-seeming man with wiry arms and a long-stemmed pipe in his hands that he waved about his head like a bailiff's rod of authority. "Look at their clothes. These ain't no streetwalkers. We lay hands on them and it'll go bad for us, I tell you."

"Do you fear man or God, old fool?" the sacrist demanded.

"I don't fear you!" declared a bull-necked man who had the look of a smith, bare-chested under a heavy leather apron. He had a long wooden staff in his hands, and he hefted it in a way that said he was willing to do violence with it. "My brother marches with the White Lions and was with them at the rivers when the sky turned crimson. If half what he says is true of what he seen, then you're setting yourself against the woman who's saved all our lives too many times. You talked to the rivermen, sacrist? Ask them what a Redlander'll do to you if he gets his hands on you. She's fought them off, her and her militia. If this is her, you'll not lay a finger on these three ladies while I stand!"

"Or even if she ain't!" declared the elderly speaker. A significant minority of the crowd seemed to agree.

"She has bewitched them!" the sacrist all but screamed, his voice cracking shrilly.

"Oh, shut up, you bloody fool!" Righteous shouted back, and the crowd growled like two wild animals trapped in a pit with each other. Some leaned in, ready for violence but unwilling to throw the first strike. The staff-wielding smith laid his pole horizontally in front of the three women and then nodded over his shoulder to a particular corner of the square.

"There's an alley down there," he said quietly. "Goes up to Silversmith's Way and past the charcoal bins. After that you'll find the high street. Please go now while you can."

The crowd was a little thinner in the direction the man indicated, and the Lace Fangs did not even ask to see if Amelia agreed. They immediately pushed that way, daggers leading and daring the few men in between to try to stop them. Soon they were past the crowd and Amelia could see the little opening between two buildings that the smith had pointed them to.

"Do not let them flee God's wrath," the sacrist screamed, seeing his prey escaping. "While they live, the dry will afflict this land. Only their blood can slake the summer's thirst!"

"You are a bloody fool," the smith said gruffly, and he stepped forward to clout the street preacher across the head. The man staggered back with a cry, and the barely restrained brawl suddenly erupted like a cloudburst. Someone launched himself out of the crowd at the smith while others threw seemingly random punches. The elder who counseled restraint went down under the upswell of violence.

Near to Amelia and the Lace Fangs, the men who had been held back by the threat of bared steel found renewed courage and surged forward to seize them. With experienced coordination, the two bodyguards thrust their ward behind themselves and held the rush at bay with continuous cuts. Backing away slowly, they fended off the hateful mob, punishing any too eager to make the pursuit. Amelia saw at least one man go down, blood spraying his shirt from a slash to his throat. Then she was at the opening of the alley, barely wide enough for a single person to walk, and as she looked down it, she saw a man waiting only a few paces back from the corner.

"This way, Duchess," he said, beckoning her to safety. "We know the way."

The man waved her towards himself, and as she looked, Amelia saw that he had a companion behind him. Seeing the second man, she was struck at how similar they were. Both wore buckskin breeks and sleeveless leather jacks, opened to show their bare chests. They were lean and sun-browned, but it was the faces and heads that got her attention. With high cheekbones and almond-shaped eyes, the two men had an almost feminine appearance, though their bearings were quite masculine in every other respect. On their heads they wore scarves, wound about like turbans, and the cloth of these headdresses was vibrantly colored.

Amelia turned to look back to Spindle and Righteous and saw that both women were blocking the entrance to the alley, holding the crowd off with curses and swift cuts. She tried to call to them, but her words turned to an inarticulate cry as one of the turbaned stranger's hands gripped her powerfully by the arm and pulled her backward. Trying to protest but unable to get her feet under her, Amelia found herself dragged down the alley until she was around a corner where the tiny thoroughfare split into multiple paths and doglegged behind a row of hutches.

"Let's do it here," one of the two newcomers said, pulling forth a dagger. Amelia made to struggle and cry out afresh, but the man's partner grappled her to himself and clapped a hand across her mouth.

"Not here," he objected. "We pass unseen."

"We pass unseen," his partner concurred.

Amelia kicked and wailed into the man's hand, even trying to bite it in desperation. His wiry strength held her fast despite her thrashing. Half-dragged, half-lifted, she was rushed further down the alley past twists and turns, and then the two assailants paused. The unburdened of the two rushed ahead while his mate waited, keeping Amelia prisoner in the cleft of a wall where the bricks had fallen in and been badly patched. It was not much of a hiding spot, but Amelia doubted they would be seen. Already, the sounds of the fray around the empty fountain seemed distant and muted.

How far have they brought me already? she wondered. Had Spindle or Righteous noticed that she was gone yet? These two ambushers had moved so swiftly and surely that the Lace Fangs might still be holding back the unruly crowd, unaware that their charge had been abducted. Or perhaps they were overwhelmed. Amelia shook her head at that notion. These two were the serpents of her dream, not the mad sacrist or his riled mob, she was sure of it. So, the lions must be coming to save her, and when they come, I must see what there is to see.

But what was there to see?

The man holding her fast had her facing away from himself, and since her initial struggle, he had made his grip vice-like such that she could not move her head even enough to see any of his arm or hand holding her mouth. His partner slunk away out of sight down the alley, and for a long moment everything seemed still, the sounds of the mob and the rest of the town's life so muted that Amelia could hear her heart hammering in her chest. Then the partner returned, a predatory expression on his face.

"It's mostly clear," he told his accomplice. "Quick dash down the street through the cisterns and then we're in the basement. We'll do it there."

Do what? Amelia wondered, fear continuing in spite of her efforts to remain calm and believe in the prophecy of her dream.

The man not carrying her leaned in so close that she could smell his breath, which was strangely fresh, like the scent of new green grass. He held up a fang-like dagger between them so that she could see her own distorted reflection in the metal.

"She says you need to be awake," he hissed at her. "Me, I'd just as soon thump you out and carry you like a bundle, but she says you need to be awake for the ritual. Sleeping folks can't despair or something like that. So, be good and this alley won't be the last thing you ever see."

The man turned away and Amelia felt herself being carried forward again. Her mind tried to sort through the chaotic spill of questions and details her captor's words had revealed. They had abducted her on orders—orders from a woman. They were to take her somewhere for some kind of ritual, for which she was meant to be conscious. That thought made Amelia shiver involuntarily, and she remembered reports of Redlander sorcery, of rites that involved torture and bloodshed. The angelic lion had promised that she would be rescued from the serpents in her dream, but did that mean she would not suffer from their intentions? Would she be rescued but only after this ritual they spoke of? Was that what she was supposed to see? Was she to be forced to endure horror? Her thoughts leaped immediately to Prince Farringdon and his wounded mind. Could that be about to happen to her?

Amelia started to struggle in her captor's arms again and for a moment it felt as if she might have caught him by surprise enough to break free. Then his partner returned and clipped her across the head with the pommel of his dagger.

"Enough!" he commanded her. The strike was not sufficient to daze her or knock her out, but it made her eyes water with the pain. She blinked a moment, trying to clear them. The dagger-wielder waited, eyes fixed on hers. "Last chance, *kreff*. Try that again and I'll knock you through the dream veil. You won't see light again until your heart's broken like a potsherd."

Amelia felt the fear clench at her throat and chest. She wanted to trust the dream, to believe in prophetic visions, but her mind was awash with terror, and her thoughts scrabbled to keep up with the myriad of strange things that swirled around her. Who were these men? Could they be Redlanders? Never before had there been even the slightest intimation that the invaders used spies or other agents. Perhaps these were supplicants to the Redlander religion, not yet fully converts but still serving its purposes. Could that be the ritual—some kind of initiation? And what did it mean that they called her *"kreff"*?

The two men stopped at the exit of the alleyway and looked out from the shadows. The street before them was open to the hot sun but mostly empty. From the little Amelia was able to see, it seemed to be a craftsmen's row of some kind—shopfronts and workshops under wide cloth awnings. Given the time of day, it made sense that there were few townsfolk about in the open. Most would be hiding from the heat in shadows until the late afternoon. The two kidnappers had a good chance of frog-marching her down the street without being noticed, especially if they were only traveling a short distance. If that happened, they would surely lose any pursuit, disappearing completely into the town. Now all sense of hope fled from Amelia and panic seized her mind. The angel in her dream had been wrong.

She blinked as she was thrust out into bright sunlight once more, and her feet barely touched the ground as the strong, slender men stole discretely down the street. Ahead, there came a sudden hammering of horses' hooves and the jingling of knights' harness. Amelia's heart leaped, but the two men threw themselves sideways into a cleft between two large clay pots, crouching down.

"*Kreff* riders, all under steel," whispered the one carrying her.

"Slow and dim-eyed," his partner responded. "We pass unseen."

"We pass unseen."

The sound of the mounted knights began to recede, and Amelia's hope withered. Her captors waited a moment more and then the dagger-wielder waved them forward once again. The man holding her made to follow, then stopped, and Amelia felt his grip loosen. Immediately, she thrust herself out of his grasp, only to feel another hand grab her and pull her free. She half staggered as Righteous pulled her out of harm's way on the way past. Behind her, Spindle was standing beside the kidnapper who had carried Amelia, her straight steel poniard biting again and again at the man's side, striking for his kidneys and other organs. From the expression on his fine-boned face, he must have been dying in agony, but he made not a sound as he slipped to the cobbles.

Righteous had caught up with the dagger-wielder, and he managed to turn to defend himself when he heard her approach. He slashed as he spun, hoping to fend her off, but the Lace Fang caught his knife arm at the elbow with her free hand. His attack checked, she kept flowing forward to bring her own blade under his arm. He tried to block hers with his free hand, but that just put his fingers in the path of her edge, and she slashed right through them. Then her blade reversed in her grip and the full length cut his throat. With a cold professionalism, Righteous turned herself and her opponent bodily on the spot so that his wound spilled blood away from her onto the ground. The two kidnappers had been slain in an instant. Their attacks successful, the Lace Fangs rapidly policed the bodies, pulling Amelia between themselves and keeping an alert watch on the rest of the street. From a nearby workshop, a puzzled man with a set of iron tongs in hand came out to look at the swift carnage.

I must see, Amelia thought, and she tried to move apart from her ladies. The Lace Fangs sought to hold her in place.

"Your Grace, we're sorry we were late," Spindle protested. "But you must let us protect you."

"I have to see," she said, and a part of her mind realized that it was an explanation that would make no sense to her ladies. Nonetheless, she shrugged at their guardian grips and crouched over the bodies. She had to see... but what? What did she have to see?

Their jacks were open and their chests bare underneath. That revealed the first important thing to Amelia. They had none of the Redlander's arcane tattoos, unless they had secret marks. Prentice had once told her that supplicants, the novices of the Redlander cult, often had a single mark somewhere near the neck. Hands trembling, Amelia pulled at their clothing but found nothing.

"Oh, damn it, not now," she heard Righteous mutter and begin to cough. She looked, and the lady clutched her stomach a moment, grimacing with sickness.

"You alright?" asked Spindle.

Righteous held up a hand and shook her head to wave away assistance.

"Just turned my stomach," she said. "I'll be right." Even as she explained though, she suddenly bent double and began to retch.

"See to her," Amelia commanded Spindle. Then the duchess turned back to the two dead men. She was concerned for Righteous, but the angel's warning was still strong in her thoughts. She had to see what there was to see. What was it?

Their faces were odd, unusual for Reacherfolk, and she was convinced they were both from a foreign people. But where? The street began to echo with hoofbeats and the jingle of tack. The knights had found them. That was good, but still Amelia didn't know what she was missing.

The turbans? she wondered. They were brightly colored, as the serpent scales in her dream had been, but what did that mean? She reached out to feel the cloth, but that seemed mundane enough.

"There they are!" called a martial voice. "Form a cordon." The horses began to surround Amelia and her ladies, the sound of them loud in her ears, as in her dream.

I still don't understand!

"Things are not settling back there," said the knightly voice. "We will evacuate the duchess and her ladies immediately."

Amelia pulled at one turban, thinking that it might hide a mark or some other secret. Hands reached down to her, but she shrugged them off a moment. The turban unwound and she saw that the man had no marks. What he did have was pointed ears, long and distinctive on the sides of his head.

Fey!

Amelia could hardly believe what she was seeing. The fey had long been gone from the Grand Kingdom, killed or driven away in crusades a thousand years ago. She reached for the other dead man's turban as more hands sought to grab her.

"Your Grace, you must come with us immediately," said the knight, reaching for her, and Amelia glanced over her shoulder to see it was Earl Sebastian. "There is a riot brewing nearby. We must get you to safety."

She turned back and tried to unwind the second turban as fast as she could. The earl was making good sense, but she had to see.

"They have the shock. See how the other loses her stomach?" said another voice. "We must act for their safety."

The earl's hands gripped her waist, leaning down from the saddle with confident strength. Amelia kept a hold on the dead fey's turban as she was hoisted into Earl Sebastian's saddle. No sooner was she there than he wheeled his mount and spurred away. Nevertheless, Amelia caught one swift glance and confirmed what she suspected—the other assailant also had the

long, pointed ears of a fey. The men who had tried to kidnap her
for some dread ritual's purpose were not Redlanders but figures
of ancient myth, remembered only in children's tales.

But was that better or worse?

Amelia chewed that question as Earl Sebastian led his detach-
ment of knights back to the castle, Lady Righteous and Lady
Spindle riding behind another man-at-arms each. Throughout
the journey, Amelia heard Righteous coughing and retching,
and in the midst of her other thoughts, she spared a moment of
concern for her lady. Could she be poisoned? Did these fey, who
were serpents in her dreams, use some kind of venom on their
blades? There were too many questions. She needed answers.

CHAPTER 13

The White Lions marched up the Dweltford road and past the town to encamp in the northern fields. There had been a time when the meadowland directly in front of the town gate would have served for an encampment, but those pastures were full to overflowing with a shantytown made up of refugees from all points of the war. Some were from the southern Reach, fleeing Redlander attacks up and down the Murr and the Dwelt. Many more had come across the mountains, down the same road the Lions now marched. Some years before, a rebel had burned out the poor hovels that once crouched under the town walls. Now, that shabby little settlement was reborn tenfold, with emigres from war and folk forced off drought-parched farms that could no longer grow sufficient crops.

Marching the militia nearly an hour further north also served another purpose for Prentice—to deter deserters. There were still a good many reforming convicts among his command. Since the drought, the militia's numbers had actually swelled because the seven years' sworn service at least came with a guaranteed meal. Even so, there were doubtless one or two former criminals who might find the chance to skip their service too great a lure. The last thing Prentice wanted to have to do was hoist some runaways by their necks. Better to keep them as far from temptation as possible.

Throughout the afternoon of their arrival, the White Lions' orderly rows of canvass tents went up while sentry posts were set, water lines established to carry to and from the much-diminished river, and the myriad other duties of an army camp were put in place. Prentice kept Solomon on the run with orders back and forth, and despite the morning's training before the march, the boy's diligence never flagged. He was away with a message to the Roars' corporals when a familiar voice caught Prentice's attention.

"Oi up, is that the high and mighty captain o' them White Lions? I thought he was taller!"

Prentice turned from watching the works to see Turley, one-time convicted horse thief and breaker of hearts, now Chief Steward to the Duchess of the Western Reach. What he saw made him smile with surprise. Years ago, Prentice and Turley had been no more than ragged, filthy criminals suffering and laboring together on a convict chain. The man approaching seemed a different person altogether from that mop-headed rogue Prentice had fought with and beside so many times. His unruly dark curls and beard were now neatly trimmed in courtly fashion. He wore fine boots of black leather to just below the knee. His trews were dark, and his paned-sleeve linen doublet was Reach blue and showed sky blue silk in the slashes. On his head he wore a fine leather hat with a cockade of dyed rooster tail.

"No, you're thinking of his old friend, a man named Turley," Prentice answered the finely dressed former rogue's sardonic question. "He was the tall one. A thief too, they say. Now he's a steward, which is almost the same thing, so I hear."

"Not in my mistress' household it bloody isn't!" Turley rumbled and came to a stop in front of his friend, glowering disapprovingly.

"Yes, well, they say he's reformed now, served his time and all that," Prentice conceded.

The two looked at each other sternly another moment and then chuckled.

"You look well," Prentice told his friend. "You're dressing better, too. Your lady wife's doing, I take it?"

Turley nodded, then put a finger inside the collar of his doublet and tugged it across a moment, as if to let heat out. "Dressing better but sweating up a storm under this, I tell you."

"Looks like."

"Don't get me wrong, it's the softest and comfortablest thing I ever owned," Turley explained. "It's like having a cloud wrapped around you, but out here in this never-stopping summer? Ugh!"

"So, stay indoors. The lower levels of the castle must be reasonably cool, away from the sun under all that stone," Prentice suggested to his friend absentmindedly. The main of his watchful attention was back on the encampment taking shape around them.

"Here, are you even listening?" Turley demanded after a moment.

"Of course, I am," Prentice lied. "What were you saying?"

"I was saying," Turley declared with a scoff, "that I'm chief steward. That means I need to be about. I can't just hide in some lower room, 'specially not with my reputation. Folk'd say I was skiving or worse, off somewhere drinking the duchess' fine wines."

"Can't have them saying that."

"No, I can't!"

"So, tell your wife you want to wear something else, something cooler."

"I do, I do, but..." Turley's voice trailed away, and Prentice gave him a sidelong glance.

"But?"

"But? But...I married a damnably fine and beautiful woman, Prentice," Turley lamented, shaking his head. "I go to her with words to speak to make myself plain." He sighed. "I plan to tell her my mind, but then she smiles with those lips and looks at me with her eyes and it all goes out of my head. Like a snuffed candle. Pfft!"

Prentice chuckled at his friend's difficulty. "The burdens a man must bear."

"Ain't that the way of it."

A wagon with no draft animals on the yoke rattled past, pushed and pulled by twenty or so militiamen while their line firsts, the most junior of all ranked men in the Lions, shouted at them to watch where they were going. Some of the men remembered to salute, but most were too focused on their task to even notice their captain watching. Prentice returned the salutes he did receive, and the wagon trundled on through the rapidly growing settlement of tents.

"We're going to need revictualing," he told Turley. "Unless the duchess has sent other orders, we will not stay long. Even for a short while, we would be a burden on the town."

"Ain't no word from Griffith, but my Dalflitch will want to talk to you 'fore you march away again."

"How's that?" Prentice asked.

"That's why I'm out here in this blasted heat," Turley explained. "She's sent me to fetch you, with a by your leave, of course, Captain Ash."

The burly man pulled his hat from his head with a flourish and sketched a reasonable courtly bow. Prentice smiled.

"She's taking her role as seneschal to the duchess seriously, I assume?" he asked. Before her journey south, Duchess Amelia had appointed Lady Dalflitch as custodian over all the Western Reach's offices.

"Seriously is only the beginning of it," Turley said, shaking his head and rubbing at his sweaty scalp. "She's got fingers in pies even I never imagined could be there. She'll do her damnedest to find the feed for your men and mounts, but that's part of what she wants to talk about."

"Not so many mounts to worry about," Prentice said.

"Aye, I noticed that. What happened to your noble companions ahorse?"

"We had a difference of opinion. They chose to ride straight south to escort her grace home."

Turley cocked an eyebrow at his friend, and for just a moment, he was the roguish charmer again, the man Prentice had saved from his own foolishness. "What reckless thing did you do?"

Prentice clicked his tongue. "Excuse me, Chief Steward? In all our history, what makes you think you get to call me out for recklessness? I remember keeping your cocky snout out of many a trouble."

"Tis true, tis true," Turley conceded. "But since you become a freedman, and a high and mighty captain to boot, you been much more the brashiest of the two of us—talking out of turn, not minding your place."

"Brashest," Prentice corrected him.

"What?"

"The word is brashest, not brashiest."

"See, that's what I'm talking about!" Turley gestured with open palms, as if Prentice had just proved his point for him. "Scolding a man for his words like that."

"I always did that," said Prentice, "since long before the duchess let us off the chain."

Turley blinked. "You know, now that I think about it, you're right. Why was I ever friends with you?"

"Because I kept your nose out of trouble, remember?"

"Ah, I knew there had to be a reason."

The two friends shared a smile. Turley looked around the settling camp. "I'm going to get out of this heat. When can I tell my lady wife to expect you?"

Prentice gave the camp one more surveiling glance before nodding in the direction of Dweltford.

"I can go now, if that suits you," he said.

"Alright."

Turley put his hat back on his head and led the way back to town. As they passed a camp sentry point, Prentice gave orders for a runner to be sent to the company sergeant and corporals explaining where he was going.

"And make sure someone tells Solomon where I am," he instructed them, "else the lad will run himself ragged trying to find me."

The sentry saluted and rushed away with the captain's commands for the company.

"Solomon's still running for you?" Turley asked as they walked down the dirt road along Lake Dweltford's former banks. In better times, the glittering waters of the lake would have washed amongst green reeds, willows, and paperbark trees, even in high summer. Now it was a shallow embankment that slipped down to sunbaked mud, a bowl-like plain settled in the midst of vales of yellowed grass, bleached almost to white. Even the mud itself was no longer the rich black of a lakebed but pale and dusty. Lines of townsfolk from Dweltford trailed back and forth across that mud to fetch water from the river proper, which had shrunk to little more than a hopeful stream, trickling through the middle of the dried plain. What had once been enough water to run boats up and down the Reach from Fallenhill in the north and then south to the Griffith Pale and down to the Murr and the Vec Princedoms was now barely enough to keep the town alive. The two men weaved their way around a crowd of lean workmen struggling under yokes to carry heavy leather buckets of water. Each man was loaded down with two or more waterskins as well, slung haphazardly about their necks.

"Most of them's refugees," Turley told him after they passed. "The duchess ordered that men was to keep water hauled to the meadows as well as the town. It's easy enough to find workers for the task, since there's hardly any other work, or not much."

"Lady Dalflitch is organizing the work gangs?"

Turley nodded. "She's over top of it all, but it's the Conclave masters she runs through most of the time. 'Course the guilds all look after their own first, so when it comes time for the unbonded and the poor, she has to be a little whip-handed. She's getting a shrewish reputation in some quarters."

"Is she not paying?" asked Prentice.

"She is, but money's not the problem. Folks can't always find food to buy to eat."

"Silver's only silver if there is something on which to spend it."

"My Dalflitch said something much like."

"It's Fallenhill all over again," Prentice muttered as they neared the town walls, stepping into their shadow but finding little coolness there. Some years back, during the siege of Fallenhill, Prentice had experienced the same problem of more money than food. Starving folk wanted to be fed, not paid.

And now it's over the whole province, he thought. How much longer did the Reach have before its people would have to abandon the land in search of food. Another half year of this accursed summer and there would be riots—first for food, then water, and then his men would be turned on the people just to keep order. *And that will be the beginning of the end.*

The pair approached the town gate where ragged folk were streaming forth.

"Bailiffs turn the refugees out at sundown," Turley explained. "Conclave made a curfew or else there are fights in all the inns and taverns."

Prentice nodded. The end might be nearer even than he feared. He was standing, watching for a gap in the crowd, when he heard his name called from the opposite direction.

"Captain Ash? Captain Ash?"

Prentice turned to see two clergymen stomping over the trodden earth toward him. One was the welcome figure of Sacrist Fostermae, bone thin with cheeks drawn and chin sharp as a horseman's spurs. The hair on his head was wispy, with a shaved tonsure, though his clothes were in better repair than the raggedy robes he'd worn when Prentice first met him, a gift from the duchess for his service. For all the time they had known each other, the sacrist always seemed to Prentice to be only one missed meal from starving to death. Nevertheless, his eyes were bright and his manner energetic and earnest.

The other cleric was much less welcome to Prentice's eyes. With close-cropped, fair hair and a body with a workman's musculature, he was as humbly garbed as Fostermae. He had a wooden leg beneath one knee, but even as he clomped uncomfortably on the prosthesis, he still projected a hardy resolution, and his expression was also clear-eyed, earnest, and open.

"Sacrist," Prentice acknowledged Fostermae with a nod. Then he looked to the other man and for a long moment but could only scowl. Finally, he forced himself to nod a second time. "Brother Whilte."

CHAPTER 14

"Welcome home, Captain," said Fostermae, tugging the thin forelock of his tonsure. "I trust you were victorious. We prayed for your success."

"Thank you for your prayers. We could have used your healing skills as well," Prentice responded harshly, knowing he sounded churlish. Brother Whilte's presence set him on edge. He and the churchman had a cruel history. Whilte had betrayed Prentice to the Inquisition many years previously, which had led to his conviction and exile to the Western Reach. That was all before the brother had lost his leg and been humbled by the experience. Whilte had repented his lies and asked forgiveness for his past actions. Reluctantly, Prentice had given it, but found that if forgiving was hard, then forgetting seemed far beyond him.

"I'm sorry I couldn't be with you," Fostermae said earnestly. "The low folk here have needed so much care. Were there many wounded?"

Prentice smiled at the simple, honest man and shook his head.

"In truth, there were not," he answered. "We never fought for the castle. There were other low folk who might have benefitted from your ministrations though. The castle was full of other refugees who suffered…"

Prentice paused as he tried to think how to describe the brutal sorcery of Halling Pass Castle. What could he tell? How could he fully communicate the horror? Were there words in *any* language that could do it?

"In war it is always the low folk who suffer most," Brother Whilte said. Prentice glared at him.

"You have learned this, have you, Sir?" he demanded harshly. Whilte accepted Prentice's fury with seeming equanimity and shrugged, casting his eyes over the forlorn crowd still leaving the town for the shanties in the meadows.

"Only a blind man or a callous one could miss the lesson," he said.

Prentice was about to snap another sharp reply at the man but bit his tongue. Whilte was right and there was nothing to be gained by provoking an argument with him. He nodded wearily.

"Well, gentles, the folk of Halling Pass have suffered more than many. If you could see your way to send some of your renegade cloister to the Pass, I think the folk there would be glad of the pastoral care."

Since returning to Dweltford from the battle of Red Sky, Sacrist Fostermae and his old friend, Solft the scholar, had become host to a small school of refugee academics and religious men and women. Nuns, monks and other clergy helped Fostermae in his ministries to the people, while Solft and other men of letters endlessly discussed and debated the possible intersections between current events, prophecy, theology, and history. The duchess, eager for every piece of useful information or wisdom to guide her rule, paid a stipend to maintain these intellectuals in their deliberations. "Renegade cloister" was as apt a description of the extraordinary religious community as any other. Many had fled not only the violence of the civil war but persecution from conflicting Church forces as well.

"You seem troubled, Captain," said Fostermae, "if I may say."

"I have many things on my mind." Prentice had always prided himself on being able to conceal his thoughts, at least somewhat, but the sacrist had never struggled to pierce the veil.

"Did something happen in the Pass?"

"Yes, something...if by something you mean rapes, murders and witchcraft."

The two clergy looked to one another grimly, then shook their heads. Turley clicked his tongue and his eyes widened in surprise.

"For true?" he asked.

"I hung an earl and gelded every last one of his knights for the crimes," Prentice told him, nodding. "Including the earl's own son and heir."

Turley whistled. "Well, that's a dark business and no mistake."

Fostermae and Whilte shared an unspoken conversation of some sort and then the sacrist turned to Prentice.

"I will leave for Halling Pass myself with the dawn," Fostermae said.

"What of your duties here?" Prentice asked, pleased but surprised by Fostermae's decision.

"Our 'cloister,' as you call it, Captain, is well disposed for those duties, although there is one issue of duty that Brother Whilte and I wish to discuss with you. A matter of some importance."

"Indeed?" Prentice's eyes narrowed in suspicion.

"You know I have been glad to serve as the White Lions' chaplain since our days in Fallenhill."

"Your service has been valuable," Prentice said quietly. Where was this circumspection leading?

"And the news I bring comes reluctantly," Fostermae continued, sparing a glance at Whilte. Prentice noticed Fostermae was clenching his hands together. He had never known the sacrist to be so uncertain in himself, so hesitant.

"Speak plain, Sacrist," he told Fostermae. "You have more than earned that right with me. You know this."

Fostermae nodded and drew in a fortifying breath. "I must withdraw from the chaplaincy. It is not my first wish, but as your own experience in the Halling Pass testifies, I have greater duties than I did some years ago when I began in the role."

"That is unfortunate, Sacrist," Prentice said. "But why the nervousness? You did not think I would be angry, did you?"

"No, not for this," Fostermae explained. "But you know that the duchess has made the chaplaincy official. Part of my stipend is for that service. And it is good for those in the militia to have prayer and guidance. So, I cannot simply withdraw from my role. For that reason, I have spoken with her grace's seneschal lady and transferred the chaplaincy stipend to another—one eminently qualified for the post, familiar with military matters more than any other clergyman in a hundred leagues or more."

"Well, that sounds perfect, Sacrist," Prentice began. Then his eyes slipped from Fostermae to Whilte and he realized the cause of the sacrist's discomfort. "Certainly not—"

"Hah! A difference of opinion!" Turley declared suddenly, snorting out a laugh. The other three looked at him in surprise. He blinked at Prentice's hard expression and smirked. "You said 'a difference of opinion.' That was why the knights all rode off. Gelding and hanging nobles for rapists, and you called it a difference of opinion. Hah."

Prentice scowled at his friend. "Did you know about this?"

"What? I wasn't listening to that last part."

Prentice turned back to Fostermae, but the sacrist held up his hands to fend off any objection.

"I have already settled the business with the Lady Dalflitch," he said. "It awaits only the duchess' approval upon her return from Griffith."

Prentice felt his jaw clench and his brow knot, but he held his anger in check. Fostermae had outflanked him and set an ambush. There was little to gain from ranting or raving. He could say no, but he suspected that if he was intransigent the sacrist would merely be just as stubborn and the whole issue would still have to await the duchess's return. That thought made him think of his wife, far away at his liege's side, which turned his thoughts around again to the victims in Halling Pass and their need. Fostermae was the best man Prentice knew to send to them, which meant he should be replaced as chaplain. As he arrived at this realization, he was met with the undesirable conclusion that the sacrist was also likely right about Brother Whilte. He was a trained man-at-arms, or had been. Who better to understand the average militiaman's plight?

As he was thinking, Prentice's eyes fell upon Whilte's wooden leg, a simply shaped piece of humble hardwood. It was the perfect symbol of the transformation Whilte claimed to have undergone. The arrogant younger son of a petty noble, facing the world with a sense of unfailing entitlement, had been replaced by this modest man, still strong and upright but with straightforward sincerity. A part of Prentice wanted to believe it was all a lie, to believe that this was some falsehood or ruse. Then it would be so easy to keep hating the man, to maintain his rage against an old enemy. But he knew that was not the case. Whilte was in earnest; there could be no doubt. He bore fruit worthy of repentance, as the scripture described it.

"You wonder if my infirmity will restrict me?" Whilte asked, noticing Prentice's regard. "I promise you, Captain, I can still step as quick as a marching man, and I am not afraid of a day's travel. I will keep up with your company and my duties day and night. I swear."

Prentice shook his head. Where was the man like Viscount Gullden and his fellows, more concerned with personal honor than what was right? For a long moment he said nothing, and Whilte and Fostermae watched him, waiting to see which way the captain would decide to go. Finally, Prentice looked to the gate and realized the exiting crowds had thinned to barely a trickle.

"No, Brother Whilte, I do not believe your missing foot would keep you from a chaplain's good service," he admitted with a heavy sigh. "I do not want to accept you, but I cannot deny there is no better candidate I know to replace Sacrist Fostermae for the role." At the look of relief on the two clergymen's faces, Prentice added, "no matter how much I might wish to."

Fostermae smiled dryly and Prentice returned the expression.

"Honest to a fault, Captain," said the sacrist, and he shook his head.

"If you say so, Good Fostermae. Now, if you will excuse us, Steward Turley and I have an appointment about the duchess' business. Brother Whilte, go to the Lions and say to the watch that you have my freedom in the camp. I will confirm it when I return this evening."

"Thank you, Captain," Whilte said, and he knuckled his forehead where his forelock would have been if his hair were not so short.

"We may be marching on a campaign to hunt bandits or Redlanders soon," Prentice continued. "You can march with that part of the company or make your way to Fallenhill where the rest are billeted as you choose."

"I will pray and see how the Lord guides."

Prentice nodded to the clergymen before turning and pointing Turley the way to the gates. They headed in through the barbican with its withdrawn portcullis and up the High Road to the castle. The late afternoon sun was almost gone, the shadows of the houses and other buildings lengthening across the streets.

"Whenever I'm out at this time, it always reminds me of that night we took the gatehouse from Duggan's mercenaries," Turley mused, looking back at the fortified wall before it was obscured by a turn in the road. "Seems so long ago and still fresh, know what I mean?"

Prentice nodded. He had many memories that seemed the same way in his mind—old but undimmed by time.

"I remember hammering on that door in the darkness," Turley went on, "and that gong farmer, Dran, lying there sucking his last breaths while his blood pooled in his chest. Weren't a good way to die."

"There are few ways that are," Prentice said with a hard tone. "Not in war."

Turley nodded thoughtfully.

"His widow still comes by the castle, you know. We always make sure she's got what she needs."

"Good."

"Her little one's a right terror, too. Near five years old and he thinks he's clever enough to steal from the cooks and stewards. They see him straight, though. We won't let him end up learning to cut purses. We'll keep him out of the bailiff's tender care."

"Is there a point to this conversation?" Prentice asked his friend without looking at him. In his mind's eye, all the captain could see was the man Dran bleeding on the cobbles and the little baby boy who would grow up never knowing his father, another orphan like Solomon and God only knew how many others. All because their fathers marched at Captain Prentice Ash's command. It was not a train of thought he enjoyed.

Turley stopped in the street and turned his solemn friend by the shoulder.

"Aye, there is a point to this talk, and you need to hear it."

Prentice stopped, surprised by his friend's forthrightness.

"You were right, I did know about Fostermae. My wife might be more cultured than I am, but she confides in me no less," Turley explained. "And you took the news exactly as I thought you might, didn't you? I saw it on your face. You wanted to tell that Whilte fella to take a high dive with a short rope round his neck. You've got history, and that's no secret. But you didn't because you knew your duty to the duchess and to all them soldiers marching under her lion flag. You feel all the debts you owe to her and to them, don't you? To every man and woman, convict and free."

"You said you had a point." Prentice felt his temper slipping. He was tired and burdened and had had enough of folk telling him about his own thoughts.

"I do, and it's this—you ain't going alone. I'm telling you that Dran's widow is fed and his boy ain't going to grow up a street thief so you can know. It's not all on you, you see? You have friends, and they're helping you with these burdens you think all fall on your shoulders."

"You think I…" Prentice's fury erupted and then faded as if blown away in a breeze. He looked Turley in the eye and smiled wryly. "You think I take on more burdens than I need to?"

"And I'm not the only one," Turley insisted.

Prentice shook his head. There was nothing he could think of to say to that. Turley clapped him on the shoulder once more and they turned to head towards the castle.

"Of course," the chief steward added after a short space, "if there's any hardship coming 'cause you cut the stones off a bunch of noblemen, then that's a different tale. You can have that crow's cage all to yourself."

"Well, of course," Prentice agreed with a smile. "You weren't even there when it happened."

CHAPTER 15

"My apologies, Captain. I really did not expect the sacrist to ambush you in that fashion. I trust you were not too inconvenienced?"

"Thank you, My Lady," Prentice answered Lady Dalflitch. "It was not a serious matter."

The two of them sat on chairs on opposite sides of a small table in the main hall of Dweltford's Conclave Council building—the Counting Hall as it had come to be known. All the major business between guilds and legitimate merchants flowed through this hall, as it was here the Conclave selectmen kept the records and register of contracts. It was in this very room that Sir Duggan's conspiracy to embezzle the Reach's taxes had probably been birthed, with Vardian Malden's midwifery, of course.

"She says this is where the deals are done," Turley had said as he led Prentice up the brick steps to enter the Counting Hall, explaining his wife's presence there. In the twilight, the way was lit by two tall, glass-faced oil lamps. "She says it's good to watch the coins change hands to see whose fingers are filching."

"Shrewd woman, your lady," Prentice agreed as they entered the doors. The inside of the hall was lit with lanterns as well, though most of the tables had already cleared as the Conclave members returned to their homes for their dinners.

So it was that Prentice, Turley, and Lady Dalflitch found themselves seated almost alone in the lady seneschal's little corner of this fiscal kingdom. Dalflitch began to pack her own documents from the day's transactions into a leather folio, and when that was done, she closed and locked the iron-bound strongbox that served as the ducal treasury while she was about its business.

"I had thought my husband might have warned you," Dalflitch added to her apology to Prentice, cocking an eyebrow at her husband who smiled with blithe innocence.

"I think he found it funnier this way," Prentice said without bitterness.

"Indeed so."

A steward of the Counting Hall arrived at that point with watered wine in a silver ewer and several cups on a tray. Once he had laid the drinks, Dalflitch directed his attention to the locked chest.

"I will see that to the strongroom now," she told him. The man went to fetch another steward and Dalflitch excused herself as she accompanied the two while they carried the chest to be stored in the Hall's stone-lined basement where several vaulted compartments were separated from each other by iron bars and heavy locks.

"She trusts them to hold the duchess' treasury?" Prentice asked, surprised given the way merchants had been so enmeshed with the previous conspiracy to embezzle.

"I wondered about that," Turley said as he took a drink from his cup. "'Parently they're all so shamed by Malden's plot with Duggan that they fall over themselves to ensure the security of that one strongbox, and they watch each other like hawks. Dalflitch says she told them if one silver goes astray, she'll see every master and merchant ends his days as convicts marching with the White Lions, and they believe her. You meeting her here probably makes the threat even more real in their minds, as well."

"Is that why she asked me to come?" Prentice could see the value of his making an appearance in that case, but if that was all he was here for, it was a waste of time he did not have.

"That's not her only reason," Turley reassured him. "Just the thirteenth bun in the baker's dozen. Frankly, I think the Conclave would just as soon have her and the duchy's money anywhere else."

Prentice could well imagine. Merchants were often despised as money grubbing and low in all their thoughts, not without some cause, but the one thing they were usually not was stupid. He took a sip from his own cup and noted the sweetness. After weeks on the march, with nothing but sparse and often stale water to drink, the Hall's wine was a pleasant surprise.

The two old friends sat quietly enjoying their drinks in the shadowy space until Lady Dalflitch returned, carrying a lit candelabra and leading a man whose dark robe and pale cadaverous face made him seem wraithlike in the evening gloom. It took Prentice a moment to recognize the fellow, even though his heavy, dark raiment made him unmistakable as a successful merchant. Even in the heat of the endless summer, the costly form of dress so declared a merchant's wealth that they were loath to give up their "uniform." It gave them too much status. As this particular merchant finally stepped fully into the lamplight, Prentice realized that he knew him, and he frowned with the recognition.

"Captain Ash, I believe you know Master Welburne?" Dalflitch said by way of introduction, and the merchant nodded his head. For his part, Prentice made a point of not standing, but he did return the nod.

"Master merchant," was all he said as greeting.

"Captain," Welburne answered, equally tersely.

Caius Welburne was the only former member of the traitor Duggan's cabal who still walked free, and Prentice was not privy to the deal-making that had caused that turn of events. Why the duchess had not had the man executed, as she had almost all the other conspirators, Prentice could not say. As far as he knew, the only other treasonous merchant who still lived was a man named Folper, who was laboring as a convict somewhere in Fallenhill, too weak and sickly to be a militiaman. At Dalflitch's invitation, Welburne took a seat, and she joined them. There was a long moment of uncomfortable silence around the table.

"Well, this is damned ridiculous," Dalflitch said finally. "Someone has to speak."

She looked to the master merchant, who had steepled his fingers together under his nose. Prentice seemed to remember it was a familiar pose the man took, thoughtful and calculating. With his dark eyes and beak-like nose, it made him appear like some kind of carrion bird, such as a crow, if a crow could be chalk white in color.

"I think it best that you speak first, My Lady," Welburne said.

"Alright. Captain Ash, Master Welburne has need of your militia."

Prentice snorted derisively but was surprised by the earnest expressions on Dalflitch and Turley's faces.

"For what purpose?" he asked with renewed seriousness.

"Master Welburne has been most forthcoming with his services to Dweltford in recent months. In fact, it would be no misrepresentation to say that without his support, the town would already be starving."

Prentice nodded. He was not surprised to hear that Dweltford's position might be dire, but he wondered how Welburne had become so central to its survival.

"The local land does not produce enough to feed the town, especially not with the shanty quarter just outside our gates," Dalflitch went on.

"They are a burden upon the land," Welburne said coldly.

"But her grace is determined to see them cared for," the lady retorted. The swiftness of her response made Prentice think this was an old point of contention between them. "It is her mistake to make and, since it enriches your coffers, perhaps we can cease to argue over it."

The merchant gave the slightest of shrugs, with such a cold expression that his manner bordered on insolence.

"How does this concern the Lions?" Prentice asked.

"Master Welburne has been able to supply food in large quantities from contacts in the Vec. It seems that while we starve, they are enjoying bumper harvests."

Prentice cocked his head in surprise. He had not heard anything from the far south for some time but had assumed the drought extended across the whole of the land.

"The farther south one goes, this false summer fades until, upon the Masnian border, a full harvest and winter have passed," Welburne confirmed. "As the Lady says, it was a bumper harvest, and they are happy to trade much for Reach silver."

"What are you bringing to the town?"

"Grain, mostly. My first caravan brought livestock, but keeping them proved difficult and too many died before they arrived. The villages and farms on the way had fresh meat but Dweltford went hungry."

"First caravan?" Prentice asked. "How many times have you done this?"

"Three, and we now await the fourth."

"Master Welburne assures me it brings salt-meat, hard-tack, dried fruits, and quality pemican that resists the heat well," Lady Dalflitch added. "Also, some other food-stuffs that can be kept long but only for so long."

"I have contracted with mercantile farms in the high-lands," added the merchant, giving more explanation than Prentice needed. "It is a type of agriculture we do not have here in the Reach, though I think to begin it, with the duchess' permission, of course." He nodded to Dalflitch, who returned the gesture with a sour expression.

Alright, so that's why you're helping Dweltford, Prentice thought. They still had not given him the answer he wanted, though.

"You have persuaded me that the master's trade is vital," he said to Dalflitch. "You still have not explained the militia's role in the process."

"The fourth caravan is late," Turley said. "They tried to come up the river on boats like it usually was, except that there's not enough flow anymore. The cargo's all down on the river, days south of here."

"I assume there's a reason you have not just sent bearers down to fetch these supplies," Prentice replied and then his eyes narrowed as a suspicious thought occurred to him. "You do not think to put the task on the Lions' shoulders, surely? We have our own duties to the duchess and the Reach."

"It's the right kind of task for a convict," Welburne muttered peevishly. It was the first time Prentice had seen the man show any kind of emotion. "At least, it was before you made them into men-at-arms."

"Absolutely not—" Prentice began to object, but Lady Dalflitch held up a hand to hold his refusal.

"No, Captain, that is not what we propose. Master Welburne knows that full well. Men have been contracted to carry, but that is the nub of the problem. They will not go."

"Why not?"

"Bandits, so it's said," said Turley.

Prentice sat up in his chair and looked his friend straight in the face. "What kind of bandits? Where have they struck?"

"When the riverboats ran aground, they sent men to find Master Welburne and get his help," said Dalflitch. "The master explained the situation to me, and bearers were commissioned and paid for. The messengers were sent to bring back word, but they never reached the boats. Instead, they encountered another member of their crew coming north. That one reported that the boats were being raided, daily, by bandits on horseback."

"Using warbows," Prentice added, anticipating that detail.

"That's right," said Turley, eyes wide. "The second one coming north had a hole in his thigh, festering, from an arrow shot. If he hadn't met his mates going back south, if they'd missed each other, for sure the fella would've died. How'd you know?"

"We have heard reports from elsewhere," Prentice said, "and seen some of their handiwork."

"And what are you doing about it?" Welburne demanded, vehemently leaning forward.

"We marched here to warn of the danger and revictual before heading straight out to hunt the dogs," Prentice retorted with a voice equal in hardness to the merchant's.

"Despite his fish-like demeanour, Master Welburne has some care for his workmen, Captain," Lady Dalflitch said soothingly. "Their plight has been working upon his nerve."

Prentice paused at that thought. He would never have credited the impassive merchant with such a level of loyalty, but it made a kind of sense now that he considered it.

"And the docksiders are sitting on my money while goodmen bleed and food everyone needs to live grows closer to rot," Welburne added.

"Docksiders?"

"The riverfolk are almost as destitute as the refugees outside the gates," said Dalflitch. "Boatmen without boats don't make much silver. They do make reasonable laborers, though, and they don't haggle too closely."

"Leastwise not until word of the bandits got to 'em," Turley added. "The mongrels are all shut up and refusing to move now. They've been paid, but the Conclave can't get enough bailiffs to enforce the contracts. A hundred or two docksiders is an army of its own, just about."

That's why you need the Lions, Prentice thought. He took up his cup and drained it while he thought the situation through. In one sense it was a Godsend. He had two problems—a witch to find and bandits to hunt. If the bandits were intent on harassing the river trade, then finding them was already accomplished for him. He could not just march his company south, however. Any bandits would likely spot the Lions coming from leagues away and simply ride off. But if his men were tied down escorting the bearers coming back with the food, then he might be able to lure riders out with hopes of catching out stragglers or making night raids. That offered possibilities.

Of course, all this meant he needed to have bearers to guard, which in turn meant forcing the riverfolk to honor their contracts. In all probability that would be almost as difficult as hunting the bandits. If he sent his Lions down to the docks to act as bailiffs, like as not all the able-bodied rivermen would simply melt away like morning mist under the sun. A large proportion of them were smugglers and tariff dodgers, shady dealers as a matter of course. They would go to bolt-holes and wait his men out, flee up and down the river. Even if the trade and cargo boats were grounded, odds were, smaller craft should be able to run and hide.

So, Prentice needed to find a way to strongarm the docksiders into acting as bait for the Lions to hunt the bandits with bows and horses without losing control over them or putting them in excess danger. Dodgy fellows or not, riverfolk were still Reachermen.

Then I've just got a witch to hunt out before she sets more men to rape and sacrifice their womenfolk, he thought sourly. He nodded to himself and then noticed the other three were watching him intently in the lamplight.

"You'll help, Captain Ash?" asked Dalflitch. Her tone was almost plaintive, and Prentice felt for her, suddenly. He realized that, like Welburne, she would be hiding an earnest concern behind her calm façade. Dalflitch's loyalty to Duchess Amelia was almost as deep as Prentice's, and she had the whole town to care for.

"I will, My Lady," Prentice told her directly as he put his cup back on the table. He stood up and straightened his sword on its belt. "First things first, we need to persuade these shirkers on the dock to honor their contracts."

"How do you propose to do that?" Welburne asked, his lips turned down. "Stretch a few necks? Put a few dozen on the chain as a warning to the others?"

"Her grace will not permit abuse of her people," Lady Dalflitch declared, not shocked by the suggestion but plainly resolute in her objection. "Punitive sanctions will not be acceptable."

Welburne snorted derisively but Prentice gestured for peace.

"Ideally, My Lady, it will not come to that," he said. "However, some threats may have to be made. We need to make sure the riverfolk know the cost of refusing to help the duchess. We need their leaders to see the future."

"Oh, aye?" said Turley. "And how do we perform that miracle?"

Prentice gave him a cunning smile and a wink. "We need to meet with an old woman."

CHAPTER 16

"Forgive my intrusion, Your Grace. I have troubling news."

Earl Sebastian bowed formally as Lady Spindle escorted him into the duchess's presence before taking her place behind her grace's chair. Amelia sat at a table in the main chamber of an apartment in Griffith Castle known as the Baroness' Rose Bower. Traditionally, it was the seat of the earl's wife, who for reasons known only to history was afforded merely the rank of baroness. Since Earl Sebastian was newly arrived and unmarried, the apartment was given to Amelia and her ladies while they stayed in Griffith. The central chamber was a solar with fine windows overlooking a courtyard garden of white and pink rose bushes, which gave the apartments their name.

"Your presence is no intrusion, My Lord," Amelia told him, and she gestured for him to sit with her as he spoke. He waved her invitation away politely, casting a glance over his shoulder at High Sacrist Quellion, who had accompanied him into the room. The clergyman was a ubiquitous presence at the young nobleman's side, it seemed.

"With your permission, Your Grace, I will not sit," said the earl, and Amelia wondered if he was afraid to offend the High Sacrist by sitting while the clergyman was forced to stand.

It is your right, Sebastian, she thought, and cast a side glance at Lady Spindle, who stood politely behind her mistress's chair with no complaint. *The sacrist should have no objection.*

"As I say, Duchess, the news I bear is troubling, and while I can spare the time to inform you, my duties will not allow me to take leisure with you."

"Very well, My Lord. What is your news? Has more trouble arisen in the town?"

It had been three days since the two assassins had ambushed Amelia, and for one of those days the lower quarters of the town had been convulsed by a riot that had threatened to consume the entire of Griffith. Acting swiftly, Earl Sebastian had moved to secure the food stores, even though they were more than half empty, using his men-at-arms to form a cordon around the town's granaries and warehouses. When the mob spilled onto the river foreshore intent on looting the food, they were confronted by a company of knights on horseback. A single charge scattered the crowd and then the violent citizens fled back into the low streets as steel-harnessed riders systematically put the unrest down. Since then, there had been reports of discontent but nothing that threatened open conflict. It troubled Amelia deeply that one wild-eyed preacher could stir up so much violence.

"The town rests, Your Grace," Sebastian said confidently. "The troublemakers have learned the folly of upsetting the duchy's peace, and even now the High Sacrist has acolytes searching out this street preacher you say stirred the original uprising."

"Acolytes, My Lord?" Amelia repeated, surprised. "Not bailiffs?"

"The man, whoever he is, is my responsibility," the High Sacrist commented, despite not being invited into the conversation between ranking peers.

"Well, when he is found, High Sacrist, you may send to me at your leisure and I will give my testimony of the incident," Amelia said, choosing to ignore the man's presumption for the sake of a smooth conversation.

"He is a clergyman and will be tried in ecclesiastical court," Quellion responded with an unexpected firmness to his voice.

"If Lord Sebastian thinks that best, I will defer," Amelia said, more confused than offended by the churchman's directness. "And when the need arises, I will present my testimony, as I said."

Now Quellion seemed as confused as Amelia felt. She tried to puzzle out the problem as she watched him reach for something to say. Apparently at a loss, he turned to Earl Sebastian and the two men had an unspoken conversation.

"Something troubles you, High Sacrist?" Amelia pressed, becoming annoyed at the clear violation of good manners, if not exact protocol.

"Your Grace, the court will not be convened on the matter of a divorce or infidelity," Sebastian explained on the clergyman's behalf, his expression twisted in discomfort. Clearly, he hated having to give the explanation he felt forced to make. "You are a woman."

Amelia blinked, surprised by the words and trying to make sense of them. Of what consequence would her sex be to this situation? Even as she formed the thought, the answer struck her.

"Women do not testify in ecclesiastical matters," she said simply. Sebastian smiled with apparent relief, but the High Sacrist merely nodded with exaggerated solemnity.

"Except where divorce or infidelity are concerned," he intoned. "I assume you are not alleging any such contact between yourself and this ragged preacher?"

He cocked an eyebrow suggestively and Amelia felt her patience with the man finally slipping. Clergy had freedoms in polite conversation that were not granted to any but the highest-ranking nobles, but this bordered on a direct imputation. She was saved from saying anything embarrassing, however, as Lady Spindle gave her own incensed response.

"Her Grace never had any truck with that fellow, either before we ran in to him on the street or after," she said with her hands on her hips. "And I'll swear to *that* testimony in any court you want to call!"

High Sacrist Quellion clearly did not like being spoken to in such a manner by a mere lady-in-waiting, but Amelia was not about to apologize to him for that.

If you don't like rudeness, then don't be rude, sacrist, she thought. She kept a stern expression on her face, however. There was no need to gloat.

"Yes, well, if that is the whole of that matter then..." Quellion offered, clearly implying that he meant to leave if given permission.

"There's only the matter of prayer for the sick or injured," said Sebastian.

"Of course," said Quellion.

"The sick, My Lord?" asked Amelia.

"One of your ladies was seen to be retching when we rescued you, Your Grace," said Sebastian. "You have not called for a healer or chirurgeon, but I was told that a herb-wife has been asked to visit. I thought perhaps your lady was ill and asked the High Sacrist here to be ready to pray. I note she is not attending you today."

Observant and considerate of you, my Lord, Amelia thought. She shook her head though.

"My Lady, Righteous, is not injured, thank you, My Lord. She has been troubled in her stomach, which is why we sent for the herb-wife."

Midwife was in fact the correct term in this case. Lady Righteous was nearly three months with child, by the wise woman's estimation, and would very soon begin to show her pregnancy. However, with Prentice's mission to Halling Pass and Amelia's own journey here to Griffith, Righteous had not had time yet to tell her husband. Amelia had agreed to keep the matter secret for their sake, but if Righteous had any more instances of public morning sickness, the secret would be out soon. As it was, if they remained more than a few weeks in Griffith, secrecy would be impossible. The same little voices that had told Sebastian about the herb-wife would happily pass on the news of a lady of the duchess's house gone into seclusion, there was no doubt.

"Well then, that hardly seems a matter for high prayer," said Quellion. Amelia was starting to wonder if the man was able *not* to annoy her, but she nodded as benignly as she could.

"Indeed, High Sacrist. You have my thanks for attending to matters so readily. You may withdraw."

Quellion twitched but managed to bow politely before turning and leaving the chamber.

"Were there any other matters you wished to discuss, My Lord?" Amelia asked Sebastian. The earl's serious expression grew even darker, and he nodded solemnly.

"At least one other, if you'll permit, Your Grace," he said. There was pain in his voice. "The Reach's company of knights martial arrived in Griffith last night."

"The whole company?" Amelia asked.

If the entire company was in the town, then why was she only finding out now? Knight Captain Gullden should have presented himself immediately upon arrival, or at least at dawn if their arrival was late in the night. It made her wonder what the news from Halling Pass could be. The last she had heard was a simple note from Prentice Ash by messenger bird. It had told only that Halling Pass Castle was retaken and garrisoned, but that there was something somber to discuss when he saw her next.

"The entire company is present, though there have been casualties," Sebastian explained.

"Viscount Gullden?"

"It is my sad duty to report that the Knight Captain of the Western Reach has been slain, Your Grace."

"How?" Amelia asked sadly.

Prentice's small report had not mentioned casualties and implied nothing of the loss of the knight captain himself.

"I am told the company was riding south from their victory in the northern pass," said the earl. "The knight captain was in haste to be available for your escort and because there was a legal matter he needed to bring to you."

A legal matter? Amelia wondered. Was that the somber news Prentice mentioned?

"On their journey south, the company followed the dried riverbed and came upon a flotilla of merchant cargo boats grounded for the lack of water. These reported to the knight captain that they had sent men to Dweltford for help in carrying their cargo farther north, but that in the meantime they had become the target of bandits. It was said that the brigands had purloined some horses from somewhere and so could ride swiftly to raid the boatmen, then steal away too fast to follow."

"This must be Lady Dalflitch's shipment," Amelia said thoughtfully. Dweltford could not afford for this cargo to be stolen or even to sit and rot on the riverbank. She wondered what her seneschal was doing about it. There was no way Dalflitch would sit in Dweltford and wring her hands.

"Apparently, the merchants' men said they had been commissioned by the duchy," Sebastian confirmed.

"What did Viscount Gullden and his company do?"

"There was some small discussion, Your Grace. Ultimately it was observed that the knights martials' first duty was to you, and since the militia would have received report of the bandits, the matter was best left to them to resolve."

My knights wanted to ride off and leave men in danger on the understanding that the militia should have heard? Amelia was infuriated by the notion, and she felt her eyes narrow coldly. The earl had more to explain, however.

"Despite this consensus, Knight Captain Gullden sought to resolve all duties, his and the militia's, and he ordered the company to ride off in the night and wait nearby, in hopes of ambushing the bandits the next day. When the brigands appeared, Viscount Gullden ordered a charge to intercept them, scattering them most effectively."

"The bandits are gone?" That prospect improved Amelia's mood significantly, but then she remembered that whatever else, Gullden did not survive this story.

"The men on horseback were driven off, Your Grace. No mere yeoman on a saddle could withstand a knight's charge, they would have known that." A confident smile momentarily lit the earl's lips, doubtless a reflection of his own pride as a knight in the strength and power of fellow men-at-arms. He quickly schooled his face to somber politeness, however. "During the pursuit, it appears that the thieves had some archers hiding to cover their retreat. Several men were shot with arrows and the hunt was called off."

"The viscount was shot with an arrow?"

"Many men were struck, it seems, but the iron heads were mostly not up to the task of penetrating steel harness. The shafts scattered on the knights' armor to no effect, except for one man, who had no gorget. He took a hit to his neck, and it bit through the mail. The wound was not mortal, but he is sickened and receiving the help of a chirurgeon to purge the infection."

"This is all good news, My Lord," Amelia said. "How then was Viscount Gullden killed? Was there some cunning on the brigands' part?"

"No, Your Grace. The knights are convinced the thieves are still hiding in whatever bolt-hole they fled to. But as he returned to his men, Viscount Gullden, having been at the forefront of the charge and getting some way ahead of the others, found his horse had disturbed a viper's nest hidden in a hole in the ground. Several of the serpents sprang forth and bit the poor animal repeatedly. The mount panicked and the sudden rearing threw the viscount from his seat. He fell and his neck was broken."

"Lord have mercy," Amelia breathed, and beside her, Spindle tutted.

"It was a tragic way for a renowned warrior to pass," Sebastian reflected, shaking his head mournfully. Amelia could understand the nobleman's feelings. All young knights wanted to die in a charge of glory, not at the hands of some petty misfortune.

"Perhaps he was robbed in his victory, but we will remember him with honor," she said, and Earl Sebastian seemed to approve of that.

"Such was the attitude of the rest his company, Your Grace. That is why they brought his body immediately south to be bestowed in his home near Griffith and to fulfil his final orders—to be available to you."

"So, the militia came swiftly to the merchants' aid?"

"They made no mention of the militia, Your Grace," Sebastian answered, cocking his head with surprise, as if Amelia had suddenly changed the subject.

"Did they at least leave some men behind to guard the boatmen and their cargo?"

"I...that is...I didn't ask, Your Grace."

Amelia stood suddenly and the earl took an involuntary step backward.

"You mean they could still be out there, waiting for rescue?"

"It is not the task of a knight to guard a merchant's wares, Your Grace."

"No, but it is their task, and duty, to enforce *my* peace!" Amelia did not raise her voice, but it was an effort.

"And they were seeking to do that by being available to escort you home. If you will remember, Your Grace, that if you were to be riding for home to Dweltford, they had a duty to inform you and your escort of the danger of brigands on horseback. It would not be the first time you had been ambushed on the Dwelt River."

Amelia cocked an eyebrow, wondering at the earl's presumption in mentioning the Redlanders' first assault on her years before. As she looked at him, she saw no anger or arrogance in his face, only a sincere commitment in his expression.

It's how you see the social order, isn't it, My Lord? she thought. In Earl Sebastian's mind, her life was worth more than all the lives of those merchants and boatmen, not to mention all the folk in Dweltford, hungry for the shipment of food. At least his thinking was based in a sense of duty instead of the dismissive self-importance that most nobles thought passed for "honor."

Amelia found herself thinking quickly. She had done her duty to win the earl's respect, and the Conclave Council here in Griffith had made it clear they would offer no more support than they were paid for. They had not even sent so much as a note to inquire after her health in the last three days. The fact that she had been assaulted on the streets was an open secret, one most senior merchants, guild masters, and selectmen would surely have been privy to. So, their goodwill was no longer worth waiting for either. Also, from a personal perspective, the duchess wanted to return her lady-in-waiting to her husband's company before her pregnancy had to be announced publicly, as well.

And now there were men in her service possibly still awaiting rescue.

"My Lord Earl, are you well respected amongst the knights martial of my Reach?" she asked suddenly.

Sebastian's eyes went wide with astonishment, and he was uncharacteristically struck dumb for a moment. Then he appeared to gather his wits and attempt an answer to her question. Amelia could tell from his expression that he thought he might be about to be insulted and wanted to steel himself. She knew him well enough already to know that he would never question her to her face. It would be too much of a violation of rank.

"I believe I am, Your Grace," he said stiffly.

"There are no unresolved vengeances between you and any others? No duels yet to be convened or honor debts to be paid? No blood that calls for blood?"

"Certainly not!" Sebastian insisted, and for the first time a tinge of indignance entered his voice. Amelia acted quickly to soothe it.

"Exactly as I expected, My Lord," she told him. "Forgive me that I had to ask."

"May I know why, Your Grace?"

"You may, but first My Lord, let me tell you that I intend to leave Griffith this very hour."

"*This* hour?"

"Indeed. My escort is here, and the unrest of the town has settled such that the streets would be safe enough, even if they were not. I will ride straight north with the entire company of knights martial and we will rendezvous with the grounded merchant boats. If they are yet there, we will assist them in offloading their cargoes for bearing north on animals or laborers and then guard them until they reach Dweltford."

Earl Sebastian seemed at a loss. He clearly had not expected to see the duchess make decisions so swiftly or so comprehensively.

You'll learn, Amelia thought fondly. And she still had to explain the other part of her plan to him, the part she imagined he might not be surprised by.

"I asked if you had outstanding matters of honor, My Lord, because I will expect you and your men to join with the rest of the knights' company."

"Of course, Your Grace." The earl bowed reflexively.

"Viscount Gullden's death is a great loss," Amelia said. "He was a good friend and a mighty warrior for the Western Reach. He will be sorely missed. However, one thing I have learned from my own experience in the recent wars and from watching others is that men-at-arms cannot be expected to wait while we mourn the loss of their leaders. As one hero falls, another must be ready to take up his mantle and rise to the example of his heroism. Earl Sebastian, your reputation in the east is impeccable. You have skill and experience. For this reason, I appoint you now as Knight Captain of the Western Reach."

"Your Grace?" Sebastian gawped. He had the humility to be completely awed by this turn of events, it seemed.

"Give me now your sword, My Lord. A full investiture will have to wait, I fear. Rushed transfers of command are becoming the norm in the Western Reach of late."

Sebastian slid his blade from its sheath and offered it hilt first. Amelia took it by the handle and rested the blade gingerly in her other palm, careful of its deadly edge. She held it up, as if offering it back to the earl.

"Earl Sebastian of the Griffith Pale, I, Duchess Amelia of the Western Reach, invest you with the rank and title of Knight Captain of the Western Reach. Take you now command of my lands' sworn men-at-arms and knights martial. Receive now the honor and obligations of my justice, the King's peace, and the defense of the realm."

Sebastian bowed his head and took the sword back by the hilt.

"We will provide you with a more formal and fitting ceremony once I return to Dweltford, My Lord," Amelia said apologetically. "In the meanwhile, go you now and arrange for us to ride as I have ordered."

"Yes, Your Grace." Sebastian bowed and turned to leave. At the chamber door, he paused a moment. "Before I go, Your Grace, as knight captain, I must mention that there were other serious matters that needed to be brought to your attention."

"Military matters, My Lord?"

"Not precisely."

"Are they matters that might wait?"

"I think so."

"Then let us discuss them later," Amelia said. "Perhaps upon the march?"

"As you say, Your Grace."

The earl bowed once more and left at last. Once the door was closed behind him, Amelia turned to her lady-in-waiting.

"I'll go tell Righteous," said Spindle. "We'll get packed right quick, don't fear, Your Grace."

"Sorry for the lack of warning, Spindle."

Her lady bobbed a quick curtsey. "Don't you fear none, Your Grace. We're nimble girls at heart. Even with Righteous up the duff, we can work right quick."

"I know you can."

Then Spindle was gone into the other rooms to pack. Amelia sat down again with a sigh. It galled her that her best men-at-arms never thought far beyond their rank. At least they were not her *only* men-at-arms anymore. She did not have to depend entirely upon her knights martial anymore with the militia Prentice had made for her, except when the militia didn't know there were folk in danger.

Thinking of Prentice reminded her of his note's warning that there was a somber business she and he had to discuss. Likely that was the same matter Earl Sebastian was hinting at. It must be serious for both men, as well as the fallen Viscount Gullden, to all want to bring it to her urgent attention. Whatever it was, however, it would have to wait.

Poor Gullden, she thought sincerely. The man had suffered many wounds in service to her land and ultimately it had taken his life, dead in a viper's pit near the dried riverbed. The images from her dream crashed into her memory like the clash of steel on steel. A serpent upon a unicorn and attended by angry horses, her knight captain dead from a vipers' nest while fighting horsemen at the river. A sudden shiver of premonition ran through her. The sooner she brought her knights north the better, she was convinced.

Amelia stood and went into the next room to help her ladies pack, ignoring their objections for her rank and status. Time was of the essence; the duchess knew that much for sure, at least.

CHAPTER 17

"The *Gilded Gunwale*," Prentice said, reading the tavern's name off the sun-bleached wooden sign over the door. "Prosaic title."

"Prose what?" asked Turley, standing at Prentice's left hand.

"Prosaic," repeated Prince Farringdon on his right. "It means mundane or normal. I think the captain meant it ironically."

"Ironicky? Well...of course...I figured that part for myself," said Turley, tutting and shaking his head.

"Forgive me, Master Steward," Farringdon answered earnestly. "I meant no disrespect."

Prentice couldn't help but smirk. It seemed the prince had little instinct for guile, and Turley's impudent sense of humor went right over his head. A Grand Kingdom noble would likely have taken offence immediately at Turley's comment, but whether all Vec nobles were more egalitarian or Farringdon was a special case, the prince was at the mercy of the chief steward's droll presumptuousness.

"Whatever the place's name, those two look serious," Prentice said, watching the burly, rough-shaven men standing either side of the drinking house's door. Both wore long chopper knives at their belts, and one was idly hefting a heavy gaff hook. The pair affected an air of relaxed boredom, but they had the swift eyes of watchful birds of prey. These men were sentries, and that fact alone told Prentice that Caius Welburne had likely given them good information. The woman they'd come to speak to was sure to be inside.

"Might as well get on with it," said Turley and Prentice nodded. The three men, accompanied by young Solomon, crossed the street under the sentries' watchful eyes. The gaff hook carrier stepped into their path, blocking the door.

"Tavern's closed," he declared with a rough accent that Prentice couldn't place. A true riverman then, likely grown up in a dozen different ports and provinces. "Ale's all sold. Nothing to drink."

"We are here to speak with the Ragmother," Prentice told him.

"Never heard of her. Piss off."

"One way or another, we are going to speak to her," Prentice insisted.

"Oh, is that right?" The one with just a knife rested his palm on its handle, his eyes looking over Prentice's right shoulder.

"Whatever comrades you think you are signaling, they will not get here fast enough to stop us killing you two first," Prentice told the man, deliberately not looking to see where the sentry was looking. The tavern thug's eyes were drawn back to Prentice's unyielding expression, seemingly against his will. Then he scanned the confidently armed party standing right in front of him as if only seeing them now for the first time. Prentice was wearing his blue brigandine and carrying his heavy war blade. Next to him, Farringdon similarly had his longsword and was wearing a white steel cuirass. Neither had the full array of their armor harness, with its leg and arm plates, but the torso protections were intimidating enough. Turley had no armor, but his polished flanged mace was propped on his shoulder as casually as a ditchdigger's shovel. Solomon had no armor either but wore his newly acquired fighting dagger on his belt as proudly as if it were the holy sword of an ancient crusading hero. The sentry gave a forced sneer.

"Maybe, but I bet we'll take the boy down 'fore you lot even get them swords out. Dockers do for blood, not honor like silk shirts."

At hearing himself threatened, Solomon put his hand to the hilt of his dagger, but Prince Farringdon touched the drummer's shoulder.

"Never reach for your blade lest you plan to draw it," the royal counseled. "And never draw it unless you plan to use it."

Solomon was plainly confused by the advice, and he looked to the other two men with him.

"That's right," Turley told him with a nod.

"Do as the prince says, Solomon," Prentice added, not taking his eyes from the thug in front of him. He hated the whole point of this ridiculous encounter. These men knew who he was, as well as Turley, and now he had made it clear the third man was the Veckander prince who lived in the duchess's castle. These men were smugglers, used to operating quietly in the shadows of the river trade. They had to know the kind of hell they would land themselves in if they made a fight of this, doubly so if they happened to actually injure one of Prentice's party. But as his wife was fond of saying, quick steel and a hard hit can cover up many a lack of wits, until they don't anymore.

Solomon saluted to acknowledge his captain's order, then put his hands by his sides. For a long, restrained moment, the two groups of men stood silently watching each other as if on the edge of a blade. Then Prentice smiled.

"We will be going in to see her now," he said and stepped forward to force the issue. The belligerent sentry looked to his mate to see if they were going to make a fight of it, but the gaff-hook man just shrugged. He used the handle of his gaff to bang twice on the door and then stood aside. It swung open and Prentice stepped into the shadowed interior.

"They give you a hard time, did they, dearie?" said the gummy elderly woman called Ragmother with a phlegmy laugh.

"Sometimes they act like they own the place. Keeps the naughty boys out."

"I didn't realize we looked the type," said Prentice, sitting across a rude wooden table from the ancient woman.

She was a hunched figure in a simple homespun dress and bonnet, her hands gnarled and swollen, her face lined and sun-browned. The woman doubtless looked like any other elder matron of the docklands, hard worked by a long life. But appearances were deceiving. She had the tar-blackened fingers, like Prentice remembered, and probably the same filthy bonnet, but he was fairly certain he could see a fine lining under her collar—silk perhaps. As Prentice watched her, so the Ragmother studied Prentice and his comrades just as shrewdly.

"Sure an' you're much prettier and cleaned up than last time we talked," she said.

"I thought you would have cleaned up more yourself," he told her, "what with Malden gone. Or was that his mistake? Did he care too much about *showing* he was king of the piers?"

The old woman's eyes sparkled, and she laughed before loudly sucking on her wooden dentures. Then she hawked and spat.

"King o' the piers is Veckander talk," she declared. "But you're right 'bout his mistake. Tarif skips got to keep their heads low, protect each other, and keep the secret—share the danger, share the silver." She looked Prentice and his companions over.

"I was a rat when we first met," Prentice explained. "Now, I'm one of the duchess' lions."

"Oh ay, I heard that much," the Ragmother said. She gave Turley a nod. "Your fella there's stepped up as well, so they say. And you keep even fancier company than duchesses now, hmmm?"

She cast a glance away from the table to where Farringdon was standing behind Prentice. He had been offered a chair, as he was entitled to by rank, but the prince had refused it. Prentice felt strange with a royal standing at his shoulder. It was such a reversal of the usual state of affairs, but he could not fault the young man's instincts. They were not out of danger just because they passed the sentries, and the fewer of them who had to rise before they drew their weapons if trouble erupted the better.

"So, what's a lion want with a rheumy old kitty cat like me?" asked the Ragmother, and she coughed into a cloth from one of her sleeves.

"Merchant Welburne's contracted riverfolk to bear for him and they have reneged," Prentice explained. "Seems someone's trying to gouge him, and that cannot stand."

"What makes that my problem, dearie?" the Ragmother asked, and her voice took on a harsher tone. "Take it up with the dockmaster."

"We say the dockmaster ain't got enough steel in his gaff to play a hand like this," Turley told the old woman. "This has your grubby paw marks on it."

"And I say it ain't my turn o' the card."

"Then someone else is playing a hand on your table," Prentice told her. "I assumed you took Malden's trade when I killed him. Is there another player on the docks with the ante to do this?" Prentice was not a true commoner like Turley or the Ragmother, but ten years as a convict meant he could talk like one just fine.

The Ragmother stared at him through slitted eyes and then let loose one of her cackles that made her seem like a mad crone for a moment.

"Oh ho, dearie," she said through her laughter. "Call yerself a lion all you want, but you are canny as a river-banker weasel. All you need is whiskers." She looked over her shoulder at a door on the far side of the taproom and started to shout for someone but was interrupted by another fit of coughing and spitting. It took her a moment to get herself under control, and she was still choking when a nod summoned another heavyset thug from a different shadowy corner. "Get Fulford in here!"

The man accepted her order without question and left through the far door. Prentice felt Turley lean close to him.

"I can't tell," he whispered. "Is this goin' well or not?"

"Too soon to say," Prentice answered quietly. He felt he had a reasonable impression of the Ragmother and her priorities, but if she truly wasn't behind the docksiders' refusal to carry supplies up from the stranded riverboats, that complicated matters a great deal more than he had even feared. For a long time, the tense parties faced each other unspeaking, Prentice doing his best to be watchful under a calm façade while the underworld mistress hawked and spat into her hankie. Suddenly, the back door burst open and a swaggering young man sauntered in. He wore breeks and a sleeveless leather jack in workman's style, but finely sewn with twined red thread through the seams. His hat was made of straw and his ankle boots leather, but both showed the same cost and craftsmanship as his doublet. This was Fulford, dressed to fit in on the river but in a way that quietly declared he cost so much more than any mere docker.

"Aye up, Nanny," he said to the Ragmother as he approached the table. "You had 'nough of these wrigglies? Want me to toss 'em back?"

"Tush you, Fulford," the Ragmother told him. She waved him closer. "I need to ask you something, grandson."

Fulford flashed Prentice a smug smile as he leaned closer to let his grandmother speak quietly to him. He seemed to choke with surprise as she slapped the expression off his face with a noise nearly as loud as the slamming door had been.

"What've I told you 'bout gouging selectmen and the Conclave, you daft sod?" she demanded. Fulford rubbed the side of his face, but it seemed more from shock than pain.

"But Nan, I ain't—"

"Oh, shut it. You're no fair-haired boy no more, and I ain't the soft touch you think I am," the Ragmother continued her scolding. Fulford scowled and cast a rapid, shamed glance at Prentice and his men. For his part, Prentice kept his own expression as neutral as he could. No need to provoke the young man by seeming to enjoy his embarrassment. He trusted the prince and Solomon to be similarly serious but gave Turley a quick check. This was exactly the kind of knife edge he liked to stir to a full barny. His friend was as calm as a statue, and Prentice was thankful.

"They come to me," Fulford said, protesting. "Riverfolk all up and down are tellin' 'bout the ghosts that ride, shootin' arrows from the bankside and takin' boaters down to the mud."

"Tales and talk," said the Ragmother dismissively.

"Maybe not, Grandma," Prentice intervened, and the woman gave him an iron glare that pulled the entire mask of her matronly persona away for a moment. No one interrupted her when she was enforcing discipline, it seemed.

Too bad, Prentice thought. He had no desire to wait while the underworld sorted out its family squabbles, and the boatmen trapped downriver certainly could not afford any delay.

"Your daft grandson is right about new dangers on the river," he went on. "They are horsemen, not ghosts, and the Lions will be moving down to hunt them at the same time the bearers go for the cargo. We will have two hundred in company, all with steel and shot."

The Ragmother and Fulford looked at him, both clearly assessing his words. She began to nod, but her grandson was not persuaded.

"We don't need their help!" he protested. "There's 'nough steel on the river that we don't need convict rogues come to our aid."

"Oh, you fool boy," the Ragmother said, shaking her head. "Was that what you was holding out for? Hiring on as guards? You are dopier than a bluefoot."

"The duchess' militia will enforce her peace," Prentice said flatly. "We have no need of guards for the task. I was ready to come down here with an offer of extra coins per bearer, as recognition for the danger, but not now. Contract breakers get no shrift with me."

"As though you're so high and mighty," Fulford sneered. He gave the other thug near the table a meaningful nod, but before Prentice could even reach for his sword, the Ragmother slammed her authority down.

"Don't be a damned fool, Grick All Fingers," she snapped at the smuggler. "Ain't no four members of your crew could take the good captain and his men here, even if they gave you the first hit free. You see that sword he's carryin'?"

Prentice forced himself to keep his expression neutral even as he felt poised for violence. Truth was, the Ragmother's words surprised him. He had no idea that the tale of his duel with Carron Ironworth and the meaning of the sword he carried would have filtered down to riverfolk. Or that they would care.

"Granny," said Fulford as she gripped him by his chin. "You aways said that kowtowin' ain't no way to run the crews."

"I know what I said boy, and you ain't been listenin' proper. You don't kowtow, but you need to remember *all* the rules. Dry-feet folk on the water? *Thems* you can footpad, if'n you feel to. Riverfolk you can gouge. Merchants, bailiffs, and the muckity-mucks? You buy them off—flash the silver. You *don't never* gouge a selectman or any Conclave member 'cause they bring the one kind of trouble you can't handle." She nodded at her guests. "The ones that dress in steel and knock on the door with swords."

Fulford sneered at his grandmother's rebuke but wasn't disrespectful enough to break her grip on his chin. Prentice wondered what it would take for him to be that defiant.

"That's the old way," he said with a sullen tone. "Now the Redlanders' come, we can change things. They kicked the muckities in their arses and we've kicked Redlanders. We can sit on top o' the heap. We can do it, I know we can! No more kowtowing."

"What's kowtowing?" Turley whispered to Prentice as they watched the exchange between the smuggler queen and her grandson.

"It comes from Masnia," he explained quietly. "It means something like tugging the forelock."

"Oh, a foreign thing then."

Prentice nodded but kept his attention on the Ragmother.

"How did my daughter birth such a muttonhead as you?" she said to her grandson. "We do it the way *we* do it 'cause that way *we* stay safe, little fool. It kept us safe and alive when Malden ruled the river, and it kept us safe long before that. Before you or even your mother was born. The Redlanders, the nobles, the Conclave, the Maldens, and all the other kings o' the piers that think they're going to take it away from us—we outlast them all. That's how it's been, and that's how it's going to be. Until you ken that, you ain't ready to run the crews. Now go and explain to the others how you cost them good silver."

She released her grip and Fulford stepped back, confused as much as chastened.

"What silver?" he asked.

"The captain lion came to deal. You heard him say it himself. Now that's off the table."

"We could still force the deal," Fulford insisted. "What are they going to do to stop us?"

The Ragmother did not answer her grandson's question. Instead, she cocked an eyebrow at Prentice. Seeing his cue, Prentice nodded with a cold expression.

"If the contracted bearers do not march with my men by noontide, I will bring the militia down to the docks," he explained, "and starting at the waterside, we will go house by house, room by room and put every man jack we find on the chain to fulfill the contract. Then we will go back to the lake and every boat, large or small, not owned by an affirmed member of the Conclave will be put to fire and burned to the waterline for smuggling."

Fulford looked aghast at the suggestion, but Prentice was not finished.

"Finally, I will have it posted on every board and every corner that any relatives of the men I've pressed into service can redeem them by offering the name of a known member of any of *your* crews. They will be able to get their men back off the chain by handing you in, and I will offer a twenty-gilder bounty on each one of your heads as an extra incentive. There won't be a tariff skip in a hundred leagues who will feel safe, and I will make sure it is your name they hold accountable."

"Bastard," grunted the thug named Grick All Fingers. His hand went to his fighting dagger, but Prince Farringdon was ready, and his sword leaped from its sheath. He pointed the long blade's tip at Grick and the smuggler froze. In the corners of the room, other men stirred, ready for violence. Turley put his hand to his mace and even Solomon drew his dagger. Only Prentice, Fulford, and the Ragmother remained still—the calm in the midst of the impending storm.

"You'd set fire to the whole of Dweltford? The town would rise. You wouldn't dare," Fulford said, not sounding quite as defiant as his words. Prentice cocked his head and gave a smile.

"As *you* said, it is a new time, and the rules are different."

Fulford looked to Grick and then around the room.

This is the moment, Prentice thought. If Fulford was going to challenge his grandmother's authority, this was when he would do it. Everything was so still, everyone holding themselves in place in case even an errant twitch became the spark to set the blaze alight. The drought made everything in the Reach a tinderbox. Then Fulford bowed his head and nodded to the Ragmother.

"Alright," he sneered as he stepped back.

"That all you have to say?" she demanded.

"Sorry, Nan."

"Don't say sorry to me. Go tell your mates whose money you lost."

Fulford scowled but accepted his dismissal, leaving the tap-room by the same door.

"He's young and eager for his inheritance, and he can't figure out why I ain't dead yet," the Ragmother explained.

"The enthusiasm of youth."

There was a long moment of silence. The Ragmother sucked on her teeth.

"You really would do all that, wouldn't you?" she asked Prentice. He did not bother to answer, and the old woman nodded to herself. "The Lioness picked right smart when she plucked you off the chain."

"That she did," Prentice agreed.

Half a candle later, Prentice, Turley, Prince Farringdon, and Solomon were all safely back on the street with the Ragmother's assurance that the contracted bearers would be ready and provisioned to march by noonday.

"Well, that was hairy and no mistake," Turley said with an exaggerated sigh. He wiped his sleeve across his brow.

"I did think we were going to have to fight our way out of there," the prince agreed. "If that young buck Fulford had his way, we would have."

"Yes," said Prentice. "He is going to be trouble."

"You think still?" asked Farringdon.

Prentice shook his head. "Not for today. In the future."

"What will you do about it?"

"What can we do?" asked Turley. "Nothin' as I can see, for now."

"We have other things to worry about today," Prentice agreed. "But we need to keep an eye out for him. In spite of his grandmother's instruction, I doubt he really learned his lesson today."

Prentice looked to Solomon.

"You, however, young man, kept your nerve well in there," he said and patted Solomon on the shoulder. "And you pulled that dagger at exactly the right time. Lady Righteous would be pleased to hear how you were ready to throw down with your fellows when it came time for bared steel."

Solomon straightened under the praise and smiled. Then he remembered and saluted his captain. Prentice returned the respect and then looked up at the sky.

"Not too long until noon. We need to be ready to march. We've lost too much time on all this already."

CHAPTER 18

The Reach knights martial rode north on the road out of Griffith in two columns—one ahead and the other behind—escorting a number of wagons and the duchess's carriage. Amelia would have preferred to ride her mount Silvermane, but her ladies, being born of low rank, did not really know how to ride, and the duchess decided it was wiser to keep close to her bodyguards after the assassination attempt in Griffith's back alleys.

"Road" was a generous title for the simple track that ran beside the diminished river. Until the drought, even the common folk used the waterway for long travel at least as often as walking. Even now, while there was still some boat traffic, a barge or other rivercraft laden with horses and armed men would struggle to find the depth to navigate. So, the ducal company was forced to ride and march. The duchess's open carriage had a cloth canopy fitted to it to keep the sun off, but even so the journey was uncomfortable, and the air was oppressively hot. As evening approached, there was little sign that there would be much relief once the sun set.

"Uggh, if I'd known I'd feel like this I'd never have wanted a babe," Righteous groaned, leaning on the side of the carriage, resting her head on the cloth of the canopy where it was pinned to the wood.

"Here, dab her brow," Amelia told Spindle, handing her lady a soft cloth and a small, brass-stoppered bottle of water. The liquid would not be cool this late in the day, but the air on damp skin might be a little relief.

"My mam used to say the sick goes away after a while and then it feels alright," Spindle told her friend as she damped her forehead.

"How long is a while?" Righteous demanded. Spindle and the duchess shared a smirk, which the pregnant woman noticed. "Ah, easy enough for you two grinnin' Gerties."

"Yes, and soon you'll have your newborn, and we can sit and envy your happiness," Amelia chided her. Righteous frowned and groaned again.

"That's assuming the little'un makes it into the world," she said grimly. "What if I can't keep him, or her, 'cause of what was done to me?"

"You mustn't think like that," said Spindle. She gave her friend a quick, encouraging hug. Righteous did not respond. Amelia frowned and felt her heart ache for her bodyguard companion. Righteous was as hardy in body and mind as any woman the duchess had ever known. It was easy to forget that she might have ordinary fears and desires like any other wife and mother, let alone a mother who had such a savage history of abuse behind her. The thought that the violations Righteous had suffered might reach up out of her past and deny her the child she was eager for filled Amelia with such disgust that she wanted to curse and rage at the world. She could only imagine how Righteous, or her husband, felt about such a prospect. She looked away to see what progress the company was making and to get a sense of how long it would be until they would stop for the night, ideally at a village with a deep well that still had good water. Her eyes lighted on something that caused her to smile despite herself.

"Lady Righteous, I've always thought that if one cannot escape a discomfort, then the next best treatment is to distract yourself from it."

"Sounds like a plan, Your Grace," Righteous responded in a sour tone. "Can you suggest something?"

"Indeed, My Lady. How about that?"

Amelia pointed out to the left of the wagon where the minstrel Bluebird was riding on a shaggy pony with bedraggled, long-faded ribbons wound through its mane. The jester was sat mostly sideways on his saddle, with his motley blue-winged arms stretched wide and one leg cocked around the saddle's pommel to keep him from falling. As he bobbed along in this unnatural posture, he produced a number of small bright balls in one hand, seemingly from the very air. Amelia assumed the man had them stored in his sleeve, brought out by sleight of hand. Righteous and Spindle shifted in their seats to join the duchess, and the ladies watched as the adroit man began to juggle the three balls one-handed. Then he tossed them over his head to his other outstretched hand, where he set them circling again. It was an impressive display, apparently some form of practice, as the tumbler showed no indication that he knew he was being observed. For some time, he continued in this fashion until his pony missed its footing on a stone and he was forced to regain his balance. Nevertheless, he caught his three balls before they fell, and Spindle applauded him spontaneously. When he looked, Amelia joined her. Righteous only nodded wanly and waved. Bluebird smiled and, flipping around the saddle in a series of movements that surely threatened to throw him to the ground, he bowed politely to his noble audience.

"You do quite well, Master Bluebird," Amelia called to him as he twisted once again to sit his saddle straight, guiding his mount closer to the duchess's carriage.

"Thank you for your kind praise, Your Grace," he returned with a jaunty wave. "It pleases me to know that you might approve of something I do."

"Did I give you cause to wonder?"

"Some cause, I thought, Your Grace," Bluebird admitted with a light manner. "At the earl's feast you seemed the least impressed with my performance."

"Your performance was impressive," Amelia confirmed readily. "I simply did not care for your second poem."

"No?" The performer seemed genuinely surprised to learn this fact. "The troubadour who taught it to me in Rose Carabost insisted it was a popular verse here in the west."

"Then you were lied to," Amelia said directly, and the notion annoyed her. If *The Gull and the Golden Horns* was not something that Bluebird had composed himself, then it meant the humiliating verse was possibly being recited all over the Grand Kingdom. Her immediate thought was that it might have been commissioned by the usurper King Daven Marcus. It was the kind of petty insult he would enjoy.

"The poem offended you, Your Grace?" Bluebird pressed, and there was a seriousness to the man's demeanor that Amelia had not seen him ever show before.

"It was clearly meant as an insult to my militia captain, Prentice Ash, casting him as the mangy mutt," the duchess explained. "It was he who defeated my renegade vassal, Liam, the man with golden horns on his helmet."

"I had no idea, Your Grace," said Bluebird, eyebrows lifting.

"It was obvious to any Reacherman, I assure you, minstrel," Amelia said. She had been happy to leave the poem's petty insults in the past, but now that Bluebird had asked after her thoughts of the night, she found her resentment was still quite fresh. She kept her tone low, but her knotted brow and harsh scowl made her displeasure unmistakable. "My lady here is the captain's wife, and she felt the insult most keenly."

Amelia gestured to Righteous, who lifted her masked head and, in spite of her sickly condition, managed to give Bluebird a cold glare. The minstrel swallowed visibly and then nodded a sincere apology.

"I crave your forgiveness, Lady," he said with a bow. Righteous only snorted and then lowered her head once more.

"I think you can count the matter settled for now," Amelia told Bluebird gently.

"Thank you, Your Grace. As to that wicked verse, I shall cast it from my memory. You shall never hear of me speaking it even once more in your lands."

Amelia wondered if that meant he might recall it to his memory again once he moved on from "her lands" but dismissed the thought as uncharitable. The potential to offend the dignity of the well born must be a constant hazard for jesters and the like. The man had apologized, and that would be enough for Amelia. The wagon continued to roll as the sky darkened toward evening and Bluebird kept his position, riding quietly beside.

"Your Grace, might I ask one more question?" he said after some time.

"What is it?" Amelia answered.

"If your captain is the mut...I mean, the hound spoken of in the tale, then who is the lady to whom the hound returns? Is it your lady-in-waiting? That would indeed have been insulting of me and I am horrified to think I would have mocked her to her face in that way."

"The lady of the verse is myself, Bluebird," Amelia told him. The man's insistence on returning to the subject kept her mind agitated, but she did not feel badly disposed towards the minstrel himself for all that. It was not his fault someone had created a poem to insult her.

"Well, that is even worse, Your Grace," Bluebird said, holding a hand to his chest. "In that case, I would have insulted your captain, his wife, and you. It implies the foulest of rumor, of infidelity at the highest level of the Reach. No wonder you and your lady were so disquieted."

"Indeed."

Another moment passed without conversation and Amelia could see torchlight ahead that indicated they had reached a travelers' inn. She and her ladies would have a reasonably comfortable sleep for the night, hopefully.

"Can I impose upon your indulgence yet one more time, Your Grace?" Bluebird asked. The man was persistent, and Amelia wondered at his ability to skirt the edges of propriety. Whether he was performing as a tumbler or speaking privately with a ranking noble, he was exceptionally skilled at risking offense without ever actually giving it.

"I think we will soon be in for the night, good Bluebird," Amelia said. "So, whatever you would ask, it had best be quick."

"Quite so, quite so, Your Grace. The *Gull* speaks of the lady having a husband, and you say the lady is meant to be yourself, yet you are unmarried, or so I am told."

"Widowed, not unmarried."

"Oh, an unhappy fate," said Bluebird. His tone was so emotionless that Amelia wondered if his talent for words had failed him momentarily. "I never imagined you might be a widow, so young as you are. I just wondered if perhaps the verse pointed to a suitor or a betrothed? It is presumptuous of me to ask and for that I beg forgiveness, yet again. I only mention it because if there is such a blessed gentleman, I might seek him out and offer my talents."

"You want to work for my fiancé, if I have one?" Amelia asked, cocking an eyebrow at the odd request. "Why?"

"Only so that by offering him my talents, I could provide a fresh verse by which to atone for the misdeed of my previous performance."

"You want to write love poems for my betrothed?"

"It is a task I have some experience in, Your Grace."

"Sounds lovely," Spindle whispered, and Amelia turned to see the masked woman smiling at the minstrel. The duchess nodded to her lady and turned back to Bluebird.

"I fear your hope of employment is in vain," she told him. Bluebird shook his head sadly.

"That is somber news indeed, if I may say so, Your Grace. A woman so young and so graced with fine and notable traits should not be consigned to widowhood."

"You are a presumptuous sort, Master Bluebird," Amelia said, smiling and shaking her head.

"A hazard of my profession, I fear, Your Grace."

"Well, I accept your words as the compliment I think you intend and encourage you not to presume too much upon my goodwill."

Bluebird bowed in the saddle once more, and as he came up, Amelia could see how much the light had faded by the shadows on his face. It was striking how completely his expression had suddenly become obscured.

"With your permission, Your Grace, I will withdraw and seek a place for me to lay my head tonight."

"Go to," Amelia said with a dismissive wave.

"And in parting, one last excess," Bluebird said as he let his mount slip behind the carriage. "I will pray that a noble and fitting man might come to you soon and plight his troth that your future might not be lonely, Your Grace."

Then he was gone, lost in the shadows of twilight.

"Silver-tongued beggar," Righteous muttered. "But at least he was more polite about it than that High Sacrist."

"Quellion?" Amelia asked her, surprised.

"Well, aye, Your Grace. Both of them wanted to comment on you being a widow, but at least the jester bloke was polite about it and wished you well."

Amelia hadn't seen the connection, and Righteous's words made her wonder just how many people in the Western Reach thought to take an interest in her marital status. She was so used to princes, kings, and high clergy presuming to tell her how and when to marry that it had been a long time since she had thought anyone might simply wish her well—the happiness of a fine match. Then she thought of Spindle's gushing appreciation of Bluebird's poetry and realized that she wasn't the only one who might long for the simple blessing of a happy marriage.

Perhaps soon, My Lady, she thought, but even as she did, the question reminded her of the limitations the two of them faced. Spindle was scarred and known for it, and Amelia was certain that the number of men she herself could choose from was so small that it was like hunting a mythical beast. Yet, she looked at Righteous and thought of how the steel-edged young woman had found herself a husband as suited to her as any man could be in Prentice. Perhaps the beast was not as mythical as she imagined. Bluebird did not seem to think so.

CHAPTER 19

"We found some tracks in the dust so we know they ain't ghosts, but whatever they are, they're swift in the saddle. We never get more than glimpses."

Prentice nodded at the scout's report, his eyes scanning the western horizon. For the last two days his men had been seeing riders in the distance as they marched alongside the dried riverbed, escorting bearers and wagons. Until last night, it seemed these mysterious horsemen were content keeping their distance, shadowing the column. Then, just before this day's dawn, some of the riders—how many no one knew for sure—had sneaked close to the encamped company and shot fire arrows into the wagons. Even with the flames to give their position away, the raiders had vanished before sentries could intercept them. Worse, at the other end of the camp, two sentries were slain, shot by unseen attackers while everyone else was distracted with saving the carts and beasts from the fire.

"What are they doing?" asked Prince Farringdon once the scout was dismissed.

"Harrying us," said Prentice.

"But why? What do they have to gain?"

"I do not know."

"Were other Redlander attacks like this?" asked the prince, and that question cut to the heart of Prentice's own thoughts.

I am not sure it is Redlanders, Highness, he thought as he rubbed his beard. The Horned Man's invasion, the first campaign against the Redlanders, had been similar to this, with the invaders attacking and then vanishing. That had been a deliberate tactic to lure a Grand Kingdom army into battle, a test of strength before the larger invasion that came down the Murr River and captured Aubrey. Were these riding archers the vanguard of a second large invasion? Prentice did not think so. They simply were not brutal enough. All the Redlanders Prentice had ever faced were too confident, too arrogant to waste their time with continual hit-and-run tactics. They moved swiftly and knew how to keep out of sight of scouts, that was true, but when it came time to give battle, they threw themselves into it, eager to come hand-to-hand.

So, if not Redlanders, bandits then?

That was making even less and less sense as the days passed. Raiding small bands of refugees or grounded traders' boats was one thing, but these riders were trailing a fully armed company. And now they had raided in the night. Prentice had assumed that marching a larger company of men with the bearers would chase these horse archers away, make them seek easier targets. That was what any typical bandit would do when faced with too many guards. Instead, it almost seemed that the Lions' presence was drawing more of the riders' attention. What the hell was going on?

"If only we knew what they want," Prince Farringdon said, and Prentice nodded.

"Well said, Your Highness. Until we do know, we will be forced to keep dancing to their tune."

"At least their harrying costs us little for now."

"Other than the lives it cost two of our men," Prentice said, not meaning to be so blunt but unable to keep the sourness of his thoughts out of his tone. The burning wagons had been saved, and with dawn over and the sun now fully above the horizon, it was time to set the company to march. The one piece of good news they had was that it looked as if they might be only half a day from the stranded merchant riverboats, but even that only increased Prentice's inner tension. If these unknown horsemen were prepared to attack his heavily armed company, what would they have been willing to do to a small group of traders? Would any of the boatmen still be alive when relief arrived?

The company marched and Prentice divided his militia into two columns, setting them, escort fashion, on either side of the hired bearers and wagons. The river flow was deepening at last, so it was no longer possible to walk in the dried bed. Prentice kept the bearers and wagons on the east bank to keep them a bit safer from arrow shots, with one of the escort columns on the opposite bank. Despite the heat, orders were given that every man was to wear his armor on the march. Even diminished, the river at least gave enough water for his men to keep from dropping from thirst.

"Long ways west!" came a sentry's shout just before midmorning, and soon a man of the Claws was wading the shallow waters to report what the west column had sighted.

"There's dust out west, Captain," he said after saluting. "Seems like riders, maybe a big company."

"I will come see for myself," Prentice told the man and followed him back across the knee-deep water flow and up the other bank. Clouds of blowflies clustered around their faces as they tromped out of the mud and crossed the dried grass to the hundred-man column on this side of the river. When he arrived, Prentice was shown to a raised hummock and pointed west. Keeping the flies away with waves of his hand, he studied the horizon. The rising dust cloud was unmistakable, and large, just as the sentry had reported. He tried to estimate the distance.

"Ten leagues, would you say?" he asked the men with him.

"Give or take, Captain," the column's lead corporal, a man named Noam, agreed.

That meant the riders were not more than an hour away, much less if they wanted to cross the distance quickly and directly. Since leaving Dweltford, sentries had sighted groups of three and four riders, and none of them had raised a cloud like this.

A hundred at least, Prentice guessed. Whoever or whatever they were, they were not bandits. Of that, he was now convinced.

"Keep close watch," he told his men. "If they come close enough that you can make them out, send to me and we will bring the second column across the river to support you."

"You think there'll be a fight, Captain?"

"We will see." Prentice still could not understand their strategy, nor did he see why they were revealing themselves like this. These riders seemed like ghosts to their victims, coming and going unseen. Why were they raising so much dust just now?

Prentice returned across the river and rejoined the march south. The wagons creaked and the insects buzzed in the morning heat. The heavy air shimmered and the stink of sweating men was almost stronger than the smell of dust and long-dead plant matter. Marching feet tramped wearily until another shout rose, a more hopeful one. The company had reached a point where the main Dwelt was joined by two small streams in short succession and its level had quickly risen until the water lost much of its muddiness. Soon after their wagons crossed the streams, as they rounded one further bend in the river the merchant boats came into view, less than two leagues away. From the distance, it seemed that there were still men on their decks, as several tiny figures leaped up and down, waving at their approaching rescuers. Prentice breathed a small sigh of relief.

"We seem to have arrived in time," said Prince Farringdon, riding up behind him.

"Indeed," said Prentice. "Can you see much from there, Highness?"

"Men on the boats are waving, I think."

Prentice was pleased. They would easily reach the boats before noon. He could order the bearers to unload the supplies and allot them through the afternoon while the White Lions set a strong defense to camp through the night. Any injured rivermen could be put in the wagons and then the whole company could begin a swift march back to Dweltford tomorrow morning. They would have to improve their sentries in the night to keep from having more fire-arrow raids and assassinations, but Prentice had ideas about that as well. It was time to get the western column back across the river. He was just about to send a runner to give the order when he heard a sentry cry from the west, followed by beat to arms on a cohort drum, echoing across the water. He looked down at the deepened river flow and realized his mistake.

"Corporal," he shouted, and the militiaman named Gennet was with him in an instant.

"Captain?"

"Take your cohort back north, now!"

"North, Captain? Aren't we going to the boats?"

"There's an ambush coming from the west," Prentice explained rapidly. "I want you to march back to where the river's shallow enough to wade across, then come back down the other bank. Meet me at the west column."

"Meet you? Aren't you coming with us?"

"No corporal, I am going for a swim."

Corporal Gennet looked at him as if he had gone mad, but Prentice had no time to explain it. The raiders had been massing all morning, and Prentice was sure he had finally understood why. They had waited until his company had reached the point where the river widened and deepened so far that it was too difficult for men in armor to cross quickly. Half his men were trapped on the wrong side of the river. Prentice had been so focused on reaching the stranded boats and keeping the escorted bearers safe, that he had missed one important possibility—that the raiders wanted him to divide his forces. Now that they had them effectively separated by the deeper water, they were attacking.

"Solomon, run to the wagons," he told his drummer. "Fetch my helmet. And take this, put it there." He handed off his partisan, the wing-bladed captain's spear.

"Here, what's going on, Captain?" demanded a strained voice, and Prentice turned to see one of the hired bearers striding up to him with a handful of others flocking behind. All were agitated. "Where are all them going now?"

The crowd of laborer's looked to the eastern escort column that had already turned about and was marching north at a demanding pace.

"They are going to cross the river to join the others," Prentice told the man, not stopping to talk but walking down to the bankside, trying to estimate the depth and distance of the swim he was contemplating. Swimming in armor was not impossible, but it was no easy task. Making a quick assessment, he stopped and knelt to unbuckle his cuisses and greaves, the steel plates that protected his upper and lower legs.

"And what are *we* supposed to do?" the leader of the bearers demanded. "We was promised protection, not being abandoned with the boats we come to off-load."

"Make straight way to those boats," Prentice ordered the man, speaking in riverfolk fashion. "Best speed. Then wait there until we deal with these bandits. We will catch up to you then."

"And what if these bandits do for you instead of you for them?"

"Do you really think that likely?" he asked the man and flashed a confident smile that felt like a bald-faced lie. Prentice was completely wrong-footed by these riders. He had no idea what was likely at this moment.

Solomon returned with his helmet and Prentice took it and then handed off his leg plates. "See these back to the wagons and then go with the bearers to the boats," he commanded the lad.

"I can swim!" Solomon protested. "I know how."

"Of course, you can," Prentice said, utterly unsure if Solomon was telling the truth and having no time to form an opinion one way or another. "But I need you to go where you are ordered. Pass my commands to the labor column and point them straight south. Once you get to the boats, you climb up on top of the tallest one there with your drum and keep watch. Stay alert and beat alarm and direction if you see anything that looks a threat. A good strong beat, one that can be heard for leagues because I will be distracted on the other side of the river. Can I trust you in this?"

Solomon saluted with such pride that a silver chain bounced out from under his collar. On the end was a little pendant that flashed in the bright sun—his silver rat, the one that had once been owned by Prentice's friend, Sir Gant.

"Watch your chain, lad," Prentice told Solomon. The drummer tucked the rat and chain away before hefting his captain's leg armors onto his shoulders.

"Come on, you lot," Solomon told the bearers as he headed towards the wagons. "You heard the captain's orders."

"There's a battle coming, and you expect us to follow a little drummer boy?" demanded the lead laborer.

"That little drummer boy has seen more battle than any five of you," Prentice said coldly. "When he brings my orders, he carries my authority, and knights and nobles have seen fit to accept my words from his mouth without complaint. Now, go to. Follow him and let me get some steel into these damn 'ghosts,' teach them they are mortal after all."

The rivermen looked to each other only a moment before moving back off to follow Solomon, who was already strutting like a cockerel in a farmyard toward the wagons. Prentice turned back to the river and drew in a deep breath. Leaving his leg armor would make the crossing easier, he hoped, but it would still be a hard swim. The flow was not as strong as it would have been in other years, but the water was muddy, and anything could be concealed under the surface. He thought about tangling roots or submerged hazards. If he got caught, even momentarily, then the rest of his armor would be a dead weight that would pull him down too fast to cast any off in time. He wanted to strip it all away, discard his boots as well. That might have made the swim safe, or safe enough, but then he would have to face those deadly horse archers virtually naked. There was no good choice, and he was about to unclip his pauldrons when Prince Farringdon rode up to the river's edge.

"Tell me, Captain, do you mean to swim the distance alone?" the prince asked. Prentice cast him an annoyed glance, but before he could make a retort, Farringdon went on. "I only ask because I have been thinking that a swim might do old Elkman here a deal of good."

The prince leaned down and rubbed his mount's neck affectionately.

"I wonder if you might let me swim him with you for the company? You could even hitch yourself to my saddle horn to give him a better workout, if you were so kind."

Prentice blinked at the prince. Holding onto the saddle horn would make the crossing child's play. He smiled and nodded.

"I would be glad to help Elkman with his swim, Highness," he said with undisguised relief. Then his expression became stern again. "Just the one crossing though, I fear. I have business on the other side."

"Oh, excellent. I will join you there, too, with your permission, Captain."

"I will be in the front-rank Highness, but you will be welcome to stand beside me."

"Very good," said the prince, and he reached over behind himself to heft his sword belt off its saddle hook and over his shoulders to settle it at his waist. When he nodded again, Prentice fitted his helmet on his head and leaped up to grab onto the saddle. Then the prince's horse plunged into the murky river.

CHAPTER 20

"Looks like trouble after all, Captain," said Corporal Noam as Prentice joined the western column in their ranks, dripping with water. The Lions were arrayed in their usual fashion, eight ranks of ten men with pikes and swords, while the twenty gunners of the Roar were at either side of the main body in two loose lines out in the open, ready to fire their matchlocks and then withdraw into the main square for protection. It was the core strategy Prentice had devised for facing knights and Redlander infantry in hand-to-hand, but looking at it now, deployed in the open on this far side of the river, his well-trained militia looked like a tiny clutch of tired, thirsty, sweat hogs.

Prentice looked out and saw that the dust cloud of the enemy riders was close now, perhaps not more than a league. He could already see the forms of individual horses in the front of the cloud.

"We are going to change formation, Corporal," Prentice told his junior officer.

"Drummer ready," Noam ordered a red-haired youth at his side. The young man had a drum on his hip and his sticks in hand. Prentice shook his head.

"This is not one we already know," he said and then stepped out several paces in front of the company, turning to face them. He opened his mouth wide and bellowed with his best town crier's voice. "Pay attention Lions, because we do not have a lot of time to get this right."

Every eye was on him, but all Prentice could think was how his skin crawled between his shoulder blades, his back turned to the onrushing horsemen and their bows. Any moment now they would come into their range, which was the problem Prentice knew he must deal with. The Lion's typical formations were designed to keep the militiamen close together so that their mass gave them strength and increased their protection. That was why they were so heavily armored and carried long pikes and halberds in the main to hold their foe at a distance, like a hedge of sharpened steel. Only his swordsmen and gunners, meant to hide inside the massed ranks and then spring forth to fight when the opportunity arose, wore lighter armor. Except they were not meant to face a force made predominantly or exclusively of archers. The more the Lions pressed together for safety, the more they would be a juicy target at which to aim. Odds were that their armor could soak up a significant number of arrows, but that approaching cloud looked like it was bringing an equally significant number of bows to shoot those arrows. There was no point making it easier on them. Prentice just hoped his men trusted him enough to overcome their instincts for safety and do as he ordered.

"Roar front and center, one line on me, three columns spacing!"

The gunners rushed from the ranks to follow Prentice's order, but once they had begun to form the line, they slowed down, unfamiliar with the new spacing. Prentice gave a quick glance over his shoulder. The horsemen were coming on and the breeze brought the first whispers of their hoofbeats.

"Come on, you louts," he shouted. "Claws, help them out. One pike and one halberd beside each Roar, face forward."

More of the militia moved into place.

"Fangs, do not think I have forgotten you! One of you each behind a man in the front rank, swords drawn and bucklers over your man's head. If they want to send us a rain of shafts, I want you ready to bat the showers away. I know it's a long time since any of us needed rain hats, but you'll remember how they work soon enough."

That drew a desultory chuckle from some of them. The Claws came up as ordered. Even as the strangely open formation took shape, with pairs of men so close behind each other they were all but embracing, Prentice turned back to watch the approaching enemy, strangely relieved to at least be facing them. The dust cloud rolled forward, and in the moment of sudden calm, Prentice could feel the perspiration trickling down his face, his neck, and his back. His breeks and shirt were soaked with muddy water, and the leather of his boots squeaked as he adjusted his weight, but neither was any clammier than the rest of his sweat-soaked body. Even with the wet cloth of his pants gripping his legs, he still felt overexposed. The thin clothing would give no protection against an iron arrowhead.

"This is certainly different, Captain," Prince Farringdon said as he stepped up beside Prentice. "Was this how you stood in the front line against Baron Ironworth?"

"Not exactly," Prentice answered, and he drew the champion sword. "Have you left your horse, Highness?"

"Down by the river, out of danger," Farringdon confirmed, explaining why he was on foot as he drew his own longsword.

"You and the prince joining the Fangs now, Captain?" some wit shouted. Corporal Noam hissed at the breach of discipline, but Prentice only smiled.

"Normally, I stand with the Claws," he shouted back in the direction from which the comment had come. "But I couldn't very well swim the Dwelt with a spear in my hands, so I am forced into the Fangs, it seems. I am not fussy."

That drew more laughter, which pleased him.

"Should join the Roar," said a gunner two spaces from Prentice's left. "We can show you how to make a real impression."

"Fetch me a matchlock and I'll gladly let you instruct me," Farringdon called, and there was a moment where no one spoke. Farringdon looked at Prentice, and when their eyes met, the prince shrugged. "What? They look like a lark!"

Men chuckled again and someone called out, "Someone get the Veckander a gun." Prentice was willing to let the ill-disciplined banter release some of the tension, and it surprised him how much it helped him as well. The riders were only moments away, however, and he signaled Corporal Noam to reestablish order. The drummer beat silence in the ranks—a simple, single rhythm—and reflexively every soldier was quiet once more. Suddenly the only sound was the buzzing of insects and the fizzing of the slow-burning long-matches that the gunners used to fire their weapons. That, and the growing hammering of rushing hooves.

"That's a lot of horsemen, Captain," said Farringdon, and Prentice merely nodded. He could see at least fifty riding roughly in a front, coming straight on to his men. There were others behind that he thought perhaps as many again, or more. Whatever these were, they were no mere gang of brigands.

"Hold your shot until you hear the order," he commanded. "We want them in close enough to hit solidly. Fangs and Claws, be ready. If they get foolish, I want the pride to spring out and punish them."

A swift glance to the north told Prentice that the other column was not close enough yet to support them. This first exchange would be theirs alone. The horses were so near now that Prentice could make out some details of their riders. It seemed they wore boots that barely reached past the ankle, and pale, undyed leather trousers. Their upper bodies seemed brightly colored, and for a moment Prentice thought that might be a sign that they were Redlanders after all, with bare chests covered in myriad tattoos. As he looked, though, he realized they were some kind of colorful chest covering, corselets perhaps. Each rider had a bow in hand, a surprisingly long one for a horseman.

As he watched, Prentice realized that this first charging line had drawn ahead of the riders behind and were angling slightly across his own force's position, traveling diagonally west to east and north to south at the same time.

One wave at a time, he thought, and was happy about that. That would mean his men should have more opportunities to fight back, his Roar more time between attacks to reload. Then the riders in this first rank rose up in their stirrups, and pulling arrows from quivers attached to their saddles, drew their bows to shoot. Even before he realized what was happening, the first volley was loosed and a second was being drawn.

They are not even slowing down.

If anything, the riders were accelerating, their mounts clearly increasing their pace to a gallop. The second volley was launched before the first one fell, and the horse archers were drawing for their third.

This is going to hurt, Prentice thought. Three volleys of arrows and the riders were barely into the Roar's effective reach. The matchlocks were powerful almost out to a longbow's range but far less accurate at that distance. It was time for the third volley, and just before they loosed, the entire line of riders seemed to twist like a ribbon in the wind, every horse spinning almost on the spot so that as they shot, they were already riding back in the opposite direction. It was a demonstration of such improbable skill that Prentice barely noticed the arrows when they fell. There were two or three pained cries, but the main of the shots thudded to the earth or rang off armor and shields. Even as that first line of riders withdrew, a second was coming on such that they passed through each other. This next line, like the first, shot three volleys and spun on the third, and their arrows struck no more perfectly than the first. One shaft did hit the prince on his pauldron, but the angled steel deflected the iron head so that the arrow clattered uselessly to the ground.

Six volleys for few injuries was no great terror, but it would not matter. The enemy never even came close. They were light horsemen and they moved with such speed that there would be no chance Prentice's soldiers could engage them if they wanted to evade. And the way they launched their shots while turning away made it clear that evasion was their preferred tactic.

Another line of riders was approaching, but Prentice could not tell if this was a third wave or the first wave returning for a second run. In a sense, it did not matter, but in the back of his mind, he was still assessing, still trying to gauge his enemy's strength. As the high-standing riders rushed in, their horses galloping, Prentice watched them let loose with one volley, then two, then drawing their bows for the third.

"Roar fire!" Prentice shouted, but at least half his gunners were unready for the order and the volley fired erratically.

"That was dung poor, you useless mongrels," Corporal Noam chastised his men. "When the captain says fire, you fire."

Prentice knew it was not their fault, but he did not contradict their officer. The truth was that the Roar had expected to do what they had been trained to do—to wait until the enemy was much less than a hundred paces distant and charging head on. These riders were something totally alien to that training. Prentice cursed himself inwardly. He should have given them a better warning.

"It's three shots and spin about on that third shot," he shouted to his men. "We won't get a better chance than that. Next line that charges, Roar, look for the turn. I will give you the order, but on that turn."

Up and down the line, Roar gunners nodded and loaded their matchlocks. One was kneeling as he did it and Prentice looked to see that he had an arrow lodged in his calf. Nevertheless, the man hefted his weapon to his shoulder loaded and waited for the order to fire. The enemy rode on again and Prentice watched, waiting. One shot, the second shot...

"Fire!" he shouted. This time the volley fired as one. Prentice thought he might have seen one or two puffs of dust where iron shot struck the ground, but it could have been a trick of his eyes in the heat haze. Not one rider even slowed down, but arrows felled two of his men, one a halberdier and one a swordsman who had the misfortune of having an arrow that was deflected by another Fang's shield hit him in the eye. The smell of powder smoke added to the discomforts of the hot, still day.

"Twenty shooting at fifty," Prentice muttered, clenching his teeth. Men were dying, his men, and there seemed little he could do about it.

"Quite the effective tactic they've developed for themselves," Prince Farringdon said conversationally. "Pity we have none of the war wagons with us. They would have evened the odds somewhat, I imagine."

Prentice scowled but nodded at the prince's observation. Having a wooden palisade made of wagons and taller than a man for them to shelter behind would have changed the dynamics of this conflict significantly. Except that the company had none of its war wagons. When leaving Dweltford, speed had been Prentice's prime concern and the war wagons were slow. He also had not considered that they would be needed. Whatever he had imagined the "ghost" horsemen to be, a horde of hundreds bold enough to strike his company openly had not been among them. The truth was, though, that even if he had had the wagons with them on the march, he would have left them on the other side of the river. Getting them across quickly would have been too difficult, with too much chance of them getting bogged or of the ambushers hitting them in the middle of the process.

So this is what we have to work with, Prentice thought as yet another hail of arrows fell. He looked around himself quickly, checking his men, the lay of the land to the south and north.

"Corporal Noam, I want you to go up to our right corner," he ordered. "Take your drummer. We're going to start slow marching to meet up with Gennet's column coming across the river. Maybe a larger number will give them more pause. Pass the word as you go up the line and I will do the same."

"Where are you going, Captain?" Noam asked.

"To the opposite corner." The left of the line was the far-thest from safety, and Prentice could not send another man there in his place. They were in this situation because of him, because of his miscalculation. Before Noam could head off to fulfil his orders, Prentice grabbed the column's drummer by the shoulder. The youth looked terrified, his eyes wide and his skin pale despite the bright sun.

"We're going to be marching an odd cadence, lad," he told the drummer. "I need about seven swift steps while those horses are riding in, then watch and when they ready for the third loose and that turn, then you beat three slow steps. That's for the Roar to fire. Can you do that for me?"

"I don't..." the drummer began, but before he could finish his sentence, another fall of arrows struck amongst them and the gunner standing right beside them staggered back screaming. A shaft had pierced his hand just where it rested on his matchlock stock, pinning it in place. Blood was spray-ing from the injury, and some landed on the drummer, all but breaking the lad's nerve. He began shaking his head in mad denial. It was a horrific situation, and the young musician had every right to be terrified. Regardless, Prentice seized the lad's chin and turned him so that they looked into each other's eyes.

"Do you know my drummer, Solomon?" he asked, and the unexpectedness of the question had the effect he hoped it would. The youth's fear paused a moment because of his sur-prise. He nodded. "Thought you did. Well, you must know how proud Solomon is of his drumming. He always tells me he is the best drummer of the company. That's why he walks with me on the march. His beat is the strongest and he knows every cadence best. Imagine how jealous he will be when he finds out you were the first to beat a new cadence, invented right in the heat of battle. And how you saved us all, even the captain and a prince, with your beat. What's your name?"

The boy was listening, a little back from the verge of panic, but when he opened his mouth to speak, no sound came out.

"His name's Mickel, Captain," Noam said.

"Well, we will call this new cadence Mickel's Arrow March. You like that?"

Mickel nodded hesitantly.

"Good man. First though, Mickel, we need your cadence. You go with the corporal and lead us north. We will meet up with the others and cross back over the water."

Noam and Mickel headed north up the line and Prentice turned to see that Prince Farringdon was helping the wounded gunner pull the arrow from his hand and weapon. The man yelped in pain as the shaft came free, then clutched the bleeding injury to his chest, using his free hand to apply pressure.

"Leave the gun," Prentice commanded him. "Just keep up, and if you get the bleeding stopped, see if you can help any other wounded."

Prentice stepped out of the line, out in front of his men once more, and started walking south along the formation. He kept watch on the approaching horse archers, careful to stay out of the way when the Roar fired. The arrows continued to fall, and more men were wounded. It took all his will not to run or cower every time another flight landed amongst them. The muscles in his unprotected legs twitched, as if they could sense their own vulnerability. He clenched his hands around the hilt of his blade and projected all the calm he could.

Then he took a hit.

A high arcing arrow fell and clipped the edge of his steel sallet helm. The impact deflected the shot and the shaft embedded itself in the wet leather of his brigandine, just behind his lionhead pauldron. It stood up like a flagpole where it had struck, and the shock of its impact caused Prentice to stumble. If he had been in full harness, with his steel gorget on his neck and shoulders, the shaft would likely have bounced off, the iron head repelled by the stronger metal.

As he regained his feet, Prentice realized all the men near him had seen the hit and they were all staring. Even the Roar had left off their firing duty to see if their commander was injured. Reaching up, he grasped the shaft and began to wiggle it gently back and forth. There was no pain, other than the dull bruising feeling of the original impact. The arrow had embedded in the leather, but the brigandine's steel plates had stopped the shot from penetrating. He wrenched the shaft out and looked at it as if with mild annoyance.

"Cheeky bastard," he said loudly and then threw the arrow away. The men near him laughed and then they began to cheer.

"Quiet in the ranks," he bellowed, and they became silent at once. "Listen for the cadence and look to your place in the formation. We're heading up to join Corporal Gennet's column. Do not get left behind, Lions, 'cause I'm the last in the rank and I am not going to turn back for you."

Prentice took the southern corner, last in the formation line, and as he did, the new cadence began to rattle. Shifting sideways and watching for arrows, the column began its quick-quick-slow march north parallel to the river at their back. Already one hundred hale militiamen had been reduced to less than eighty uninjured, and Prentice still could not yet see Gennet's force approaching. Thankfully, it looked as though few of their casualties were fatal, and Claws and Fangs, with no hand-to-hand fighting to do, were helping the wounded keep up. It was a tense business, and Prentice was pleased his men held their nerve so well. If they panicked and tried to run, he had no doubt they would make easy prey for the horsemen.

"You should keep to the middle of the company, Highness," he told Farringdon as the prince kept to his side. "That would be safest."

"The Lions rally on their captain," Farringdon replied enigmatically. "I will be safe enough wherever you are. Besides, how many arrows can they have? They must run out eventually."

We can only hope, Prentice thought and sighed. At least they were keeping at too great a distance for the masterful accuracy their enemy had shown when they ambushed the refugee caravan. But knowing that these "ghosts" could move unseen when they wanted and could choose to shoot volleys or to snipe like champion marksmen, another irrefutable truth was becoming clear. The riverboats were not random victims of bandits; they were bait, deliberately harried to remain in place until the riders' true target arrived—Prentice and the Lions. This was an ambush. These riders had planned it this way all along, and Prentice had marched his men obligingly right into the middle of it.

CHAPTER 21

Arrows fell and Prentice's cohort was down to little more than sixty uninjured by the time Gennet's relief cohort came close, a league north and marching near to the old bank of the river. Prentice heard a call announcing their approach and risked stepping out of line to look for them, doing more calculating of the times and distances in his mind.

"If they are really cunning, they will try to stop us joining up," he said, mostly to himself, but the prince heard him.

"They've shown themselves quite canny so far," he agreed.

Prentice could not argue with that observation. The question was, what would be the better response—to continue the defensive march or rush toward the second cohort and link up as fast as they could? He shook his head. There were too many wounded to rush now. The injured would fall behind if he tried to order a forced march, and despite what he had told the cohort already, Prentice would never leave a wounded man behind if he could help it. Certainly not since the flight from the Red Sky battle when he had expected his wounded to be offered honorable parole by the enemy, and instead the forces of the usurper had butchered them all in a frenzy of bloodlust. This cohort could not be made to rush now, but Gennet's could.

"Pass the word to Mickel," he told the man standing next in line. "Beat rally on the standard. Loud as he can. Corporal Gennet's men need to hear him."

The man turned to his neighbor.

"Rally on the standard, Captain?" asked Farringdon, clearly perplexed.

"Rally is the fastest movement, Highness," Prentice explained, but he understood the royal's confusion. The cohort had no standard. In fact, the entire company that had marched on this mission had no pennants or colors of any kind with them. The White Lions' blue and white battle standard had been left behind in Dweltford. There hadn't seemed a need to bring it because there wasn't going to be a battle. Prentice rolled his eyes at that thought. Nevertheless, he hoped in the absence of the standard, Corporal Gennet would interpret the drumbeat as a call to rally on the commander, who would normally be found with the standard. As the prince had said, Lions rally on their captain. It was the best he could do, and Prentice was relieved when he heard Mickel begin the summoning beat. Then he turned to watch the enemy.

"If they move to keep us separate, do we let them, or do we press to break through?" asked Farringdon. It was a good question. Prentice chewed the inside of his cheek as his eyes searched the riders to see how they would respond. To his surprise, they seemed uncertain what the arrival of the second cohort meant for their plan. At least that was what Prentice assumed, as they rode a distance away and ceased their shooting for a time. The captain looked back and forth between his coming men and the lax-seeming enemy. The distance between his two cohorts closed and then they were linked up, Corporal Gennet ordering his men to join the existing formation and pushing along the ranks to salute his captain. Corporal Noam joined them, his left hand wrapped in a bloody rag and looking to be missing a finger or two. He saluted readily though, and the officers and prince all took counsel together.

"Nice of them to stop so we could come together like this," Gennet said with a nod to the riders sitting their horses in line about four hundred paces distant.

"They are resupplying," Prentice said, noticing that two or three horsemen were riding up and down the line and handing over large objects from stacks on the backs of their saddles. "Fresh quivers full of arrows, I would wager."

"Ah well, that's not so nice, I s'pose."

"We need to step swift," Prentice told them. "Use this delay to make as much distance as we can. I want to get us back across the river and down to the boats and wagons. There will be better cover to hide from arrows there. Pass the word, every hale Fang and Claw helps with the wounded. No one gets left behind."

"Even the dead, Captain?" asked Noam.

Prentice hissed, but he did not begrudge the man his question. It was fair enough.

"We will leave the dead for now," he said, his lips twisting as though the words themselves caused him pain. "But we will come back for them on the return march. And only the dead. Make sure any with even a breath still in them are given the best chance to keep up."

"The healer's with 'em now," Gennet confirmed. "Mayhap some'll get their strength back in short order, if his talent's as good as the old chaplain's."

"Chaplain?" Prentice asked, his mind taking a moment to catch up to his corporal's meaning. Gennet pointed into the center of the formation where a fair-haired man with a wooden leg was kneeling down to lay a prayerful hand upon a wounded militiaman.

"Brother Whilte?" Prentice said as he approached the chaplain at his work. "I had not realized you were with us on the march."

"I have been keeping out of your way, Captain, if you'll forgive me," Whilte answered, only looking away from his healing labor for a moment. "We can talk about it later, if you like. I have work to do."

"Of course," Prentice said to him, and he moved on to ready the quick march back to the fordable part of the river. Even as he did so, he could not resist casting a second glance at the chaplain who solemnly ministered to the injured. The power of healing was a gift from God, or so it was said, but that did not mean those with the gift were saints. Some of the best healers Prentice had ever known were grasping skinflints, or petty account keepers, charging hard coin for every ministration. Even so, Prentice wondered that the divine Creator would put the gift into the hand of such a man as Whilte. Then he shook his head. It was none of his concern who had the gift, and since Whilte was here now, risking his own life to serve others, it was only churlish to hold old resentments against him.

I want to put my own past behind me, Prentice thought. *Why should other men or women not desire the same?*

He was brought back from his reverie as the warning shout went up anew. The horse archers were in motion once more.

"Lions, we make for the fordable river!" he commanded and turned to take his place once more on the south-most end.

"That's my post, Captain," Gennet said to him, "if you'll allow. You should be in the center. Best for commands to be heard."

Prentice blinked, then nodded and made his way to the middle of the formation. The archers began to ride in.

"Roar, single volley, at the middle of their line each time they make the turn. The rest of us, march on the cadence."

Men around him nodded and they watched and shuffled, doing their best to help carry or drag the wounded with them. The arrows fell and the Roar fired. A small cheer went up as a rider fell, slain, his horse running off by itself. The next wave saw two more fall, as well as their mounts, and that line of horsemen rode off in a different direction.

"We've changed their mind, do you think Captain?" asked Farringdon.

"No, Highness, I do not." Prentice nodded to the north and sure enough, the second wave had peeled away to block their march to the shallow water.

"They mean to intercept us."

"And divide our fire."

"What can we do?" asked the prince.

"What we have been doing," Prentice said flatly.

Now the waves of riders, charging, shooting, and spinning away at the edge of the gunners' effective range continued from two directions. One or two were struck, but soon the Roar's ammunition was starting to run low, while more and more militia were struck and wounded.

"We can't march into much more of this, Captain," Noam came to tell him, and Prentice knew the corporal was right. All around him he could see the fear and tension on his men's faces. Their nerves were stretched to the limit. Soon they would surely break. More than half of them were injured and at least twenty were slain. From the looks of the ground behind him, Prentice knew they were still a league or so from the proper shallow water where the river was no more than calf deep. Where they were now, the flow was near to one of the feeding streams, and about waist deep—not deep enough to force his men to swim but enough to make crossing slow and difficult, and to make them easy targets. However, if his men had to try for that last league's distance to the shallower water, he doubted their courage would last, even if their bodies could brazen the arrows. And of course, there would be nothing to stop them being followed and shot down on the other side of the water.

"Pull back to the riverside," he commanded. Crossing now was the best of a bad set of choices. With shouted commands, the ranks began to move backward the short distance to the river and men started helping their wounded mates down the shallow ridge of the river's old bank, now just a waist-high rise in the earth. That would be where they would have to make their stand.

"The most wounded go straight to the water," Prentice ordered. "Highness, if you would be so kind as to lead them, fast as you can make way, straight to the cover of the boats. Brother Whilte, go with them."

The prince accepted the order without question, and the chaplain looked up from the man he was helping carry to nod his acquiescence.

"The rest of you, here's our rampart in reverse."

Prentice pointed to the steep little rise in the ground.

"I want Roar lined against that earth like it was the wall of the wagons," he explained. "Claws, beside them with pike up so the beggars won't try to overrun us. Fangs, use your bucklers. Grab spares from the wounded and go one each hand if you can. Play umbrella for us, bat away this iron-headed rain they keep sending our way."

The militiamen who were staying followed his orders eagerly, each man obviously glad for some hope of cover, small though it was. In truth, in this next phase they would be in less danger than the wounded trying to make the crossing. Prentice sheathed his sword and took up a wounded man's buckler shield to hold over the head of a Roarsman. Smoke from the man's burning long-match stung his eyes as he leaned over gunner and weapon.

"What if they cross the river, too?" asked the Roarsman of his captain.

"Then they will make slow-moving targets while they wade the waters, and I expect the Roar to feed them iron shot for all the arrows they have made us eat!"

"Sure, we can do that, Captain," the man said with a grim, battlefield smile. It looked like the kind of smile Prentice's friends always said he had.

Not surprising, he thought. *How many battlefields have I stood on now?*

"What if they go further upriver to cross out of our range, Captain?" the Roarsman went on. "What if they cross and come back and take to us from that side?"

Prentice looked at the man and blinked. He had done everything he could think of. He had no other plans, no other options, and no more gallows humor to share. They were down to their last. If this enemy had another resupply of arrows and the patience to keep up with the current tactics, inevitably they would kill every last man still at the river. He looked to the sky and thought about the possibility that they could survive until night and sneak away in the dark. Sundown was still half a day away and Prentice did not believe they could survive that long.

"If they do that, my man," he said at last, "I hope you have said your prayers this morning, because you and I will be standing tall before our Lord in very short order."

"Had to happen someday, I guess," the gunner said with a shrug, and he went back to sighting his musket against the incoming horse archers.

The next wave began its ride in, and Prentice hefted the buckler to his shoulder, ready to play bat-away with the arrows. Then something strange happened. The oncoming line began to falter in parts, some riding on a distance while others reined in more quickly. Prentice wondered what they were doing as a mere spatter of arrows fell, some even in the water behind them. Not a single man was struck. Prentice risked standing somewhat and noticed the archers standing tall in the stirrups themselves, looking somewhere to the south-east across the river. As he turned to follow their gaze, Prentice heard the blast of a war horn and was astonished to see a column of knights in full harness, pennants flying, lances in hand, riding up the east bank—the Reach's knights martial, and as many men-at-arms again, it seemed.

The steel-clad company flashed in the sunlight so that they were almost blinding to look upon. They thundered a short distance north past the point where Prentice's men were taking cover and the wounded were crossing. There they turned west and plunged into the river, churning the shallows to foam as they made short work of their own crossing. Then the powerful mounts were climbing the opposite bank and forming on the run into small fighting companies of twenty to thirty. These charged straight across the open ground at the horse archer lines. The bow-wielding ambushers shot one haphazard volley and wheeled about, plainly unwilling to face knights ahorse. The remaining Lions gave an earnest cheer to see their salvation.

"Every man across the Dwelt right now," Prentice bellowed, and he felt his voice almost crack. His throat was hoarse, and his lips were dry. The arrival of the knights martial was a God-send, but they were not safe yet. Needing no more encouragement, the remains of the company plunged into the river and waded across the mucky flow, some even picking up wounded friends still laboring slowly against the water as they went. As he stepped through the shallows, Prentice dipped his hand down and took mouthfuls of dirty water to wet his lips and sooth his parched throat.

Once across, he paused on the east bank and looked west to see how the knights fared. It seemed that their presence alone was enough to cause their attackers to quit the day completely, or at least for some time. They were riding a long way west, as far as Prentice could see. It seemed strangely sudden, but the battle was over, at least for now. Watching his men following his orders to head south and meet up with the bearer column and the stranded boats, Prentice felt a sudden release of tension, and he sank almost unthinkingly to the grass, sitting on his haunches and resting for a moment. He took his helmet from his head and let the still air touch his sweat-matted hair. It was little relief, but he closed his eyes to enjoy it regardless.

He sat like that for a long moment until the sound of hooves drew his attention. Looking at the opposite bank, he saw a small cadre of men-at-arms in the finest of gilt armor. In their midst was a ranking knight with dark hair tied behind his head in the noble fashion. The knight's helmet was hung on his saddle. It had a long feather plume, as black as the man's hair. He was clearly in command, and he pointed as he gave orders to the men about him, who accepted them with bows and then rode away to fulfil them. Prentice assumed they were being told to continue harrying the archers and, if possible, find where they were encamped and track them to their base of operations. At least, that was what Prentice hoped he was telling them to do. It was what he had wanted Viscount Gulden to do in the first place so that an ambush like this would not have happened. Then it occurred to him—where was Viscount Gullden, and why was he not in command? He remembered the penny prophet's words the day the knights martial had quit the militia and stood as the commanding knight and his closest companions crossed back over the water.

"Well met and well come, My Lord," Prentice called as the handful of noblemen rode up the east bank not ten paces from him. As one, the tiny entourage gave Prentice the disdainful look that some yeoman called "the nobles' glance." He almost expected them to ride past him, but the commander reined them in and looked Prentice up and down.

"You are one of her grace's militiamen, I take it?" the dark-haired noble asked. Prentice bowed, the correct respect from a patrician, a high-ranking townsman, to a noble. The leader cocked an eyebrow.

"I am, My Lord," Prentice said and was about to introduce himself, but the noble dismissed him with a wave.

"Take cheer, yeoman, you have been rescued."

Then he put his spurs to his horse once more and they started off. Prentice was happy to let them go. It galled him to hear them say the Lions had been rescued, and he felt his teeth grind, no matter how true it was. Nevertheless, Prentice's curiosity got the better of him and he called after the withdrawing men-at-arms.

"Your pardon, My Lords, but is Knight Captain Gullden with you?"

The lead noble looked to another knight riding beside him on the right, a man of similar age to the young leader but with a softer aspect. The leader had dark hair and strong lines in his cheeks and jaw. The right-hand man had a slightly more rounded face and soft brown curls. He reminded Prentice of the usurper prince. The right-hand man detached himself from the rest of his master's entourage and rode the few paces back towards Prentice.

"Viscount Gullden is gone to glory," the man-at-arms said disdainfully. "His body waits in state in Griffith Cathedral. Earl Sebastian is Knight Captain of the Reach now."

"And whom do I have the honor of addressing?" Prentice asked the man, feeling his ire rising at the knight's supercilious attitude. He knew he was tired, and the relief of surviving the battle was making him brasher than was wise. Turley would have been proud of him.

"I am Sir Tarant, you impudent rodent, Earl Sebastian's boon companion and most trusted man."

Prentice noticed that Sir Tarant had no interest in learning the name of the man addressing him.

"You and the new knight captain have my thanks, and the thanks of the White Lions, but I must counsel you that calling a man a 'rat' might not be the insult you think it is, here in the Reach."

"Sir Tarant?" Earl Sebastian called over his shoulder. "Come you now. I must report this victory to the duchess. She will not want us to tarry."

Sir Tarant sneered at Prentice and then wheeled his mount around and rode after his lord. Prentice wanted to throw another verbal jab after him, but a key piece of information wormed its way into his fatigue-slowed mind.

The duchess is here? he thought. Drawing a deep breath, he steeled himself and trotted off south to rejoin his men and his liege lady.

CHAPTER 22

The ground near the west bank of the river where the transport boats were stranded bustled like a village on market day. The hired bearers had already been formed into work teams and were beginning the heavy labor of unloading the rivercraft. The knights martial and their accompanying servants were setting tents for the nobles to sleep in, and off by themselves were the filthy and bloodied Lions, tending to their wounded and fetching their own supplies from wagons so they could eat and take a moment's rest.

Prentice marched wearily into the camp and considered which of his next priorities was highest. He needed to see to his men, to assess their wounds and losses and decide what that meant for their effectiveness. He expected they would need at least a day for Whilte and any others with chirurgeon craft to treat all the wounded and sort the lesser injured who could return to service from those who were so infirm they would have to ride back to Dweltford in the wagons. He also had to see to the labor force, make sure they kept the off-loaded supplies safe, especially from night raids with fire arrows. The knights may have driven the "ghost" riders away, but that did not mean they would not return in the night to cause more havoc.

As he thought about it, though, Prentice knew these other tasks were already being undertaken and what he should most likely do was find the duchess and report to her. It was not something he was looking forward to, as it would mean outlining to her the events in Halling Pass, the witchcraft, and his judgement of the rapists. Likely she would already have heard something, but it would have been from the mouths of the nobles who disapproved of his actions. He trusted that the duchess would not turn on him without hearing his side of a story, but who knew what trouble had been stirred since the knights martial had split from the militia? He was about to start off looking for her grace when a feminine form strode toward him from between two clutches of bearers wrestling barrels into a stack—a woman in a pale green dress and wearing a half mask of black lace.

"I thought I recognized the form of my husband," declared Righteous as she approached, her head cocked quizzically to one side. "And good thing that I do know that shape because I wouldn't recognize him from the mucky state of his armor and uniform. You look a right filthy mongrel, Prentice Ash. I'm a duchess's lady, and your presentment reflects on me, you know. How can you go about like this?"

"I used to be a convict, Righteous," Prentice answered his wife. He cast an eye over himself. There was dust, mud, and blood. He was filthy.

"So did I," Righteous snapped, rejecting his objection. "You don't see me getting all grubby every time I go out of doors. Do I look like you?"

She fixed him with an arched eyebrow of mock disapproval, and he laughed.

"Oh wife, you look glorious," Prentice said, and he meant it. He opened his arms to embrace her. "I have missed you so."

Righteous held back. "You're absolutely filthy, you wretch. I'll not let you near this dress. Spindle'd have my hide if she heard I let you touch it in that state. She works well hard to make these for us."

"A kiss then?"

Righteous's eyes narrowed, and she frowned. Then she gave him a suspicious smile, as if he had some ulterior motive.

"Alright," she said. "I suppose I've missed you enough for one kiss." She stepped close to him, lips pursed, but before she reached him, she clutched one hand to her mouth and the other to her stomach. "Oh, hells..."

"Sweetheart, what is...?" Prentice managed to ask before his wife bent forward at the waist and proceeded to be loudly sick all over his boots. Righteous half rose and raised one finger to tell him to wait for her to explain, but before she could say another word, she was forced back down and threw up a second time.

"I am not that filthy," Prentice protested, but his wife reached up and put her hand on his mouth. From there she moved it to his shoulder and used him to steady her weight as she stood back up. Her face was pale under the mask, and her expression showed that any sense of playfulness was now banished from her mood.

"Don't be daft," she muttered, her lips twisting in a frown at the taste of bile in her mouth. "This isn't 'cause of you, leastwise not now. Just give me a moment. It usually passes after a moment."

Prentice was becoming concerned. "Usually?" he asked. "How long has this been going on?"

"Since you left for the Halling Castle, I guess," Righteous told him.

"Have you seen a healer, an apothecary?"

"Herb-wife looked me over in Griffith."

"And what did she say?" Even with the fatigue of the march and battle on him, Prentice could feel nervous tension rising in him again, this time born of fear for his wife's health. If only she would not force him to play questions to find out what was wrong. It was like pulling teeth.

"She said, husband, that it was quite normal," Righteous told him.

"Normal? What did she mean, normal?"

"Normal for how I am. For the way I'm in."

Righteous put both hands on her belly, fingers splayed. She looked down meaningfully at herself and then back to him. Prentice stared a moment at her hands on her bodice. His battle-weary mind felt slow, but all the other priorities that had been burdening his thoughts dropped away swiftly, nonetheless.

His wife was pregnant? Righteous, his love, his swift-edged, savage hearted, wounded wild rose was pregnant?

She wasn't showing yet, that was clear, but that did not surprise him. The march to Halling Pass and back hadn't been more than a month. She could still be early in her term. Because of the injuries and mistreatments Righteous had suffered in her life, she had assumed she would never be able to bear children, and Prentice had always accepted her belief. He loved her dearly regardless. Yet now there was a child coming to them? Now his mind that only a moment before had been moving slower than the drought-cursed river boiled and churned with confused emotions like the swiftest rapids.

For himself, Prentice had spent many years expecting to die a convicted man on the chain, destitute and forgotten. Then he became a man-at-arms for the duchess, and he hardly had thought for anything else. Even his love for Righteous had been found in the lee of that service. It was nothing unusual for a man of his age and situation to have a wife who was expecting; it was simply something he had never considered. Now, faced with the unexpected reality, he found an endless swirl of thoughts in his mind. He plucked one at random from the turmoil, and as it happened, the wrong one.

"How?" he asked.

Righteous cocked a disdainful eyebrow at him. "Oh, how do you imagine?"

"But we have been apart...and..."

"Stop right there, husband!" she told him, holding up her hand again. "You ain't normally so stammery as this, so I'm going to pretend you've lost your mind, temporarily like. But if you ask the next question I think you're about to, I'll make it so this'll be the only babe you ever sire. Am I clear?"

The sudden threat, strange but sincere as it was, brought Prentice's confusion to a halt, and he took the moment to put his thoughts in order. He reached out and took her hand, careful not to touch the sleeve of her dress, and kissed it.

"You are a wonder," he told her, blinking eyes that were unexpectedly moist.

"Are you happy, husband?" she asked, all playfulness and belligerence still gone for a moment.

"More than I can ever remember being."

"You know I might not come to term," she whispered. "I been praying every day and eatin' what the herb-wife says, but with my past..." she paused to draw in a shuddering breath. "I might break your heart."

Prentice looked into her eyes. "It is your heart to break," he told her solemnly. "Sworn to you in joy and sadness 'til death."

A tear formed in Righteous's eye, and she clasped his hand with both of hers. It took all of Prentice's will not to wrap his arms around her and just enjoy the experience of being an expectant father with his wife.

"Does the duchess know?" he asked quietly. Righteous nodded.

"There he is!" an angry voice nearby declared.

Prentice and Righteous both turned to see a knot of knights no more than a dozen paces away. Some were dressed in armor, dusty from the recent action against the horse archers. Others were stripped down to their arming doublets or mail. At least three were youths, little more than pages, wearing only their surcoats and looking like they were trying hard to seem as menacing as the older members of the angry band. From their expressions, it was clear they meant trouble. Prentice scanned their faces, not recognizing many, but in the center was the disdainful Sir Tarant. The knight had his longsword drawn in his hand.

"That one?" the nobleman asked of his nearest companion, his expression one of furious disbelief. "I know him!"

The knight next to him nodded and reached for his own arming sword to draw it forth. The others hefted blades and the pages carried metal-bound cudgels, like those used for weapons training in armor.

"What's this about, husband?" Righteous asked Prentice quietly, releasing his hands and reaching inside one of her sleeves, no doubt to draw a fighting blade of her own.

"I am not quite sure, wife," Prentice replied, equally quietly. He scanned the aggressive pack and then quickly glanced about at the rest of the camp. Not interfering in the actions of armed nobles was second nature to lower-born folk, but Prentice hoped that some of his militia might see the situation and come to his defense. In the meantime, he put his hand to the hilt of his own blade. At any other time, it would be taken as a provocative gesture, but he had a sense that whatever was happening was already too far gone to worry about that.

Sir Tarant strode up and pointed his blade tip straight at Prentice's face. The other men with him began to fan out beside their leader, forming a semicircle around the couple. As some of their number began to extend the circle around behind Prentice, he felt his wife shift herself until she was standing almost at his back.

"You! You're the dog who dared to have men of birth mutilated? Insolent *rodent*!" Sir Tarant emphasized the word. "My cousin Balfour is unmanned on your order. He'll never sire children and is lucky he can even still walk."

Ah, that is the issue at question, Prentice thought. *Oh Lord, deliver me from cousins.*

"I do not know your cousin, Sir," Prentice said flatly.

"Oh? Do you not? And yet by your order he had his manhood removed! You know *that*, don't you! I'll have your bollocks for his. He can feed them to his dogs. Then we'll track the convicts that dared to carry out the order for you and flay them alive!"

"What did you do, Prentice?" Righteous asked in a shocked whisper, but Prentice did not answer her. He kept his main attention focused on Sir Tarant while with the edges of his vision he tried to remain alert for any other overeager retainer hoping to prove his loyalty by making the initial strike. He did not think they would. He was becoming increasingly convinced that Sir Tarant would lose control of his temper first.

"The man was a rapist," Prentice said, and Sir Tarant looked almost ready to swing.

"The hell he was!"

"We've come to arrest you, man called Ash," another of the posse said, and from his expression, Prentice wondered if he were seeking to find a more peaceful resolution than the bloodshed Sir Tarant was clearly set upon. God bless the man if he was. Prentice was almost certain he would not get his wish.

"Arrest me? For what charge?"

"Sedition against the sumptuary order," said the man at Sir Tarant's side.

It was all Prentice could do not to scoff. He wondered if the knights martial had spent the whole ride to Griffith and back trying to devise an actual crime with which to charge him. Sedition against the sumptuary order was an ordinance so old he had never heard of it being tried. In essence, they were accusing him of criminally undermining the social fabric of the Grand Kingdom. If the men in front of him were not so ready to do violence, he might have actually laughed at them.

"And who brings this charge?"

"We do!" declared Sir Tarant, nodding vehemently as if he were making an ironclad argument. "We do, and we come with the order to arrest you from the new Knight Captain of the Reach. The weak-handed former captain has been replaced with a true man of rank. As a man under arms, supposedly, you will answer to the west's preeminent martial authority."

"The new Earl of Griffith has summoned you to answer the charge, Ash," said the more reasonable knight. "We're to bind you for trial."

"And what? Am I to have an unfortunate accident while in custody? You've brought quite the armed company to effect my arrest. Is there some 'fear' already circulating that I might not come willingly?"

Several of the armed band smirked murderously, and Prentice knew he had hit upon the "secret" plan they had in mind. The reasonable one was not committed to the conspiracy, though, it seemed. He shook his head.

"You will be brought to trial. This is all according to law," the man insisted.

"Of course, if you were to resist your lawful arrest, we could not be held responsible," Sir Tarant added, to the naysayer's dismay. The furious knight waved the point of his blade back in forth in front of Prentice's face, still more than a pace away but close enough that it would be almost impossible to dodge. Prentice wanted desperately to draw his own blade. He felt so vulnerable, but he knew if he did, it would be the spark to this tinder.

"You do want to resist, don't you?" Sir Tarant mocked. The reasonable knight put his hand on Tarant's arm, gently restraining.

"He's favored of her grace, man. We can't do it that way. And we're in the middle of the camp. No one would believe he did it. You have to trust me. This isn't like in the east. He's her man. It won't wash this way."

Sir Tarant gave the man a sneer, obviously disdaining his caution. Behind himself, Prentice felt his wife shift her weight, and he was afraid she might be about to do something foolish as well.

"I think I might go seek out my mistress," she said loudly, and Prentice breathed an inward sigh of relief. The duchess's intervention was the best possible solution. Before Righteous could move off, though, Sir Tarant turned his ire upon her.

"Stay where you are, whore," he all but spat. "After I'm done with rat-killing, I might want some recreation."

Now Prentice did draw his blade, in a smooth flowing motion that brought it straight to high forward guard, its curved edge ready to slash directly down on Sir Tarant.

"Call my wife a whore again," Prentice told the nobleman in a tone like forged steel, "and see if you can get the whole sentence out."

"At last," Sir Tarant said, and he set himself into a fighting stance, the others around him also bringing their weapons to the ready. Prentice felt the cold rush of clarity within himself that personal combat drew out of him, and he shifted to make the first strike. All thought of a peaceful resolution was gone. Baron Ironworth's champion blade was going to draw blood once more.

Then a commanding, feminine voice split the hot air. "Captain Ash? Lady Righteous? What is happening here?"

Duchess Amelia stepped between Prentice and his target, and without a moment's hesitation the Captain of the White Lions lowered his sword and went down on one knee before his liege lady.

CHAPTER 23

Duchess Amelia looked at Prentice on his knee, his drawn sword held with only one hand, and Lady Righteous standing behind him. In front of him, Earl Sebastian's lieutenant, Sir Tarant, was holding his longsword at the ready, as if he meant to execute the kneeling captain. The duchess was reminded of a day, years before, when Prentice had been attacked by three squires with truncheons, set by a rebellious retainer to beat him to death. Then, he had been as dirty as he was now, and the violence had only been stopped by her intervention. For that matter, that had been the second time Prentice had been on his knees in her presence as a nobleman threatened to execute him. The similarity of so many situations struck her that she almost wondered if life were repeating itself again and again.

"Rise, Captain," she said to Prentice, "and explain to me what is happening."

"We are bringing a seditious rebel to justice," Sir Tarant declared as Prentice stood up, not allowing him a chance to answer for himself. Tarant's longsword tip remained pointed at Prentice's chest. The knight seemed so intent on thrusting it home that Amelia wondered how long the man could restrain himself. It might be that her intervention had not been enough for Sir Tarant. Amelia looked over her shoulder where Earl Sebastian was accompanying her, along with High Sacrist Quellion, and behind them both, Lady Spindle and two of her houseguards. She noticed farther away that a dirty but competent-looking pack of White Lions was gathering, weapons to hand, watching the entire affair. If Sir Tarant was the kind of hothead other young knights Amelia had known were, her camp was about to erupt into bloodshed. She swallowed and gathered her nerve.

"Earl Sebastian," she said loudly, "I know we live in strange days, but is it the fashion in the rest of the Grand Kingdom now for knights to wave naked blades in the face of their lieges?"

"No, Your Grace," Earl Sebastian answered shamefacedly, and he looked to his sworn man. "Tarant! Tarant!"

It took a moment for the earl's words to penetrate the knight's focus on his prey, but at last he blinked and looked to his knight captain. "What?"

"Put. Up. Your. Sword." the earl commanded vehemently. "The *duchess...*" He let the word hang and Amelia was thankful for the discipline he maintained over his liegemen as Tarant finally nodded and turned his sword away.

"Now, explain this to me, Captain," the duchess said, reiterating her command.

"You want him to—" Sir Tarant began to object, but he was cut off by a hiss from Sebastian.

"These men have come to arrest me, Your Grace," Prentice said simply, as if that would be sufficient explanation. Amelia waited a moment, but he did not elucidate.

Oh, for God's sake, Prentice, she thought. *You could make it a little easier for me.*

"For what charge?" she pressed.

"Sumptuary sedition."

Amelia felt herself blink with surprise. Since becoming duchess and ruler of the Reach in her own right, she had made much study of laws and could scarcely believe Prentice's words.

"You sought to overthrow the righteous order of society under God?"

"That is the charge." Prentice nodded at Sir Tarant and his accompanying armed men. Sir Tarant straightened his shoulders and gathered his dignity.

"The arrest order came from the knight captain himself," the knight said formally, and he looked to Earl Sebastian over Amelia's shoulder.

"Knight Captain?" Amelia asked.

"I can confirm, Your Grace, the order is mine," said Sebastian.

"And why did you give it?"

"Because your man of the militia there has done something monstrous, Your Grace," the earl answered. "And as the Reach's military commander, it fell to me to execute justice for the crime."

Amelia sighed. She raised her eyes to heaven for a moment, then blinked at the bright sunlight. Looking down again, she pressed her fingertips together and scanned the crowd of angry men.

"Several times now, Gentles, I have asked for an explanation of this fracas that disturbs my encampment, and at every turn I have received only obfuscation and equivocation. It is not good enough. Captain Prentice, speak you plain and explain this to me."

Prentice looked ready to answer, but Earl Sebastian spoke first. "Your Grace, if you require a summary of the matter, I will be glad to give you—"

"Are you Captain Prentice?" Amelia asked, cutting across the earl's words. His blank expression showed astonishment, but that did not stop him answering her question.

"I am *Knight Captain*, Your Grace," he replied, clearly thinking the answer explained and justified his intervention.

"And I am Duchess of the Reach, mistress in my own domain. If I require you to speak, I *will* give you leave."

Earl Sebastian seemed shocked by such a level of rebuke, but he nodded his head to accept her command. Behind him, the duchess noticed that Quellion was looking on, not quite as offended, but clearly not approving.

Does he ever approve of anything? Amelia wondered. That was a question for another time, and she turned her eyes back upon

Prentice. With a nod, she indicated he should explain the whole incident to her as she required.

"Your Grace, the campaign to Halling Pass was a complete success," he began, and Amelia was sure she was about to hear the tale behind the troubling news of which Prentice, Gullden, and Sebastian had all hinted.

"When we liberated the castle, however, we found that Earl Yarmass, who had conquered it in the name of the usurper, had quit the strongpoint rather than fight to hold it against a besieging force. We pursued him and his retainers through the pass and found that Knight Captain Gullden's company had captured them. Yarmass and his men had offered their parole and it had been accepted."

"This sounds like good news, Captain," Amelia said, wondering what fateful twist was waiting in the tale.

"It was, Your Grace, or at least it would have been were it not for the earl and his men's conduct during the time they held the castle."

"Nobles take liberties; it is the way of war," Sir Tarant said impetuously, but another hiss from Sebastian and Amelia's own cold glare drove him back to silence. She was pleased at least that Earl Sebastian did not need her encouragement to put such claims away. She did not like the thought of nobles taking advantage of her people and simply justifying it with the claim "such is war." Prentice was waiting for her signal, and when she nodded, he continued.

"This was not mere debauchery or wild living, Your Grace," he said, and Amelia was struck at the icy glare in his expression. In all her time of knowing him, she had only seen Prentice so hateful a handful of times.

"Earl Yarmass and his men had brought a woman into the castle who called herself a witch. Promising these men vitality and magical power from her sorcery, she prompted them to the rape, murder, and mutilation of every woman in the castle they could find, including the lady of the fief and her daughter. The blood of the slaughter was used for pagan rituals too foul to describe."

Standing behind Prentice, Righteous hissed audibly at this revelation.

"Fables!" Sir Tarant said dismissively. "Dread tales to frighten peasants."

"I was *there,* Sir, and I saw it all," Prentice said in a voice so hard it made Amelia shiver a moment in spite of the heat.

"Who else saw it?" she asked. She turned to the other knights standing by Sir Tarant, one or two of whom she knew by face as men of the Reach, not the new arrivals who had come with Sebastian. They would have been in Halling Pass. "Did you?"

"Not everything he says," one of them answered awkwardly, as if embarrassed not to be able to refute the whole of Prentice's story out of hand. "But I did see the lady and her daughters' bodies. They were..."

The man's voice trailed off and Amelia wondered how horrifying the treatment of the women must have been to cause men-at-arms to have such emotional reactions—Prentics's fury and this man's shame. She remembered the morning of the Battle of the Brook, when Baroness Stopher had been found chained naked in the brookside reeds and how it had enraged Prince Mercad's army. Honorable men, sworn to defend the weak by force, *should* respond to such abuses with violence, Amelia felt. And when these crimes were committed by men who were so sworn, furious anger was surely the natural response.

Realizing all these things in a single moment, Amelia quickly started to foresee how this story would probably end.

"What did you do, Captain?" she asked Prentice.

"I ordered the Lions to put the perpetrators bound under your law, Your Grace," he said.

"You had them castrated!" Sir Tarant almost shouted, and the knights and men-at-arms with him nodded angrily.

"I wanted to hang them all!" Prentice spat back, his iron control slipping for just a moment. Amelia was surprised to see it, but just as it happened, she noticed him cast a backwards glance at his wife and she knew. Of all the sins of men, the one that Prentice would most struggle to forgive was rape because of what Righteous had suffered.

"I trust you need hear no more, Your Grace," Earl Sebastian urged quietly. "No need for you to subject yourself any further. As knight captain, I can dispense judgement to the issue."

Amelia turned to look at the nobleman. "Are you serious?" she demanded sharply before she could control her tongue. Sebastian had not composed a reply when she turned back to Prentice. "Why did you not confine them for trial, Captain Ash? Why the rush to judgement?"

"The mutt got a chance to bite and did," said Sir Tarant.

Prentice sneered at the man's words but did not answer him. Amelia ignored the interruption.

"It was my intent to hold them for trial, Your Grace, but matters were complicated. And Earl Yarmass confessed."

"Confessed?" Amelia repeated, and she heard Sir Tarant and Earl Sebastian speak the word as well. Obviously, this was a detail the Reach knights had not shared with the rest of the martial nobility.

"Yes, Your Grace. He confessed to me in front of witnesses. That is why he was hanged."

"He confessed to save his son from the noose!" the Reach knight insisted. "Men of rank do not hang!"

"Sir Haravind had forsaken his rank when he attacked her Grace's captain after giving his parole," Prentice retorted.

"Parole you had already violated! And Sir Haravind demanded trial by combat."

"Is that what that was? Rushing at me with a stolen longsword? Does that pass for judicial combat these days? Is that what is left of the honor of Reach nobility?"

A collective indignant hiss arose from every man of rank that crowded around this strange public conference. Amelia was sure that if she were not present, they would cut Prentice to pieces right here. As it was, she wondered how much longer her presence would restrain them. Prentice was never normally this provocative. She understood his motives, but she wished he would stop. Even so, she found herself sharing his indignation. So far, she was struggling to even find fault with his actions. She would likely have ordered something similar herself in his place.

"Captain Prentice, it seems that though you acted peremptorily, you punished those who transgressed my peace and justice as liege of the Reach. As such, there can be no case of sumptuary sedition for such actions. I find that you acted in accordance with my law and thus, in retrospect, grant my authority to your judgement."

That dealt with the legal niceties of Prentice's actions but would only inflame the knights and nobles around her. Almost without thinking, Amelia took a half step closer to Prentice and prepared herself to run towards the White Lions gathered close by if the knights lost their self-control.

"My Lord?" Sir Tarant demanded of Earl Sebastian, his anger mixing with an almost pleading tone. The earl nodded to his man and then addressed the duchess directly.

"Your Grace, with all respect and honor, this is not right," Sebastian said forcefully but keeping his tone calm.

"Is it not, My Lord?" Amelia asked him. "Why not?"

"It was a usurpation. The matter should have been brought to your court for judgement."

"And I have just told you that on this evidence, my judgement would have been the same."

"Your Grace would have had a nobleman hanged?" Earl Sebastian was plainly shocked by the notion, but he still kept his temper better than his lessers, it seemed.

"Perhaps not," Amelia conceded, and she gave Prentice a downcast glance. It was the only slight disapproval she could show towards him. "However, My Lord, let me assure you that regardless of the method, as chief perpetrator in this hellish tale, Earl Yarmass would be no less dead and his son and retainers no less permanently punished."

"I understand your feelings, Your Grace. Nevertheless, the cool-headedness of a trial might have allowed for other possibilities more suitable to the dignity of all participants."

"Such as what?"

"Well, wergeld for a first—" Sebastian began to explain, but Amelia cut him off.

"*Wergeld*?" she demanded in a loud, harsh voice that felt almost shrill in her own ears. Wergeld was a longstanding tradition from the earliest days of the Grand Kingdom whereby noble victims of crime could demand and receive payment as recompense rather than forcing judicial punishment upon a perpetrator. It was associated with the concept of battle forfeits and was the basis of the contemporary process of nobles ransoming back their prisoners of rank after a battle. In essence, the earl was suggesting that some of Yarmass's men might have *bought* their way out of punishment. The notion infuriated Amelia.

"What wergeld would you offer for women raped and murdered and sacrificed to demons and false gods, My Lord?"

Earl Sebastian was taken aback by the question, but before he could regather his thoughts, the duchess turned to the clergyman behind him.

"High Sacrist, what say you?"

"You...Your Grace?" Quellion stammered, clearly surprised at being drawn into the confrontation, especially at this tense moment.

"What weregeld would you think should be levied for the rape and slaughter of ladies in their own home? How much for truck with witches and priestesses of false gods? Is there enough silver in the world to buy back a man's defiled soul after such sins? And would the God of all Creation accept such a payment? What are silver coins to the one who adorns his city with streets of gold and his crown with stars?"

Quellion looked as if he were trying to think of answers for her questions, but he wisely did not actually voice any of them. Amelia cast a scalding glance over the gathered nobles and their men-at-arms.

"For *this* you disturb the peace of my camp? To punish my captain in the name of men who defiled themselves and the virtue of an entire community of women, all in the service of a witch, an enemy of God and thus of Mother Church. This will not stand in my domain. The matter is judged and concluded. If a man, any man, draws so much as a distempered breath over these issues, let alone a blade, he will have forfeited his title, his lands, and his good name, and will end his days on the chain. Am I understood?"

"Your Grace, it is too much," Sebastian urged, less forcefully than he had been speaking before. He had the decency to seem at least somewhat shamed by Amelia's words. Nevertheless, she would brook no objections, no half-hearted assent.

"No, My Lord," she said, her own voice calming again as well. "It is barely enough. Women of rank were violated, even if you and your men care nothing for the lower orders. And yet you want to punish their avenger. Today you have cared more for the honor of monsters than the lives and bodies of good folk. They could have been your mother or sister, Earl. Would you care the birth of the man who cut their rapists down then? Would you feel anything other than disappointment you had not swung the sword or tied the noose yourself?"

Amelia fixed Sebastian with a straight look, pressing him to answer her question. He held her gaze for a long moment, then shook his head slowly.

"No, Your Grace, I do not think I would be so concerned had it been my mother."

"It is good that you speak so truly, My Lord," Amelia said. She addressed the whole tense crowd. "Now, Gentles and others, to your duties if you please. We must gather ourselves to see these supplies north as swiftly as possible. My capital, and all its folk, of *every* rank, go hungry while we dither!"

Amelia looked disdainfully at the men who had gathered for violence until they turned and headed away. Then she felt the knot of tension loosen in her belly and she breathed an involuntary sigh of relief. She turned to Prentice to see that Righteous had moved around to stand directly in front of her husband, staring into his eyes.

"Did you really neuter a whole pack of noblemen? For rapin'?" the lady-in-waiting asked Prentice.

"Yes, wife, I did," he told her quietly.

"Damn, I love you, Prentice Ash." Righteous stood on her toes and kissed her husband devotedly. The two held each other close for a moment and then Righteous stepped back, the dirt from Prentice's face smeared on her cheek. "Oh bugger, me dress!"

"It'll come clean, Righteous," Amelia told her. "When you two are ready, come to my tent and we will speak and get you something better to wear."

Chapter 24

"There's no need to apologize Prentice," Amelia told her captain as he stood in her tent. "As I said, I completely agree with your actions. You have my full approval."

"Thank you, Your Grace," he said with a short bow. "Even so, I am sorry that I did not have the chance to explain things to you before that disorder found me. I suspected that something like that might happen."

"Well, it's over now," Amelia said, and even as she did so, she recognized the look in Prentice's eye. She knew what he was about to say, even as he said it.

"Until the next time."

"Indeed. Are you so sure there will be a next time? You don't hope the matter is settled?"

"I hope, Your Grace, but hope alone has not usually been enough, has it?" Prentice answered.

Amelia smiled dryly and nodded.

"I hoped you were going to run some steel through that pompous twit," Righteous said as she emerged from behind a cloth screen, Spindle beside her. The two had chosen a clean dress for Righteous to wear, and Righteous was straightening the faun-colored bodice and fanning out the undyed linen skirt. "I was ready to set to with you. Good thing I didn't chuck."

"Me too," said Spindle.

"Ladies!" Amelia said in a gently chastising tone, but Righteous was not chastened.

"What? Fool like that would've looked good wearing my bodkin in his eye."

"That 'fool,' Lady Righteous, is a man of rank, a sworn knight martial of the Reach, and the knight captain's right-hand man, no less," Amelia insisted.

"So? He was sidin' with rapers and pagans. Whatever he gets, he deserves."

Spindle breathed in a reproachful hiss and Amelia noticed Prentice give his wife a raised eyebrow, but Righteous was unrepentant.

"Whatever he deserves, I need him to help keep peace in our lands. Look about us, My Lady. The drought bleeds us dry, the Redlanders are still rampaging about our lands, and now would-be witches and pagans rise up to slaughter in the name of dark powers. We need the knights and nobles, and knights always have one eye upon their own pride and honor. You taught me that, Prentice."

"I remember, Your Grace," Prentice said, looking down thoughtfully.

"And the trick has always been to get the nobility to see their honor and pride as the same as mine," Amelia continued. Prentice shook his head. "You disagree, Captain?"

"Herding cats, Your Grace," Prentice said wryly.

"Herding cats? Are you speaking about us Veckanders again, Captain?"

They all turned to see Prince Farringdon standing just inside the tent flap. He bowed respectfully to Amelia.

"I beg your pardon, Your Grace, but there was no guard outside your tent to announce me, and when I heard the voices here inside, I felt it safe that I would not catch you indisposed. I wanted to present my respects and apologize for my delay in doing so. My mount Elkman took fright in the recent affray and I had to chase him down."

"I accept your apology and your respects happily, Highness," Amelia replied, returning his bow with a nod of her own. "Welcome to our camp, such as it is. Tell me, why did you think Captain Ash was speaking about your people?"

Prince Farringdon looked to Prentice, and it was the captain who explained. "His highness once described Vec politics in such terms, Your Grace. He told me that trying to unite the princes was like herding cats. It seemed to fit your experience with the nobility just as well."

Amelia found she agreed. How many supposedly trusted sworn men had turned on her for their own ends like proud housecats, living in the warmth of her household but ranging off at night on their own business and obedient to none but their own whims? She thought about the traitors like Sir Duggan and Baron Liam, as well as the usurper King Daven Marcus, and now this supporter of his, Earl Yarmass, who had seized her border castle and done...unspeakable things. All these men, ostensibly sworn to the good of the land, the kingdom, and the people.

"Herding cats—an apt metaphor, Highness, well done," she muttered.

"I would like to claim the credit, Your Grace, but the expression comes from a tutor of mine. A much wiser man than I, who sadly did not survive the invasion."

Amelia smiled gently at the prince. How many of the nobles in the Grand Kingdom would so readily share credit for something as small as a witticism? None of the list she had just had in her thoughts, of that she was sure. Perhaps Earl Sebastian might be modest enough to do it, but she could not think of many others.

What I need is more nobles like you, Highness, she thought, then realized that she was staring and looked back to Prentice.

"The politics of the Reach aren't going anywhere," she said, clearing her throat. "In the meantime, perhaps you should give me your report of this morning's battle."

"Battle would be a generous title, Your Grace," said Prentice.

"Oh, and what title would you give it?"

"Ambush." Prentice's tone was bitter and his expression harsh. "A damnable beartrap, and I stamped our foot right down hard in it."

He blames himself, Amelia thought, and she looked quickly to Righteous. Prentice was such a guarded man in so many ways that it was often surer to track his emotions through his wife, who was always in tune with his thoughts and easier to read. Righteous's expression, however, offered no more insight.

"Was it that bad?"

"They lured us to the best point for their assault and then made the most of it," Prentice explained. "By the time I recognized what their plan was, it was too late to do anything but weather the storm, badly. If Your Grace's forces had not arrived, we would not have survived, I am convinced."

Righteous clicked her teeth disapprovingly, but before Amelia could ask any other questions, the prince intervened.

"With respect, Captain, I don't think you're being fair on yourself," he said quietly but firmly. He turned to Amelia. "May I, Your Grace?"

Amelia nodded her permission. Farringdon turned back to Prentice.

"From the moment we learned of these archers ahorse, Captain, you were insistent that we would need our own horsemen, the knights martial, to ride them down. It was Knight Captain Gullden who insisted on separating from the militia and leaving you with only men afoot to hunt these raiders. *You* had the right of it."

"Thank you, Highness," Prentice told the prince. "Even if we had had the knights martial with us on the march the whole way, the outcome might well have been similar, or even worse."

That surprised Amelia. "How can you say that?" she asked. "You just said that it was the arrival of the knights ahorse that saved you today."

"That is true, Your Grace, but I think the enemy rode away because of other reasons."

"Such as?"

"Your Highness, you are a man trained to fight from horseback," Prentice said to Farringdon. "Would you tell us your opinion of these mounted raiders?"

Farringdon blinked a moment, then scratched thoughtfully at a healing cut on the side of his face.

"Well, Captain, if nothing else, they are as unlike knights ahorse as I could possibly imagine. For all that, they are masters in the saddle, there can be no doubt."

"Are they that good?" Amelia asked, and unbidden she had an image from her visionary dream enter into her mind—the horses down by the river, angry and bound to the will of the serpent on the unicorn. Almost without considering it, she was convinced that these riders were the horses in her dream.

"Your Grace, they shoot warbows from the saddle while riding at the gallop," the prince explained. "In all my life, I've neither witnessed nor heard of such skill. Have you, Captain?"

"I remember reading a few passing accounts of peoples in the ancient past when at Ashfield, Highness, but other than that, I know of no one anywhere in the world with this skill."

Like the spiritual figures in my dream, Amelia thought. *Animals that stand for peoples, beasts that represent spiritual forces, such as the serpents that stood for the two fey assassins.*

Amelia had to share all this with Prentice, since he was the only other one she knew of who had such dreams or visions, but she wanted to do it privately. Word that the duchess was speaking of oracles in her sleep could easily fan all kinds of rumors in troubled times like these.

"They use it to great effect," the prince was saying as Amelia returned from her own thoughts. "Riding in like that and then away, shooting their shots and never engaging at a range their enemy might like."

"Knowing that, Highness, is there any reason to think they could not use the same tactic on knights in harness and saddle?"

Prentice asked. Farringdon took the question seriously, thinking for a long moment.

"No, there would be no reason the tactic wouldn't work on knights."

"But the knights drove them away," Amelia insisted.

"That, I think, is the captain's point, Your Grace," Farringdon said. "Knights can charge, and their destriers are powerful, but they are not built for the speed that these raiders use. Add to that the weight of steel a knight would need to protect himself and his mount from those arrows, and the horse archers could ride circles around knights for hours, if not all day."

Prentice was nodding.

"So, you are sure they had some other reason for retreating?" Amelia asked him.

"I am not sure they even consider it a retreat, Your Grace. I think they would see it as only another part of the battle."

"But the battle is over."

"Only by the way *we* judge battles, Your Grace," Prentice explained. "They may see it not as a matter of a day or even many days, but of weeks or even longer."

Amelia stepped to her camp chair and sat down, considering this information.

"You think they will be back," she said, not needing Prentice or the prince to confirm her words. "The reports I have from the riverboats is that they prefer to raid at dawn and sundown, but sometimes they come at night. Do you think they will this night?"

"I could not say for sure, but I think we must assume they will," Prentice answered her.

"What can we do if they do come?" Before anyone could answer that next question, Amelia had a more important one suddenly occur to her. "Why haven't they wiped the boat crews out by now? They have riders enough to nearly butcher two militia cohorts and, by your assessment, are unfazed by a full company of knights in harness, so why haven't they slaughtered the riverfolk to a man?"

"That question is the one that disturbs me the most," said Prentice.

"You think the boats were bait?" the prince said, and it impressed Amelia how swiftly his thoughts tracked Prentice's meaning. The mind-damaged young royal who had been lurking in her castle for nearly a year, barely present most days, was rapidly being replaced by this competent figure. She wondered if it was Prentice's tutelage or if the prince was simply healing back to the strength and competence he'd once had before the Redlanders' tortures. Possibly both. It boded well for other folk who fell into the invaders' clutches.

And for my land as a whole, Amelia thought.

"Bait for what? For myself? A kidnapping for ransom?"

Prentice rubbed his chin but shook his head.

"If they were knights, Kingdom men, or Veckanders, that would make some sense," he said. "But we know they are not. Also, they would have to guess that you would come in person to lead forces against them."

"She is the Lioness," said Righteous, which said it all in a sense. Amelia already had a reputation for taking the field with her armies. It would be no great assumption to think she might ride to the rescue of the riverboats. She also liked the idea that her concern for her people might be taken as a given by her enemies.

"You are right, my wife," Prentice agreed. "But if they were Redlanders, what would they want with ransom? Whom could they negotiate with for it, and what would they do with it if they received it?"

"They did not ambush Her Grace," Farringdon observed, and Prentice nodded again. "They fled from *her* forces, at least temporarily."

"That was the other observation that struck me," the captain concurred. "The Lions seem to be the ones they worked to ensnare."

"Or they were after Prince Farringdon?" Amelia asked as the notion occurred to her suddenly.

"Me?" Farringdon asked, surprised. Prentice only nodded pensively, clearly not caught out by the notion.

"I think that is a possibility, Your Grace, but again, assuming the prince has a ransom, with whom would they negotiate for payment? No, none of these seem likely."

"Then what is, husband?" Righteous demanded, her impatience apparently finally overwhelming her sense of decorum. "We all know you already have a deep inkling in that shrewd head of yours."

Amelia smiled as Prentice said nothing but waited for his liege to correct her lady-in-waiting. He was so exacting in his dealings with her, even when his wife was involved. It filled Amelia with a deep affection for both of them.

"We all think she's right, Captain Ash," Amelia said, taking Righteous's side. It was typical of Prentice to never reveal his thoughts at first but to walk his hearers to the key questions and let them devise the answers for themselves. "Why do you think they waylaid your cohorts as they did?"

"I think it was a test, Your Grace."

"Like the Horned Man's campaign?"

"Similar," Prentice agreed with a nod. "We know the Redlanders seem to have no use for spies or scouts. They march fully armed and sortie by battle. I think these riders are allies of the Redlanders, if not a new form of the invaders we have not seen before. Knowing that the invaders' brotherhoods and beast-men have been bloodied by the White Lions, I think they are testing a new tactic against us. They wanted to lure the Lions into battle to test our array against their horse archery. If I were them, I would consider it a very successful test."

"This cannot be a new tactic," Farringdon objected. "This is not a skill and strategy that could be developed in a season or even a year. Those riders would have to have been riding from birth and shooting from the saddle since childhood."

"That is why I think they are allies rather than Redlanders themselves," Prentice answered. "If the invaders had horse warriors like this all along, I cannot imagine them not deploying them from the start of their campaigns."

"That makes sense," said the prince.

Amelia, however, was hardly listening again. In her mind, a new connection was coming together, linking her prophetic dream with the current circumstance. She remembered from years before a conversation she had had with the hermit prophetess, the Widow in the Wood. The little woman had told Amelia a history that included the clannish folk who would become the Redlanders and their pact with true fey from the ancient forests, and how the alliance had broken. Prentice's talk of allies made Amelia wonder—what if the pact had been restored?

"Gentlemen, there are facts you have not considered," she said suddenly, and Prentice and Prince Farringdon fell silent. "You have not considered them because you do not know them."

Then, she carefully relayed every facet of the Widow's tale that she could recall, as well as overcoming her reluctance and outlining her dream the night before she was attacked in Griffith. Lastly, she told the prince and captain of the two fey assassins during the riots, describing them in detail.

"You never told us about that dream, Your Grace," Spindle said with a concerned tone. "It sounds like a frightening and burdensome thing."

"There was no need, dear Lady," Amelia said. She was touched that in all this, Spindle's concern was that the duchess had been carrying the burden of a dread experience by herself.

Amelia looked to Prentice, who was plainly digesting all this new information. "What do you think, Captain?"

"I think we need to capture some riders to question," he said as if he were discussing what to eat for dinner. "And then we need to track these horse folk back to where they live. We must know for sure their motives in all this."

"We will need the knights martial if we are to have much hope of taking any of these fey riders prisoner," added Farringdon.

"Assuming the riders are fey," Amelia said. "For now, we have only my dream, a pair of assassins who showed no motive, and a story from a dead wise woman. It's hardly an array of solid facts."

Prince Farringdon nodded, acknowledging the duchess's assessment of the situation.

"Well, whichever way it turns, we will need men ahorse to find out," he said. "Which makes me wonder why the knight captain is not here. Is Viscount Gullden still at odds with you, Captain?"

"There's a new knight captain, Highness," Prentice explained. "Viscount Gullden died, thrown from his horse after it was bitten by a viper."

"The prophecy," the prince breathed, plainly astonished by something Amelia did not understand. Prentice nodded, though.

Another prophecy? she wondered. Or did the prince think Gullden's death was somehow prefigured in the Widow's story?

"That is only part of what you have missed while chasing down your wayward horse, Highness," said Prentice, and Amelia was happy to let him tell the full tale of Sir Tarant's attempted arrest, if only to get to the question of why there was prophecy about Viscount Gullden and his apparently-not-unforeseen passing.

CHAPTER 25

The next morning, the task of distributing supplies for bearing back to Dweltford was interrupted as Prentice redirected the riverfolk to breaking up the boats. Planks were pulled up and then nailed into long sections like squared decks, detached from their craft and carried away as portable wooden walls. There were hardly enough of them, but they might offer some protection for the marching workers if the archers returned to attack in force. The sections of artificial cover took the day to construct and then were loaded onto the wagons, since they would be too heavy for men to carry, and dragging them would cause them to break apart all too easily. In the end, there was nothing left of the riverboats save their ribs, half sunk in the baking mud, like carcasses picked clean by scavenging animals.

"That much weight of wood is going to make for slow going," Prince Farringdon observed.

"Speed is no use to us now," Prentice answered. "We would never be faster than those riders. They will run us down no matter what. Better we try to be strong than swift."

Prince Farringdon responded with no more than a shrug.

With all the preparations, there was no opportunity for the company to leave that day, which made the bearers and their foremen further upset and fearful. The riverfolk naturally wanted to be gone as soon as possible. In spite of their urgency, however, none of them was willing to leave without escort, especially once they received word of how badly mauled the White Lions had been in their skirmish with the "ghosts." Come sundown, the camp watched, waiting uneasily to see if the raiders would come again in the night.

"Same set again, Solomon," Prentice heard Prince Farringdon instruct as the youth finished a sequence of moves with his training pole.

Having done everything he could think of until the time to march came in the morning, Prentice had decided to take a moment to drill with his war blade on a piece of clear ground in the late afternoon. Solomon came to do his own drills, and seeing them, Prince Farringdon asked if he might join them as well. After a quarter of an hour or so, Solomon had nearly bounced with excitement when the prince offered him some pointers for his training, after asking Prentice's permission first, of course. To intervene between an instructor and his student or a knight and his squire without first asking would have been the height of bad manners amongst men-at-arms. Duels could be fought over such things. Prentice was happy to give his permission since it freed him to concentrate on his own repertoire, and so Solomon received his first "royal" lesson in arms.

"Wait, wait! Where are you thrusting?" Farringdon asked.

"Uhhmm...forward?" Solomon answered with a shrug.

"Well, yes, obviously, but where on your man?"

"I don't understand."

Farringdon moved around and stood next to Solomon. He pointed to the empty air in front of them.

"There is your enemy. Can you see him?"

"I...don't...?" Solomon looked from the prince to his captain, but observing the moment from the corner of his vision, Prentice made sure to keep out of the exchange.

"The best form of practice is always against an opponent," Farringdon explained. "Even when you drill alone, your opponent must be with you."

"How can my opponent be with me if I'm drilling alone?" Solomon asked. The prince rubbed the lad's head.

"You must conjure him for yourself, here in your mind. Imagine him, see him even though he is not there, and then train as if he opposes you. Never just wave your weapon about. It's not a toy and you are no longer a child. Every move must have a meaning. Can you do that?"

Solomon nodded, though hesitantly.

"So, again, where were you thrusting?" Farringdon asked.

"His...chest?" Solomon answered.

"Show me."

Solomon repeated the thrust and when he reached the greatest length of the movement, Farringdon caught it and held it in place.

"Not bad, not bad," the prince said. "If your man had no armor, he might be in strife. But what if he was wearing a cuirass, like a White Lions sergeant? Or a knight in full harness with breastplate, gorget, and spaulders? Where would you aim then?"

Solomon shrugged.

"Come, let's ask the captain if we can have his help."

Prince Farringdon released the training weapon and led Solomon to Prentice as if they were crossing a vast field rather than a handful of paces.

"Captain, may we ask a favor?"

"Certainly, Highness," Prentice answered, and he let his arms drop from technique. He was a little embarrassed to realize how welcome he found the interruption. Baron Ironworth's hero sword was perhaps only a quarter-pound heavier than a typical knight's longsword, but much of that weight was farther up the blade, shifting the weapon's center of balance and making it much more demanding to wield effectively. The difference in shape and weight made the weapon excellent for heavy slashes and chopping, but it wore out Prentice's arms faster than he would have liked. Ironically, another of the reasons the blade's weight was a challenge was the lingering injury to his shoulder that Prentice had taken in the very honor duel where he won the weapon.

"How may I assist you, gentlemen?" Prentice asked, pausing to wipe the sweat from his hands on his cotton undershirt. The heat was too great to practice in his doublet.

"Perhaps, Captain, you could demonstrate for us," said Farringdon. "Something simple, like quartering the cross on half tempo?"

"Just the straightforward drill?"

"So that young Solomon might see how it goes."

Prentice nodded and took up stance. Quartering the cross was a basic sword drill which used the classic eight cuts that were the basis of every knight's training. There were subtleties of course, but the basic drill was well known. By asking for *on* tempo, the prince wanted Prentice to step with each strike, similar to the way Solomon was training to advance and retreat with his practice staff. Half tempo was to be at half the usual speed. As Prentice executed the eight techniques one at a time, the prince explained them to the drummer.

"Diagonal slash downward—that's to the throat. Rising back again on the same line? That attack would come up in a man's armpit."

Solomon looked at the prince in surprise.

"You don't think the armpit's much of a target?" Farringdon asked but didn't wait for an answer before explaining. He grabbed Solomon's arm and, lifting it, poked his fingers into the lad's own armpit. "It's not easy to hit, but there's more blood pumping through there than you might think. And it's very hard to protect. That's why so many knights wear a mail hauberk under their breastplates and why even the White Lions will line that part of their buff coats with a patch of mail, or failing that, a thick pad of leather. It's hot and uncomfortable, but it might well save your life."

Solomon was absorbing every word, his attention rapt. Prentice continued his techniques until he reached the last.

"And finally, the thrust," said the prince. "Where did that one go?"

"The eyes?" Solomon replied.

"Yes, eyes are a goodly target if your opponent has no helmet or if you are supremely skilled. But the throat is an easier target, and just as deadly. If your enemy has no armor, then the belly is good enough. A blade through his innards and he will not likely recover, even if he lives through the fight."

"It seems so simple," said Solomon.

"It is, but don't be deceived. On this simple foundation can be built an array of complex and difficult techniques—difficult to execute and devilish to defend against. Would you like to see?"

"Yes, please."

"What say you, Captain?" asked the prince. "Ready to put away the drills and do some sparring?"

"If you would like, Highness."

Prentice felt strangely peaceful and was glad of this moment in the midst of the chaos that beset the Reach, its liege lady, and her people. Weapons training was simple, and straightforward, requiring only concentration. It left his mind little space to wander or worry. It was like the cold calm he felt when he was fighting for his life, and it was a simplicity that he doubted would ever lose its appeal.

Prentice and Farringdon faced each other, and the prince drew his own longsword.

"Touches at half tempo?" the prince asked, and Prentice nodded. There was no point going full pelt with live blades in training, and heavy strikes would only mean the weapons would need resharpening at the end, not to mention the risk of a fluke cut. "You can take the first pass, if you will, Captain."

Prentice came in, using the basic cuts he had just demonstrated. His blade rang on the prince's, and at last the passage was done. Prince Farringdon was chuckling, and Prentice gave him a raised eyebrow.

"Well, Solomon, clearly the captain is both better and faster than I am."

"Highness?" Prentice asked with a half-smile.

"If that is your *half* tempo, Captain, I shudder to think what facing you at open tempo would be like."

Prentice acknowledged the compliment with a nod and smile of his own.

"You see, Solomon, even when you train hard," the prince went on, "even when you come to be very good, there will be some who are truly great, and they will defeat you every time. The legendary Lord Ironworth was such a man, and your Captain Ash is as well. Do not doubt it."

Prentice was almost embarrassed by the compliment and was pleased when Solomon asked his next question, keeping the subject on training and not foolish hero worship.

"How do you beat a man like that?"

"You cannot, not easily," said the prince, but that was not acceptable to Prentice. It sounded too much like surrender.

"You keep close to your mates, Solomon," Prentice declared. "That is what Lions do. Three good men are the equal of all but the greatest of the great, and ten ordinary men are better together than even that. That is why we train with the pike and halberd. They are simple weapons but in numbers too hard to defeat. A lot of simple is better than a little of great."

"But what if it's just one to one?"

"Then you use whatever you know or can think of," Prentice told him. "All your strength, speed, courage, all of it. No point dying with something held back."

"That's good advice, Solomon," the prince concurred.

Solomon nodded thoughtfully, and then looked up. "How will I know if I'm holding something back?"

"That is what training is for," said Prentice. "Not just for learning the technique but for working yourself hard, to your limits even. Then, when you face your enemy, you will know what you have left and whether to yield."

"What happens if you yield?"

Farringdon looked to Prentice. The captain shrugged, letting the prince answer.

"Well, it depends on what sort of enemy you yield to. Some are honorable and will expect no more of you than that you quit the field and promise to make no war against them for a year and a day. Others will take you prisoner, exact a ransom from your relatives, or strip you of your valuables. The worst will not let you yield."

"Or else will let you, then kill you anyway," Prentice added. "That is why you should be careful to whom you yield. Only ever to foes who have deserved reputations for honesty and honor."

Solomon frowned and shook his head.

"I don't think I would yield to those men in the tavern at Dweltford."

Prentice and Farringdon shared a smile.

"Good man, Solomon," Prentice told him, then looked toward the setting sun. "I think that is enough training for today. Clean up, put your staff away, and find some dinner. You will need your strength in the morning."

Solomon saluted and Prentice returned it. As the drummer turned to go, he had one last question.

"Will the riders attack again tonight, Captain?"

"You let the captain worry about that, Solomon," Farringdon counseled. "You look to your rest. Tomorrow will say whether we were attacked in the night."

Solomon saluted the prince as well and then trotted away.

"He's a valiant lad and true," Farringdon observed.

"And you are an excellent instructor, Highness," Prentice ventured.

"A generous assessment, Captain, but it is all wisdom learned from better men, I fear. Little by my own efforts alone."

"Highness, if you will permit me, the time comes when a man has to own his own wisdom, no matter how he earned it. It is one thing to honor our teachers and another..."

Prentice's words trailed away as he noticed a trio of knights nearby watching him and the prince. The three were only dressed in tabards and boots, not even wearing breeks on their legs, but they still wore their sword belts, blades in their sheaths.

"A problem, Captain?" the prince asked. Prentice did not take his eyes off the three men-at-arms.

"I do not know, Highness. I just wonder how long they have been watching us, and why?"

"Perhaps they wish to admire my teaching style as well."

Prentice smirked at the prince's joke but kept watching the trio.

"Do you know them?" he asked.

Farringdon shook his head. "They do not look like any I have been introduced to, but it is late, and the light is not good."

It was true; already the sun was almost fully beneath the horizon. The Rampart was out in the sky, along with the first stars, and much of the nearby light was already from watchfires. Presently, the three knights moved away, back into the main of the camp.

"What does that bode, do you think, Captain?" Farringdon asked as he checked his blade's edge for damage and then returned it to its sheath.

"Hopefully nothing," Prentice answered as he tended to his own weapon. "But I will keep an eye out until I am sure."

"Two enemies to watch for in the night then?"

"At least. This is the Western Reach, after all, Highness. It is why the duchess labors so hard to make peace and prosperity for her people."

"Her efforts deserve better," the prince said with surprising vehemence.

"Yes they do, Highness," Prentice agreed. "They certainly do."

CHAPTER 26

"It is a sound plan, Your Grace," Earl Sebastian said, and Amelia was relieved to hear him do so. She had half expected him to reject the proposal out of hand as recompense for her siding with Prentice in previous days. The first rays of dawn were cresting the horizon, bathing the camp in orange light, and soon they would be marching north. She was giving the earl her orders at the front of her tent while the camp readied itself to travel.

"And you are happy to execute it, Knight Captain?" she asked.

Earl Sebastian cast an eye at Prentice who stood to one side, not speaking. It was Prentice's plan that the duchess had committed her forces to following, but he had insisted that he should not be the one to present it.

"He will have to accept you as captain of the militia eventually," Amelia had said, but she knew Prentice was right in the meantime. "Eventually" did not mean overnight.

"I will see that your commands are obeyed to the letter," said the earl.

"I am pleased to hear it."

For a long moment Sebastian stood, unspeaking. He was wearing his arming doublet and hose under a tabard. As soon as this conversation was over, his squire and page would help him into his plate harness and a long, hot day of riding ready for battle would begin. Amelia did not envy him. She gave Prentice a quick glance before asking the earl one last question.

"You do understand our purpose in doing this?"

"The capture of as many of their riders as possible," he said. "For interrogation. As I said, Your Grace, a sound plan."

"Do you have no questions or objections?" Amelia asked. "You do not seem exactly happy with my orders."

Sebastian sighed and then looked to Prentice as well. The duchess thought the earl looked like he was assessing, weighing opinions in his thoughts. She wondered whether it was their strategy or something else that occupied his mind. Presently, he sighed heavily a second time and looked back to his liege. Amelia met his rich, brown-eyed gaze and was struck at the depths of thought she saw in his expression.

"It displeases me to think that this matter could not be accomplished by your knights alone, Your Grace," Sebastian said in a tone of honest discomfort. "Nevertheless, I think the militia captain is correct and we will be best served if we use both foot and knights ahorse to try to pin their forces. Even if we could do it by horse alone, and I think we can, there's no reason *not* to use the militia since we have them. Doubly so, if, as it is claimed, these archers are looking to test your footmen's mettle."

From the earl's expression it seemed to Amelia that Sebastian did not like the idea that Prentice's men, and not his own, would be the raiders' intended targets. Prentice had warned her to expect as much.

"If he is like most knights of the Grand Kingdom, Your Grace, then it will gall his pride not to be seen as lord of the battlefield," he had warned her the evening before as he outlined his plan. Amelia was glad for the warning now that she stood with Earl Sebastian grinding out his agreement, as if following her orders was physically painful for him.

"Then I will keep you from your duty no longer," Amelia said when she was sure he had no more comment to make. The earl accepted the dismissal with a bow and withdrew.

"You were right, Prentice," she said when Sebastian was out of earshot. "He did not like to be told his place in a plan he was not consulted on in the making."

"He is accustomed to leading, Your Grace," Prentice said quietly, "and to being consulted. An earl of the Grand Kingdom has few equals in any arena."

"He's not been an earl more than a month."

"But he has been readying himself for the part his whole life."

Amelia could not fault that reasoning. What concerned her was, now that the earl had his noble rank, would he use it against her? Up until the last few days, Sebastian had seemed a little formal but otherwise unfailingly loyal. Now, with the matter between Prentice and her other knights unmasked, it felt as if his loyalty was in question, or at least somewhat strained. She had been through this before—her sworn retainers resenting her relationship with Prentice, the former convict heretic. In a sense, it was a repeating pattern. She only hoped that in time Earl Sebastian would come to accept that she had the Reach's best interests at heart, his own included. Until she could persuade him or, failing that, win the direct loyalty of the men under him, she felt like she was back where she had been when Baron Liam rebelled against her. Although, perhaps not in exactly the same place. She had a better reputation amongst her people and the wider nobility of the Reach now than she had then.

I am still the Lioness, she thought, but nearly laughed at the idea. Heat-draggled and forlorn, Amelia felt less like a lioness these days and more like a seamstress, fighting to hold the ragged cloth of her land together as it threatened to unravel in her fingers. She followed Prentice as he led her through the awakening camp, and everywhere she looked she saw that same weary, sun-bleached desperation in the faces that looked to her, tugging their forelocks. *God bless us all and curse the drought.*

The one-legged chaplain, Brother Whilte, clomped over the dry ground to Prentice and tugged his forelock to them both.

"Are things ready, Brother?" Prentice asked the clergyman. Given the little she knew about the chaplain's history with Prentice, Amelia had been astonished to learn the man had replaced Sacrist Fostermae. Righteous had been livid, offended on her husband's behalf. Spindle had more than half seriously had to talk her Lace Fang comrade out of doing murder. All Prentice would say of the new chaplain's placement was that Fostermae had "made a persuasive case."

"Things are being readied, Captain," Whilte said respectfully. "But reassure me, please, that you do not mean for wounded men to be marching with you? That thought would trouble my conscience more than a little."

Amelia thought she heard Prentice sigh a little, but he still answered the chaplain's question.

"Under no circumstances do I want a wounded man in that cohort, chaplain," he said. "Not even the walking who are just a bit scratched or bruised. They must only *look* like they are on their last legs. Make sure they are bloodied and bandaged but nothing tight. Any rags they have on must not impede their movement or else be easy to throw off. Have the hale swap damaged gambesons for good ones and sound armor for dented. We want the predators to think they see the weak and the lame, the vulnerable separated from the herd. Does that trouble your conscience, Chaplain?"

"No, Captain. And in that case, this is for you, for your 'wounded' head." Brother Whilte held out a loop of dirty, white rag that looked like it had been cut away from the hem of someone's undershirt. There was already a large patch of blood on it, and Prentice fitted it around his head like a bandana. Brother Whilte went off to help the other members of Prentice's "wounded" cohort dress for their next mission.

"With that around your head, you'll not be able to wear your helmet," Amelia observed.

"That should make me seem more authentic."

"Your wife would not approve."

"My wife disapproves of much that I do," Prentice answered her, but Amelia could not accept it.

"No, Prentice, she does not. You know that, don't you? She loves you."

Prentice nodded with a half-smile but did not say anything more. He looked to the west where the shadows of night were retreating.

"Somewhere out there is your salty sea, Your Grace," he said almost wistfully. "I think I would like to see that one day."

"Survive this day and I'll give you all the time you need to explore it," she promised him. "When do you think they will come?"

"I half expected them last night or here at dawn. That they have not yet makes me wonder. Perhaps in the midmorning like the ambush two days ago. They also might wait until evening to make sure we are at our weakest and most tired."

"Then you might have a long day ahead."

"I would say so, Your Grace. With your permission."

He bowed and withdrew. Once he was gone, Amelia made her way to her carriage and mounted up, the Lace Fangs already waiting for her. She gave the order to a nearby squire that she was ready to depart, and the word was passed down the company in short order. In her time as duchess, Amelia had marched with more armies and convoys than she had ever imagined she would, but none of them ever readied itself to depart as swiftly as this one. Long lines of riverfolk bearers and other servants, nearly bent-backed under sacks and barrels, and knights ahorse in full panoply ranked to ride escort for her carriage and the wagons carrying the improvised shelters and wounded. Lastly, walking in the rearguard, was Prentice's cohort of militia mummers, acting the part of the walking wounded, supposedly too injured to make any kind of strong defense.

The plan was that as the day progressed, this cohort would shuffle and stumble and ultimately fall about a league or so behind the main column. They were to be bait, hopefully drawing the horse archers close to the river to attack them. Once an assault began, Earl Sebastian was to lead the knights martial directly west, crossing the river and riding out behind the raiders, thus catching them in a pincer between the knights and Lions. The great risk, of course, was that in order to keep from being spotted too soon, the knights would have to ride very wide and not too fast so as to not kick up too much visible dust. In that period, Prentice and his men would have to endure the archer's deadly shots.

That was only one of many parts of the plan that Amelia did not like. She was comforted, at least, that Prentice intended to keep to the east side of the river.

"We would be a juicier target on the other bank, but I think we might be too obvious like that."

"You will at least take some of the constructed pavises to hide behind," Amelia insisted, referencing the improvised cover from the riverboat planks. A pavis was a free-standing wooden shield, large enough for a man to stand behind and typically used by archers in sieges and the like.

"We will not look weak if we are carrying extra loads of wooden planks, Your Grace," Prentice had said, shaking his head, but when Amelia gave him a look of stern disapproval, he relented somewhat. "Let us take one of the wagons. We can store some slats on the baseboard and then load a few Roarsmen on top to loll out the side and look even worse wounded."

It was hardly enough to ease Amelia's discomfort, but she was thankful he gave even that much allowance to her concerns. As the morning's journey got fully underway, the duchess reached over and squeezed Righteous's hand comfortingly.

"He'll be alright," she said. Righteous nodded but frowned and looked away without speaking. Amelia hoped it was only morning sickness.

Soon the sun was fully risen, and the blazing light struck the march. Everyone's throat was parched, and every tongue tasted dirty. Around midmorning the first sentinel's cry went up and

Amelia peered at the west horizon. Sure enough, there was a column of dust rising into the air. The fey horsemen—Amelia was becoming more certain that was what they were almost by the hour—were once more shadowing the caravan.

"Not long now," she whispered to herself, but her ladies with her heard her and nodded. Righteous hawked and spat.

"Make 'em hurt, my love," the pregnant lady muttered, then retched over the carriage's side.

CHAPTER 27

"They have to have seen us, Captain," said Prince Farringdon, gazing westward from his saddle. "What are they waiting for?"

"Evening perhaps, Highness," said Prentice, but he wasn't convinced that was the right answer. By mid-morning when his cohort had heard the first warning cry about the raiders, they had already "slipped" a good four or five hundred paces behind the main column—not quite far enough to make them beyond rescue, so he did not expect an attack at that moment. He passed the word for the company to march slower yet and doubled the number of men he sent back and forth to the river for water. He wanted them to keep their eyes out for enemy scouts, but they were to seem like wounded men too desperate to march without extra drinks. Now it was mid-afternoon, they were at least a league behind the column and had spotted only scout riders through the thirsty grasses. The main enemy force still kept its distance on the horizon.

"Evening will not be a good time to face archers," the prince said. "Not with the sunset in our eyes."

"I am well aware of that, Highness."

"Of course. I am sorry."

Prentice accepted the prince's apology with a nod, then adjusted his false bandage around his head. Looking up and down his cohort of false-forlorn, he was happy that his men were enduring the march as well as could be expected. He imagined that, if anything, they were frustrated by the enforced slow pace. The afternoon wore on, and it was an hour before sundown by Prentice's estimate when a squire rode down from the main column with a message.

"Her Grace and My Lord Sebastian wish you to know they plan to make a stop presently and you are to attend them as soon as your own slow company rejoins the rest of the camp," the young knight in training said, not even bothering to dismount or offer Prentice any other form of acknowledgment.

"You may tell the duchess and the earl that I have received their instructions," Prentice told the petty messenger and then dismissed him with a wave. The squire wheeled his mount about and all but galloped away, as if he feared any association with the marching footmen. The company continued their slouched advance until, with sundown almost upon them, they closed the gap to the camp. Prentice found he had to forcibly keep his jaw from clenching with the tension. In one sense, the closer he and his men drew to the rest of the company, the less danger they were in, relatively speaking. It was still sundown though, the preferred time for an ambush. Looking west, the sun was turning from gold to orange, and the light made it harder to see if the enemy's dust cloud was still there. It took a long moment's searching, but he spotted the cloud, smaller and farther to the south. As the sun was going down, so the cloud was diminishing.

"Are they going to ground for the night, Captain?" said Prince Farringdon. "Or have they lost track of where we are?"

"They know exactly where we are, Highness," Prentice told him. The enemy had slipped back and were now hiding their movements. Prentice finally understood why they had let their dust cloud be seen all day. Just as he and his men had been trying to lure the archers to attack, they had been trying to lure the knights out into the western grassland to destroy them there. Prentice was sure of it. It seemed his militia was not the horse archers' only focus.

When the two companies were fully reunited, Prentice made his way to Duchess Amelia's tent, finding her in conference with Earl Sebastian and his man Sir Tarant in front of the small cloth shelter. Prince Farringdon accompanied Prentice to the meeting as well. Everyone was dusty and unkempt, the men-at-arms stripped of their armor but with their sweated hair still plastered to their scalps. Duchess Amelia maintained a dignified stance, but even she seemed flushed in the warm evening. No fire had been lit since the only food they had easily to hand would not need cooking. Prentice himself chewed a half-round of hard tack between sips of muddy water.

"Our quarry didn't take your bait, Captain Ash," the earl said in a direct tone of neither praise nor criticism. Sir Tarant sneered but held his tongue. "Perhaps they are too canny to fall into the trap."

"Or they fear we are too cunning for theirs," Prentice said, keeping his expression controlled.

"What do you mean by that?" Sebastian demanded with knotted brows.

"Only that we do not know yet exactly what they are doing, My Lord."

"Hunting calls for patience," Farringdon offered earnestly, "especially if the quarry is cunning, as this one surely is. It is too soon to know if the trap will work."

"Perhaps they need worthier bait," Sir Tarant snapped.

"If you want to put yourself at a distance from aid in hopes that the enemy falls on you full force, Sir, you do not need my permission," Prentice told the man. It was a foolishly provocative thing to say, and he regretted it immediately. He should be watchful, not prideful. The duchess needed that from him, as did the whole company. The Lions were not going to defeat these archer horsemen by themselves. Sir Tarant stirred, as if he meant to reply to Prentice's caustic comment, but Earl Sebastian held out a hand to stop him.

"Captain Prentice, what do you think? Will they yet come tonight? Earl Sebastian thinks it's unlikely," said the duchess.

"I think the earl is right, though until we are within sight of Dweltford, night raids will always be a risk."

"I meant only that they would not attack us in force, this night, Your Grace," said Sebastian. The duchess accepted his explanation with a nod.

"And I meant no criticism, My Lord," Prentice said, forcing himself to a graciousness he did not feel. "I think your instinct is correct. Before sundown their force looked to have dropped back south of us."

"So, we've outrun them," Tarant said with a snort of disgust.

Prentice forced himself to say nothing but was pleased when Sebastian shook his head.

"Their horses can run rings around us, Tarant. We'll never outrun them. They've dropped back for another reason."

It impressed Prentice to see the earl's thoughtfulness. It was obvious the man was more than a typical young nobleman, impetuous for blood and glory.

"They are hunting us," Farringdon said suddenly, apparently making the connection in his own mind. "Like a pack after a herd."

"I think so, Highness," Prentice said with a nod.

"We put the wounded at our back, and they plan to run us down from that direction, take the weak from the herd first," the prince continued.

"I think that is what they have decided to do now that the knights ahorse have not rushed out to engage them on their terms."

"Is that why they have been putting up so much dust?" asked Amelia, and Prentice nodded again. "I did wonder, given the reports of them moving like ghosts, why they were letting us see where they were like that."

"An excellent question, Your Grace," said Prince Farringdon.

Earl Sebastian looked from the duchess to the royal with a fleeting expression of suspicion.

Well, he dislikes Veckanders, like other Kingdom nobles, Prentice thought when he noticed.

"So we could have ridden out to engage them after all," said Sir Tarant.

"And engaged them on their terms," Farringdon responded.

"Kingdom knights aren't afraid of a hard fight, Veckander," Tarant spat back.

"Neither am I," said the prince. "But that doesn't mean I want to walk into the wolf's den and face his entire pack by myself."

Sir Tarant sniffed derisively and turned his face away as if disgusted.

"You say, Prentice, that sight of Dweltford is our marker," the duchess said in the sudden lull in the conversation. "That means we have at least two more days' march ahead of us with this enemy hunting behind us. The question now becomes, do we continue this stratagem or try something else? Earl Sebastian? What say you?"

"We still have captured none of them, Your Grace," Earl Sebastian answered. "That is still a worthwhile goal, and in that, the militia captain's plan is yet sound."

"If they're thinking to ride us down, let's put the knights martial in the rear and show them their mistake," said Sir Tarant, returning to his main desire. Clearly Tarant was the more typical type of young knight.

"If the knights ride in the rear, the enemy will simply not engage," said Prince Farringdon.

"And the column will be safe," said Tarant.

"Until they circle around ahead of us and attack elsewhere. You don't seem to grasp Sir, the nature of the enemy we face. If we don't lure them in, they will always set the terms of the engagement."

"What I can't grasp is why I should even listen to your half-witted prattle. You're the worthless get of an upstart bastard who couldn't even keep grip of his rebel holding south of the Murr. What do you know of war that I couldn't learn from my horse's arse?"

Prentice heard the prince suck in a harsh breath and wondered if there was about to be a challenge of steel. Sir Tarant had only said what most Reach nobles probably thought of Farringdon, but his honesty did not excuse the offence. He was moving to draw his own blade and to get the duchess out of the area of conflict when Earl Sebastian surprised him.

"Sir Tarant, apologise," he commanded.

"To a Veckander? Never," was Tarant's reply.

Sebastian did not accept it. "To Her Grace. The prince is her guest and you have insulted him. It is unacceptable. You will beg her forgiveness and then excuse yourself."

"But he's a Veckander—"

"Do it!"

Sir Tarant clenched his jaw and stiffly forced himself to bow. As he rose, he addressed the duchess.

"Your Grace, I...beg...your forgiveness for...insulting your guest."

Duchess Amelia nodded her acceptance. "You may withdraw, Sir," she told Tarant, and the knight walked into the darkness. The duchess looked to the men remaining. "Clearly this has been a long day and difficult. I suggest we all go to our rest and prepare to follow today's plan again tomorrow."

"With your permission, Your Grace," Prentice said, "I would like to propose one adjustment to the plan.

CHAPTER 28

The copse was almost dead, the tall trees maintaining no more than handfuls of green leaves at the tips of branches that were spindly, like crones' fingers. The trees had survived the long summer with deep roots in a cleft of sandstone that formed between two undulations flanking the water's old course at one point in the journey north. In past years, the Dwelt had flowed straight through the small cluster of hills, filling the entire gap between the stones save for this tiny patch of dirt where the ghost gums grew straight. Anyone who had never travelled the Dwelt by boat would have no idea it was there, hidden in the midst of the low hills. Now, of course, the river's dry bed was all but a road with a stream down its middle, a low valley that saved the laboring bearers from having to walk the long way around the hills. The column reached the rolling landmark around midmorning and had passed through in less than an hour.

Except for Prentice and his chosen cohort.

"What happens if they don't come this way, Captain?" a man asked Prentice as they lay close to the ground under a smothering piece of hessian. The entire ambush party was concealed under sacks that had been hastily split and stuck through with fallen branches and dead leaves, lying at the foot the copse. It was an improvised camouflage that would not fool close examination, but it was the best "bait" the cohort could prepare quickly, and Prentice just had to hope it would fool the hunting horse archers long enough to spring the trap.

"If they ride around the hills, the column will give us the signal and we will just have to run to catch up," Prentice told his man.

"Is that all? I was afraid we were here getting hot and thirsty for no good reason," the man answered.

"You'll get all you can drink from the river soon enough, Treff," said Corporal Gennet, hiding some distance away on the other side of the complaining man.

"Oh lovely," Treff grumbled. "I always liked me a cup o' fresh mud!"

Men crouched under hot cloth or hidden behind trees and rocks chuckled at Treff's grousing humor.

"That's enough o' that, damn you lot," Gennet hissed. "This is supposed to be a bloody ambush, not a harvest festival."

Prentice let the corporal enforce discipline a moment, but when all was quiet again, he gave the man Treff a wry grin and a wink.

"I will make sure you get a chance for a double ration, Treff. The duchess never denied a man an extra mouthful of mud."

The chuckling began again, and Treff tapped the side of his nose to the captain, a gesture to show that they both shared credit for the good humor.

"But for now, you lot all do as your corporal says and shut your damned mouths."

Silence fell once more. A patch of humor was useful to relieve the tension, but this stratagem needed stillness. There were a hundred little signals that could catch the eye or ear of a skilled hunter. The birds needed to sing, and the insects had to be buzzing the right way. All of that required that the natural world forget it had seventy armed cutthroats lurking in its undergrowth. They had the advantage that they had not had to hide their tracks, but other than that, they had to think like hunters and be as still as the trees they hid beneath.

This ambuscade party was not quite the same as the one who had slouched along as false wounded the day before. Prentice had ordered Gennet to go through and specifically look for ex-convict Lions who had been transported for affray and similar mischief—anyone familiar with close-quarters combat. In the tight confines of this gully, there would be no possibility for ranks to maneuver. The Lions would not be using their usual open-field tactics. For that reason, he left most of his pikemen behind, taking just a roughly equal arrangement of halberdiers and swordsmen, Fangs and Claws to leap straight into the skirmish. The Roar would open the dance, then hold back and harry the riders who tried to escape. It would be a bloody business but ideally short. If his wife had not been pregnant, he might even have asked her to join them. This kind of melee was her specialty, after all. As soon as the fight began, Prince Farringdon, who was stationed at the north end of the short valley, would ride to give the word to the Reach knights who were waiting just beyond. Then they would charge in and force a surrender. Farringdon had begged leave for the "honor" of carrying the message. Prentice wondered if it was simply to save from any arguments over a Reach knight being placed under his command.

No more than half a candle had passed when the first sounds of unusual movement came through the gully from the south. Prentice realized he had been listening for the jingle of horse tack, such as knights and Kingdom riders would use, and so did not at first recognize what he was hearing. It was a susurration, like the movements of a stealthy animal, but it grew and was magnified by the echoing rocks. Even so, it was quieter than ten horses should have been, let alone a company of a hundred or more. It was a long while before the sound even exceeded that of the river's diminished flow, mere muddy stream though it was.

Ghosts indeed, Prentice thought, impressed despite himself.

Soon, the first of the raiders came into view, and the duchess's vision was confirmed. They were fey—lithe, muscular-figured men with long, point-tipped ears and almost impossibly high-boned features. They wore their hair shaven on the sides of their head, which made their heritage even more obvious. On their torsos they wore corselets of what Prentice guessed was glued or waxed linen, lighter and weaker, but stiffer than a typical man-at-arms gambeson. Their arms were uncovered, doubtless to make shooting their bows easier, but they had buckskin leggings and boots. Bright ribbons were woven through their hair and around their reins and stirrups, and their corselets were sewn with complex embroidery, as were the covered quivers that hung from every saddle and into which were fitted the deadly warbows.

Prentice watched closely to see if any of the cunning riders spotted his men. The plan was for his diminished cohort to wait until the enemy had passed, then to burst out and cover any possibility of retreat south. If they were spotted, though, that would be the end of that hope. So Prentice watched his enemy to see how closely his enemy watched. The column ahead had been ordered to scatter the occasional bloodied rag or weapon into the riverbed as they passed through the gully to give the impression that the "wounded" cohort had not stopped. Prentice hoped it would be enough.

The enemy trotted past in double file, as orderly as the most well-trained knights. Not a single one let his mount's hooves splash the stream. They never spoke that Prentice saw. One of their number, a straight-backed elder with hair so pale it seemed almost silver in the sunlight, rode up beside the line.

An outrider or an officer? Prentice wondered. The man's skin was the same leathery color of his comrades and his face seemed no more lined than the others, but there was something that spoke of age about the fey man. The fellow leaned close to one passing rider, but Prentice could not hear anything they said, or even if they spoke, assuming they spoke the tongue of Kingdom folk. The elder rider cast his eyes over the rocky hills above him and down the run of the dried river. Then he peered directly into the bare shadows under the copse of trees. Prentice had the sense that the fey could actually see him, that their eyes were meeting.

He knows.

The fey man's expression widened with recognition even as Prentice leaped up, throwing off the hessian. The captain had no idea what little clue had given them away, but it was too late. At the same moment the rider was shouting a warning to his company, Prentice was bellowing his own order.

"Fangs out!"

The command echoed around the gully, and the White Lions sprang from their ambush with a fury. The plan had been for the Roar to start the fight, but while the gunners could lay in wait with their weapons loaded, they could not have had their matches lit while they did so. There was just too much chance that the burning wicks would have given them away by the smell of their smoke. So, the Roar were waiting with unlit long-matches, with one of them holding a hot coal in a closed pot for quick igniting. That would take time, and since the company had lost the initiative, they would now be late into the fray.

For their part, the fey riders reacted quickly, breaking their formation as they wheeled their horses to face the revealed foe, sand and water spraying about. Some went for their bows, while others drew long-handled, double-bitted axes. The nearest, though, fell almost immediately as the frustrated and heat-burdened Lions surged upon them.

"Roar, get behind them, Claws in support," Prentice ordered, and then he was in the thick of it. He had his champion blade with him in its sheath, but he began the combat with his partisan, and the long, wing-bladed spear leaped in his hands, thrusting and slashing. He knew his men were outnumbered. They did not have the full surprise they wanted, and they had to keep the enemy engaged long enough or the fight would be nothing but pointless bloodshed. And there was no more time for thought. This enemy had ambushed his militia and tried to draw the knights ahorse into another ambush. Now the fight was on the Reach's terms, and the battle was begun in earnest.

CHAPTER 29

"Damnit man, combat is joined already, I tell you," Duchess Amelia heard Prince Farringdon shout as she approached the waiting company of knights martial. Men-at-arms flashed in polished steel and the mounts waited ready, in one ranked body, no more than three hundred paces past the opening in the hills where the river once entered. When the flow was at its height, they would have been standing no more than a hundred paces from the western bank.

The duchess had been in the saddle all morning, choosing to ride Silvermane rather than in her carriage. The spirited mount suited her own fractious mood. She had spent the time since the column had started off again at dawn riding up and down the line of march. Once they had cleared the gully, Amelia gave orders for the column to progress more slowly, and she remained at the tail, watching for the signal rider, much to the consternation of the dozen knights who had been detached from the rest of the Reach's noble men-at-arms to be her personal escort. If the fey riders somehow avoided the ambush or in some other way conspired to attack the main column, these twelve men had strict orders to take her grace directly to Dweltford, not sparing horse or rider until she was safe. Amelia had scoffed at the idea, but both Captain Prentice and Earl Sebastian had been adamant.

Nonetheless, as the caravan crawled north away from the little hummocks of rock, so mundane-seeming and yet now so crucial to their strategy, Amelia watched the gully mouth constantly. Near her, the captain's chosen drummer, Solomon, rode standing on the back of a loaded wagon, hand shading his eyes as he watched as well. It was he who spotted Prince Farringdon riding to take the message at first, though when he shouted, Amelia soon picked out the motion of the prince's horse. Then she had watched and waited and...the knights martial did not move. She waited some more and still they did not ride to close the trap. It might have only been moments, but in her tense state, Amelia felt as if it were hours. Prentice had deliberately reduced the size of his company so that they could hide. That meant that the knights' additional strength was crucial to success, yet here they were, dithering. And so, the duchess had spurred Silvermane southward at a near gallop, daring her escort to object. She arrived in time to hear Prince Farringdon all but pleading for the Reach nobles to fulfil their part of the plan.

"What is this, Gentlemen?" Amelia demanded as she reined in her mount. "Prince Farringdon has brought you the word. The battle is begun. Can you not hear it?"

It was true. Even with the rock walls forming a barrier to sound, the shouts of battle, the clash of steel, and the crackle of the Roar firing echoed over the land.

"As the prince has been told, we are waiting, as we were ordered," said Sir Tarant from his charger's saddle. The mighty beast snorted and shifted, apparently stirred by the sounds of battle and ready to move, but its rider held its rein fast.

"What order?" Amelia pressed. Sir Tarant said nothing, but the man beside him, who had also been with him during the abortive attempt to arrest Prentice and whom the duchess now knew as a baronet called Helpman, gave a response.

"Your Grace, word came that these horse bandits were skirting around the hills to the east. *Knight Captain* Sebastian told us to wait here while he rode to investigate."

Amelia did not miss the emphasis Sir Helpman put upon the words "knight captain," nor did she mistake their implicit rebuke to her interfering in military matters. It was obvious what was happening, and she wanted to scream at them for the shame of it. They were using the strict letter of their orders to justify deliberately not obeying the greater imperative. The longer the fight in the hills went on and men continued to die, the greater the chance Prentice would be one of them. She was sure that was their hope. It made her sick to her stomach.

"Well, Sirs, perhaps I will fulfil your duty for you and ride to the aid of my Lions. If I am slain, then you can explain to all and sundry how the Western Reach lost its liege and leader."

"The Reach would not be leaderless for long," Sir Tarant replied, and Amelia nearly gasped with the audacity of it.

****

A fey horseman leaned almost fully out of the saddle to slash at Prentice's neck with his axe, but the blow only caught on the lionhead of the captain's pauldron. Before the rider could regain his saddle, Prentice swung his partisan in a counter-arc to the axe strike. The target was too close, though, and the long-edged spear point missed, but the weapon's pole did thump into the rider like a hit from a cudgel and the adroit fey nearly tumbled backward out of his saddle. Then the horse had galloped past, and Prentice had a space to breathe in the middle of the chaos.

This was going on too long. At least a quarter of the ambuscade were dead or dying. Twice that many fey looked to have fallen as well. The point had been to force a surrender, but the second half of the trap had yet to spring. If this went on much longer, it would be nothing but a slaughter.

Where were the knights martial?

Nearby, two Claws hacked a rider from his mount with their halberds and there was a ragged volley of gunfire from southwards down the gully. Prentice turned to see his Roar, or at least half of them, trying to maintain their skirmish line across the rock-walled space. They were too exposed, however, and at least two went down as he watched, struck with arrow shots from riders who had gotten past them and then wheeled to shoot.

"We need to guard the Roar," he shouted to the halberdiers and pointed them to the gunners. At that moment an arrow hammered into the back of his brigandine, embedding itself between the steel scales under the leather, just below his left shoulder. He was knocked to the ground, hitting his head on the former riverbed. With a face full of dried dirt, Prentice spat sand and dust, trying to regain his feet. Someone put their hand under his shoulder and hefted him upward. Sparing no more than a glance to thank his fellow, he started staggering toward the line of gunners who needed protection, snatching at any Lion he passed and pointing for them to follow. He shouted orders, but they seemed swallowed by the echoing cacophony of battle that rang off the steep stone walls, like raindrops into a raging ocean.

The chaos of the combat shifted again, and Prentice was thrown sideways as a horse's flank bashed against him. He managed to keep his feet by using his partisan like a walking staff to lean against a moment. He cursed aloud as he scanned the warring crowd, looking for a better overarching sense of the battle. This was exactly what he had wanted to avoid—a brawl rather than a strategic action with no tactical structure and no way to enforce any. It was just a tempest of steel and flesh, wild and disordered. That was why they needed the knights to swing the tide in their favor.

Prentice looked for a rock, a rise, even the body of a fallen horse to jump on and look over the heads of the affray. He couldn't find anything like that, but as he searched, he felt a cold rage wash through him. It was akin to the hard-steel focus he felt in personal combat when the frenzy of battle strangely focused his mind but more so. This was the same sensation, increased unto a total purity. It was similar to when mere happiness rose to sweet joy, or when sorrow's bitterness intensified to heartbroken mourning. Suddenly, all around him the clamor seemed to retreat, sounds dimmed, and dangers diminished. He was still in the midst of the battle, but it seemed so insignificant compared to what he felt within—an unyielding, tempestuous fury at injustice, like the pure storm of the deepest ocean that would scour the whole world of life so that no evil might hide. Cold, dark, and overwhelmingly powerful, it flooded around Prentice so that he could barely stand it. Only once before had he known this rage: when the angel had fallen on the beast men at the Battle of the Brook. Then Prentice heard the angel lion's roaring voice thundering through the gully.

"Beware! She comes."

****

"It was a ruse, Tarant," Earl Sebastian declared as he rode up to the waiting knights martial. He paused to bow to Amelia, and his troubled expression showed he did not like her so close to danger. "Your pardon, Your Grace, but you should not be this near to the conflict."

"I'm no closer than any of these men here," Amelia responded, making no effort to keep the acid from her tone. Only a moment before, Sir Tarant had very nearly spoken treason, and from the expression of the knights gathered with him, not one of them was offended on her behalf. The duchess could scarcely believe it. She had thought it was Earl Sebastian who would be a resistance to her authority, but he at least knew to hold his tongue and keep to his place in the social order. Would she ever be free of nobles who sought to erode her position and her rule?

A problem for another time, she told herself. For now, the battle was crisis enough.

Earl Sebastian looked to the leader of Amelia's escorts.

"See her grace to safety at once," he ordered.

"And in the meantime, My Lord, what will you be doing?" she asked as the escort leader reached for her reins to steer Silvermane to follow with his bodyguard company. Amelia wanted to object to being dismissed and to bring Sir Tarant's treasonable comment to the earl's attention, but the urgency of the Lions' need far outweighed hers.

"We are riding now to complete the plan. Victory is close at hand."

"Well, I am glad this dithering is finally at an end," said Amelia, her disdainful glare falling on Sir Tarant and Sir Helpman.

"Your Grace!" Sebastian declared in loud disapproval. Amelia knew then that this was a step too far for even the earl's stringent sense of decorum. In his eyes, she had just insulted his men, implied they were weak, or slow, or even cowardly. She could read it in his face.

She did not care.

For a long moment of disbelief, the earl studied her. Then his handsome features soured and his moustache twitched. It was the closest to an angry sneer she had ever seen on his face.

"You must withdraw for your own safety, Your Grace," he told her stiffly. "We must ride now to the battle."

"Do not let me delay you," Amelia said in return. "Enough time has been lost already."

"Men of the Western Reach, with me!" Sebastian shouted and led the mounted company away at a gallop, the knights martial shouting huzzahs as they rode with him.

Men of the Reach, with him? Amelia thought. It was an ominous notion in her mind.

"Do not fear, Your Grace," the knight leading her escort told her as they began to canter back toward the rest of the caravan, still making its way up the nearly dry wash of the Dwelt. "Earl Sebastian is a great commander. He will wrap the battle up speedily. You will see."

"Do I look fearful?" she demanded of the man-at-arms as she let her scowl reveal the depth of her ire. Nevertheless, she actually was afraid—just not for herself.

****

In the way of visions and angelic visitations, Prentice somehow knew what was coming up the gully from the south even before it rounded the bend in the rocks. As if it cast some kind of unseen shadow that the angel's words revealed to him, he knew it was there. He heard the hoofbeats on the dried riverbed, even as he wended his way through the melee. The fury he felt scalded his veins like the burning touch of icy water in the deepest high mountain winter—cold like the Reach had never known even before the drought cursed it. He was the edge of the scythe and the battle around him no more than harvest-ready grain.

Charging southward, Prentice speared an archer launching arrows into his Roar line. The fey warrior toppled sideways from the saddle without a cry. Another rode at Prentice full pelt from the right, but the captain only ducked under the slashing axe that aimed for his head, then switched his grip on his partisan and hacked at the rider's neck before he could ride past. The White Lions' captain was focused on the southern end of the gully, and nothing would interdict his path.

Then it emerged—a horse, but nothing like the swift ponies that the horse-archers rode. Taller at the shoulder than a man and as powerful as the greatest knightly destriers, the pale-coated beast tossed a mane of matted, filthy hair. It snorted like any other equine, but its breath was foul. Prentice knew it even at a distance. Its eyes were the color of drying blood, angry and hateful, not with the righteous rage of the lion, but with an accursed bitterness. And from its forehead projected a single ivory horn. Once perhaps, the spike-like protuberance had been fine and glorious, like a temple tower, but this one was filthy and from it hung tatters of rotting flesh.

The unicorn, Prentice thought as he charged toward the beast, remembering the story of Duchess Amelia's dream. When the duchess had told them her vision, Prentice had had a conventional idea of the mythical creature in his mind. This was not that. He had imagined a beast of near divine beauty, so pure only a maiden's love could tame it. This fearsome monster was some perversion of that image—beauty corrupted and turned to bloodlust. Suddenly, Prentice understood the rage of the lion within himself. This beast coming at him was purity twisted into an abomination, an affront to God and all creation.

Upon the unicorn's back rode the cause, a single woman, seemingly too small to control so mighty a beast or, indeed, to be in so wild a conflict. She rode with her hands dug into her mount's filthy mane, like a raptor's claws on its prey. Her skin was marked with the tattoos of the Redlander cults, and she was adorned only in filthy rags of badly cured leather. Seeing them, Prentice knew at once they were of human skin. That was the way of visions, and now this whole battle had that feeling for him. This combat was taking place not only on the ground of the dry riverbed, but also in some other, more spiritual realm. He was no more than fifteen paces from the unicorn and its rider when Prentice first saw the woman's face clearly, looking straight into her slitted eyes. Her fanged mouth twitched as she saw him as well.

"The Ashen One," she hissed.

Still call me that, do you? Prentice thought. He had first heard that name when he faced two Redlanders in the ruins of Fallen-hill, when the ashes of that charnel pyre had covered him from head to toe. It was from them that he had his battle name. None of that mattered to Prentice at this moment, though, because as he met the woman's reptilian gaze, he knew two things with utter certainty—first, that this was a serpent priestess, a bestial sorceress of the Redlanders, and second, that this was the witch who had promised power to Earl Yarmass and his men. Even as he came on, that calm part of his mind that stayed still in the midst of the raging storm wondered how many of those vile skins that hung about her had been taken from the women of Halling Pass. Of course, the rider of so corrupted a creature of beauty would practice a sorcery of degeneracy and blood sacrifice. It would take rape and brutality to pervert as pure a thing as the unicorn so completely. In one last moment of clarity, before the practical reality of battle reasserted itself, Prentice knew that he would never rest until this minister of depravity was stopped and her influence on the world ended. He would not forget his duty to the duchess or his family, but he could not allow this serpent witch to live.

Of course, that did not mean he had to be foolish about it. He had men right here, right now, who could help.

"Roar, about face, fire!" he bellowed as he charged past the gunner's skirmish line. Only four of the remaining gunners were loaded and ready to obey, but they turned as commanded and at least one of them shouted in terror as he saw the fell beast bearing down on them from behind. The four matchlocks fired desperately, but only one iron ball struck home, scoring a long wound on the unicorn's flank. Then the beast crashed into them, lowering its head and scattering them with its charge. As it reared back, a man screamed, impaled on the bloody horn and lifted bodily into the air before being thrown away with a toss of the mighty head.

Prentice stepped closer to strike, but the unicorn's movement caught him wrongfooted, and he could not bring the partisan blade to bear. He settled for cracking the beast across the snout with the butt end of the pole. It recoiled from the strike. Almost at Prentice's shoulder, another Roarsman fired straight at the witch. Prentice did not see if the shot went home, but the serpent woman opened her mouth wide and hawked to spit her venom. Prentice tried to push the man clear but had to dodge away himself, and the toxic spittle sizzled like acid as it struck the gunner on his hands and weapon. Then his cry of pain rose to a scream as the burning long-match ignited the flammable poison and he was engulfed in fire. Prentice threw himself clear, tumbling into the bloodied stream as the fire ignited the gunner's powder still hanging from his bandoleer. Smoke, flame, and sparks burst out, like a macabre fireworks display, and the melee seemed to thin out around the unfortunate man who was dead even before his body finished falling.

Scrambling for safety across the stream, Prentice struggled to get to his feet as he looked through the smoke for the witch and unicorn. He was tired and sore and desperately thirsty. A sudden moment of despair threatened to overwhelm him. Here he was again, on the verge of defeat a second time in a few days. Again, he needed the knights to ride to his aid. Worse yet, here he was in a bloodied trickle of water, facing the same foes he had been fighting since the riverbend village, with the same bitter hatreds. The rage had left him and he nearly collapsed to the ground, exhausted.

No, he told himself. *Not the same. Never again the same. If they know me and hate me, then let them fear me as well.*

With iron determination, Prentice forced his legs under him and took his weapon in hand once more. He turned at the sound of pelting hooves, but before he could defend himself, a fey rider spurred his mount to a leap and cleared Prentice's height as if he were no more than fence in a field. Looking about, Prentice realized that the other riders were fleeing as well. Suddenly, he recognized a hunting horn echoing down the gully walls. It had been blowing for some time, he thought, but his ears had been ringing from the exploding powder and he had not noticed. At last, the hammer of destriers at the charge and the jingle of tack washed through the surviving Lions. The knights of the Reach pelted past, pursuing the fey. Of the witch and her unicorn there was no sign.

Prentice rested on his weapon a moment and looked about him at the carnage. Dead Lions lay about amidst slain riders and fallen horses. The sand was stained rust-red with drying blood, and the sudden stilling of the noise of battle was replaced with the moans of the wounded. The air stank of all the detritus of war, wounds and filth, with the added horror of the venom-burned Roarsmen's roasted flesh. Prentice wanted to throw up, but there was no fluid left in his parched body.

"Are you yet alive, little convict captain?" a prideful voice called, and Prentice looked to see Sir Tarant approach from among the last of the charging knights martial. He sneered down as he reined in his charger. He had an arming sword in

hand, but no shield. "Too much to hope for any other outcome, I suppose."

Prentice only stared at the knight.

"Still, butchered by archers a second time?" the knight
went on. "Your militia is getting a reputation for needing to
be rescued by true men-at-arms, it seems."

"No more than you will cement your own reputation
for being late to the battle if you don't catch up with the
rest, Sir," Prentice said coldly. He saw the indignance in Sir
Tarant's expression and noticed the sword blade twitch in the
man's hands. Prentice did not care. In spite of the breach of
protocol, he stared straight at the nobleman, willing him to
make the swing. He was sure his partisan would be faster. It
had the reach and was made for fighting horsemen. Of course,
if he did kill Sir Tarant, here after the battle, it would make
matters a thousand times worse for the duchess. At the very
least, she would have to dismiss him or even have him exiled,
and that only if she was not forced to have him executed.

Still, he did not care.

Make your stroke, Sir, he thought. *See if God favors you
avenging the honor of a rapist who would serve that demonic
priestess for the promise of power.* The angel's voice was gone,
the moment of spiritual warfare passed, but still the coldness
of the ocean deluge remained in the depth of his soul.

Some of the other knights rode back from the south, leading captured fey horses with enemy bodies slung over their
saddles. Seeing them, Sir Tarant lowered his sword with a
slow deliberateness.

"You will keep," he said with hateful vehemence and
spurred his horse to join his fellows.

"Do not wait too long, Sir," Prentice muttered watching
the knight's back. "You are not the only one who seeks my
blood."

"Sorry, Captain, did you say something?"

Prentice turned to see Corporal Gennet approaching.

"Nothing important, Corporal. Let's see to our dead and wounded. We also need to find any wounded riders we can and secure them as prisoners for the duchess."

"About that, Captain," Gennet answered, and he had an embarrassed look on his face.

CHAPTER 30

"Not. One. Prisoner?"

Amelia's tone made it clear what she thought of that news. Yet again she was meeting with her leaders outside her tent. From where she stood, she could just make out the lines of bodies, the slain from the battle, where they were laid out on the ground south of the caravan's night camp. They were not far from a farmstead, and the herald of the march had said he would secure the little settlement's buildings for the duchess to sleep in. Amelia had nearly ordered the man flogged. As it turned out, the farmstead was abandoned, several of the buildings burned out, and now the lair of half-starved livestock gone feral.

Like the rest of us, was all Amelia could think when she was told. Now she looked at the dark lumps on the ground and tried to hold her tongue against the exasperation she felt grinding in her thoughts. So many slain and nothing achieved.

"None surrendered, Your Grace," Prentice said simply. "I had hoped to at least take some of their casualties captive, but that was not to be."

"How?" Amelia demanded. "Are they so frail that not one of them survived his wounds?" Amelia could hear how cruel her question sounded, but she found she had no gentleness left within her. As the drought was draining her land of water and life, so it was draining her of compassion, or so she felt.

"We saw many of them gathering their wounded to take them away," Earl Sebastian answered. "Many rode off two to the saddle."

"Two to the saddle, My Lord? And yet even so burdened, my knights ahorse could not run them down?"

"Their mounts are swift, and they dress more lightly for combat than we. It is the way of all Redlanders."

"I know this, Earl Sebastian," Amelia said, turning to face him. The sun was going down and their conference was bathed in flaming orange light. "I know it because we have faced the invaders out of the west for years now. Moreover, even if we had not, we had Captain Ash's warning that unless the militia were engaged to—what was your phrase, Captain?—pin them in place? Unless they were pinned in place, we were warned that the knights martial would never catch them. And so it was. Our knights ahorse were too slow—slow to the fight and slow in the pursuit."

Earl Sebastian stiffened visibly at Amelia's criticism. He drew in an audible breath, apparently keeping himself from speaking out of turn. It was the kind of self-control that Amelia had seen in some exceptional men, including Prentice, and generally she admired it, but in this instance she refused to let it soften her demeanor. She held the earl's eyes with an expression of harsh disapproval. Despite his restraint, she could read from Sebastian's face that he was wrestling with his thoughts. He wanted to speak and yet held back. Then he looked down, took another breath, and Amelia knew he had decided to take the fetters off his tongue.

"Your Grace, what happened today is one of the unfortunate exigencies of battle," he said in clipped tones, keeping his voice measured. His tongue was unfettered, but not off the leash, it seemed. "A squire who was out-riding for us on the east flank was certain he had seen movement under a long ridge. Given the danger of being outflanked and the vulnerability of the caravan, it was essential that the report be confirmed. A knight captain is often needed in many places at once on a battlefield."

"I do not see why your man Tarant needed you at all," Amelia told him.

"How say you?" Sebastian retorted quickly, before remembering himself and adding, "Your Grace?"

"Sir Tarant knew our stratagem and that the signal would be brought by Prince Farringdon. What need had he to await your return once word came that the fey were engaged in the gully?"

Now that the enemy had finally been faced at close quarters, that their bodies had been seen and the signs were unmistakable, no one had any trouble referring to the enemy as fey. It was the one consolation Amelia had from the day; she could speak the truth without fear of being thought a mad woman.

Sebastian blinked as if he could not quite believe the duchess's question.

"He needed to await my assessment whether the east flank was a true action or a feint, Your Grace," he said, his voice taking on a harsher tone.

"Surely that question was answered by the prince's message? You do not have to be present for my men to follow a simple plan that they already understood, do you?"

"The plan was not in question, Your Grace, only the circumstances. There were uncertainties..."

"Was the prince's message not clear?" she asked.

"Not the message, Your Grace, but..." Sebastian paused, obviously seeking a way to politely say what he thought. Amelia had no more patience for Sebastian's good manners. Men were dead.

"So, the message was clear but untrustworthy? Or was it the source? Was it that my knights cannot trust Captain Ash's word or a foreign prince's?"

"Your Grace...please?" Sebastian said with a grimace, his voice full of pain.

"Please, what?"

"Your Grace, confusion happens in battle! Even your p e..." Sebastian paused and cast a glance at Prentice. "Even your militia captain would acknowledge that. This divided command you have maintained may seem fair to you, but it only fosters that confusion. You respect this man's experience and ability. You need to respect mine as well."

"Have I not?" Amelia replied. "Have I not made you Knight Captain of the Reach?"

"Have you, Your Grace?" Sebastian answered her. "In the army of any other ducal house, the knight captain would have no equal and answer only to the duke—a clear chain of command, as rank demands, not the confusion that your fondness for men afoot has created."

"There was no confusion when Sir Gant or Lord Gullden commanded."

"Was there not, Your Grace?" Sebastian challenged Amelia, and it was clear that not only were the fetters off, but the reins were held loosely on the earl's words now. He was speaking his unvarnished thoughts. "If there was so much natural coordination, then why were knights martial and militia separated when the viscount fell? Why was he on the way to guard and support you while your militia *dithered* at your capital?"

Sebastian pointed at Prentice.

"As long as you let yeomen like this one command above their station, confusion will be inevitable, and days like this will be the result. Your knight captain offers quarter and then your militia favorite revokes it, humiliating your own nobles and rendering their word worthless. Who will yield to any of us now, knowing our forces do not honor parole? What of the other traditions of war that keep combat from becoming mere slaughter?"

"Have you ever known the Redlander's to seek quarter or offer parole, My Lord?" Prentice said without emotion. "Did they today?"

Sebastian looked straight at Prentice, and his hand rested on the hilt of his longsword as he did so. Amelia had a flash of uncertainty, but the earl made no more threatening gesture than that. He turned back to the duchess at last.

"Again and again, he fails in reverence, speaks and acts above his station, and you indulge him, Your Grace. This is what makes for confusion in your armies and makes failures like today inevitable. As long as you refuse to curb his arrogance, it will be as sumptuary sedition. This is an afront to the right order under God, and you are the cause, Your Grace. Men are dead and their deaths are laid at your feet."

Amelia nearly lost her own self-control at that moment. She glared at the earl and felt her body tremble with the urge to cross the distance between him and slap his face. Only the thought that he too might completely lose his restraint held her back. The days when she feared a bondsman assaulting her out of pride were supposed to be long past, but right now, she did not want to tempt fate.

"The bearer foremen tell me we are only a day or so's march from the south bank of Dweltford Lake," she said, swallowing bile and clenching her teeth. "That means we will likely be able to reach the town itself by midnight if we make good time. We will be marching hard tomorrow. Go now, tell your men and get your rest."

Sebastian bowed, accepting her command. "Your Grace—" he began, but she cut him off.

"Get out of my sight! Speak no more words to me this night, My Lord. Just go."

The earl bowed once more and then left. Amelia watched him leave and realized the sun had finally fully set. She shuddered as the tension within her unclenched, and she sighed. In years gone past, such an encounter would have set her close to tears, and she realized she did, indeed, want to cry but not for herself and not for fear. Now she was too angry to be afraid, but Earl Sebastian had been right about one thing—men had died this day, and they deserved someone to weep for them. She looked at Prentice.

"Was there anything you wanted to add?" she asked in a harsher tone than he deserved. The captain showed no umbrage, though, and merely bowed his head respectfully.

"I think you said everything this night needs said, Your Grace. With your permission, I must bury my men."

"Oh, God in heaven, Prentice, of course," Amelia said, and tears almost did overwhelm her self-possession. Earl Sebastian's assessment was wrong, and the duchess was sure that Prentice would agree with that, but he was correct about one thing—the men who died had perished in her name. She had a responsibility to them, even as they were laid in the ground.

"I will attend to that duty with you, Captain. They are my men as well."

Prentice bowed and escorted Amelia in the direction of the grave digging. With so many bodies to inter, graves to dig, and prayers to be prayed, it would likely take most of the night.

I'll sleep in the carriage tomorrow if I have to, she thought. Tonight, the Lioness would mourn with the pride.

CHAPTER 31

"Lord, we commend unto you these souls fallen in service," Brother Whilte prayed over the graves as the torchlight flickered in the night breezes. With so many having needed to be buried, dawn would not now be long away. Prentice and his men would find little rest before they marched again. Likely, the captain would get none at all. Still, Prentice was resolved. It had been a promise he made to his men during the siege of Fallenhill—every Lion who fell would be buried and remembered, from the least to the greatest.

No one said anything specific, but Prentice knew how important it was that the duchess stood with them through the night. He knew because he felt it in himself and could see it reflected in his militiamen's faces. She had seemed confused when he asked her to take a cup, but she cooperated, holding it at his direction. Prentice reached down and scooped a handful of dirt and spilled it into the held cup. Then, he turned to Corporal Gennet and took a stoppered clay bottle from him. He pulled the cork and poured gin into the cup as well, mixing the dirt into an alcoholic mud. Prentice knew it was a strange-seeming gesture, but water just didn't feel enough.

"A cup of the duchess' finest mud," he shouted as he turned back to face his men. "Treff was promised, and the Lioness keeps her promises."

He gestured to one of the nearby graves, and although she clearly did not fully understand, the duchess followed her cap-

tain's direction and poured the mud from the cup onto
the freshly turned earth. She looked up in surprise when
suddenly every Lion present, the ones hale enough to stand,
began to beat the ground with the butts of their weapons or
to stamp their feet. Even the ones assigned to gravedigging
hammered down with their shovels. Prentice was surprised
himself when he realized that the pounding had taken on a
rhythm, and he recognized it as the beat to arms, the signal
for every Lion to take his place in the order of battle and
prepare to march. The Lions had formed up to send off the
dead for their last march to their final rest. At the other
end of the line from where Prentice was standing, a lone
drumbeat went up to keep the rhythm strong. It echoed into
the dark night, and nobody seemed to want it to end. At last,
Prentice raised his hands and the rhythm fell away to silence.

"The dead have nothing more to fear and no more work
ahead of them," he shouted. "We have no such luxury. Go
now to your duties, and every man do his best to get some
rest as well. At dawn, we march for Dweltford and will not
stop again until we rest under its walls."

Corporal Gennet saluted and turned to enforce the captain's orders. The drum beat "dismissed to duties," and
Prentice nodded. It pleased him to hear Solomon still at his
post. The other drummer, Mickel, had taken a wound in the
first ambush and was now lying in a wagon somewhere with
the main of the caravan. Soon enough, Prentice was standing
alone with his liege by the gravesides. He would have liked
to give the duchess a moment of silence to reflect, as well as
wanting something like that for himself, but for all that they
seemed broken by the day's combat, the fey riders might still
seek retribution. It would only take one or two to attack by
stealth and he and Duchess Amelia would both be dead.

"If I may, Your Grace, we should see you back to the camp
proper," he said.

The duchess was staring at the fresh graves and did not at first respond. Then she nodded and allowed herself to be escorted away.

"It is strange the things I promise men, Prentice," she said quietly as they walked.

"Pardon, Your Gra...oh, the cup of mud?" he replied with a half-smile. "That was a joke on the battlefield. Something that helped calm some nerves. It just made a useful gesture to signal your loyalty."

"I do not disapprove," she told him. Then she sighed heavily and rubbed her hands together, not from cold he was sure, since even the nights were warm during this unending summer. It was more as if she were trying to clean them, rubbing away a stain that could not be seen. "I must offer them more than mud and a grave, though. I must give them more, mustn't I Prentice?"

"Your Grace?" he asked as she turned toward him, her expression earnest almost to desperation in the darkness.

"Make sure they know, Captain Ash, there are no poor widows or lonely orphans in the Lions," the duchess said in a rush. "I will provide. God bear me witness, I will bankrupt myself to provide. No man or woman who dies in my service goes to their grave to be forgotten. They must know that! I need them to know."

"We know, Your Grace. We know."

Prentice bowed his head, ostensibly in respect, but really to break eye contact. He loved his wife and would never betray her, but he felt such deep regard for this noblewoman that the emotions had the power to confuse him, if he let them. That, he would not do.

They walked side-by-side, not speaking for a time, and were almost to the duchess's tent when she stopped again.

"The man Treff, he died today?" she asked. When Prentice nodded, she went on. "I know it sounds strange, but he wasn't alone, was he?"

Prentice could not help another wry smile.

"In truth, no, Your Grace," he said and shook his head. "We found him with one hand around a fey man's throat and the other on the rider's axe, stolen and thrust into the enemy's belly. Treff had three arrows in his back. It was these that killed him."

After the ambush, Prentice and the White Lions had discovered that another unique feature of the enemy fey was the saddle axe they typically carried as a hand weapon. The head was double-bitted, with a blade on either side, and the arcs of those blades were flatter than a Kingdom knight's battleaxe. The arc's shape reminded him of the Rampart across the sky, a gentle curve. The blades extended past the end of the haft and met as two points that, taken together, looked very much like fangs. It was those points that Treff had shoved into his mortal foe as he died.

"Not before he took the enemy in front of him down with him," she said softly. It was a warlike thing to say, but her gentle tone made it sound as if she was trying to persuade herself of the truth of it.

"Actually, it looked like the fey took his own life, Your Grace."

"How say you, Captain?" The duchess's eyes were wide with disbelief.

"The way I saw the wound and the hands on the blade they were struggling over, the fey rider drove the steel home himself when he realized that he could not get out from under Treff's body. That is the other reason we took no prisoners, Your Grace. I have at least two other reports of injured riders taking their own lives rather than be captured."

He watched the duchess shaking her head in horror. She rubbed at her eye a moment, he thought perhaps to brush away a tear.

"So, our plan never had any real chance of success," she said, her voice cracking with agony. She beat at her chest with her fists. "They were never going to surrender. They died and our men died in vain."

"Your Grace, no," Prentice said. Risking the shame of breaking protocol in public, he wrapped his arms around her and rapidly bustled her into her tent before anyone else in the camp noticed. Inside, it was almost completely dark, but there was one tallow candle shedding its oily glow on a small wooden stand. Both Spindle and Righteous were awake, sitting upon cloths on the ground. Righteous saw the duchess in her husband's arms and cocked a jealous eyebrow until she realized that Duchess Amelia was crying.

"Her Grace grieves," Prentice said before any real suspicion could grow. "She needs your aid, Ladies."

The Lace Fangs leaped to their feet and rushed to attend their mistress. Just that action of care seemed enough for the duchess, and her tears dried quickly. Nonetheless, she allowed herself to be escorted to her bed and sat there while Spindle fussed over her. Righteous also tried to help, but the duchess pushed the lady toward her husband.

"A bad one today, was it old man?" Righteous said as she came to her husband and laid her head against his chest.

"It truly was, love," he answered and wrapped his arms around her. "We lost more than half of us by day's end."

"I wanted to be with you."

"I am so glad you were not," he said, and he put the palm of his hand on her bodice. Her stomach was still flat, but just the knowledge that their baby grew within stirred his heart. The sweetness of the moment poured over him and he stood still to let it happen, like standing under a waterfall, fresh and clean.

"What was the total butcher's bill, Captain?" the duchess asked, using a handkerchief from Spindle to wipe her eyes.

"Today and the first ambush comes to sixty-eight men killed since we marched from Dweltford, Your Grace."

"A third," she said, and for a moment it seemed she might lose control of her emotions once more. Then she swallowed and kept her calm.

"Another third or more are wounded, too," Prentice reported, deciding to share all the worst news in a rush. "We return with just over fifty men fit to fight.

"All for nothing," she said, but Prentice shook his head.

"Not for nothing, Your Grace, though we paid the premium price, have no doubt. Still, we have learned much more than our enemy would have liked, believe it."

"Such as what, Captain?"

"For a start, we know they are not ghosts, and for all their mysterious skills, man for man, they are far from invincible. On their own terms they are superb, but when we get them in hand-to-hand, they have no true advantages over us. We had seventy today, and though we lost over thirty, easily twice that number of riders lies dead in that gully. We did not achieve our goal of capturing prisoners, but we bloodied them harshly, Your Grace."

"Was it worth it?" the duchess asked, and it was clear from her tone she did not think it could be. Lady Spindle offered her a cup of watered wine and she accepted it dejectedly as she waited for Prentice's answer.

"As I said, Your Grace, we paid the premium, but that is not all we learned. I saw your serpent on a unicorn today."

Righteous pushed herself away from her husband to look him in the face, and all three ladies' expressions showed their surprise at this revelation.

"You been seeing visions again, too, husband?" Righteous asked him. He smiled at her but shook his head.

"Not quite. It was more like at the Battle of the Brook," he told them.

"You saw the angel as well?" Duchess Amelia asked.

"No, Your Grace, but I heard its voice. It warned me of what was coming with the fey. The unicorn's rider is a serpent priestess, one of the Redlanders. I am sure she is the one leading these fey riders, Your Grace, or if not, at least lending them her power.

Perhaps it is how they pass so easily unnoticed in the land. We know that some Redlander forces have that power."

"The Widow of the Wood said the fey had broken their alliance with the Redlanders," the duchess reflected, and her mood quickly shifted from mourning to thoughtfulness.

"If it was broken, it has been renewed," Prentice said flatly. That seemed obvious. "Also, Your Grace, I cannot explain how I know it, but I am certain this serpent woman is the witch Earl Yarmass brought into Halling Castle."

"Of course, she is," the duchess said with grim resignation. "How could it be anything less horrifying?" She scowled as she appeared to consider the implications. Normally, Prentice would have let her think this through for herself, but something was pushing him to reveal one more thing, something personal.

"Whatever else we do, Your Grace, this witch must be stopped," he said, more directly than anything he could ever remember saying to her grace before. The resolve within him would not allow anything less. "I must stop her."

"Are you asking me or telling me, Prentice?" she asked him quietly. It was clear she had heard the unyieldingness in his tone.

"Please do not force me to choose, Your Grace."

Duchess Amelia looked into his eyes, and Righteous and Spindle looked back and forth between them, like patrons in a tavern house frightened an argument was about to come to blows.

"She rode a unicorn?" she asked.

"And dressed herself in the skins of men and women she has sacrificed," he added.

"How do you know...?" she began to ask, then stopped and shook her head knowingly. "Dreams and visions, ay, Captain?"

"It is the way of things when the Redlanders come, Your Grace."

Finally, the duchess nodded.

"Very well, Captain, go to. I will see people fed and find a way for us all to survive this drought. In the meantime, you find this witch and put an end to her in my name. If God is merciful, we will find out that this summer is a curse she has put on us all and we will end it with her blood."

"It is worth hoping, Your Grace. I will begin the search as soon as we are returned to Dweltford."

"Good. In the meantime, Lady Righteous, take the next spare hours before dawn with your husband. It is likely they will be your last for some while."

"Thank you, Your Grace," Righteous said, and Prentice felt grateful as well. He took his wife back into his arms and they left the duchess in her tent.

CHAPTER 32

The footsore caravan reached the old southern bank of Lake Dweltford near to sunset and tromped on down into the dried mudflat that was once its bed. There was a road they could have joined by following the old bank around to the east some way, but there was little point. A straight path across the flats was the shortest distance, and it was easier to eat the dust than walk the longer path. Near midnight the entire company reached the dead ground between the docks and the castle island. The grounded riverboats loomed in the dark, though several of them had lamps lit to guide the caravan. Soon, the hard-won food supplies were being formed up in stockpiles and readied for distribution.

As soon as the caravan had come abreast of the Dweltford walls, Earl Sebastian had asked leave to take the knights martial farther on to encamp in nearby fields, and Duchess Amelia had granted it. In better times, knights and nobles might have been billeted in the castle and the town, but a company this size was too large for Dweltford to absorb. Once the knights ahorse were gone, Prentice urged the duchess to go as well and to return to the castle.

"I will stay and oversee the distribution of foods," she told him. When Prentice respectfully objected, she sought to stand firm. "If we wait even until morning, half this store will be spirited away in the dark, lost to the hands of ruffians and footpads."

"I do not deny that, Your Grace, but burglary is not our only fear tonight," he insisted. "Look to the dockside. That must be nearly half the town."

He pointed to the raised stone jetties and docks where a huge crowd of all kinds, men, women and children, stood in the night. They carried lanterns and candles, tallow wicks and rushlights.

"That, Your Grace, is desperation manifest. Believe an ex-convict when he tells you he knows the sights and sounds of it. If all goes well, we will distribute these supplies and folk will return to their homes peacefully with hope to live another month or so. If not, that mob will tear our small contingent apart to get something, anything, of that food before others do. You can see the Conclave have sent bailiffs to keep order, but..."

"But they might be as likely to steal as any others," the duchess observed, understanding his reasoning.

"In days as desperate as these? I would be surprised if they did not," he said. "Then there are the bearers themselves."

"You think they will steal the food after being paid good silver to bring it here?" The duchess was clearly disgusted by the notion.

"I can assure you, Your Grace, the discussion will have been had in many quarters during our return march. Starving families cannot eat silver. The riverfolk are almost a people apart to themselves, and smuggling is a tradition for them. If they have not started squirreling small barrels and sacks away already, they soon will. I have sent runners to summon fresh cohorts of the White Lions from their encampment, Your Grace. Until they arrive, we walk a narrow beam with a violent fall on either side. Please, go to the castle."

The duchess considered his words for what seemed like an eternity, then she agreed and told her carriage driver to take her back to the castle. The steward with the reins did not bother to try and find a way into the town and across the bridge, but rather simply drove the carriage's team straight up onto the raised flat that was once the rear half of the castle island and through the open walls. Prentice watched them go, relieved that his liege and his wife were now as safe as they could be, but he also realized that the drought had essentially robbed Dweltford Castle of its prime defense. With the water gone, access to the rear of the castle, which had no permanent gate, was open to the world. If the fey decided to attack in force, they could potentially ride up into the castle's main bailey before anyone even knew to stop them, not to mention the access for thieves and the like.

"Wondering about the rear of the castle, Captain?" asked Prince Farringdon as he approached out of the night. He was limping, favoring his left leg.

"I was, Your Highness," Prentice replied. "I have also been wondering what happened to you." He knew the prince had not been killed, but he had not seen or heard from him since the battle.

"Had a try at running down one of those horse archers," said Farringdon with a pained smile. "Fool thing to do, really. That fey man shot Elkman right out from under me, and I fell like a lump. Hurt my hip. Your healer Whilte has looked to it and says I'll recover, but until I do, I'm quite the slow snail, I fear."

"Glad to see you still can walk though, Highness," Prentice told him, but already he was looking to the crowd on the docks. Hearing shouts echoing in the night, Prentice moved around a grounded river lighter to see a section of the lakeside where a fight was developing. It looked as if one or two townsmen had tried to jump down surreptitiously but had been caught by the bailiffs, and now they were being dragged back while the crowd jeered. It was impossible to say for sure, but it seemed as if the mob did not even agree who they were for or against—some upbraiding the bailiffs as bullies and some the dock jumpers as cheats.

"We may have a problem soon, Highness," Prentice said without taking his eyes off the crowd. "Better you find somewhere safe if you cannot move easily."

The prince offered an objection, but Prentice did not hear it as over the rooftops of Dweltford, the drumbeat of marching Lions echoed through the night. It rang off the town's walls, and soon columns of militia appeared, some on the dockside coming through the town by way of Castle Road while another cohort marched through the shadows under the castle drawbridge and quickly out onto the mudflats around the stockpiled supplies. At the edge of his vision, Prentice thought he saw some folk steal away from the amassed barrels and sacks, doubtless a few making good their one chance of theft before it was taken away. He thought about ordering men to try to hunt them down but knew immediately there was no point. Riverfolk would know how to hide in the night too quickly for even a cohort to find. Ultimately, they would not have stolen too much, at any rate.

"Good to see you back, Captain," Sergeant Franken said after he saluted his commander. Beside him, Markas, the company standard bearer, was carrying a blazing torch on the end of a long staff and saluted as well.

"Good to be back, Sergeant," Prentice told his men. "We are going to take full charge of these victuals and see to it they are fairly distributed. Pass the word that we brook no theft or affray. No murder, but anyone who makes trouble or tries to take more than their share will be held for trial."

"Figured it'd be somethin' of that sort, Captain. I telled the men as much."

"Excellent."

With the Lions to enforce the peace, the Conclave's bailiffs set about ordering the crowd to come and take their share of the supplies. Looking at the numbers, Prentice only hoped there would be enough. Of course, if only some went hungry, they would be a smaller number to bring to heel if they became violent. It disgusted him to think in such brutal terms, but here, so close to the end of this wretched duty, he was resolved to aim for as near to fairness as he could. Perfection was the enemy of the good. Of course, as he watched the bailiffs about their task, he knew that there would already have been a brisk trade in bribes, favors, and promises. There would be some at the front of the line less deserving than others, but there would also be no way to prove it.

"We need to put a share aside for the almsgiving," Prentice told his men. "On the duchess' command."

Duchess Amelia had given no such order, but Prentice knew she would have if she were present. Almsgiving through the church parishes was often the only protection the poorest of the poor had against the miseries of their existence.

"I'll see to it, Captain," said Markas, and he planted the torch staff in the ground for his commander's light before moving off to see the poor folk's share secured.

"Just one thing more, Captain?" said Franken.

"What?"

"As we were marchin' over, we passed some folk in steel on horses."

Prentice gave a short, snorting laugh. "Do you mean the Reach's knights martial, Sergeant Franken?"

"I s'pose I must, Captain," Franken agreed. "Only they seemed much less colorful than knights usually is. Covered in a lot of dirt, and you could see that even in the night, with only torchlight."

"They have seen a lot of dusty riding."

"Well, they were sure givin' orders like nobles ahorse, Captain. Commanded us to clear the road for them and make them way."

"They are going to encamp outside the town as guests of the duchess," Prentice said.

"I figured. Looks like they're headed to a patch of pasture just north of the refugees' huts out of the town gates. Not sure how they figured it in the dark, but there's a good well there. Some of our boys've been usin' it at times, and the refugees like it cause they don't have to cross the lake flat to go to the river."

Prentice shook his head as he realized why the sergeant was telling him this story.

"Odds are a squire or two were sent as heralds to scout out a suitable space to camp men and horses, Franken. It would never have occurred to them to check if the locals were inconvenienced by their arrival."

He thought about the implications a moment, sucking his teeth and looking down at his aching feet in his well-worn boots.

"Pass the word to the whole company—while we camp at Dweltford, that well is forbidden to the Lions. Make sure everyone hears it."

Sergeant Franken saluted. "I'll do that, Captain. With your say-so, I'll go now and make sure the rest of the cohorts is set to watch for theft and what-have-you."

"I say so, Sergeant," Prentice said. As Franken turned to go, he added, "And make sure the men doing sentinel duty on the camp boundary watch out for trouble between the knights and the locals. If it comes to blows, we want to know about it *before* we get drawn into it."

"Will do, Captain."

Prentice watched the lines that formed as the hungry citizens of Dweltford waited for their share of the limited available supplies. It would be long hours before this duty was concluded, another night where Prentice would have almost no sleep. He would have to take some extra time on his cot come the morning or he would likely collapse before the end of the next day. In the past, he had worked himself nearly to death in service to the duchess. That was when the worst they had to fear had been the machinations of the usurper and his pet, Baron Liam. Evil as those men were, they were nothing next to the witch who now hid somewhere in the shadows of the Reach. With his mistress's authority to the mission, Prentice would not stop until the serpent woman was found and slain, and for that, he would need his whole strength. Alien as it was to his character, that meant he would need to rest.

CHAPTER 33

T he division of foodstuffs proceeded through the night with no more strife, and Prentice was thankful to reach his tent with the rest of the Lions just before dawn broke over the Azure Mountains in the distant east. Exhausted as he felt, he briefly contemplated simply walking up into the castle and finding a space beside his wife, whichever bed she was in. It was a tempting notion, but he resisted it in the end.

When the Lions march, so do I, he told himself. For over a decade as a convict he had slept in straw and on barn floors, chained to walls and posts. A night in a cot under canvass was no great hardship. He shed his armor, boots, and doublet, and then fell asleep in his clothes.

The tent was baking hot inside, like the air close to a roaring hearth, when a noise inside it awakened the sleeping captain. At first, he was merely instinctively awake, with the alertness for trouble that a dangerous life breeds. It was unlikely any convict who survived their term on the chain ever completely forgot the habit. The blistering sun backlit the canvass so that everything was only partly shadowed, and Prentice could see an obscure little figure hunched over his open strongbox. There were few possessions in all the world Prentice valued that he could not carry with him on his person, but his strongbox stored his extra clothes and a handful of items he had accrued since he was freed, as well as a small number of coins. In the security of the Lions' camp, he seldom bothered to lock the chest, and watching the interloper, he felt no fear of loss. He did, however, resolve to punish the cur's audacity.

Moving carefully, Prentice readied himself to spring out of his cot. Nonetheless, the wary thief heard the creaking of the wood and rushed immediately for the tent's entrance.

"Stop," Prentice shouted, more from reflex than expectation of being obeyed, and so he was surprised when the thief paused at the tent flap. His surprise gave way to shock when he recognized the outline of the figure against the outside light. "Solomon?"

The young drummer flinched at the mention of his name, then bolted from the tent. Ignoring the stiffness of his limbs, Prentice flung himself after the youth. Once his head was out of the tent, he shouted with his battlefield voice.

"Drummer Solomon, stand fast!"

In spite of himself, Solomon came to a halt, doubtless out of the similar reflex of daily obeying any order given in that tone of voice. Anyone on a battlefield who didn't respond in such a manner did not live long. As with so many of the Lions, obedience was virtually an instinct for the drummer. He hung his head in shame as Prentice stalked up to him. Towering over the young man, the captain stretched his arm and flexed his aching shoulders and back, trying to wake his body up to the same level as his anger.

"What have you taken?" he demanded.

Solomon held up something in each hand. In his right, he had a pair of reinforced leather training gauntlets that belonged to Prentice's wife Righteous. When she visited him in leisure times, husband and wife would often train together, and she left the gloves for that purpose with him to save her carrying them back and forth. They were worn but strong and serviceable. In his left hand, Solomon had Prentice's dagger, the one Righteous had given him the day he faced Baron Ironworth.

"I needed gauntlets," Solomon said in a pleading tone, and his voice cracked. "Prince Farringdon says it's only a fool who goes against a live blade with bare hands if he can avoid it. Please, Captain, it was only to borrow. I was going to bring them back."

For a moment, Prentice was reminded of the night the usurper Daven Marcus killed the king, the night Viscount Gullden had lost the tops of two of *his* fingers. He had said exactly the same thing about live blades and bare hands. Then he realized something else, and he blinked in the scalding sunlight as his eyes fell on Solomon's left hand.

"Where is your dagger, Solomon? The one I bought you?"

"They took it," Solomon answered, still looking away.

"Who took it?" Prentice asked, but Solomon did not answer. "Look at me, Drummer! Who took your dagger?"

"Noble boys," he said, looking up as commanded. His eyes were red, as if he had been crying, and he had a bruise growing next to one of them. "Some of them pages that ride with the knights ahorse, like. They jumped me on the road, down the edge of the camp towards Dweltford."

"They stole your dagger?"

Solomon nodded.

"And you were going to get it back?"

"I don't care 'bout that," Solomon said with hateful venom, and he looked away in disgust. It took a moment for Prentice to realize that the lad was disgusted with himself.

"I don't deserve it," Solomon continued. "But...but they took Sir Gant's rat." His voice caught in his throat. "You trusted it to me, and I let them take it. I'm so sorry, Captain. You got to believe me; I didn't want to let them. They pinned me down to take it and I was going to snatch it back when they let me up, but one of 'em kicked me in the guts, and I wasn't tough enough. I didn't fight to my limits. I'm so sorry."

"Oh, lad," Prentice said, and without thinking he wrapped his arm around Solomon's shoulder. Then he stepped back. "How many were there?"

"Five, Captain," the youth answered with confidence. "I'm not a great counter, but I know the little numbers on account of drumming and counting rhythms."

"And you by yourself?" Five to one were bad odds in any fight. Prentice felt his own disgust, but not for Solomon. He also wondered at the cause. Entitled youths might have preyed upon a passing young man for a fancy, but Prentice felt a suspicion that there might have been more to it. "Do you know why they attacked you? Did they say anything?"

"One of them was like a corporal to them all, in charge" Solomon answered. "He said he was page to someone called Sir Helpman and that he was going to be his squire on his next birthday. He said I had no right to a dagger or any jewels. He said it was sumpty law, and as a noble he was supposed to take it away from us uppity peasants."

Once he heard Baronet Helpman's name, Prentice had no doubt about the truth of Solomon's tale. Even as it made him furious to hear, he might have been inclined to encourage Solomon to put the whole matter behind him, to swallow his pride and learn the lesson to watch out for the predatory self-interest of Grand Kingdom nobility.

But there was the matter of the silver rat. It was a simple little thing and not worth very much. Nonetheless, there were barely twenty such pieces of jewelry in the whole of the Reach, and each one had been earned in blood. Prentice had one of his own and had shed blood over the very one he had entrusted to Solomon. That changed things. It made the whole event a matter of honor—honor to comrades that Prentice had as much stake in as Solomon. As captain of the militia, maybe even greater stake.

"You should have come to me with this, Solomon," he told his drummer firmly. "I cannot have a Lion who steals from me go unpunished. You will be doing discipline drills for days, I promise you."

Solomon nodded his head. Discipline drills were long periods of marching and weapons training at maximum intensity. They were a moderately harsh form of punishment that had the added advantage of improving the recipients' skills as members of the Lions.

"As a fellow Rat of Dweltford," Prentice went on, "I most certainly would have lent you my poniard to get yours back. You only had to say, and my sword was yours to call upon as well, lad. Lady Righteous would fall over herself to draw steel and help get your rat back."

Solomon's eyes were wide.

"You'd kill them page boys for me?" he marveled. Prentice smiled benignly and shook his head.

"It will not come to that, I think, this time, Solomon. However, I will go with you now, and we will recover what is yours by right."

And perhaps some of your dignity as well, Prentice thought, though he knew that was actually the more difficult proposition. He tried to keep his own emotions in check, but he knew that under the protective front he was maintaining, his own anger seethed at the casual injustice being visited on this loyal youth.

CHAPTER 34

"This has to be deliberate," Prentice said as he reached the edge of the White Lions' camp and saw the knights martials' encampment. It was less than a hundred paces from the edge of one to the start of the other. After the conflicts between the two groups in recent days, it just felt provocative for the noble men-at-arms to position themselves so closely. For his part, Prentice would have rather they kept completely separate. He thought about the order he gave Sergeant Franken for the Lions to stay clear of the knights martial and realized the command was both more necessary than he had imagined and at the same time, less likely to be successfully obeyed. The two armed groups, ostensibly in service to the same liege but quietly hostile to each other, were within shouting distance of one another. The whole situation was one bad bottle of rotgut from turning into a brawl or, worse yet, a pitched battle.

With Solomon following quietly on his heels, Prentice crossed the tiny strip of no man's land between the two camps. Feeling like he was stealing into an enemy bivouac, he paused a moment and considered sending for an escort. There were militia sentinels in sight, it would only take a short while to fetch them. Of course, such an action could be taken as a provocation in itself. As he contemplated the implications, Prentice found himself reviewing his circumstance in the light of what he knew about Earl Sebastian, the new knight captain, on whose order the location of the camp would have been chosen.

The earl was proud but competent. During the march, Prentice had seen the man in conferences with the duchess. Clearly, he had no love for the notion of the White Lions, or for their reputation for standing against men of rank, even if those men were enemies of his liege. Even so, the earl never seemed to make choices that deliberately risked any men, and despite his dislike, he accepted the wisdom of using armsmen afoot when they had them. The duchess had told Prentice of his explanation of the delay that left his militiamen to be slaughtered in the gully ambush. The captain was certain that delay was not the earl's intention, that it was more likely a conspiracy of his lieutenant Sir Tarant. The earl seemed too scrupulous to resort to that kind of treachery. In fact, if he was the earnest man he seemed, it was possible that he simply did not suspect his underlings. Tarant, Helpman, or some other offended noble could have concocted the report of flanking horse archers, and Lord Sebastian might just be too trusting to question it. Prentice was reminded of a saying a teacher of his had told him many years before: "Do not attribute to malice what can be adequately explained by stupidity."

Perhaps it was the same for the two camps. Earl Sebastian clearly saw his authority as knight captain extending over both military forces, so he might well have simply ordered the knights martial to camp near the Lions for convenience. In more amenable circumstances, it would make perfect sense. Prentice decided to give the Reach's new knight captain the benefit of the doubt and put the issue out of his thoughts. He was still angry, but he knew that such feelings could poison everything if he let them, only making a bad situation much worse.

"Come on, Solomon," he said as he led off again. Nearby there was a line of horses tied to stakes and eating straw. A pair of pages who looked about ten years old were rubbing one of the beasts down. Prentice turned to Solomon and pointed the boys out.

"Were they amongst your ambushers?"

Solomon was almost indignant in his reaction. "They're still children, Captain. The ones that put me down were like to my age or older even."

"My apologies," Prentice said wryly.

"You want something yeoman?" one of the two pages called out. Both lads had stopped in their chores and were looking at Prentice and Solomon as if they were lurking ruffians up to no good. Prentice realized he was just wearing his shirt and trousers, having not bothered to fully dress before coming here, but the two boys had to know he was from the militia. Yet the one addressing them did not hesitate to speak like a master to servants.

"We seek the tent of Baronet Helpman," he told the lad, doing his best not to be annoyed at the casual disdain. This was a child who knew no other way. Blaming him for his place in the social order was pointless. The two pages looked at each other and then the speaker pointed to a spot farther along the edge of the camp.

"He's got a tent in up that way, with all the others that've got Reacher-blue ribbons hanging off them. You know that color?"

Prentice nodded and led off once more in the direction they had been pointed. Solomon came alongside him, and Prentice was surprised when he heard his drummer mutter under his breath.

"We're Lions, aren't we? Loyal members of her grace's militia. 'Course we know what color Reach blue is. My bloody uniform is Reach blue."

"Quite so," Prentice whispered to him. "The lad was being a twit, but for the rest of this, I need you to hold your tongue, Solomon."

"Aye, Captain," Solomon replied quietly and saluted gently.

They wended their way between tents and guy lines, hardly drawing any attention, probably seeming no more noticeable than any of the hundreds of other servants and retainers servicing the noble force. Nevertheless, Prentice felt fully on edge when they found the open space and campfire around which a half dozen tents flying blue ribbons from their poles were set in a loose circle.

"That's him," Solomon said, and he pointed to a young man who looked about fourteen years of age—easily of an age to take his testing to become a squire. He was sitting on a log, scrubbing at a piece of armor steel with handfuls of sand—a rerebrace, protection for the upper arm, by the look of it. The page had dark hair in a bowl cut, sunburned cheeks, and a wide mouth. He was wearing a tabard in his master's colors—wide diagonal slashes of white and green separated by thin stripes of red. Solomon had not described the lad and Prentice had not thought to ask, but as soon as he laid eyes on him, he knew he was the one. Dangling from a chain around his neck, the silver rat glinted in the morning sunlight.

"Are you lost, Captain?" asked a voice, and Prentice looked to see Baronet Helpman emerging from one of the tents. His hair was wet, and he was drying his hands, as if he had just washed them. The baronet was wearing his house colors, just like his page.

"Thank you, no, Sir," Prentice replied and bowed his head, forcing himself to keep the precise niceties. It might be possible to resolve this issue simply, as a matter of youthful high spirits gone too far. He doubted it, but he had to try that path first. His loyalty to the duchess demanded at least that much. "But we are here to recover something that was lost."

"Indeed? What?" Sir Helpman's tone was hard and dismissive.

"Something it looks like your page has found, Sir."

Sir Helpman looked to the lad who was still polishing but making such a show of it that Prentice was sure he was, in fact, listening to every word.

"Kirkin, get you over here!" the baronet ordered his page, and the boy cast the rerebrace aside as he jumped to his feet and ran the short distance. Sir Helpman took hold of the silver rat pendant and held it up as if he had never seen it before, then looked to Prentice.

"Is this what you lost?"

"Not I, the lad," Prentice said, nodding to Solomon.

"How came you by this, Kirkin?"

"I traded for it," Kirkin said so quickly his tongue nearly tripped itself up. The lad seemed inordinately proud of himself.

"Traded what?" Helpman asked.

"Gin."

"Where'd you come by gin, boy?"

"Some of the newcome boys from the east found it," Kirkin said. "They offered it to me. But I never touched a drop." The youth shook his head with exaggerated emphasis. "I was just explaining to the lads that we pages shouldn't touch hard drink 'til we are sworn, like we promised, when this fellow happened up and offered this silver thing as payment for the whole bottle. So I traded. After all, it's not my duty to keep the low-born from foolish dissipation. It's an ugly thing, but it might be real silver. I thought I could have it melted and made into a ring."

Foolish dissipation? Prentice mused, and he nearly scoffed at the words. Whatever kind of page the youth was, he was a terrible liar.

"There you go, Captain. Not lost, sold," said Helpman with a sharp-edged smile. "Is there anything else?"

"Kirkin is lying," Prentice said, returning the baronet's smile with a steely one of his own. Helpman bared his teeth in a hateful grimace, but there was a knowing gleam in his eye.

"You are quick to throw insults at your betters, Prentice-called-Ash," he said, scoffing at Prentice's battle name. "But I will humor you. Kirkin, are you lying?"

"No, Sir, never," Kirkin insisted with almost over-performed earnestness. "The boys I was with, they'll all testify it's the truth."

"Testify?" Prentice asked and he felt the cold anger stirring within. "The louts who helped you rob my drummer? Why would I trust their words?"

"Have a care, Captain," said Helpman. "I know some of the lads my page is speaking of. They are a little brotherhood, sons of men of rank, all soon to make their vows as squires. They will begin taking to battlefields and seeking their spurs. Their fathers will not thank you for defaming their characters. And when they are knighted, they might retain a grudge for staining their honor. You know how rash the young can be." Helpman opened his arms wide and shrugged as if he was explaining a sad truth. "Nonetheless, if you would take this matter to the knight captain as a question between two lads in martial service, of sorts, that would be your prerogative. I know the earl is a righteous judge, but I would not expect much goodwill after all the contempt you have shown to the traditions of law and the relations between those of birth and those of...your station."

Hands clenched at his sides, eyes like slits, Prentice stepped closer to the smug noble man-at-arms.

"You are not a newcomer to the Reach, Sir," he said quietly through gritted teeth. "You know the reputation attached to those rats. I know you know the tale, Sir Helpman. Solomon knows as well, and he carries it by right of honor. He would sooner die than give it up."

"What I know about those lumps of silver is that they are paraded around by a clutch of uppity yeoman and ex-convicts who should be cuffed for the filthy curs they are, not cosseted like lapdogs for the duchess."

At least the baronet had not insulted Duchess Amelia, for if he had, Prentice doubted he would have been able to keep himself from striking the man right here. As it was, the nobleman's use of the word "uppity" told him everything he needed to know. It was the same word Solomon said that the boy Kirkin had used when he was attacked. This entire situation was a plot of Sir Helpman's, Prentice was certain.

"Now, former convict and heretic, if you think to take this matter further, you must speak to the knight captain."

"He is not the only one..." Prentice started to say, but Helpman cut him off.

"Oh no? The duchess? Is that what you were going to say?" Sir Helpman's expression took on a cruel cast with a cocked eyebrow. "We all know you're her favorite, but how long will that matter, do you think? The Reach withers and she dithers. And you keep stirring more trouble for her. Already there is talk, quiet whispers that a husband had best be found or else she will estrange the rest of the nobility still alive. You are not her salvation, Prentice. You are the wedge that splits her off from her true peers, the ones who will actually win this war for her."

Prentice wanted to scoff again, but Sir Helpman was right about one point. There *was* division between his Lions and noble men-at-arms sworn to defend the duchess and her peace. In a sense, it did not matter if it was his fault or theirs, the division was there and the weakness it fostered cost his men their lives. The entire purpose of the Lions had been to give Duchess Amelia a loyal force that would empower her to defend her lands and bring the nobles to heel. That was the problem. As long as the two forces existed, they would be forced to be at odds, and petty moments like this would repeat themselves.

As Prentice contemplated this grim realization, Sir Helpman backed away a step, shrugged with a self-satisfied smile, and turned to go back into his tent, the matter clearly resolved in his mind.

"I'll be a squire soon," Kirkin said to Solomon with a sneer. "When I am, don't let me catch you on a battlefield, little rat boy. You won't make it home that day." Then the page turned back to his seat and sat down to resume his polishing. He looked up from the work to wink smugly at them.

"I'm so sorry, Captain," Solomon said quietly. "I should've fought harder. Run quicker. Something. You trusted me with that and it's so precious. Better I should have died. How will I face Sir Gant now, him knowing I've lost his honor."

Prentice looked at Solomon in horrified shock. The lad meant in the afterlife. He wondered how he would face Sir Gant in the world to come. That was a horrific burden to lay on a young man. Prentice wanted to explain that the afterlife would not be like that and to reassure him that Sir Gant would have nothing but welcome for him, but this was not the place for that conversation. Worse, though, was the vile dishonor this supposedly honorable man was teaching his page. Bad enough that Sir Helpman held his rank more important than truth or righteousness, but he was teaching the next generation of nobility the same venality and encouraging the same abuses that had made Prentice's life a misery since his first days at Ashfield.

"This is a bad day, Solomon," he said. "And it may get much worse yet, but know this: Sir Gant had nothing but the utmost respect for your courage, as do I. Now, do you trust me?"

Solomon nodded solemnly. There was a sadness in him but no tears in his eyes.

Good, Prentice thought. *No self-pity just yet.* His own storm-cold fury was fully enraged now, so that the heat of the sun was barely recognizable to him. He had a plan, one which almost no one he knew would approve. Kirkin and Solomon were both too young to be enmeshed in the loathing that swirled around them because of their masters, but it was too late now.

Prentice stepped around Solomon and took one of his wife's leather gauntlets from his belt where he had put them after retrieving them from his drummer. He stood over Kirkin.

"Stand up," he told the page.

"What?" Kirkin shielded his eyes from the sun as he looked up.

"I said, stand up," Prentice repeated in a command voice, the volume rising. Kirkin stood uncertainly, more than a little intimidated. He cast an eye past Prentice, most likely to see if his master was watching. Prentice did not look for himself, but

Kirkin's restored confidence made him think Helpman must be still nearby.

"What is it now convi...?" the page started to ask, mimicking his master's disdainful manner. His words were cut off, however, when Prentice slapped that glove across his face full force. Kirkin bent sideways at the waist from the force of the strike, and behind him, Prentice heard Sir Helpman give a cry of objection. He ignored it.

"Kirkin, page to Sir Helpman of the knights martial," he said in full voice, holding none of his own contempt back, but still in complete command of his temper. "Solomon, drummer of the White Lions is a servant of her grace, Duchess Amelia, of approved character and known to her by name and honorable service. By his testimony, I name you a thief, a liar, and a coward. In his name and as his second I charge you to appear in the open ground between the two camps at noon to answer the charges or be ascribed a coward for the rest of your life."

"What the bloody hell are you playing at, convict?" Sir Helpman shouted. "Do you think this is a game?"

"If there is a game, then it is yours, Sir," Prentice replied whirling on the baronet. "You dealt the cards, and we all play our hands."

"You expect boys to fight an honor duel?"

"You made it clear that Solomon's case would not get a fair hearing if it was taken to Earl Sebastian, and you virtually threatened to stir treason amongst the knights martial if I asked the duchess to intervene. What other course is there in this question?"

Sir Helpman opened and closed his mouth in disbelief. Then his eyes narrowed, and he wiped the sweat from his face with the back of his hand.

"Your little brat has no standing to challenge," he said with an acid tone. "He has no noble rank."

"Neither does your page," said Prentice, meeting the nobleman's hateful glare. "When he left his father's house, to swear on to you, he forsook any previous title until he won his spurs as a squire or quit your service. That is the path of chivalry."

"Do not think to sermonize me on the ways of knighthood, you convict bastard." Sir Helpman's sword hand twitched, and Prentice readied himself to intercept if the nobleman tried to draw his blade. "I will not let Kirkin take part in this ridiculous folly."

"Very well, Sir. It is your right as his master," Prentice told him, then turned to look straight at Kirkin who was still holding his face where he had been slapped. "Know this though, boy—if you are not there at noon, we will count the charges proven and I will inform her grace before nightfall. Your master might defend your name and claim that you shirked the challenge because of his command, but everyone you meet from this day on will know. They will see the stain in your soul, and you will see it in their faces. The shame will never leave you."

Kirkin let out a despairing sigh and Sir Helpman put his hand to his sword hilt. "You bastard!" he said hatefully.

"Draw your blade if you must, Sir," Prentice said without the slightest fear. "But make your first strike count. We are speaking on a matter of honor, and the White Lions are camped not a hundred paces from here. Even if you take me, I favor Solomon to reach my men before you can stop him. He is fleet of foot. Then you will have civil war on your hands. You know you will."

The knife-edge moment stretched out, and Prentice watched for the tell-tale signs that Sir Helpman was about to make a fight of it. He only had his poniard with him, the blade he had taken back from Solomon, but Prentice was certain he could get it drawn and defend himself long enough for Solomon to make it back to camp. As he expected, though, it did not come to that. Spitting on the ground with furious disgust, Sir Helpman took his hand from his sword's handle. He looked to his page then back at Prentice.

"Noon then."

"We will await you at the appointed place," Prentice replied. Then he took Solomon by the shoulder and turned him to walk out of the knights martial camp.

"Am I really going to fight a duel?" Solomon asked in a quiet voice full of a wretched mix of emotions. Prentice still felt the hard-edged fury dominating his own feelings, but he gave the young man a squeeze on the shoulder.

"Yes, you are."

"What if I die?"

"Then you will be able to face Sir Gant with full confidence and honor, young Solomon," Prentice said, and it took all his will to keep his tone steady, so great was the hate within him. He hated the social structure that empowered the self-indulgent privilege of nobles like Helpman and Kirkin; he hated that so many men could not be made to see the difference between pride and honor; he hated that the only solution he knew to problems like these was violence; and most of all, he hated himself for allowing so fine a youth as Solomon to find himself in this murderous situation.

CHAPTER 35

A melia slept much better than she expected to and awoke when the light through her chamber window lit the room with shafts of gold. She had not realized how tiring she had found the rapid march from the south. It was also a relief to know she was safe from the marauding fey, a fact she felt ashamed to have to admit to herself. Her safety came at the cost of too many peoples' lives and sufferings. That grim reflection banished the sleepiness from her mind, and she forced herself up in bed. From the bustling elsewhere in her apartments, she could hear Lady Spindle about her morning duties, readying clothes, jewelry, and hair dressings for the mistress's day. Gone were the days when Matron Bettina ran her mistress's chamber. The elderly lady-in-waiting was living a much quieter life, sleeping elsewhere in the duchess's household these days. Looking about, Amelia could not see Lady Righteous, but she was more surprised to see Lady Dalflitch sitting at the chamber's one table. Poised and straight backed, the raven-haired beauty was the figure of elegance she always was, but there was a pensive look on her face, and her features seemed somewhat drawn and pinched. For the first time since Amelia had met her, Dalflitch was showing signs of her age.

"Good morning, My Lady," Amelia said as she swung her legs out of bed and found her ladies-in-waitings' truckle still extended from under the bedframe. She reached down to put it

CHAPTER 35   307

back but found herself caught awkwardly half-standing on the lower mattress.

"Oh...your Grace...I...good morning," Dalflitch stammered, uncharacteristically tongue tied, as she broke from her own reverie and quickly stood up to help put the truckle away. From the garderobe, Spindle appeared and was plainly alarmed to find her mistress wrestling with the furniture.

"We will do this, Your Grace," the Lace Fang insisted, somehow managing to hand her mistress a morning robe to cover her linen slip while also working the truckle back into place under the duchess's bed. "I'm sorry, Your Grace. I left it because I thought the noise would wake you."

Amelia shook her head.

"It is no trouble, Ladies," she said to them both, embarrassed for their embarrassment. At last, the simple if cumbersome chore was complete and Amelia pulled her robe over her shoulders. She made her way over to the table and took the chair opposite Dalflitch's while Spindle returned to preparing her grace's wardrobe for the day.

"Righteous has gone down to make sure the kitchen is ready with your breakfast meal, Your Grace," the Fang said, explaining her partner's absence. "She'll like be back in a short piece. Matron Bettina has poked her head in once as well, but she said that she would be ready for whenever you summonsed her."

"The days march on, whether we are ready for them or not," Amelia said to herself and then tutted at her own thoughts. She was the only one in the room who had had the chance to sleep as late as she had. She looked to Dalflitch. "Well, My Lady, it is good to see you. What word of our town in my absence?"

"Your town swelters and thirsts, Your Grace," Dalflitch said flatly. Her tone was weary, and Amelia could well imagine the burdens on the Reach's effective ducal seneschal having to manage the withering domain. "However, the supplies you brought will go a long way to alleviating hunger for a time. I have word from the Conclave that the entire stockpile has been distributed with the help of the White Lions."

"Was there much violence?"

"Hardly any, I am happy to report. Two men will go before magistrates this morning for minor affray, but no more than that."

That is a mercy, and a near miracle in itself, Amelia thought.

"Thefts?" the duchess followed up, and her lady gave an apologetic frown.

"Probably, but none reported."

"So, either the thieves were too good to be noticed, or..."

"Or, with everyone so much closer to the edge of desperation, the honest folk identify more readily with the thief who skims a little extra for themselves."

Amelia shook her head, but in her heart could not fully condemn the people who might act so desperately. Spindle handed her a pewter cup with watered wine, and she sipped it thoughtfully. Dalflitch politely waved away the cup Spindle offered her.

"So, I suppose the next question is how long the supplies are likely to last." Amelia said after another moment's thought.

"Honestly, Your Grace? I think even four weeks would be optimistic," Dalflitch answered soberly. "In four weeks, Dweltford will need another such caravan of foods, and then another one four weeks after that. Worse yet, if the drought goes on as it has, each caravan will have to bring more and more. The crops around us are failing, even the ones we have dug extra works and wells to support."

"How long until it all collapses?"

"I don't know how I would even calculate such a thing, Your Grace," Dalflitch said, shaking her head. "But if I were to guess, I would say a season, or what a season once was."

"Is there nothing else we can do?" Having drained her cup, Amelia found herself twisting the metal stoup anxiously in her hands. She forced herself to put the cup down on the table, banging it more loudly than she meant.

"For the Reach as a whole, I think we are doing what we can, Your Grace," Dalflitch told her. "For Dweltford itself, the best thing we can do is send the militia and knights martial away."

"We have marauding horsemen raiding our lands, My Lady. Have you not heard yet?"

"I have, Your Grace. Still, those two large forces are draining food, and worse yet, water from Dweltford. To extend the town's life, the best thing will be to put some of them at much greater distance."

Amelia chewed over her lady seneschal's suggestion. As the fey raided her people, the militia and knights were needed to hunt them down, but since the land struggled to even support the people, the large military was almost as great a threat to those same folk.

Between the devils and the drought, Amelia thought.

"Where would we send them?" she asked.

"The militia could return in the main to Fallenhill, at least, Your Grace. Word from the north is that near to the mountains, with runoff from the heights, they have had close to a true growing season. They are still drought-stricken, but there is enough food to sustain the village and garrison some while more. Just sending the Lions back to their training grounds would relieve the town vastly."

"And leave me more completely at the mercy of my nobles," Amelia reflected bitterly.

"Your Grace?"

"Have you not heard of the further conflicts between the Reach's peers and my militia?"

"After you went to bed last night, the Lace Fangs regaled me with a rather bloodthirsty tale of revenge exacted by your militia captain, Your Grace," Dalflitch confirmed. There was an unmistakable twinkle in her eye as she did. Amelia was not surprised. There were no ladies of her chamber who had not suffered at the hands of an arrogant nobleman or five. Not one of those women would shed a tear for Yarmass and his rapine company.

"Well, regardless of how deserved the punishment, the peers of the Reach have decided that Prentice exceeded himself in executing it," Amelia mused. "They have made it clear that when the present crisis is resolved, if not before, they will expect the White Lions brought to heel like a pack of unruly hounds."

"While the nobles themselves bark and bay like the worst curs?" Dalflitch reflected.

"Quite so, My Lady. If I must send the Lions away, that will only confirm to the knights martial that they are the irreplaceable ones, the ones without whom my rule cannot continue. Prentice and I raised the Lions specifically to overcome that hubris."

Dalflitch nodded, understanding the politics of the situation exactly, as Amelia expected she would.

"So, if we keep both forces here, the town starves faster," the lady seneschal synopsized. "But if you send the Lions north, you are at the mercy of the peers. What if you dismiss the knights martial?"

"Imagine the affront to their honor they would take from that?" Amelia said, smiling wickedly as she did so. The idea had its appeal, even though she knew it was politically unthinkable. "If I dismissed each peer to his own holdings, I might never get them to come back. Marshalling them to war once more would cost me more favors and promises than getting that caravan up here from Griffith did. In fact, it's a wonder that more haven't simply quit the company ahorse and returned to their own lands."

"I suspect a deal of that has to do with your new knight captain, Your Grace. He has a reputation as something of a war hero, apparently, the kind of man other nobles wish to follow in hopes of glory. You picked well there, I'd say, even with all these attendant problems."

"You are remarkably well informed, My Lady," Amelia marveled. The caravan and the Reach's two competing militaries had not been in Dweltford more than a day, and already Dalflitch knew so much. Were there any secrets safe from her?

"You retain me to know things, Your Grace, and I am thankful for my place in your household. I will not fail you."

"Indeed not. Well then, my shrewd retainer, what is your advice?"

Dalflitch considered the question, and while she did, Amelia waved Spindle over.

"Find a steward and tell him we are ready to break fast," she told the waiting lady quietly. "Then come back and help me with my hair. The time has come to make me presentable for the day's business, I think."

Spindle curtseyed and hurried out. Amelia looked back to Dalflitch and cocked an eyebrow. "Well?" she asked.

"The two main problems are hunger and these grumpkin riders, are they not, Your Grace?"

"They are fey, My Lady, and I assure they are most real. Do not make the mistake of thinking the reports of them are exaggerated. These are neither grumpkins nor nixies, nor any other creatures from children's tales. Knights and Lions both have struggled to bring them down on the field."

"Forgive me, Your Grace," Dalflitch said, bowing her head. "I didn't mean to be so flippant. However, my main point stands. Hunger and the raiders. So why aren't the raiders hungry? Or are they raiding for food as well?"

Amelia had not fully considered the question that the raiders might have been driven purely by the desperations that beset the rest of her lands. Now that she did, however, she was sure that was not their prime motive. They looted from their victims, she had heard, but there was no pattern of food theft at the core of their actions. And the way they moved and fought showed no signs of the weakness and desperation that hunger produced in her own people. Amelia shook her head.

"They are not so hungry," she said.

"So, it follows that there are sources of food somewhere out where these raiders hide," Dalflitch continued. "Perhaps there are lakes or springs of fresh water between here and the salt sea that we have not yet discovered. Or perhaps they are able to simply range far enough to find sufficient food even with the scarcity of the drought."

"Assuming they even eat what we eat," Amelia said dejectedly. The thought that the fey might be so different from ordinary folk that the drought did not even affect their food situation was a dispiriting one.

"*Not* grumpkins or nixies, remember, Your Grace?" Dalflitch chided her mistress politely. Amelia nodded at the good-natured reproof and then gestured for her lady to continue.

"I think it's most likely they can range farther to gather the food they need, and if *they* can, then so can knights ahorse, surely."

That seemed a reasonable conclusion to Amelia.

"So, why should you not send the knights martial to hunt these fey riders?" Dalflitch went on. "That is a fair duty for men-at-arms and would take the burden of feeding them from Dweltford's back."

"And then I could send the militia north."

"Yes."

"Leaving Dweltford unprotected?" Amelia mused, but Dalflitch was ready for the objection.

"Not really. The knights martial will be ranging but will never be too far away, in truth. Also, you could reasonably retain a single cohort of Lions to defend the castle and town. I understand there has always been a plan for a home garrison, a kind of Lioness' Own cohort. Make it official. A hundred men-at-arms are still a burden on the town, but much less crushing than the one we labor under at the moment."

Amelia considered the proposal. It was a compromise with a number of unpleasant possible consequences, but it was as good as anything she could think of for herself. She nodded, and at the same moment there was a knock at her chamber door. It opened and Matron Bettina entered, leading a pair of stewards with trays laden with breakfast. Simple fare but wholesome, and Amelia was surprised at how welcome she found it.

"Alright, My Lady," she told Dalflitch. "After I break my fast, let us begin to put this plan into effect."

"As you say, Your Grace," Dalflitch said with a bow of her head and stood to make it easier for the stewards to serve on the table. "Oh, while I think of it, Your Grace, a happier little piece of business. A minstrel arrived last night, an odd man, all in motley."

"Master Bluebird," Amelia said, and she smiled at the prospect of the poet tumbler's entertainments.

"Yes, he said he had met you, Your Grace. He begged a spot to rest in the kitchens and a chance to sing for his supper. I granted it to him, if you do not object."

"No, I do not," said Amelia. "He is a merry talent, and his fooling will be most welcome, I think, to lift sullen spirits."

"That was what I hoped. Of course, with some food now in the town, spirits will lift naturally for a time anyway. And once we get the knights martial and White Lions separated, we can expect the tensions there will ease as well."

"Most likely," Amelia agreed, taking a first spoonful of the simple porridge that tasted like it had been made with ewe's milk but was flavoured with something sweet as well. A berry liqueur perhaps? She settled down to enjoy one last moment to herself before going about the business of the day. Having discussed their options with Lady Dalflitch, Amelia had some sense of peace about what she needed to do. Between the drought, the fey, Prentice's witch, and the endless politicking of her peoples, at least she could take some action to resolve some of the tensions between her knights and her militia. And better to get it done now, before some new problem reared its ugly head.

CHAPTER 36

B y noon, Prentice and Solomon were standing in the middle of the gap between the two camps, along with Sergeant Franken, Markas, and twenty or so other militiamen. Prentice had not asked for the attendants, but when word of what was to happen spread, the number of interested parties grew with surprising swiftness. They stood in the open sun wearing hats or scarves to protect their skin, even though most were already sun browned like tanned leather. Markas had asked to bring the company standard, but Prentice thought it would be too provocative. Besides, by the strict standards of Kingdom law, this should be a private matter.

There was an odd air about the group of militiamen as they waited with a mix of anticipation and resentment. In order that they would not be too fractious, Prentice commanded a space cleared on the ground for the duel—something to keep idle hands from turning to mischief. That did not take very long, though, and Prentice was ironically glad to see Sir Helpman and Kirkin approach from the nobles' camp.

Of course, I might not be so relieved in a short while, he thought, recognizing what was about to happen.

Just as Prentice and Solomon were not alone, so the baronet and his page were accompanied by about a dozen members of their own camp, including two or three knights, with their longswords and house colors, and four youths, all about Kirkin's age, whom Prentice was sure were the gang that had ambushed Solomon originally. He half expected to see Sir Tarant or even Earl Sebastian, but neither was present. He was wondering about the implications, as well as observing that one of the approaching party was carrying a long, cloth-wrapped bundle, when he heard a friendly voice at his shoulder.

"I have to say, when I left my beautiful wife in her bed this morning, this is not even near to what I expected the day to bring."

Prentice turned to see Turley there in his fine garb, his eyes well shaded under his expensive hat and its long, jaunty feather.

"Solomon landed his'self in a touch o' bother, has he?"

"Sir Helpman's painful little page landed Solomon in the bother," Prentice said, nodding at the approaching noble and ward.

"Oh aye, looks the type," said Turley. "Did you want me to try and smooth it over?"

Prentice gave his friend a disbelieving look.

"What?" Turley responded with a shrug. "You may be all fancy spoken, but I spend much more time in noble households than you do nowadays. I've picked up a lot o' the knack of speakin' to folks of rank." He gave Prentice a sly wink.

"Have you indeed?" Prentice said, smiling at his friend's sense of humor in spite of himself. "Not enough time to realize that the peers of the realm do not favor themselves to be called 'folk,' though."

"Well, I never said I'd learned everything!"

"Why *are* you here?"

"Oh, thanks."

"You know what I mean," Prentice said. Turley nodded and his smile dimmed, the closest the roguish man ever came to deadly seriousness.

"Duchess sent me," he said. "She's got fresh orders for you and the Lions, so my Dalflitch says. I'm to escort you straight back to the castle. 'Course, once I heard what was happening here, I had to stick around and see it. It's just a pity your Righteous ain't here. She'll be livid when she hears she missed it."

"She is pregnant and should not be out in this heat."

"Well, sure, she spent half the morning with her head in a privy, but it's not like she's even showin' yet. She won't be taking to a birthin' bed any day soon."

Prentice recognized his friend's sense, but he was not really listening. The noble contingent with Sir Helpman had lined up on the opposite edge of the improvised dueling ground. Now the baronet and his page stepped forward into the middle of the space and waited. Prentice tapped Solomon on the shoulder, and they went out as well. Turley followed along on his own initiative.

"Who the hell is this?" asked Sir Helpman.

"I am Turley of Dweltford, Chief Steward in the house of her Grace, Duchess Amelia," Turley said with a level of authority Prentice had never heard him express before.

"He is here to observe and report back to her Grace," Prentice lied. "That the forms are observed."

Sir Helpman shrugged and did not bother to introduce himself to Turley.

"Alright, Prentice, let's be about this foolishness. Is your boy resolved to blood, or can peace be found between these two?"

Prentice turned to Solomon.

"If the page, Kirkin, will admit to the theft of my rat and return it with an apology, I am willing to call the matter finished," Solomon said, using exactly the words Prentice had taught him for this moment. His voice shook a little with nerves, but otherwise he was admirably clear-spoken and audible. Sir Helpman turned to his page and gestured for him to answer Solomon's offer.

"He sold me the fool hunk of silver for a fair price," Kirkin declared with the kind of disdain that only youth and privilege can attain. "If he wants it back, he can pay me its value. I was going to have it melted down for a ring, I'm sure the same jeweler can fix a ready price for us. Not too costly. After all, it's just meaningless metal."

Hearing those words, Prentice knew that Sir Helpman had coached his charge, just as he had Solomon. He was about to comment when Turley loudly cleared his throat. Everyone present looked at the tall man and saw that he was tapping his finger on his chest, pointing at the silver rat pinned to his own doublet. He gave Helpman and Kirkin a knowing glance and then cast his eyes at Prentice's chest where the captain had his own silver rat hanging openly from the chain around his neck.

"Is this supposed to be some form of intimidation?" Sir Helpman demanded.

"Intimdatin'? Certainly not," said Turley. "I just thought your young charge there ought to know exactly who he was speakin' *to* and what he was speakin' *about*, before he said somethin' he might regret. But don't let me interrupt. I'm just here to observe."

"Well then, observe and keep your observations to yourself," the baronet snapped. He turned to Prentice. "They cannot be reconciled, it seems."

Prentice nodded.

"Then it is time to name terms."

"Solomon is resolved to see the matter judged fully," Prentice said, and the words tasted foul in his mouth. Two boys, barely teenagers were about to fight with live steel, possibly to the death, and the niceties of the duel called it "to see the matter fully judged." It disgusted him. "He will fight to the conclusion but will give quarter if it is asked."

"Kirkin is resolved the same," Sir Helpman confirmed, then flashed a smug smile. "As the challenged party, Kirkin claims the right to name weapons. He chooses longswords."

The baronet waved over his shoulder, and the member of his entourage carrying the wrapped object stepped up and pulled back the cloth to reveal a pair of knights' longswords with unadorned steel fixtures, pommel, and crossguard—serviceable but unimpressive weapons. The companion knight offered the two blades openly, without scabbards.

"Please inspect them, if you wish, to ensure there is no treachery. Kirkin has the right to choose first, but he foregoes that since he is forced to provide both weapons—assuming your boy has no longsword of his own?"

Prentice's own champion blade was the closest thing to a longsword in the entire White Lions' camp, and with its long, slightly curved and single-edged blade, no knight would consider it a true longsword by any stretch. This was all just a cunning snub, another way for Helpman and Kirkin to intimidate Solomon, as was choosing the longsword. It was the kind of maneuver Prentice had been anticipating, though he had not guessed this one precisely.

Formally fulfilling his duty as second, Prentice took each blade by the hilt and felt the weight. He looked for warps and with care checked the edges all the way along from ricasso to tip. There was nothing to pick between the two swords that he could tell and so he chose one of the two and handed it to Solomon, hilt first. Sir Helpman handed the other to Kirkin, and the two parties returned to their respective sides of the dueling ground.

There was no going back now.

CHAPTER 37

Prentice held the longsword while Solomon stripped himself to the waist. Across the dueling ground, Kirkin was doing the same. With their bared limbs and pale chests, the two lads seemed so scrawny, both too young and unready for this wretched business. Prentice handed Solomon his wife's gauntlets.

"I thought we weren't allowed armor," the lad said. Prentice pointed to Kirkin, who was fitting gauntlets of his own.

"Gloves are allowed. The bare skin is to let blood show. If you had gambesons on, you might both take a mortal wound before anyone watching even knew it. It seems more dangerous like this, but actually it is safer, after a fashion."

Solomon accepted his captain's explanation with a nod. Prentice cast another glance over his shoulder and saw Sir Helpman giving his page the longsword. Kirkin was a little taller than Solomon, having obviously had his first growth spurt toward manhood. Even so, the longsword was almost three quarters the boy's height and as he hefted the weight in his hands, Prentice realized the baronet's mistake. Kirkin was still too young to have trained with a full-weight longsword. Up until now he would have been using blunt, youthful practice weapons. He had almost certainly been taught all the right techniques, but the weight in his hand now was too much for him.

"You always said the longsword was hard to master," Solomon said quietly. He was watching as Kirkin brought the weapon into guard and went through some basic cuts, ostensibly feeling the weight of the sword and limbering up. Prentice looked from the page to his drummer. Solomon was too inexperienced to see what Prentice could see—that the page was overmatched by his weapon. Solomon saw a young knight-in-training wielding a knight's signature weapon. Prentice saw a combatant who was going to use the right techniques for the weapon but not for who he was.

"Are you ready, heretic?" Sir Helpman called. "Kirkin stands prepared."

"One moment, Sir," Prentice answered, holding his hand up. "My man will pray a moment. It is his right."

"Good thinking. He's going to need it."

A condescending chuckle ran through the noble crowd. Prentice ignored it, leaning down to whisper to Solomon, who had put his hands together for prayer. The captain put his own hand on top of Solomon's.

"We will come to that in a minute," he said. "Firstly, are you afraid?"

Solomon began to shake his head, but as his eyes met his captain's he stopped. Then he gave a small, shamed nod.

"Good," Prentice told him, and the lad's eyes went wide with surprise. "Only a fool is unafraid of death. Better you recognize it in yourself now than when you face Kirkin's steel. Too many men tell themselves they have no fear, but then it sneaks up on them in the middle of the duel and unmans them. Good that you have it out of the way. Now, this is how you are going to fight."

He held the longsword out flat, and Solomon reached for the hilt.

"No, not like that," Prentice said. "That way is for a longsword."

"Isn't this a longsword?"

"Not to you. In your hands it is just an oddly shaped short pike. Do you understand?"

Solomon shook his head. Prentice pointed to two spots on the blade.

"Rear hand here, lead hand there. Just like when you drill."

"Won't I cut myself on the blade?" Solomon asked, looking where Prentice wanted him to place his front hand.

"The gloves will protect you, that is what they are for. Also, keep your lead back a little, near the ricasso."

Solomon put his hands where he was told and reflexively set himself in the Lions' fighting stance. That made Prentice smile. He leaned even closer to his drummer's face.

"Now do not let that lout fool you, Solomon. He is not a knight. He is a boy playing at being a knight with a sword that's too big for him. You are a Lion. You have marched with us, stood with us on the battlefield. Fight him like one of us. He will have the reach on you to start because your 'pike' is an odd one. Stay out of his way, let him tire himself out. Keep moving fast and wait for the best moment to strike. You've seen the prince and me do that."

"What if he's faster than me?"

"Then he will cut you. Do not let him do that."

"This seems a long prayer, convict," Sir Helpman called. "Are you hoping for sundown to save you? Or are you aiming for doomsday?"

Prentice shook his head without looking.

"Ignore them. They are just trying to scare you," he said.

"*They're* trying to scare *me?*" Solomon seemed to find the idea strange.

"Of course. Kirkin's terrified of you. He needed four mates with him just to knock you to the ground. You don't think this whole thing is turning his bowels to water?"

"I never..."

"Yes, well, now you know. We cannot delay any longer. Do you have any favorite prayers?"

"I don't know any," Solomon said, shaking his head. "I just say amen like, when the chaplain says to."

"Well, let me pray for you." There were all sorts of formal prayers Prentice could remember from his time at the academy, but they all felt bloodless in his mind now. He decided to improvise. "God in Heaven, Lord over all Creation, this is Solomon, my brother-in-arms. He has been robbed and abused. You send your angels to fight demons and devil-men. You make filthy rats into mighty lions. Judge now between Solomon and Kirkin, and vindicate my brother. In your Son's name."

Solomon blinked at the captain in near disbelief.

"You say 'amen' now," Prentice told him.

"Amen."

Then Prentice stepped aside, and Solomon made his way cautiously into the middle. Kirkin stepped forth, swinging the longsword in his hands with long cuts so that the blade swished through the air. Several of the knightly crowd laughed as they saw the way Solomon held his own weapon.

"Look out Kirkin, he thinks he's going to stick you with a pitchfork," one of the other pages shouted, and he was rewarded with chuckles and a pat on the back from one of his fellows.

Ignore them, Solomon, Prentice thought. *They know what half-swording is. Only the idiot boys think you're making a mistake.*

Kirkin feigned a swing at Solomon, but the drummer did not even flinch. Prentice was proud of his nerve.

"That's it, Solomon," someone on the Lions' side shouted. "Show 'em what kind o' steel a Lion's heart is made of."

Solomon was momentarily distracted by the encouragement.

Eyes on your man, lad, Prentice thought, but it was too late. Kirkin had seen Solomon's eyes look askance and picked the moment for his first assault. He charged in, using a passage of cuts from exactly the basic repertoire Prentice and Prince Farringdon had demonstrated to Solomon days earlier. The cuts were reasonably well executed, but even at this initial stage of the fight, the longsword's weight was slowing Kirkin down. Unless, of course, the lad was just not very fast.

Solomon fended off the assault without too much trouble, but being forced to retreat so quickly, he nearly tripped over his own feet. If it were not that Kirkin had also worked himself so far out of position that he had to reset his balance, he would have easily caught Solomon with a follow up cut.

Prentice tutted loudly.

"He did alright," Turley said, coming up beside his friend.

"His footwork's better than that," Prentice retorted. "I make him drill it often enough."

"Oh aye, I don't doubt. But the boy's fighting for his life. Give him some credit."

A sudden flash of fresh anger made Prentice give his friend a harsh glance, but he did not dare take his eyes off the fight longer than that. Turning back to the duel, he knew that he was not, in fact, angry with Turley. He was angry with himself. Any wound, any blood shed from Solomon's skin would be on his conscience, and Prentice found himself almost shaking with the effort of not rushing in and striking the boy's opponent down himself. He wondered if this was how loving fathers felt when they watched their sons make the harsher transitions from boyhood to manhood. He had no real way of knowing. All his own harsh transitions had taken place under the tutelage of weapons masters and military instructors. His own father had offered him nothing but a set of obligations to the family.

Kirkin followed up with another passage, and another, and yet another still. Solomon, true to Prentice's advice, kept fending the cuts away, maintaining distance. The knights' laughter began to turn to open jeers, and the Lions in responses were trying to encourage Solomon to make an attack of his own. Prentice wanted to shut them up.

Let the boy fight his own battle, he thought. Kirkin had a smug smile on his face, but already the heavy weapon was starting to seriously fatigue him. He barely had the strength to hold his guard, and the point was now aiming at the ground in front of him most of the time.

"Come on, Solomon, give him a thump," someone shouted near Prentice and the captain hissed his disapproval, but it was too late. Prompted by the encouragement, Solomon tried to step into Kirkin at exactly the same moment that the page was lifting his sword to start another passage. By sheer fluke, the two lads engaged their blades. Then Kirkin's flat bounced off Solomon's gauntlet and the point leaped up and bit him in the cheek. The drummer recoiled with a pained cry, staggering away from his opponent. Kirkin watched him go, breathing heavily from the stress and exertion. Then, when he realized he had made a successful cut, he lifted his sword as if in triumph and was greeted with applause from his side. The Lions groaned in disappointment, but Turley quickly stepped into the dueling ground and held up his hands for peace.

"A moment to assess, Gentles?" he asked in accordance with dueling tradition, as if he had presided over a hundred such judicial combats. Sir Helpman nodded, and Prentice also assented, then stepped up with Turley to see to Solomon's wound. The drummer hissed in pain as Turley examined him closely. Blood was trickling down his bare chest, and Prentice helped him sit back on the ground as Turley pressed at the cut. Solomon whimpered.

"Oh, tush, lad," Turley chided. "You been grown-man brave up to now. Don't go all babyish at this point." He thrust a finger into Solomon's mouth and the lad flinched a moment in pain. "I say, boy, looks like you been well lucky. He hasn't taken out any teeth and you still got both eyes. I'm sure it hurts like a bastard, but keep it clean and you'll have a flash scar to intimidate your enemies and impress the girls."

The calm pronouncement seemed to help Solomon's fears, and he hardly even twitched as Prentice pressed a clean rag onto the wound to staunch the blood somewhat.

"I'm so sorry, Captain," Solomon slurred, talking with the uninjured side of his mouth. "I thought I could get him."

"You nearly did," Turley encouraged him.

"There's no shame, Solomon," Prentice said, but the lad hung his head.

"Time to go, sirs," Baronet Helpman declared loudly, clearly for the benefit of the Lions' side of the duel. "The matter has been resolved."

Solomon's head snapped up and his eyes met Prentice's. It was a moment of intense communication without words, and Prentice had never felt a stronger connection to this orphan lad. He was not just a drummer or messenger anymore. The captain realized this youth was his ward, as fully and honorably as the sworn relationship between knights and their squires. Closer even. If Solomon wanted it, Prentice would give him his name and take him into his household like an adopted son. If he died today, Prentice would see him buried as Solomon Ash.

"I haven't given it everything yet," Solomon said with a resolve that would have done any grown man proud. Prentice nodded and stood.

"Wait a moment, Pren…" Turley tried to object, but Prentice was not listening.

"Sir Helpman," he shouted at full volume, "Solomon says that he is willing to continue."

CHAPTER 38

The knightly crowd were already turning to go, offering Kirkin their congratulations. From within their midst, Sir Helpman emerged, his expression conveying utter disbelief.

"What say you?" he demanded.

Prentice took a handful of steps towards the baronet. "Solomon says he is ready to continue."

Helpman crossed the rest of the intervening distance and leaned close to speak to Prentice quietly.

"For God's sake, man, blood has been shed. Is that not enough?"

"That is not for me to say," Prentice answered. "Solomon does not consider the matter resolved."

He wondered at the noble man-at-arm's reluctance for the duel to continue and suspected that for all his aristocratic arrogance, Sir Helpman was professional enough to recognize what Prentice had—that it was sheer good luck that had granted first blood to Kirkin.

"Is your jumped-up pride so stiff-necked?" Helpman ground out in a furious whisper. "Can you let no matter go? They are just lads. Must one of them be crippled or die over a little piece of silver?"

"You should have thought of that before you set Kirkin and his mates to ambush my drummer," Prentice growled back, and the flare of hostile surprise in Helpman's eyes confirmed that the words were true. The baronet's expression hardened, and he sneered with undisguised contempt.

"Very well! Let your brat pay for your sins," he said and turned back to the surprised nobles still gathered around Kirkin. All faces looked astonished as they heard Sir Helpman explain that the duel was not yet concluded.

"There you go, Solomon," Prentice heard Turley say, and he looked to see that the rag on Solomn's wounded cheek was being held in place with an improvised bandage. He nodded at the running repair and then looked back to the noble and his page. It was clear they were discussing strategies, just as Prentice and Solomon had before. Prentice watched closely, trying to read their lips or divine from their gestures what they were plotting. Beside him, Solomon took hold of the longsword once more and it was clear that he was weary, the wound paining him so that he squinted and winced.

"He will try to feint you out of position," Prentice told Solomon. "Expect him to aim low often to try to lure your guard down too much. He will want to repeat the same strike he knows he has made once already. Do not let him fool you. Fight your fight. Ignore every other noise and voice. It is just you and him now. When he makes an opening, leave nothing back."

Solomon nodded and stepped once more onto the dueling ground. Even with the bandage, blood dripped down his jaw and streaked his chest. Kirkin took up his sword once more, the point still hanging low. The page looked at his opponent, and Prentice could not fully read his emotions. He seemed to be looking at the blood, and he was clearly afraid while trying not to be. Perhaps Kirkin was wondering whether, if their roles were reversed, he would have the courage or heart to come back onto the field.

Solomon held his stance as before and waited for Kirkin to come on. The longsword swept low, as if aimed for Solomon's legs, but nowhere near close enough to strike. Kirkin tried again, exactly the same. There was no cheering this time. Both groups were somber, knowing that since first blood had not been accepted, this duel was forced now to a much more brutal resolution.

Kirkin swept low a third time, much closer, and Solomon was forced at last to deflect the incoming edge. Kirkin tried to follow up after the deflection, but Solomon shuffled away cleanly, his long-drilled footwork serving him well at last. He waited for Kirkin to come on again. Now Solomon looked less as if he was afraid and more like a canny predator, waiting for his prey.

It's over, Prentice thought, like a chess player who knows that the final set of moves can have only one resolution. He even felt a momentary flash of pity for Kirkin, who was suddenly no more than a pawn in his master's hateful game.

Kirkin came with a low sweep once more and Solomon did not retreat but blocked the strike with a low horizontal block. This was the move Sir Helpman had told his page to watch for, and Kirkin reversed his strike to bring it up over Solomon's lowered guard. The fatigued lad was slow, though, and Solomon was ready for the move. Wielding his own sword like little more than a steel bar, he lifted it quickly to intercept the overhand blow, and at the same time stepped in, barging bodily into Kirkin. The page was knocked off balance and as he staggered backwards, Solomon followed up, slamming his weapon's pommel into his opponent's chest with a resounding blow that had to have cracked ribs. Kirkin fell backwards, his sword flying free from his grip, and as he fell, Solomon leaped on top of him. Switching his hands around, he pointed the longsword's tip at the fallen lad's face like the point of a spear.

"Yield!" Solomon shouted, his words slurring and blood spraying from his lips onto Kirkin's face.

"I yield! I yield," the beaten boy screamed, his voice cracking with emotion. "Oh God. Please don't kill me! I yield."

"Confess," Solomon demanded, his weapon held with the point directly over Kirkin's eye. He sat with his full weight on the boy's chest and Kirkin began to cry through the combination of fear and the pain of his injury. "Confess what you did, you thief."

Solomon's words were thick with the damage to his face and his swelling lips, but no one misunderstood what he was saying.

"I confess," Kirkin all but screamed, terror and shame overwhelming him. "I jumped you. Me and the newcome boys. Sir Helpman said we should give you a thrashing to teach your convict captain a lesson. Take you both down a peg. He treats you like a squire but you have no right. Neither does he. It's all against the sumptuary laws, and you needed to be shown your place. Please, don't kill me. I yield. It was all Sir Helpman's fault!"

Solomon held the sword's point over the broken lad's face a long moment, and Prentice wondered if he would kill him anyway. The laws of dueling would allow it, though it would probably cause all manner of other problems—problems of exactly the sort that had brought matters to this point. No matter what he chose to do, though, Prentice would have his drummer's back.

"Return my rat," Solomon slurred at last. "Give it back, and we're square. Just like I said."

"Sir Helpman has it," Kirkin said and looked to his master with a pleading expression. Solomon looked over his shoulder at Prentice, and the captain wanted to laugh with pride. All the niceties were being observed. As Solomon's second, Prentice crossed the dueling ground and held out his hand. Sir Helpman glared at Prentice in fury and looked to his companions, but none of them met his eye. Kirkin's admission had shamed both page and master, and none of the nobility present wanted any share of that dishonor. Already one or two on the edge of the crowd were slipping away, heads down. Odds were good that most of the knights martial would shun Sir Helpman once word of this event spread.

Prentice waited, and Sir Helpman finally handed over Solomon's property. With the recovered chain in hand, Prentice stepped to the two boys and helped Solomon to his feet. He took the sword from the young man's grip and handed it off to Turley, who had also joined them. Then he slipped the silver rat on its chain over Solomon's head and embraced him like a father to son, pressing him so close that the running blood stained Prentice's shirt. Prentice let him go and turned to his own militiamen, who were watching with awestruck faces.

"Solomon of the White Lions," he shouted and the whole of them cheered. They rushed forward and seized Solomon up, lifting him onto their shoulders. "See he gets to the chaplain for healing immediately."

The crowd of Lions headed back to their camp, chanting Solomon's name and hoisting him into the air. Prentice smiled as he watched them go. When they reached the camp's edge, he looked back and realized he was virtually alone. The knights and pages were gone, Sir Helpman and Kirkin with them. Only Turley remained. The chief steward reached into his doublet and pulled out a flask. After taking a swig, he offered some to Prentice.

"How old were you the first time you fought for blood?" he asked as Prentice felt whiskey burn the back of his dry throat.

"Sixteen, I think," the captain said as he handed the flask back. "I did a lot of fighting my first year at Ashfield. Trying to prove myself. You?"

"I don't really remember, exactly. There was this ostler, big fella but kinda slow. We went at each other with sickles, and I got lucky, took off his ear. I think that was the first time. I figure I was about sixteen or seventeen summers then."

Prentice nodded wearily.

"Well, Solomon has both of us beaten on that score now."

"Tough little beggar," Turley observed. "Thank God."

Thank God, indeed, Prentice thought. Solomon would be a hero to the White Lions now. They would be telling the tale up and down the Reach for years. Prentice was happy for him; he deserved it. Nevertheless, the captain was certain this would not be the end of the matter, not really. After all, Solomon had ultimately been in this position because of him. Sir Helpman's real target had always been Prentice. The hatred that had prompted the whole affair still existed in the Reach's noble men-at-arms. They would likely soon seek for a new way to pay him back for all the many slights they felt he gave them just by serving his mistress and her lands.

"Oh, well," he said with a shrug and allowed himself a smile. That could be for later. Right now, Solomon was the victor. He looked at Turley. "Weren't you supposed to be taking me to see the duchess?"

CHAPTER 39

"Two days to ready the Lions and then we will be able to march north, Your Grace," Prentice was saying when a steward rushed from the far end of the Great Hall to the high table where Amelia and her close staff were planning for the militia's departure to Fallenhill. The air was sweet with the aroma of a bowl on the table, filled with a concoction of eucalypt oil and herbs to keep flies away. Looking up at the man's footfalls, the duchess noticed Earl Sebastian and two other knights, one of them Sir Tarant, waiting at the other end of the hall. Nowhere in the Reach was truly cool in this unending summer, but the great hall's high ceiling, with its high, vaulted roof of hardwood beams and thick clay tiles, was at least less warm than the outside. The three newly arrived knights' ruddy faces and sweaty demeanors were a clear reminder of that fact. Amelia looked down the long, shaded space, lit only by fragments of afternoon light through shuttered high windows, and watched the steward bring his announcement.

As etiquette required, the steward first brought the news to his senior, Chief Steward Turley. When Amelia waited and watched for Turley to announce the new arrivals, she was surprised to see him instead raise an eyebrow in Prentice's direction.

"Something you and the captain wish to share, Chief Steward?" she asked, and Turley flinched before tugging his forelock respectfully.

"No, Your Grace. Pardon me, please."

His wife, Lady Dalflitch, tutted from where she sat at the table, and he straightened himself to a formal posture.

"Your Grace, Knight Captain, Earl Sebastian and your sworn men under his command, Sir Tarant and Sir Valbey Laster-mune, request an audience. Shall I admit them?"

Amelia nodded and Turley left the table to escort the three knights the length of the hall. She knew from experience that the distance from the main door to the high table could feel like leagues at times. Even so, she felt she had barely a moment to look at Prentice to divine what matter there had been between he and Turley before the noble men-at-arms arrived. Prentice's face was its usual neutral mask, and he respectfully rose to his feet as the knight captain and his men approached.

"Your Grace," Sebastian greeted Amelia with a bow. The two men with him bowed as well. "You know Sir Tarant; may I present Sir Valbey?"

The third knight bowed as he was introduced, his long, loose hair falling about his head such that he had to wipe it from his face as he straightened up.

"Sir Valbey, you are a Lastermune, I am told," Amelia said, and the man's eyes flashed brightly at being recognized. "Are you related to Earl Lastermune?"

"My grandfather, Your Grace," Valbey explained. Looking at him, Amelia saw the resemblance to the venerable noble she had met in King Chrostmer's court.

"Well, no doubt you do his name and line proud."

"He is not an easy man to make proud, Your Grace," Valbey said breezily. "But thank you for the compliment."

Amelia nodded and looked to the earl. Pleasantries out of the way, time to get to whatever business this was. She resisted the temptation to give Prentice one more quizzical glance.

"Did you have something you wished to say, My Lord?"

"Your Grace, that man has flouted the martial discipline of your domain, yet again." He pointed at Prentice, though

Amelia doubted anyone in the hall would have been confused about who he meant.

"I am not aware of him having done it one time yet, My Lord, let alone yet again."

Earl Sebastian looked away, as if unable to believe that the duchess would say what she did. The more often she saw him like this, the further Amelia was convinced that the earl was growing to want nothing so much as to see her captain brought to heel. War was noblemen's business in his mind, and while he was mindful of her station and her achievements, he would not truly be happy until she put Prentice out of that business and then returned to womanly duties. She wondered how much the High Sacrist Quellion coached the young nobleman's viewpoint. At least Sebastian was enough his own man to not need the churchman with him absolutely every time he met her.

"There has been brawling and affray, Your Grace," Sebastian explained grimly "between men of the knights martial and your militia. The noble ringleader, Sir Helpman, has been disciplined. The militia side of the disarray was instigated by the man called Prentice, and I come now to insist that similar discipline be laid on him as well."

"For God's sake, Sebastian," Amelia said, exasperation making her forget some of her good manners, though not beyond the privileges of her rank. "The 'man' is Captain Prentice Ash. You know his name and title as well as everyone else here. Do you think by pretending you do not we will all forget?"

Sebastian sighed and shook his head.

"No, I suppose not, Your Grace. However, regardless of the names and titles he enjoys, he must be disciplined. As knight captain, it is my duty to see it done."

Brawling and affray? Amelia thought. That was a serious charge. If one of Prentice's men struck or, worse yet, injured a ranking peer, he would be in for serious punishment. If it were a convict still working off his sentence, the man would have to be put to death. The prospect troubled Amelia more than a little.

"What do you say in answer to this charge, Prentice?"

"There was no brawling, Your Grace, and the only affray was when a gang of noble scions bushwacked my drummer and robbed him."

Amelia was shocked by that assertion, and while she noticed that all three noblemen scowled at it, none of them rushed to refute it either.

"So how does this come to be named a brawl?" she asked.

"Because his drummer boy played at a duel with Sir Helpman's page and nearly killed the poor lad," Sir Tarant spat, pointing his own accusing finger at Prentice.

"There was no play," Prentice answered the knight with a growl in his tone. "The two fought an open duel, and the little snot you call a 'poor lad' was given quarter once he yielded and confessed his crime."

"He's still a boy, you filth. His nerve cracked, is all."

"Then his master should not have sent him to rob a White Lion."

It sounded as if the two men were about to come to blows right here in the hall, but Amelia was still chewing the more incredible notion of a duel.

"You set two boys to fight a duel, Prentice? A true duel?"

"All the forms were observed, Your Grace," Turley interceded. "I made sure of that."

"You were there, too?"

When Turley seemed to realize that the duchess might not approve of his involvement any more than she did Prentice's, he ducked his head and tugged his forelock again, making a show of saying not one word more.

"There really was a duel?" Amelia asked Prentice again and he nodded.

"There was, Your Grace."

"Two boys were forced to brawl in the hot sun," Sir Valbey scoffed.

"With live blades, according to all the protocols of dueling. Blood was shed and honor observed," Prentice said. "In what way was it not a duel?"

"Your drummer boy's an orphan, from what I hear," Valbey answered the question. "A gutter rat has no standing to duel."

"No less a page who has foresworn his birth to seek his spurs," Prentice countered. "Sir Helpman accepted the chivalric principle in this regard."

"A fine point of law, I'm sure," Sir Tarant sneered.

"I thought we were discussing points of law," said Prentice, and apparently recognizing they were outmaneuvered on the issue of the duel's legality, the two lesser knights fell silent. The sudden quiet felt loaded with menace, all the same.

This is why I must separate them, the Lions and the knights, Amelia thought. *Until we do, we'll just keep having incidences like this.*

She had no doubt that Sir Helpman had probably been the instigator behind the whole incident and wondered what kind of discipline the earl had already exacted for his role. Amelia liked Solomon, and the thought of him fighting for his life against another boy his age sickened her to her stomach. Could Prentice not have found some other solution? She closed her eyes and pinched the bridge of her nose for a moment, head down. Then she met Earl Sebastian's irate gaze.

"It does not seem to me that the matter is as straightforward as you present, My Lord," she said, choosing her words carefully. "I might be more willing to accede to your demand if I understood your position better."

"You want me to tell you what I will do?"

"No, My Lord. If I accept that your charge is just, I will not interfere with the execution of the discipline you choose to enforce. I appointed you knight captain. I will not undermine you."

Amelia forced herself not to look at Prentice. She knew he would understand why she was saying what she was, but it tasted like betrayal, and the bitterness soured her stomach further.

"That is...good...to know, Your Grace," Sebastian said, obviously surprised by this open show of support. "In the simplest terms, this 'duel' should never have taken place."

"What should have happened instead?"

"Your man, the 'captain,' should have brought the matter to me. As knight captain, it is my place to judge over military discipline in the Reach. That is another 'fine point of law' which I am sure he understands."

Sebastian glared at Prentice, speaking the last words through gritted teeth. The two knights with him were likewise hateful in their expressions.

"Sir Helpman assured me I would not get a fair hearing," Prentice told the earl. "I believed him."

"You did not trust the earl's honor and honesty? He is a peer of the realm," Valbey growled.

"So is Sir Helpman. Which one do I trust?" Prentice's simple answers were so calmly delivered, but Amelia could tell he was only inflaming their wrath. It occurred to her that he might be doing it deliberately.

Damn it Prentice, I need your calm to serve the peace, not undermine it.

"You trust the earl, who is knight captain," said Tarant. "Why?"

"Because I am the ranking noble," Sebastian said.

"So was Daven Marcus, once," Prentice said in a voice that chilled Amelia's soul despite the warm air. She was about to chastise him for going too far, but Sebastian finally lost his self-control.

"Enough of this nonsense," he shouted, using a voice that was clearly meant for battlefields and parade grounds. It echoed off the high walls and roof. "This cur runs too wild, Your Grace. I insist you dismiss him or else dismiss me! I will not serve beside this reprobate upstart one moment longer."

There may have been a time when Amelia would have found such an outburst unnerving, and she would certainly have wondered how she could soothe her retainer's inflamed temper. Those days were past.

"You do not *insist* to me, My Lord," she said with imperious resolution as hard in its way as Prentice's cold steeliness. "I am duchess. This is my domain, and I am finished with these disruptions to my rule!"

She turned, looked to the table and took up an almost finished document.

"I have here my warrant, Knight Captain, that only awaits my seal." Picking a piece of sealing wax from the planning detritus elsewhere on the table, she ran it through the only lit candle nearby and dripped some on the warrant document. Then she pressed her signet ring into the wax and made it official. She held it out.

"Take this now and your command of the knights martial. Seek you out these fey riders and purge them from our land. Every camp and village, any hole or burrow where they lurk. Go you now."

Sebastian looked at the proffered sheet suspiciously, then glanced at Prentice.

"You are sending *me* away from *him*?"

"I am commanding you to the task for which you are most suited," Amelia told him bluntly. "Captain Ash, I am sending on other duties, including marching the White Lions back to their garrison in Fallenhill." She added that last detail as a sop to the earl's pride, letting him know that it was not only he and his men who were being ordered away from Dweltford.

"If this task is not to your liking, you are free to quit my service."

"His loyal men would go with him," said Sir Tarant, but Amelia only shrugged at that.

Earl Sebastian stared at the warrant a long moment, and then he stepped forward and took it from Amelia's hand. He bowed.

"I will do my duty," he said formally, his temper seemingly back under control. "And when this enemy is slain or driven away, I will return."

"And I will gladly welcome your victorious return when you do," Amelia responded, holding herself stiffly upright, her voice steady and imperious still.

Sebastian bowed once more and led his men from the Hall. When they were gone, Amelia looked at Prentice and then at Turley.

"Sorry, Your Grace," said the steward, and his wife snorted with disgust.

"I'll say you are, husband," Dalflitch said with affectionate disdain.

Amelia turned to Prentice. "And I think you need to tell me a story, Captain."

CHAPTER 40

It was mid-evening when the duchess finally dismissed her retainers from her apartments. They had retired there to sup while they finished discussing the plans for the town's next few months and listening to Prentice's report of Solomon's duel.

"Her Grace was none too pleased to hear about the lad's face," Turley said as he, Prentice, and Righteous made their way down the gallery stairs to the castle's main floor. "I could've told you it'd be that way."

"And yet you never said a word about it while we were out in the fields," Prentice observed. Turley shrugged.

"Aye, well, I got swept away in the excitement o' the moment, is all."

"You were not the only one."

Behind him, Prentice heard his wife give a derisive sniff.

"You two are lucky to get off lightly as you did," Righteous said archly. "If t'were mine to judge, I'd a had you both against a post and a lash laid on your backs."

"Been there," Turley responded with a flippant smile over his shoulder, but when he saw her furious expression, he turned back without another word. The trio descended the rest of the steps in silence. At the bottom, Turley turned to head toward the kitchens, while Prentice made to go the other way to the castle's gate, nodding a bare farewell. Already, his plans for the next few days were rising to occupy the main of his thoughts, although he did want to say a proper goodnight to his goodwife before he went back to camp.

"Say, Prentice, you going back to Fallenhill, it's got me thinking," Turley said before he left them.

"About what?"

"About them fey we saw hanging when we first got to the town that day, when that fella Lord Dunstan wanted to do you in."

Prentice blinked, his thoughts caught by Turley's memories. The Redlanders had hanged a dozen or so people outside the gates of the town during their first campaign, as well as burning the rest of the town's population alive. Among those hanged victims were four pointed-ear folk that Prentice had thought were probably fey. Back then, the notion had been no more than a curiosity, but in their current circumstances, it was a useful piece of additional information.

"I had forgotten about them," he admitted and cursed under his breath.

"Yes, well I'm not surprised," Turley went on. "You used it as an occasion to mock me, as I recall. That's such a habit for you that I wouldn't expect you to remember every specific instance."

"You make it so easy," Prentice commented reflexively, but his thoughts were now almost fully gone, considering the implications and adjusting his plans. The duchess had dispatched the knights martial to hunt the fey and commanded the militia back to Fallenhill, but she had been noticeably vague about what she expected him to do after that. Prentice was certain she had not forgotten his commitment to hunt the serpent witch on the perverted unicorn. That was still what he planned to do, and Turley's hanged fey were possibly an important clue.

"You should have mentioned those fey of yours to Earl Sebastian," Prentice told his friend in an insincere tone. "He is sent to hunt them, after all."

"Well, the fella lit out before I got me a chance," Turley said with a flash of a grin. He stepped aside as a maid slid through their group about some late-night house business. "I s'pose you'll have to look into it, Captain o' the Lions."

"Yes, I will."

Prentice shared his friend's moment of wicked humor, but he knew that if he discovered any more useful information he would have to send a letter to the earl. The duchess had separated her two forces, but if the fey were based somewhere around Fallenhill and Prentice did nothing to help the knights martial find them, the affront and petty rivalry would only grow worse.

"Right, well I'm off to me bed," Turley said at last. "I figure my goodwife will have finished with her document scribblings by now, or soon enough. I never knew a lady or any kind o' woman born as fond of a quill as her."

He gave them both one last smile and headed away down the hall. Prentice turned to Righteous, who was standing a little behind him, one foot still on the bottom step.

"Would you like to take a moment together?" he asked her. "It will be some time before we see each other again after I go north. Your belly will probably be well full by the time I come back. I do not think the duchess would begrudge us a few hours. Perhaps a walk in the 'part-light?'"

"No, I don't think that'd be such a good idea," she said distantly, looking away from him.

"I would like your company before I go."

"No, not tonight." She turned to head back up the stairs, but Prentice caught her by the arm and stopped her going.

"You are not happy, my love?"

Righteous whirled on him, her place on the higher step making her close to equal to his height. "Oh, you kenned that all yourself, did you husband? Your flash canniness give you the 'sight into my soul, did it?"

"What are you going on about?" Prentice had hoped for a short, pleasant moment with his wife in the relative cool of the evening before heading back to his tent. After the day's many pressures and conflicts, one loyal instant had not seemed too much to expect. He was apparently mistaken. What he had no idea about was why.

"You are angry at me?" he asked.

"Damn straight I'm angry," she answered in a harsh whisper, poking one finger into his chest. "I'm fit to cut you, I'm so fuming at you!"

"For what?"

"Oh, you don't know? You so smart and so confident and making all the decisions for everyone, and you can't tell why your goodwife might be filthy with you?"

Prentice blinked and shook his head.

"How could you?" Righteous demanded. Prentice was about to say that he did not even know what she was talking about, when she went on. "He's just a boy! A boy! And you throw him into the teeth of the nobles like a chewed bone to a pack of mongrels. You're s'posed to keep him safe."

"Solomon?" Prentice asked, finally starting to understand at least a little.

"Yes, Solomon, your poor scar-faced drummer. Hardly a babe and you got him getting' cut for some fool honor."

"Solomon marches next to me in battle and you have never said a word about it," Prentice said, thinking to point out the obvious foolishness of fearing one danger for the youth and not the other.

"That's not the same thing!"

"How is it not?"

"It just isn't, alright husband? And if you can't see it, then I *really* don't want to go walkin' with you in the night."

Prentice smiled a moment, thinking he had a better grasp of what was going on now. "Dear wife, could it be that this is your pregnancy talkin...?"

He never finished the sentence as Righteous whipped a hidden blade from somewhere and held the point in front of his eyes.

"Don't you bloody dare! I am fit to add to your scars, mark me Prentice. Don't you dismiss me as just a madwoman with child. Don't you damn well dare."

Despite her harsh words, tears glistened in her eyes. Nonetheless, Prentice had no doubt his wife would cut him to make her point if he pushed her. He looked down at the blade—a slender, dark shape in the shadows.

"Solomon is already in his first growth to manhood," he said quietly. "His limbs get gangly by the day. He will have to start shaving soon. How old were you, wife, the first time you held a man at knifepoint like this? Were you even as old as him the first time you cut someone, Cutter?"

Righteous's head jerked as he used her old street-fighting name.

"It's not the same," she protested, but her voice was a brokenhearted whisper.

"Why not?"

The blade slowly lowered, and Righteous laid a hand on her bodice.

"I sick up every morning and cry myself to sleep wanting for you every night," she said, looking down. "I do it and I know I'd do it every day and night 'til doomsday for this little one growin' in me. I console myself, saying you're away for the duchess, that you're making the land safe for me and our littlun. This might be the only one we get, and he or she is more precious than gold. You know that, don't you?"

"I know," Prentice said solemnly.

"And you love that boy, I know you do. Everyone knows you're fond, but I see the father in you when I see you with him. I dream that's how you'll be with ours. And then...and then you go do something like this. You're supposed to keep us all safe."

"You keep yourself safe and the duchess beside. You are a Lace Fang."

"Course I do, but we're not fools, Prentice. We keep safe in here because you keep the Reach safe out there."

Prentice thought of the serpent witch, the fey riders and all the men who had lost their lives on the march up from Griffith, not to mention all the other Lions who had lost their lives under his command.

"The Reach is not so safe as that," he said bitterly.

"It's a damn sight better than it would'a been without you," Righteous answered back. "But I can't face the thought o' you throwin' our littlun to dogs."

"I will do what *you* plan to do, my love," Prentice said and meant it as a promise.

"And what's that, old man?"

"I will protect them with the whole of my breath and blood. I will work and teach them all that I know. I am a man of war; it is my trade, and I will teach what I can of it. Just as I know you will not let any child of ours grow past their toddling without knowing how to shank a man."

Righteous smiled shyly but nodded.

"But the day will come, as it came for Solomon today, when they will step out from under their father and mother and become their own person. Solomon's day came early, and he will have a scar such that he will never forget this day, but he is become his own man. You should have heard how the Lions cheered him."

That thought made Righteous smile a little more widely.

"I *am* a little raw that I missed it," she admitted.

"I told him you would be," Prentice said, returning her smile. "Also, I am going to send him to you."

"What? Why?"

"Because you are correct, he is like a son to me. I realized that today. With that cut on his cheek, he cannot march with the Lions. The wound could sicken, and he might die of an infection. So, with the duchess' permission, I will leave him in your care. Surely you can use a runner while you grow fatter."

Righteous slapped his face with her free hand, and he was glad. It meant she was not so angry anymore, though she still had her dagger in her other hand.

"So, he's like your son and you're going to use him as a servant for your wife?"

"Certainly not. He will do chores, like any other lad his age, and I will ask Lady Dalflitch to teach him his letters. You, I know, will hammer dagger skills into him, and likely drill him in sword and buckler. Pregnant or not, you are the best instructor I could leave him with."

"Is that all?" Righteous's voice was softening, and she slowly lowered her blade.

"Well, if the duchess takes an interest, there is no end of subjects she could tutor him in."

"You've thought about all this, have you?"

"Who, me? The one who is 'so smart and so confident and making all the decisions for everyone'? Of course, I have. I tell you, darling wife, the day will come when Solomon will take command of the Lions, if that is what he wants."

"And what about our child, or children?"

"If they are a boy, they can learn command from him and take it up after him. He will be fifteen or so years the senior, you realize?"

"And what if it's a girl?"

"She can marry if she wishes or, if she takes after her mother..."

"Yes?" Righteous was only a finger's width from her husband. Prentice could feel her breath on his neck.

"If she takes after her mother, she can learn command from Solomon and take it up after him."

"You're going to be a good father to our children, aren't you, Prentice husband? Promise me—taken into our house like Solomon or born of our blood—promise me you'll be a good father."

"The best I can be," Prentice promised her and then took her into his arms. He enjoyed the moment's embrace and did his best not to think of how little he truly knew about fathering. Most especially, he tried not to think about what he knew from his own father's example. Little as that was, he wanted to follow after almost none of it.

CHAPTER 41

P rentice woke with the dawn watch-change drum and broke his fast with hard tack and goat's milk. Even with the new supplies, water was at too much of a premium to waste on a morning meal. The milk tasted like it was souring and he guessed that it was already a day or two old. Odds were the milkers—cattle, goats, and ewes—were all giving much less these days. Spitting to get the taste from his mouth, he left orders with Franken and the other sergeants to begin preparing to march for Fallenhill at dawn, the day after tomorrow. Then he left to speak with Duchess Amelia's brood of pet scholars.

The southern quarter of Dweltford was mainly given over to a district called the Weeps, so named because it was where the foulest of businesses were congregated—dyers, slaughterers, tanners, and fullers. The stench in the area was so strong it was said to make the eyes water; hence, the name of the district. On the boundary of the neighborhood on a street called Edger's Row, the scholars who had taken refuge in the Western Reach from the internecine strife in the rest of the Grand Kingdom had bought a little building for themselves. Built of wood and two floors high, it backed onto a single-storied tannery, which had become the little academy's sole supplier of vellum. The scholars themselves, an odd assortment of clergy and scribes from various towns and provinces in the Grand Kingdom, slept in communal quarters on the upper floor. The bottom floor was split in two. Most of it was filled with tables and tiny desks, as well as a small but growing library of academic works, legal treatises, and other tomes. The rest of the ground floor that had once been the building's kitchen was where the academics conducted their experiments in making their own paper from flax pulp, so far with little success. The increased difficulty in acquiring material because of the drought was further hampering their self-education in the craft. Nevertheless, it was from this endeavor that the building acquired its name from the locals of the district. It was called the Paper House.

Prentice arrived at the Paper House while the sun was just clearing the town walls, but already the air was hot and thick with the smells of the district's trades. Coupled with the taste of sour milk still in his mouth, it made his stomach turn. He knocked on the wooden door, but there was no answer. He knocked again. Trying the latch, he found it unlocked and stepped inside, hoping to escape some of the heat and smell.

Instead, he was almost bowled over by a new set of aromas so heavy that they caught in the back of his throat and made him cough. Looking about in the dimness, he could see that every available rafter and hook was hung with flowers, herbs, and all kinds of aromatics. Bundles of lavender the thickness of doorposts were tied to wooden pillars, while dried rosemary branches shed their needles in small clouds when he shut the door. Clearly this was all an attempt to keep out the district's stench, but it seemed to Prentice to merely replace one problem with an adjacent one.

"Captain Prentice, welcome. I thought I heard a knock," came a voice from Prentice's left, and he turned to see the scholar Solft, Sacrist Fostermae's old friend and the Paper House's unofficial leader, coming downstairs. The wood creaked under his footsteps as the heavy-set man made his way gingerly to the ground floor. Pale, with his hair in a simple bowl-cut like a youth's, he was nonetheless dressed in a fine silk blouson and soft cotton trousers. Even without the money the duchess provided to the Paper House, Solft was a man of personal means, being from a respected family in Lower Otney.

"You seem tender, Master Solft," said Prentice. "A good night's drinking was it?"

"Certainly not, Captain," the scholar objected. "We had a late night last night because Pawley saw fit to expound Meerenmachter's fourth treatise. Since the only translation the House had was an old Kastrian text, that meant translating on the go while proving Meerenmachter wrong."

"You never did anything of the sort," called a voice from a far corner of the open floor. Through the dimness and clouds of herbs and flowers, Prentice could just make out two men in black robes seated at a desk and poring over an open tome.

"Hush, Pawley," Solft called back. "And you and Xander there should get to your beds."

"When his thick skull gives way to reason," Pawley responded, and he fell back to quietly debating whatever points had kept the scholars awake through the night. Prentice was an educated man, but he had barely heard of Meerenmachter and would not have been able to tell the fourth treatise from any other of the man's works. He also could not read Kastrian.

"I am here to ask you some questions, Master, if I may," he told Solft. "History mainly, though you might have to lead me through some legendaria as well."

"Fascinating," said Solft, and he turned away, stepping to a nearby desk. He picked up a little metal object. "There it is."

He turned back and Prentice saw that the object was a gold pin, like a guildsman's pin, in the shape of a feather quill.

"Keep losing the dashed thing," Solft explained. "But it digs into me while I'm writing. I have to take it off at times."

"You could wear it from your ear," Prentice ventured.

"A pin in my ear, Captain? What would that look like in the Guild Conclave?" The scholar shook his head and then waved Prentice to follow him as he made his way to a shelf against one wall where there were thick folios tied with twine. "Excuse me a moment. I will fetch a lantern, so we may read."

Solft left the room and returned a moment later with a lit oil lamp with fine glass panes. It glowed softly and he set it down on an upturned barrel near the shelves.

"Have to use closed lanterns," he explained. "Can't have open flames with all this debris in the air. Catches too readily." He waved at the room and the floating particles.

"You do not think to remove some of the cause?" Prentice asked.

"Have you smelt the air outside? Ugh, the stink!" Solft shook his head. "This makes it bearable. We just have to be careful. After the second fire, we decided closed lights only."

"You've had fires?" Prentice looked about for signs of damage, but he could not find any. Solft noticed his quizzical expression.

"Oh, small things, but frightening enough in a scriptorium like this. We dealt with them both quite swiftly. You might not think us brave, Captain, not like your men. And truth to tell, we'd all likely surrender our purses to a determined toddler armed with a soup spoon. But I assure, there's not a man here who wouldn't throw himself into the hellfire breath of a dragon to save a precious text from the flames."

Prentice knew the man meant what he said. Master Solft had already shown a proclivity for risking his life for the sake of his research during the campaign against the Redlanders on the Murr River.

"So, what history do you wish to discuss? Or better yet, what are your questions?" Solft asked.

"What can you tell me of the fey?"

"Aha, so it's true?" Solft said excitedly. "The little folk have returned out of legend!"

"Well not so little, it seems for a start," Prentice observed. "The ones we have seen are about men's height, perhaps a little shorter and lither, but not by much."

"And they ride ghostly horses, I'm told."

Prentice shook his head. "Quite mortal ponies, I fear, Master. No more than that."

He decided not to mention the unicorn or its rider. Like so many of his sort, Master Solft was clearly a man who liked to acquire and share tidbits of information. Were it not for his professional interest, he would be an inveterate gossip.

"Well, that's a little disappointing, but never mind."

Solft turned to the shelf again.

"You'll be wanting history from the crusade period, then," he said as he ran his finger across the gathered volumes. "Not quite as ancient as my lesser-kings research, but still not something we have a lot of works on. Any specific questions?"

"I need any information about where the fey might be hiding here in the west."

"That's rather obscure, Captain." Solft's brow knotted in thought.

Prentice nodded, accepting the scholar's pessimistic opinion. He was here only because of what the duchess had said about her conversation with the prophetess in the west—that the Redlanders and the ancient fey had once been allies in the far past. If that was the case, then whatever the two groups had been like at that time might be the basis for whatever was going on now between the witch and the raiders. Other than Turley's recollection of four hanged fey from years past, the only evidence Prentice had to go on was the brutal ritual at Halling Pass Castle.

"Even the slightest clue might help," he said. "Also, anything about witchcraft here in the Reach. Even, well, fey tales."

Prentice shrugged his shoulders and gave a half smile. *Fey tales* was the term Kingdom folk gave to a story that was obviously false—made up, scary yarns—since the fey were supposed to have been hunted into extinction. If the fey folk were back, fey tales was no longer a fitting term for pure fictions.

"Ah, Halling Pass as well?" Solft said, deducing more of Prentice's subject than the captain wanted. Shaking his head, the leader of the Paper House pointed to the two quietly debating sages in the corner, raising his voice to be heard across the distance. "Pawley's our man for Redlander rites and paganism, though. He's an intractable pain in my posterior when it comes to ancient heresies that he knows too little about, but when it's word of witchcraft or the invaders, he's best in the House."

"That's 'cause I'm not too proud to drink with vagabonds and serfs," Pawley shouted back. "They're appalling liars and tellers of tall tales, but they also hear and see things their betters pretend are impossible."

"If you will forgive me, Captain," Solft said as he led the way to where Pawley was seated with his debating partner, "but I heard that Earl Sebastian and the duchess' knights martial have been dispatched to hunt the fey. The entire company rode out in the night."

Prentice had passed the vacated encampment on his way into the town. Whatever frustrations Earl Sebastian felt about Reach politics and Prentice's "jumped up" status, he had no hesitation fulfilling his orders when they were given, it seemed.

"This is a related matter—" Prentice began to explain, but before he could go on, the door banged open and a muscular, bald-headed man in a plain homespun tunic and no leggings or hose thrust himself inside. He had simple woven straw sandals, like a serf just off the farm, and his legs were dirty and mud streaked. At least Prentice hoped for his sake that it was mud. In the Weeps, it could easily be something much fouler.

"I almost had him that time, I swear," the man said, shaking his head. "Beggar turned down an alley I've never seen before. One day soon, brothers, I promise...aye-up, sorry, I didn't realize we had gentle visitors." The man approached and tugged his forelock to Prentice, who returned the respect with a simple nod.

"Captain Prentice, this is Arosten, formerly Brother Aroste
n..." Solft began to introduce the man and then stopped.

"Formerly Brother Arosten of the Holy Inquisition," Prentice finished for the scholar. The exact details of Prentice's history with the Inquisition were not well known, but his previous status as a heretic was. It was obvious why Solft would
be nervous to introduce the captain to a former Inquisitorial
soldier, but he need not have bothered. "We have met, Master
Solft, during the flight to Griffith after the Red Sky. Well met,
Arosten."

"Fear not, Solft," said Arosten. "The captain knows I have
given up my vows and burned my tabard." He offered an honest
hand to Prentice, who took it, though not eagerly. Arosten had
come to the Reach at the same time as Brother Whilte, and while
Prentice still struggled to forgive Whilte his past involvement
with the corruption in Mother Church, he had found it somewhat easier with Arosten since they had no personal history.

"No longer a soldier but still chasing men through the
streets?" Prentice asked. "A thief, was it?"

"Worse. A liar. A perfidious preacher of the worst water."

Prentice cocked an eyebrow. "You are no longer an agent of
the Inquisition, you do know?"

"I do not need you to tell me, Captain," Arosten responded,
but with no malice or resentment. "I am just another humble
yeoman and servant to the Paper House. But I am also a citizen
of the Reach now, and I will not stand by while some penny-prophet defames the duchess."

"Was he at it again?" asked Pawley. Arosten nodded angrily,
and as he did, he seemed to notice his filthy state. He started to
brush himself down.

"On the street corner near fuller Wanmer's when the guildsmen were on their way to work. Cheeky beggar!"

"There's an itinerant preacher, apocalyptic sort, keeps turning up around the low quarters," Solft explained. "Harsh times
like this drought tend to breed his type. At first he just called

for repentance. Usual sort of thing, benedictions for bread. But lately he's started blaming the drought on the duchess. Talk of her being a rebel, a widow who will not remarry or withdraw to a convent. Other less flattering things. Mostly folk have nothing to do with him, but he keeps showing up."

Prentice nodded. It sounded like the same itinerant who had prophesied over Viscount Gullden—a prophecy that had come true.

"He's nearly been thumped more than once, and if I get my hands on him, he'll wish he had been."

"You seem quite earnest in your distaste," Prentice observed, wondering at Arosten's intensity. "Why does he offend you so?"

"Do you forget, Captain?" Arosten said under raised brows. "I know the kinds of churchmen who will stir this sort of trouble, foment unrest the ordinary man neither needs nor can afford, all to further their own petty power. The kind of men who would back the Kingslayer and his claim to the throne. I don't care how humbly a dog dresses himself; when he calls the people out against their liege lady, he serves the schemes of the heretics who currently call themselves the patriarchs of God."

It fascinated Prentice to see the zeal of an inquisitor, or a former inquisitorial soldier, at least, now fully turned against the Inquisition itself.

"Yes, well, perhaps next time you'll catch him," said Solft, apparently uncomfortable in the face of Arosten's forcefulness. The lead scholar then returned his attention to Pawley. "Getting back to the subject at hand. The captain wants to hear what you know about magic and fey here in the Reach."

"History or contemporary?" Pawley asked.

"Both."

"Well, if he's ready to set himself to study, I could teach him the lot in about four or five years. How's his Prior Glashaen?"

"Not as good as it once was, and it was pretty shabby back then," Prentice answered. Prior Glashaen was an ancient language not spoken since the days of the Grand Kingdom's founding. It was said to have originated in the most primeval of times, in the Bright Age, before the mountain was cast into the sea. Prentice had been taught a little of it at Ashfield and never mastered it. "Also, I do not really have the time to come under your full tutelage, good master."

Pawley snorted with disgust.

"He needs a few main questions answered or given hints, Pawley," said Solft, sounding exasperated. "Can you not make the effort to truncate your teaching methods?"

Pawley started to shake his head and then stopped to look at the nearest window, as if only just noticing that it even existed.

"It's nearly midmorning," he declared, and lay his head back to yawn. He scratched at himself. "I need to get me to bed. Alright, Solft, have the fella leave his questions and I'll write out my answers for him. I trust he can at least read in the Kingdom tongue?"

"This 'fellow' is Captain of the White Lions," Solft said in a gentle but chastising tone. "He is Academy trained and close advisor to her grace, Duchess Amelia, our patron."

"Fine, so he can read my notes when I'm done writing them."

"Be done by sundown tomorrow," Prentice told the cantankerous sage. Pawley looked ready to give the captain the same disdain he showed Solft, but Prentice fixed him with a hard glare. The scholar tried to meet his eye for a moment, then ducked his head and tugged his forelock.

"If you would accompany me, Captain," Solft said politely, indicating another nearby desk. "I will fetch ink and quill for you to write your questions for my foolish brother-scholar."

CHAPTER 42

After the hectic planning and difficult confrontations of the previous day, Amelia found herself somewhat at a loss for anything to do. Dalflitch was seeing to financial matters somewhere and her husband was about his duties with the household staff. Righteous had awakened feeling better than in many recent days and Amelia set she and Spindle at leisure to plan dresses more suitable for the near future when Righteous's pregnancy would become more obvious. After spending an hour or so with the two women, Amelia started to feel cooped up and excused herself to wander the castle.

On the ground floor she heard laughter echoing from the kitchen and followed the sound to find Bluebird entertaining the cook-staff with a juggling act. Coming up quietly, she discovered him at the center of the room, standing one footed on a stool while he kept a spoon, a cup, and a small sack of something looping into the air. Cooks and kitchen maids clapped and cheered, but after a moment those nearest noticed her presence and stopped. They bowed their heads and tugged their forelocks in respect, and the heavy solemnity soon spread over the room like ripples from a rock thrown into a pond. When the room was ultimately silent, Bluebird realized his audience's mood had shifted and he looked about to see the duchess overseeing proceedings.

"Greetings, Your Grace," he said with a simple bow. "We were distracting ourselves from the morning's drudgery."

"Do not let me stop you," Amelia said, but looking to the stilled servants, she realized her presence was restricting their pleasure. Feeling like an unwanted burden, she nodded to the room and withdrew. Turley would have known how to disarm that uncomfortable moment, she was sure, but unfortunately he was not in the kitchen at present.

Heading back the way she had come, Amelia took a different turn around another corridor and found herself going further down stone stairs to the castle's under level. It was cooler here, and in days gone by it would have been damp. Now it was as dry as the rest of her drought-ravaged land. These rooms would normally be below the water level of the lake. Sadly, one had to go deeper into the Reach than this to find moisture these days. She was about to turn down into the cellars when she noticed the other short passage to the chapel crypt where her husband's sepulcher lay. She walked the few paces in that direction and stroked her fingers across the carven hardwood doors with their inlaid silver cross. It was hard to make out in the dimness, but now that she was this close, she saw that the doors were open, and there was a wan light coming through the crack.

Amelia's reflexive thought was one of indignance, that someone had trespassed on this sacred place where her husband's remains were interred. This was a family place, reserved to those of her line. If she must be a stranger in her own kitchen, could she not at least have this place to herself? Before she even knew what she was doing, she threw open the doors. Mounted against the opposite wall from the door was a graven marble figure of the redeeming Christ, arms out wide, welcoming the penitent into heaven. It was an appropriate iconography for a chapel crypt. Even in the poor illumination, the marble statue seemed almost to glow.

The light itself originated from a single oil lamp on the ground in front of the statue. Beside the lamp, a shadowed figure knelt, head bowed in prayer. It took Amelia a moment to realize that it was Prince Farringdon, and she felt a sudden rush of shame at her thoughts and emotions. After the statue of Christ, the rest of the crypt was bare by comparison, its stones dressed in flat planes. The carved corners resembled vaulting pillars, but they were unadorned as well. All but one of the grave niches was unoccupied; the crypt was little more than ten years old, as was the castle above it. In that time only one lord had died, Amelia's fallen husband Marne. His sepulchral casket was now carved with his likeness on the lid and with his name and title above the alcove. That was why she felt so possessive of this little room, but seeing the prince at prayer, she remembered that it also served as a place of holy contemplation, quiet and cool.

Not wanting to disturb the royal, she tried to withdraw, but it was too late, it seemed. Farringdon looked at her over his shoulder and then wrestled himself awkwardly to his feet.

"I am sorry, Your Grace," he said readily, bowing uncomfortably, apparently injured. "I was taking a moment to beseech the Lord. If you wish privacy to pray, I will leave."

Amelia held up her hand.

"Stay, Highness. Surely there is enough space for us both to seek our Father in Heaven."

Farringdon gave a thankful nod and smiled. Amelia returned it, and for a moment they stood facing each other uncomfortably. Looking down, she noticed he had a leather folio in hand, stuffed full of documents. One handwritten sheet was outside the folder, stacked on top.

"You write your own prayers, Highness?" Amelia asked out of curiosity, pointing to the document. Farringdon shook his head.

"No, Your Grace, it is a letter from home. The merchant patrician, Master Welburne, brought it to me. It came with the recent caravan."

As he explained, Amelia drew closer, and she noticed that the prince's eyes were wet with tears.

"It is unwelcome news, Highness?"

"Yes, Your Grace." The prince looked down at the sheets in his grasp and sighed, a bitter sound that caught the duchess by surprise. "It is news from Aubrey. I am told that the drought is not quite so heavy as it is here, but that matters little to my peo...to the people there. Those who survived the invasion still have not recovered. The land barely grows them enough to feed themselves, and the wreckage of the town proper is now home to packs of vermin so vast that they torment good folk even in broad daylight."

The prince paused in his account and the images in Amelia's mind caused her to shudder at the thought.

"Worse yet, your enemy, the usurper king, Daven Marcus, sent a small force across the Murr to claim the province for himself. Apparently, they were cut off from their supply by men-at-arms from another Grand Kingdom noble called Lark-Stross, who seized Aubrey bridge behind them. Trapped on the south side of the river, the usurper's men were then attacked by another prince of the Vec, Prince Kal Harn-Zade. The battle harmed the people further, as battle is wont to do. Harn-Zade took the province and claimed the town for himself. Now my uncle, Prince Garrodmin, has raised a banner against the occupation and another battle besets Aubrey."

Farringdon looked down and shook his head pityingly.

"You do not favor your uncle to reclaim your domain?" Amelia asked, touched by the prince's sincere concern for his homeland.

"Uncle Garro isn't doing this for me, Your Grace," the prince explained. "He is a gentle-hearted man who would rather breed his horses than fight a war. He is doing this for factions in his own court, I promise you. They do not prompt him on my behalf. And still the low folk will suffer."

Amelia was surprised at how like her own nation's politics the Vec's were—the ambition, the predatory conquests.

"Nobles should rule for their people instead of clambering over their backs to claim glory and riches for themselves," she said without thinking, then ducked her head in embarrassment. She had not meant to chastise the prince or his people in his moment of worry. "Forgive me, Highness."

"Good Lord, Your Grace, there is no need!" Farringdon seemed astonished by the notion that the duchess should apologize to him for any reason. "Your every word was entirely correct. I weep and pray for the folk of Aubrey, but I would not shed a tear if God threw my uncle and all the other avaricious Vec rulers down from their thrones and had them cast into the flames."

The prince surprised her then by slipping his folio under his arm, stepping close, and clasping her hands in his own. It was something the young man's father had once done, entreating her to help his people when they'd been conquered by the Redlander army. The familiarity of the gesture caused a sweep of emotions to crash over her for a moment, and she did not even think to pull back.

"I recognize you, Your Grace, your earnest labor for the whole of your land, lowborn or high. I watch your heart break as the Western Reach sweats and bakes, and I know you would cut your veins and spill your own blood if it would save one thirsty child's life. I have heard what is said, how the peers whisper their hateful ambitions against you, and how penny prophets issue petty proclamations against your young widowhood and blame the drought on God knows what. But, Your Grace, I kneel here and I pray, 'God, send us more nobles like Duchess Amelia.' Let fools scoff, but she is the Lioness, and her pride is her people."

As if suddenly realizing the intimacy of their closeness, the prince released Amelia's hands and stepped back. She reached up and touched her face where a tear of her own had fallen, wiping it away with her sleeve.

"Thank you, Highness," she said, swallowing a lump in her throat. "If only more of the Western Reach thought as you do."

"More do than you might imagine, Your Grace. And as I am protected by your hospitality in my effective exile, I find I count myself almost as one of them. After all the trouble that princes have given your Reachermen, I hope you will not be offended that I like to consider myself one of them, at least in an honorary capacity."

"Offended, Highness? No, I think I am flattered."

"That makes me glad to hear. Now if you wish privacy, I will withdraw, but if you can bear another praying beside you quietly, I would kneel before the Lord with you."

Amelia had not exactly thought to pray, only to escape the grim heat and its burdens for a time. Yet, if this foreign prince could weep before God for his people then why shouldn't she?

They both knelt before the statue of Christ, but before she bowed her head, she had one more question for the solemn royal.

"You say you consider yourself like unto a Reacherman, Highness. Is that why you would not call the folk of Aubrey 'your people'?"

"No, Your Grace, not precisely," Farringdon answered her, not lifting his head from the attitude of prayer. "My father died to save me and his people. I am still alive and hidden in safety far away. I do not deserve to call them my people, not until I have expended myself to save them as my father did and as you would, if they were your people."

"Would you really do that?"

"If God grants me the chance. It is what I pray for most earnestly."

It comforted Amelia for a moment to imagine she was not the only one who thought they could not do enough for the people who trusted them. No wonder Prentice and Farringdon seemed to be growing in affection for one another.

CHAPTER 43

"I t wasn't this bad when we was sieged in Fallenhill that first time," Markas muttered under his breath but loud enough to be heard nonetheless. Revictualling the White Lions, even for the short march north to Fallenhill, was turning into a greater undertaking than Prentice or any of his staff had anticipated. Food was not as desperate as it had been only days before, but no one in the town was eager to part with any of their new supplies. Prentice had expected the merchants to gouge him for every extra guilder they could get, but even amongst the Conclave members, there was a reluctance to trade away precious food for mere coin.

"You can't eat silver," was the protest heard in every quarter.

"I was there, Markas, remember?" Prentice reproved his man. "You know damned well it was worse than this."

"Yes, Captain!"

"But not by much," Prentice added and patted his standard bearer on the shoulder. Markas nodded, and Prentice left him to his duties supervising the movements of wagons and fetching water from as far afield as possible. At least with the knights martial having ridden off, his men had access to a second well reasonably close. Prentice walked through the dusty encampment and turned when he heard the clomp of Brother Whilte's wooden leg.

"Good morning, Captain," Whilte called as he rushed to catch up to Prentice.

"Morning, Brother."

"I bring you a delivery," the chaplain said, and as he reached Prentice, he held out a folded packet of vellum. Prentice cocked an eyebrow.

"Your researches," Whilte explained, "from scribe Pawley. I met with him earlier this morning and he asked me to bring this to you, save you the bother of fetching it yourself."

Prentice accepted the document with a nod of thanks and began to unfold it. He thought about Whilte's words as he did so. It was barely midmorning. The chaplain must have been into the town very early to have already met with Pawley. Then he looked at Whilte and noticed the man had soot stains on his clothing.

"Did you sleep the night in a hearth, Brother?"

Whilte looked himself over and chuckled. "No indeed, Captain. Looks that way, though. No, I was in the town because there was a fire. Pawley and a few of his brethren were burned. Unpleasant for them, but thanks-be-to-God not life threatening."

Prentice half-listened as he perused the notes Pawley had made for him.

"Was there a fire at the Paper House?" he asked. After Solft's comments only the previous morning, had several scholars already burned themselves exactly as their leader predicted?

"Apparently, yes. The master of the House is most vexed. It seems your man Pawley was the cause, at least indirectly. After preparing your notations, he attended a local tavern. There he fell to drinking with an eccentric fellow and the two returned, singing drunk, in the early hours. While dancing a reel on the ground floor and waking the whole house, it appears Pawley knocked over an open flame and the paper quickly took fire."

An open flame? Prentice thought. *Pawley must have been truly drunk to bring a candle or the like into the Paper House.*

"The scholars fought their darnedest to save their home, though. They used everything they could, even grabbing noxious fluids from the tanning vats in the next building, what with water being so much more precious in the drought. It did the job, but the stench set a new standard for the Weeps, I think. All the books saved will smell like a privy for years, I'd say.

"At any rate, they called for me to tend the injuries and now I act as messenger."

"Thank you, Brother," Prentice said sincerely.

"You are welcome, Captain. Now, if you don't mind, I'll go make sure I'm ready to head north with the rest of the company. Some of the men want me to show them the basics of chirurgeon craft, but I still haven't persuaded them of the importance of keeping everything out of the dirt."

"A dirty bandage will stop the bleeding just like a clean, but you will wish it hadn't when the wound festers. Clean. Clean with wounds whenever you can," Prentice recited from memory.

"Master Wellspar's exact words," Whilte said with a smile. He and Prentice had sat under the same instructor at the Church Academy in Ashfield. Then it seemed the chaplain remembered what recalling their past together would bring back and he frowned, ducking his head and tugging his forelock. "I'll leave you to your work, Captain."

Prentice watched Whilte leave and put his memories back in their cell in his mind. Then he scanned Pawley's notes. There were some historical references that were nothing specific and one two-line account of a combat in one of the passes over the mountains during the crusades against the fey. It spoke of fey and "allies" fighting to escape west. Prentice thought those allies were likely to be the early Redlanders, whom he was also convinced were Solft's renegade "lesser kings."

There were other notations as well—a woman found guilty of witchcraft in a northern jungles town near Quenland that Prentice had never heard of. She was accused of marrying a fey man, but it was determined that her husband was, in fact, just a foreigner of unknown ethnicity. One of the other references

that did catch Prentice's attention was a translation of a
verse from a folk song. Prentice wondered if Pawley had
got it from his minstrel drinking partner, in which case it
was probably total fiction made up last night rather than
originating in the ancient past.

The verse was simple enough and warned of making pacts
with fey creatures. *You will burn,* it cautioned, *your house,
your town, your land, if even one bargain you strike with these.*

"Well, the land certainly burns," Prentice muttered. "But
who struck the bargain?"

He put the papers into his purse and continued with the
business of the day. All the time, though, his mind kept
drifting back to the question of pacts made with fey. Were
these the kinds of pacts men made with witches that led to
rape and human sacrifice? If they were, then clearly hanging
the man who took responsibility was not enough to break
the curse. Of course, the drought long predated Earl Yarmass
and his men's vile paganism, and not all the perpetrators had
been equally punished. In spite of himself, Prentice gave a
scoffing laugh. After all the trouble gelding Sir Haravind and
his fellow rapists had caused, to think it was not a violent
enough outcome to purge a curse was an irony too cold even
for the reformed heretical convict.

"Well, a laugh is welcome," a voice said. "But typically I
have to jest or fool for it first."

Prentice looked to see Bluebird standing nearby in his
motley with an enormously broad-brimmed hat flopping
about on his head.

"You must be sweating a storm under those heavy rags,
Master Fool," Prentice said, wondering why an entertainer
was out here with his camp and not somewhere cooler, like
the castle. His men certainly did not have time to stop and
make merry. The newly arrived entertainer treated Prentice's comment as rhetorical.

"I was wondering if I could ride with your company on the morrow, good Captain?"

"Why?"

Prentice's blunt question caused the tumbler's lips to twitch a little, as if an honest smile tried to push its way past his mummer's comic expressions.

"In truth? To see the whole of this land. I came from the south with the earl and then accompanied the duchess to her ducal seat. Farther north, I hear there is a barony yet to see."

"The barony was burned by the Redlanders," Prentice told him. "The baron and his people with it."

"And now the whole Reach burns, too. Well, sunburns at least."

Prentice smiled suspiciously. Bluebird's words were a fairly ordinary witticism, but what caught the captain's attention was the cold-heartedness under it.

"There are no nobles and few taverns to sing for in Fallenhill. You would do better business staying here."

"I respect your opinion, of course," the entertainer said with a half bow that showed no more than a passing relationship with true respect. "Nonetheless, I have asked the duchess' permission, and I think I will see my plan through. I trust I can count on your protection as her representative?"

"You can, of course."

"Excellent." He bowed more deeply this time, his motley blue wings fluttering from his arms. "Do not fear, I do not eat much, and I can find my own nests to sleep in. And who knows, perhaps I will make more coin than you think. Soldiers in camp have pay to hand and little to spend it upon. I know the Church fathers disapprove almost as much of me as of a flock of doxies, but truth to tell, any place a brothel can make a coin, so can I."

Prentice had no doubt the man was completely correct. He nodded and Bluebird turned to leave, his arms waving in the air and his "feathers" flapping. Watching him go, Prentice saw a number of the Lions pause to laugh as the waving became a dance that ended in a spectacular tumble which seemed to injure the performer not in the least.

Witches, fey, nobles, and now fools, Prentice thought, shaking his head. *Almost makes me pine for the days of fetters and chains and overseer's whips.*

Suddenly he imagined how Turley would respond to this self-pitying thought, and he could almost hear his friend's voice as if he were standing right next to him.

Pine for their convict days? Not bloody likely.

CHAPTER 44

The smoke over the walls of Fallenhill, not to mention from the village at the foot of the slope beneath the fortifications, was visible from leagues distant. Rising from forges and smelters, as well as a whole population's worth of cookfires, the sight still reminded Prentice of the town's brutal recent past and his own winter starving inside its walls. As the Lions marched around the last bend in the road through the forest south of the town, the captain was struck by how different it all looked.

The village, which began as refugees forced to labor for Baron Liam and his besieging force, was now a permanent settlement of hundreds. It swelled by much more on market days, essentially taking over the commerce of the northern province from the old town. That was because while the fortified walls of the old Fallenhill still stood, the inside was now the home and training base of the White Lions. Having sent messengers ahead, Prentice knew the fortress would be ready, but he was surprised when he saw a garrison cohort lined up to welcome the rest of the Lions home. The drums rattled and the one hundred finely dressed men held their weapons at "present arms." A corporal named Sedgemark, one of several in charge of training new recruits, called for the salute as Prentice drew even with the honor guard, and the captain paused to return it.

"How goes it, Corporal?" he asked, waving for the rest of the company to continue its march inside Fallenhill's walls.

Markas, with the Lions' banner, stopped beside his captain, while Sergeant Franken led them in.

"I think it's well, Captain," Sedgemark said eagerly. He was a younger man, with wispy fair hair and freckles on his cheeks. For all his childish appearance, however, he was an excellent Fang, with unusual aptitude for sword and buckler. He was also uncommon among the corporals as one of the only ones, other than Gennet, who was not a former convict. A Reacherman, he had signed on when his father died of pox and his brother took the main of the inheritance for himself, including the family farm. "We're training the newcomers as they swear themselves in."

"Good man," Prentice told him.

"Can I ask, are you back for long, Captain?"

"We will be here some time, but I cannot tell you how long yet. How is the fortress for food and water?"

"Water's not too dire," Sedgemark explained. "We had a frustrating few days a while back when it looked like some of the wells might be drying up."

"How did you deal with that?" Prentice asked.

"With buckets and spades, Captain. We sent men down all the wells and got them dug as extra deep as we could to find more water. It started out as a punishment duty, but once men realized it meant time down in the cool of the earth out of the sun and closer to water, they soon started to volunteer."

"And food?"

"Not terrible but getting dicier. The miller up in Grey Cleft was bringing us flour made of some kind of wild high-pasture grain, at least that's what he said it was, but he also says there's no more growing up there now. Of course, there's flocks of sheep and goats all over the hills, but even that's not easy pickings anymore."

This was all good news as far as Prentice was concerned, but it was clear Sedgemark was nervous about the state of affairs.

"How much longer do you think this dread summer will go on, Captain?"

"As long as God wills, Corporal."

"And how long can we last?"

"Longer than Dweltford will, that is for sure." Prentice looked away down at the new-grown village and tried not to think about it empty again, abandoned to the drought. "Take them inside Corporal."

Sedgemark gave orders to his drummer. The beat rang out, the cohort turned on their heels, and marched in at the back of the rest of the column of returning Lions. Prentice followed them and stopped just inside the gate to marvel. If the newly sprung village was a notable change to the little vale, then the space behind the walls was miraculously transformed. Gone were the ruined remains of the burned town, as well as the rude long-huts that Prentice and the first of the White Lions trainees had huddled in through that winter's siege. Now, there was a pebble-lined road straight down the center of the fortress ground, joining itself to a broad parade field that took up one whole half of the area. The other half was occupied with neat rows of barracks, long buildings constructed of mortared stone and wooden beams, with thatched roofs and white-washed walls. At the other end of the road, smoke rose from the forges, originally built into the town's fallen keep and now grown to a thriving metal-working district the envy of any large city, providing the Lions' weapons, armor, and tools.

As Prentice watched, the entire militia company concluded their march on the parade field, their officers bellowing orders and dismissals. The hot, weary ranks fell out and went looking for their billets or just something to drink. Some greeted friends who had been in the garrison, while one or two simply sank down in the nearest piece of shade they could find. Sergeants, corporals, and line firsts issued orders, and the whole process moved with a natural flow that was not ill-disciplined, even if it might seem disorderly to the untrained eye.

Time was when I did not dare turn my back on any of them, Prentice thought. *Now the whole thing almost runs itself.*

He knew that that was not quite true, but he was surprised how relieved he felt knowing he did not have to fear a convict's knife in his back. Of course, as the long dry went on, the ties of loyalty and discipline were going to unravel. He would need to look for projects to set the Lions to, between marching and drilling with weapons, to keep a sense of purpose high and bored men from plotting ill.

Then there was also his own sense of purpose driving through Prentice's thoughts—the witch from Halling Pass. After four days marching north to plan his next moves, and finally away from the politics of the Reach and conflict with the peers of the realm, it was time to go on the hunt. Despite all the delays and the minimal leads available to him, Captain Prentice Ash was still resolved to pursue the serpent priestess and her horned horse to whatever bolt hole she had found for herself. Let Earl Sebastian hunt the fey wherever he would, Prentice would rest once the witch was dead.

So first, he needed to find fresh signs of his prey.

CHAPTER 45

"I ain't exactly sure what it is yer askin', Captain," the big-bellied man named Grice said as he stroked his long, grey-streaked beard. He was the village headman, having stayed since the days when Baron Liam indentured all the local settlers. Grice had been a farmer then, but his skill with both woodworking and metal was great, so now he made his living as a cooper, producing water and powder barrels for the fortress. "Are you really wanting folks to tell you kiddlings tales and ghost stories?"

"Not quite," said Prentice. "What I am looking for is anyone from the mountains, high-country folk, who knows local stories of mysterious things."

"Sounds like what I said," Grice replied and frowned as he folded his arms. The yeoman leader clearly thought Prentice was on some kind of fool's errand, and Prentice did not blame him.

After considering the few facts he knew for sure, Prentice felt that there were two apparently conflicting threads of information. The first was the behavior of the riders themselves. They ranged over the open west beyond the Dwelt and even into the ground between the river and the mountains. They could pass almost unseen but were sometimes noticed, giving them the legend of being like ghosts. Whatever traces a ghost left, those would be best located by Earl Sebastian's own stalking pack, and there was no point in Prentice pursuing that.

The other two confirmed sightings of his prey were in the mountains, though. The witch was at Halling Pass even while Prentice's forces had besieged the castle, yet she had left without being seen. Cunning and eldritch as the fey riders were, Prentice was convinced that she could not have left the castle and gone into the Reach through Halling Pass while his men were occupying it. That meant she had left by some other mountain path, one that neither he nor his men knew anything about.

The only other time fey had been conclusively sighted was at the burning of Fallenhill, being the Reach town furthest north and closest to the Azures. That made him think there were good odds the fey lived somewhere in those mountains. It made a strong kind of sense when he thought about it. A village on the open grasses would surely be seen eventually, no matter how arcanely it was hidden. Signs would be noted, trodden-down grass as the riders went back and forth if nothing else. But in the mountains, a man could stand less than a league away from a substantial settlement and the intervening rocks and ridges might mean it was never even noticed, except for perhaps some smoke and other lesser signs. So that was what Prentice was looking for—the unknown and unexpected things that the high-country folk of the Azure Mountains dismissed as ghost stories, tales to frighten children. Of course, that sounded like a fool's errand to straightforward men and women like Grice the Cooper, village headman.

"Don't know much as folk would say," he explained to Prentice with a shrug. "Mountain folk ain't talkin' folk, you know? We had that blue butterfly fella come through the village the other night, and he said we were the quietest he'd ever fooled for. I don't see why that's our problem. All he did was dance and chuck things from one hand to t'uther. What's all that about?"

"Well, thanks to you anyway," Prentice said and nodding, headed away. Grice turned back to his work, but after a pause, he added one more thought.

"O'course, there's the miner's guild folk up in the gulches and gorges," he said. "They're a different sort in a lot o' ways. They keep to themselves, but they like a sing and a drink of a night. Maybe they tell the kind of fey tales you're lookin' for."

Prentice nodded again and considered the advice. The miner's guild dug the silver and iron ore out of the mountains that made the Reach so wealthy. They worked hard, lived close to their holes in the rock, and only came down out of the mountains to trade their ore, pay their taxes, or quit their trade. Prentice had suspected that at some point he would have to make a journey into the mountains, but now he was certain that was his next step. Returning to the fortress, he started putting together his plan. Firstly, he would need a guide and an escort force.

"A guide shouldn't be hard to scare up, Captain," Corporal Gennet commented when Prentice told him his plan. Gennet was the officer Prentice wanted to command the escort. "But a force that size? Is that necessary, if you'll pardon me askin'?"

"You have seen them, Gennet," Prentice replied. "If the fey are up in the high-country, I do not want to be alone when I find out for sure."

"Oh, for certain! I just, I don't' know. Horsemen in mountains? It just don't make much sense to me. Open ground, long arrow flights—that I understand. I seen that work and it's nasty. But, I mean, knights don't do much good ahorse on steep slopes."

"I think we have established that whatever these fey riders are, they are not our grandparent's men ahorse."

"Well, no argument there, Captain." Gennet nodded at last and saluted. "I'll get you three lines ready to march at dawn. The boys have had a few days to rest, and some are probably even ready to head out again. We've got a good few who are at their best marching somewhere and fighting at the end of it. They don't do so good in camps and forts like this."

"Go to, Corporal," Prentice told him and was glad. If there were militiamen in the Lions who got antsy after only a few days' rest in camp, then it would do discipline good to get them out roving over the heights searching for settlements of mystery folk. Prentice was less pleased a little while later when Brother Whilte asked to join the expedition.

"Why, Chaplain?"

Whilte shrugged. "The men are eating hearty and resting in clean barracks, and the ones still carrying wounds are well tended. There is little for me to do. Fallenhill can spare me a handful of days to see to the pastoral needs of the high country. Prayers and some healing, perhaps. I hear that mining is a dangerous occupation. Who knows? I might even find some younger families who've never had a chance to say proper vows. I might get to perform a wedding or two."

"We will be hunting, Brother, not rambling," Prentice cautioned with raised brows. Whilte returned the captain's knowing look with one of his own.

"Have I slowed you down one pace yet, Captain?"

Prentice shook his head. The man had a point.

"No, Brother, you have not," he conceded. He considered for another moment. "I think your plan is a goodly one. It is precisely the kind of service of faith that Sacrist Fostermae would have rendered in the same place. Tell Corporal Gennet you will be marching with us and to make sure supplies are packed for your needs. Anything you can find in the fort or village before the dawn that you think to need, buy it and send the account to the quartermaster. The Lions will cover the cost."

Whilte tugged his forelock and withdrew. Prentice watched him go and felt a snap of the old anger in him, a memory of the vicious loathing he had once held for the former nobleman. That was all it was though, a memory. The truth was that Whilte was humble, faithful, and devout—everything Prentice admired in Fostermae and wanted in a chaplain for his men.

This is a difficult teaching, Prentice recalled from the words of scripture. Yet he was finding that perhaps he could forgive a truly penitent foe, even one as bitter as Whilte had been. He just hoped the Halling Pass witch on her unicorn did not try to repent to him. That would surely try his Christian charity a step too far. His champion blade would find her heart before she even got the first words out of her mouth, of that he was certain.

CHAPTER 46

"Will it be possible to gather that much food so quickly, Master Welburne?" Duchess Amelia asked the elderly merchant as they concluded negotiations for the creation of another caravan to ship more supplies to Dweltford as soon as possible.

"It will be more of a challenge, Your Grace," Welburne said with a polite bow. The shutters on the windows of the Great Hall were completely closed against the afternoon's blistering sunlight, but the air was still stultifying, and even the normally cadaverous merchant was red-faced and sweating. He pulled a silk from his sleeve and wiped at his brow. "As you may expect, I have already adjusted my prices accordingly. Extra cost aside, it will also take more time to assemble than the previous."

"Well, as soon as you may, please commence the work. Lady Dalflitch will ensure the silver is in your purse by sundown."

Amelia nodded to her lady-in-waiting sitting beside her at the high table. Dalflitch returned the nod, but there was a knowing look in her eye. Amelia and her seneschal had already had a conversation this morning about the state of her treasury. Coin had always been the one resource her lands had never wanted for, but now the drought was drinking that away as well. If the prices remained the same, the duchy could afford to purchase one more shipment after this, and not so large as this one. Then, she would be bankrupt.

Too bad, she thought. *My people cannot just save their money and go hungry. Better to spend it and save their lives.*

"I have already presumed upon our bargain and sent word to my factors in the Vec to begin the process," Welburne told her.

"You are to be commended for your industriousness," Amelia said, though she wondered what the man would have done if they had not been able to settle on a price.

"Thank you, Your Grace."

Welburne bowed and folded the duchess's instructions away into his long black coat. Even thin as he was, Amelia thought the man must be only one climb of a flight of stairs away from collapsing with heat exhaustion. She expected him to withdraw but was surprised when he had a follow-up request.

"With your permission, Your Grace, I would speak a moment privately with your lady-in-waiting? We need not leave the hall, only find a quieter part of it. No chaperoning will be required."

Amelia was surprised by the request, but it seemed benign enough.

"By all means, Master," she said and turned to Dalflitch. She was astonished though, when Welburne held his hand out to Lady Spindle, standing her usual, quiet vigil with Righteous at Amelia's shoulder.

"If you would honor me with your company, Lady?" Welburne said.

Eyes blinking under her mask, Spindle seemed even more surprised than Amelia. She took a step to move around the high table, then looked back at the duchess uncertainly.

"I gave my permission, My Lady," Amelia said. "Fear not, we will keep a sober watch from here."

Spindle curtseyed, moved around the table, and walked with Master Welburne away down the hall until the two stood near one of the enormous hearths, long empty and swept clean.

"What is that about, do you think?" Amelia asked her remaining ladies.

"I would not hazard a guess, Your Grace," said Dalflitch quietly, plainly as mystified as her mistress.

"He was one of the ones that done for your husband, the duke, wasn't he, Your Grace?" Righteous asked, watching Welburne with slitted eyes behind her own mask.

"Yes, Righteous, he was a member of Duggan's conspiracy," Amelia confirmed.

"And yet he's still alive and free."

Amelia knew Righteous disapproved. After all, the conspiracy's other instigator, the merchant and criminal gang leader Malden, had nearly beaten her own husband to death. If Righteous had had her way, every member of the treasonous compact would have rotted in a crow's cage after she had made some choice cuts in their flesh to get the process started.

"We know he has your pardon, Your Grace, but I do not know the story behind it, if you would be willing to share it," Dalflitch said more tactfully.

Amelia smiled mournfully as she considered whether to tell the tale. She quickly decided that there was no reason to not.

"Master Welburne did not flee, like the others in the compact," she said, giving Dalflitch the main of the story. "He waited in his home, and while we were suffering under Daven Marcus' vile attentions, My Lady, and Liam had Prentice and Lady Righteous cooped up in the ruin of Fallenhill, Caius Welburne sat under house arrest by the Conclave bailiffs. By some means, I don't know what but I suspect some bribery, he persuaded them not to put him straight on a convict chain, as I had ordered."

"Cunning bugger," muttered Righteous, but Amelia ignored her. A fly buzzed lazily through the sultry air, and the duchess batted it away. The bowl of repellent herbs had not recently been replenished.

"When I returned, he arranged to have himself brought to a meeting of the Conclave at a time when I would be there. With a number of guild masters and selectmen speaking on his behalf, I was persuaded to allow him to plead for his freedom."

"Did he at least get down on his creaky knees?" Righteous asked.

"No, but if I had insisted, I think he might have."

Righteous scoffed loudly, but Dalflitch "tsked" equally audibly. The lady seneschal was plainly interested to hear the whole of the tale.

"Master Welburne told me he had been coerced into the compact," Amelia said.

"I take it he had persuasive evidence, Your Grace?" said Dalflitch.

"The complete accounting of the conspiracy, every guilder, even letters from the previous seneschal, as it happens, making it clear how the conspirators managed to corrupt the duke's treasurer and draw him into the treason as well. Master Welburne is something of an institution in our town, it seems. His silver backs part of nearly every large deal done in Dweltford. The conspirators forced him in with them because if they had not, he would likely have discovered them anyway, and that was a risk the venal Malden would not take."

"Yea, but how, Your Grace?" Righteous pressed. "If he's such a straight dealer, how'd they make him deal in with 'em?"

"Master Welburne has almost no relatives, save for a nephew in Rose Carabost. The man is an upright and successful guildsman in his own right, apparently, a carder. Caius and his nephew are reasonably close in affection, and the merchant also thinks highly of his nephew's wife, a sweet thing by all accounts, but also a Thrice Fristian."

"Dear God, poor thing," Dalflitch whispered. Righteous, however, did not understand.

"What's that? What is it?"

"The Fristians are...were...a minor local sect in the Church in Carabost," Dalflitch said somberly. "Some while ago they were condemned as heretics and forced to renounce their beliefs. I don't know the details, but the Thrice are the offshoot of their faith who refused to recant. Most were put to death, but there are rumors that some simply hid amongst the common folk, changing their names, marrying out of their sect."

Amelia nodded.

"Somehow, Malden discovered the secret about Caius' niece by marriage and threatened to send word to the authorities in Rose Carabost," she explained. "We've all seen Prentice's scars. Would any of us give a loved relative over to the cares of the Inquisition?"

"I wouldn't give 'em a mongrel cur that I wanted to see dead," Righteous averred, and Amelia wasn't sure if she meant a person or an actual dog.

"So Welburne told you all of this...?" Dalflitch began, and Amelia finished for her.

"He trusted me with the secret, yes, knowing I still had the power to throw him on the chain. He begged my forgiveness and committed to accept whatever judgement I rendered. He's got the bearing of a cold river fish, but he seemed horrified by Malden murdering my husband. Once he knew for sure that Malden was dead, he longed to confess, I think."

"A better man than he appears, then," Dalflitch reflected. "Shrewd with a piece of silver, though, I assure you, Your Grace."

Amelia had no doubt. With the burdens on the land, more than half the Conclave's higher members had left Dweltford to other, greener places where they had holdings. Not Welburne. Still, what did he want with Spindle? Her sewing perhaps?

The three ladies sat watching the two in conference when another pair arrived at the main doors. One was a steward in household livery of blue and white. The other took Amelia a moment to recognize as the High Sacrist Quellion. His presence caught her by surprise. She was so used to him accompanying Earl Sebastian everywhere that she had assumed he would be with him even now on the hunt for the fey.

Welburne and Spindle paused their speaking as the steward escorted the senior churchman along the length of the hall, watching them pass. Then the steward announced Quellion, and Amelia waved the sacrist to the table.

"Your Grace, I bring you the outcome of my investigation into the street preacher in Griffith."

Investigation? Amelia thought. *I'd forgotten about that.* In truth, with so many more significant issues requiring her attention, she hardly cared what happened to the man.

"Then please present your findings," she told him.

"The preacher was indeed ordained, a member of the Crucian order."

That meant nothing to Amelia.

"He willingly confessed to the details of his encounter with you and your...ladies in the streets."

The High Sacrist's pause was tiny, fleeting, and likely involuntary, but Amelia noticed, nonetheless. She looked askance at Dalflitch who cocked an eyebrow to show that she had heard it too. Behind her, she thought she felt Righteous shift her weight, but thankfully the Lace Fang held her tongue.

"Since he was speaking out of right order, I have had him chastised and sent to other pious duties," Quellion continued, then stopped speaking. Amelia waited, expecting more of this "report."

"Well thank you, Sacrist," she said eventually when it became clear there was nothing more. She waited again, ready to dismiss him when he asked, if he truly was finished.

"Your Grace, there is one other thing, if you will allow me," Quellion finally began afresh after his long silence. He was uncharacteristically anxious in his manner this time, and it made Amelia wonder what he planned to say now.

"I am hesitant to bring it up, but my duty as a senior spiritual leader in the Reach presses me to do so. I do it against the express request of Earl Sebastian, which troubles my soul, but my higher duty is to God and Mother Church."

So, Sebastian has some influence on you *as well,* she thought. *Good to know it's not all one way.* Then she considered the fact that the High Sacrist was defying the earl's wishes. Not so much influence after all. She nodded and waited for Quellion to reveal what "troubled his soul."

"Your Grace, the preacher in Griffith spoke out of turn, but he spoke to an important issue."

"He called myself and my ladies 'whores,' Excellency," Amelia said, her voice turning to ice that almost seemed to freeze the heat-hazed air between them in place. "What *important issue* did that speak to?"

If Quellion recognized how dangerous the conversational ground he was venturing onto was, it did not show in his manner. Having confessed his discomfort in defying Earl Sebastian's wishes, he was now returned to full confidence, it appeared. Reproving noblewomen was not something that troubled his conscience.

"Your Grace, your public mourning for your late husband, the Duke Marne, undoubtedly does you credit, even as a mere show," the High Sacrist expounded. "And obviously the land experiences troubles that can only be overwhelming to one of your inexperience and sex. You should recognize, however, that your status unnerves your people and your peers."

"Which part of my status is it that troubles them most, do you think Excellency? My inexperience or my sex?" Amelia felt her fingers digging into the arms of her throne-like chair, the honor seat that she had inherited from her husband and signal of her authority in this hall. It was her literal seat of power. She was afraid that if she did not hold herself back, she would seize something from the table and throw it at the man. The only thing close to hand was a silver water ewer, and she was certain it would make a satisfying thump when it hit.

"Your widowhood, Your Grace," Quellion went on in his condescending manner, blissfully ignorant of his impending encounter with a piece of tableware. "You are yet too young to take to a cloister and the Reach needs an heir."

"You are not the first to have said as much, Excellency," Amelia told him. "Nor is this the first time you have hinted at the issue. Are you so sure I have not heard you?"

"The duchess has the finest of hearing, Excellency," Dalflitch added supportively. Her words caused the churchman's lip to twitch into an almost sneer.

You don't approve of her talking to you, do you? Amelia thought. She considered that fact a moment and realized the churchman almost certainly knew Dalflitch's reputation as a notorious wanton and former mistress of Daven Marcus. *Is that why you think the street preacher's attack was possibly justified? Do I not keep sufficiently chaste company for your sensibilities?*

"I had hoped, Your Grace, that by now you would have heard for yourself, for the sake of both your reputation and your immortal soul."

"My reputation and my soul?" The ewer was seconds from taking flight.

"When you sent Sebastian away, I despaired, but you also packed the other captain off, so I am left to wonder what the true impediment is?"

"True impediment to what? To finding myself a husband?" Amelia demanded.

"To finding your way clear to accepting Earl Sebastian, Your Grace."

Amelia blinked. The conversation had just taken an unexpected turn.

"Accepting him as what?" she asked. Dalflitch laid a gentle hand on Amelia's, and she turned to her lady to see what she wanted to say. Before Lady Dalflitch could do more than give her a pregnant glance, Amelia's mind caught up to where Quellion was taking the conversation. "Accepting him as a husband? Is that what you mean?"

"Of course," Quellion answered, clearly annoyed that he had to spell it all out. "Who else would you consider? You can't marry the *reformed* heretic, we both know that. Even if you wanted to, I am told he has a wife."

"Yea, me!" Righteous said, pointing a thumb at her chest. "I'm carrying his child."

"Truly?" Quellion responded, then shrugged his heavy shoulders. "I suppose that's not so surprising, and it makes the question simpler, surely."

"The question?" Amelia repeated. "The question of wedding myself to Earl Sebastian?"

"Precisely so," Quellion said with the air of a frustrated teacher pleased that his slow-witted student finally seemed to be catching on. "The loss of your husband was plainly a deep shock, hero that he was. Then you have had to suffer the continual further distresses of the painted invaders, Daven Marcus' depredations, and his rebellion, seizing the throne. I can only imagine the pains his accusations caused you, insinuating treason on your own part as well."

His accusations were as nothing compared to his rape and pillage, you pompous fool, Amelia thought, and she was certain her growing contempt for Quellion was visible in her expression, if the man only paused to look.

"As a high churchman, Your Grace, I cannot approve of the methods you might have found to console yourself in your confusion and grief, but I do understand them. You would not be the first of your rank to fulfill their needs, but you cannot allow it to go on. Turn from the pleasures of your chamber and seek a righteous companion in the noble life which God has allowed to you. The Reach needs an heir, and he must be legitimate."

"Don't you dare suggest my husband lies with Her Grace one more time or I'll show you the color o' your innards, holy sacrist man or not!" Righteous declared with venom, her voice rising such that Welburne and Spindle paused in their conversation to look once more at the high table.

"I do not quail from your threats, convict slattern," Quellion said with the serene confidence of a man who believes his own holy status renders him immune to the violence of the world, as if God had no place in his kingdom for martyrs. "Now hold your tongue or you can join your 'husband' in learning what it feels like to be put outside the bosom of Mother Church."

Suddenly Amelia felt her own anger drop away, replaced by the terror that Righteous would leap the table and slit the man from groin to throat. She put a restraining hand on Righteous's wrist. Dreaming of smacking Quellion with a silver jug was one thing; letting him be butchered in the middle of her Great Hall was something else again.

"Your words are quite direct, Excellency," Dalflitch said with quiet menace.

"I have tried subtlety and seen it fall upon deaf ears—" he began to protest, but Amelia cut him off.

"Direct words and premature," she said with a firm tone. "Regardless of the newly acceded earl's worthiness as a potential husband, Excellency, I cannot accept a suit of marriage before it is even pledged."

That revelation seemed to take the wind from Quellion's sails, and he paused in his arguments, blinking and looking down in confusion.

"He hasn't yet proposed?" he asked, more rhetorically than of Amelia. She answered him anyway.

"He has not. Perhaps this is a matter you could take up with him. In fact, Excellency, perhaps you could explain why you are so sure he wants to marry myself or any other."

"But that is why he retained the silly minstrel," Quellion said, "to write poems to woo you with. The earl is a man of action and resolve. Feminine fripperies do not come readily to his hand or tongue."

"The earl has already shared his plans with you?" Dalflitch asked, leaning forward in her chair and cocking an eyebrow. "And he had this in mind since before he crossed the Azures for his investiture? He's quite the presumptuous little hound, it seems."

"No more than any other in this chamber," Quellion retorted. "He would not be the first one in the Western Reach to marry above himself. At least he would be unusual amongst them as being first born to high peerage."

That was enough for Amelia, and she thrust herself to her feet. She was prepared to make no further effort to hold back her disgust at this arrogant, condescending fool. He had accused her ladies of being whores and suggested that her most loyal captain was nothing more than a lapdog bedwarmer, and now he was accusing her of having ambitions above her station in her first marriage. She wondered for a moment if the man even knew the difference between insult and persuasion. Did he bless the sick by spitting in their faces, or order drinks by throwing rocks at the taverner?

"You have delivered your report, High Sacrist," she said through gritted teeth. "You may leave now."

"These are not questions you may simply dismiss, Duchess."

"Get out of my house, Excellency, and do not ever return unless I call for you!"

"Your rejection will not still my words," Quellion protested "It is my duty to God and Church to counsel you in holiness for the sake of your soul and your land. The rumors of witchcraft and debauchery will only grow if you reject sound doctrine."

"I am well situated with instructors in sound doctrine, you obstinate ass," Amelia spat back, her patience finally slipping enough to force her to insult the man. "Many are the sincere and humble sacrists who preach God's word in my lands, and they are all welcome counselors."

"You do not surely mean that heretic scriptorium in your fell district, Your Grace? I have heard of them and their words. When this war is done, Mother Church will have to purge their infection from the west."

"Get out!" the duchess commanded him. "Get out before I summon guards. I do not lack for theological guidance, but if in future I do, I will not need to invite your return, Excellency. By your own report, penny prophets are abounding in the Reach these days. I will need only step out into the streets of my beleaguered town and surely I will be beset with religious teaching of at least as high a quality as you offer. So, you may go!"

Quellion's lips turned in a bitter frown and he withdrew without bowing, huffing down the dais steps and striding from the hall alone while his escorting steward ran to catch up.

"I said it before, and I say it now: Cheeky git!" Righteous said, and Amelia would not have been surprised if she had spat on the ground in contempt as she said it. Dalflitch's reaction, however, did surprise her.

"Cheeky git is right, My Lady," she agreed, "and fool enough to think he could push Her Grace around on the strength of rumors alone. He'd be laughable if his kind were not so common."

"My Lady?" Amelia said, aghast but nonetheless smiling at Dalflitch's assessment. She heard Spindle returning up the short stairs and looked to see that Master Welburne had gone as well.

"You don't know what you missed, Spindle," Righteous said as the other Lace Fang returned.

"No?" Spindle asked in a distracted fashion.

"The High Sacrist registered his disapproval of the duchess' widowhood," Dalflitch added by way of extra explanation. "He was deeply interested in Her Grace's marital status. Indeed, of her whole household, it seemed."

"Caius, too," Spindle said enigmatically.

"Master Welburne also asked after my marriage?" Amelia clarified, astonished.

"No, Your Grace, mine. He's asked me to wed."

CHAPTER 47

T he mine, such as it was, was little more than a cleft hacked out of the side of a ravine wall. Orange-red streaks in the otherwise grey rock showed where lodes of iron ore were embedded between other minerals. The metal rusted so readily on contact with air and water that when deposits were near to the surface, they were almost unmissable. The deep mountain cleft rang with the hammering of picks as men hanging from rope harnesses attacked the rock face, sending chunks the size of a person's head dropping onto a huge pile of rubble, there to tumble to the ravine floor where other miners gathered and assessed the pieces.

"We used to refine it to bloomery right here," the mine foreman was explaining to Prentice as they watched. The wiry older man pointed to the low stream behind them. "There was good clay in that water, refreshed from the melt further up the mountains. Not so much now. And ever since your man in Fallenhill took over, there's not so much need."

"My man?" Prentice asked.

"Masnian fellow, fussier than a housecat what's gone off fish and milk."

"Yentow Sent?"

"That's him. After three loads of him telling us our blooms ain't 'up to his standard,' we stopped bothering. He couldn't talk us down a price 'cause that's set by the guild, that is. So if he don't like our refining, he can do it himself."

"He does," Prentice confirmed. Yentow Sent took his position as a true master smith as a matter of utmost seriousness. His fixated oversight of every aspect of the process of smithing and smelting was rapidly becoming legend in the north of the Reach. As long as he kept turning out weapons and armor in the amounts and quality that the Lions needed, Prentice was inclined to indulge the man's professional vanity. These miners had a similar attitude, it seemed.

"Tell me again, Captain, what is it you're looking for?" said the foreman.

Prentice outlined once more the kinds of information he was seeking. This was the second mine he and his men had stopped at, along with numerous high-country farmsteads, asking at every stop for signs of the fey. So far, he had been told all the usual fey tales, the kinds repeated from one end of the Grand Kingdom to the other of wild dwellers hiding in forests and abducting children in the night. Witches tended to feature in stories that involved bonfires in the wild and more snatched children. No one had anything specific to the mountains to share. Most were more concerned to discuss whether the presence of Prentice and his men heralded the coming of ducal tax collectors into the high country and how poorly that would be received by the locals. Hardy and independent-minded, Azure Mountains folk did not take kindly to excessive oversight by far powers, or indeed, any oversight, it seemed.

"I ain't seen no fabled things in my time in the mountains, Captain, and I been here ten or more years now," the mine chief said with an apologetic shrug. "I ain't even seen one of these painted westerners folks say are hounding the rest of the Reach. *They* sound like fey tale to me, and if it weren't that I was told by folks I trust, I wouldn't believe anything I heard about *them*."

"I wish I could disbelieve, yeoman," Prentice said, shaking his head. "But I have fought far too many of them to doubt."

The foreman looked nervous for a moment and tugged his forelock.

"No disrespect, Captain," he insisted with a fraught expression. "Like I said, I do believe in 'em. I didn't mean to make light of men-at-arms doing the fighting or nothing."

Prentice shook his head. The last thing he wanted was for the man to be afraid of him. He decided to change the subject.

"How long can you last here with the drought? Her Grace, the duchess, is bringing foods and other provisions up from the south. I can speak to her people, if you have need."

"Nah, Captain," the foreman said, his nervousness easing. "'Tis hard work, but we don't want for much up here most days, 'cept women, and I figure Her Grace ain't gonna send us no doxies, huh?"

"No, I would not think so," Prentice agreed, smiling.

"Well then, not much else to ask for. We got some trapper folks keep us well in meat, and fur in the winter. We save 'em having to go the whole way into Fallenhill and keep 'em from havin' to pay the tariffs if they did."

Prentice almost laughed. The fellow was terrified of accidentally calling Prentice a liar to his face but did not hesitate to discuss tax evasion with him.

"Of course, food's a little scarcer nowadays, though nothin' like lowland folks is facing, and since the..." The foreman trailed off a moment.

"Something wrong?" Prentice prompted him, looking about to see if something had happened in the mine works.

"No, no, Captain, only I think I might have a story for you after all. See, we used to have more mouths to feed for a half season just before the drought started. They were another crew, silvermen mostly, but they were happy to hit the rocks with the rest of us. They stopped in to dig with us, but they had just left their own works up north some leagues. They had some funny superstitions, like never letting tools out of their sight."

"Superstitions?"

"Aye. Some of us took it amiss when they started, like they were accusing us of being thieves. There weren't no account to be like that, seeing as how we're all guildsmen. Miners don't thieve from miners, or they don't stay miner's long."

Prentice was familiar with the pride of the mining guilds. Entrusted with handling most of the precious metals in the Grand Kingdom, as well as the minting of official coinage, the masters of mining were more ruthless with malefactors of their profession than even the harshest magistrates.

"Anyway, when we called them on it, they said it was a long habit from working their wash up north. They said anything left unattended would get taken and they were certain it was nixies or some other mountain water spirit. Since we work here by the water, they had the same watchfulness. At the time, I figured they were just making an excuse for themselves. Are you saying there might actually be something in the water, Captain?"

Prentice shook his head, then looked at the stream flowing at the bottom of the ravine. The water's rock bed was clearly visible, even at this distance. Anything in there, even small fish, would be easy to see.

"I wouldn't think there is too much hiding in those waters. But if these fellows were so certain there were fell spirits in their stream, why go mining up there?"

"They said they took silver, copper, and all sorts of things out the dirt up that way," the foreman said. "For that kind of load, I'd sure put up with a couple of thieving nixies, wouldn't you?"

"I suppose so." Prentice wasn't too hopeful about the foreman's tale, but it was still the best clue he had heard since coming into the high country. "Tell me, if the diggings were so good, why did they leave?"

"They were using the wash to pan the sands, but then it dried up, so they couldn't pan no more."

"The drought got to their wash?" Prentice asked.

"Nah, like I said, Captain, this was before the drought. They left *here* cause of the drought, so they were already here that half-season when it started. Unless, of course, the drought started with their wash first; 'cept that can't be right because our

stream didn't show for long after word of the dry happened and
there was still a winter before they left us."

"Can you show us where this dry wash was? Can someone
guide us?"

"None of us has been there that I know, Captain, but I can
give you easy enough directions. The other lot never kept secret
where their diggings were. They were loyal guildsmen, after all.
Also, there's a farmstead up there, lone farmer. Look for the
smoke of his fire. He's the only one for leagues." The foreman
paused and then his brows lifted. "Why, Captain? Do you think
there really is a nixie?"

"I doubt it, but we will look it over anyway," Prentice told the
man. In his mind, he was thinking of Pawley's notes, especially
the injunction against making pacts with the fey because of the
curse that would come upon your land. He could not help but
wonder, what if the drought really had begun in that mountain
stream wash worked by miners and haunted by unknown creatures—capricious creatures skilled at keeping out of sight and
haunting mortals like ghosts. And what if, when the Horned
Man led his forces out of the west, some of those same fantastical
creatures had snuck out of their mountain holdfasts to make a
fresh pact with the Redlanders, a pact that now bound them to
serve the serpent witch and her unicorn?

It was a long bow to draw, but Prentice was sure he had the
right of it. The land was accursed, and there was a secret hidden
in that mountain wash that he and his men would have to search
out.

CHAPTER 48

Amelia was dreaming again. She recognized the signs more easily this time, but that was not as comforting as she might have hoped. She was out under the night sky, with the Rampart overhead, blazing almost as brightly as a silver sun. Other than the sky above, Amelia did not at first recognize anything else about where she was. It was as if she stood in the midst of a vast bowl of black glass. Then she saw ripples and she realized she was standing on the surface of Lake Dweltford, not as it was in this time of drought, but how it was when it was full of water. She was walking on the water. In dreams like this, miracles were possible as well, it seemed.

From out of the darkness, Amelia heard hoofbeats and she looked for the horses and the serpent on the unicorn that she now knew was the image of the witch who led the raiders, just as the horses stood for the fey with their deadly bows. Arrows flew around her, thrumming from unseen archers and falling into the water. Where they struck the surface it dried instantly, as if every hit splashed away some of the water and the lake itself had only the depth of a puddle. Not one shaft hit the duchess herself, though some flew by closely, causing her to flinch. When the lakebed was fully parched, the riders became visible, and their hooves beat the dust as they rushed by her, as in her first dream. The serpent on the unicorn ran with them, but in the midst of them now, hard to see behind their shielding forms.

The horses thundered past, and in their passage the ground hardened further until the thick mud cracked like shattered glass. Then the herd wheeled about and returned. In the shadows at their feet, a pack of hounds appeared, nipping and yelping. The feuding crowd of beasts overran Amelia once more, and she felt herself losing her patience.

"I have seen all this!" she shouted into the night, and she meant both in her previous dream and in the mortal realm where her land was dying. Visions were of no use to her if they provided no guidance.

"You have seen, but have you heard?" the rumbling voice of the angel Lion spoke at her shoulder. Amelia turned in surprise and fell on the mud as she recoiled from the mighty creature. More than once, Prentice had told her of the angel, describing its appearance, and nothing he had said prepared her for its majesty. It was the height of a pony, but twice the size of one for all that, heavy muscle and sinew rippling under its snow-white fur. Its mane glowed, as if made from moonlight itself, and its eyes were the darkness of the night sky between the stars. Eons had been witnessed by those eyes that had been old when creation began. The angel lifted its paw and pointed at the herd, claws like polished obsidian emerging from its softly furred toes.

"See, she hears her doom coming in the mouths of her own lying prophets," it said.

At first Amelia thought it was speaking of the man who confronted her in Griffith or of the others Quellion had mentioned. Then, the serpent poked its head above the fracas and looked to the far north. From that distance, Amelia heard a lone lion roar, its challenge echoing off the mountains. It surprised her when the serpent burst forth from the mass of animals and stampeded north on its unicorn, quickly followed by the rest of the herd and then some of the hounds, these with rams' horns on their heads.

"Prentice," she whispered, knowing that he was the one true lion in the northeast. What was he doing? How had he managed to provoke the serpent witch again if she was still out here, hunting and being hunted by the hounds. Were they not her knights ahorse? Although, what were these hounds with horns? So much of the imagery of the vision was clear to Amelia now, and yet some of it still mystified her, and she felt she understood too little of its ultimate meaning.

"His fate is not in your hands," the angel told her. "The serpent's prophets have called down the fire and sword. They must now suffer the ashes and the drawn blood."

Amelia had no idea what any of that could mean, except that Prentice was called Ash, but whose blood would be drawn? His? Before she could ask, the remaining pack of hounds turned on her. As in her first dream, they came for her, but this time she could not see any defender hounds. Was that because she had sent the knights away? Had she dismissed her protectors against some other true enemy?

"You will not be dry forever. Best to seek higher ground," said the lion, and then it was gone. Even as it disappeared, Amelia felt the mud beneath her grow moist, then sticky, and then it softened to a cloying morass. For a moment she was delighted at the thought that the water would return, that the drought would break. The mud kept rising, however, and it felt like it would suck her under if she did not move to higher ground as she was warned. Looking about, she saw Dweltford Castle sitting high on its rock. Thrashing through the mire that rose and rose but still did not run to clear, life-giving water as the lake should, Amelia pressed toward her home and its saving height. Behind her, the hunting hounds bayed and snapped, and the one glance she spared over her shoulder at them told her they were struggling as much with the mud as she was.

Amelia reached the edge of the castle high ground. She was about to climb out of the muck that threatened to sink her, but she looked and saw that her way was obstructed by a large throne made of different metals and covered with pelts and furs. The throne blocked her path into the castle and on it sat the peacock that had ridden on the back of a hound in her first dream. Its feathers were iridescent and seemed to change color continually in the moonlight.

"You cannot sit here," it said in a mocking, sing-song voice. "This is a throne for two."

The hounds behind Amelia were drawing closer, even as they were still drowning in the murk. Their slavering jaws snapped as they drew close. A softer growl sounded nearby, and Amelia looked down to see another dog, this one filthy and bleeding from wounds, sitting at her feet between herself and the throne with the peacock.

"There's no crown for that one," the preening bird said. "It can no more sit here than in its home."

"To hell with you," Amelia said with a sudden rush of fury. She swatted at the peacock with her hands and the bird took flight, cawing angrily. At that moment, the hounds behind her sprang, and to escape them, she threw herself onto the throne, dragging up onto its seat and pulling her legs behind her. Then the hounds leaped, and Amelia awoke, her face pressed against her pillow.

I saw and I heard, she thought as she looked out her bed-chamber window at the rays of dawn's light. *But I am not sure I understood.*

It was a puzzle, which did not overly trouble her. Given time, she was sure she could decipher its meaning. Her only fear was that she had no idea how long she had to do so. It was a comforting thought that the drought would end, and the Dwelt and the lake would flow with water again. It was less comforting to think that that would be a flood in which she could drown.

CHAPTER 49

T he farmstead was a simple affair, typical of any number of similar homes in the high country. A single, low, stone-walled hut roofed with sod that was now so dry that even the wildflowers that once grew out of it had withered and blown away in the wind. The humble dwelling crouched under a cliff face at the back of a mountain pasture that would likely have been truly pretty before the drought had afflicted it. Half a league away was a cleft in the rocks, out of which came a dry wash. Beside the evaporated watercourse were piles of broken earth and two deep, hand-shoveled pits—the remains of the miners' works.

Prentice led his troop to the farmstead in the middle of the day. At this altitude, the air was not so hot as it was on the lowlands, but it was still not cool, and the continuous uphill rising meant the entire company was weary and thirsty when they arrived. Meaning to call out to anyone in the farmstead to reassure them of their friendly intent, Prentice was beaten to the punch. A farmer in a sleeveless leather vest and kilt, with a straw hat and scarf on his sun-browned head, emerged from inside the hut and waved at them.

"You lion fellas lost? Or you running off from your sworn service?" he asked as he tapped a pipe on one hand to clear the bowl. "It's a long way from Fallenhill up here."

"We are here in obedience to the Duchess Amelia," Prentice told the man. "We mean no harm to you or your family, only to ask some simple questions."

"Don't got no family," the farmer said simply. He tucked his pipe away in a pocket on the front of his vest. "It's just me and has been since those shovel-slingers packed up a while ago."

"If it's just you, then it must not be so hard to find enough water, what with the drought."

"Not so hard," the man agreed. Prentice could well imagine that it would not take much to slake the man's thirst. Like typical Reachermen who worked the land, he was brown as a nut and lean, but even more so. He was so thin that he could almost be on the brink of starvation, though he did not move like he was suffering. Prentice looked over the area and wondered how little was needed to feed one such slight person and whatever animals he kept. Not that Prentice could see any. Perhaps they had already been sacrificed to the exigencies of survival.

"What's your questions?" the farmer asked.

"Simply, I want to know about the nixies the miners said they were tormented by."

"Nixies?" the farmer repeated and spat on the ground. He shrugged. "Don't know nothing about nothing like that."

"No? The miners said that they had tools and things taken by pranksters and will-o-the-wisping. You have no problems of that sort?"

"I don't dig in the earth or filth up the waters with tailings. Maybe the spirit-folk don't hold no grudges against me."

"You think the miners made the spirits angry?" Prentice asked.

"Didn't say that," the farmer replied.

Like most educated men, Prentice took stories of spirit-folk with a large pinch of salt. Of course, the irony was not lost on him that such was exactly what he was asking after. Generally, Grand Kingdom folk either had Prentice's reflexive skepticism or else a wariness born of fear—if not fear of the strange folk of tales, then fear of what one would be thought of for not being wary of such things. Either one did not believe in spirit folk or did not want to know. This farmer did not strike Prentice as having either position.

"Perhaps we could go inside," Prentice said quietly and then called over his shoulder. "Brother Whilte, could you step up here?"

"Why would you want to do that?" the farmer asked as Whilte approached.

"Brother Whilte is our chaplain and healer," Prentice explained as the one-legged man drew closer. "He has been treating the infirm and injured while we travel the high-country."

"I don't have any problems like that," the farmer said.

"He also blesses hearths," said Prentice. Next to him, Whilte made a sound that made it clear he was confused. Since coming into the mountains, Whilte had treated a number of injuries and sicknesses, but he had not once "blessed a hearth."

"What's that then?" the farmer asked suspiciously.

"A prayer of benediction to God. The duchess has commanded it to ensure that the holy power counteracts the burden on the land from the unending summer. It only takes a moment."

Next to him, Prentice could feel Whilte's tension, but he was thankful that the religious man did not voice any objections. The farmer watched him warily for a long moment, then cast an eye over the rest of the sweaty troop.

"Alright, be quick," he said eventually with a shrug.

"The rest of you take a rest," Prentice told his men. "This will not be long."

The farmer pulled back the leather curtain at the threshold and allowed Prentice and Whilte to follow him in. The floor had been dug out so that it was possible to stand under the low roof. Two uprooted trees, their branches dried out and repurposed as rafters, held the sod and thatch aloft. The inside was spartanly appointed, and the small stone hearth was readily identifiable in the midst of the space.

"There it is," the farmer said, pointing to the fireplace. Prentice pointed Whilte towards it and the chaplain played along, though unenthusiastically.

"My name is Prentice Ash," the captain said as Whilte stood near the scorched stones. "What is your name?"

"Why do you need to know?" the farmer retorted in a surly tone.

"It will help the blessing take better," Prentice lied. The man was unpersuaded.

"I'm not that concerned if it takes or not," he said. "Just get on with it."

"Yes, certainly," Prentice said. Then he fixed hard eyes on the man. "And you will need to take your hat and scarf off."

The man started at the order and one hand went almost unbidden to his hat's straw brim. Prentice drew his dagger and pointed it at the slender farmer's chest. The captain easily outmatched the man, overshadowing his height and significantly outweighing him.

"Captain Ash, what is this about?" Whilte asked, having clearly reached his limit for deceptions and mummery.

"Just one more moment please, Brother," Prentice said without looking at him. "Our host is about to unmask himself for us."

The farmer sneered. "There's no such thing as a blessing for the hearth, is there?" he asked ruefully. Prentice shrugged and the farmer took off his hat and then his scarf. "Was that what gave me away?"

"You have a farm with no animals and no crops," Prentice said.

"There's been a drought."

"And there is no sign you have done anything to fight it. No channels in the earth to redirect water, no moving crops closer to the last trickle coming down the wash. Just you and the abandoned mine."

The farmer slowly unwound the cloth around his head, which looked as if it had been put in place inside out, since the underside was significantly more colorful than the cloth had appeared beneath the man's hat.

"Show me," Prentice told the man, and the farmer lifted the hair on the side of his head, first on the right and then on the left. Under the unremarkable brown locks, each of the man's ears was strangely mutilated, with rough, ugly scars across the tops. Prentice looked from the disfigurements to the farmer's face once more.

"Works well enough at a distance," he said with a shrug. "But when them miners came in, I had to hide it like when we go south sometimes. Too many curious questions. Your folk cut and burn each other for the bastard joy of it. I can see the marks on you under your collar. But a couple of trims to my ears and everyone one of you have to ask. It's like the elders say—a thousand years and you still haven't forgotten to hate us."

"Good Lord," Whilte declared, suddenly understanding. "You're a fey?"

"He's one of the quick ones, is he?" asked the "farmer."

"He is too sincere to see lies in others. I am not so pure, more of a mongrel that way. So, what is your name?"

"You going to kill me if I don't tell you?"

"Do you really want to find out?"

The "farmer" drew in a deep breath, then shook his head. "Suyeer."

Prentice turned to Whilte. "Our new friend Suyeer here is a sentinel, isn't that right, Suyeer? How far from here is your village?"

"We don't have villages. We're not like you."

"Settlement, canton, hole in the damned ground," Prentice said dismissively. "Wherever it is that your elders meet and that you are the watchman for. How far is it?"

"Far enough and hidden enough that you will never find us."

"How do you contact them? You have a way to warn them, don't you, when armed men like us roll up on your false farm?"

"There's a signal."

"Well make it," Prentice said. "Your elders, leaders, whoever is in charge when your mistress is away. Call to them."

Suyeer spat on the ground, and his eyes flared angrily. He looked at Prentice's drawn dagger. Prentice expected the fey man had a fighting dagger of his own somewhere close to hand, if not on his person. That did not frighten the captain, but he would hate to have to use his own blade to defend himself now.

"They'll come and pepper you and yours with so many arrows that they'll call you *gresper*. Do you know what that word means? It means hedgehog."

"They can call me whatever they like, but do not doubt they will find us much harder than hedgehogs to kill. But you already know that. I told you my name and you know who I am, don't you? You live a long way from Fallenhill, but you do not need Reachermen to hear of me from. She has already told you to watch out for the Ashen one, hasn't she?"

"She tells us a lot of things."

"Well, send for your elders and I will tell you something different. Something better than what she has told you."

CHAPTER 50

"Three weeks passed already?"

Amelia stood alone at the opening at the south end of the castle's lower bailey, speaking to no one but herself. Ahead of her stretched the long flat of dried grass that had once been a fine green sward, beautiful for picnics and tourneys, surrounded on three sides by the protective, glittering waters of the lake. Now it was just a small plateau of beaten dust that dropped away to the wider flat of the desiccated bowl.

This is the place, she thought. This was where she ended her dream, with the hounds in a mire in front of her and a peacock on a throne behind her. Looking south, Amelia tried to picture the waters rising in the lake again, imagining the gleaming beauty of how it was, but her mind rebelled and all she could see was the engulfing muck of the mire from her dream. The level rose and threatened all to drown.

As she stared south, Amelia could make out the fading dust cloud of the next caravan of bearers. Three weeks had passed already, and her dream was the only change she had seen in her province's state of affairs. Master Welburne had received word that the next load of supplies would be ready as scheduled, and Amelia had sent word to Captain Prentice to dispatch another escort for their safety. The Lions had arrived at the march but with word that Sergeant Franken had sent them. Captain Prentice, the duchess was told, had gone into the mountains some days before, and no more word had yet been heard from him. Corporal Noam had the leadership of the new escort, and a letter written in a very rough hand begged leave to reassure her grace that he was a loyal and competent man for the task. Noam had marched with the captain on the previous escort and there was no other with more experience against archers ahorse. This time the caravan left with several wagons fitted to carry pavises made to cover the soldiers and bearers against arrows. The fey riders were still at large, and the knights martial had not yet brought them to heel.

That last notion had made Amelia laugh when she considered the hounds of her dream. For she was convinced the dogs were knights, and it made sense to her. Hounds were for hunting, wild instincts tamed to men's needs. What better way to envisage men-at-arms than as killers tamed to the service of society. Yet in her dream, they turned against her.

Was that the message of the dream that I must learn? she wondered. Are the knights untrustworthy? That brought another scoffing laugh to her lips.

Of course, the knights were untrustworthy. Just as hungry hounds might turn to bite their masters' hands, so the peerage would turn on her in their hunger for honor and glory. From the first day the Redlanders had invaded, the duchess had seen it played out again and again. It was almost a pattern in her life now. As if they were hounds, she fed the nobles from her hand, rubbed their heads and praised every little loyal action, and still the cur within them always lurked. Earl Sebastian seemed better than most, more willing to bite his tongue and know his place, but that was only while he dreamed of taking the seat beside her. Could she marry him? With no legitimate prince or king to speak to the issue, the matter was completely Amelia's to decide. Strangely, that only made it more difficult, not less.

At one level, the earl was the perfect candidate. He was of an age with her, vital and full of life. He was strong, proven in battle, and of the appropriate rank in the peerage. As duchess, Amelia had a right to expect to marry a prince, a duke, or, as in this case, an earl. Anyone lesser than that might be permitted. After all, she herself had been a commoner when her beloved Marne married her, but it would mean controversy. And with the earl fixed on the seat for himself amidst all the other chaos, if she chose another, it would only smash what little control she had over the peers of the Reach.

Suddenly, the words of Bluebird's verse from the feast in Griffith, *The Gull and the Golden Horns*, arose in her thoughts, and she recalled how the lapdog mutt in the tale had been supposed to be Prentice. If she had not understood the implication before, High Sacrist Quellion's confrontation now made it clear. Elsewhere in the Grand Kingdom, and likely in much of the Western Reach, people assumed that Prentice was a dalliance, a forbidden romance to console her in her young widowhood. That thought did not make her laugh.

Even if she had been inclined to defame her late husband's memory with such an indulgence, she was certain Prentice would never have allowed it. He would have gone back on the convict chain before submitting to that, doubly so now that he had his own wife who adored him and whom he would not hesitate to die for. That did make her laugh. Amelia imagined that if she even intimated a longing for Prentice's company in her bed, she would awake the next morning with her bedsheets soaked crimson and Righteous's favorite dagger thrust into her heart.

"That one cannot sit here," the preening peacock had said, as directly as Quellion had said it to her at the high table. Damn him and all the others who thought her so debauched. He did not ask her if she were dallying; he simply assumed it. He even excused it as a noble's right to indulge themselves a little. The theologian in him should make up his mind. Was it a shame or an entitlement?

Her anger was cast aside as a man surprised her, staggering out of the building to her right, cursing loudly and waving his arm around him in pain. The building was the huge stone barn where the transported convicts had once been chained before being sent to their various soul-purging labors around the Reach. She had assumed it was empty now as no convicts had been transported over the mountains since the civil war began. Amelia expected that any criminals convicted in the Grand Kingdom proper these days were simply drafted directly into the war to become rogues 'foot and thrown directly at knights as blade fodder in the time-honored traditions of *chivalric* warfare. It took her a moment to realize that the filthy man cursing before her was Prince Farringdon. He was bent over in pain, clutching at his left hand a moment. Then he stood and realized he was not alone.

"Your Grace, please forgive me," he said earnestly but still wincing in pain. He bowed himself over again, the courtly gesture mixed with a goodly dose of discomfort. "I had not realized that you were there. Your pardon."

"Of course, Highness," Amelia replied virtually by reflex. "Are you injured? Should I send for a chirurgeon or healer?"

The prince flicked his arm about, waving the fingers at the same time.

"I think I will be alright, Your Grace," he said, still grimacing despite his protest. "Dashed thing caught my fingers and squeezed them like a vice. Still, I don't think they are broken. Just hurting like the devil."

Amelia found herself smiling and wondered why for a moment, then realized that the prince's honesty was strangely refreshing to her soul, especially with her thoughts so vexed by the politics of the realm. Prentice was honest, and she missed it, but his was the fearless honesty of a predatory animal—a lion, in fact. He might hide himself away, but he rarely pretended to be something he was not. His company was too often a cold kind of comfort. Everyone else around her, loyal or not, was a guarded creature to some degree. That did not mean they were all as untrustworthy as the peers of Reach and Realm. Amelia knew she could trust Dalflitch or Turley, Righteous or Spindle, but none of them would be straightforward with her and each had their secrets.

Not so the prince, it seemed. Hurt, he cried in pain and made no boast of enduring it or claim of pity for it. Alone, he accepted his solitude, and in company he was polite and open, regardless of the ranks he stood amongst. A man who could rightly claim himself of birth above all men, and yet here he was, happily filthy in only his undershirt and breeks, feet bare and hand stinging.

Refreshing indeed.

"What is the dashed thing that squeezed you, Highness?"

"In here, if you'll allow me, Your Grace," said Farringdon, and he ushered her through the enormous rear doors of the convict barn. Inside, there were three of the White Lions' war wagons lined up beside one another. "I shared some notions with Captain Prentice a little while ago for improving his wagons and he kindly allowed me these three to experiment with since they were too heavy for the mud and too slow for the quick march to fetch the supplies from the riverside. That was the previous march, I should say." He pointed southward out the open barn door. "But the new caravan had no liking for them either, it seems, so I can still tinker."

"And what tinkering is it that injured you so?" Amelia asked, astonished yet further at the prince's humility. She tried to imagine any royal, or for that matter any peer or petty noble she had ever met, submitting themselves to craft labor like common guildsmen. No wonder he was so filthy.

"I've been trying to pull the yoke pole metal free of the...um," he paused and pointed at the place where the nearest cart's yoke was attached to the rest of the wagon by a wrought-iron hinge. "Free of...the jig...thing. That's what I've been calling it, the jig, though I am reasonably certain that is not the correct name. The pole can be freed and by one man. I've seen it done once, but for the life of me I cannot figure the art of it. And the stubborn thing sees fit to punish me for my failed attempts."

"Goodness," Amelia said, following the prince's explanation but having no helpful thing to offer from her own knowledge. Her merchant father had understood wagons and wagoneering, but he had never shared aught of it with her. "Couldn't a farrier help you?"

Prince Farringdon smiled politely.

"I think a cartwright would be of more use, Your Grace," he said without the merest touch of condescension. "But sadly, your lovely town has only two such craftsmen, a pair of brothers I believe, and both of them have just departed with the bearer caravan going south now. They were signed on to make the journey as fast and secure as possible, repairing any damage to the carts on the way. A master merchant from the Conclave commissioned them, I am told."

Amelia had not been told, but taking the cartwrights with him was the kind of thorough planning that she was learning was typical of Caius Welburne. The man probably didn't even roll over in bed at night without considering the business implications.

"Do you think you will be able to do the work without these cartwright brothers, Highness?" she asked. "I would not insult you to suggest otherwise, but if you need extra hands, I can send some servants to your aid."

"You are very kind, Your Grace, but your servants have enough duties to concern them, I think, and strange as it may seem, I rather like the challenge of defeating this problem by my own effort."

"Then I will distract you no longer, Highness," Amelia said and turned back toward the barn door.

Prince Farringdon called after her. "If I may, Your Grace, would you like some company?"

"I thought you were of a mind to continue wrestling with the wagons, Highness?"

Farringdon gently kicked the nearest wagon.

"I think we can say this rebellious fellow has won this round," he said with a smile. "He will keep, but with my fingers smarting like this, I think I am best off taking a break."

"Then you would be welcome company, Highness," Amelia said, and she offered him her hand to escort her. He moved to accept it, but reaching out his own fingers caused him to wince once more. Amelia felt apologetic, but the prince only waved away the moment.

"Perhaps if I take your other hand, Your Grace?"

Amelia smiled and they switched sides, heading out into the hot light.

CHAPTER 51

S uyeer gave his signal out in the yellowed pasture, whatever
  it was, since neither Prentice nor his men could discern it
from him simply standing there. Then he told them to wait.
So, they did. They camped overnight, clearing a wide space of
earth for their cookfires and keeping them small. Any stray spark
would have set the whole upland pasture to tinder in seconds.
The dry wash had just enough of a trickle to slake their thirst
and the ground was thankfully not so hard-baked under the
grass that they could not sleep.

Just after dawn the next day, the first three fey rode up on
sure-footed ponies like the ones ridden by the raiding archers,
if a little smaller. Prentice stood to speak with them, but they
ignored him and conferred with Suyeer. Once they had spoken,
the new fey took to the other side of the farmstead, sitting out of
sight like children making a show of ignoring a friend they have
come to dislike, or nobles shunning a fellow fallen from grace.

"These are just the first," Suyeer said when Prentice asked
about it. "They won't speak to you until all are gathered. Be
patient."

Initially, Prentice suspected that the fey sentinel might have
been plotting some kind of ambush but quickly dismissed that
notion after two more groups arrived—one pair and a clutch of
five. If the fey folk wanted to assault his little group, it would be
more sensible to gather into one company somewhere secret and
safe, then attack in force. Also, as he watched them, he saw they

were like the elder rider he had seen during the ambush in the gully. In fact, these were even more lined and aged-seeming than that outrider had been, and their hair was more silvery than any of the other fey he had seen. Some of them also seemed a little paler, though most were still brown from a life in the sun.

"How many do you think will come, Captain?" Corporal Gennet asked around midafternoon when the number reached fifteen. "Only, they'll outnumber us soon if this goes on."

Ironically, the more that arrived, the less worried Prentice became about conflict. These were not a single governing group coming together but an array of leaders of different groups gathering in a rare fashion. All of them had axes on their saddles, even the three women fey, as well as bows and quivers in purpose-built cases that hung on the backs of their saddle-tack. Nonetheless, they took no martial posture, posted no guards, and left their bows with their mounts at a distance, though several carried their axes with them. If they feared conflict, or plotted it, they were taking an awful risk not all having their best weapons to hand.

What persuaded Prentice most, though, that these were representatives of different clans and not a united nation was the scarves that they wore around their necks. Brightly colored, indeed the only bright things they wore, they were distinctively patterned like the embroidery of the horse archer's corselets, or for that matter, the Redlanders' tattoos or even Kingdom nobles' livery. Yet, despite the complexity of the patterning, each smaller group—pair, trio, or the like—that arrived together all wore the same pattern. The weaving was not decorative, Prentice was sure; it was a clan marker to pick strangers from family across the mountains. He wondered how many of the same patterns he had already seen when the archers had been riding at his men.

The recognition that there were internal partitions within the fey also encouraged Prentice that his own hopes would be realized. It was possible, of course, that whatever breakdown of structure the fey peoples practiced—whether clans, houses, or some other order he could not name—they nonetheless acted as one group under one leadership, a king or council of some sort. Suyeer said they had no villages, and their elders all seemed to be arriving separately, but what Prentice needed to know was whether they were always so disunited. Were they as factional as the Grand Kingdom, or was united action the norm regardless of familial loyalty? In essence, he needed to know if the army of riders harassing the Reach was typical or the result of an outside influence—specifically, the witch on the unicorn's influence.

Near sundown, Suyeer came to fetch Prentice from his men, telling him that he could only bring one other with him to meet with the fey elders.

"The priesty one," the fey sentinel insisted, indicating Whilte. "You can bring your weapons if you want."

Given that the space between the two groups would be no more than two or three hundred paces, Prentice was not too concerned about the meeting turning treacherous, though his wariness was piqued momentarily when he saw all the elders going to their mounts. He relaxed when each one unfastened his or her saddle and dragged it over to form a circle around a single tended campfire. Each elder sat on their saddle like a conquering king upon a throne, and a single gap in the circle was left. It was to this gap that Suyeer brought Prentice and Whilte and let them stand. Over twenty pairs of almond-shaped eyes regarded the two militiamen with a disinterested curiosity that made Prentice want to smile. They all frowned as if they wanted to know nothing about the captain and his men, but they were all listening and watching intently, nonetheless. The message was clear—we are curious and wary about you, but we don't want you to know we are.

"How do we begin?" Prentice asked Suyeer, but the false farmer shook his head and stepped back out of the circle.

"You called the meeting," he said as he went and leaned against the back wall of his hut. "You begin how you want."

Prentice shared a puzzled glance with Brother Whilte, but it was clear that the chaplain had no answers of his own for the question. Prentice cast his eyes over the gathering.

"I am Prentice Ash, Captain of the White Lions and servant of the Duchess Amelia of the Western Reach," he said, deciding that an introduction was probably the best beginning. "How should I call you?"

"We know who you are," said one fey man, with a green-and yellow-colored scarf about his neck. "We saw the day you were given that name, when you wrestled in the cinders of old Fallenhill. And we saw you take the head of the Horned Man."

"You see much," Prentice told him.

"Our scouts see so much more than you *kreff* imagine," another one told him. "And what our scouts see, we all see. We pass unseen."

"We pass unseen," the entire gathering repeated, almost like a chant.

A motto or a prayer? Prentice wondered.

"'*Kreff*'? Is that your word for me or my kind?" he asked.

"All lowlanders and the ancient mortals, unseeing since the Writhing Earth, are *kreff*. In our tongue it is the word for creatures who cannot see and do not know they are blind," a fey woman with a voice like the wind through dry leaves answered from the other side of the fire.

"You still have not told me your names, or how I should call you," Prentice said, starting to become annoyed. He was doing his best to be diplomatic and respectful. If this crowd of unfamiliar leaders had only gathered to lord their mysteriousness over him, this was nothing but a waste of time—time the Reach did not have.

"We do not give our names to *kreff* or any others for a thousand years," the woman explained in her breathy tone. "You know Suyeer's name only because you held him at the end of your blade."

Diplomatic and respectful, except for that bit, Prentice thought and nodded ruefully. Were they going to hold it against him?

"I apologize," he said and bowed his head to the assembly. If the gesture meant the same to the fey that it did to Kingdom folk, it did not seem to have much impact on their demeanors.

"For folk who do not share much of yourselves, you speak our language well," Whilte observed.

"We pass unseen," the woman answered, and the phrase passed amongst them all once more.

"You watch us? Close enough to learn our speech, and you say for a millennia?" Prentice mused out loud. "Our presence here, now, must make you uncomfortable."

"We pass unseen," they all repeated, but Prentice was sure he saw some uncertainty in their expressions. The arrival of the miners and other Grand Kingdom frontiersmen over the last generations must have come as more than a mild shock. Until now though, they had remained unseen.

"Have you come to hold us all at knifepoint?" asked the green-scarfed fey who had spoken first. "We know your kind hate us. You have your religious hunters who speak the name of a merciful god and yet show no mercy. Are they amongst you, behind you, driving you to our slaughter?"

"I have served such men," Brother Whilte answered before Prentice could say anything. "It is a shame that I have repented of. I did not know their evil until I had seen my own. Now I repent."

"Repent," the fey said, as if he recognized the significance Whilte invested in the word. Perhaps it was one that both languages shared. The elder was not impressed by it though. "It is easily said, not easily done."

"No, it is not," Whilte agreed. "It cost me my leg." He slapped the wooden stump beneath his knee.

"A crippled *kreff*," muttered another who had not yet spoken. "Doubly useless."

"Perhaps, but better crippled and blind than a servant to merciless men," Whilte retorted with pride. "Better to be weak and righteous than strong and wretched."

That seemed to touch something in the circle of fey, and the mood shifted somewhat. Prentice wondered what it was but knew that any guess he made would be no better than plucking ideas out of the air.

"Sit," said green-scarf, pointing to the ground. Prentice helped Whilte sit on the earth with his wooden leg, then sat cross-legged himself.

"I think we've just passed some kind of test," Whilte said quietly.

"Thanks to you," Prentice acknowledged. "I wonder what that means for us now?"

CHAPTER 52

Sitting on the dirt, it occurred to Prentice that he was now lower than the elders on their saddles, but perhaps that was a good thing. They were letting him show them the respect he had been trying to conduct himself with, sitting at their feet. It was a position of humility he doubted any Kingdom noble would accept, although Prince Farringdon might. Duchess Amelia, too, he realized as he thought about it, especially if it were for the good of her people.

"Tell us why you have come," said the fey woman with the sighing voice. "Truly and fully."

"We seek…" Prentice began and then he stopped. He wanted to be diplomatic, but he felt a strong pressure to be honest. These were not a folk who loved clever words and convoluted speeches, he was becoming sure of it. With a nod, he resolved to be completely truthful with them.

"Vengeance," he said flatly. "Vengeance and justice against a witch who sheds blood and befouls even the land she walks."

"Hah! This one still serves the merciless ones!" declared the fey who had called Whilte a cripple.

"Not so," said Prentice, and he sat up to unbuckle his brigandine, pulling it and his shirt over his head. Then he pushed up on one knee and turned to show them all his back with its savage scars. "I know their cruelty better than everyone who sits around this fire, and all the fires within a hundred leagues."

"If you know them as enemies," asked green-scarf, "then why do you come amongst us naming us witches, as they do? Why do you use their words with us?"

"Because I do not name *you* as witches," Prentice said and took a breath for a moment. He was about to take the main risk, to gamble everything on an obscure reference from an ancient scholar and a handful of half-formed impressions from battles with an enemy he hardly ever saw close at hand. "I name the serpent from the Redlands as a witch."

For the first time since Suyeer had brought him over, the council of fey elders looked more uncomfortable than hostile. As Prentice had hoped, whatever else the serpent priestess was to these folk, she was no beloved ally.

"So, if you know she is not of us, why do you come seeking her here with us?" another of the circle asked.

"Because we cannot find her, and *you pass unseen*."

Those words struck home, and Prentice was both pleased and surprised as the gathered council fell instantly to arguing with one another in their own tongue, speaking and gesticulating forcefully. He tried to track the flow of the debate, but it was quickly fruitless. Not only did he not understand their tongue, but even their gestures and facial expressions were not the same as Kingdom folk—as *kreff*.

"We appear to have broken a dam, Captain," Whilte whispered as he, too, watched the vehement conversation ebb and flow around the circle.

"Or lanced a boil," Prentice countered and Whilte seemed to like that notion.

"A moment of pain to bring enduring relief," he said pensively. "It is worth hoping for."

Prentice raised a hand to quiet the chaplain and his eyes narrowed as he watched closely. The fey disputing was now mostly swirling around green-scarf, with several individuals making a statement to him, each in turn, and then receiving a stern nod as if to say they had been heard and now should be silent for the others. Finally, the voices stilled and the night was quiet, with only the crackle of the fire and the buzzing of insects. Prentice waved an annoying fly from his face and realized that not one of the fey seemed beset by pests as he and his men were. Since the drought truly set in, flies had been virtually ubiquitous. They were the lesser scourge of every summer, and now, as so much rotted under the heat, they were pestilential in their swarming. But the fey seemed not to notice them, or perhaps the flies did not notice the fey.

How unseen can they be if they wish? Prentice wondered, but it was an errant thought. His main focus was on the fey in the vibrant green scarf, for he was now certain this one was a senior of some kind, an eldest amongst elders in some way.

"How much do you know?" the eldest asked him with a straight gaze.

"Too little," Prentice admitted. "Worse, we have forgotten much that we once might have known. Until they came from the west, we had no idea there could have even been Redlanders, and their ways are alien to us completely. We knew nothing of you either, save for stories so old we thought them false."

"We pass unseen until even in your memories you have not seen us," said the elder.

"But our sages have watched and seen the turning of the worlds since the Earth Writhed," said the sighing fey woman. "We have seen and do not forget."

"When did the earth writhe?" Whilte asked with sincere confusion. Like the chaplain, Prentice did not recognize the phrase specifically, but he had a good idea.

"When the mountain was thrown into the sea, I think Brother," he said and Whilte's eyes went wide with surprise and awe.

"You remember back to the Bright Age and the judgement of lesser heaven?" he asked in wonder. "Only the scriptural era and Far Jerusalem are more remote from us."

"Our sages remember," the woman asserted.

"What do you know?" the eldest asked Prentice again.

"We think that a curse was pronounced," Prentice ventured, "on you and on the lands of those who made pacts with you."

There was an audible hiss from the sighing woman, and two others beat the flats of their palms on their saddles. Lord only knew what that signified.

"The curse is on *them*!" the eldest said with a new passion in his voice, and he leaned forward angrily. "They lied and broke all faith with us. Stealing our secrets, they insisted we flee with them across the bitter water, and when we refused, they sought to make us slaves. The forests they felled and our hope they stole. Like the carrion bird of the east, so they would be kings of iron over all of life."

Prentice listened to the eldest's words that flowed like a recitation of ancient wisdom and was sure he was hearing the fey version of the same history he and Duchess Amelia had been slowly unfolding since the Horned Man first invaded. He had the pieces from his own visions and Solft's heretical history. There was the tale told by the Widow of the Wood, and now the fey account, preserved by their sages. He regretted not sending for Solft or even the crochety Pawley to come with him on this expedition. Their knowledge would have been invaluable. Perhaps in coming days, if everything else went well here, the Paper House might send a delegation because even though Prentice knew these revelations were fascinating, what he needed was a specific piece of information.

"What was the curse? Specifically?" he asked.

"We will not speak the words to you, *kreff*," said the eldest, but there was much less malice in the word this time, as if it were simply a recognition of fact, like calling a man a Masnian or a Veckander. Prentice and Whilte were not fey, so they must be "*kreff*."

"You pass unseen," Prentice said again.

"We pass unseen," the circle pronounced, and Prentice nearly recoiled with shock. He lowered himself carefully back off his knees, nervous that he might fall on his bum otherwise.

CHAPTER 53

"You speak a truth," said the fey woman.

"And you have seen us," the eldest added, and several faces turned hard expressions on Suyeer, barely visible in the edge of the firelight. There was another short pause and Prentice wondered if he was supposed to say something. He looked to Whilte, but the eldest spoke first.

"The Untrue came back across the sea, and our sages knew them," he said. "We sent our envoys to the *brakkis effar*—the Horned Man, you name him—to tell him we remembered the old breaking. For a thousand years we have hidden until we pass unseen even in memory, but we let him see our envoys to say just once that we would pass unseen for him and his force. Let the faith-breakers and their demons fight the merciless merciful ones. We take no part."

"The Horned Man did not take kindly to that message, did he?" Prentice said.

"Hanged upon our own trees, that is their curse for us," said the woman elder. "As if our bodies need to touch the earth to find rest for our souls." She seemed to mean the words as a kind of scoff, but there was a hesitancy in her expression that made Prentice think she did not quite believe them herself.

"He broke our envoys and asked them only one question," said the eldest. "Where was the Ashen One?"

That made Prentice start with surprise. He remembered that the Horned Man's army had seemed concerned to find this figure of an "Ashen" man, and that they had fixated on himself as that figure, but it was just a fool superstition, he thought. After all, what was he that they should fear him? It was a silly title that sounded brave when he needed to inspire men for battle, wasn't it?

"They fear you," the eldest said. "No fire will burn you away, they say. If they do not slay you, they will not have their vengeance. Their fell sages tell them this as a *nevaas*, a future remembered. They hate you."

"They are not the only ones," Prentice muttered, but next to him, Brother Whilte fixed on something else the eldest had said.

"A future remembered?" he whispered. "Is that prophecy, do you think? Can the Redlanders have prophets of their own?"

"Ancient Baal had prophets, so the scripture teaches."

"Indeed so."

"We saw our envoys die and knew the Untrue were as they had ever been," the eldest continued. "Then we saw their *brakkis effar* fall to your hand and we learned a new fear. We came across the mountains and refused the bitter sea to pass unseen in the mountains, the hills, and the grass. After a thousand years now, you *kreff* come across the mountains and take the land. More and more. You fight your wars and bind your own kind with iron chains. Like ants you are. We pass unseen, but eventually, when ants cover the whole of the ground, even the unseen are stung. You were a broken thing, bound under their iron, and yet you slew all. A mere *kreff,* yet you slew *brakkis effar* and your own iron wearers. Our young said we must strike, or else if we waited, you would kill the Untrue and turn upon us next. The elders told them to wait and see; we pass unseen. They did not hear us. They learned to fear you as the Untrue learned. And then she came to us."

There was a bitterness in the eldest's tone that made Prentice think he was ashamed to have to recount this story. The ancient past was fresh and certain in the fey elders' minds, it seemed, but recent days had them confused and unsure. The Redlanders' invasion, their return from self-imposed exile across the western sea, had surprised the fey as much as the Grand Kingdom, if not more. Even as the eldest continued the story, Prentice could guess what this next phase would reveal. Just as the invasion and the affliction of the land made the folk of the Grand Kingdom vulnerable to apocalyptic preachers and penny prophets, so it must have made the fey vulnerable to the savage and cruel gospel of the Blood Sects, the religion of the Redlanders, the *Untrue*.

"The serpent came amongst us slowly, as they always do, patient and tasting the air," the eldest continued. "She saw us, and the young let themselves be seen. She told them of a new way, the old curses broken and the iron tyranny of the carrion bird ended."

"What is the carrion bird?" asked Whilte.

"The Eagle of Denay," Prentice said and hushed his companion. This was the moment he needed to hear best. There was a truth here he could not let pass unseen.

"The young listened to her and showed her the way amongst us. We pass unseen, but she was allowed to see. Her promise was sweet, and she tasted the fear in the air amongst us. The Untrue are ever untrue, the elders said, but we were not heard. This was new, she said. Before, the Untrue had stolen secrets; now they brought secrets of their own. Before, they had enslaved and stolen. Now, they offered gifts and free friendship, she said. So, the elders were told they were wrong, that they saw things that no longer were. A new pact was forged, and in the next moment we who pass unseen grieved. What matter if we pass unseen when our grief is visible from the earth up to heaven."

He opened his mouth, and a strange, multi-tonal ululation came forth. It was not an animal-like sound, but it was not like singing either. It was as if a natural sound, a sound of the pure forces of the world, had been turned into a kind of music. The entire circle took up the grieving cry, and for a moment the night echoed with a sadness touching and alien to mortal men like Prentice and Whilte. As he listened, Prentice wondered what the rest of his men thought about it. He hoped they would not take it amiss. This council still had the potential to go badly, and a mistimed intervention by his escort would likely be the sort of thing to tip it in that direction.

As suddenly as it began, the mourning ceased. The eldest looked directly at Prentice through the red light of the diminishing fire.

"You *kreff* bind with chains of iron," he said with a tone like a pronouncement. "She has bound us in chains of blood. At first only the fooled tasted the blood she shed and the power she bound them with. Then, an elder sage was taken to her altar and the binding was vast. The sage looked the serpent in the eye and cursed her, mother to false mother, but it was too late. That shed blood took power over us all."

"Then the drought came on the land," said Prentice.

"That much you have seen," the eldest told him solemnly. "Now console our grief, tell us what *else* you have seen. Tell us or we will pass unseen away, our blood drunken away by the thirsty earth. Not since the Earth writhed has there been such fear upon us."

Prentice thought about his answer carefully, and then he raised himself up on one knee.

"We are *kreff*," he said first, willing to begin where they were. Pride was not going to help him here. This was their land, and if they wanted to, they could have ignored him and his men. They could have hidden away and "passed unseen." They had already humbled themselves, in their own eyes, by even meeting with him.

"We have not seen much, but not because we are willfully blind. The carrion bird and merciless preachers of mercy put blinders on us. Now, the Redlanders have returned. That much we have seen, and in seeing we also have learned to fear. Amongst us, though, we have also seen something else, something new to us, though we say that there is nothing new under the sun. Still, this is new to *us*."

Prentice paused and looked at each face around the circle.

"You ask what I have seen," he went on. "I tell you I have seen the lion that stalks by moonlight, whose mane is like the ribbon across the night sky and whose eyes are the dark between the stars."

He looked up at the sky where the glittering band of the Rampart shone from east to west on the northern side.

"We saw the lion, when he burned the *brakkis effar*, when you took the Horned Man's head," the fey woman said, her voice almost like a whisper. "But he only roars in our dreams from a distance. We have not seen him amongst our people. Do you bring him to us?"

"I have spoken to the lion in dreams and waking," Prentice explained, and he cast a glance sideways to see Whilte looking at him, as astonished by this revelation as by everything the fey had already said. Prentice gave his chaplain an apologetic shrug. He turned back to the fey. "I have spoken to him, and he has shown me things, but I do not bring him with me. He walks as he wills and no chain, iron, or blood could bind him unless he chose to bind himself."

Several of the elders seemed to approve of Prentice's words, and he felt confident to move to his conclusion. This was the do or die moment.

"You saw me bound under the iron chain," he said. "Then see that I am bound no more by a chain, only by my word to our Duchess Amelia. She is no elder sage, but she has also heard the lion in her dreams. He calls her to be a young mother, a mother to a new land."

That was cheating and Prentice kept from looking at any one person, chaplain or fey, in the eyes at this point. The claim of mother to a new land was an adaptation of the prophecy the Widow had given the duchess in the west. It had nothing to do with the lion, as far as Prentice knew, but if the lion was an angel of the Lord, or even the Lord himself in angelic form, the prophecy and the lion came from the same heavenly source. Hopefully, God did not think Prentice was cheating too much.

"In her name, as a true mother and breaker of chains, I ask you to trust us," Prentice said. "See us and see that we are true. Let us end the witch and the curse and make something new under the sun."

He drew out his champion sword and held the point at the fire. Not one of the elders so much as flinched at the bared steel.

"I took this sword from the last good man I ever hope to fight. I will bear it against all who hate my duchess, but for her allies I carry it to defend their every drop of blood. Allow us to unbind you from the witch and I swear I will never wield this blade or any iron over you."

The elders looked to each other then, and as the fire was dying still, Prentice could hardly make out their features. He wondered if the fire were allowed to fully die, would they simply vanish into the night? Would they pass unseen and leave his proposition unanswered?

"You want a new peace between us and the *kreff*?" the eldest asked.

"I want the *kreff* in the west, between the mountains and the river, to open their eyes and see. I want you to pass unseen or be seen as you choose, and to know no fear. I want you to come see the mother of a new land and see a new thing birthing. Midwife it with us. Then we will not fear you and you will not fear us."

"We do not fear you now," the one who called Whilte cripple said, more churlishly than with genuine defiance.

"Your young men do," Prentice countered. "They ride for her, bound by fear and blood. I know now they are bound because she whispers the same promises to men who dress in iron—carrion bird's men. Let me end that, end all of it."

"We have seen, and what you say is good to us," said the eldest, and many around the circle slapped their hands on their saddles. "But..."

For the first time there was real hesitancy in the fey's manner.

"But what?" Prentice urged, but the fey did not or could not answer. Then Prentice realized their problem. "But you are bound. Bound to her? Is that it?"

"There is life and much power in blood for those who do not fear the judgement of heaven. She has bound us by blood. We have sent no messenger, but be assured, she knows you have spoken to us. Even across vast distances, we can speak of her, but not defy her."

Oh, damn it all, Prentice cursed inwardly. *What was the point then?* A long night's conference at the end of a trek into the mountains and all he had to show for it was a series of simple facts he could likely have deduced for himself, given enough time.

"Your duchess young mother is a breaker of chains?" asked the eldest.

"She put off mine," Prentice answered wearily, hardly listening anymore. He was weary and felt defeated. He needed a good night's rest and a new plan in the morning. Perhaps he could send for Solft immediately. The scholar might have better luck getting useful intelligence out of these fey. Prentice no longer had the patience for it.

"The serpent who you call a witch has not come on behalf of her people," said the woman fey, her voice stronger than it had been before throughout the whole evening. "She is a false mother who seeks to birth her own land here. She claims to have the power to break the ancient curse of the Untrue, but still the land bakes dry. If she is the false mother and we have none who can stand against her, then perhaps your duchess young mother is the true. We have watched you bleed, and the arrows of our young have bled your folk in the serpent's service, and still you speak of a new way. I see you, White Lion, and you are true. The witch binds us to her secrets, but think, and you will see what you already know. The sun drinks the life of the land and there is life in the blood. Where must she go to slake the sun's thirst? See what you have already seen."

With the same clarity as he had in his dreams and visions, Prentice suddenly knew where the witch was.

"Thank you," he said earnestly. His fatigue temporarily washing away in the relief of puzzling out the secret, he half stood and then paused and dropped back to his knee. He sheathed his sword and looked around the circle. "I will hunt the serpent witch and take her head, as I took the Horned Man's. When you are free, come to me if you wish, and I will take you to Duchess Amelia."

"If you do this, we will let her see us," the eldest said. "Go now *kreff* and beware. Others who should not see are seeking you now. She knows of our meeting and will see you if you let her."

The elders then stood and took their saddles away into the night. Prentice heard them saddle their ponies and ride off. He poked at the near-dead flames of the fire.

"In all my days I never thought to 'see' something like that," Whilte said and rubbed his crippled leg where the stump was pressed against the wooden prosthesis. "They didn't say where the witch is, but you seemed to get some kind of clue from them anyway. Is that right?"

"I believe so, Brother, I believe so."

Whilte clearly anticipated more information, but the hopeful energy that Prentice had been feeling a moment before was ebbing swiftly. He was so tired that he almost felt he could lie down here and sleep now without even bothering to return to the safety of the rest of his men. He certainly did not have the strength to explain everything to the chaplain right now. He heaved himself to his feet and helped Whilte up with a groan.

"Not now," he said. "In the morning I will make it plain."

The two men made their way back carefully in the dark to where the Lions were waiting watchfully for their leader's return.

CHAPTER 54

"Damn it," Lady Dalflitch cursed as she half rushed, half fell out of the door to Amelia's apartment in the castle. The lady-in-waiting all but collapsed against the opposite wall, knocking her usually perfectly fitted coif askew and causing her skirts to gather and tangle about her legs. All of this would have been indignity enough for the elegant lady, but it also happened right in front of her mistress.

Amelia was returning from the ground floor solar to ready herself for the evening, having sent her ladies ahead of her, when Dalflitch exploded through the door.

"Are you hurt, My Lady?" she asked Dalflitch, who looked up at her in shock more than pain.

"I am quite fine, Your Grace," Dalflitch responded quickly, straightening herself up and rearranging her skirts. Amelia pointed discreetly to her lady's headwear, and Dalflitch reached up to resettle the pearl-laced piece back into place.

"You are bleeding," Amelia said in alarm, and she pointed again, this time to a fine trace of a line on Dalflitch's collarbone. The lady reached up and touched it, coming away with a sheen of crimson on her fingertips.

"A minor accident, Your Grace. Think nothing of it." Dalflitch fetched a kerchief from her sleeve and placed it to the cut.

"Well, let us see to it immediately," Amelia insisted, and she pushed the door to her apartments open to usher her lady-in-waiting inside. Before they could enter, however, they were confronted with the sight of a chair and table knocked over while Lady Spindle was pressing back into a corner of the room near to the window and Lady Righteous was standing facing her, back to the door. Spindle's mask was knocked from her face, and her scarred flesh was on display, even more flushed than the rest of her visage. The sound of the door drew both Lace Fangs' eyes, and as Righteous turned to look, Amelia could see past her shoulder that Spindle had a blade to hand and was half pointing it—at Righteous.

"See, Her Grace is here now," Righteous said. "Put that sticker up and let's have an end to it. You don't want me to have to take it off you."

"Maybe you couldn't," Spindle answered defiantly, and Righteous seemed to lose her temper for a moment.

"Don't fool yourself, Tress," she all but shouted. "You come a long way and you're a dab hand at cuttin', but I'm still your better, and if you have to find out the *hard* way, it *will* go hard for you!"

Spindle's defiant stance mellowed somewhat, and her poniard lowered a little, but her expression, if anything, grew angrier.

"Why d'you call me that? I'm Lady Spindle! That's my name. I earned it. Why say 'Tress'?" she demanded, her voice cracking with emotion. "You think o' me like she does! Like you all do! I'm just bagatelle to the lot o' you!"

"Oh, don't be bloody foolish," Righteous answered her. "I call you Tress cause I've known you since you were Tress, and when you go back to actin' like old Tress instead of Lady Spindle, then I'll damn well call you that! What, you think my man don't call me Cutter again when I say or do something as witless as this? Cause he does!"

"What on earth is this all about?" Amelia asked, astonished at the rising clamor amongst her normally demure chamber attendants. At her question, Spindle burst into tears and slumped against the wall, sliding down to sit like a weeping child.

"Just an accident, Your Grace," Dalflitch said again, slipping past Amelia toward the overturned furniture. Amelia noticed that she and Righteous shared a meaningful glance.

"An accident...?" Amelia began to ask, but Righteous talked faster.

"Nothing you need to worry about, Your Grace. Bit of frayed nerves, is all."

"Yes, frayed nerves," Dalflitch agreed. "Frayed nerves and a thoughtless word. A matter we can resolve without troubling you. If you permit me a moment, I will have the room restored to order—"

"Oh, for God's sake, shut up!" Amelia was not sure if it was her concern for these three women whom she loved like sisters and who were clearly at odds over something or if her own frayed nerves were robbing her of her own temper, but she had had enough.

"You all keep secrets, but do you think that is a mystery to me? You think I do not know how two will watch and cover with excuses while one of you sneaks off to take a moment with your husbands? And soon you'll have to fit Spindle into your rota of absconders, and she can have you two make excuses for *her*."

She waved her hand over the disheveled room.

"But this is not that. One of you has cut Dalflitch and I cannot allow that to be covered over with deception. Violence in my own chamber against a lady of rank? She is of birth, you know this."

"It's not like that, Your Grace," Righteous protested, looking back and forth to the other two. Spindle had her head buried in her hands while Dalflitch stood shamefaced.

"I...insulted Lady Spindle," the elegant lady-in-waiting admitted. "The fault is entirely mine."

"Insulted?" Amelia asked, knowing the matter could not be that simple. Her attendants routinely traded playful barbs and double entendres that drew so close to insult that it was a marvel they did not take offence more often. Amelia could hardly imagine how brutal the verbal exchange must have been for Dalflitch to call it an insult or for Spindle to reach for a blade to avenge it.

"T'weren't exactly an insult, Your Grace," Righteous clarified. "It's just..."

"Yes?" Amelia pushed.

"It's just, she said that Spindle's marriage, Welburne like, that he, that he was only marrying her cause she was your chamber lady. For the influence, like."

"I never said *only*," Dalflitch added. "I said it, but I never said he was doing it only for that. I'm sure...I *know* he has more than that intent. Babies for a start. He wants an heir."

"Until he sees my face," Spindle all but wailed, and beat her palm against her scars a moment while more tears ran down her cheeks. Suddenly, the subtext of everything that had happened felt open and bare in Amelia's mind. However hopeful, exciting, or worthy Caius Welburne's proposal was to Spindle, somewhere in her mind she was terrified that he would marry her and, having unmasked her on their wedding night, spurn her for her scars. Dalflitch's comment, coming from the loveliest woman any of them had ever met, so beautiful that she had wooed nobles and princes as a matter of professional pride, must have stung Spindle's deep fear. Amelia felt a sudden rush of compassion for her lady. She moved over next to Righteous and crouched down to take Spindle's hands from her face. One of them still held the fighting blade, which gave Righteous a moment's consternation, but even as she objected, Amelia was gently removing the weapon from Spindle's grip.

"Let's give this to Righteous for a moment, shall we?"

She handed the blade over her shoulder, never taking her eyes off Spindle.

"Tell me, Lady, what if you *were* still just Tress with none of your history?" she asked her. "No conviction and transportation. No ravishment or wounds. Just ordinary Tress, the seamstress. What if a young man came to you one day and said he wanted to marry. He had heard you were a great seamstress, because you are, and he counted that a valuable skill in a wife. How would you feel?"

"Proud, I guess," Spindle said, wiping her nose with her sleeve.

"Indeed, you would, as well you should. But would you be offended if this man only counted you plain to look on?"

"I might not like it."

"But if he was loyal, worked hard, stayed home, and had no wandering eye?"

"I s'pose if he stayed faithful there'd be nothing to complain about."

"Exactly," said Amelia. "So, what is the difference between that and Master Welburne seeing your scars?"

"But scars ain't plain, Yer Grace." As Spindle's emotions had risen, so her attempts to speak in a higher manner diminished. "You see me. I'm ugly."

"Well, Master Wellburn's no fine figure of a man himself," Amelia joked, and both Righteous and Dalflitch smiled.

"Easy for you three," Spindle still objected. "None of you's ugly."

"No? Thank you, Spindle," Amelia said, pretending the words were meant as a compliment. "But I think you are missing the point. As fair as I may be, and there is more debate than you seem to admit, do you think I would have made a match with my husband if not for my dowry? Without the silver my father made, Duke Marne, beloved though he was, would never have looked twice at me, would he?"

Spindle nodded a little, and Amelia went on.

"Or consider Lady Dalflitch. She is as fair as any woman I have ever known, as well as cunning from birth and, by all accounts, as skilled in love as any decent woman has a right to be."

Dalflitch tutted in mild offence, but Amelia gave the lady a cocked eyebrow and dared her to object to the characterization. She did not.

"She has made matches for herself and even had the love of a prince, such as it was, yet I assure you, for all her loveliness, she could not make Daven Marcus spare even a single breath to speak with her of marriage."

"It's true, Spindle," Dalflitch agreed, and Spindle returned the beautiful lady-in-waiting's earnest smile a little hesitantly.

"What about Righteous?" Spindle asked, somewhat playfully now that her mood was comforted, and her tears were drying.

"Righteous?" Amelia said, glancing over her shoulder. "Isn't it obvious? You've seen Captain Prentice, and you know the mass of scars he is under his clothes. What has the lady said her husband looks like? A half-chewed ham? If that is not proof that love overcomes scars, My Lady, then what is?"

Righteous shrugged affably as the duchess stood and offered Spindle her hand to help her up.

"No, Your Grace, you shouldn't," Spindle objected, but Amelia insisted. When they were both on their feet, Amelia hugged her lady.

"Master Welburne is a calculating man, Spindle," she told her. "But he is not disloyal and not quite as cold as many think, I'd say. I would not wait around for sonnets and swooning, but once he cleaves to you, expect that he will not be faithless."

There was a knock at the open door, and Solomon poked his head around it. The first few days after the drummer had been left behind, he had been sour in mood, not to mention in pain in his face. Soon though, Righteous had judged him fit to start learning, and in the weeks since he had begun to know the castle and run about it like any other page. He was so useful as a messenger to the duchess that Amelia had rewarded him with one of the castle's master keys, giving him access to all but Dalflitch's treasury, which had been moved back to the castle from its place in the Conclave Hall. After her run-in with

Quellion, Amelia had not wanted Dalflitch traveling back and forth in the town for fear that another street preacher might do something foolish. Solomon's cheek wound was healing well enough that he wore no bandage as he stood in the doorway, but the scabs were not fully gone, and the underlying scar was fresh and angry red.

"See, Spindle, facial scars are all too common," Amelia said, gesturing to Solomon. "Indeed, they are almost becoming a mark of high service. Given the loyalty of the three scarred faces currently present, I could wish that more of my Lords and Ladies were so marked and for equally good reasons."

She waved Solomon into the room, but as she looked, she noticed that the lad was breathless, a sign he had run here at full pelt, and there was an expression of deep anxiety in his eyes.

"What is it?" she asked him.

"There's a messenger come from Fallenhill," Solomon said, saluting the duchess like she was an officer of the White Lions. "It's bad. He says the captain...the captain's gone missing."

CHAPTER 55

"**S**he needs blood to perform her sorcery," Prentice told Whilte and Corporal Gennet as they marched beside him.

"We sure seen enough o' that at Halling Pass," said Gennet grimly.

"The life is in the blood, so the scripture says," Whilte observed from a theological perspective. Prentice thought he remembered the reference, but he had no idea how that might help him in this specific instance. In truth, he did not care exactly how the witch extracted power through blood sacrifice. What he wanted to know was how to take the power away from her.

"At least now, we know how to hunt her," he muttered, but the two men with him had no idea what he meant.

"How's that, Captain?" Gennet asked and he looked to Whilte, who shook his head to show his ignorance as well.

"She needs shed blood for power, that much we know," Prentice mused. "And that matches with what we have seen elsewhere. In Aubrey across the Murr, the serpents forced neophytes to sacrifice their own family members to enter their foul creed. That's a lot of blood for a seemingly small transition. But I saw arcane power made from simple tracings of spells on the ground. Folk struck dead just by crossing a line of writing in dried blood."

"How then do we measure her power?" asked Whilte.

Prentice shook his head.

"I do not think any of us could say for sure, unless we sold our souls to whatever gods they worship, or if they had some holy writings we might steal from their temples."

"Unholy writings, you mean, Captain," said Gennet.

"Holy to them, unholy to us," Whilte differentiated. The corporal nodded with the solemnity of a man attending a church sermon.

"Bad stuff, either way."

"I keep thinking of something Earl Yarmass' son, Sir Haravind, said when he attacked me," Prentice went on. "He said the witch had promised him vitality and power. That is why he felt confident to attempt so wild an assault, I would think. He expected something magical to empower him from the women he helped rape and butcher."

"A dark blessing of sorts?" said Whilte.

"Maybe he figured he'd be a wild power, like them beast men?" offered Gennet. "Maybe he saw himself sprouting fangs and claws or something? Growing big like them bull-men at Red Sky."

Prentice nodded and touched his finger to the side of his nose while pointing, as a gesture of shared understanding.

"I think you have the quarry's scent there, Gennet," he said. "I wonder if Haravind thought she had turned him into some kind of beast-man. The way he swung the sword about, as if he could sweep men aside like ninepins."

"He looked like any other ordinary bloke to me, I mean, other than he was a noble knight, like," said Gennet.

"Perhaps she gave him the power, but it didn't take," offered Whilte.

Prentice looked down at his feet as they continued to march, thinking. The ground under them was rocky, all broken and pebbled, as they made their way beside the diminished mountain stream.

"We're almost to that mine camp," someone in the line said happily behind Prentice, the man's voice echoing faintly off the stone walls of the ravine around them. "Hope they got some o' them hares in the pot like they had before."

"They weren't hares, they was rodents," another said.

"I don' care what they was. It was tenderer meat than I had in years. You tried the stringy rubbish the butchers in Dweltford are passin' off as coney?"

There was a round of communal grumbling at the current state of the Reach's meat markets, but Prentice hardly listened. He was looking at the terrain and realizing the iron miners were only around the next bend in the stream. That meant they were a day and half's straight march from Fallenhill, since they could cut out much of the wandering they had followed on their way up into the hills.

"I'm considering, Captain," said Whilte after another moment. "If the magick did not take to the man, then how much blood would she need, do you think?"

"As much as she could get," Prentice answered without really concentrating. In his mind, he was already composing some of the orders he would have to give to Sergeant Franken when he got to Fallenhill, as well as a message to the duchess to update her on his investigation.

"Maybe it's not the quantity but the quality?" offered Gennet. "Like, you know, vermin versus hares. 'Course, sometimes it's got to be quantity, since there's so many of their damned magicks everywhere. I mean if they use it in their markings and writings, is it in every tattoo they stick on their bodies? And their sails all painted intricate like. That's a lot o' blood, no matter the quality."

"You think that she needs lots of dead and noble dead as well?" Whilte asked. "I might have agreed with you once, Corporal, but as your chaplain, let me assure you that the Lord God in Heaven does not value a prince's soul above a pauper's. He died once for all, that all might be saved, even a thief beside him on a cross."

Gennet tugged his forelock to the chaplain and let the matter drop. Prentice appreciated Whilte's fair-minded theology, but he could not help but wonder if Gennet was at least partly correct. He thought about the bitter multitude that had fallen under the Redlanders' violence. Fallenhill had been burned alive, one and all, but in the midst was Baron Stopher, chained to a cross and cooked in his ceremonial armor. Prince Farringdon's father, Forsyte, was nailed to the pinnacle of the dread pyre raft used to call down the Red Sky. At every turn, it seemed, the Redlanders loved bloodshed in numbers, but still they reserved important figures for special torment. Even the noble mistress of Halling Pass and her daughter had been especially violated, as if more abuse after that much horror could extract a further power.

But it does not always take, Prentice thought. The notion connected with another in his mind—the theological idea, long discredited in his beliefs, that those born highest were the best of all humanity. The peers of the realm loved the pretense that their birth was a measure of their virtue, but at every turn they made a lie out of that thought. Nobles protected themselves and exploited their position as much or as little as their consciences allowed them, just like any other folk—high, low, or in between. Some sought the highest values and tested themselves against stern ordinances of character, like Prince Farringdon. But for every such *noble* nobleman, there were a myriad of Daven Marcuses, Yarmasses, and Haravinds.

And over it all, Mother Church taught maintenance of the righteous order, even when it produced no righteousness. "Merciless preachers of mercy," that was what the fey had called the Church, and Prentice could think of no better description. He rubbed at his armor, where his skin beneath the scars from his time in the hands of the Inquisition's "mercy" started to itch involuntarily.

"Shouldn't we be there by now?" a man on the march asked. "I can't hear nothin'. Have they packed up and gone off already?"

"Damn it, no hares for us," said the complainer for good meats.

Prentice's heavy thoughts slowed him down a moment, but he realized that his men were right. They should have heard the miners working the stone with their tools by now. He pricked up his ears and then heard an unexpected sound—singing. It was faint and gentle, blending into the natural sounds of the mountains like any other birdsong or animal calls. Yet it was a human voice, there could be no doubt. Prentice listened as attentively as he could, trying to pick the meaning, but it was certainly in a tongue he did not know. At least he did not think he knew it. The more he listened, the slower his thoughts seemed to become. Soon it felt like he was wading in deep water, his legs too heavy to lift and step.

"Do you hear that?" Brother Whilte groaned, but his words seemed to come from far away.

"Oh, bloody hell," Corporal Gennet exclaimed as a number of men collapsed in the line of march. Some of their fellows tripped over them, and then lay across their comrades as if passed out from drink. Gennet himself went down next.

"Sorcery?" Prentice gasped. He tried to turn away and draw his weapon, but it felt like he was swimming through treacle. His knees buckled, and the sweet singing cloaked his mind like a blanket. He felt the cool of the pebbles against his cheeks as he slid to the ground to lie flat. It was a feat of strength just to keep his eyelids open.

Ahead, a small group of folk stalked along the stream bank. Prentice watched their doeskin-garbed legs and low-booted feet coming towards him as if through a distorted glass. He heard the sound of a blade being drawn.

"No," said a voice, and Prentice realized it was the strange singer, no longer singing but giving orders. "The song works because it only brings sleep. The power within him rouses for battle. Try to use steel, and I will not be able to restrain him, him or his men."

What power? Prentice thought, but he could not form the words.

"Besides," the singer's voice went on, "your mistress wants him alive. And leave the others, too. Steal if you want but no deaths. When they awake, there will be only mystery and no certain response. Kill them all and the rest of the lion pride will be stirred against you."

"We can outride them," hissed a different voice with an accent foreign yet familiar to Prentice's ears. He wanted to turn his head, to see who was speaking, but even keeping his eyes open had become too difficult.

"You can outride them, but what of your fellows up in the farther mountains? Aren't you doing all this for them?"

"We are doing this for her," said the foreign voice.

"And in so doing, you are protecting them." The singer was giving orders, but he was not their leader, exactly, it seemed. Prentice felt hands grab his body and lift him from the stones.

"We will bring this one, too," said the foreign voice. "She likes the ones with power."

"Suit yourself. Just keep your knives and axes in their sheathes."

Then the singer began to sing again, and Prentice felt his mind pushed further and further downward, until even the song faded and he slipped away into darkness and silence.

CHAPTER 56

"He's not dead? You know that?" Righteous said for the fifth or sixth time.

"No one is arguing with you, My Lady," Amelia responded, trying to remain patient with her lady bodyguard. Righteous's devotion to her husband was laudable, but merely refusing to believe he was dead until his body was found did not help the current situation much. In the days since word of Prentice's disappearance had arrived from Fallenhill, Amelia had given permission for the sergeant in charge to send numerous patrols into the mountains, looking for him. The original escort who had marched with him returned from the mountains remembering almost nothing of their time there. All they knew for sure was that they awoke beside a mountain stream one morning and Captain Prentice and Brother Whilte were missing.

"Let me and Righteous speak to these militiamen," Spindle said in what Amelia had come to know as her killing voice—a low, pitiless tone that contemplated any form of violence to achieve its ends. "'Specially this corporal. He's got more to tell than he's letting on, I'll wager."

"Corporal Gennet is a loyal man, and true," Prince Farringdon objected. "At least he always seemed that way to me. If he says he doesn't remember what happened, then I would believe him."

"That was the sergeant's impression as well," said Amelia, holding up the two letters she had received from Franken, the

first detailing Prentice's disappearance and the second outlining his further searches. Prentice's men had been questioned at length, including the corporal, and although
Franken had not used the kinds of judicial torture that were
common in other parts of the Grand Kingdom, it was clear
from his letter that he was not lax either. She cast the two
letters onto the high table and slumped backward into her
chair. A single beam of light penetrated a crack in the high
shutters and reflected on the glass insert of the table's surface
where the captured war banner of King Kolber was still preserved. The beam played painfully in her sight, and Amelia
closed her eyes against it, rubbing her temples.

"And what of the scholars that Prentice spoke with before
he left?" she asked. Hoping to learn some clue of where
in the mountains Prentice had been going before he disappeared, Amelia had sent Turley to Master Solft and his little
academy. What the steward had discovered was equally as
mysterious and as troubling as the captain's disappearance.
For three nights running, a mob had gathered, stirred by a
religious rabble rouser to try to burn the Paper House to
the ground, claiming that it was their heresy that must have
prompted the drought as a curse from God. Turley said that
when he arrived there was only one member of the house
present, a former knight named Arosten. He had told the
duchess's chief steward that with the regular threat to their
precious texts, the scholars had resolved to sneak out in the
daylight hours in small numbers, smuggling important parts
of their library with them. Arosten alone remained to try to
protect the house itself, but the scholars were in hiding.

"They are gone, as near as we can tell, Your Grace," said
Turley. "Gone to ground."

"The word has been passed to the rats," said Righteous,
"to keep watch and help them out if they surface."

"Which is to the good," Lady Dalflitch said. "But they are
few. Master Welburne has persuaded the Conclave to set bailiffs

to try to find them and bring them to the castle for their safety, but..."

"But what, My Lady?" Amelia asked without opening her eyes.

"Bailiffs are not normally welcomed anywhere, Your Grace," Dalflitch explained. "They keep the peace, but they also collect the taxes and let their palms be greased. There have always been quarters where the bailiffs would not walk alone at night. Such parts of the town have become dangerous for them in the day as well. I think the rising tensions have given many a sense that the normal order is slipping or gone for good."

Sumptuary sedition from the greatest to the least, Amelia thought. Earl Sebastian would doubtless tell her to condemn the whole of Dweltford, except that in her eyes, he was no less a guilty party than the rest. In all likelihood, the earl would lay responsibility at her feet. High Sacrist Quellion certainly would, blaming her unmarried status for everything.

"The dockside, in particular, is unruly," Dalflitch said. "Two bailiffs tried to settle a dispute between river crews that was getting violent. The crews turned on the bailiffs, beat them, and threw them off the docks. One of the two did not survive."

"That'll be the Ragmother's whelp's doing," Turley muttered.

"Who is that?" Amelia asked, opening her eyes.

"A nasty young man of frustrated ambition named Fulford," said Farringdon. "A riverfolker who thinks he should run Dweltford, and, I suspect, the whole of the Western Reach."

"At least," Turley agreed with a sneer. "He could rule from here all the way to Masnia and still not be satisfied, I'd say."

"Fancies himself another little Daven Marcus, does he?" Dalflitch asked with equal contempt.

Oh Lord God, another player and another faction I must consider? Amelia thought, and she felt a sudden deep urge for Prentice's presence. His advice and strength would be such a consolation.

"My town is a nest of vipers," she whispered, and a sudden image of the vicious serpent from her dreams rushed into her mind. It was so hateful and terrifying, and it made her start with its vividness. For a moment she thought it was another vision, such as she had had when the Kingslayer had feasted his court right here in her hall, but it was not. It was just a rush of fear, and it had the strange effect of striking her mind like a splash of cold water to her face. She almost laughed at that notion, since she could hardly remember what cold water felt like. She sat up in her chair and adjusted her bodice and sleeves.

"No, they are not vipers," she said in a tone like a pronouncement. "They are like unto a flock, hounded on all sides, and in their fear, they bite and kick at each other and at the shepherds seeking to bring them to safety."

"We had a stampede one night during the siege at Fallenhill," Righteous said somberly. "That sure felt a bit like this."

"Stuck in the middle of a whirl out of control," Spindle added. "Madness and noise and animals gone crazy, slammin' themselves to death. Yeah, a bit like this."

"How did you survive?" asked Dalflitch.

"We gathered around the safest spot with poles and torches to drive the herd away. Then we just fended 'em off until they run themselves out. Fire was driving them crazy, but when the rain come in the morning, that put out the fires."

Amelia put her hands, palm down, on the table.

"Well, I will continue to pray that morning brings the rains to end the fires of this drought," she said. "As I'm sure you both did that night."

"I don't think I had time enough to pray, Your Grace," said Righteous.

"I sure did," said Spindle and the two exchanged the chuckles that only comrades in arms who survived the same testing experience can.

"Yes. In the meantime, I am not content to let my people stampede against themselves until they are dead," Amelia continued. "Not while I can think of anything else to do for their good. So that is what we need now—plots, plans, any devising that we can put our hands to, to put our land back into order."

"Including finding my husband?" Righteous asked.

"Especially finding your husband," Amelia reassured her. "He is a resource I do not like doing without."

"I agree, Your Grace, that we must devise new plans to hold together what remains of your lands," Dalflitch said quietly, almost fearfully. It was such an uncharacteristic public lack of confidence on the lady's part that it almost threatened to knock Amelia back into her fears.

"I only worry," the lady seneschal went on, "that perhaps we no longer have enough pieces to put things back into right order."

"Then we shall have to find new pieces," Amelia said, determined to hold to her resolve and not give way to fear or self-pity.

"Perhaps what you need, Your Grace, is a new order," said Prince Farringdon enigmatically. Amelia looked at him and shook her head in good-natured wonder.

A new order? What would such a thing even look like?

CHAPTER 57

Prentice's chest and stomach were in agony as he bounced along, slung over a horse like a sack of grain. A rope that bound his wrists was looped under the mount and tied to his ankles as well, so he had no chance of escape. He did his best to control his motions and reduce the pain, but the position they had him in gave him so little purchase. He had no way of knowing how long the eldritch song had left him unconscious, but he knew he'd been in motion for a day and a night since he awoke. He had thought to pretend to still be asleep for a while, to try and spy on his captors, divine any secrets they might let slip, but they had been aware of his wakefulness almost immediately. By the time they stopped at the end of the first day a waterskin was offered to his lips and he was so thirsty that he simply took it in his mouth and drank as much as they allowed him.

"Fear not, *kreff*, we'll not let you die," said a fey voice. "She wants you more than she even wanted an elder."

"I thought it was only women she hated," Prentice said through dry lips, coughing dust turned to mud with the water he had just drunk. His comment earned him a cuff across the head, but the fey then moved on.

"Her hate is nothing like ours after a thousand years of cowering from you," the fey said at a greater distance while there was a coughing and spluttering, mixed with a splashing sound. Someone else was getting a drink. Another prisoner?

"We will put you on your own iron chains," the fey continued as the other prisoner took his one life-giving drink for the day. "Then you will fear us for a thousand years."

"To bind us with iron, you let her bind you with blood?" Prentice challenged. The other prisoner choked off his drink and cried out.

"Captain Ash, is that you?"

Brother Whilte? Before Prentice could respond, there was the hiss of a blade coming from a sheath.

"Shut your cripple mouth, *kreff*. Him, she wants. You're just extra. Make so much as a whisper and my blade will drink you dry." There was a horrid gurgling sound and Prentice feared the fey was slitting Whilte's throat.

"If she makes you so free, why do you still fear me?" Prentice demanded as loudly as he could, not able to raise his voice to a shout with his head hanging down so awkwardly, and his chest and stomach in so much pain. He hoped to draw the fey away from killing Whilte. He was rewarded with having his head wrenched upward painfully so that his eyes met, upside down, the face of their tormentor. He was like any other fey Prentice had seen—deeply tanned skin, long straight, fair hair, shaved at the sides to reveal his ears. His eyes were a rich, emerald green, and on his high cheekbones there were sigils, like Redlander magical writing. These did not look like tattoos, but rather more temporary, like face paint. Did that mean these fey were not a part of the Redlander cult? Not converts but something else? Perhaps the writings were the spell by which she bound the riders. Would wiping off the paint break the spell? Given that merely touching other Redlander writings had resulted in death, Prentice was not eager to experiment.

"I do not fear you, *kreff*," the fey growled, his face so close to Prentice's that spittle fell in his eyes. "You are *palpolon*, saddle baggage, nothing more to me."

"You fear her, and she is *brakkis effar*. I have faced and slain them," Prentice taunted. "I took the head of the Horned Man. If you fear her and she fears me, then *you* fear me!"

The fey laid his long knife on Prentice's throat, but at that moment another fey voice called out. It was not the voice that had sung the sleeping song, but it was the one who had spoken with that one.

"Leave him, Hanrayr!" the second fey commanded. With instant obedience the fey named Hanrayr withdrew his steel and stepped away, violently dropping Prentice's head so that it struck the horse's flank. The response was so immediate that Prentice assumed it had to also have the force of magick behind it. After a moment, the face of the elder fey outrider who's eyes penetrated Prentice's ambush at the gully appeared in front of him, gripping his head as cruelly as Hanrayr had.

"I know you," Prentice said, his head ringing from the combination of the simple thump and his hunger and thirst.

"You saw me as I saw you," the elder confirmed. His cheeks had similar writing upon them to Hanrayr, if perhaps a little more complex-seeming. Prentice could not tell for sure. His vision was blurring.

"She does not allow you to pass unseen," he told the elder.

"Who are you, that you speak our words and know of our ways? For a thousand years we have passed unseen."

"I am something new, I think, or an old thing that was broken in ages past and forged anew by God."

As soon as he spoke those words, Prentice felt as if something he had known for a long time but not fully understood was suddenly completely in his grasp. There was a new purpose coming upon this land, this Western Reach, a new place full of vibrancy that connected two lands with ancient corruptions—the Grand Kingdom and the Redlands. Like the heat of the forge, so the drought was tempering the land and readying it for its purpose. Soon the quench would come, and the Reach would know itself for what it was meant to be. The Widow of the Wood had told

Duchess Amelia that her descendants would sit upon a throne. The Reach was that throne, Prentice knew that now, somehow, but he was sure the serpent witch knew it too. She was trying to subvert the Reach's purpose. As Amelia had freed him and he had built her a new army, the White Lions, so the witch perverted the true purpose of the land, making an army for herself with which to seize the throne of the Reach. Just as Duchess Amelia made a way for men to leave their chains behind, so the witch made a pathway for her followers into further slavery and binding.

And somehow Prentice knew, looking into the elder's eyes, that this eldritchly bound fey understood the same thing. The duchess and the witch, the righteous and the unholy possibilities of the Reach.

"You ask who I am?" Prentice said to him, the power of revelation giving sudden strength to his voice. "I am one who has suffered at the hands of the merciless preachers of mercy. Look at my scars and see that I was broken but am yet here. They claim the words of God fall from their mouths, but they lie. God sees all. If he spoke his words to them, he would tell them of you, and you would not pass unseen."

"You want us to turn from her lies to theirs?" the elder said with a contemptuous glare. "She lied to us *and* to them. Are you any different? She and they have power in their promises. Do you?"

Who is "them"? Prentice wondered. Who else was playing a hand on this table?

"I have seen power from Heaven," Prentice said. "But you must test my words for yourself, as I have done."

"So you speak for God who sees all, who made all at the beginning?"

"Not *for* him," Prentice said, shaking his head and feeling the pains still there. "He has messengers who speak for him. He does not need me. But I have seen *them*. I have walked with the Lion in the moonlight, servant of the holy God. You have heard him roaring in the night, and I have heard him speak. When I took the Horned Man's head, he came to my aid and slew the *brakkis effar* with thunder and fire. Your people saw that day."

"Can you summon this lion to your aid?" the elder asked.

"I cannot summon him. He walks where he will. But I have learned to trust the word he brings, and I trust that God will send him when the need is there."

"You speak our words and hopeful words, *kreff,*" said the elder with an expression that seemed to mix anger and sadness. "But she spoke words with great power, and we have listened to her. For a thousand years we have passed unseen."

"But not unseen by the Lord who sends the Lion, I know it." Prentice felt almost like he was pleading now. "If God can reach down into the coals and pull out a piece of old iron like me, reforging it into a weapon, then what can he do for you? Perhaps the witch has enslaved you to prevent you from coming into something better, something new. Perhaps even a land where you can pass seen and be known without fear."

"If you could summon the Lion, then maybe I could believe you *kreff.* I have seen the beast that she summoned and how she has made it like herself. Show me the Lion in the moonlight and I will see you then."

Then the elder dropped Prentice's head again and he passed out from exhaustion and discomfort.

CHAPTER 58

"Your Grace, may I have a word?"

Amelia turned from her pacing on the Great Hall dais to see Prince Farringdon entering from a side door. The duchess had received word that a small company of knights ahorse had arrived at the town gates, and that Earl Sebastian was one of them. Where the rest of the Reach's knights martial were to be found, there was no mention.

"Is your need urgent, Highness?" she asked, and noticed that he had his longsword and belt hung at his waist, though he wore no armor.

"Not too urgent, Your Grace," Farringdon began, then noticed she was looking at his armament. "The unruliness in the streets and docks is growing, Your Grace. Twice now I have intercepted bravos thinking to sneak in the castle through the back and perhaps thieve something of value."

"More likely they come for food," Amelia said reflexively. "Though we have no more than anyone else."

"A castle speaks to treasures, no matter the form imagined, I think, Your Grace."

Amelia nodded at the prince's wisdom. "What was the matter you wished to discuss? I have word that Earl Sebastian will soon be here, and I do not know why he has come. My guesses do not give me much comfort."

"Well, since the *stampede* has not yet abated," the prince said, drawing on the metaphor from days before, "perhaps having a few knights returned to help defend your seat of power will be of benefit."

Amelia cast a swift glance at the main chair on the other side of the high table. Her "seat" of power.

"If only I can afford the cost," she said before looking back to the prince and then to the main doors of the hall. Shouldn't the earl be here by now?

"You should not have to pay for loyalty you are already owed."

"I cannot raise an earl, that he should owe me his loyalty, if I do not rule correctly in his eyes," Amelia said. "Only a prince or king can raise a knight or baron in his lands, and higher ranks are all to king alone reserved. They may owe me fealty, but only if I stand myself in their good stead.

"But come, Highness, the earl must draw near soon, and I will have to meet him privately. The Lace Fangs are on their way, but you should not be here. I suspect it will be sovereign issues of the Reach the earl will wish to discuss."

"Well then, Your Grace, in short, I was thinking to ask your permission to move those three war wagons to block the rear access to the castle. And if you will permit me to suggest, perhaps your castle garrison could sleep at nights in their tents in the lower bailey instead of the barracks."

"Move the wagons and the garrison, Highness? Why?"

"To secure the castle's rear, Your Grace. You can draw the bridge and protect the main gate at night, but as I said, the most brazen are already trying to sneak up in ones or twos. There need only be one rabble rouser on the docks one night to gee a hundred or more up, and a mob will be through that gap and in here to tear your home apart in an instant. The lake was a goodly moat when it was full. Now it is little more than an open invitation."

"Oh God," Amelia said, her hand to her mouth. She had thought to defend her castle against fey horse archers, not her own people in riot. "This is why I need Prentice. I *never* even thought, but I know he would have. Or even the earl. Oh God, why must I never have nobles I can fully trust?"

Amelia felt her nerve slipping, and she thought to call for some wine, but there were no stewards about. She had sent them away to let her meet Earl Sebastian in private. In truth, she had half expected she might have to beg him to return and put the unrest in her capital down for her, as he had in Griffith. She had not wanted to do *that* with any witnesses.

"Pity we are not on the Masnian border, Your Grace," Farringdon said pensively, and Amelia looked at him as if he had just grown a second head.

"What on earth do you mean?" she asked.

The prince smiled and shrugged. "As much as I consider myself now at least part Reacherman, I forget how much you are not a Veckander, Your Grace. Masnia is a very stable kingdom, but from time to time an army commander will declare himself a warlord, and taking loyalty from his king's own banner army, raise a banner against his leader's throne."

"He splits the king's army?"

"Indeed, like the shattering of the Grand Kingdom, in a sense, but he has no noble title or lands of his own. That is why they call him a warlord. Such a one is often driven into the mountainous lands on Masnia's northern border, which is the Vec Princedom's southern border. That's a problem for the Vec, since he will raid from us as soon as from his own people. The solution we came up with was to prompt him to join us, to welcome him into the fold, as it were."

"You make him a prince?" Amelia asked, her nerve calming a little as Farringdon led her on this distracting excursion through Vec politics and history.

"A prince cannot make another a prince," Farringdon answered, "just as you cannot make a man a knight or any other form of noble. It takes a king."

"The Vec princes made themselves when they broke away from the Grand Kingdom. They were earls before that."

"That is true, Your Grace," Prince Farringdon conceded. "But that was the one and only time. Each of the signatories to the Grey Hill Compact has sworn that there will be no new princedoms in the Vec ever. Every prince swears to uphold the oath on his accession. So instead, they created a new title—that of Archduke."

"What is that?"

"An archduke holds his lands as a duchy, except that within them he has the powers and authority of a prince. He has no rights in the councils of princes, the few times they ever gather, and cannot make war on another prince without bringing the entire Compact down upon his head. When the second archduke they created tried to take Gelon by force, it was one of the few times the princes have willingly acted as one."

"They made him a duke...sorry, an archduke, and he thanked them by trying to conquer one of them?"

"It was a contentious time in our history, Your Grace," Farringdon said with a strangely accepting shrug. "The princes were so at odds with each other, fighting their own private wars, that I don't think he imagined they could unite against him. He was mistaken."

"Your princes unite under a king though," Amelia said, thinking of Kolber's invasion that had been the making of her dead husband's title. "No new princes are permitted, but kings are?"

"A king is not a prince," Farringdon answered, tilting his head and shrugging as if that explained everything.

Amelia shook her head in wonder.

"What happened to the other archduke, the first one?"

"He was captured by forces of the Masnian king he had rebelled against. His little domain was absorbed by the Vec. Into Gelon, as it happened."

"This Gelon seems a..." Amelia paused to think of the best word. "Contentious place."

"Not normally, Your Grace. But when warlords arise..."

They shared a moment of distracted good humor, before Amelia looked once again to the main door. Still, Earl Sebastian had not arrived.

"So, are you suggesting I become a warlord, Highness?"

"As the Lioness, aren't you a little bit already?" he joked with her, and when she saw the mischief in his expression it made her almost laugh out loud.

"No, Highness, I am not. I am my husband's widow, defending his domain and his name."

Even as she said it, Amelia realized that it was no longer the whole truth. In the first days of the invasion, it had been true, and during Prince Daven Marcus's execrable crusade west. But her role in the Western Reach had grown beyond that now. Her title of Lioness felt a little threadbare and weather-beaten in these days of drought and domestic turmoil, but it was *her* duchy now, not just her husband's in trust. Nonetheless, she was no warlord.

"You think I should become an archduchess?" she asked, speculatively.

"It would solve some of your problems," Farringdon said, sharing her tone and expression. "An archduke is equal unto a prince in his own lands and can raise or dismiss nobles at his, or her, pleasure."

"A prince can only raise knights, baronets, and barons, though."

"Vec princes have many of the powers of kings in their own domains. They can raise earls, counts, and dukes, if they like."

"Rights they claimed for themselves while not taking the titles of actual kings?"

"The Compact Founders saw that as a step too far. Of course, since then, one or two have tried."

"King Kolber being the most recent," Amelia said with an amused snort. The original Vec princes, whom Farringdon called "Compact Founders," were known as rebellious earls in Grand Kingdom histories of the period. One nation's presumptuous rebels were another nation's fathers of restraint and humility. It was not unlike the condition the Grand Kingdom found itself in at this time. Depending on where in the civil war one stood, the throne in Denay was either empty or occupied by a Kingslayer usurper, or else sat by its rightful king, cruelly unacknowledged by seditious nobility. It made Amelia want to laugh, and suddenly she could not think of a reason not to. She was tired, beset, and so worn through with worry that her feelings felt like a gauzy cloth.

So, she laughed, a long, slightly hysterical laugh that threatened to take her breath away. Then it did. She felt lightheaded for a moment and made to lean against the high table but misjudged the edge. Suddenly she had slipped to the floor, half kneeling, half leaning against the table's edge with her head. And giggling like a child. Prince Farringdon moved to see that she was alright, but his look of concern only made her laugh more. Soon he was smirking with her, but still offering his hand to help her back to her feet. Amelia nodded and took hold of her emotions. She arranged her skirts so that she would not tread on them as she stood, then took the prince's hand. He stood, to help her up, but before Amelia could join him, there came a bellow from the other end of the hall.

"What can this be?" Earl Sebastian shouted as he charged from the main doors up the hall. He did not look like he had come directly from the road but was clean and wearing the ceremonial mail and surcoat in which he had sworn his oath of fealty. He had taken time to change and clean himself after arriving in town, it seemed. Some way behind him and making no attempt to keep up with the earl's charging pace came the red-faced High Sacrist Quellion.

"My Lord Earl," Amelia said politely as Sebastian stormed toward the dais. She motioned surreptitiously to Prince Farringdon. "Perhaps you might leave us, Highness."

"Stand knave," Sebastian commanded.

"You think to order my guests in my house, My Lord?" Amelia asked, almost exasperated to find they were immediately back on the same terms they had between them when he left.

"Spare me your indignation, duchess of lies," Sebastian spat at her. Amelia drew back in shock. They were *not* on the same terms, it seemed. The restrained Sebastian of previous days had been replaced by a nobleman prepared to speak his mind.

"For weeks, I have ridden the length of this land of yours," the earl went on. "I have eaten dust and drunk the mud that passes for water in this heat, hunting a foe that hardly any can see sign of. But I have consoled myself with the knowledge that I have been given this chance to prove myself. I will defend this land, my new homeland, and return victorious to plight my troth. Yet I have been cozened!"

"I have done no such..." Amelia began to protest, but Sebastian talked straight over her.

"Good Quellion wrote me, summoning me to the capital, saying that the town is in uproar. The people are on the verge of rebellion and the duchess hides in her chamber, disporting herself in whatever lewd or corrupt fashions, who could say? Even with what I have seen, I could scarcely believe it. Yet his Excellency has never lied to me, so I have rushed back, hoping to find him mistaken."

"The High Sacrist has been commanded from my home," Amelia said, giving the churchman an acid glance. "I do not see how he presumes to comment upon anything that happens here. How would he know?"

"And yet you confirm the very core of your error," Sebastian retorted. "For what reason would you eject a holy man from your presence, if not to conceal some sin? Could it be debauchery or something viler? Could it be witchcraft as the rumors insist?"

"That is a foul lie and vile accusation not worthy of the least dog," Prince Farringdon interjected, pointing an angry finger at Sebastian. "A peer of your rank should know better."

With a smooth sweep, Earl Sebastian drew his sword.

"Keep your tongue, foreign snake, or I will do God's work and send your heretic soul to your masters in Hell."

"You dare draw your sword in anger in my hall?" Amelia demanded. She had imagined this would be an unpleasant encounter, which was why she'd wanted privacy, but outright rebellion had not occurred to her. In this age where princes slew their fathers on the very throne they wished to inherit, perhaps there were no limits to rely upon anymore, even in men like Sebastian, completely committed in their hearts to the upholding the old "righteous" order yet still able to violate its most basic tenets. Out of the corner of her eye, Amelia noticed the side door open again, quietly. She prayed it was the Lace Fangs, but she did not risk looking to see for sure.

"I will do more than draw, *Duchess* Amelia. I will draw and cut for righteousness. You have played the merry widow too long, and the land suffers for your self-indulgence. I demand you repent, turn your face to God and Mother Church, and accept my hand in marriage."

"Are you mad?" Amelia retorted.

"What? Have you pledged your hand to the rebel prince?"

They both looked to Farringdon, who had his hand on his own sword hilt. Would he be swift enough to draw and defend her if Sebastian made an assault, Amelia wondered. She hoped so.

"Was that what I witnessed when I entered?" Sebastian continued his accusations. "The heretic playing man-at-arms for you was not enough? He is dead or gone at any rate, so I hear. Are you widowed twice already and looking for a third?"

"You are a worthless cur!" Amelia spat at him, drawing herself upright to look straight down on the earl, as she had once done when she judged the rebel knight Sir Duggan. "I would never marry you."

"You will!" Sebastian pointed his sword directly at Amelia. There were only three or four steps between them, yet she refused to flinch. Out of the corner of her eye, she saw the prince moving gently closer to interdict. "You will accept my troth, or I will cut you out of that honor chair and take it for myself. And God will hono—"

His last declaration was interrupted as what looked to Amelia's strained mind like two flying bundles of laundry suddenly crashed into him, knocking the earl sideways. His sword rang on the flagstones as it was sent flying from his grip, while Righteous and Spindle wrestled with him, trying to pin him in place. For all their skill, the earl's was their equal, and he had the advantage of strength and mass on them. The three grapplers broke apart and came to their feet, the Fangs with fighting knives in hand and Sebastian having reflexively drawn his armor-piercing rondel dagger.

"I will hang you convict whores in crows' cages from the tallest steeple in Dweltford," he told them hatefully, "as a lesson to all the slatterns of the town to repent."

"Not before you face me, My Lord," Prince Farringdon said as he came to stand beside the Fangs, his own longsword drawn now.

"So be it," Sebastian declared, apparently ready to trust his skill and armor against three opponents, even without a helmet and wielding only his dagger. Behind him, though, High Sacrist Quellion reached out a cautioning hand on his shoulder.

"No, My Lord," the religious leader said sternly. "There is no need for this now. The sin is fully unmasked. She either gives herself to heretics or rebels or, most likely, both. It is sin gross enough now to remove all restraint from the peers. We can go to them and observe the forms."

Sebastian nodded and took a step backward. He looked to Amelia over the head of her three protectors.

"I go now, Amelia, liar and slattern. When I return, I will have the true army of the Reach at my back. Run, hide, send your pets to fight—it will not matter. At sundown that day, you will no longer be duchess."

Amelia bent down to pick up the earl's fallen sword, the blade he had sworn upon when pledging fealty to her in Griffith not so long ago. She held it up in his sight.

"You are a proud man, Earl," she said coldly. "I hope this piece of pride is not too dear to you, for you have forfeited it this day."

"I will have it back upon my return."

Then the earl backed away down the hall, the High Sacrist hiding behind him the whole way. For a short space, the Lace Fangs and the prince kept guard, but soon they let the distance grow, and at last the earl and his spiritual counselor reached the main doors and withdrew.

"You should order your houseguards to arrest them, Your Grace, if I may presume to advise you," said Prince Farringdon.

"Not now, Highness," Amelia said wearily. She felt like a rag that had been rung out too many times. Had she really been laughing only a moment ago?

"We need to get ready to fight knights then, I guess," said Spindle. From elsewhere in the castle, servants and houseguards who had been ordered to stay away were carefully poking a head or two into the Great Hall to confirm the shouting was all over and done.

"I fought knights before," said Righteous. "Even cut me a baron once."

"We were all there," said Spindle, but she and Righteous shared a smile.

"Quiet now, please, Ladies," Amelia told them, feeling so quiet within herself that any speaking seemed almost too loud for a moment. She looked at the elegant weapon in her hand and hated it. She dropped it upon the stairs and suddenly remembered the care taken with the point during the earl's accession ceremony.

"Highness, may I have your assistance?"

"Of course, Your Grace," Farringdon said, and he stepped up to her, sheathing his own sword before coming too close. Amelia pointed to a spot halfway up the blade lying at her feet.

"Place your boot there, if you would, Highness."

Farringdon did as she asked, and she next pointed at the weapon's pommel.

"If you would grasp that and pull up with your full strength, please." Amelia's voice was almost preternaturally calm after the tension of the last moment. She watched, emotionless, as Prince Farringdon pulled the elegant blade against his heel until the steel was irrevocably bent, like a corner. Then she looked to a steward standing cautiously just inside the side door. She waved him over.

"Take that," she said, pointing to the ruined sword, "and have it mounted over the drawbridge barbican, high up so the earl may see it when he comes back in rebellion."

The servant tugged his forelock and removed the longsword as instructed. Amelia then made her way around the high table to the honor seat and sat in it serenely.

"Thank you for your assistance and advice, Prince Farringdon," she said as in the tone of a pronouncement. "Go now and do everything you think right to make sound the castle's defense. Command my forces in my authority however seems good to you."

"I will, Your Grace," the prince said and left immediately.

Amelia was left in her seat with only her Lace Fangs close by.

"Ladies, I hope you know I consider you worthy of the highest of honors," she said, her voice still emotionless. "I am sorry you were so insulted just now."

"Tis alright, Your Grace," said Spindle earnestly.

"We don't blame you," Righteous added, and the two bodyguards exchanged a swift, worried glance.

"I am glad," Amelia said to them with neither happiness nor sadness. She only stared into the hot air of the hall, a single tear wending its way down her cheek.

CHAPTER 59

P rentice awoke, lying on a hard earth floor. He flexed and groaned, his body sore in many places, but deeply gratified to no longer be slung over the back of a horse. His armor had been stripped from him, as well as his shirt and boots, but he still had his trousers. Pushing himself to sit up, he found that his wrists were still bound and the rope itself was tied to a hook in a wall. There was a pair of large wooden doors no more than three paces from where he sat.

Oh wonderful, he thought drolly. *All these years and back sleeping bound to a wall again? Some folk go their whole lives and never experience this.*

"You are awake at last, Captain," Brother Whilte said from somewhere behind Prentice. "I was beginning to fear you might be badly hurt."

"Not terribly, thank you, Chaplain," Prentice said with another groan. Flies tickled at his face, but with his bound arms, all he could do was toss his head fruitlessly. "Good thing the rest of the Lions aren't here to see me sleep in like this. They will think their leader has gone soft."

"Not exactly, Captain."

It was a lame jest, Prentice was willing to concede that, but something about the somberness of Whilte's response drew his attention. He levered his body about awkwardly, unable to pull his hands far from the wall and not yet limber enough to get to his feet. He looked in the opposite direction and saw that Whilte was tied to a hook in the same wall only a few paces further along into the building. It was the long wall of a large, rectangular building with a high roof. Made of sandstone blocks, plastered, and whitewashed, the building's roof above was thatched, though the bundles were thin and rotted. Light showed through in places.

A little beyond Brother Whilte's spot on the wall were the remains of a simple rood screen that had once separated the building's vestibule from its main chamber, though most of that wood was smashed to kindling, its relief carvings indistinguishable. Beyond that was the source of the chaplain's ill mood. Ten corpses, at least, lined on the floor, but with no respect or order. Mutilated, it would have been all but impossible to identify the men save that they all wore tatters of the same uniforms, the blue and cream of the White Lions. These were Prentice's men, and in the gloom he could make out that each one had his own weapon, a sword or a halberd, or the end of a broken pike, shoved through his body, as if pinning it to the packed earth floor. It was a brutal defilement, attended by a swarm of flies so thick they were like a cloud of fog near the ground. Prentice was suddenly thankful for the relatively small number of the pests that actually took the time to annoy him.

"That is grim," he said, and then his eyes met Whilte's. "Trust me when I say that outside has been worse."

"What?" the chaplain demanded. "How can you know...? Do you know where we are?"

"I do."

Prentice closed his eyes and leaned his head against the stone wall. After his meeting with the fey elders, he had had a short list of possible places the serpent witch would be hiding, and this had been at the top of it. He smirked as he realized that he was only being falsely humble saying that to himself. He had been all but certain it would be here.

"Well," Whilte said with quiet impatience. "Where are we?"

"We are in a church," Prentice said without opening his eyes. "At least it once was. A parish church in a village so humble that it had no name of its own."

"Had?"

"Not while I was a convict here."

"You served here on the chain?" Whilte asked. From his tone, it was clear the religious man had been sitting some while awake and alone with his thoughts. Prentice had seen men and women experience it many times, as well as going through it himself once, long ago—the first time in imprisonment, confused, uncertain and not yet adjusted to having so much of one's basic freedom taken away. Thoughts frayed as they worried at the lack of information. Where am I? Where are my jailers? How long will I be here? What happens next? The mind had not yet apprehended the new reality. It was the key marker that separated the old hands from the fresh meat—the longing for freedom versus the resignation that freedom had now become as rare as...as rare as rain in the drought.

"What happened here?"

"Some of the Horned Man's first raiding parties attacked the village after they ambushed the duchess and her escort returning from a journey to the Vec," Prentice explained. He outlined the tale of Sir Dav's failed counterattack on the Redlanders, the flight to the church, and the slaughter of the villagers. Prentice had hardly thought of that day much in recent years. His tally of horrors found under the Redlander's hands was too great now to give this one much precedence, but now that he was back, crouching by the wall as he had that long, terrible night, he found the memories fresher than he would have expected.

Whilte listened quietly to the tale. Prentice ended by describing the grave-digging and the duchess's promise to pay the sacrist a stipend to tend the graves.

"I have heard this tale once before from Sir Liam's mouth," Whilte said, "but he neglected to mention the grave-digging and the lonely sacrist. I wonder if that is him, up there?" He looked through the nave and past the brutalized Lions' bodies to the church's small altar. It was difficult to make out, but on the stone it looked as if there were human bones, scattered, but still bloodied and bearing strips of near-mummified flesh.

"I would expect." Prentice wondered how long ago he had been killed, and if it was the serpent witch herself who'd done it. He doubted that somehow. He had seen how the beast men, the *brakkis effar*, responded to the touch of sanctified ground—the first time in this very church, as it happened. The more he thought about it, the more Prentice was convinced the witch would have had someone do the murder for her. She would most likely have sent the murderers in to shed the blood and defile the ground to try to make it safe for her foot to tread.

"How did you know it was this church?" Whilte asked after a moment. "I mean, how many little churches, one exactly like the others, are there up and down the Reach? Why are you so sure this is the one?"

"When the fey elders told us that the witch used blood and she planned to bind this land to herself, it became clear. Whether it was quality or quantity, she would need a lot. The Redlanders summoned the Red Sky with Prince Forsyte's death, but that did not grant them control over more than Aubrey really, and then only for that night."

"I thought the Red Sky led to the drought," Whilte countered. "Did the death of the prince not have the power to blight the whole of the west?"

Prentice shrugged. "A Vec prince's blood with power over the Reach? I wouldn't think so. No, the drought is the older curse. Remember, the fey are suffering under it just as we are. I think the witch is in a race with the curse. If she binds the land with blood sacrifice, she thinks she can lift the curse of the fey, making a pact with the Redlanders again. I wonder if she can."

"And so you think she has come here for the what...*extra* blood...shed by the Horned Man's coming?" It was clear Brother Whilte found the whole question abhorrent. Prentice did not blame him.

"I think she wanted Fallenhill initially," Prentice said thoughtfully. "It was by far the worst atrocity of the original invasion. That might have been why she was in the north in the first place. She might not even have originally thought to make contact with the fey in their hidden settlements."

"A strange turn of events, but it would make a perverse sense, Captain," Whilte said, tracking the captain's thoughts more clearly now. "She goes north to find a town made a charnel house and instead sees Fallenhill transformed into a renewed settlement."

"Or else closed to her because of the siege," Prentice added. "We have no idea how long ago she did this. Perhaps she only thought to recruit a few fey to get her into and out of Fallenhill secretly while Baron Liam had us cooped up in there."

There was a shift in the buzz of the cloud of flies, a sudden rise in intensity, and Prentice shivered at the thought that they might have suddenly noticed the living prisoners. The notion that they might assault them both en masse made him sick to his stomach, and he spat bile on the ground quietly. Whilte seemed to notice the flies, too, and for a moment he was quiet, but then he continued the conversation in a whisper.

"Could Fallenhill somehow still serve her purposes, do you think?" he asked. "We were ambushed on the way back there."

Prentice thought for a moment. The witch was using the fey to move through the Reach in stealth. They could get her from the far north Azures to Halling Pass, all the way south to this village and to raid the river trade. The Redlanders had some similar magicks, but they must not be as good as the fey or she would not have bothered to bind the fey to herself in the first place. And if all she needed was blood and a place like this, what was the point of Halling Pass and binding Earl Yarmass to her cause? For sure, that would have been her intent. She did not promise Haravind a cure for his sterility in a mere quid pro quo. There were still so many factors Prentice did not understand.

"I do not think we need to fear for Fallenhill, Chaplain," Prentice whispered back. "If the fey were in the area, they pass unseen."

"They are fond of that phrase. They say it the way a knight might say 'for throne and church,' and we have seen what that simple loyalty has produced in the civil war. Two mottos that govern many lives. How many more peoples are entangled in simple-seeming ideas from which they cannot escape?"

Whilte's words reminded Prentice of what the elder had said when he was tied to a horse—the intimation of another player at the table with their own hand of cards. Whoever that was, they had spoken with the fey or with the witch because the elder had called them liars, just as he said the witch was. So, who were '*they*'?

There were still so many factors Prentice did not understand. In the meantime, though, he now knew where the fey riders were based. He and Whilte needed to devise a way to get that information to the duchess or the knights martial as quickly as possible. The fey would likely melt into the wilderness before any force could conquer them, as they always did, but their witch needed the power of this place. Once the fey were driven off, work could be done to purge the land, as had been done with Fallenhill and as Fostermae was now doing in Halling Pass. Then they could look to hunt her down, knowing better the signs and forms of her sorcery. If they were lucky, she would try to stay, make a stand of it, using her blood-binding to force the fey to fight. Then Prentice would see her shredded by Roar iron-shot.

Chapter 60

Lady Dalflitch looked down at the letter in her hands one more time. It was definitely Caius Welburne's writing, even though it was scratched in charcoal rather than the ink he typically used for correspondence. In truth, the rough paper was beneath his usual standards as well. It troubled her. She was folding the note away when the door to her little counting room opened and her husband entered, followed closely by Lady Righteous.

Turley had discarded his usual fine doublet for a Lion's gambeson, undyed white like a simple militiaman, though he had lobstered, steel gauntlets on his hands and a polished steel gorget around his throat. Dalflitch wondered where he had acquired them. He had never been a member of the Lions to have them issued to him. As well informed as the lady made a point of being, her husband's canny resourcefulness still had the power to surprise her, which was part of what she loved about him—that and his manly features. He may have been low born, but he was far from unhandsome.

Righteous was also dressed in Lions' armor, pursuant to her rank as corporal in the militia, including her trousers and leather boots. Unusually, though, the Lace Fang was also wearing a brigandine, the type of leather jacket with metal pieces studded to its inside that her husband the captain wore. Her typical lace mask was replaced with an open-faced salet helmet.

Both Turley and Righteous were heavily armed—he with his flanged mace and a dirk at his belt that could easily have passed for a small sword, given its length, and she with her backsword and buckler like any other Fang. That being said, Dalflitch counted at least three small daggers on Righteous's person at various points, as well, and she suspected a number more were present though not visible.

"I didn't think you liked to wear body armor," Dalflitch observed to Righteous.

"Normally, maybe not, but things tonight could get tight, and I'm not just lookin' after myself anymore, am I?"

She patted her belly over the heavy armor. Dalflitch nodded, fully understanding. Of course, Righteous would want to protect her abdomen now that she was carrying another life within. Doubly so, the lady seneschal imagined, since it was entirely possible the unborn would be her last connection to her lost husband. Unless tonight's note was true.

"Is that it?" Righteous asked, looking at the folded paper in Dalflitch's hand. Dalflitch held it up for her to look at, but Righteous only cocked her head to one side. "Don't ask me to read it. I ain't got that many letters. That's Prentice's talent."

It was so rare to hear Righteous use her husband's name that for a moment it caught Dalflitch by surprise. She was so used to the Lace Fang impudently teasing the captain that Dalflitch wondered just how anxious she must be for his safety.

"You tell us what it says, my lovely," Turley told his wife quietly. Dalflitch gave him a wan smile and nodded.

"I'm fairly certain that this is from Master Welburne," she began. "He's had men scouring the town for members of the Paper House and says that he has located one, the head scholar, Master Solft, along with a rescued stash of lost documents. More importantly, he claims that he can lead us to Captain Prentice."

"And you believe him?" Righteous asked her directly. There were days when the two ladies-in-waiting teased each other mercilessly, mocking each other's perceived deficiencies. When they had first met, the mocking had also been born of thinly veiled contempt. Now, though, the two had a hard-forged respect for each other's strengths. Each one looked into the other's eyes and knew that this night's work would require the best from both of them. Righteous was not questioning Dalflitch's estimation, only asking for confirmation.

"I do not know whether everything he says is genuine, but nothing in this note rings false," Dalflitch explained, giving her best estimation. "He also says there's been a roving gang of rowdies that drove away the bailiffs he had with him as guards."

"Lots of hungry folk turning on the bailiffs, so I hear," Turley said.

"Half of 'em are no more than footpads with the Conclave's blessing," Righteous said coldly. "They deserve what they get."

Lady Dalflitch knew the duchess would hate to hear her civil authorities held in such contempt by one of her ladies, nor would Duchess Amelia approve of mob justice. Nonetheless, Righteous's comments were essentially true.

"Well, Master Welburne's particular bailiffs have been driven off," Dalflitch went on. "So he's taken shelter in a small warehouse and sent us this note, begging for rescue."

"Seems an unbanked throw," Turley mused, using an expression from tavern skittles games for something straightforward. "But you've got your suspicions, lovely?"

"I do, husband. The note asks specifically that we not send more bailiffs or the castle cohort of the Lions, supposedly because of the fear that a pitched battle will result with the mob. There's already been a number of small fires throughout the town in the last few days. It is the sheer mercy of God himself that a proper inferno hasn't swept from the docks to the walls and consumed the whole lot, tinderbox that it is."

"So, he's thinking of the town?" asked Turley.

"Or he wants to get someone from the castle into a trap," said Righteous.

Dalflitch looked at them both over the steady wax candles. Although she still maintained the air of a wealthy lady accustomed to only the finest things, Dalflitch actually lived mostly sparsely, using wealth only as an illusion to hide her thoughts. Let people see the dresses and the jewels and misjudge the mind in the body they clothed. One item of wealth she did indulge herself in, though, was candles. She always had the finest wax candles she could obtain and would spend much to get them. Her life involved a great deal of reading and writing, often late into the night, and she could not abide the smell of tallow lump wicks.

"What do you two think?" she asked them both.

"Smells like a bushwhackers' setup to me," said Turley. "But for what purse? How does he know you won't just send some minor steward?"

"Because the note is addressed to her grace directly."

Turley balked at that revelation.

"Hold on there, wife. We don't have authority to intercept missives to the duchess. This is close to treasoning, you know."

Dalflitch shook her head.

Righteous's eyes narrowed shrewdly. "It's a fiendish well-seasoned bait if tis a trap."

"That was my thought, My Lady," Dalflitch agreed.

Turley's mind seemed still caught on the notion that they were discussing this behind the duchess's back.

"How does a letter to her grace make for bait?" he demanded.

"Husband, for a former lecher and former convict, you are much too trusting a sort," Dalflitch told him, shaking her head.

"I always had Prentice to watch out for me."

Righteous thumped him on his shoulder.

"Think it through, you big lout," she chided him. "It's sent to the duchess so someone important can be sent back *by her*—someone the seneschal here, or the chief steward, can't send on their own account. Remember, almost all of Welburne's business is with your wife. He's met the duchess all of what, three times? And at least two of them's been to do with her husband's murder. No, a merchant like him would go back through the name he knows best if he had to make a fast contact. That's her."

She pointed at Dalflitch.

"If he's sent to the duchess, he wants someone commanded to get him that only the duchess can send," Righteous continued. "And he only wants one or two, or no more than four at most. That's a number that can be jumped down a dark alley in the 'part-light.' Like you said, it's got the sniff of a bushwhackers' setup, but what we don't know is for who or what."

"He asks for an escort," Dalflitch says, "but not too many. It makes me think he wants someone from her grace's chamber."

"Or her grace herself," Righteous suggested.

Dalflitch doubted that. "Perhaps, but counting on her grace's compassion to come to the rescue of a man who once conspired against her? Christian forgiveness or not, that is a great deal to expect of a merciful noble."

"So, who else?" asked Turley.

"Other than the Prince Farringdon or Lady Spindle, the only other targets I can imagine are all in this room."

"Farringdon? What? For ransom?"

"Ransoming the prince makes a kind of sense," Dalflitch agreed. "Snatch a heavy bag of silver and make a run for the east or south in the chaos. But Welburne has an overflow of silver. Unless he thinks to clean out every last guilder from the treasury before abandoning the Reach for good, he has more than enough coin just by doing the business he's doing."

"Spindle?" asked Righteous, but almost immediately shook her head at the idea. "Nah, he's already wooing her. What need's he got for snatching her?"

"That leaves we three," said Dalflitch. "And you two are silver rats, rats of Dweltford, who would walk through fire and steel for Captain Ash."

"So it's got to be one of us two?" Righteous mused.

"Or both."

"Why?" Turley asked.

"I do not know, but I intend to find out," his wife told him. "And you two are going to come with me."

"What for, if it's so like to be a trap?" Righteous asked. "Why not just make the safe play and not step into it?"

"Because, Lady Righteous, there is still an outside chance that the whole thing is on the up-and-up, and if there is even a remote possibility of finding your husband alive and well, I would never forgive myself for not taking it. And because, despite my husband's fears, I would never act on something like this without Duchess Amelia's express permission. She has told me that if there is any chance this mission matter might be resolved safely, I am to pursue it with her authority."

Righteous nodded with an expression of gratitude on her face. Dalflitch returned the gesture and then stood, putting the note into her sleeve and beginning to snuff the candles.

"When did you two become such close companions?" Turley asked as the three made their way to the door. "I thought you were always as chalk and cheese to each other."

"Says my illiterate, horse-thief husband," Dalflitch bantered. "Whose closest friend is a scholar patrician and captain of men-at-arms who once trained to be a Church knight."

"What's that got to do with it? We were both just convicts when we met! We still got that between us."

"And Lady Righteous and I are both women."

Turley shook his head as he held the door for the two women to leave. Righteous gave him another thump on the shoulder as she passed him.

"It's alright, big fella. We don't know what she sees in you neither. Now let's go see if this merchant can lead me back to my husband so I can give him a piece of my mind, puttin' me through this kind of worry. I'm pregnant, doesn't he know!"

CHAPTER 61

E ven with the Rampart in the sky, the moon and stars, the streets of Dweltford were darker than Dalflitch had even imagined. The overhanging roofs and narrow lanes closed out so much of the light that she felt as if she was almost underground, lost in a maze at the bottom of a deep pit, the only natural light too far overhead to ever be reached.

I wonder if this is how Duchess Amelia feels sometimes, she thought.

Almost old enough to be the duchess's mother, certainly the age of an eldest sister, Lady Dalflitch had the deepest regard for her liege lady. She could never imagine another woman, not even herself, holding so well to both her dignity and her resolve through the seemingly endless sequence of crises that beset her lands. If not for Duchess Amelia's mercy after they had been pointless enemies in a war for Daven Marcus's affections, Dalflitch was sure she would be dead in a pit somewhere in the western grasses, or else trading her waning charms for smaller and smaller favors, like an aging strumpet.

There was a flash of yellow light as her husband unveiled a hooded lantern for a moment to gain his bearings in the stygian streets. His bear-like frame was lit in silhouette, and Dalflitch had another moment of appreciation.

If not for her Grace, I would never have had this husband, she thought, *this rogue who is a truer man to me than all the nobles I flitted between through all my younger years.*

The lamp was shuttered again, and Turley led off down a corner to the right. Dalflitch followed, her hand out to touch his back as a guide. Behind her, Righteous was the rearguard, though how the Lace Fang never lost track of them, Dalflitch had no idea.

"How are you two so confident in this darkness?" she whispered after her slippered foot caught on yet another cobble and she stumbled against Turley, barely keeping herself upright.

"It's hardly our first times," Righteous said quietly and much closer than Dalflitch had realized she was. It sounded almost as if the Fang's lips were right on her ear. "You get used to it."

"Lord, I hope not," the lady seneschal breathed. "I suppose I should be thankful, though. I don't want to imagine the kind of filth I'm stepping in. My slippers will be ruined, for sure."

"I told you, my lovely, you should've worn boots," Turley whispered from the dark ahead of her. "Or waxed covers, at least."

"And I told you, husband, that I do not own boots. As to covers, you never fetched any for me when I asked."

"Because I was hoping it would discouragize you from this night's work. I was hoping you would leave it to me and Righteous."

"Fat chance of that," Dalflitch said with vehemence, barely even noticing her husband's creativity with the language, even though normally it made her roll her eyes. "I've been dealing with Welburne all this damned summer. If he means to play me false now, I intend to look in his eyes when he does it."

A fury burned within Dalflitch. Despite the story the duchess told about why she pardoned Caius Welburne, it was Dalflitch who had been drawing the merchant further and further into the duchy's affairs. That meant that whatever he did, if he did do something amiss, the responsibility ultimately fell on her. She could not bear the thought that he might have been dealing from the bottom of the deck this whole time.

They stopped again as loud voices echoed across the roofs and around corners from a nearby street. Ahead, a dogleg in the road came into view as what sounded like a small gang with torches moved past on a parallel road. Three or four voices spoke in low but hostile-sounding terms. Then the scattering shafts of light disappeared around the dogleg and the street was darkness again. The trio paused, waiting to see for sure that they were gone.

"I'd say that's some of the folk searching for Master Welburne," Righteous muttered.

"If it is, they're headed the wrong way," Turley reflected. "The address his letter give us is off to the right, up here."

Again, they started, Dalflitch following her husband still by touch. She marveled at the confidence he had in moving through the shadows.

"So how often do you two make your way down dark alleys together?" the lady seneschal asked, her tone more churlish than she meant. She was mainly annoyed at the discomfort in her stubbed toes and ruined footwear. She hadn't meant to sound like she was accusing the pair of anything untoward. She had more faith in her husband than she was even comfortable admitting, and if any woman loved a man more devotedly than Righteous loved her Prentice, Dalflitch could not imagine it. If any other man than the captain tried to lay a hand on Righteous, Dalflitch was sure the Lace Fang would cut off his fingers and present them to her husband on a necklace. Prentice Ash would probably wear it too.

"Down dark alleys together?" Turley repeated, and Dalflitch could hear the mischievous smile in his voice. "Just the one time, my lovely, I swear. The night we met, weren't it Righteous? Or should I call you Cutter?"

"You do and you'll regret it," Righteous snapped back, but her voice also sounded more roguish than angry.

"Don't fear, goodwife-o'-mine," Turley reassured Dalflitch. "It weren't nothin' like a tryst or even a pleasant stroll in the night air. Lady Righteous there was still going by Cutter and dressed like a skinny lad."

"She still does at times," Dalflitch retorted, trying to sound as lighthearted as her companions, but feeling the tension knot in her stomach.

"Well, we was all dressed in sewer muck that night," Righteous added. "What did Sir Gant call it?"

"Ditchwater," Turley said.

"That's right, ditchwater. He and that other bloke got a mouthful comin' through that drain."

Turley and Righteous shared a quiet chuckle, and Dalflitch smiled herself. Their relaxed comradeship was comforting at a time like this.

"He was one of the good ones, Sir Gant," said Righteous, and Dalflitch imagined that the lady was shaking her head remorsefully.

"Yea," Turley agreed. "I miss him sometimes."

"Prentice does, too, I think. He doesn't say too much about it, but I'm sure he does."

They fell quiet then for a space. Over the rooftops a sound like a scuffle echoed, but it seemed a long way away. Turley unshuttered the lantern once quickly, to confirm their location. They were at an intersection of several alleyways not far from the docks.

"Well, I was more worried than I like to admit, but I think I've got us here," Turley muttered. "We were down here a fair bit with Prentice when we had to get the bearers to march for the town's provisions. What was the sign that note of yours said to watch out for, lovely?"

"A sign with three whitewashed triangles," Dalflitch explained, "over a shed that looks like half a stable."

Turley pulled back the lantern's shutters quickly once more. "Then that's it there, I'd say."

Sure enough, the light revealed the sign they were looking for, not four doors down the narrow street from where they stood.

"If we're going to do this, then this is the hour," said Dalflitch. Behind her she heard Righteous's backsword drawn from its sheath.

"You two don't have to do nothin' if you don't think," said the Lace Fang. "But I'm going in there."

"Don't worry, Good Lady," Turley said, uncharacteristically respectful of a sudden. "I'll no more abandon him than you."

"Righto. Keep that lantern open but under your cloak. We might need some light right quick if this is some traitor's defraudation. If it's too hairy, we'll likely need out fast and we don't want to trip."

"No, indeed," Turley agreed.

"Last chance to sit this one out," Righteous said to Dalflitch.

"Not this night."

"Good girl."

The three of them stalked forward, more easily able to find their way by the open lantern light that was pressing out from under the edges of Turley's cloak. The lamp was hooked around his bad wrist by a loop of wire, while his mace was in his good right hand, sitting on his shoulder and ready to hammer down on any attacker who might come at him out of the shadows. Righteous had her sword in her right hand and her buckler shield fitted to her left. With her helmet on her head, in the bad light, she could have been any other small-statured White Lions corporal.

They stalked to the building's door and paused. There was no lock on the latch, and when Turley tried it, the portal swung open slightly. He looked back at them and Dalflitch shrugged. He pushed it a little further and listened.

"Master Welburne?" Dalflitch hissed into the shadowy interior. "Master Welburne?"

"In here," a voice came back out. "Quickly, and watch out with that light."

The trio hesitated on the doorstep, but there was nothing more to do or say. Either they went inside or they didn't.

"Quick now, or you'll get us all killed," the voice in the dark pressed. Shrugging again, Dalflitch tapped her husband's elbow and urged him inside. Then she followed, and Righteous came at the last, pulling the door behind them. Inside, Lady Dalflitch was surprised to find they were not standing in a room or a warehouse space but rather a narrow corridor with no other doors leading off from it except one at the far end. By Dalflitch's estimate, the corridor probably ran the length of the block and into the back of a building on another street on the far side.

"Smuggler's door," Righteous said, nodding in recognition.

"Where's our boy?" asked Turley, but as he did so, the door at the other end of the corridor opened, seemingly of its own accord. Down the narrow passage, Turley pulled back his cloak as he went, releasing more light, though the motion was awkward for his lame arm in the tight confines.

They paused at the next door and looked in. By the fractured shards of lantern light, the next space more closely resembled what Dalflitch had expected originally—a barn-like space with posts supporting a high roof, stacked about with boxes, barrels, and sacks. There was a smell of straw, as well as something sweet and alcoholic. The three of them had moved no more than two or three paces into the warehouse when the door behind them suddenly slammed shut and a crossbar was heard to lock into place. They whirled to look, but there was no one near the door. It had been closed from the other side.

"Oh dammit," Dalflitch's husband cursed under his breath. "I just figured exactly where we are cause o' where this spot must back onto."

There was a loud metal clack, and the covers of a larger hooded lantern were pulled back, lighting the center space quite well. Dalflitch blinked, and then as her sight adjusted to the sudden brightness, she looked straight into Caius Welburne's own beady eyes. He was seated on a barrel against the opposite wall, but he did not look comfortable. His wrists and ankles were bound and there was a cloth gag tied across his mouth.

"Ye're in the back rooms behind the Gilded Gunwale, dearies," an aged, cackling voice said. "Sorry 'bout this."

CHAPTER 62

The church door swung wide and the hot light of the setting sun bathed the vestibule. Prentice turned his head away from the sudden rush of light, but before he did so a large figure was silhouetted in the doorway. He also positioned his body to hide the marks of his attempts to loosen his bonds from the wall. So far, he had actually achieved very little, but the scratches in the whitewashing were quite visible. It looked like the task would take some time but Prentice was patient.

Then the sudden rush of air through the open door disturbed the flies and the swarm rose like a cloud of pestilence, filling the air. Prentice kept his mouth shut and his eyes pressed closed, but he could feel hundreds of the foul insects crawling over his face, at his nose and ears. He blew air out his nostrils and shook his head to keep them off, until gradually the swarm diminished and he guessed that the main of the insect mass had flown past and out into the open air. As the buzzing receded, Prentice heard Brother Whilte coughing and spitting, doubtless as afflicted by the flies' passage as he was. Whoever was standing in the doorway seemed unaffected because they made no sound.

"That's what I like to see," said a voice that was somewhat familiar to Prentice's ears. "A dog cowering at its master's feet, where it belongs."

Prentice turned his head and risked looking upward, but the sun's rays around the figure still made recognition impossible.

"Good Lord in Heaven, what happened to you, man?" Brother Whilte asked, clearly horrified by something.

"Shut your cripple mouth, feeble priest," the newcomer commanded, and as he moved in the light, Prentice caught better sight of the man.

"Haravind?"

Earl Yarmass's gelded son looked hatefully down at Prentice, and as he did so, the captain saw what had shocked Whilte. On the left side of his face, the young knight looked much as he had when Prentice met him in Halling Pass. On the right side, he had been transformed into something unhuman. The bone of his nose rose to join with his brow, so that on that side of his face it looked more like an animal's snout than a nose. His fair-haired beard on that side did not stop on his jaw and chin, as on a man. Instead, it rose all the way up his face, curling like animal fur into his hairline where an enormous, curved ram's horn sprouted from his temple. Prentice's mind could scarcely understand what he was seeing. It was as if a half of a man and half of a mountain ram had been heated together in burning coals and then incompletely forged, so that instead of one new thing, he remained only two badly welded pieces. He was like a Redlander beast man in the middle of a transformation from mortal to creature but trapped there.

"You do not seem well, Sir," Prentice said to him with mocking calm. The half-transformed knight's animalistic features flared with fury, and he reached down to seize Prentice by the throat, hefting him up as far as the rope tying him to the wall would allow. He held Prentice there one handed, his grip threatening to choke the breath from the captain's body. In whatever way the transformation had failed to give Haravind a proper shape, it had nonetheless bestowed him with prodigious strength.

"Do I not, cur?" he demanded, and Prentice realized why he had not recognized the rogue knight's voice when he came in.

Even his throat had undergone some change, it seemed. He no longer sounded as he once had. He held Prentice close.

"Take a good look, you jumped up churl. When it is finished, I will have power like you cannot imagine. Already you are like a ragdoll to me."

"And all it cost you was your honor, your freedom, and your soul," Prentice retorted. Haravind slapped a backhand across Prentice's face without dropping him, and his head rang with the force of it.

"It's going to cost you all of your lifeblood," the knight said through sneering, barely human lips. He punched Prentice in the belly, and with this strike, dropped him to the ground. Prentice didn't bother trying to keep his feet but collapsed to the floor against the wall, still trying to cover his preliminary escape attempts from discovery.

"See this?" Haravind demanded, and Prentice turned his head to see Ironworth's blade in the man's hairy, half-transformed hand. "It finally has a worthy master."

"It had one from the start."

"Is that right?" Haravind smacked the sword's pommel against Prentice's head so hard that he bounced off the wall. The pain was tremendous, and Prentice thought he might black out. "How does it feel? Do you like its sting?"

Prentice tasted blood from where he had bitten his lip. "Not really," he muttered and spat some of the crimson on the floor. "But it's not the first time I've tasted it."

"It's going to be the last thing you ever taste," Haravind sneered, and he leaned down to lay the edge on Prentice's throat. Even with only a half-human appearance, the captain could read the hate in Haravind's eyes. The errant knight's loathing was barely restrained. One more challenging word and he absolutely would slit Prentice's throat. Prentice said nothing but held Haravind's gaze without fear. He had faced death too many times to cower from this fool. He felt the steel of Ironworth's sword begin to slide ever so slowly along his neck, the sharpness starting to bite almost painlessly into flesh, so fine was the edge.

"Haravind!" someone shouted from outside the church. The blade stopped moving, but Haravind still held it in place.

"I could do it now," he whispered, venom dripping from every word. In spite of his assertion, he still did not finish the barely begun cut.

"Haravind!" the shout sounded again, more commanding. Prentice saw in the errant knight's eyes the power that that voice had over him. The more he was called, the more he longed to rebel, to finish the stroke and spill Prentice's blood. But he could not. The sorcery that transformed him ruled him, and while he loved the might it imbued him with, he knew it also made him a slave, and that he hated almost as much as he hated Prentice. It was all there in his barely still-human expression. Haravind finally removed the sword and stood upright.

"A hell of a thing, is it not, to be on a chain?" Prentice said in a quiet voice. "To live your life at the whims of others? The convict iron bound my body for years. She's bound your soul with blood. The duchess released me; can anything set you free?"

Haravind twitched, and Prentice imagined the man was making one last attempt to kill him. Then he relaxed and sheathed the sword.

"She has made me a god. What do I care about freedom?" he said finally in a voice that sounded as much wounded as defiant. "You tried to make me half a man, and with your blood she will make me more than any man. I will be her champion and bathe this land in blood for her. The drought will break, and she will be queen."

"She will need a better army than a company of fey archers and a handful of knights led by a failed *brakkis effar*," Prentice told him. "Dweltford castle has high walls, and strong."

"Dweltford is a catch-fire waiting for a spark," Haravind said contemptuously. "And her castle? What do we care for that?

Your duchess is not a lion, you know? She's just a broody hen that won't lay, and there's a cuckoo in her henhouse. It's just a matter of time. You or the upstart bitch—it's only a question of which one dies first. And don't think to see her in the afterlife cause once I drain your veins, your soul will be mine forever."

Haravind's threat to Prentice's soul hardly even registered with him. He was caught on the claim of a cuckoo in the henhouse. An intruder, hiding their intent. Who was it? His first instinct was Earl Sebastian, but Prentice doubted that. Sebastian was an ambitious nobleman, no doubt, but Prentice could not believe he was serving the serpent witch. Sir Helpman was the next he thought of, since he was apparently a relative of Haravind's, but that made too little sense as well. It had to be someone who had access to the castle right now. Someone not sent away and not suspected.

Prentice was still musing when Haravind dropped two heavily full waterskins on the floor in front of him.

"One for you, one for him," he said, pointing at Whilte. "You drink it. Her orders. She wants your blood to flow when we cut you, and if your veins are dry, it won't do. So drink up."

Prentice looked at the two skins and wondered if they were poisoned. He was sure Haravind's boasts were not empty threats. The witch planned to bleed them both, but that did not mean she wouldn't drug them first. He was considering which was more powerful, his thirst or his caution, when Haravind stepped in close again, bent down, and suddenly dragged his foot out from under him. Before Prentice had any idea what was happening, the errant nobleman stood again and then stamped his foot down heavily on the side of the ankle. Prentice cried out at the sudden agony, and Whilte called out his name in concern. The snap was loud and the break obvious.

"Just in case you thought you were going to escape. She wants you whole, but she doesn't need you hale," Haravind said coldly. Then he left. Prentice watched him go, huffing in deep breaths to try to control the pain. The church door swung closed, and just outside in the last of the daylight, Prentice saw the blood-bound fey elder, watching with pitying eyes.

"So much for escape," Prentice said through gritted teeth once he heard something laid up against the church door outside to keep it closed. The burning fury in his ankle was bringing tears to his eyes.

"Good Lord, man, how do you feel?" Brother Whilte asked. He shuffled forward, but the point on the wall where he was bound was too far away for him to reach.

"I do not feel well, Chaplain, I concede that much," Prentice answered trying to sound flippant rather than agonized. There was one rule for suffering that he had learned after years as a convict and surviving the tortures of the Inquisition—actually long before that, if he was truly honest with himself. Pain was of the body, suffering was of the soul. His injuries might defeat his flesh, and one day old age would, if nothing else, but he refused to surrender in his heart.

"Never let the bastards see you bleed," one of his fighting masters had said, long before he went to Ashfield. He had forgotten, but it came back to him now. Prentice knew his younger self had not truly understood the meaning at the time, and though he had forgotten the words themselves for years, they were a principle he realized he lived by still. They were as true to him as the fey's "passing unseen."

"I've never healed without laying on hands," said Whilte, wrestling with his bonds. "I will pray, but I do not know what will happen." His voice was laden with care, and Prentice was surprised at how strangely comforting it was, how comradely. He took up one of the waterskins and tossed it the short but uncrossable distance between them.

"There you go brother; your share."

"Why should we? If her purpose is only to make it easier to bleed us, why should we give her the satisfaction?"

Prentice nodded. *Never let the bastards see you bleed.*

"Because our bodies need the water," he told Whilte. "Whether she means it to make us better sacrifices or not, it is to our benefit. Tomorrow they may slit our throats, but sufficient unto today are the problems of today."

Whilte reached out and took the waterskin, shaking his head with a rueful smile.

"I am the chaplain, Captain," he said. "I should be quoting the scripture to you."

Prentice tried to say something clever back, but the pain shooting up his leg made it come out as a strangled moan. He leaned back, huffing and sweating, and uncorked his own skin. The water inside was warm and tasted of earth, but it seemed otherwise like any other well water from the droughty land. Of course, there could easily be poisons he could not taste. In the end, he decided he just did not care. He swigged the fluid and swallowed it thankfully. When he paused to take a breath, he heard Whilte laughing quietly to himself.

"Brother?" he gasped. The last light of day was fading, and they were now in deep shadow. It was not the first such night he had spent in this church with bloodthirsty warriors just outside the door. The previous time had been ironically less painful, though.

"Forgive me, Captain," Whilte said with a genuinely apologetic tone. "I did not mean to make light of our estate. I only laughed at my own arrogant folly."

"How so?"

"What kind of a fool must I have been to imagine you were a heretic?" the chaplain said. "We sit together, I as chaplain, and I find myself wishing I had your patience in suffering." He gave a self-effacing snort of amusement.

"It is patience hard learned, Brother," Prentice told him. "And I *am* a heretic. I was when you accused me but only in my heart. Your lie was simply that I had told anyone." Prentice took another drink.

"You are merciful, Captain."

"You are repentant, Brother."

They sat together in silence for a long time.

"If Mother Church is so compromised, as we know her to be," Whilte said at last, "what does it mean if someone is a heretic at all?"

"I do not know," Prentice admitted. The *merciless preachers of mercy*, that was what the fey feared—the Inqusition—and Prentice understood that fear. They were the Church's tool for *creating* fear. But there was also Sacrist Fostermae, who was earnest, compassionate, and true of faith. Or Whilte himself, arrogance turned to penitence.

And what of me? Prentice asked himself. *Angry so long, forged in fires of hate and tempered in suffering, but strong for all that—strong enough to help build a throne.*

What weapon feared the fire that forged it?

These questions were too deep for Prentice's exhausted mind. He was in pain. He was wounded. And tomorrow he was likely to die. Any questions left after that he could ask the Almighty when he stood before the judgement. In the meantime...

In spite of his pain, Prentice slipped into a troubled sleep, Brother Whilte's whispered prayers sounding in the darkness.

CHAPTER 63

Amelia sat at the high table in almost total shadow. A single candle rested on the glass inset, some of its light reflected but no more than enough to create a little island in an inky sea. She was not alone, but her only companion was Lady Spindle, dutifully at her side. Amelia knew that Dalflitch, Righteous, and Turley were all in the town to escort Master Welburne to safety. Dalflitch had explained the purpose of the mission before leaving, and Amelia had willingly given her permission for them to go. There had been a moment where Righteous and Spindle had discussed the division of their service. Of course, Spindle wanted to go to her betrothed's rescue but had quickly conceded that Righteous had the greater claim. There had never been any question that at least one of them would remain to protect the duchess.

The main doors at the end of the hall opened and a figure bearing an iron lantern entered. Amelia saw that it was Prince Farringdon escorting a White Lion. The pair approached the table and the prince bowed, while the Lion, a corporal of the Claws by his armor, saluted.

"Your Grace, may I introduce Corporal Genet," Farringdon said, and Amelia nodded. "The corporal is arrived from Fallenhill at the head of a cohort."

"Sergeant Franken says you might need us," the corporal explained. "We weren't too pleased to be called off the search for the captain, but we know our duty." He nodded and then seemed to think he might have spoken out of turn. He looked to Prince Farringdon and then back to the duchess.

"You are welcome, and your loyalty is as precious gold to us, Corporal," Amelia told him. She could hear the weariness in her voice.

"I have sent the cohort down to the lower bailey, Your Grace," Farringdon explained, "to combine the two we have as one force."

"Good," was all Amelia could think to say. She wanted to sound of good cheer, but it was beyond her.

"Their arrival is timely, Your Grace," Farringdon added, "as there seems to be some disturbance in the town, and we've seen torchlight moving on the lakebed."

"Disturbance, Highness? Worse than other nights of late?" Amelia asked.

"I do not know of worse, Your Grace, but a large crowd, truly. Larger than any other we've seen so far, I'd say."

Amelia sighed. Her most trusted retainers were in the town at this moment, and the largest unrest yet was stirring there. Worse was the torchlight on the lakebed, for she knew what that meant. That was Earl Sebastian and her rebellious knights martial. As he set to make the castle as secure as he could for her, Prince Farringdon had persuaded Amelia that it was inevitable the earl would attack the castle at the rear. The gate bridge was a narrow point and too easily drawn against trouble. The lake was gone, but the castle's island was like a highpoint now, too difficult to ascend except at the southern end. So that was where the war wagons and the Lions were encamped, their improvised palisade covering against the inevitable invasion.

And now there was torchlight on the lakebed.

"When will they attack, do you think, Highness?" she asked.

"After dawn, I expect, Your Grace."

"Then we have some hours yet?"

Farringdon nodded but also shrugged. He was educated in warfare and strategy, as any noble would be, but he lacked Prentice's experience and instinct for the fight. He was doing his best, and Amelia was grateful for it, but she could not shake the feeling that this would be her last night in this castle. The hounds and the peacock would throw her off the throne soon.

"If we have such time, then I will go to the chapel to pray," Amelia said. After all, the plans that could be made had been. There was nothing else for her to do.

"If it please you, Your Grace, I will go with you," Farringdon said. "If an attack comes, Gennet here may send for me."

When the attack comes, Amelia thought, but she nodded her permission for the prince to join her. He dismissed the corporal and then waited as Amelia made her way around the table. She gestured towards the Great Hall's side door.

"Through the kitchens will be quickest," she said. Farringdon and Spindle followed her as she carried her one candle down the hall until they emerged into the brighter light of cookfires and lamps that were the castle kitchens. In spite of the brightness, however, the space was oddly empty, a sign of the lateness of the hour. Amelia realized that she had never been in the kitchens at this time of night, and its quietness felt odd indeed. As she looked down the long tables, she realized that apart from a burly scullery maid who was scraping a large pot clean with a bundle of straw, the only other person present was the tumbler-poet Bluebird, who was sat upon one of the workbenches idly plucking at a wide-necked lute. It had been weeks since she had seen him last, though she knew he had been about the castle.

"Are you alone, master minstrel?" she asked.

Bluebird looked about, as if surprised to discover how empty the kitchen was.

"So it would seem, Your Grace," he said and he bowed so low that his head was almost level with the table top. "I was seeking to cheer your kitchen staff in this difficult time, but it appears they have left me for their beds. All save one diligent lass, at least." He nodded in the direction of the scullery maid.

"It is a late hour," Amelia said, not really of a mood to engage in Bluebird's usual badinage.

"I could sing for you, Your Grace, if you wish. Since we are both awake. Well, you and I, and your attendants."

Bluebird's gaze perused the prince and the Lace Fang standing behind Amelia.

"No, thank you, minstrel," Amelia said curtly with a wave of her hand, "unless you know some hymns or spiritual songs. I am on my way to pray in the chapel crypt."

Bluebird cocked an eyebrow.

"As it happens, I do, Your Grace."

Amelia paused, surprised by the assertion. It seemed so ridiculous that such a clownish man would have any connection with the dignity of high religion. Bluebird appeared to read the surprise upon her face.

"Not every hour is suited to fooling, Your Grace," he said by way of explanation, stepping off the workbench. "There are somber times when even a blue tit must sing a mournful song."

"I do not know if this is a time yet for mournful songs, Bluebird, but if you could sing something to soothe the soul in a dark hour, then you are welcome to join us at prayer."

"I can do that, Your Grace, gladly," Bluebird said, his usual jaunty tone now replaced with a more suitably serious manner. "Especially since my other songs this night have already soothed my audience to sleep."

Amelia nodded and then continued her short journey across the kitchen, down the passage and stairs to the chapel crypt. Leading the way, she pushed the door, finding it unlocked as usual these days because she was so often here to pray. The candlelight glinted off the silver inlay in the wood as she passed. When she was sure Prince Farringdon was holding the door, she moved swiftly to the other side of the chapel to light the extra candles at the foot of the marble statue. The other three followed her in as Amelia heard Bluebird speak with a hard tone utterly out of character.

"A crypt? Fitting for a final prayer, I would say."

Amelia turned to ask what he could mean and was in time to see him lock the chapel door. When had Bluebird acquired a key to the chapel? Even as she watched, she was horrified to see him spin like a wild dancer but with much darker intent. Using his free hand to catch Lady Spindle's wrist, he barged his other shoulder into her back, throwing her off balance to crash headfirst into one of the stone niche edges. She crumpled insensible without even a cry. Amelia had not even time to shout a warning before the minstrel's motion turned him about to face Prince Farringdon. To the prince's credit, he noticed trouble in the darkness and managed to get his hand to his sword hilt before Bluebird's instrument slammed into the side of his head. Staggered, he had no chance to defend himself, and the minstrel followed up with blow after blow until the lute was smashed to kindling and the prince was slumped unconscious on the floor.

CHAPTER 64

"Well, that went better than I feared," Bluebird said, his tone light and playful once again.

"Treachery," Amelia shouted at the top of her voice. "Help! Treachery!"

Bluebird gave her a disdainful smile.

"Go on, get it out," he said, encouraging her cries. "Let it *all* out. No one will hear you. Your castle sleeps, Your Grace, a sleep that *you* certainly cannot wake them from. So, vent your fears. I do not mind."

Amelia made to call for help again, and then stopped, her eyes narrowing. She would not give him the satisfaction. Instead, she stepped back against the statue pedestal and took back the candlestick. She held it out in front of herself defensively, even though it was a poor weapon at best, and given the ease with which he had dispatched her protectors, Amelia had no delusions she could actually defend herself against him.

"You could have killed me at any time," she said. "You've been unsuspected in my home for weeks. Why now? Why this night?"

"Lord Sebastian will assault in the morning," Bluebird said breezily. "It will be an easier task by far, and much less bloody, if you are already dead, little duchess."

"That still doesn't answer my question," Amelia persisted. She kept her eyes on the minstrel assassin while hefting the weight of the candlestick in her hands. Could she throw it at him and get past in the distraction? The door was locked and that would certainly slow her down.

Bluebird sighed and then flicked at his motley sleeves, as if they were suddenly uncomfortable. He looked down at his outfit and then back to Amelia.

"Believe it or not, it's even hotter than it looks," he said with a grimace. Amelia blinked in disbelief. He was pausing in his assault to discuss the comfort of his clothes? Then he seemed to recognize the incongruency himself, for he cocked his head in a gesture of wry amusement. He flicked one sleeve again, and a narrow poniard blade dropped into his hand, the fine edge flashing momentarily in the spare light.

"As to your question, Duchess, it is a matter of the order of things. No need to kill you if you'd showed the least sense and gone to the earl like you were supposed to."

"So, your master Sebastian has sent you? I would not have expected this from him, even now," Amelia said, shaking her head in disappointment. She was shocked when Bluebird released a laugh drenched in utter contempt.

"The good and earnest earl would likely die of apoplexy if he knew what I was doing here," the minstrel said, his sardonic smile widening.

"Quellion then?" Amelia asked, voicing her confusion. Bluebird found that notion equally amusing, it appeared.

"The High Sacrist? I'm certain he imagines he is mastermind enough to make a play like this, but let's be honest, shall we? He's more of a useful fool than most of them at his level, sending his street preachers out to try to shame you into marriage like an idiot farmer who sets fire to his barn to kill the rats inside. I'll admit, the fire he set was useful for distracting you a while, but it is getting out of control now. We need Sebastian's steadier hand on the reins before the High Sacrist burns the whole of Dweltford down."

"*Whom* do you serve, then?" Amelia demanded, finding herself so incensed at the minstrel's casual disdain that she was forgetting to be afraid of his bared steel. He off-handedly accused Quellion of deliberately stirring sectarian violence to undermine her rule, as well as admitting to fostering Earl Sebastian's ambitions to the level of open rebellion. Yet he claimed neither was his true loyalty, so whom did he serve? Daven Marcus? Was this all a plot of the usurper?

"We have a little while until dawn, Your Grace," Bluebird said quietly. "The earl will not attack until there is light to see by. Knights do not fight well in shadows. Of course, when they find your body dead on the battlements, slain by your own hand, it will make the whole affair quite swift, I think.

"As to your question, even if I were not sworn to secrecy, there wouldn't be enough time to reveal to you the myriad mysteries that govern this world, not enough for you to understand. Console yourself with knowing that you are merely another piece in a strategy that has kept the Grand Kingdom safe for a thousand years."

Amelia had a sudden flash of insight, connecting the minstrel's grandiose boast with something she and Prentice had learned from the scholar Master Solft long ago.

"You helped the eagle, the royal family," she said, referencing the ancient history that no one truly understood anymore—no one save Bluebird and his masters, it seemed, whoever they were. "You usurped the original white lion and put the eagle on the throne in Denay. Then you turned on the other kings and their fey allies, driving them west. Did you know they lived? Did you know they could come back? And with such powers?"

Bluebird blinked with surprise at her questions, and the poniard rose to point at her such that Amelia thought he was about to strike. Then his hateful glare melted back into his mocking smile, a little more rueful than before.

"Your pets at the Paper House, of course," he said disdainfully, shaking his head, discerning for himself the source of her insight. "We keep secrets and have kept them for centuries. Yet curious fat ferrets with a love of ink and parchment keep finding them out. You could not believe how many libraries have been burned for the sake of the Grand Kingdom, yet still the 'paper houses' spring up like weeds in the coming Eden. I will have to see that they are finished with later today, I think."

"The scholars have already gone to ground," Amelia said.

"I know. The seeds are in the wind again, but when they land they will sprout, and we will pull the weeds. We've been doing it since the beginning you know. We've become very good at it."

"The fey must have been a surprise then," Amelia said. Judging the distance from where she was to the door and the minstrel assassin's skills, she had little hope of getting past him. Her only chance, she felt, was to keep him talking until someone arrived. Even with all the chaos in the town—Quellion's "burning of the barn"—there was a chance Turley and Righteous might be back soon. Or perhaps one of the White Lions down in the lower bailey might come looking for Prince Farringdon. It was all she had for now.

"Not really," Bluebird responded to her comment. "We've known they were there for centuries. There have been the occasional contacts as well. They have learned to fear us, or more accurately, have not been permitted to forget their fear. And every now and then, they have been useful, as in recent days. We let the serpent come and stir them up because it was useful."

"*You* set fey loose upon the Reach?"

"No, we just didn't stop the witch when *she* did. We may even have helped a little."

"Why?" Amelia was horrified at the casual way he spoke of setting her people at odds with an ancient enemy, murderously at odds, when her people were already on the verge of starvation.

"You were too enamored of your role as the Lioness," Bluebird told her. "You were letting the *wrong* people run amok. You needed prompting to remember the right order of things."

"You set fire to my barn to kill the rats?" she asked rhetorically, mocking him with his own words, and his mask of humor slipped once more. He fixed her with a cruel expression.

"You were the twit who let your 'rats' have the run of the barn in the first place. Better to burn it than let the farm be overrun as a whole. But fear not, I have much greater control of my flames than the righteous fool and his street preachers, though I have helped them as well, once or twice. Nothing like a prophecy fulfilled to give weight to religious panic."

"You killed Lord Gullden?" Amelia asked with a gasp. What were the limits to this man's evil, or to his power, for that matter?

"The vipers and a fall from a horse killed the viscount. But the curse that drew them to him? That was mine. Words have power, Your Grace. That is why we have to burn so many of them."

Amelia fell quiet then. She was terrified, and feeling more and more as if this was to be her last night alive. It reminded her of the night she had spent hiding in the church when the Redlanders arrived. Nonetheless, her fear was not ruling over her, not as it might once have. Now she felt a growing frustration. For years she'd been fighting to keep her Reach together, as if holding onto its pieces by her fingernails, and now it seemed she'd never even realized the extent of the forces fighting against her. And still the land thirsted in the heat.

"I suppose you have a plan for the drought," she said, trying to seem inscrutable but fearing she just sounded bitter. "Or will you tell me now that that, too, is your curse, just another flame to burn out the rats."

"The drou...?" Bluebird began, as if the brutal dry was something he hardly remembered. His expression turned cunning and then rueful again. "Oh, I wish I'd thought of that. How heartbreaking would that have seemed if you thought I had that kind of power? You would truly have despaired, wouldn't you? No resistance in you, then."

Amelia remembered the words of the fey assassins who had planned to kill her according to some order from the serpent witch. They had said that she had to be awake to despair. She wondered why. Why did her sorrow matter so much?

"The drought is the witch's problem, for now," Bluebird said, shaking off his regret for having missed a possible clever lie. A matter of professional pride? "Either she can break it, or she cannot. We will allow her the one attempt to try, since the sacrifice she wants to make suits our plan. Then, whether she succeeds or not, we will find her out and put an end to her fantasies. We will not topple a wayward lioness duchess just to have a serpent witch-queen take her place."

"The drought is not from the Redlanders either?" That was the fear that had sat unspoken in the back of Amelia's mind since the furious summer had first started to run long. It was a terror she had not wanted to admit, and now that it was debunked, assuming Bluebird wasn't lying, she felt herself strangely relieved.

"The Broken Kings? God no! Even if all their sects were to combine, like they did in Aubrey, I doubt they could do this. The witch doesn't think so, I'll tell you that. She's been up and down the Reach, splashing blood around like an infant with its bathwater, trying to break the summer's grip. It took the whole craft of that ridiculous mythical horse of hers just to bind the fey. She says the blood of the right hero is what she's lacking, so I gave him to her, but I have my doubts."

"Gave him to...?" Amelia's confusion was suddenly spiked through with fury. *Bluebird* was behind Prentice's disappearance? She felt her will harden to unyielding steel.

Best strike true with your dagger, master assassin, she thought. *For if I survive this night, I swear you will not.*

Spindle shifted slowly, groaning as she moved, and Bluebird looked down at her a moment.

"Robust little thing, this one," he said, and he gave Spindle a swift kick in the side that could easily have broken a rib or two. The fallen lady groaned, a muffled sound, but there was no flinching in her. She seemed to be rousing but was still too unconscious to be any real help.

"I think our time draws to a close, Your Grace, or would you prefer to die as Amelia? I see no reason to be cruel about this."

"Cruel?" Amelia repeated and shook her head. She doubted this man even understood the meaning of the word, except in the abstract.

"Yes," Bluebird said with a pleasant smile and a nod of his head. "In fact, I feel quite indebted to you at the moment. I so rarely get to discuss my work openly. Since my true performance is so secret, I typically can only receive applause from myself, and self-praise feels so indulgent, not becoming of a true agent of Mother Church but an occupational hazard, I fear."

"How burdensome your life must be," Amelia whispered, wondering if she had ever hated anyone as she hated this man at this moment. Bitterness was still swirling through her thoughts when there was the sound of someone trying the latch on the door. Amelia looked up in sudden hope.

"It is locked, remember?" Bluebird said disdainfully without turning to look. Then there came the further sound of a key being fitted into the lock, and Amelia gave the minstrel a derisive sneer of her own. Without hesitating, Bluebird crossed the distance between them and stood beside her, one arm around her shoulder to keep her from moving and his poniard point pressed against her bodice.

CHAPTER 65

"So, *you* are the fabled Ragmother," Dalflitch said as she regarded the elderly smuggler queen. Beside her, the lady seneschal felt her husband shifting his position.

"We ain't alone on this side o' the room," he said, apparently making out dangers in the deeper shadows.

"Three or four this side too," said Righteous, and she adjusted her stance as well.

Dalflitch fixed her eyes on the Ragmother and did her utmost to ignore the gathering threats around them. There was nothing she could do about them anyway, and the real crux of the problem was in front of her. They were in the lair of a beast now, best to aim for the head. That was why she was surprised when the Ragmother had another coughing fit, and as she lifted a cloth to her mouth, she did it with both hands. The elderly woman's wrists were tied together. She was as much a prisoner as Caius Welburne.

"Well, you've got us here, ready to make a deal," Dalflitch said. "But who am I dealing with?"

A sneering hiss came out of the dark behind the Ragmother's right shoulder, and a young, well-dressed dockworker followed it into the light.

"You were right, Nan," he said, leaning down to pat the Ragmother on her shoulder. "A fine dressed lady and she ain't the least bit scared. She really don't know the kind o' hazard she's facing. River bluff and she's sunk, and like any other gull, she ain't got no idea."

Dalflitch never took her eyes off the Ragmother.

"This popinjay is Fulford, I take it?" she asked.

"Me grandson," the Ragmother said with a sad shake of her head.

"Bit of a jump-up, is he?"

"Spoilt brat, more like, but ask me again when this is all over. Maybe he's got a trump card in this fool hand o' his."

"He'll need one," Dalflitch said, sounding more confident than she felt. Any moment now, this whole affair was going to turn bloody. She was all but certain of that. What she wanted to know was whether this ambitious criminal actually had any useful information she could pry loose before he had to be put down. Assuming, of course, that Righteous and Turley were up to the task. There was always a good chance they were all about to die.

"Oy, you two," Fulford said, clearly annoyed at being ignored in the midst of his own ambush. "I didn't get you here to have a knittin' circle natter. You are in all manner of vulnerabilities, you daft prancer. Are you so blind-stupid that you can't see that?"

Turley growled at the insult to his wife, but Dalflitch merely turned a cold glare on the would-be smuggler boss.

"Very well, young man, it's your room. What's the deal you have to offer?"

Fulford folded his arms, smug now that he was the center of attention. In one hand he had a gardener's billhook, the tightly curved, sickle-like tool that yeomen and rogues often tied to the end of a long pole to form the typical fighting bill. It was a common enough piece of steel for a lowborn man to carry, but this one was polished like a proper sword and looked as if it had never been turned to a tree branch in its life.

"There is no deal for you, prancer," Fulford said with complete satisfaction. "The deal was done to get you here. You have no idea what your pretty face was worth to some folk. And we get to keep your purses and your flash clothes. Wonder what we can get for your silks and play armor. The big lug's doublet I might get resized for myself. I rather fancy the look."

Dalflitch cocked an eyebrow at him, but before she could say anything more, Righteous huffed a sigh of lost patience.

"Enough of this bloody flimflam," she said with a tone of exasperation and disgust. "You said as you had information. So where is my husband at?"

"What?" Fulford asked, obviously still pleased with himself but confused for a moment as to who Righteous might be talking about. Then it seemed to dawn on him. "Oh, you're the convict captain's slut."

"Have a care, grandson," the Ragmother muttered, but that only earned her a cuff with Fulford's backhand.

"Quiet, old woman." He turned to Righteous. "I knew you were all useless up in your castle playing princesses, but I never knew what fools you were into the bargain. He's dead, doxy. Isn't it obvious? Your convict man is *dead*."

"Then where is his body?" Righteous demanded tautly.

"How the hell should I know?" Fulford said with a broad, mocking smile.

"Then you're no use to me."

Righteous executed a smooth, lunging strike, her lead foot stepping a long distance, and the point of her sword piercing Fulford's throat. The movement was so swift that it seemed the smuggler had to think a moment to even realize it had happened. She twisted the blade a half turn and then stepped back, pulling the tip out with a gush of crimson. The young thug's eyes went wide with horror, the whites plainly visible even in the sparse light. He dropped his billhook and clutched futilely at his neck with both hands. His lifeblood poured out through his fingers, running down his chest and stomach. In mere moments, his body lost strength and he collapsed against his grandmother, his head leaning on her lap as he died.

For a long instant the only sound in the smugglers' warehouse was Fulford's gurgling death throes. Then like the kind of cloudburst the Reach had longed for for so long, chaos erupted. Emerging from the shadows where they were skulking, dockland criminals charged into the lantern's glow. Most were carrying long knives or heavy gaff hooks, though one had an ironbound cudgel with large studs down its sides. With assailants coming from all directions, Dalflitch dove for the only space she could think might be safe—the little gap between the two barrels where Welburne and the Ragmother were tied in place. Crouching between the two, Dalflitch heard the Ragmother cooing something to her grandson as he died in her lap. She was unable to make out the exact words in the turmoil, but it made her think of the kinds of things a mother said to calm an upset child. It made the lady seneschal feel oddly like an intruder, and she turned her attention to the brawl.

As best she could count, Dalflitch thought there were about seven more smugglers in the crowded space. That meant that before Fulford had caught the sword-thrust, the ambushers outnumbered their targets four to one. Dalflitch had no delusions she would have counted in their calculations. Four to one should have been good enough odds for any ambush, and if they had jumped to the attack straight after the trio came through the door, it would all be over now. But Fulford had wanted to show his brass. He had wanted to prove he was flash enough to take over from his grandmother, and in that he had underestimated them. As someone who lived her life in the gap between appearances and realities, Dalflitch almost pitied these fools. They would be the only victims of Fulford's ambitions this night.

Turley was swinging his heavy mace about in long sweeps, the flanged head tearing and biting into flesh and smashing the bones beneath. The weapon made accuracy unnecessary against unarmored opponents, especially in the close confines of the shadowy warehouse. Whenever one of his opponents was too quick and made to strike after a dodged swing, he deflected it with the lantern in his bad hand. Dalflitch nearly panicked when such a blow cast a splash of burning oil in the air, but it landed on a section of floor where the scuffle had scattered the straw and only left the dirt underneath. It occurred to her that the four that had thrown themselves at her husband—now three as one crumpled—should still overwhelm him, but there was a notable lack of enthusiasm in their attacks. They were hesitant, and she knew why. All of them had to be wondering what it meant that their ringleader was dead. This was a powerplay, and their side's player was gone. Who were they fighting for now?

With the longer and swifter blade, Righteous was faring even better than Turley. One of her opponents was down already, his feet just visible at the edge of the light. Another was hanging back and looking behind himself, doubtless plotting his escape. The Lace Fang's last foe was the cudgel wielder, and from his wrathful assault it seemed he was determined to avenge his fallen boss. He kicked straight at Righteous's stomach and hefted his ironbound weapon overhand to bring it down on her head. Being so much smaller though, Righteous let her armor take most of the sting out of the kick and it's force lifted her up and out of the way of the falling cudgel. She landed adroitly and made a quick thrust for her opponent, but the range had become too great. He deflected the edge comfortably. Righteous made to move to her left, but the cudgel hammered at her shield side, and she was forced to dodge to the right instead. The move put her into an awkward corner, and before she could see a way out, her opponent was swinging hard again, this time for her head. She desperately sought to deflect the attack with her buckler, while ducking low as well.

The cudgel all but blasted through her shield like a cannonball, but since she had managed to duck slightly, the rest of the blow only deflected off the angled point of her helmet peak. Nonetheless, Righteous cried out against the brutal hit, and her foe sneered at her while his weapon finished its swing by smashing a divot in one of the warehouse roof's pillars. The thug's triumph turned to terror as he looked down and realized that while she had been deflecting and absorbing his attack, she had laid a cut against his inner thigh. Already her sword's edge was clean through his trousers and she stepped past him, turning her slash into a draw cut that went through the meat of his leg, all the way to the thigh bone. The man fell to the ground like a dropped sack and there was a sickening sound of rushing fluid as the severed artery bled him dry in so few moments he never even cried out. The scuffed earthen floor was awash, and the sudden fresh quiet was enough to end the little battle. All the other thugs fled, vanishing into the shadows.

"Come back here, you cowards!" Righteous shouted, trying to follow them, but struggling to see exactly where they'd gone. She banged on the walls, trying to find the doors they had fled through by feel. "Come back and tell me where my husband is, you bastards!"

Turley went to calm Righteous, and Dalflitch turned to the Ragmother. She was stroking Fulford's face, her skirts wet through with his blood.

"I told you, my fair-haired boy," she whispered to him. "We can't rule like they do. Shadows keep us safe and scare the gulls, but t'ain't everyone is 'fraid o' the dark."

Dalflitch left the grieving woman and looked to Master Welburne, removing his gag.

"Are you well, Master?" she asked.

"I...well enough," he said working his cheeks and jaw now freed from the discomfort of the rag.

"I take it they forced you to send the note?" Dalflitch asked him, her eyes looking straight into his, still suspicious for treachery. The reedy merchant held up his hands, and Dalflitch saw that one of the fingers on his left was bent at an unnatural angle.

"I thought to bravely refuse, but I was not equal to their persuasions, I fear," the merchant said regretfully but without shame.

"We need to go, lovely," Turley said over Dalflitch's shoulder. "They're rabbiting now but might get their pluck back soon enough. Best we are gone before that."

"Can you walk?" Dalflitch asked Welburne.

"To leave here? I will crawl if I must. Or you can have your steward there carry me if you're in a hurry.

"He can't carry you," Dalflitch told him. She looked at the Ragmother. "He's got to carry her."

"What's this?" the old crone demanded, and Turley gave his wife a quizzical look that said he was equally surprised by the statement.

"You're short one heir, old woman," Dalflitch said heartlessly. Fulford may have been the inept mastermind behind this night's tragedy, but as far as the lady was concerned, the Ragmother was the one responsible. She'd raised the cosseted twit to be such an ambitious fool.

"Short one heir and your little duchy of shadows is in disarray. What are the chances you even survive another day?"

"So leave me to die then," the Ragmother said with equal harshness. "What's it to you?"

"Oh no! You may not know where Captain Ash is, and I doubt you know the whereabouts of any of the Paper House scholars, but *I* am not done with you yet."

"Enough nattering," said Righteous, her sword still in hand and eyes scanning the shadows. "If we're bringing her, then bring her."

Turley made to grab the elderly woman, but before he did, Dalflitch had one last question.

"Can you keep your tongue, or do we need to gag you?"

The Ragmother's eyes were still wet with tears, but her expression had taken on the shrewd cast of the lifetime smuggler queen once more.

"You'll do it, too, won't you, dearie?"

Dalflitch held up the gag she had taken from Welburne. Far from being intimidated, the Ragmother nodded approvingly.

"A pride of lionesses, alright," said the old woman, and then she held her hands up for Turley to heft her over his shoulder like an old bag of her namesakes. Dalflitch borrowed one of Righteous's daggers to cut Master Welburne free, and once he was on his feet and reasonably stable, considering his ordeal, she indicated to the Lace Fang to lead them off. Righteous nodded, taking back her dagger. She turned toward the door they had come in by and then turned back, looking at the Ragmother.

"How do we open it? Can we from this side?"

"Oh aye, deary," the old woman said happily, a mad hag once more. "There's a release for the bar near the floor. Looks like a loose carpenter's peg. Push it in and up, and the bar slides back."

"Clever," said Righteous and she turned back to the door. Before she could take another step, however, she touched her hand to the side of her helmet where the cudgel had been deflected. She winced loudly and then bent over to vomit all over the floor.

"Oh God," she muttered. "Why did I ever want to get pregnant?"

CHAPTER 66

S olomon poked his head around the door and one hand reached through to tug his forelock. He was starting to remember the correct forms of respect.

"Forgive me for disturbing you, Your Grace, but the corporal sends for Prince Farringdon."

"Excellent, lad," Bluebird said, tightening his grip on Amelia as a warning. "Run and say that the duchess will send the prince to him in a short while. She must speak with him first."

Amelia felt her breath catch in her throat. If she shouted a warning, she had no doubt Bluebird would sink his blade between her ribs and then kill Solomon as well. Strangely, it was fear for the loyal young man, not herself, that clenched Amelia's heart. She had hoped to see Righteous or Turley at the door, not this orphan lad whose face still bore the unhealed mark of his service to her. Looking at his youthful features in the sparse candlelight, Amelia silently prayed Solomon would accept Bluebird's odd speaking out of turn, that he would run away and live.

It was not to be.

"Go on, lad," Bluebird urged, his typical good-humored manner starting to sound strained and resentful. "Don't keep your corporal waiting."

"No, I don't think so," Solomon said, and he moved farther into the room as his eyes ranged about, taking in the whole scene. The candlelight was dim enough that the youth might have missed the two insensible bodies lying in the shadows from the door. Now that he had entered fully, there was no chance that he had not seen them. Amelia's heart sank in despairing admiration as Solomon drew his dirk from his belt and took a fighting stance.

"Release Her Grace and step away from her, master minstrel," he said calmly.

"Oh, lad," Bluebird said, shaking his head pityingly. "I had heard you were brave. How unfortunate."

Solomon advanced a careful step, looking so like Righteous or Prentice but with the ungainliness of youth and inexperience. She could see his teachers' influence in his motion, but he lacked their practiced smoothness and poise. Next to her, Amelia felt Bluebird's weight shift subtly. The minstrel had that poise, and she had no doubt Solomon was stepping into his doom.

Not alone, she thought. *I will not let you die alone, Solomon.*

While Bluebird was distracted momentarily, Amelia thrust straight at his face with the lit candle in her hands. She hoped to set him alight, his hair or his motley, but the wick end jammed straight up under his chin. He was burned, but the flame was extinguished in the same moment. Flinching with a grunt of pain that seemed strangely poor-spoken for the normally poetic man, Bluebird pushed Amelia away a half-step while keeping hold of her. Solomon charged into the sudden opening, but the expertly trained man intercepted the young man's thrust with his own dagger and, one-handed, managed to hook the attacker away so that Solomon cried out and was cast sideways into the shadows.

We need Prentice, Amelia thought despairingly, trying unsuccessfully to wrench herself free. Her captain was now the only one she could imagine as the equal to this vilely cunning assassin. Bluebird turned his eyes on her, and she knew he was going to use the small space created by Solomon's deflection to complete his mission. Amelia readied herself for the blade when several things happened at once. Bluebird screamed in sudden agony, his amused expression transformed to a terrifying rictus. His right leg seemed to buckle under him, and Amelia looked down to see Spindle, having crawled along floor and rammed her own poniard to the hilt through the back of the assassin's knee.

That was the last thing the duchess saw of Bluebird before she felt herself suddenly hammered and lifted up from behind. She was torn from Bluebird's grip and borne toward the chapel wall beside the statue of the Messiah, held there by a body behind her. She felt hot breath on her neck and a pressure that pushed her deeper into the corner.

"Forgive my impertinence, Your Grace," Farringdon whispered in her ear, his voice sounding slurred. "Please do not resist. We must keep you safe."

The prince was shielding her with his body. From the way he stood, she was reasonably sure he was barely conscious and upright himself, but what he had, he was giving. Amelia hated being pushed away, unable to see as she heard the melee behind her. She knew it was swift, but the uncertainty and the darkness made it seem to never end. Then it was quiet. She waited a moment to see if it meant her peril was more or less before turning. Farringdon lifted himself away from her, and as he did, he lost his footing, half slipping against the statue's pedestal and almost knocking over one of the remaining candles. As he straightened up, Amelia could see the blood seeping down his face from wounds in his scalp.

"Oh, Highness, you are injured," she said and immediately felt insipid.

"Quite so, Your Grace," Farringdon said with a weak smile. "Only, thank God he had that lute in hand. If he'd a real weapon ready, I think we would be having this conversation in the afterlife."

He slipped again and used both hands to keep himself upright. Amelia thought to treat his wounds and looked about the room to see what other damage the assassin had wrought. Of

Bluebird there was no sign, but Spindle was standing, leaning on the doorframe. She had her dagger in her offhand and her other palm pressed against her side, gasping for breath.

"Solomon, you daft child, get back here," she called down the hallway, but her voice sounded breathy and weak. She bowed her head as she leaned forward in more pain.

"My Lady?" Amelia asked as she came up to Spindle to see her condition.

"Sorry I took so long, Your Grace," the lady-in-waiting told her between pained gasps. "I was trying to be canny, pick the right time without giving away that I was coming to. Then that mongrel put his boot to me, and it was all I could do not to make a sound like. He was so fast that first pass, I didn't want to give him any chance to get ready for when I made my move."

"You have nothing to apologize for, My Lady," Amelia reassured her. "I am delighted you even live. When I saw your head strike the wall, I was sure that was the end of you."

"Not sure it isn't yet," Spindle said, blinking her eyes and wincing at the pain in her head. There was no blood on her face, as there was on Farringdon's, but as Amelia looked closer, she saw a large lump on the lady's crown, seeming to swell further even as she watched. It must have been excruciating.

Suddenly Solomon appeared in the doorway, carrying a reed torch fetched from somewhere else in the castle, presumably. He saw the duchess and smiled broadly for a moment before frowning and bowing his head, saluting like a White Lion, his dirk in his fist as he did so. There was blood on the blade.

"I'm so sorry, Your Grace," he said earnestly. "He got away. I tried to run him down, but God-in-heaven he was fast, even with Spindle's sticker in his knee. I did lay my blade on him one time, though." He held up his dagger's bloodied edge proudly.

Amelia stepped up to him, clasped his face in her hands, and kissed his forehead.

"You are the bravest and most valiant lad I have ever known," she told him, and it seemed in the candlelight that he blushed.

She smiled at him for a long moment, then released his face and looked to her injured attendants. "Bluebird is loose in the castle. He must be captured."

"I saw one of the houseguards, Your Grace," Solomon said. "I told him you wanted the minstrel brought to you in chains. I know you didn't say it, but I thought it was what you'd want. Is that alright?"

"It is, indeed, sweet Solomon," she said to him.

"Good man," Spindle added.

Farringdon limped the short distance to join them and awkwardly rubbed at Solomon's hair, though in truth the young man was starting to be too old for such a gesture.

"No wonder Captain Ash thinks you'll be captain yourself one day," the prince said, and Solomon's eyes went wide with wonder.

"He does?" the drummer asked, but before anyone could answer, Turley appeared in the corridor behind the lad. The chief steward was as disheveled as everyone else present, and there were small sprays of dried blood across his clothing, but when he saw the condition of the duchess's entourage, he looked horrified.

"I were comin' to tell you we brought Welburne back safe, Your Grace, and a prisoner," he said with earnest concern. "But what happened here?"

"The minstrel Bluebird is a hired assassin," Amelia told him. "He made an attempt on my life. I am safe, but the man has done our friends no small injury. He has escaped into the castle somewhere. Odds are that he will flee, but Solomon has informed the houseguards in case he tries to hide and make another attempt."

"Not in my bloody house he won't," Turley said, already turning to go. "I'll get the whole staff up looking. No one sleeps this night until I know every room is searched for this dog." He paused in his indignant storming away to turn back and tug his forelock. "With your permission, Your Grace?"

"He's not a dog, he's a peacock," Amelia said distractedly. When Turley gave her a confused look, she smiled and nodded. "Go to, Chief Steward, but be warned. Bluebird said that he had cast a spell of some sort to make the castle's retainers sleep."

"Well, I've got a magick spell of me own that's guaranteed to wake the deepest sleeper," Turley said, and he swung his open palm through the air, mimicking slapping a person awake. Before Amelia could counsel him to mercy, he was already off to rouse the household. Amelia turned back to the injured prince and Lady Spindle.

"Now we must get you to a chirurgeon, or better yet a true healer," she said.

Prince Farringdon shook his head.

"With respect, Your Grace, Lady Spindle and I can see to ourselves. You have been called by your corporal. You must go see to the Lions."

"Of course, Highness," Amelia told him, and she turned to Solomon. "Lead off. Take me to my militia."

CHAPTER 67

Prentice stared at the darkness and wondered if he was dreaming. He was lying on his back and his ankle was in agony. There was no comfortable position to lay it in, and he was sweating with the pain of it. Nonetheless, the 'part-light coming through the missing thatch in the church roof seemed especially bright to his eyes.

Perhaps not dreaming, just hallucinating from the pain? he thought.

Across the short distance in the inky space, he thought he could still hear Whilte's whispered prayers, and that was a comfort. Throughout his many years on the convict chain, Prentice had lived through nights like this with pain and exhaustion and nothing but fear of more with the coming dawn. But there was one difference this time. This time, he was not angry with God. It was not that there were no injustices in his condition or that he was at peace with the evil in the world. Those things pricked his indignation as cruelly as they ever had, but he no longer felt alone in his suffering. As a convict, falsely condemned and tormented far beyond even his fellow convicts' sufferings, it had once seemed that God had singled him out for a fate worse than all others. Even now, his experiences felt grimmer than many he had known or heard about. But granting all that as true, he did not resent it because he knew now that it had a purpose. He knew that bitter as every moment of it had been, it had not been a waste, and it was not meaningless.

"The blade does not fear the fire that forged it," he whispered, a kind of prayer of his own. If not for what he had been through, too many things he valued would not be. The Horned Man's invasion might have been much worse. The duchess might not even have survived, or if she had, she might well have been married to a weak and treacherous cur like Duggan or Liam. And even if all those were not true, if not for his life on the chain, Prentice would not have met Cutter Sal, helped her to become Lady Righteous, and married her. She was the wild delight of his heart, and even if everything else had an acceptable outcome, Prentice would not give up his conviction if it meant not having her. She was worth all the moments he had spent on the chain.

It was such an odd thought, and it made him smile in the dark until another shift caused new pain in his ankle, and he winced and hissed. He laid his head back and tried to sleep, but he felt drawn to watch the bright moonlight through the holes in the thatch. He lay like that for what felt like a long while until he thought he must be falling asleep after all. Then he realized that his eyes were not closing but the silvery light beyond the damaged roof was diminishing of itself. He wondered what it could be—an eclipse of the moon? But such a thing would not have much dimmed the Rampart's light. For a dread moment he feared another dark sorcery, like the ritual that had turned the sky to blood over Aubrey, but he doubted that as well. After all, that had taken an unthinkable sacrifice of the kind the witch was apparently holding him for. If she had the power to dim the moon and stars, the witch wouldn't need him, would she?

Prentice was still contemplating these questions when the church door opened silently, unlatching seemingly of its own accord. Outside was dark, darker than usual night, and it took Prentice a moment to realize the sky was overcast. It had been so long since he or anyone had seen clouds over the Reach. Had the witch found a solution to the drought?

All at once the entryway to the church blazed with light, and Prentice beheld the angelic lion, pale as snow and brighter than the full moon. Only once before had he received a visitation of the creature while awake, and he knew it was significant that he was not dreaming now. The creature padded its way into the church until it was right next to him. Its presence seemed to fill the vestibule.

"You are not afraid," it said to him in its fathomless voice.

Prentice shook his head.

"And are you yet angry?"

He thought about the question. "Yes," he said finally with a sober nod. "But not as I was."

"Good, then the steel that was hard-forged has been well-tempered, too. Come, you must leave this place."

The lion laid its paw on Prentice's ankle, and the pain was healed instantly. He almost laughed with the relief of it but was distracted as Whilte gasped from deeper in the nave.

"It's true," the chaplain said with awe.

"You can see him?" Prentice asked.

"A shape standing next to you, akin to a lion, but made entirely of glorious starlight?" Whilte said, nodding. In the brilliance, his face was lit with religious ecstasy. Prentice turned to the angel.

"Why cannot he see you as I do?" he asked.

"Not every gift is given to every man or woman. And blessed are they who have not seen and yet still believe."

Prentice smiled at the gentle rebuke in the angel's recitation. He bowed respectfully.

"It is time to go," the angel said again, and it turned about and led the way out of the church. Whilte quickly joined Prentice and held up his hands.

"Our bonds have fallen away," he said with delight. "And your foot is healed."

Prentice nodded, and the pair followed the angel into the night. Above them, the clouded sky shut out all light, but the divine glow lit the fallen village like a silvery day. In the open square in front of the church, the ground was still disrupted by

the myriad sharpened spikes that had been driven into the earth
to murder the original villagers. The rest of the village was no
more than a ruin, however, with few stones left on one another,
and the beams and branches used to construct them were gone,
likely poached for fires.

On the ground beyond the forest of spikes and amongst the
tumbledown huts, the fey riders slept with their heads on their
saddles like awkward pillows. The angel led Whilte and Prentice
amongst the sleepers. For a moment, Prentice feared they might
awake and catch them, but he only needed to glance at the
lion to know that for the foolish thought it was. He looked the
sleeping fey over and picked out the elder who led them. He
wasn't the one the witch had slain to bind the whole nation
to her, but he was important, nonetheless. Prentice was sure of
that. He found himself drawn to the sleeping fey man and saw
deep pain in his expression, a bitter sadness that seemed to cover
him like a heavy blanket. Prentice looked down as he stood over
the elder, and it seemed as if the blanket stretched over all the
riders, perhaps over all the fey in the Reach. At one level it was
such a fanciful notion, yet Prentice was sure it was true.

As he was contemplating this, Prentice heard a snuffling
sound, like an animal sniffing at the ground for food. He looked
and saw about ten figures, humans and half-human like Haravind, who slept in their midst. Their sleep was fitful, and it was
Haravind who snuffled, as if it were almost too difficult for him
to breathe. For the price of his power, he would know no peace,
not even in sleep, it seemed.

Then Prentice froze in fear as beyond the sleeping,
half-beast-men he saw something moving. It was the unicorn,
and beside it, cross-legged on the ground, was the serpent witch,
draped in her human skins. The sorcerous woman had two
bodies freshly killed laid out in front of her—one fey, one human. She was mutilating the corpses with a dagger of bone
edged with metal and throwing sliced pieces onto the ground
at the unicorn's feet. At her command, the creature rolled in

the dirt, which was ugly red even in the moonlight. It reminded
Prentice of how the dirt had looked that first morning, turned
to a crimson mud that stained everything the color of rust.
The beautiful creature was being forced by the witch to defile
itself further. As he watched, Prentice's horror-filled fascination
overcame his fear until the witch paused in her ritual and looked
about as if she had heard something. The slitted serpent eyes
stared straight at him for a moment, her gaze sickly yellow despite the light. Like the color of the blooded earth, her *brakkis
effar* eyes were too much their own stain to be washed by the
angel's glow. Nonetheless, it was soon clear that she could neither see Prentice nor Whilte and the lion.

"She truly cannot see us," Prentice whispered.

"We pass unseen," Whilte said, happily enjoying the irony
of being able to do so. While Prentice understood that feeling,
something in the chaplain's words crystalized in his thoughts.

"Time to go," the angel commanded and turned to lead them
away from the village.

"No," Prentice said, almost without thinking.

"What?" Whilte asked, astonished and fearful.

"I cannot leave like this," Prentice said, his eyes still on the
witch and her ritual.

"Captain, truly we must leave. If we stay, they will put us to
death. We can escape now and flee to Dweltford. Then we can
return with the full might of the Reach. Your ankle has been
healed. This was your plan."

Whilte did not sound desperate exactly—how could he in
the presence of a divine rescue?—and he was clearly thinking in
practical terms, not wishing to miss the opportunity to escape.
Even as they were speaking, the witch stopped in her ritual once
again and her serpentine tongue, long and forked, flickered out,
tasting the air. Perhaps if they stayed too long, even the angel's
power would not be enough to conceal them.

Still, Prentice looked about, and he could not simply leave.
Yes, it made the most sense to escape and return with an army,

but that was just more bloodshed. Would that not play into the witch's hands? He looked back at the fey, trapped under their blanket of despair, and the venal knights, evil by their own hearts' desires but also bound by false and vile promises. Suddenly he was struck with the memories of every time he had been marched onto a battlefield as a convict rogue—despised, abused and thrown into the cauldron of blood and steel. The same despair that crushed these ancient riders who had hidden themselves away a thousand years also oppressed the heart of every convict. Prentice knew their plight, and he would not fight them if he did not have to.

Before he even knew that he was doing it, he had turned in place and started marching back toward the church. Behind him, Whilte rushed awkwardly to keep up on his wooden leg.

"Captain, what are you doing?" he asked, his voice taking on an even tauter edge. Angel or not, the chaplain was becoming panicked by his leader's behavior.

"They are as convicts to her," Prentice said, explaining in his own fashion but not caring if Whilte truly understood him. "She will fashion a throne of blood for herself and throw them upon the pikes to achieve it. They mean no more to her than the rogues mean to a Kingdom knight."

"So let us fight her and overthrow her plans. Let us fetch the Lions and defeat them."

"They'll flee," Prentice said without turning at the top of the church steps. "They will hide for another thousand years, and that is just another form of transportation over the mountains."

"Captain Ash, Prentice, you're not making sense," Whilte protested. He laid his hand on Prentice's shoulder to try and hold him back. Prentice turned to him and saw the angel lion standing, watching behind. His eyes met the divine messenger's, and for a moment he felt almost drowned in the infinity of those depths. Then he forced himself to look at the brother directly.

"I was lost and forgotten in conviction, Brother," he said in a hissed whisper, even though the angelic protection still seemed to shield them from discovery. "They bound me with iron, and I was worth even less than the chain they held me by. I was like the tailings from the miner's smelters, the leftovers, the waste. Lost and forgotten. A discarded man. And I was content that way..."

He paused a moment and shook his head. That was not true. He had not been content. He had been bitter and enraged, a clay vessel full of the wine of wrath. He had not been content, but he had not been looking for anything else in life, either. For death alone had he waited.

"I was nothing, and that was how I saw myself," he continued. "Then the Horned Man and his scouts came, and they feared what they saw in me. I do not know why, and in truth, I do not care. Perhaps they are deluded, and I really am just another worthless man cast into the cauldron of war. But even if that is all I am, I cannot bring steel and fire upon other men who are trapped in the same worthlessness."

Prentice looked at the sleeping enemy and the witch going about her eldritch ritual. Whilte followed his glance.

"What does that all mean?" the chaplain asked.

"It means...it means...that I think this is a different kind of battle we face now," Prentice explained as best he could. "Most of war is heart and sinew, sharpness of steel and hardness of will. Tactics and strategy will out. This is different, something of the realm of spirit and magick. The witch curses the land and flesh and binds the souls of her slaves."

"Our battle is not with flesh and blood, but with principalities and powers?" Whilte breathed, quoting the apostle. Prentice nodded.

"In this moment, I am certain that is how it is."

He looked over Whilte's shoulder at the angel again, but it only regarded him with its usual regal aloofness. He nodded to it and then turned on his heel once more to enter the church.

"So, what will you do?" Whilte asked.

"I am going to bring her fears upon her, if I can, and stand against her power, not her slaves. She is the one we fight, not them."

"They will defend her. You will have to fight through them to get to her, and you cannot fight them all by yourself."

"You are here, too, Brother," Prentice joked quietly. Whilte leaned down and slapped his wooden leg.

"*We* cannot fight through them all by *ourselves* either, Captain."

"We will not have to," Prentice told him with a confidence he did not fully feel. He looked into the dark of the church and stepped inside, only to realize that the glow of the lion did not go with him. He looked once more to the divine creature.

"I am not sent to fight for you," the angel said, its voice rumbling down to Prentice's bones. "I am to set you free and lead you to safety. No more than this."

"I cannot take safety if these are left in chains," he told the magnificent creature. It bowed its head and shook its mane in a gesture he hoped was like a nod. He glanced at the darkness of the church. "Can you spare me a light, at least?"

Suddenly, there was a lit torch in a sconce just inside the door. Its warm yellow glow was so much dimmer than the angel's radiance, but it was comforting all the same. Prentice nodded his thanks and took the torch from the wall. Holding it ahead of himself, he began to stalk down the aisle of the nave. The swarm of flies rose up in its dark cloud, disturbed by the flames but not driven back by them. The pestilence hounded Prentice's face and bare flesh, crawling over the blood from the myriad little cuts and grazes he had acquired in recent days. Only a pace behind, Prentice heard Whilte coughing and spitting at the insects as they assaulted him as well.

"Thank you for coming with me," Prentice said.

"I am one of your men, Captain," Whilte responded, batting at his face with his sleeve. "We would follow you into hell, one and all. I hope you realize."

"Ideally, it will not come to that."

When they reached the first militia corpse, Prentice pulled forth the weapon that pinned it in place, a broken piece of pikestaff nearly six feet in length. He was hoping for a usable weapon, but as he held it up, it was clear the steel head was badly bent and useless for fighting. He handed it to Whilte.

"What is this? I am past the need for a crutch, Captain."

"Consider it your prophet's staff, if you like."

Prentice moved along, passing bent swords and a halberd with a broken haft, until he came to a full halberd, buried deep in a man's chest. He wrenched it free and, inspecting the head, found it whole. The edges were likely blunted, but serviceable enough. He handed it off to Whilte as well.

"Are you not going to fetch one for yourself?" the chaplain asked, and Prentice smiled for the first time since the angel's original appearance.

"That one *is* mine," Prentice told him. "I just need you to carry it for me."

Whilte gave him a confused glance, made strange by the swarming cloud between their faces, but Prentice merely turned away and made his way to the altar at the end of the nave. The bones on the stone platform looked more forlorn than frightening in the firelight, but Prentice had not come for the sacrist's remains. He was just one more victim of the ancient curse that afflicted the Reach. All Prentice could do for him now was to attack the powers that had spilt the poor religious man's blood.

Or else add mine and Whilte's blood to his, Prentice thought, shaking his head. Moving past the altar, he started to search the floor, rifling through the debris there and finding collapsed thatching, broken pieces of rood screen, and a fallen shutter from one of the high windows. Then he found what he was looking for—the church bell, still in its hardwood frame. A piece of heavy brass a handspan across, the bell was mounted on a stand that the sacrist would carry out the door to ring and call the faithful to worship. Remembering the sacrist's small frame and looking at the solidity of the wood, Prentice suspected the last rector had needed help to move it.

He hefted the frame upright and then positioned himself to take the weight on his shoulders. When he was confident he could carry it and the torch at the same time, he lifted it up and began to lug it towards the door.

"What are you doing?" Whilte asked.

"When the Horned Man's army faced us at the Battle of the Brook, his lieutenant or chosen man or whatever he was, stood with the Fallenhill city bell and rang it to keep time, waiting for us."

"I remember."

"It was an impressive feat of strength and fearlessness," Prentice said. "We are going to borrow a page from his book."

"You can't be serious. You can barely lift the thing."

"Thank you for your support, Brother."

Prentice ignored Whilte's doubts and kept trudging toward the door under the weight of his burden. He was certain now that the last sacrist had had help to move the thing in the past—likely the help of two men, in fact. As the door drew closer, it felt as if the flies were becoming thicker, and Prentice smirked as he took it as a form of encouragement.

Do you fear what is coming, oh Lord of Flies?

Soon enough, he had reached the door and brought the hardwood stand out onto the church steps. The bell hummed quietly as he set the whole thing down, but not so loudly that their enemies might have heard it.

"What now?" Whilte asked.

"Now, Brother, we do what we have been called by God to do," Prentice told him. He exchanged the torch in his hand for the halberd he had asked Whilte to carry for him. "For you, that means to pray, earnestly, with all the heart within you."

"What if we fail?"

"Then it will be in the service of something new and better, Brother," Prentice told him. "And ours will not be the first or last blood spilt on this ground."

Whilte nodded with grim resolution and stepped aside, holding the torch high and the pikestaff in his other hand. Prentice hefted his halberd and then looked to the angel.

"Thank you," he said, and he tugged his forelock. This creature was heroic and militant in its way, but he had a sudden feeling that he was unworthy even to salute this messenger of God. "If by the mercy of the living God there is anything else you might do, please do. If not, I give thanks for the grace shown to my brother and me."

Prentice was surprised at his own words for a moment. He had meant to name Brother Whilte by his title, not to call him an actual brother, but as he looked to the man who had once betrayed him into fire, steel, and blood, he knew it was true. It made him smile. If God could reconcile him to this man whom he had hated for half his life, then defeating the hellish powers of a serpent woman and her array of servitors, monstrous and eldritch, should be a mere trifle. He turned away from the angel and swung the halberd. The silvery light vanished so that only the torch flame remained, and the flat side of the halberd head struck the brass bell.

CHAPTER 68

Amelia followed Solomon out into the lower bailey to find it transformed into an armed camp, tents and stores crammed into every corner. Torches and lanterns hung from every conceivable point, making the still shadowy space reasonably well lit, but the darkness in nooks and crannies made Amelia wonder, and she looked up to realize that the Rampart could not be seen. The sky above was densely overcast. She nearly gasped at the sight. There had not been a single cloud over the Western Reach for at least a year.

Wondering what the change in weather could mean, Amelia followed Solomon as he wended his way through narrow gaps in the crowded space that formed distinct walkways. Militiamen were rushing back and forth so that Amelia was regularly jostled, but Solomon began to call for men to make way. Soon, the militia began to stand aside at their approach and salute as they passed. When the duchess and her young escort arrived at the rear of the castle, the three war wagons were already in place, lined across the opening in the walls. The Lions' blue and cream standard was raised on its pole over the middle wagon and Amelia headed there but was redirected by a line first to a spot between the wagons. She and Solomon crossed the final small distance to find Corporal Gennet standing out in front of the wagon line.

"What is all this, Corporal?" the duchess asked, and she was surprised to see that the entire ground in front of the wagons was a hive of activity. Groups of militia, aided by some of Turley's stewards and other household staff, were developing a second, lower barricade, made of upturned tables, barrels and boxes. Waist high, there were already several lines of Roar manning the growing defense, with Claw pikemen standing their usual guard behind them ready to fend off any assault.

"It's Prince Farringdon's orders, Your Grace," Gennet reported, saluting. "He says it'll let two lines o' Roar fire at once, the ones on the wagons over the heads o' these ones in front. If things get too hairy out here, then the Claws cover the retreat back to the wagons. The prince says it's just like a castle defense. If the knights get their blood up and overrun the first line, there's still the second line to 'fall back to.' That's what he called it."

"Very good, Corporal, but what did you call me for?" Amelia asked.

"Actually, Your Grace, it was the standard bearer, Markas."

The duchess looked to the standard, but the corporal pointed to a spot near the growing front barricade and escorted her there. Markas was holding an iron brazier lantern on the end of a pole, but even without its light, he was distinctive to the duchess by his white "noose" lanyard. Even though she understood its true significance, the sight of it always made Amelia uncomfortable. He saluted when he saw her approach.

"Your Grace, the enemy wants to speak with you."

Amelia looked south to where the land dipped away. The night there was lit by an enormous firefly swarm of torches and other lights. Not since the night the docks had prepared for Daven Marcus's crossing had the Dweltford lake been so brightly lit. To one side were the knights martial, clearly visible as their polished armors glinted in the lamplight. They had banners and pennants on lances, but the colors were indistinguishable at this distance, even with the torches. On the other side, the space between the docks and the castle was filled with a crowd of folk in a variety of yeoman and guildsmen's attire.

Amelia could not be sure, but it seemed as if there were a number of women amongst them, and she hoped her eyes deceived her, but she also felt she could make out some children there.

"My enemies?" she said as she scanned the strange host at the edge of the darkness.

"They sent a herald up a short while ago, Your Grace," Markas explained. "With the captain not here and only a corporal in command, they figured I was the best one to speak. The toff said to tell you the earl would 'observe the forms,' whatever that means."

He shrugged and Amelia nodded for him to go on.

"So, he said he wouldn't stay, but I was to wave this lantern back and forth when you come to talk. He also said I was to lower it if you didn't come down, and they would take it as surrender."

"He said that?"

"Actually, what he said was too disrespectful for me to repeat, Your Grace." The standard bearer frowned, shamefaced. "But he seemed to think it was like that you would be hiding in the castle somewhere all night. Most impolite he was about it, in point of fact."

"Well, I am here now, master banner-bearer," Amelia said with a weary sigh. She was tired of petty insults. "Wave your lantern...no, wait!"

Markas stopped himself before he began to give the signal and Amelia turned to command Solomon, sending the lad off with a nearby steward. It would be a quick task, and Earl Sebastian and his rebel army could bear a quarter hour's further delay. She watched the crowd and the horsemen down on the lakebed while she waited.

"Knights to one side and rogues foot beside them," she muttered to herself, recognizing the structure of the earl's little army. "Except these are not convicts forced to the fight but zealots stirred to hatred and rebellion by the servants of Mother Church."

"They're mostly just a hungry levy, Your Grace," Markas said quietly. Amelia looked at him suddenly, and he bowed his head apologetically. "Not to speak out o' turn, Your Grace, but I know what it is to be hungry. A body'll do desperate foolish things when food grows short. We still have to fight 'em, course, just I don't think they means to rebel, is all."

"No, perhaps not."

Amelia was aware of only some of Markas's personal story, told to her by Prentice, but she knew he was a survivor of Liam's siege of Fallenhill where the first White Lions had almost starved to death. For a long moment of silence, she kept watch southward, barely noticing as a warm breeze set the flame in Markas's lantern dancing, until she smelt something on the air. It took her a moment to realize what the unfamiliar thing was; it was moisture, the promise of impending rain.

My dreams come to pass, she thought, and remembered the image of the peacock, now driven from her throne. She wondered if that meant the lake would fill with water again. Could rain refill a whole lake before the earl attacked? Or even in a single night? The concept seemed inconceivable, but it must have seemed so to the pharaoh as well, on the banks of the Red Sea.

Solomon returned, bearing Earl Sebastian's bent sword taken down from the gatehouse. Two lines of militia were summoned to act as Amelia's close bodyguard, and then she gave Markas the word to give the signal. Soon enough, a small cadre of knights martial were geeing their horses up the slope to their meeting. Earl Sebastian was in their center, with Sir Tarant at his right hand and High Sacrist Quellion at his left.

"Come to ask me to marry again, Earl Sebastian?" Amelia asked him when they were close.

"Never again, strumpet," Quellion declared, but Sebastian held up his hand for silence.

"It is over, Amelia," he said, not bothering with her title. In one sense it was clearly a calculated slight, but in the face of open rebellion, the duchess could no longer care about such fripperies. "The only thing that remains is to demand your surrender according to the chivalric forms."

"You are mistaken, Earl," Amelia shouted so that everyone could hear her. "We have one more thing to discuss. You are in open rebellion, My Lord, although as such, I suppose you are no longer entitled to that epithet. Nevertheless, for this you will be judged, stripped of your title, and exiled from the Reach on pain of death."

Sebastian shook his head ruefully and Quellion openly scoffed.

"Fool girl," Sir Tarrant derided her loudly. "How many times did you want your pretty rogues to fail you before you learned your lesson? Stubborn bitch."

Pretty rogues? Amelia thought. That was all Sir Tarrant thought of the Lions, that they were just another rabble of peasants to throw into the battle to smooth the way for the knights with their bodies. He saw their armor and their weapons, better than any rogues had ever had, but could not see the truth past his prejudices. It was a blindness that had cost many knights their lives already. *Tonight will be no different.*

"We have rogues of our own," Tarrant continued to boast.

"You have my vassals, levied to revolt against me."

"They are driven by zeal for God and justice to throw down a whore in her temple," Quellion countered, but Amelia refused to even look at him. The wind was picking up, and the smell of rain was stronger. It would have been a source of joy if not for this confrontation. Quellion seemed to take it as a sign of God's favor.

"Can you not see the clouds? Can you not sense the coming flood to wash your sin from the land?" he shouted, sermonizing. "What good your infernal fire sticks if the wicks won't light from the rain, Jezebel?"

Call me witch as well and you'll have covered all the options, Amelia thought contemptuously, but Quellion's last assertion gave her a flicker of uncertainty that doubled as the first rain in over a year began as a fine mist and fell upon them all.

"See, slattern Amelia, your time as duchess and the curse you laid upon the land is at an end," the high churchman proclaimed with a wide gesture of his hand.

Amelia looked down and let the warm drizzle drip upon the back of her neck. She wanted to undo her hair and let it fall loose, to be wet and washed for the first time in too long. She longed to tip her head back and capture a drink of fresh water. First though, she had to finish her duty to her people. She raised her head and looked into Sebastian's shadowed features. He returned her gaze attentively, and it occurred to her that he actually thought she might surrender after all, even at this late stage.

"Earl Sebastian, you say that you wish to observe the correct forms," she shouted, blinking water that beaded on her eyelashes. "Then let us observe them."

Amelia turned to Solomon and received Sebastian's bent blade from him. She held the ruined weapon up in both hands.

"That sword has been in my family for six generations, wretched woman," Sebastian said, pushed finally to a rare slip of temper.

"Then you should be thankful I have denied it to you," Amelia interjected before he could say any more. "Otherwise, its honor would have been stained with the shame of your rebellion."

Sir Tarrant snarled and his horse stirred under him so that he was forced to tighten his grip on the reins. Quellion shook his head as if he could not believe Amelia's actions. Sebastian only scowled in fury, his lips curled in a hateful sneer. Amelia threw the sword over the heads of the men in front of her and it clattered on the improvised barricade before falling to the earth out of sight.

"As a rebel," she continued, "your title, your lands, and your place in the Western Reach are forfeit. Your rank as Knight

Captain of the Reach is revoked, and any man-at-arms who rides under your command, if you assault my castle, will be under sentence of death for rebellion and treason. However, I will be merciful. If any knight sworn will lay down his blade and forsake the knights martial-in-revolt, I will spare them, and their family will yet retain its rank.

"Also, in accordance with the forms, if any man lay down his arms now, or in the coming battle, he will receive quarter. No member of your revolt will die or be robbed if they will but yield."

Sebastian held her gaze for a long moment and Amelia stared back, unafraid. Then the earl turned about and ordered his entourage to return to their lines. Before he left, Sir Tarrant leaned forward in his saddle.

"It will be me, you know that, slut?" he said so savagely that even through the strengthening rain, his spittle was still evident. Amelia thought he looked like a lower-born Daven Marcus, and that made her smile coldly. "I'm the one who'll find you in your bolt hole. I'll cut you in quarters for what you've done to him."

"Better men than you have tried, Sir," Amelia said, and she let her smile become a sneer.

Sir Tarrant wheeled his horse and rode to join the rest of his master's company when he realized that two of them were still left behind.

"Come now, you two," he shouted at them, waving his hand. "It's time to end this at last."

The two knights on horseback looked at him and then each other. One still had his helmet on, but he removed it, hooking it on his saddle. Nodding, the pair dismounted, drew their swords, and knelt in the mud. One of them looked up at Amelia.

"Duchess Amelia, Lioness of the Reach," he shouted, "I am Sir Urrimahd. This is my brother-in-law, Baronet Petar Lime. We are from the Pale. We have ridden for the Reach in this turbulent season and have found our souls troubled no matter which way we rode. Nevertheless, we cannot in good conscience ride against you as our liege under God. We ask your forgiveness and surrender ourselves now to your mercy."

Both men symbolically cast their swords away from themselves and bowed their heads once more. In spite of her offer of quarter to anyone who yielded, Amelia was astonished by these two knights' show of repentance. It took a real effort for her to overcome her surprise.

"Take their swords," she told her militia guards, and Lions rushed forward. Their eagerness worried her for a moment. "But do not lay hands on these men. They are of birth and have offered their parole honorably. Do not defame me by mistreating them."

The militiamen accepted the command without question, and after the two discarded blades were collected, the noblemen were permitted to stand of their own accord.

"I must ask you to quit the field, gentles," Amelia said to them. "You are welcome to shelter in the castle until the day is decided, or even to observe the battle if you choose. Please stay clear of the conflict, though, since I cannot vouchsafe your wellbeing with all my other duties. Also, and with no imputation, I warn you that if you are seen to take up arms against me again this day, no one of my service will be permitted to offer you quarter a second time."

"We understand, Your Grace," Sir Urrimahd said after looking to his brother-in-law. The two knights marched back through the battle wagon fortifications, and Amelia watched them go. Once they were out of sight, she was pleased to see Turley arrive, along with Prince Farringdon.

"How fares the state of my home?" she asked.

"I don't think he's in the castle anywhere, Your Grace," Turley said, referring to Bluebird. "Sure, I don't know every little corner a bug like him might hide, but I've got folks to every place I can think of. There ain't no sign. He was dripping blood awhile, but even that trail's gone cold."

"Good enough for me this night, Chief Steward," Amelia told him. The castle secure behind her meant she could concentrate on the battle in front of her, at least for the few hours she thought it would take to win or lose her seat. She looked at the prince and saw that while his injuries had been tended somewhat, the blood on his face had only been wiped away and there were smears still at the edges.

"Are you quite well enough for this, Highness? Shouldn't you be inside?" she asked him.

"I am counselld to rest, Your Grace, and I can do that as easily on the back of a wagon as in a chair in the solar," he responded cheerily. "I heard some of your speech to the earl. May I compliment you on its dignity?"

"You may, Highness."

They shared a smile that was sincere but still somewhat bittersweet. In the current circumstance, how could it be anything else?

"This rain's alright, I'd say," said Turley, as if discussing the weather on a market day in the village.

"Well needed," Farringdon agreed, "but poorly timed, I fear. Your Grace, with your permission, I would like to withdraw the militia from the first barricade."

Amelia looked at the improvised barrier only a few paces away, now almost completed.

"You do not trust it, Highness?"

"It is what I hoped, Your Grace, but I didn't anticipate the rain. If we leave the Roar out there in the open, the rain will dampen their powder and snuff their long-matches. They will be worse than useless, and if there is no need for them there, the Claws can be withdrawn as well."

Amelia nodded. It impressed her that Farringdon had immediately seen in the rain the same threat to her forces that Quellion had, but his solution did not fully console her.

"What of the gunners upon the wagons?" she asked. "Won't they be equally disarmed by the rain?"

"It won't be ideal, Your Grace, especially if it builds to the kind of downpour we probably all hope it will, but they have wooden shelters and other parts built exactly for the purpose of protecting their powder. They will be useful a good while yet, I promise you."

Amelia nodded her permission and Farringdon gave the order for the barricade to be abandoned. Militia and servants withdrew, and the duchess and prince followed. She found herself escorted to an improvised stair built of boxes and up onto the left-most wagon to watch the initial phase of the battle from there. She looked over the south, trying to gauge by the torchlight exactly what Sebastian was up to. Wondering how long it was until dawn, she looked to the eastern horizon, and then up into the darkened sky.

The rain kept falling and was becoming heavier, she was sure.

CHAPTER 69

The brass tone of the bell rang out over the ruins of the village. Each time he struck the metal, Prentice drew his halberd back to ground it beside himself, as if in a sentry position. It was a piece of simple theater, and he felt a little foolish doing it, but if nothing else, it helped him keep a calm, even tempo. The whole point of this act was to demonstrate his fearless nerve to his enemy, which would be thoroughly undermined if he rushed the space between the ringing of the bell because of fear.

By the third peal of the bell, the entire of the enemy camp was awake. The witch had not been asleep herself, but somehow it still took her a long moment to become alert to what was happening. Perhaps her magicks forced her into some kind of trance that was hard to clear from her mind. Perhaps it was a lingering effect of the angel's protection.

Prentice rang the bell twice more, then stopped, sure that every eye was upon him. Haravind's half-men pawed at the earth like the angry rams they were merged with. The fey looked at him with cold disdain, too weighed down in their misery to be afraid of a single armed man and his torchbearer. Prentice saw their elder in their midst, and his eyes met the ancient fey's. He thought he read despair in that gaze, but he did not have any time to look for more than that.

"You!" the witch hissed at him, her tongue flickering. She had stood from her bloody ritual and was beside the neck of the unicorn. Her hands were reaching up into the filthy mane, grabbing at the strands. The creature whickered at her touch and shied, but it did not fight to get away. The witch's hands dragged its neck downward and she pulled herself up onto its back. Once she was there, the unicorn's temper seemed transformed, its fearful hesitancy gone. Now it was as violent-seeming as the ram-men, snorting and tossing its head.

"The time has come for this to end," Prentice declared, watching the serpent woman carefully. He felt this was the turning point. If she decided to spit her venom, he was at his most vulnerable. Even if she missed him, there was a good chance it would strike Whilte or the torch he was carrying. The fire that resulted would likely engulf them both, and this little folly would be over.

"Surrender to the duchess and live," he shouted, "or face me and die."

The witch laughed, a frighteningly bright and feminine sound from so inhuman a figure. She looked to her servitors and waved them toward him disdainfully. Prentice turned back to the elder, and he met the fey's eyes directly.

Oh Lord in Heaven, he prayed silently, *let me show them the Lion.*

Prentice had no way to describe what happened next, but a power came upon him such as he had never known. It was like the cold rage he felt in battle, but so all-consuming that he almost wanted to hide from it, even though it was in him and he was in it. It was no rush of mere strength or wild might such as Haravind received from the witch, Prentice was certain of that much. This was an inevitability that had never been denied, even when it was hidden. This was the truth that was sung by stars, the supreme authority that had thrown the mountain into the sea. He opened his mouth and spoke a single word.

"Yield!" he commanded them, and the sound rolled out of him with the voice of the Lion. The glorious light blazed around him for that one moment, and the word thundered through the air such that the cursed earth itself seemed beaten down by its force. Haravind's beast-men all fell backward, some actually knocked from their feet, to lie flat upon the ground. Haravind himself was forced down onto one knee. The witch's unicorn shied and whinnied in terror, and she was forced to cling on desperately or else be thrown.

"Kill him," she screamed as her mount wheeled about in panic.

The fey and their elder were stood fast, as bewildered as men awakening suddenly from a strange dream. Some blinked their eyes, and a number looked to their leader.

"We have seen you," the elder said quietly, but somehow Prentice heard him.

"Kill him! Kill him now!" the witch cried out, finally getting her bound beast under control beneath her.

"No!" the elder declared, and he swayed as if an invisible blow had struck him in the head. His bow was sticking up from its case in his saddle behind him and he used it to steady himself.

"Oh, I'll damn well do it! His blood is mine anyway," Haravind shouted. In spite of his eagerness, it took him a long moment to push himself up from his knee, as if the power of the Lion's roar still lay upon him. Finally, he was standing, and he drew the champion's sword. "Come on, brothers, let's claim his power for ourselves."

Sword held high in one hand, Haravind led his men in a charge at the church steps. Prentice readied himself, close to the edge of the top step to allow the maximum room to move or fight a withdrawl into the church itself if they threatened to overwhelm him. Then, there came the song of a bowstring thrumming through the air. Each fresh hum was punctuated by a thud as a feathered shaft struck home. Haravind and his men paused, turning to look behind them as one after another they fell to deadly arrows from the elder's bow. Not every shot was fatal, and the elder's hands visibly shook as he loosed each shaft. Some arrows bit into throats and chests, but as many landed in arms and legs or other non-lethal locations. At last, the elder nocked another arrow from his saddle quiver, but before he could draw the string, he collapsed to his knees, holding himself from falling flat only by clinging to his bow like a walking stick. The other fey lifted their voices as one and uttered the ululating mourning song that Prentice had heard at the council in the Azures. Slowly, the elder's eyes fluttered and closed, and he slid to the ground, seemingly dead from his final effort of resistance against the spiritual tyrant who had bound his people. Nonetheless, in his one short moment of mutiny, he managed to kill or injure seven of Haravind's companions. The errant knight snarled at the betrayal and stood indecisive as to which enemy he wanted to attack first.

Prentice was not so confused. As soon as he realized that the bowshots had been at the beast-men and not himself, he surged down the church steps. Ten to one, with fey archers in support, had been suicidal odds he faced only by holy resolve. At three to one odds, he was willing to try his skill. Even as the elder was slipping to the ground, Prentice reached the bottom step and slapped the spike of his halberd into the back of Haravind's head. It was a lighter attack than he wanted, and it seemed to mostly bounce off the heavy ram's horn, but that did not matter too much because Haravind was not Prentice's true target for this pass. He wanted the leader aside so he could get to his underlings, to exploit the surprise the elder had bought for him to its fullest.

After the halberd struck Haravind, Prentice continued its swing into an overhand chop that fell on the shoulder of one of the two other standing beast-men, the axe blade biting deep, like splitting a log. Blood sprayed from the wound and the man staggered back, dead before he even realized he had been struck. Using the halberd like a pitchfork or bargepole, Prentice guided the dying man's body towards his comrade. The other beast-man saw the motion and tried to deflect the body, but that only helped Prentice to wrench the axe blade free of the corpse. As the space between them cleared, the beast-man sprang forward at exactly the same moment Prentice thrust the halberd's spear point straight for his throat. The force of the two motions all but tore the errant knight's head from his shoulders, and Prentice dodged free as this enemy fell dead as well. He brought the halberd around in guard just in time to see Haravind recovered from the hit to his head and lusting for blood.

"Hit me from behind?" he bellowed, and his voice sounded even more inhuman than it had before. "I always knew you for a secret coward."

"You are a half-man who rapes women in their homes and bathes in their blood as he butchers them," Prentice retorted, the full coldness of battle now rushing in his veins. "You cannot imagine how I do not care what *you* think of me."

Prentice had meant the "half-man" to be a reference to Haravind's bestial status, but as he said it, and by the expression on the man's face, he realized that Haravind took it as a reference to his impotence and lost manhood. Bellowing again, the knight errant charged forward, swinging the champion sword in great horizontal sweeps. Prentice retreated, using the halberd to deflect the strikes, but even so, the force of each blow vibrated up the weapon's haft, causing his hands to ache. Incompletely transformed or not, Haravind's sorcerous strength was prodigious.

Still withdrawing, Prentice suddenly found himself in amongst the field of spikes protruding from the ground. In one sense they offered a defensive opportunity, but their height interfered with the length of his weapon and made it harder to wield. He was forced to hold the halberd higher, like a pike, to clear the intervening obstacles. A halberd was not built to be used like that, and the heavy head almost instantly made Prentice's old shoulder wound ache. He felt the sweat dripping down his face and the wooden haft slick in his hands. He had not eaten in days. He was hungry and sore and tiring; Haravind seemed as wildly strong as ever.

After several interchanges, dodging amongst the wooden points, Prentice's weakening arms had managed to swing and land a handful of ineffectual strikes, the force of each attack either absorbed by Haravind's thickly enhanced skull, or on one occasion, by a misjudged wooden spike that deflected an axe blow at the last moment. For his part, Haravind kept lunging and swinging wildly, consumed with the desire to slay. Then Prentice thought he saw an opening, and he swung a narrow-arced cut in a small gap between spikes. Unfortunately, it coincided exactly with Haravind stepping into that gap, so that instead of the axe biting into the beast-knight's side as Prentice intended, it went past him, and the monster was only struck by a part of the haft. He barely grunted as he absorbed the blow and then used his left hand to seize the halberd and twist it out of Prentice's grip. Hefting his sword one-handed, halberd trapped in the other, Haravind swung a massive downward blow that would have split Prentice in two had it struck. Instead, it bit deep into the mud right beside Prentice as the captain stepped to the side and forward, slipping to the outside of Haravind's sword arm. He gripped at Haravind's wrist and slammed an elbow strike into the back of Haravind's limb, hoping to break it at the joint and disarm the knight errant in turn.

On an ordinary man, the technique would likely have succeeded, but Haravind's bones were like iron and his grip unyielding. Treating Prentice as if he were an annoying child clutching at his hand, Haravind merely threw his arm wide so that Prentice felt himself cast backwards through the air. More from reflex than intent, he held his grip on the beast-man's wrist, essentially to keep from falling. It meant, though, that the full weight of his body pulled backward against Haravind's one arm, and even with his massive strength, the beast-man was thrown momentarily off balance, falling against a wooden spike. The point bit into his flesh just below his shoulder blade, not deeply but drawing some blood. Seeing the opportunity, Prentice released Haravind's wrist and grabbed for his neck from behind. Under other circumstances, Haravind's eldritch might would have made short work of Prentice's wrestling, but being tipped backward and caught on the spike for a moment so that he could not easily work free enough to get his balance back, there was nothing he could do to resist. Prentice heaved downward with all his might, and Haravind snarled, then screamed, as the wooden spike was forced all the way into his chest and punched its way out through his ribs, impaled as the villagers had once been.

Prentice slipped in the dirt and took a moment to get his feet back under himself. Then he moved around and retrieved the champion blade. He looked Haravind in the face and was surprised to see he was not yet dead.

"I will be a god," the errant knight said, his lifeblood bubbling out of his mouth with the words.

"You are a fool," Prentice told him, and with a single swing, he clove Haravind's head from his shoulders. He rested a moment then, leaning on another of the spiked posts, head down, breathing in gasps.

"Kill him!" the witch was screaming, over and over again. Prentice looked up to see her still seated on the unicorn and waving her arms in the air in a frenzy. The fey's ululation had ceased, but they were not moving to act for her. "You are mine! I will be queen! Obey me! Kill him."

Prentice stepped out from the field of stakes and faced her across the blooded earth of the ruined village square.

"You want me dead," he said, sword pointing at her, "come and do it yourself."

CHAPTER 70

"Here they come!" someone on the wagons shouted, and every militiaman held his weapon that little bit tauter that a ripple of motion passed along the line. The rain was coming down in a steady fall now, and off in the east, the cloud-banked sky was beginning to get light, though ever so slowly.

At the slope end of the castle's back meadow, first a column of knights ahorse and then a mob of yeomen appeared, clambering up from the lakebed. A single Roar gunner fired to no effect.

"Hold shot," Corporal Gennet commanded, and a shouted apology sounded from somewhere on the line.

"Sorry. Misfire."

"I'll misfire you, you beggar!"

"They're picking their lines of attack," Farringdon said to Amelia as he watched the knights' leaders giving orders. "See, they have told them to leave a gap on the west side."

"Why?" she asked, determined to understand everything she could of what was going on around her.

"If they are planning to use your levied townsfolk as they would any other rogues, Your Grace, then I would guess their intent is to have the crowd assault the wagons and either try to overturn them or just push them aside by sheer mass. If they succeed, the knights will ride down that channel at the side and charge into the gap opened for them."

"Damn them." Amelia had loathed the Grand Kingdom's traditional tactics for as long as she had been duchess, seeing their murderous waste of life. Even so, the fact that these were free folk being driven by desperation to let themselves be used like the lowest of the lowly sickened her. She found herself wondering for a moment if she would care as much if they were merely convicts but realized she already knew the answer. Of course she would. That was why the White Lions had been mustered in the first place.

The rain was turning the dusty ground to mud, and she felt her dress clinging to her. The townsfolk began to stride forward, improvised weapons in hand, slipping on the mirey ground and urged on by rabble-rousing clerics, easily distinguished in their number by their cassocks and shaved heads. These men carried large crosses and shouted words that were not typical in religious men's mouths.

"They certainly love staining my reputation," she muttered.

"Brother Whilte says you're a gift from God for the ordinary militiaman," Gennet said. "He says there ain't no righter or juster noble in all the Grand Kingdom."

Amelia looked at the man in wonder. He noticed and tugged his forelock.

"Just saying, Your Grace. Them's ain't the only type of churchman."

She looked back to Prince Farringdon and Turley. The Chief Steward gave her an encouraging and entirely inappropriate wink while the prince nodded.

"There you go," he said. "Who said the common man was of one mind?"

"Indeed, Highness."

The crowd had reached the outer barricade and were either climbing over it or else trying to break it apart. With all the Roar pulled back to the wagons, Farringdon had passed the order for the first barricade to be their signal to begin firing. Twenty matchlocks spat fire, smoke, and iron shot, ripping into the townsfolk. At least half that number fell, and the uninjured already across the barrier charged at the wagon line, enraged. Still being urged on by their rabble rousers, they crossed the short distance and began to batter at the wooden defenses or else aimed toward the gaps between wagons where pike-and-halberd Claws stood in disciplined lines, ready to hold them off. More pikemen thrust their weapons over the top of the wagons into the pressing crowd.

Watching from her position on the wagon on the left-hand side of the line, with the castle's town-side wall looming over her, Amelia felt surprisingly safe at first. She had stood on battlefields before, even on a wagon line, but never this close to the seething melee of an assault. Still, she watched with strangely little fear as only a pace or two away and down from her, people shouted and died.

Suddenly, one bold member of Quellion's townsfolk levy managed to get purchase for his hands and feet, climbing above the melee with unexpected speed. Up against the wood as he was, the man was inside the reach of the pikemen's points, and there were no halberds or Fangs to stop his climb. Poised for a moment on the wagon's edge, Amelia saw he had a knife in his mouth. He took it in his hand and was readying himself to spring when Farringdon struck the man a brutal cut across his shoulder and knocked him backward off the edge. As he fell, he must have thrown his knife in a last-ditch attempt to attack, for it looped up and then clattered harmlessly on the wood. It inspired others, though, as for a moment the falling raindrops were joined by an array of tools and hard objects, thrown from the crowd—knives and gaffs, belaying pins and iron boat hooks, even a tackle block with a length of rope still threaded through it. In their armor and helms, the Lions on the wagons hardly noticed the clattering fall, but not so protected herself, Amelia shied away until she realized that Prince Farringdon had once more interposed his body between her and danger. A wooden belaying pin rang on the backplate of his cuirass, and he grunted with the hit but was otherwise unhurt.

"This cannot be good for your healing," she said to him quietly as they crouched close together.

"Where you need me, Your Grace, there I will be," he answered her.

Amelia was moved by his pledge and wanted to send him away, or even go away with him if it would keep him safe. Her loyalty to all the other militia drove her to stay and face the danger with them, though. She was the Lioness, and they were her White Lions. If she must face battles like this without her Captain Ash, she would remember his example and follow it, at the very least. Even more, she wanted to be seen, right here at the front, just to prove Sebastian and Quellion wrong when they expected her to cower in the castle. All of these thoughts must have been visible in her expression, because before she could say a word of it to Farringdon, he nodded to her and looked behind the wagon to Solomon, standing dutifully in the back ranks.

"Solomon, run now and fetch me a shield," Farringdon commanded. "And see if you can find a helmet for Her Grace's head."

Solomon saluted and dashed away.

"My thanks, Highness," Amelia told him as he straightened up a little and allowed her to do so as well. He remained standing mostly in front of her, though the number of tossed weapons seemed to have diminished. Sooner than she would have expected, Solomon returned with a helmet of the same type that the Lace Fangs favored when they armed for full battle and a knight's heater shield, with a white field and two chevrons—one emerald green and one Reach blue—and a riverboat in their midst.

"The helmet is Lady Spindle's, Your Grace," Solomon explained. "She had me bring it here to be ready if you needed her down in the midst of the battle. The shield is from one of them knights that surrendered from Earl Sebastian's men. He gave it me when he saw me searching. With his compliments, he said."

"I must thank him when this is done," Amelia said as Farringdon fitted the shield to his arm so that he could cover her more readily when other thrown items came their way. He had already batted away a lit but guttering brand while she was fitting the salet to her head. It astonished her how much the noise of the conflict was dulled in her ears, and she suddenly understood even better why men on the battlefield needed drums and trumpets to signal each other. The reduction of noise was at once a relief and a little unnerving.

The ugly conflict was yet ongoing, and the rain was getting worse so that even as the overcast sky was lightening with daylight, the entire field of combat still seemed dark and frighteningly confused. Amelia was looking south, trying to see what the earl and his knights—*her* knights, actually—were doing. Would they charge soon? Apart from setting one of the wagons rocking a little for a time, the yeoman levies seemed to be doing very little actual damage and suffering brutally for the privilege. Then a Roar gunner pushed past her and jumped off the back of the wagon to the ground. Looking around, Amelia realized that the Roar were not shooting anymore. Corporal Gennet was consulting with the prince on his other side. When she leaned in to listen, Farringdon explained the situation.

"The rain's soaking the powder, and none of the Roar can keep their long-matches lit, your Grace. The corporal just asked permission to withdraw them. They will be set to fetch and carry, taking the wounded off the line."

"Do we have many wounded?" Amelia asked. Farringdon smiled and Gennet shook his head.

"Nothing to force a man to quit the line yet, Your Grace. We're holding fine and dandy, even without the Roar. In fact, my guess is them levies is down to 'bout half their number already."

"Perhaps not that little," Farringdon said. "But they are suffering, and we are not."

Those are my *people,* Amelia thought. The entire point of having a trained militia was so that her populace did not have to suffer pointlessly like this.

"I thought Earl Sebastian was a great war hero," she said bitterly. "What is he waiting for?"

"For the tactics his ancestors have trusted from time immemorial to work, Your Grace," Farringdon said, and Amelia smiled at him.

"That's like something Captain Ash would have said," she told him, and he bowed humbly in response.

"You flatter me, Your Grace."

Amelia nodded, but her somberness reasserted itself immediately. She looked from prince to corporal, inviting them both into open conference.

"These are the desperate and hungry," she told them. "Do not doubt many will be refugees, already driven out of their homes once by war. Others are good folk too hungry to think clearly and desperate for a way to feed themselves or their children. I will not suffer them to be slain for the earl's hubris or my good name. What can we do to take this battle to the rebels directly? You are my men-at-arms; what do you advise?"

Prince Farringdon looked a moment to the corporal, who seemed a little overwhelmed. Amelia couldn't blame him. Only a few years ago, the man had probably been a sheep thief or a drunk who'd gotten into one too many tavern brawls. Then Gennet nodded and his expression grew resolved.

"Advance," he said simply and looked to the prince for confirmation or correction. Farringdon nodded and repeated the word.

"As simple as that?"

"It's what the captain would do," Corporal Gennet insisted. "They ain't breaking us, not even close. If we push, they'll be forced back, I swear it, Your Grace. We're holding them off, and it ain't even costing us. We can advance, close file, like we did against Baron Ironworth's knights. We broke knights in full plate that way. These are townsfolk. They won't hold."

"And what about the knights still ahorse?"

"We're trained to deal with them, too. Unless this earl's got a secret trick hidden in the lake dust, there's nothing here we ain't ready for, Your Grace."

Prince Farringdon nodded when Amelia looked for his opinion.

"Very well, Corporal, Highness, go to and let us push the victims aside so that we may reach the true perpetrators."

Corporal Gennet jumped down and started to give orders. Amelia was surprised to see Solomon snap to the man's side, and having received orders, pull up a drum from the ground and begin to beat upon it. The lad was so calm, so ready to turn his hand to any duty on the field. As loathe as she was to accept the horror of children turned to soldiers, she could see why Prentice would trust this lad to defend his own honor and the honor of her militia.

In the gaps between the wagons, the Claws shifted their posture, and at Solomon's drumbeat, deadened somewhat by the rain but still echoing off the castle walls, pole and pike soldiers began their one-step, one-thrust advance. Almost immediately, the levies in front of them drew back in fear. As the Claws began to move ahead of the line of the wagons, Fangs came out from behind them to scour the sides of the wooden battlement clean of assailants. Swords bit, and townsfolk who had been shouting in battle lust began to scream in agony and terror. Soon the wagon line was free of assaulters and the White Lions had formed two lines of their own across the same front. If the levies were organized and pushed back, this would be too weak a formation to hold them long, but no matter how they shouted religious reassurances of victory, the rabble-rousing clerics could not inspire the townsfolk to throw themselves at the disciplined blades. As if the rain itself was washing them away, the levies melted from the Lion's advance, and soon they were fleeing en masse. The militia kept its discipline, and whoever did not or could not flee was held and passed back to the Roar who were now policing the battlefield behind their comrades.

At the outer barricade, the line paused and Corporal Gennet asked for his liege. Amelia met him as he stood beside what looked like a piece of a horse's stall from the castle stable.

"We can hold here if you like, Your Grace, but I think we should keep going."

Amelia was happy with that, but looked to Farringdon for his opinion, nonetheless.

"Sound tactic, I think, Your Grace," the prince concurred. "The townsfolk are broken. I doubt they'll be reorganized for another assault anytime soon, if ever. If we press forward toward the downslope, we force the knights to engage or cede the height to us. Either is a useful outcome."

"Very well," Amelia agreed. "Have Markas bring the standard. I will march beside it."

"Your Grace?" Farringdon was clearly surprised by the command. Corporal Gennet looked positively stricken. He clearly had no desire to see his liege in that much danger. Amelia knew better, though.

"The earl wants me dead or captured so that he can hang me himself," she explained. "If I am in sight, I guarantee you he will not simply withdraw for a more favorable ground."

"Very good, Your Grace." The corporal could not fault her logic, but he clearly did not like it.

CHAPTER 71

T he witch hawked her foul venom and made to spit at Prentice. They were not close, but he had seen other serpent women discharge their poison such distances before. He braced himself, fairly confident that he could dodge it when it came, even as tired as he was feeling. Her mouth distended to inhuman proportions, her fangs dripping ichor, and then she spat. Prentice found himself wrong-footed. She had guessed which direction he planned to dodge, perhaps from reading his body position or the movement of his feet. Whatever the cause of her intuition, she spat to follow his motion, and the venom was going to catch him in mid-move. As it came on though, Whilte shouted from the church steps.

"No!" was all he said, though his voice echoed over the ruins. The spit of venom broke apart in midflight so that by the time some of it nearly reached Prentice, the gobbet had become a mere mist that simply fell to the dust harmlessly.

Prentice looked to Whilte and saw his own astonishment reflected on the chaplain's face. The brother was still holding up the torch in one hand, and in his other he was lifting and pointing the piece of pike that Prentice had handed him, holding it exactly like a prophet's staff in a stained glass or illuminated text.

The witch snarled in fury and made to hawk another gobbet, but Whilte reflexively pointed his "staff" at her and commanded her again. "No!"

The noise in her throat stopped up as if she had choked on the venom, and she clutched at her chest a moment, even beating her fist against her own ribcage. Happy to accept the moment's deliverance, Prentice smiled and then took a stance once again, silently inviting the witch to attack him. She surprised him by pulling her mount to the side and charging straight at Whilte. Prentice bolted in the same direction, but the unicorn was naturally swifter. Its hooves clomped up the stone steps, and it reared to plunge. Whilte held his ground fearlessly, and they seemed frozen there in Prentice's sight for a moment. Then Prentice threw himself at the serpent witch to remove the threat by taking the rider as he would with any mounted man-at-arms. His sword never even reached her, but he did save Whilte, since the unicorn twisted as it fell, not striking the chaplain with its horn, but using its shoulder to bat Prentice aside in defense of its rider. It was a feat of agility that even the nimble fey ponies could never have achieved. The mythic creature followed up with a thrust of its horn that Prentice deflected with the edge of his blade by sheer fluke. The force of the hit knocked him back down the stairs, the strike of horn on blade ringing like a hammer-blow on a smith's anvil.

Prentice tumbled down the stairs to the ruddy dirt, his only focus on keeping hold of his blade. He managed to come awkwardly back onto one knee and forced the sword into a high guard. It seemed the witch was caught in indecision now, as Whilte had taken Prentice's intervention as a chance to withdraw to the door of the church or else had been knocked there by the unicorn's motions.

Make up your mind, bitch, Prentice thought as he slowly retook his feet. His body ached, his breathing was harsh, but he still felt strong enough for this fight if he had to be. Of course, a little more assistance would not be unwelcome. He looked to the fey, hoping that some others of them would be willing to rebel and shoot their enslaving mistress for him. They stood by, not helping either side, but fixated on the conflict. Perhaps only the elders had the power to openly rebel. If simply taking no sides was the best they could manage, Prentice would make do with that much.

The witch made up her mind and spurred the unicorn to charge down on Prentice. It was a short distance, and Prentice had faced knights' charges, not to mention beast-men and cannon fire. Yet this felt like waiting to receive an avalanche or a vast tidal wave. Akin to a pure force of nature, stand or run, it would destroy him, regardless. He set himself to move, but even as he dodged, the beast twisted again at the end of its charge, its deadly horn chasing him and scouring his back. He screamed in pain and rolled over the dust to find himself once more under the shadow of the stakes. Scrabbling on hands and feet, he rushed into the hedge of spikes and hid a moment. The unicorn and its rider prowled back and forth at the perimeter like a predatory animal, watching him as he took a breath and worked to get the pain under control.

"Hide as you like," the witch told him, and strangely, her voice was like a young girl's again. It was disconcerting. "I can wait. The land gives us strength." She patted the unicorn's neck. "We will not rest. Come out now or wait and die in your sleep. Matters nothing to me. And then I will show them what it means to defy their queen."

She cast a disdainful glance over the waiting fey. Prentice felt as if he could almost sense the war within the secretive people, hopeful defiance against crushing despair. It was the war in every convict. But while she looked to them, Prentice had eyes only for the unicorn and his met its bloodshot gaze truly for the first time. In that moment he felt the same conflict in this beast. In every respect, it was as much a convict as he had ever been, bound in ancient, unbreakable chains and forced into war and death for a cruel and tyrannical master. Whether a mortal was righteous or wretched, they should not be enslaved to fight the wars of others, and as so this creature should be beautiful and free, the spirit of the land, to grow and be as the Creator intended. Instead, it was enslaved to blood and slaughter, and in its eyes, Prentice was sure that he saw its true heart just for one moment and knew that it would rather die than be this.

I cannot free you, he thought, and it grieved him. He felt a single unexpected tear form in his eyes, and it seemed there was one in the unicorn's eyes as well. Then the beast tossed its head and the moment was broken. Blood-stained hooves stomped the earth. The witch smiled down upon him with contempt.

"While you live, the land is enslaved," he said, looking to her but speaking to her mount. "Its folk are accursed and rain cannot fall. The fey have rejected the liar's pact. I am sorry."

"I'm not," the witch said, and she watched in glee as Prentice moved slowly forward, his back aching where it was cut, blood running down and dripping at his feet. Slowly he emerged from the hedge of stakes, carefully choosing his spot on the perimeter. The witch had withdrawn slightly to let him emerge. Perhaps she thought he planned to make a dash for freedom and wanted the pleasure of running him down. It didn't matter to Prentice. He set his feet and waited. The unicorn prowled back and forth a moment, like a hungry wolf in reach of its prey, and then it sprang.

Even knowing what was coming, Prentice was barely fast enough to get to one side. The horn led the beast, and it turned aside to chase him as before, but he used his sword to deflect the lance-like thrust away from himself and straight at one of the stakes. Still in mid-air, the unicorn managed to twist itself, catlike, to near safety. The stake's point only scratched the beast's skin-draped flank. The rest of the spikes behind this one on the perimeter meant that the creature could not simply bound away, though, and it had to turn about in place to avoid any more points. That was easily within its agility, but it was also a slow maneuver, and Prentice only wanted that one extra moment. The champion sword, forged at Baron Ironworth's direction to be forward-heavy for chopping into the adamant bones of *brakkis effar* and other enchanted creatures, crashed down on the unicorn's neck like a headsman's axe. It was a brutal, ugly thing to have to do, and Prentice hated the witch who forced them to this. A creature like this should be free, and he steeled himself with the thought that the only freedom he had to offer it was the freedom of the grave—"for the dead have passed beyond the sufferings of this world."

The unicorn's forelegs collapsed beneath it and the witch screamed as she was thrown sideways, falling from its back. Prentice ignored her and swung the sword overhand to end the poor creature's misery. With his second strike, the beast fell utterly dead, its neck almost completely severed. As the blow struck, the heavens roared with thunder and a cloudburst opened that drenched everything in moments.

Rain.

The desperate need of the Western Reach and now it was as if a whole winter that had been held back was released. Prentice felt the filth and blood being washed from his body and watched as the sorcerous carrion on the unicorn's corpse started to sluice away, but he had no time to contemplate any of that. As if the slain equine were no more than a lump of rock, he scrambled over it to throw himself at the witch. She was clawing her way through the sudden mire that the dusty ground had become. Some of the badly cured skins she clothed herself in were slipping away, tangling her legs a moment. Prentice landed in the mud on the other side of the unicorn and immediately lost his footing. He was exhausted, and his body was wounded. Nevertheless, he swung from his knees; his enemy was so close. He wanted nothing but to end this witch and purge the land for his duchess, for the women slain in Halling Pass, for the fey and their lost elders, and most of all, for his wife and child.

The blade's tip caught the witch on her foot, and she screamed again with terror and agony, but she managed to crawl on all fours like a lizard through the torrential rain and gripping mud. Prentice wanted to hunt her, to run her down, but the cold downpour was already draining the last strength from his limbs. He tried to get his feet under him but only slipped to the ground again. Another attempt threatened to pitch him facedown when Whilte caught him suddenly, holding him like an old friend.

"Peace, Captain, peace," the chaplain shouted in his ear. "It's done. She's done. Her power is broken. Surely the land is freed."

I certainly hope so, Prentice thought, though he could not rise to a smile at it.

"Come, let's get you in out of this rain so I can look at your new wounds," Whilte told him.

"Are you joking, Chaplain?" Prentice asked, even as he was accepting the man's help. "I have had enough of being out of the rain to last me a lifetime."

"Don't be ridiculous, Captain," Whilte chided him, and with his arms wrapped carefully around Prentice's chest, he helped him to his feet. The rainfall was so heavy it was like a weight on their backs, and they were walking ankle deep in water when they realized that the fey were moving around them. Prentice was not sure what to expect, but he was still surprised when he saw four of them carrying their elder's body. He was even more astonished when he realized the elder still lived, because as the four bearers drew closer, the elder opened his eyes and looked at Prentice. The fey did not interfere as Whilte helped Prentice up the church steps and into the vestibule. In fact, they followed, and as Prentice leaned against a wall and slumped down agonizingly, leaving a crimson smear on the whitewashed wall, they placed their elder in a similar place beside him. Then the fey left, silently but insistently drawing Brother Whilte with them. The chaplain allowed himself to be taken, apparently not alarmed, but sparing Prentice a glance. Whilte's torch had been thoroughly dowsed by this point, but the greyness of the overcast sky told that it was full day by now and there was just enough light in the vestibule to see by. Water rushing in through holes in the roof scattered the swarms of flies.

"I saw the Lion in you," the elder whispered, his voice weak and hard to hear over the downpour. "I saw and I heard it speak with your voice."

Prentice nodded, but there was nothing he could think of to say.

"The blood is unbound, and the liar's pact ended," the elder continued. "There are words in our tongue for thanks that is deserved, but we have no way to speak them to *kreff*. In a thousand years we have passed unseen by your kind and needed to thank you for nothing. But I have told them that what they might owe to me, they now owe to you. What the other elders owe to me, they owe to you."

The elder reached over and patted an exhausted hand on Prentice's shoulder. Prentice did his best not to flinch from the pain in his own body.

"Do not mistake me," the elder said, looking into his eyes. "You cannot be a king to them, and by the Creator's will, they will never allow themselves to be bound as she bound us, but you will have an elder's voice. They will see you and let themselves be seen. You are now to them *kreff enkreffra*, 'the blind one we allow to see us.'"

"I...uh...thank you," Prentice told him.

"It is deserved," the elder said and closed his eyes. "Now I will rest with my ancestors and not go to them in chains. You have done well for us."

"I may yet ask for much in return," Prentice said. Already he was imagining the usefulness of having the fey riders on the Reach's side. Would it be possible? Or would they fade back into the mountains for another thousand years after this? Might they agree to serve? And could he ask them, after what the witch had done to them and forced them to do? The Redlanders were still about the rivers in the south and the war in the Grand Kingdom proper was sure to spill westward again soon. Could he in good conscience drag them back into conflict?

He knew the answer to all those questions. For the duchess and the new thing she was making in this land, he could and he would. Nevertheless, he felt he owed the elder one commitment.

"As you go to your rest, take this with you to your ancestors," he said. "The *kreff enkreffra* you leave behind will honor your people. I will ask of them, but I will never ask a pledge that they do not word for themselves. They can decide what they will offer, and whatever they will not offer, we will not ask."

Prentice knew he was speaking on his duchess's behalf without consulting her again. It was a bad habit of his, but he was convinced that in this case, as so often before, she would honor his words. He hoped the elder had heard everything he said, because as he finished, the fey's head dipped low and he sighed out his last breath. Prentice laid back against the wall and called for Brother Whilte.

Chapter 72

The knights martial chose to cede the upper ground, withdrawing onto the muddy flats while the Lions occupied the top of the slope, barring access with a single oblong formation of five ranks of thirty-five men. It was a position almost as dominant as the one they had had behind the wagons. The militia standard was planted next to some trees at the town-side corner of the slope, and Amelia stood beside it with Markas and Prince Farringdon. Turley had withdrawn to the castle to assist with the prisoners and keeping order there. Solomon had his drum and was with Corporal Gennet in the center of the formation—the position Captain Ash would have taken if he were here.

"It looks like they want to draw us out onto the flats," Amelia observed. "Does Earl Sebastian think to get us in the open and encircle us, do you think, Highness?"

"That's likely to be his hope, Your Grace," Farringdon responded.

As they watched, a small band of men-at-arms rode up to the base of the slope and made a fuss of challenging the militia, shouting insults and denouncing them as convicts and cowards. They were in full steel harness themselves, but their mounts were not as barded for war as many of the other knights martial. That confirmed Amelia's suspicion in her mind. They were the lighter coursers, who would fall back to the rest of the knights martial if the Lions came down the slope. Amelia's militiamen impressed her with their calm discipline. Not a single one called back, and all held their positions in the ranks. Everyone could see that these men-at-arms were bait to draw the footmen down onto the flats and into the teeth of a full charge.

And still the rain soaked them all.

The shouting continued, and as it did, Amelia found herself ignoring the words and studying the men and their mounts, comparing them to the rest of the rebel company farther out on the increasingly muddy flats. For years now she had read everything she could lay her hands upon to learn of war and statecraft. She had listened to every word Prentice spoke and questioned him at length when she did not understand. He had always told her that she should have wise advisors she could trust, but she also had to know for herself so that she could choose poor advice from excellent and all qualities in between. Prentice was not here, but she had a stout corporal who knew his duty and a prince and standard bearer who also knew the captain's wisdom and who also had their own experience to add.

So, Amelia asked herself: what did she know? What could she see?

The knights issuing the challenge were standing their horses at the base of the slope, and it would take their mounts less than ten climbing strides to reach its top. They would not be even halfway before they encountered the points of the forward-most pikemen, and if they passed those, every next step would bring them into range of yet more sharpened steel. The more heavily armored men and riders might trust to their protection and try to bully through, making a hole for their comrades, but surely the more armored, the slower the going uphill and out of the mire. Looking down, she saw that even these lighter-armored coursers already had stains splashed up to their bellies, and their fetlocks were black with fresh mud.

That caught her attention. Knights ahorse were heavy cavalry, there was no way for them not to be, but these who were taunting bait were the lightest that could be expected. Yet even they clearly had sunk to almost their knees in the mud just to reach the bottom of the downslope. The others farther out in the flats, weighed down by an additional fifty or more pounds of steel barding, must be almost swimming in the mire already. Amelia was struck with the memory of the final parts of her dream. Her first thought was for her people, and she looked to the docks where the broken remnants of the townsfolk levy were lingering amongst the grounded river boats. Some were seated on the docks to watch, as if this was a summer tourney, even though the rain was so heavy that it created a spraying fog over her town where it bounced off roofs and walls. The folk still down at lakebed level seemed to be ankle deep themselves already.

Amelia cast her eyes up the docks to where the castle draw-bridge and barbican were clearly visible. She had half expected the earl to try to distract her forces with a second assault there, but none had materialized. It was calm and seemingly deserted along all the parts of the bridge, Castle Road, and the north docks that she could see. Then she looked down under the bridge, where the exposed stone footings looked like stout cousins to a cathedral's flying buttresses. Farther down on the lakebed under the arches, Amelia saw black water flowing forward, and it filled her with the ominous dread of her dreams.

It was no more than a ripple, barely ankle height. By no means was it the mighty waves that swept pharaoh's chariots away. But it was water, free-running water. The tiny-seeming wave rushed on, gathering speed as the channel between the docks and the castle island concentrated its flow. Even by the time it reached the first grounded boat, a second ripple was pouring down the channel, and more would be coming. The lake was returning to life, dried death washing away in deceptively gentle rinses of black water. When they realized what was coming, the townsfolk began to cry in panic and wade for the lake edge that had not been a shore for a year now.

"Corporal Gennet," Amelia shouted as loudly as she could over the rain. "Stand ready. They will come soon and desperately. Any that seek quarter and surrender their blades, we rescue from the mire."

She couldn't be sure the corporal heard her over the drumming of the rain. His helmet likely blocked shouts at this distance as well as hers would. Nevertheless, she saw Solomon beat his drum, his hands rising high over his head and slamming down to force the wet skin to ring out its full sound. After this much rain, the instrument would likely need to be fully reskinned.

"You think they will try to force a resolution now with the rain, Your Grace?" Farringdon said loudly, close beside her. Amelia nodded.

"If he hasn't seen the danger yet, I cannot imagine the earl will miss this waterflow for long. If it keeps up, and it seems the rain *is* keeping up, he and his horses will be up to their stirrups in water within the hour. That is not a position he will wait to find himself in, I think, Highness."

"No, of course. He might withdraw, make for the banks of the lake. Perhaps seize the town while we are here."

Amelia had not thought of that, and she felt a sudden rush of panic. She remembered the riot in Griffith and Sebastian's calm readiness to ride knights through the streets. It felt like a real possibility.

"If we see that start to happen, Highness," she told the prince, "I will need you to take a cohort swiftly back through the castle and over the bridge. Turn straight right off Castle Road and down the dockside. See if you can block their entry or even capture them."

"At your command, I will," the prince answered.

As she watched though, she was sure Sebastian would make a final assault. He had resisted facing odds he did not like all through this attack, willing to wait to fight in his preferred fashion, but she did not think he had the desire to drag his rebellion out beyond this day. Unless this rain stopped now and the drought returned tomorrow, he would have lost the key motivation that was driving her people to join him in his uprising. Prentice had once told her that there was a moment in every battle where it was won or lost, a turning point where the right decision could swing the pendulum. He even said that sometimes that moment happened before the battle was begun, which made no sense at all to Amelia. Watching this battle, mere skirmish though it really was, she realized they were now at the turning point. The next move would determine who won and who lost, and that move was Sebastian's.

The second ripple of water reached the knights ahorse, no more than fifty paces from the southern shore of the castle island, which was rapidly regaining its status as an island. A horn sounded from the earl's company and the "bait" horsemen withdrew while the rest of the company geed their horses forward through the mire. Mighty destriers carrying men and arms labored to lift their legs out of the mud that was already under a shallow level of water. The company pressed themselves towards the castle and its defenders, but their progress was exhaustingly slow.

"You've already lost, My Lord," Amelia said sadly as she looked down at the earl's standard in the middle of his company. The proud and disciplined men-at-arms could not even maintain their formation, so difficult was it for their horses to wade forward. The rain drummed on their steel plate, and their plumes and pennants, banners and caparisons all hung limp or clung to them awkwardly, making movement even more difficult.

The first of the knights martial reached the bottom of the slope, but there was not enough space for them to order themselves for a charge. The initial group were forced to come up the slope in small numbers, just to make space for those behind to exit the water. Without many comrades beside them and with no way to build up speed or power riding uphill, even for that small space, the knights stood no chance. Some tried to force their way through and managed to break some initial pike points on their armor or with their weapons, but ultimately the steel hedge was too much, and even the most heavily protected lacked the strength to force themselves and their mounts through it. As they failed, they were either felled or driven back, and they crashed into the others behind them, still hoping to make their own attempts. The knights martial of the Western Reach were broken before making even a single concerted charge.

Some few at the rear tried to swim their horses around the others to find a way out of the water and up the steeper slopes at the island's sides, but Corporal Gennet saw them and dispatched his rear-most rank to act as an independent unit to force the one or two hopeful horsemen back into the water. On the muddy slope, men-at-arms knocked from their mounts, trapped between pike and halberd above them and the press of horse flesh behind, began to wrench their helmets off and throw away their swords, to beg for rescue from the crush. Fangs, waiting for exactly this moment amongst their pole-armed comrades, seized those knights and dragged them into the back ranks where they were forced to their knees and commanded to surrender officially. Amelia smiled to see that happen and then watched, amazed, as if like the slow toppling of a stack of boxes that grew faster as they fell, the surrenders became a rush. It seemed like some of the riders at the back resisted for as long as they could, refusing to accept the inevitable, though perhaps they simply could not find a way out of the water over the fallen horses that thrashed at the bottom of the slope. Already it seemed that some of the poor beasts must surely be doomed to drown.

"Your Grace," Solomon shouted at Amelia's elbow, and she turned to him in surprise. "Corporal's compliments, but if you could join him with the prisoners. Some of them are demanding the right to surrender to you directly."

Amelia nodded, even though she wanted to laugh at the ridiculousness of the idea. Rebels too proud to trust or obey her were now too proud to surrender to anyone but her. Whatever chivalry was or had been, it would have to change. Her land would have to change. This mad foolishness could not be allowed to continue unchecked, war or no war, Kingslayer on the throne or not.

She followed Solomon. Markas and Farringdon came with her to where Corporal Gennet was overseeing the small crowd of armored men, all with heads bared and bowed, kneeling in the rain. They were a forlorn-seeming group, with frustrated expressions. Ironically, they were quite clean as the rain sluiced from their bodies the mud that had been their undoing. Nodding to the corporal, Amelia removed her helmet and felt the fresh, cold raindrops soak her coif and hair anew. She scanned the kneeling men-at-arms, looking for Earl Sebastian. His surrender should make an end of it. There was no point starting with his underlings.

Even as she looked, she saw Sir Tarrant rise up from the second rank of prisoners, lifting an arming sword from the muck where he had apparently concealed it. He threw himself toward her, sword ready for a lethal downward cut, and all she could do was watch him come as if all time had been reduced to this one unending moment. His blade was only partway through its slash when Prince Farringdon's longsword swept forward and caught it. The prince's quillons locked with Tarrant's own crossguard, and he turned the slash away and down so that the force spent itself in the mud. In one smooth motion, Farringdon followed up with his shield, slamming its edge into Tarrant's face, cracking his cheekbone and knocking him senseless to the ground. One of the Lions' Fangs threw himself on the knight, pinning the man's arms. The other Lions keeping watch made a show of having their weapons ready to suppress any further violence. Before anything else could happen, though,

Earl Sebastian stood in the midst of the prisoners and held his hands over his men.

"Peace!" he shouted. Amelia met his eyes, and it was clear he was wracked with shame and furious anger—at his defeat, at his man's shameful attempt at assassination, or even at his own rebellion she could not say. In truth, she did not care, not now.

"Highness...?" Amelia said, turning to the prince, still a little in shock by the speed of this whole final moment of the battle. The prince looked to her and grounded his sword in the mud. Then he tapped the side of his head where a small scar could be seen near his temple.

"I resolved never to be caught napping in a moment of truce again, Your Grace," he said.

"Thank you," she told him, then looked back to the prisoners. "Corporal Gennet, let's see about getting these men's surrenders, starting with that one."

She looked directly at Earl Sebastian, and two halberd-wielding Claws escorted him out of the crowd to kneel at Amelia's feet, now in shame in the rain as once it had been in honor in the chancel of Griffith Cathedral.

CHAPTER 73

D uchess Amelia sipped at a toddy of rum and honey with an intoxicating array of spices and herbs, her fingers gripped around the warm-glazed cup. Had it only been three days ago that the land had baked and sweated? One morning of standing in hard rain and now she had a cold. In spite of her aches and runny nose, it made her smile to think about. She would gladly suffer a hundred colds if that was all it took to bring her land out of the burden of endless summer. In the two days since the drought broke and Earl Sebastian was defeated, there had been almost continuous rain, although not always as heavy as that first morning. Lake Dweltford was almost waist deep at its banks, so it was said, and already skiffs and other small boats were going about their old business. Amelia suspected a number of riverfolk simply took their boats to the water for the joy of doing so. If the water continued to rise, the heavier barges would be refloated very soon, and the river's full commerce could be restored.

This morning the rain had abated and the sun had come back out, but it was the pale, watery sunshine of a true winter's morning, and even now as noon passed, clouds were gathering again on the horizon. Amelia stood at the solar window, warming cup in hand, watching the last of the glinting of sunlight on the water and tasting hope with every sip of her toddy.

Of course, the town was still hungry, and there were still the legal matters of the rebellion to deal with. It would be a full season or more before growing would be reestablished, but the rivercraft afloat would be able to bring provisions swifter and fresher by far than Dweltford had known for so long. Prices would go down again. The fields around the town were already sprouting the tiniest of green shoots. Within weeks there would be the beginnings of enough feed to restore thirsty and famished livestock.

The rebellion was a more complex problem. Of course, there was also the grim necessity of providing a funeral for Captain Ash as well. She had not had the courage to raise the notion with Lady Righteous, but the duchess was becoming convinced he was dead in a shallow grave somewhere, never to be found, another one of the accursed Bluebird's victims.

Behind her, Amelia heard footsteps and turned to see Prince Farringdon enter the solar. He was dressed warmly in a doublet and woolen hose, but he seemed not to have taken a cold as she had. He bowed formally.

"You sent for me, Your Grace? Forgive me my delay; I was seeing to the horses, helping assess them for injury." The destriers and coursers of the surrendered knights martial had all been forfeited to the duchess as spoils of war. They were being pastured to the north of the town, near where the White Lions had camped. The prince's estimation of them was yet another useful service he was providing to her without comment or hesitation.

"I *asked* for you, Highness," Amelia corrected. Even as a duchess in her own lands, she had no true right to summon a prince to attend her, at least not yet. "I wanted to discuss this notion of an Archduchy with you. I have some questions."

"Anything I can help you with, of course. Most of what I know, I have already shared."

Amelia nodded. She stepped away from the window to the table and put her cup down, running her fingers over several of the codices and legal commentaries she had stacked on top.

"There is no precedence that I can find in all of Grand Kingdom law and history for the creation of an Arch Duchy," she said. "I have consulted also with some others, including the Lady Dalflitch, whose knowledge on such matters is surprisingly diverse."

"I thought the lady was much engaged in conversation with an older woman these days, Your Grace," the prince said. "Leastwise, that was what I was told."

"She is, but that is a 'legal matter' of an entirely different breed and character," Amelia told him. She had had two conversations with Dalflitch about the old woman who was now being held under house arrest in the Conclave House. Her lady-in-waiting assured her there was a method to her madness, but Amelia still did not fully understand exactly what service the woman Dalflitch called the Ragmother was supposed to perform for her. Still, there was no one whose cunning Amelia trusted more than Dalflitch's, and Dalflitch insisted she was but an amateur next to this elder madwoman.

"So, the question that arises, Highness," she continued, "is how is it done?"

"Done, Your Grace?"

"How is an Archduke made?"

"How is anything done at the highest levels of law and tradition, Your Grace?" Farringdon asked rhetorically and shrugged. "Either it is done, as it has always been done, or else those at such a level agree to act as if it has been. Once, there had been only earls of the Grand Kingdom south of the Murr. Then they formed their compact at Grey Hill and all agreed to treat each other as princes."

"But the throne in Denay refused to acknowledge them as such," Amelia objected. Farringdon shrugged.

"It never stopped them," he said matter-of-factly. "The Masnian crown was happy to name them what they wanted. Kings and mercenaries from Aucks accepted them as such and made treaties under those names and titles."

"So, to rise to the status of Archduchess with all the rights and responsibilities thereto, I only have to take it for myself and then persuade or force someone of similar or higher level to treat me as such."

Amelia sighed at the arbitrary-seeming nature of it all. Could it be that all it took for a man to be a king was for him to call himself one and then get others to agree with him? Wasn't that what Daven Marcus was trying to do? Perhaps it did not always involve bloodshed, but perhaps it did. She was honest enough with herself to realize that if not for having her own army and being in the midst of a civil conflict, she would never even consider the radical political change she was contemplating. Amelia was still thinking when she realized that the prince was staring at her. His expression was deeply thoughtful, and she found herself meeting his gaze, momentarily fascinated.

"You have something to say, Highness?" she asked quietly.

"You know I have long enjoyed my sojourn here in your lands, Your Grace," he said with slow deliberateness, as if carefully choosing words to express important thoughts. "And I have been contemplating a broad number of subjects while here. I believe I have a solution to your problem."

Before Amelia could ask him to explain, Turley rushed into the chamber, almost falling over in his haste. He caught his balance and tugged his forelock breathlessly.

"Beg pardon, Your Grace, but you must come."

"Chief Steward?" Turley's lapses in protocol and manners were becoming fewer and rarer, but this was one time Amelia wanted the choice whether to be disturbed. She was about to dismiss him, but he spoke too swiftly for her.

"You got to come, Your Grace. It's Prentice. Captain Ash." He paused to catch his breath again.

Amelia's felt her own breath catch hopefully in her chest and saw that Prince Farringdon's expression reflected her own emotions.

"He's alive?" she asked, smiling.

"You could say that, Your Grace," Turley answered.

"Well, where is he?" she demanded, becoming frustrated for a totally different reason than a moment before.

"That's what I'm saying, Your Grace. You got to come see him. He's outside the town. I got someone saddling Silvermane for you."

Amelia shook her head in wonder. A part of her wanted to demand a full explanation, but Turley's enthusiasm was infectious. She spared one glance for the prince.

"Will you join us, Highness?"

"If the captain is alive outside the walls of Dweltford," he answered, "you would have to command me directly not to go. And forgive me, but even then I doubt you could prevent me."

Amelia almost laughed at that comment, respectfully disrespectful and strangely charming into the bargain. Waiting only for a warm cloak to be fetched for her, she allowed herself to be escorted to her horse and took the saddle, with the prince on his own new mount beside her. An escort of Lions was already drawn up as well and marched on either side of the two horses. All along the route to the town gate, Amelia tried to make Turley explain more to her of what was going on, but he was distracted, calling for way through the crowd. The townsfolk seemed to share his excitement for some reason, and they were filling the road and slowing the otherwise short journey. Amelia had a moment of apprehension when she thought that some of these folk had likely been amongst the levy that Quellion and his churchmen had stirred against her or were of the criminal element that had taken Master Welburne hostage at Bluebird's direction. Would one of them try to attack her in the confusion of the crowd? As she looked about, though, she could not see any unhappy faces. Whatever this was that involved her militia captain, it was in keeping with the new atmosphere of hope that the rain had birthed in her people.

They reached the main gate of Dweltford, and Turley led her through the barbican and into the open. Opposite the walls of the town, the vast refugee encampment was firming itself into a permanent settlement, an extension of the capital that would soon be as populous as Dweltford itself. Amelia knew she would have to commission works to improve the area and make it into a genuine district in its own right, but she also had plans for the rest of the Western Reach that she expected would draw many of these folk away to settle elsewhere. She was astonished as she looked to see that a vast crowd was gathered on the edge of the shantytown, all watching the road. At first, she thought they may have gathered to see her or the prince, but then she looked to the south and gasped in disbelief. There was Prentice, sitting upon a rugged-looking pony, which was odd enough, but he was riding at the head of a long column of horsemen in pairs, each one a fey with warbows on the backs of their saddles. For a moment she could only remember these mysterious warriors as they had been when they harried her people on the march. Then Prentice put his heels to his mount and walked it forward. He sat the animal as awkwardly as any other horse she had ever seen him attempt to ride.

"Your Grace, greetings," he said, and Amelia realized that Righteous was already out here, standing just at her husband's stirrup. The Lace Fang was beaming, and it made Amelia smile just as broadly to see it.

"Duchess Amelia of the Western Reach," Prentice shouted. "I present the fey folk of the Azure Mountains. Recently freed, they have come to make peace and pledge themselves to you and the Reach in service."

Amelia felt her eyes go wide and had to force herself not to gape. Prentice smiled at her, as if he recognized her emotions and found them amusing. Before she could say anything, one of the fey riders, a stern, slender-looking figure with tanned skin and long ears visible on the shaved sides of his head, rode toward her.

"If you are the duchess mother who births a new way," he said in a serious tone, "then we see you and permit you to see us."

Amelia looked to Prentice, wondering if he would explain what that meant, but he only nodded, giving her the signal to trust him for now and agree. She was sure he would unfold it all to her when the time was right.

"Thank you," was all she could think to say at first, but then added, "I thought I had seen you before, but I think this must be the first time, truly."

It was true. In spite of the blood and conflict between them in the past, this meeting felt fresh and full of promise. The fey man nodded with the same serious expression, but Prentice smiled approvingly.

"With your permission, the riders would camp in the north fields," he asked, and she nodded.

"We have a fresh herd of warhorses there," she told him. "Your friends might feel well at home."

It was Prentice's turn to seem surprised, and that made Amelia want to laugh.

"You are not the only one with a tale to tell, Captain," she said. She looked to Prince Farringdon beside her and felt herself suddenly caught in his gaze once more, though this time it was a lighter, more joyful, laugh-filled experience. He was clearly as excited and amazed to see Prentice and these fey as Amelia was, but when she gave him her attention, he returned it with full intensity. In that moment she knew what he wanted to discuss with her, and she thought she knew what she would say, but that would have to wait just a little while.

"I'm afraid you've been upstaged, Highness," she said. "We will have to finish our conversation later. Does that suit you?"

"Of course, Your Grace," Prince Farringdon replied and bowed in his saddle.

CHAPTER 74

"The whole place smells like a wet dog," Righteous whispered in Prentice's ear, and he had to work to suppress a smirk. Seated at the high table with the duchess and her closest retainers, the Captain of the White Lions had to project a certain dignity. He was wearing his best woolen doublet and a fine, thick cotton shirt to shield his aching body from the cold, but with so many folk crowded into the Great Hall, he was starting to feel uncomfortably warm.

The dense crowd was the cause of the smell that offended Righteous's sensibilities, such as they were. No matter how finely dressed people were, and they were all dressed in their finest, the persistent rain made it impossible for most of them to arrive here without becoming soaked, or damp at least. From the high table back, half the hall was filled with rows of benches on either side of a central aisle. Every possible space there was filled, and beyond that, the hall was crowded with ordinary townsfolk standing, watching the proceedings with fascination. Though mostly a place of honor, the benches themselves were not all even, especially with the front right corner being given to the chained gang of imprisoned knights, wearing manacles and fetters and looking dirty, dejected, roughly dressed, and totally out of place amongst the finery of the rest. They had been held under canvass on the castle's back meadow since the day the drought broke, and this was the first time any had been indoors since then. Most had been model prisoners in that time, though two had conspired to escape and swim for the shore. They had been run down by fey riders on patrol before they even found the road. They were brought back with shafts through their thighs, and one had sickened and died two days later. Chained and broken, even now the prisoners were watched over by five full lines of White Lions, adding their armored bulks to the press of the crowd and forming a clear cordon around the defeated.

On the other side of the hall, the benches were occupied with the worthies of the Western Reach, including black-robed members of the Conclave, their gold guild-master pins flashing on their breasts or collars. Of them, Caius Welburne was the most prominent, sitting in the front rank. Prentice had heard tell of the merchant master's pledge to Spindle and understood they would be married in a matter of days. He hoped they would be happy, though more for Spindle's sake than Welburne's.

Also seated on the front bench were three elders of the fey, with their brightly colored saddle blankets draped over the benches beneath them. They had wanted to bring their own saddles into this courtly audience to sit upon, as was their right in their own councils. After some earnest negotiations, a compromise was reached where they sat upon their own clan colors, but a single saddle to represent all of them was placed in front of the first bench on the first step of the dais as a place of esteem for the proud and ancient people.

"This pledge will stand between us in honor of peace made and blood shed for its cost," the duchess was saying to the three elders, and Prentice looked down at the gift they offered to her as the marker of the pledge. It was Haravind's head, preserved with wax and mounted on a stand made of steel rods that twisted around and held the macabre trophy in a claw-like grip. The duchess pointed to the head in its stand and then turned to the prisoners.

"Look you now on Sir Haravind," she said to them with a voice as cold as the freshening winter outside. "Rapist, murderer, rebel, worshipper of false gods, and servant of our people's enemies. Look at his horn, his teeth, and snout like a beast's. This is the 'man' whose honor you counted so worthy that you sympathized with him and brought division to my lands in his name."

Her eyes scoured the former knights martial, many of whom at least had the decency to look ashamed. One or two even looked genuinely sick at the sight of the monstrous head, and Prentice was glad. They hadn't even had to see him when he was alive.

"This head now stands as the marker of the honor of Reach nobility," the duchess continued. "It shows without doubt that the rot that besets the Grand Kingdom proper has infected the body of the peerage here as well. The nobility is sick, sick unto rebellion and perversion. When a limb is this diseased, it is beyond the healer's art to restore it. It must be cut away. And so it will be, here and now."

The duchess paused and looked to the only knights seated at the high table—the two men who had repented on their knees on the day of battle. Prentice looked at them as well, seated at the opposite end from himself and his wife. They seemed earnest men and proudly dressed in house colors, but their emotions were clearly mixed. They knew what was coming, as everyone at the high table did.

"Sir Urrimahd and Sir Petar Lime both recanted their rebellion and begged my mercy. They have received it. They will both retain their ranks, and their families will retain their titles. As for the rest..."

She turned once again to the prisoners.

"You are rebels, with your rebellion witnessed and attested fully. As such, your ranks and titles are all stripped from you. From this moment you are serfs, without family names or any rights under law. Your wealth is forfeit, and your lands and titles revert to the duchy. I will hold them in trust to dispose of, or dispense with, as I see fit."

That caused a ripple of disquiet amongst the prisoners and, Prentice thought, several of the other worthies gathered. The former nobles were merely resentful that they had lost so much status, but many of the other surprised folk were likely aware of the important legal portent of the duchess's words. The "dispense and dispose" phrase had distinct meaning and was a right that was reserved in Grand Kingdom law to the throne in Denay alone. Duchess Amelia using that phrase was giving the educated in the crowd a preview of what was coming. She was acting as if she had the king's right to create or abolish noble titles at will.

"If my punishment seems harsh, I remind you that the traditional reward for rebellion is a headsman's blade, and even if I let that pass, I would be within my rights to send you now in chains to serve a full conviction as the least of all men. However, I relinquish that right for myself and for my descendants, now and forever. Convict servitude is hereby abolished in the Western Reach."

That caused a much greater stir, especially on the left side of the hall. There were undoubtedly many patricians and wealthy folk who had long depended on the free labor that the institution of conviction provided. Although the convicts had recently been redirected to rapidly build the White Lions now that membership in the militia was also open to volunteers, many of those wealthy folk had probably expected convict labor might soon become available once again.

"Service in the White Lions will still be a purging pledge, but those who cannot serve my militia as men-at-arms will be given other roles in service to the duchy. The slavery of the convicted to ordinary citizens of any rank is now ended. There will be no convicts made in the Western Reach and none received from elsewhere."

The entire hall buzzed with this news, no doubt wondering what this would mean for the magistrates, for the laws, and the relationship with the rest of the Grand Kingdom. What would the kingdom proper do when it could no longer farm the cost of its legal system out to the Reach? The duchess allowed the conversation to hum for a time and then looked to Turley, standing by on the dais's top step with a brand new brass-shod staff of authority. It was especially crafted to make a loud noise when struck upon the ground, and when Duchess Amelia gave her chief steward a nod, he hammered it loudly on the flagstones. The voices died down.

"You rebels will be the first to receive the attention of this new law," the duchess told them. "You may pledge now to join the militia and serve the seven-year sentence to redeem your crimes and to leave then as yeomen. If you refuse the pledge, you will be marched from here to the border of the Reach and banished into exile under threat of death. As a convicted Reacherman could never return to the Grand Kingdom, so an exile will never be permitted in the Reach again."

This was a part of the plan that Prentice did not favor. He recognized the usefulness of trained men-at-arms in the Lions, especially if they could be taught to fit with the new military practices, but he worried that a clutch of ex-nobles might form a canker sore in his militia company, spreading resentment, undermining discipline, or even seeking possible revenge. Ten former knights would make a fairly effective assassination squad if they chose. He did not want to awaken one night to such a group in his tent.

The duchess had fixed Earl Sebastian—now *former* Earl Sebtian—with her cold glare.

"Sebastian, there is something you wish to say?"

The defeated nobleman had been deliberately sat in the front of the prisoners. This was a piece of political theater the duchess had planned, and again Prentice did not approve. The earl was charismatic and well spoken. There were times in history where a defeated foe, given a chance to speak, had taken much of the sheen off a victory, even won enough favor with crowds or courtiers to reverse a liege's judgements. An arrogant fool like

Duggan or Liam could be relied on to play their role to perfection, spitting insults and acting the deserving rebel. Former Earl Sebastian might not be so obliging.

With a sour expression, but uncowed, Sebastian stood in his place, the chains on his wrists clanking in the quiet. The entire hall was listening with bated breath. Only the fey seemed politely attentive. Everyone else present was rapt.

"You have no right to do these things," Sebastian said flatly but loudly, his voice echoing in the rafters. "You are not a king, nor even a queen. You do not sit the throne."

"There is no king at present," Amelia replied. Prentice knew she had been rehearsing this conversation for days to be ready for whatever Sebastian might say. He and Lady Dalflitch had done their best to help her prepare. "As the throne is bereft, so the Reach is bereft of a worthy nobility. For that reason, I am pressed to make *this* declaration."

The duchess reached down to the table and took up a piece of heavy parchment, filled with dense writing, several signatures, and at least two wax seals. She held it up for everyone to see.

"This is the charter of the Archduchy of the Western Reach," she pronounced in a voice as loud and clear as Sebastian's. "By its ordinances, I make known that from this day forth I am Archduchess Amelia, sovereign within the boundaries of the Western Reach, with all the rights and responsibilities thereof. I am announcing now that Reach law *alone* governs this land. There is a throne now in Dweltford, and I and my descendants will sit it by right of blood. A copy of this charter will be sent to the heralds of the courts in Denay and Rhales, as well as one to the Patriarchs of Mother Church and another published in the Vec. When a rightful king sits in Denay, we will offer fealty to him, and our arms will march in defense of the Grand Kingdom against foreign enemies, such as the Redlanders who yet plague the lands. In all else, the Reach stands by its own authority, makes its own laws and treaties."

She held the document out to Sebastian.

"Would you care to read it for yourself?"

"Mere words on a piece of paper," Sebastian sneered.

"As are the King's Law," the duchess retorted. "As are all laws and charters. Recent events have proven that laws and traditions are empty words unless there is steel to enforce them and silver and gold to pay men to wield that steel. The Reach has steel, silver, and men. We invite any who doubt our rights to this charter to come and test us."

Sebastian shook his head, looking disgusted and sad at once.

"They will never accept this. No one will accept this. When the civil war is done, you will be scoured from the land. The Redlanders will crush you, or if they do not, some heretic opportunist 'prince' from the Vec will snatch this folly out from under you. You will see."

Prentice nearly scoffed openly at the man's pig-headed devotion to old beliefs about the social order. No wonder this otherwise insightful leader had been ready to charge him with sumptuary sedition. He was in for a dreadful shock.

"We have seen the Redlanders off more than once," the duchess told Sebastian, and there was a rumble of approval through the free members of the crowd. "We have become quite adept at it. As to the rest, perhaps this will answer your concerns."

She looked to one of the benches, and from amongst the seated worthies, Prince Farringdon stood and moved to the aisle. He was dressed in livery, with a velvet doublet dyed bright green with three gold rings and a farring—an ancient coin that was his namesake—rendered in grey thread on a divided field with white stripes dexter. It was the heraldry of the Vec Princedom of Aubrey. Murmurs of curiosity accompanied him as he walked toward the foot of the dais. Turley hammered his staff on the flags again.

"Pray silence for Farringdon, Prince of Aubrey," he shouted, and the room became hushed like an empty chapel.

"Archduchess Amelia," Farringdon began, "many are the thanks and praises I could bring to you, and with your permission in the future, I shall. But for today, I have one question: will you give me your hand in marriage?"

The Great Hall erupted.

CHAPTER 75

Most of the noise was surprise and wonder, excited conversation that any crowd caught unawares might have. Some, though, was indignant, and a strong thread of the uproar was openly hostile. Turley's staff rang out again and again, but it took what seemed an age for the crowd's ferment even to lull a little. As it did, though, one voice began to emerge strongly.

"Whore! Slut! I knew you were a strumpet of the devil!"

It was High Sacrist Quellion, chained in amongst the other rebels, though carefully not in a spot close to Sebastian. He was standing now, and his sermon voice was loud and clear as he pronounced curse and insult upon the newly created archduchess. During the uproar, Prentice had stood also, ready to play an anticipated part at this point.

"Lions, gag that man," he bellowed as loudly as if he were on a battlefield, and even Quellion heard him. "And if he resists, cut his tongue out!"

"You would dare gag Mother Church? I am a high churchman," Quellion shouted back in sheer disbelief, though his voice cracked just a little.

"You are a rebel, sentenced to exile," Prentice continued to shout. "Whether by the new charter or the King's Law, you have no Church authority here. You fomented rebellion, and at her grace's discretion, your neck's for the noose. Now be silent or be silenced."

Quellion's mouth opened as if to speak, but a Fangs swordsman had come to stand beside him and took him roughly by the elbow. The militiaman had a dirk in his other hand, and at the sight of it, the clergyman grew pale and closed his mouth. Prentice turned and bowed to the duchess. She nodded and looked back to Prince Farringdon, waiting patiently at the foot of the steps.

"Highness, I can bear witness to your character, and your service to the Reach has been much appreciated," she declared loudly. "But you are a Veckander, and though your rank of prince is fitting, your status as a rebel to the Grand Kingdom makes a marriage between us impossible."

Prentice could see the fascination in the faces of all Reach folk present, seated or standing. Some in the crowd of commoners at the back were jumping up and down, hoping to get a better glimpse. They were witnessing history. This was the most momentous change the Grand Kingdom had experienced since the Vec earls had broken away centuries before. They may not have all quite understood, but everyone in the Great Hall sensed it.

"I know our history, Your Grace," Prince Farringdon declared loudly, "and the barriers that prevent our joining. That is why I offer this wedding gift."

He drew his longsword and laid the blade down on the first step between Haravind's head and the fey saddle. Then he went down on one knee before her.

"I, Prince Farringdon of Aubrey, hereby repent and renounce the rebellion of the Grey Hill Compact and the establishment of princedoms south of the Murr River by my ancestors. I bow my knee now to the throne of the Archduchy of the Western Reach and pledge my fealty to you as your vassal under law and thus to any throne to which you are pledged. If you will accept my hand, I will wed to you as your Marquis Consort, husband in heart but not in law. Our children would be your heirs, not mine, the seat yours, not mine, and should you perish, I will be

Marquis Widower with no rights, claims, or authority beyond a father with his children.

"This is my pledge to you because of your beauty, because of your glory, and because in all the world I love no other as completely as I love you."

Prentice frowned at the prince's final words. They were extemporized and did nothing to put paid to the rumors that the duchess had been having affairs up to this point. Only the first part of the speech was supposed to happen. Nonetheless, seeing the prince's expression, Prentice could hardly fault the man. He really did love Amelia, that was clear.

Prince Farringdon turned to the crowd and unlaced his doublet, pulling it over his head and holding it up.

"Regardless of the archduchess' answer to my pledge, the princedom of Aubrey is no more. The town and its lands are now of the Western Reach. Let Reach law rule there."

He dropped the heraldic garment to the floor and symbolically put his foot upon it. Then he turned and looked back to his newly declared love. Prentice could not see her face, but the happiness in her voice was unmistakable.

"Yes, Marquis Farringdon, I will take you as my husband and be your wife."

Awe and breathless shock ruled the crowd then. Most of the faces Prentice could see were fascinated, with no more position than happiness to be present. The now-untitled former nobles looked too bewildered to remain angry. Return of Vec fealty to Denay had been the crusader dream of the peers of the Grand Kingdom since the day the earls seceded. Now it had been achieved, even if only to the extent of one frontier province by the liege they had rejected. It was an honor all of them would have died for, and not one of them would taste its glory. Even Quellion's expression had changed, his self-righteous indignation colored by astonishment. What was an achievement for the peers was equally so for Mother Church. Every year since the Vec secession, sacrists had preached sermons that called for a moment like this. In this one sincere, loving pledge, Amelia, First Archduchess of the Western Reach, had achieved what no Grand Kingdom noble had before and none alive could deny. She had expanded her authority and lands legally, and to attempt to deny it would be to risk legitimizing a Vec prince's claim on his own lands. If Amelia was not Archduchess, then Farringdon's repentance was not real and his province was still a princedom. It was a set of legal niceties that the many Grand Kingdom nobles might try to simply ignore, but as Archduchess Amelia had already pointed out, she had the steel, the silver, and the men to back her charter. Any who wanted to deny her could come and press their claim if they dared.

To end the awestruck silence, Turley banged his staff one last time and shouted the pronouncement his wife and his liege lady had scripted for him.

"Archduchess Amelia, redeemer of the Vec! Archduchess Amelia, sovereign liege of the Western Reach! The Lioness! Huzzah!"

He shouted another huzzah, and by the time he gave a third, the crowd had taken it up. The Great Hall thundered to the rafters with the cheers. Prentice looked down at the three fey elders, the only ones not standing or cheering. Even so, he could read their expressions, and there was a satisfaction there. They were a quiet and serious people, but they recognized and approved of the importance of this moment. He met their gazes and spoke to them, even though he knew they could not hear him over the applause and praise.

"I see you, and you see me. Now we have seen a new thing birthed on this land. We have midwifed it. Let us go from this place and break more curses together."

The celebrating spread out from the castle until it overwhelmed the whole happily wet capital, and though there was not enough food for folk to feast, they did drink, and dance, and sing, and forget that for so long they had been thirsty.

Epilogue

"**B**rother Cerulean, come in. How's the leg healing?"

The man named Cerulean limped into the lamplit chamber, watching the shadows behind every pillar and stone vault rib. He hated the name Cerulean. He felt it was a foolishness that he would much rather do without. However, servants of the Inquisition's inner cadre did not get to choose their own names, and if they wished to advance, they did not make any bones about the ones they were given.

It was not his name that put the man Cerulean on edge, however, nor was it the still-healing wound in his knee. It was the fact that members of the inner cadre who failed at their missions so thoroughly as he had done did not typically survive their next visit to this chamber, known to the very few who did know of its existence as the Vault Above the Pit. It was so named because it was so deep underground that it was said that the only thing below it in the earth was Hell itself. God was in his heaven, but the leaders of the Inquisition carried the keys to the gates of Hell.

Or so it was said.

Brother Cerulean crossed the chamber to the enormous table called the Master's Bench. Constructed of ancient, dark hardwood, the singular piece of furniture could easily have sat forty or fifty people, fifteen down its long sides and ten at its ends. As far as Cerulean knew, a single meal had never been served at it, and instead of a typical wooden surface, its top was inset with a single sheet of impossibly thin iron onto which was etched a complete map of the entire known world, with the Grand Kingdom at the center. The table was an artifact of the order's founders, made with techniques no longer remembered. If it were ever lost or destroyed, it would be beyond the skill of current craftsmen to replace it. In this regard it was akin to the brat king's beloved cannons. The unbroken chain of masters of the Inquisition had conducted their business from this table since the founding, consulting a map that had never failed to inform them truly, at least until the Broken Kings' descendants—the Redlanders—had sailed back out of the west five years ago.

Cerulean made his awkward way around the Master's Bench and presented the one man seated at the table with a folded document packet.

"This is the king's copy?" he asked Cerulean as he took it.

"Yes, Sanguine," Brother Cerulean answered. The Inquisition's secret master, its *true* master, not the fool patriarchs who thought its purpose was to enforce their paltry understanding of Church Law, was named only Sanguine. It was a reminder to each one who held the post that their true purpose was to preserve the purity of the blood of the Grand Kingdom and its ruling family.

This Sanguine was a short, dumpy man with a soft, grey-haired tonsure, who looked most like the comfortable rector of a small but prosperous parish, kindly and content in life and without an ounce of ambition. Cerulean knew it was a lie, as utterly untrue as his own motley was when he went about as Bluebird, the clever and entertaining nobody. Sanguine had the cunning of a spider in its web and even less mercy for the Inquisition's enemies, or for anyone, Brother Cerulean imagined.

Sanguine unfolded the document and read it by the lamplight, carefully studying every word, examining the signatures and the wax seals. As he waited, Cerulean scanned the other documents already on the table. Amongst the journals, reports, and notes was another large sheet of vellum, seemingly the true replica of the one the master was reading now.

"Well, it is the same exactly," Sanguine said at last, laying down the new document next to its doppelganger. "Same words on the copy to the patriarchs. I expect to receive a description of the one she sent to the Rhales' court in the next few days. Likely it will be as precisely the same and correctly worded. Give the bitch her due; she observed the forms."

Sanguine was silent for a moment, but Cerulean did not take it as an invitation to speak.

"And the drought is lifted?" the master said at last.

"That is the word. River traffic is bringing them all they need until the growing seasons are reestablished. She's throwing silver around like a farmer sowing seed."

"She's smart enough to know that silver's worthless if your peasants starve out from under you. Dammit, if only that horned animal had killed her in that first ambush. We'd have the whole Reach under our hands by now."

Cerulean doubted it would have been that simple. Having been to the western frontier himself and seen how rough and ready life and politics there were, he had a grudging respect for the new archduchess and her continued rule. He did not say that, though, either.

"What about these retainers and bodyguards of hers? How good are they?"

"I'm still limping, aren't I?" Cerulean answered slightly churlishly, and Sanguine shot him a disapproving glance.

"And that captain of hers? He put the witch's binding beast down by himself, did he? So much for a human sacrifice to bind the fey and the land to her forever, making her a bloody queen in every respect." Sanguine snorted derisively. "Studied their damned blood sorcery half my life and still can't figure how she thought that was going to work. Of course, if it had, snatching the fey back out of her hand would have been very useful. I suppose we must accept that's washed away now, too."

"They have their own priests back in their homeland," Cerulean offered, speaking of the Redlanders and the source of their magickal knowledge. "The few I've captured and interrogated seem to think there's a whole swathe of prophecies that are supposed to be fulfilled or headed off during this invasion of theirs. The witch was adamant that whoever slew or bound the 'Ashen Man' to themselves would rule the Reach. Whoever did not would fall under his steel. Her words."

"Barbaric twaddle," Sanguine said, snorting again. "And you say she's fled to that magic lake of theirs up the headwaters of the Murr."

"Last I heard."

"Well then, I think we will leave the west to itself for now. Whatever the *arch*duchess thinks she's doing with the fey, that'll fall apart soon enough. Trust the fey folk and find their blade in your back. Slaves or corpses are the only safe fate for that lot."

"As it was from the start," Cerulean agreed. Distrust of the fey was an article of faith for all the inner cadre. Use them or destroy the ancient foe, but never trust them.

"In the meantime, good King Daven Marcus has grown bored sitting on his ancestor's throne and tormenting the city fathers of Denay," Sanguine said, sarcasm dripping from his lips at the mention of the Kingslayer's name and title. The Grand Kingdom's capital had resisted the murderous brat king for almost a year of siege, and when he finally conquered them, his first act, at the same time as having himself officially crowned in a lavish ceremony, was to have all the members of the city's Guild Conclave arrested and imprisoned. He'd spent the months since torturing them and randomly murdering their loved ones. If the city had not hated him before he captured it, there was no doubt now where the people's feelings lay.

"He's going north to teach Lastermune some proper respect," Sanguine continued. "Good luck to him. How the earl yet clings to life is a mystery that I will be glad to have resolved.

However, the *good* king lacks the men-at-arms and has demanded the Inquisition provide them to him."

"Demanded?" Cerulean cocked an eyebrow. Like all inner cadre members, he found it droll when the meaningless acted as if they had actual power. He and Sanguine shared a moment of true, if cold, amusement.

"We are going to beg his forgiveness," Sanguine explained, "but our poor beleaguered brotherhood has suffered at the hands of heretics and rebels so much more than we anticipated. Nonetheless, we have scraped in the corners of our coffers and managed to put together a small mound of hacksilver for him. We offer it as loyal servants that he might hire mercenaries to cover his manpower needs. Perhaps, if he does not think us presumptuous, we would even gladly introduce him to some reliable men-at-arms for hire in Aucks. The money's already in two chests upstairs waiting with an escort. You'll take it to him when you return this fable."

Sanguine handed back the king's copy of the Reach charter. Cerulean received it with surprise.

"You're sending me?"

"Not as Bluebird, obviously." Sanguine glanced mockingly at the still bandaged knee. "Tell him you're a close advisor to the patriarchs. They've offered your services as a mark of respect to use or not as he chooses."

"I...uh...yes,...uh...of course." In spite of all his self-possession, Cerulean could not help being relieved to discover he was going to live. He was not especially afraid to die, as such, but if it was at Sanguine's order, it would likely be an excruciatingly long and creative ordeal. Sanguine smiled like a predator with its prey.

"You lost a lot at the table in the west, Brother Cerulean," he said, "but you were sent to gamble for the whole pot. It may be your fault you lost, but not your fault you lost *big*. There're still some coins in your purse, though, and cards in your hand yet to play. In the meantime, let us sit you down at another table with lesser stakes 'til you get your confidence back."

"Thank you."

Cerulean turned and left. There were no bows, tugged forelocks, or other gestures amongst this most secret part of the Grand Kingdom. Honor was for fools and the dead. The reprieved agent of the Inquisition found himself smiling quietly and even feeling a desire to laugh as he awkwardly limped the torchlit steps to the surface. He would go to his new mission and apply all the craft he had been trained with, all the experience he had in secrecy and mystery. He would redeem himself in the eyes of his masters. And then, if God answered his prayers, he would return to the Western Reach and crucify the new archduchess, her foreign husband, her captain, and every man and woman they loved. The crosses would line the road out of her precious town, which Cerulean—Bluebird—would watch burn to the ground. Then he would see what "ash" was left after all that.

GLOSSARY

The Grand Kingdom's social structure is broken into three basic levels which are then subdivided into separate ranks: the nobility, the free folk, and the low born.

The Nobility

King/Queen – There is one King, and one Queen, his wife. The king is always the head of the royal family and rules from the Denay Court, in the capital city of Denay.

Prince/Princess – Any direct children of the king and queen.

Prince of Rhales – This title signifies the prince who is next in line of succession. This prince maintains a separate, secondary court of lesser nobles in the western capital or Rhales.

Duke/Duchess – Hereditary nobles with close ties by blood or marriage to the royal family, either Denay or Rhales.

Earl; Count/Countess; Viscount; Baron/Baroness – These are the other hereditary ranks of the two courts, in order of rank. One is born into this rank, as son or daughter of an existing noble of the same rank, or else created a noble by the king.

Baronet – This is the lowest of the hereditary ranks and does not require a landed domain to be attached.

Knight/Lady – The lowest rank of the nobility and almost always attached to military service to the Grand Kingdom as a man-at-arms. Ladies obtain their title through marriage. Knights are signified by their right to carry the longsword, as a signature weapon.

Squire – This is, for all intents and purposes, an apprentice knight. He must be the son of another knight (or higher noble) who is currently training, or a student of the academy.

The Free Folk

Patrician – A man or woman who has a family name and owns property inside a major town or city. Patricians always fill the ranks of any administration of the town in which they live, such as aldermen, guild conclave members, militia captains etc.

Guildsmen/townsfolk – Those who dwell in large towns as free craftsmen and women tend to be members of guilds who act to protect their members' livelihoods and also to run much of the city, day to day.

Yeoman – The yeomanry are free farmers that possess their own farms.

The Low Born

Peasants – These are serfs who owe feudal duty to their liege lord. They do not own the land they farm and must obtain permission to move home or leave their land.

Convicts – Criminals who are found guilty of crimes not deserving of the death penalty.

Military Order

Knight Captain, Knight Commander & Knight Marshall – Every peer (King, Prince or Duke) has a right to raise an army and command his lesser nobles to provide men-at-arms. They then appoint a second-in-command, often the most experienced or skilled soldier under them. A duke his Knight Captain; a prince his Knight Commander; and the King his Knight Marshal.

Knights – These are the professional soldiers of the Grand Kingdom. All nobles are expected to join these ranks when their lands are at war, and they universally fight from horseback.

Men-at-Arms –A catch all term for any man with professional training who has some right or reason to be in this
group, including squires and second and third sons of nobles.

Bannermen – This is a special form of man-at-arms. These
are soldiers who are sworn directly to a ranking noble.

Free Militia – The free towns of the Grand Kingdom have
an obligation to raise free militias in defence of the realm.

Rogues Foot – A rogue is a low born or criminal man and
so when convicts are pressed into military service, they are the
rogues afoot (or "on foot") which is shortened to rogues foot.

Other Titles and Terms

Apothecary – A trader and manufacturer of herbs, medical
treatments and potions of various sorts.

Chirurgeon – A medical practitioner, akin to a doctor or
surgeon, especially related to injuries (as opposed to sickness,
which is handled by an apothecary).

Ecclesiarchs – ruling members of the Church. Their ranks
correspond (very roughly) to noble ranks. The ecclesiarchy
refers to the power of the Church where it rules with its own
power, like a nation within the nation. Monasteries, churches, cathedrals and the Academy in Ashfield are all part of the
Church lands, where religious law overrides King's Law.

Estate – A person's estate can be their actual lands, but
can also include their social position, their current condition
(physical, social or financial), or any combination of these
things.

Fiefed – A noble who is fiefed possesses a parcel of land over
which they have total legal authority, the right to levy taxes
and draft rogues or militia.

Frater – brother (from the Latin word)

Hoi Polio – the common folk

King's Law – This is the overarching, national law, set for
the Grand Kingdom by the king, but does not always apply
in the Western Reach.

Magistrate – Civil legal matters of the Free Folk and Peasantry are typically handled by magistrates, who render judgements according to the local laws.

Marshals/Wardens – Appointed men who manage the movement of large groups, especially of nobles and noble courts when in motion. They appoint the order of the march and resolve disputes.

Physick – A term for a person trained in the treatment of medical conditions, but without strict definition.

Proselytize – Attempt to convert someone from one religion, belief, or opinion to another.

Pugilist - A professional boxer.

Provost – (short for provost marshal) junior officers assigned to sentries or patrol for the purpose of military discipline. In the case of the White Lions militia, the typical rank of a provost is a Line First. Roughly equivalent to military police duty.

Republicanists – Rare political radicals, outlawed in the Grand Kingdom and the Vec who seek to create elected forms of government, curtailing or overturning monarchical rule.

Seneschal – The administrative head of any large household or organisation, especially a noble house of a baron or higher.

Surcoat – The outer garment worn by a man-at-arms over their armor. Typically dyed in the knight's colours (or their liege lord's colours in the case of a bannerman) and embroidered with their heraldry.

Te tree – A tree, known for its medicinal properties.

The Rampart – A celestial phenomenon that glows in the night across the sky from east to west in the northern half of the sky.

About Matt

Matt Barron grew up loving to read and to watch movies. He always knew he enjoyed science fiction and fantasy, but in 1979 his uncle took him to see a new movie called *Star Wars* and he was hooked for life. Then *Dungeons and Dragons* came along and there was no looking back. He went to university hoping to find a girlfriend. Instead, the Lord found him, and he spent most of his time from then on in the coffee shop, witnessing and serving his God. Along the way, he managed to acquire a Doctorate in History and met the love of his life, Rachel. Now married to Rachel for more than twenty years, Matt has two adult children and a burning desire to combine the genre he loves with the faith that saved him.

Learn more at:

mattbarronauthor.com

Also By Matt Barron

Rage of Lions

Prentice Ash

Rats of Dweltford

Lions of the Reach

Eagles of the Grand Kingdom

Serpents of Summer

The Mantis and the Mirrored Sky

MORE FROM PUBLISHER

Be sure to check out our other great science fiction and fantasy stories at:

bladeoftruthpublishing.com/books

Made in the USA
Middletown, DE
26 November 2023

43596114R00359